They live under the diabolical, watchful power of John Murray Eden, whose only wish is to control them . . .

Mary's secret love for John's most bitter enemy brings a cruel revenge . . . John's frail wife, Lila, forced to bear his heir, suffers a most devastating fate . . . Harriet, imprisoned in a world of self-imposed darkness, will suffer forever for an act of long ago . . . Dhari, John's seductive Indian mistress, drawn to his trusted advisor, must make an agonizing choice . . . Elizabeth, despite years of devotion to John, is threatened by his arrogance and violence.

THE WOMEN OF EDEN

"Murder, rape, incest, mayhem, mutilation, romance, a chase and a love story have all been stirred together with great skill. Treat yourself to this delightful concoction."

Best Sellers

Also by Marilyn Harris
Published by Ballantine Books:

THE EDEN PASSION

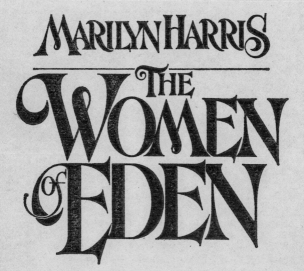

MARILYN HARRIS
THE WOMEN OF EDEN

BALLANTINE BOOKS • NEW YORK

Library of Congress Catalog Card Number: 79-19757

ISBN 0-345-28965-X

This edition published by arrangement with
G.P. Putnam's Sons

Manufactured in the United States of America

First Ballantine Books Edition: January 1981

For Judge and Karen and John

There is a destiny now possible to us, the highest ever set before a nation to be accepted or refused. . . . Will you youths of England make your country again a royal throne of kings, a sceptered isle, for all the world a source of light, a centre of peace, mistress of learning and of the arts, faithful guardian of time-honored principles? . . . If we can get men for little pay to cast themselves against cannon-mouth for love of England, we must find men who also will plough and sow for her, who will behave kindly and righteously for her, and who will bring up their children to love her. . . . This is what England must either do or perish. . . .

John Ruskin
1870

Nature has given women so much power that the law very wisely has given them little.

Dr. Johnson

❧

London
May 10, 1870

OUT OF ALL the futile activity of her day, only these moments made sense, when behind the discretion of a small white lace mask, she could forget the muddle of who she was and what she was.

Standing safely in the shadows of the red velour stage curtains of Jeremy Sims Song and Supper Club off the Strand, Mary Eden looked over her shoulder at her two watchdogs. Old Jeremy Sims was there as was Elizabeth, her surrogate mother who triumphantly had taken the place of her real one, who still resided in semiseclusion at Eden Castle.

Mary looked closer, newly impressed with how pretty Elizabeth still was. Nearing fifty if she was a day, but petite and elegant, adored by men and women alike. It had been Elizabeth who early on had taught Mary that every human being had a right to at least a portion of their own life.

Then why the need for debate? She really couldn't understand Elizabeth's hesitancy. A quite respectable place this was. Not at all like the East End music halls, where the female entertainers bared their breasts completely and lifted their skirts beyond their garters. No, here Jeremy Sims insisted on decorum, and the ladies who performed were required to possess modesty as well as natural charm.

As her anger blended with confusion, Mary turned and looked directly at the two in confrontation, aware at first glance that rotund old Jeremy was waging a good argument on her behalf. And why shouldn't he?

Since that first night eight months ago when Mary had badgered Elizabeth into letting her do one song for the gentlemen, Jeremy Sims' Thursday-evening clientele had increased threefold. In fact, now certain club members only attended on Thursday evenings. Mary knew this for

1

a fact and was proud of it. And she knew further why they came. It was to see her, to hear her crystal clear voice singing the songs of their childhood.

But she knew they came for something else as well, for she'd taken careful note of their faces in the smoky semi-darkness of the club, old men mostly, their cravats knotted like nooses about their necks, staring at the flowers tucked between her breasts.

"But it's such a risk, Jeremy." Elizabeth frowned. "If John were to find out—" She broke off in what apparently was genuine fear, and briefly Mary recognized a disappointing hypocrisy.

"Then why did we come, Elizabeth?" she demanded, allowing a sharpness to fill her own voice. "Why did you help me to dress, saying how much the gentlemen would like this gown? And why didn't we just stay home and do our French grammar or our needlepoint, or count the carriages that pass by our window?"

Looking into Elizabeth's anxious face, she saw not the independent woman she loved more than life itself, but merely an extension of John Murrey Eden, the benefactor who gave generously with one hand and took with the other.

As Mary continued to gaze at Elizabeth, a strange defiance shook her. She was twenty-one. She was educated, polished, groomed, brushed. She could speak three languages, could do figures, could play the pianoforte. She could sew, could organize servants, could sit a horse, could drive a carriage, could navigate her way through the most treacherous table conversation. She could smile on cue. She had never wept in public. She could decant wine, balance books, quote Shakespeare, Aristotle, Plato and Homer.

Yet—

She had never been alone with a man other than Richard, her brother, or John, her cousin. She had never felt a man's arm about her, never experienced the sensation of a kiss, save brotherly ones. She had never been permitted to walk in the park alone, or enter a public room alone, or ride a train alone. She was checked in each night and let out each morning like a prisoner. She was permitted to use her natural talents such as her rare clear voice only when it suited others. She was permitted to speak, think, walk, act, talk, only when it suited others.

The inventory was deadly and took a deadly toll. Without hesitation and only vaguely aware of the two staring at her in apprehension, Mary lifted the mask in her hand with the intention of affixing it in place, all the time speaking with a calmness which belied her inner turmoil. "We came here tonight, Elizabeth, for one express purpose, the same purpose which brings us here every Thursday evening, for me to indulge in the harmless activity of singing for Jeremy's gentlemen. I promise I will break no law. The songs are innocent. The mask is in place. No one will know or even suspect that I am the property of John Murrey Eden."

The delicate white mask *was* in place, and on that note of defiance, and since neither of the watchdogs seemed inclined to say anything further, and since Betty Merkle's cockney jig was winding down, now was as good a time as any to take the stage, to receive that first heady sensation of seventy-five men staring at her through the smoky haze.

Oh, how she loved it all, the sense of the spotlight, the sudden quiet, the feeling of power! But as she started toward the small stage she felt a hand on her arm.

"Mary, I beg you. Please, not tonight," Elizabeth whispered, "the risks are too great."

"Perhaps it would be best if the songbird remained silent." Jeremy nodded vigorously. "Elizabeth has a point. With all the big doings at Eden Castle, all the publicity, if you know what I mean . . ." And he grinned stupidly and left them with a silence even more confused that before.

While Mary was trying to digest this nonsense, Elizabeth stepped close again. "Please, Mary, let's return home, where we should have remained in the first place. I'm sorry for initially agreeing and then changing my mind. But I had no idea the club would be so filled." Her hand lifted in an attempt to remove the mask. Mary stepped back, prohibiting contact.

Obviously Elizabeth saw defiance. "Please," she begged. "John has enemies. You know that as well as I—scribblers who would like nothing better than to spoil the Eden Festivities for him." She drew so close that Mary saw beneath the face powder to the lined face of a fifty-year-old woman. "Please," Elizabeth begged, "neither you nor I must provide them with the weapon they so sorely need."

In the impasse, Mary heard Betty Merkle's pianoforte grow quiet. There was a polite scattering of applause, as though the gentlemen were withholding their enthusiasm until there was something worthy of it.

With the weapon they so sorely need......

Was she now a weapon? She'd played a hundred passive roles on John's behalf. But a weapon? That didn't sound so passive. And what was it to her, the Eden Festivities, the Restoration of Eden Castle? And that foolish painting for which she and Lila and Elizabeth and Dhari had sat for an interminable number of days, gowned in Roman garb while Alma-Tadema recorded for all time "The Women of Eden."

Now commencing this coming Monday, they were facing a fortnight of public display so common that anything she might do at Sims Song and Supper Club paled in comparison.

"Mary, please," Elizabeth whispered.

So! It was to be as it had always been, John's will stated and obeyed.

"No," Mary said simply, backing away from Elizabeth's reach, a bit regretful of the consternation in that beloved face. "No," she repeated, adjusting the bodice of her pale blue gown to reveal more of her breasts.

She was almost to the edge of the curtain now, and they were both starting after her, Jeremy Sims, mountainous on one side, his ruddy face contorted with embarrassment, and Elizabeth on the other, her earlier gentle persuasion abandoned and replaced by a stern demeanor.

"Mary, I forbid you!" she said, full-voiced, loud enough to carry to the front tables of the club.

But Mary was resolved. No force on earth could have kept her from inhabiting that empty stage. Oh, she was aware that she would have bridges to mend later and she would have to endure Elizabeth's hurt. But anything could be endured, even the dreaded fortnight at Eden, if for just a moment she could be someone else, the young woman with the lovely voice known only to the club members of Sims Song and Supper Club as "Maria of the Mask."

"Mary, please—" Elizabeth called a final time. Was she weeping? Surely not, and even if she were, Mary would have to deal with it later.

She stepped forward, lifting her head so that the light from the candles in the wall standards shimmered on her hair. A sudden hush fell over the crowded room, the gentlemen looking up from their platters and glasses as though an apparition had appeared before them.

As she reached the center of the small stage her excitement accelerated. The applause started low, then gradually increased, sweeping over her with the same medicinal effect as the headland breezes off Eden Point.

Just behind the red velour curtains she saw two figures clutching at each other as though they were weathering a storm. No matter. She was incapable of dealing with that problem now.

All at once, behind the safety of the mask, Mary blew out the light of her customary identity, touched her breasts in a revealing gesture, moved delicately among the shadows, and felt like the silver balloon that she remembered launching into space off the quay at Mortemouth when she was a child. . . .

Out of all the furtive activity of his day, only these moments made sense, when for a brief period of time he could indulge in a vision so lovely that all the secretive dealings and natural confusion that accompanied a double life fell away and left him with a sense of deliverance.

Seated at his customary front table in Jeremy Sims Song and Supper Club, Burke Stanhope glanced over his glass of port toward the pianist. Would she never cease? And where was little Maria of the Mask? He looked at his watch. Half past ten. Generally she had appeared before nine.

Be patient, he counseled himself. She was worth waiting for. Looking out over the crowded club, it occurred to him that he wasn't the only one waiting. For a Thursday evening the club was mobbed, every table occupied, an all-male audience of varying ages, yet a circumspect and decorous gathering. With one exception. He peered at a front table located at the opposite end of the stage, where four young men had been consuming copious quantities of spirits for the better part of the evening.

Over his shoulder, Burke spotted Henry, his waiter. With a familiarity based on six months of patronage, Burke summoned him to the table. "What's the delay, Henry?" he called out, his American accent seeming to resound over the crowded room.

The skeletal old waiter shook his head. "Don't rightly know, Mr. Stanhope. I've had others making the same in-

quiry." He swiveled his long neck about. "I can't even locate Mr. Sims to pose a formal inquiry for you." Then, in
the manner of a tolerant headmaster, he comforted, "Not
to worry, sir. I'm sure the young lady will take the stage
soon. She's not one to let us down, now is she?"

Amused by his feeling of a child being mollified, Burke
drained his port and sent Henry scurrying for a fresh decanter. As the pianist launched forth into a spirited rendition of a cockney jig, he lowered his head into his hands,
the sense of a lost schoolboy still strong within him.

He was grateful for one thing, that John Thadeus Delane had not accompanied him here tonight as had been
their initial plan. Fortunately a minor crisis had kept Delane in his editorial office in Printing House Square, thus
sparing Burke the humiliation of trying to explain his unreasonable obsession for a masked young woman.

From the table at the opposite end of the room a burst
of laughter erupted. A questionable joke apparently had
found a receptive audience. Burke looked up to see the
four drunken men in uncontrollable laughter. Almost envying them their fun, he watched a moment longer, then
again he rested his head in his hands.

Without warning, as was happening more and more
frequently, the sense of his splintered existence swept over
him and he felt empty, like a house long since deserted. It
was astonishing how clearly he saw the image of his childhood home, Stanhope Hall outside Mobile, Alabama. Effortlessly he saw the colonnaded portico, the long line of
leafy elms which led to the house, a little boy in old-
fashioned clothes curled in a cool, shady corner of the
swept porch, writing words on the back of one of his
father's old cotton ledgers.

The thick curtain which separated the past from the
present lifted. The five-year-old boy was replaced by the
thirty-five-year-old man, though the sense of loss and confusion remained, the central mystery being what in the
hell was he doing here, not just here in Sims Song and
Supper Club, but in London, nursing a weak mother who
had refused to return home after the disgrace of defeat,
who had successfully recreated the old fantasy by bringing her favorite Negroes with her, and who in her own
mad way was generally placid and harmless as long as all
about her refrained from speaking aloud one name:
Abraham Lincoln.

"Here you are, sir." As Henry placed the decanter of port on the table, Burke nodded in thanks, filled his glass and drained it, knowing the price he'd pay come morning, but filling it again anway.

Come morning! There was a dreaded thought. A jostling ride with John Thadeus Delane in his carriage to a place called Eden on the North Devon Coast, where apparently with hundreds of others they would be forced to endure the arrogance and ostentation of John Murrey Eden.

Burke knew the name well, having dealt with it countless times in his column, which he wrote anonymously for the *Times*—another example of John Thadeus Delane's macabre sense of humor. For the last five years, at Delane's insistence and on his sacred promise never to reveal Burke's true identity, Burke had written columns for the *Times* under the pseudonym of "Lord Ripples."

At first it had started as a lark, something to relieve the tedium, to amuse editor Delane, who had been kind to the entire Stanhope family on their difficult passage through the American Civil War. But three years ago both Burke and Delane had become aware of the interesting fact that thousands of readers were buying the *Times* just to read and become outraged by Lord Ripples' writings.

In fact, the public had named him. An angry Englishman had written a letter to the editor after a particularly vitriolic column in which Burke had dared to criticize the length and intensity of the Queen's mourning for Albert. The letter-writer had demanded the immediate identity of the scribbler who dipped his pen into the placid, superior English landscape, causing ripples.

The very next morning, with a journalistic instinct that amounted to genius and with a wisdom of human nature that informed him that the public loved to hate at least as much as they loved to love, editor Delane had christened Burke Lord Ripples, had given him a free journalistic hand and had instructed him to seek out and graphically describe every boil, sore and tumor on the English national body.

To this day, no one but Burke and John Thadeus Delane knew Lord Ripples' true identity, that he was a displaced American whose father had sent the family to England in the early sixties for the dual purpose of escaping the carnage of the Civil War and in an attempt to

plead with the cotton mills of the Midlands to lift their
barricade on Southern cotton, a sympathetic gesture
against slavery which had threatened to do greater econ-
omic damage to the South than the marauding armies of
the North.

Again Burke drained his glass of port. What matter
now? It was all ancient history, the South defeated, his
father trying to salvage what he could after commanding
Burke to remain behind in London with the mad Caroline.

Sunk in thought, Burke was scarcely aware of the cessation of noise from the pianoforte. The first sound which
summoned him back was the drunken laughter of the four
young students, which echoed over the now quiet club. He
cast a quick glance in their direction. Why was Jeremy
Sims permitting such behavior? Then he looked toward
the stage and caught a flare of a pale blue gown, as though
someone had started out from behind the stage curtain
only to be restrained.

He sat up in his chair. What in hell was going on?
Would she appear or not?

Then she did. The flare of the pale blue silk gown grew
and became a full apparition, the young woman pausing
beside the stage curtain as though the weight and expect-
ancy of men's eyes had disarmed her. But it didn't last
long, for then she was moving, a picture of grace, the
gown fully visible, light blue very fine silk wreathed with
ropes of seed pearls, while in her golden hair floated two
soft plumes of lilacs, another fortunate plume nestling between her breasts.

In that peculiar way that the imagination will seize on
trifles, Burke found that he could not take his eyes off
the lilacs, the way they moved with each delicate inhalation
of breath.

He was aware of the applause increasing about him,
the gentlemen responding with delight to the vision on the
stage. And once again he was struck by the phenomenon
known as Maria of the Mask. There were any number of
establishments in London where these gentlemen could
even glimpse a thigh, the hundreds of music hall entertainers whose every song was an open invitation for se-
duction.

Then what was the attraction of this rather shy young
girl who conducted herself more like a noblewoman than a

music hall entertainer? And why the mask unless to conceal an identity which, if revealed, could cause embarrassment, or worse?

Now she was looking back at the audience with the greatest serenity, all traces of the earlier timidity gone, as though at last she had found her natural habitat. And Burke was aware of the silence in the room, a quiet so intense that he closed his eyes and imagined the large club empty except for a pulsebeat of longing and expectation.

Opening his eyes so as not to miss a moment, he saw her incline her head to the pianist. The melancholy musical introduction only enhanced the mood. She stood with such ease that she might have been a beloved daughter merely performing for a doting family at a Sunday-afternoon musicale.

It was that innocence, and yet— There! Notice that gesture, her right hand, passing over the blue silk bodice, cupping briefly about her breast as though offering it to the gentlemen.

At some point in the remarkable performance Burke was no longer witnessing the needs of others. His own were sufficient to keep him occupied, the tension building as the song reached its climax, all the ugliness of the world disappearing before the beauty of her voice and face, the promise that with her the act of love would not be carnal sin but rather an ethereal flight to paradise.

She was moving in time to the sorrowful melody, informing them of unrequited love and a broken heart. Slowly she walked to the front of the stage and looked sorrowfully out, as though pleading with the stunned gentlemen to take the place of her dead lover.

Burke began to wonder how much they all could endure. Impulses were churning within him, the young woman shining through his secret fantasies. All men dreamed of such a woman, the temptress concealed within the lady, the unspoken promise of sin issued through the lips of an angel.

Suddenly there was a disturbance on his far right, merely a scuffling at first, then a stumbling upward, an impatient figure rushing the stage, one of the drunken students, his hands reaching out.

It was several moments before Burke could bring himself out of his spell, and when he did he saw the student mounting the stage, looming large over the young woman, who apparently was so surprised by the approach that she made no move to withdraw.

Then he was upon her, his hands planted on those small shoulders, his body obscuring her. Burke heard the shocked protest of the audience, the gentlemen still not believing what they were seeing, their dream obscured by pawing hands.

The pianist screamed, and Burke thought he heard another female scream, though he was certain that it had not issued from the lips of the young woman. From where he sat, she seemed to be indulging her attacker, whose hands were now moving over her breasts, and apparently finding the fabric of her gown an obstacle, he gathered the silk in one angry fist and jerked downward.

At last aware of her predicament, the young woman commenced to struggle and, as Burke started toward the stage, he saw old Jeremy Sims rush out from the wings, his fleshy face ruddy with shock. Accompanying him a few steps behind was a petite graying lady, whose eyes reflected the horror of the ugly scene.

"I say!" Jeremy blustered, approaching the drunken youth, one pudgy hand reaching out to dislodge him from his position over the young woman, who in the attack had been forced to her knees.

Now Burke commenced running toward the stage, confident that Jeremy Sims, overaged and overweight, would be no match for the young man. Just as he stepped over the row of foot-candles he saw the student turn from the young woman kneeling at his feet, draw back his fist and drunkenly take aim at Jeremy Sims. A lucky first strike sent the old publican stumbling backwards, crashing into a set piece of forest scenery.

Burke had seen enough, as had everyone else in the club. He was aware of all the gentlemen on their feet, a few rushing toward the stage, all shouting instructions, none of which he needed. To the continuous siren of the pianist's screams, he approached the scene with confidence and lifted the student by the collar of his coat, angled him into position, then delivered a blow to the side of his jaw which sent him sailing over the foot-candles and crashing into the front row of tables.

Burke looked down on the young woman and in the process caught a glimpse of one lovely breast. But it was not the breast that held his attention. Rather it was the look of excitement on her face, as though she were pleased with herself for having brought the young man to such a fit of passion.

Burke's scrutiny did not last long, for shouts from the audience informed him that the student was rising again, and within the instant Burke jumped down from the stage and met the belligerent while he was still in the act of coming up. Again he lifted him by the collar of his coat, drew back his fist and sent it shooting forward with such force that he heard his knuckles crack against front teeth, saw two small white objects fly out of the young man's mouth, accompanied by a flow of blood.

Flattened and senseless at last, the young man's friends came to retrieve him, and with the alarmed waiters holding back the outraged gentlemen, they lifted him and carried him from the club.

With the crisis safely passed, the indignation of the gentlemen knew no bounds, and for several minutes Burke found himself surrounded by congratulatory and wrinkled faces, a few assuring him that they had been more than ready to back him up in the event that he had required their assistance.

Rubbing his bruised knuckles, Burke assured them that all was well, dismissed their congratulations and noticed unprecedented flushes on their pallid cheeks.

But at this moment the rejuvenation of senile old men was not uppermost in Burke's mind. Still haunting him was the image of self-satisfaction on that beautiful young face. If she had thanks to give, these he would gladly receive along with her name and perhaps her card and permission to call on her.

As he turned to receive her grateful thanks, to his disappointment he saw the stage empty except for the still sprawled though recovering figure of Jeremy Sims. With a feeling akin to panic, Burke ran back up on the stage and looked into the wings, confident that the pianist and the older woman had merely led her to a position of safety.

But the wings were empty, the backstage door ajar, letting in a cool draft of the early May night as well as the sound of a rapidly retreating carriage.

Still suffering from the irrational feeling that thanks were due him, Burke ran through the opened door where a weak spill of fog-encircled gas lamps spread before him.

He saw the carriage just turning the far corner, departing rapidly.

Suffering anew that peculiar sense of loss over something that had never been his, he turned back into the dimly lit wings. As he reached the edge of the curtain he was aware of his bruised knuckles bleeding. Pulling a handkerchief from his waistcoat pocket, he was in the process of wrapping the damaged hand when he heard his name.

"Mr. Stanhope?"

He looked up to see a wobbly Jeremy Sims being helped to his feet by two waiters. Once up, the large man insisted that he needed no support and started toward Burke, rubbing the side of his face and instructing the waiters to see all the gentlemen out to their carriages, then to lock the doors of the club for the night.

His duties of proprietorship completed, he stumbled past Burke and sat in a straight-backed chair, the disaster that had befallen his respectable club clear upon his face.

"My God," he muttered, shaking his head. "Never in twenty-seven years has such a scandal befallen Sims," he moaned, his words muffled by the swelling of his jaw. "Ruined," he pronounced melodramatically, looking up at Burke for the first time.

"Not ruined, Sims," Burke countered, amused. "I predict your membership will increase threefold, particularly if you can lure your masked beauty back."

"Oh, no," Sims replied, shaking his head, his triple chins waggling like aspic, "I'm afraid we've seen the last of little Maria. They'll never permit her to return, not after—"

On an impulse of hope, Burke asked, "Whom do you mean by 'they'?"

"Oh, list them as you like," Sims said despondently. "Her cousin for starters, her brother, her mother—"

The fog cleared and the old man realized what he had almost done. Abruptly his manner changed. He stood with dispatch. "I want to thank you, Mr. Stanhope, for your intervention. I'm afraid most of Sims' patrons are beyond the art of physical defense. I shudder to think what would have happened if you hadn't—"

Burke dismissed his gratitude and considered probing again for the identity of the young woman. The reference to a cousin and a brother and a mother were of no help whatsoever.

Just as he was ready to pose another question, he saw Jeremy Sims move past him as though to avoid the unasked question. "Please, Mr. Stanhope, I insist that you seek medical attention for that." He pointed toward the bruised knuckles, which were showing blood through the white handkerchief. "And I insist further that you send the bill to me."

"It isn't necessary," Burke declined, following after the man, wanting only one gift as long as the man was in a giving mood. "Mr. Sims!" he called out, halting the man in his laborious progress down the narrow stage stairs. "There is one favor you might perform for me, if you will. The young woman—I had hoped to inquire about her well-being—but she departed so rapidly. If you could supply me with her name and place of residence, I'd be most grateful."

Only then did he turn to confront the ashen face of Jeremy Sims, whose supply of gratitude apparently had just run dry.

"Oh, I couldn't possibly do that, Mr. Stanhope. It's quite out of the question, totally impossible, not to be considered."

His protest seemed excessive, and still he wasn't finished, his manner growing even more flustered as he commenced backing away. "No, no," he repeated, "not possible, not at all possible. You see, the terms of the agreement were—oh God, no. You must understand that it is not possible. Now, if you will excuse me, one of the waiters will fetch your carriage."

With that he was gone, making his way through the crowded tables as quickly as his girth would permit.

In astonishment, Burke watched the whole performance, amazed at the speed with which the normally blustery old proprietor had gone from a position of generosity to one of—what? Fear?

Why would the identity of the unique young woman cause fear, unless she was performing without someone's knowledge, a very important someone who could cause trouble for—

"Mr. Stanhope, your carriage, sir."

It was Henry, drawing near, appearing to view Burke with new respect. As the old man held his cloak, he whispered, "Good show, sir. It's been a long time since I've seen such forthright action. But as I told me mates, it's a shame a colonial had to do our fightin' for us."

Out on the dark rainy pavement, he saw his carriage waiting patiently. His driver hopped down from his high seat to open the door. "Quite a scuffle, was it, sir? According to the other blokes, it was rape, that's what it was."

"Nonsense," Burke scolded. "Just take us home the quickest way possible." He slammed the door behind him and settled back into the cushions, grateful for the dark privacy of his carriage.

So much for little Maria of the Mask. Of course she must have known that the drunken student would be stopped. So what was the risk? Convinced now that her innocence was as staged as everything else, Burke relaxed further against the cushions, his mind running in several directions: to the mansion in Mayfair, presided over by the madwoman; to the midday carriage departure tomorrow in the company of John Thadeus Delane and a fortnight's ordeal in the presence of that most offensive Englishman, John Murrey Eden; to the current column by Lord Ripples still in his typing machine, this time his target the hypocritical treatment of the Irish by the high-minded English Parliament; to that little five-year-old boy sprawled lazily in the corner of the broad cool portico, the Southern heat heavy upon him, the complete confidence that his world of grace, of sultry nights and pungent magnolias would last forever.

The discomfort of his injured hand increased, joined now by an ache at the base of his throat, his sense of homelessness growing.

The last image before he closed his eyes and gave himself completely to the rocking motion of the carriage was of a plume of lilacs nestling in the soft curve of two perfect breasts. . . .

It wasn't that Elizabeth hadn't known fear before; she'd known it plenty of times in her life. But apparently the security and peace of the last nine years at Eden Castle with John, where she was treated with as much dignity as the Countess Dowager, had made her soft.

Now eyeing Mary sitting calmly on the edge of her bed, chattering with Doris about the grim events of the evening, as though she had just returned from a fête, Elizabeth saw it again as though it were just happening. Then an image of John appeared before her, his reputation ruined, Mary's honor compromised, all brought on by—Elizabeth herself.

The perception was unbearable and she reached out for the mantelpiece in an attempt to steady her trembling hands.

Apparently Mary saw the weakness and smiled. "Doris, I think your mistress needs the tending. Look to her. I'm fine."

Incredulously Elizabeth asked, "Do you have no conception of what almost took place tonight?"

The question seemed to delight Mary, as though after the silent carriage ride home and the rapid ascent to her bedchamber on the second floor of the house at Number Seven, St. George Street, what she wanted most in the world was a chance to talk about the events of the evening. "Oh, nothing happened, Elizabeth," she soothed, one hand toying with the pearl clasps which held her long hair atop her head. She worried them loose; a shimmering cascade fell to her waist. She lifted her chin as though the weight of hair had pulled on her head. In the tumbling disarray the sprigs of lilacs fell into her lap. Gently she scooped them up. "Nothing at all happened," she repeated to the flowers, that maddeningly serene smile still on her face.

From the mantel Elizabeth watched the performance. And it *was* a performance. For the last nine years that she had known Mary Eden, and certainly for the last six when she had been assigned as her guardian, Elizabeth was aware that with the exception of a few unguarded moments, everything the young girl did was a performance. Her only reality was that of her imagination.

Through the gloom of the midnight room Elizabeth continued to watch her with a mixture of love and concern. And fear. At twenty-one the young woman was beautiful and growing more so. And more important than that, she was becoming aware of her beauty and even more aware of the mysterious power she could exert over people.

Averting her eyes from the object of her thoughts, Elizabeth was forced to confess that she too was a willing pawn. Had there been one occasion in the last six years when she'd pronounced a firm no to the young woman?

Oh, in the beginning she'd seen to it that Mary accomplished her lessons, the demands of the various tutors, and broadly speaking she had taken that shy little animal of thirteen who had grown up without a mother's love or a father's and had converted her into a polished, finished, beautifully groomed young woman. But for all her efforts, what was the result? A polished, finished, beautifully groomed little animal.

As though all at once to rectify the indulgences of the past, Elizabeth stepped forward. "Get dressed," she commanded, puzzled that the sight of Mary clothed only in her chemise annoyed her.

Mary looked up. "Dressed?" she asked, still fondling the lilacs.

"Yes, dressed. We're leaving for Eden tonight."

It was an insane suggestion, though the first protest came not from Mary but from Doris, the plump little maid who had served Elizabeth for over twenty years.

"Are you daft?" Doris exclaimed, speaking with an ease which normally pleased Elizabeth. She had never wanted a classic mistress/servant relationship. Her own murky beginnings precluded that.

But in the face of the blunt question, Elizabeth found herself longing for the submission of a true servant. "Not daft, Doris," she said, leaving the mantel in an attempt to stir the lethargic room into action. "I made a simple command. We are leaving for Eden tonight. See to the trunks. I'll inform Jason that we will require the large carriage, and—"

"See to the trunks!" Doris exploded. "There's a good six dozen gowns in that dressing room," she sputtered, "and as many bonnets and boots. And those are just Mary's."

Retreating, Elizabeth murmured, "Well, when can you be ready?"

"Sunday morn as planned," Doris said patly, her fleshy arms folded over her breasts in a stance of pure stubbornness.

Annoyed, but conceding that the woman was right, Elizabeth moved back to the mantel. It was while her back was turned that she heard Mary's voice.

"It's my fault, Doris," she said with mock contrition. "Poor Elizabeth just wants to whisk me out of London while my virginity is still intact."

The vulgarity only served to fan the fires of Elizabeth's anger. "At the rate you were going tonight, that loss may come sooner than you think and under circumstances that you may not find very pleasing, I can assure you," she snapped.

From where she stood she saw the young woman leave the bed. Her manner altered, became playful. As she stood at the center of the room, half-naked, she shook her long hair off her shoulders and proposed, "We'll let Doris be the judge of the seriousness of the evening. Agreed?"

Without waiting for a reply, she dragged the large chair to the center of the room, then pulled Doris forward who, giggling, sat on the edge, enjoying her role in the theatrical.

Once everything had been arranged to her satisfaction, Mary folded her hands before her. "Now, Doris," she began, her voice filled with glee, "there I was, center stage with hundreds of men watching me, singing that silly song about the woman looking for her lover's grave. . . . ."

Standing by the mantel, Elizabeth watched, annoyed, as Mary directed the entire theatrical, even commanding Doris to force her to her knees, which reluctantly the woman did, glancing back once at Elizabeth to see how the theatrical was being received.

But Doris was the only one concerned, for Mary apparently had fallen victim to the power of her own imagination and was now insisting that Doris tear her chemise.

"Right down the front, Doris—that's the way he did it, and I could feel his hands on my skin. Wet they were, and strong. Oh, tear it, Doris, just as he did."

Repelled though fascinated, Elizabeth had seen enough. "Stop it!" she commanded, reaching out in an attempt to bring Mary to her senses.

"No," Mary protested. "That's not the way it happened. The gentleman from the audience came next. He lifted the drunk and knocked him halfway across old Jeremy Sims' club. Oh, it was fun, Doris. You should have seen it."

"Stop it!" Elizabeth scolded sharply, sensing that the girl was on the thin edge of hysteria.

"And he was so nice," Mary went on, determined to re-enact the scene in full, beads of perspiration glistening on her forehead. "He looked down on me," she whispered, "but not at me directly. Oh, no, Doris, his main interest was my torn gown. Like this it was then." And because no one would tear her chemise, she performed the act herself, baring her breasts. "Oh, for ever so long he stared at me." She smiled. "I prayed he would lift me up and carry me away." In a spinning, rising gesture of rhapsody she whirled about, the chemise dropping completely free of her body, her arms outstretched, unmindful of her nakedness.

Shocked, Elizabeth tried again to halt the mad whirl about the room, her eye in the process falling on Doris' colorless face as she beat a safe retreat to the corner of the room.

But when after three commands the young girl didn't hear, Elizabeth forcibly caught the whirling shoulders and delivered a stinging slap to the side of the flushed face.

The spell was broken, but something else had taken its place. In the watery, hurt eyes that looked slowly up, Elizabeth saw something she'd never seen before, a need that was painfully deep and a frightening degree of hate for the one who had brought her back to the chamber of that house filled only with females.

Then both expressions were gone and there was a strange lifelessness on Mary's face as though the shock of the slap had been too great. Slowly she looked down at her wrists where Elizabeth held them together.

"No need."

Elizabeth released her, beginning to feel remorse. In all their years together she'd never struck Mary. Why had she done so now? With the need for apology heavy upon her, she lifted her hand to comfort.

Slowly Mary backed away, three red finger marks blazing on the side of that smooth cheek. Elizabeth watched her progress back to the bed, her hands reaching out, as though she were moving blindly through her humiliation.

When the tears came, they were scarcely recognizable, merely a low panting as though she were reaching deep inside for her last breath.

Incapable of watching such grief, and convinced that she had contributed to it, Elizabeth hurried to the bed, lifted the sobbing girl into her arms and held her close, the sobs not diminishing at the contact but increasing.

"Oh, I hurt, Elizabeth," she wept. "I hurt so much."

Elizabeth pressed Mary's head to her breast, understanding the hurt, but understanding as well the need for Mary to have the courage to face it. Yet how unfair. When Elizabeth had been Mary's age she had known dozens of men.

But Mary—

At the thought of her hopelessness, Elizabeth gathered the girl closer in her arms and with a nod of her head dismissed Doris, who already had seen too much. As the door closed, leaving them in private, Elizabeth commenced to rock gently, in an attempt to relieve the hurt and the emptiness.

"There," she whispered, kissing the nape of Mary's neck, smoothing back the long hair, wondering for both their sakes how long it could persist. How often she had spoken to John of the problem.

The girl is lovely. Men do look at her, and one day one will—

Then would come John's slow-rising anger, reminding Elizabeth that he had entrusted Mary to her, that she was to "keep her busy, refine her, keep her safe."

As the memory of those foolish words filled Elizabeth's head, Mary's sobs served as an appropriate counterpoint.

Keep her safe!

How was Elizabeth supposed to do that? No, it could not persist. As far as she could see, John had two options: either find a suitable husband immediately, or else place Mary under lock and key.

With effort, Elizabeth stood and released Mary to the custody of the pillow. "You must sleep now," she said, drawing the coverlet up over her.

Exhausted, Mary lay back, her eyes searching Elizabeth's face. "I love you so much," she whispered.

"And I, you."

"I'm sorry for what happened tonight," she murmured, a residue of tears clinging to her dark lashes. "I didn't mean to cause trouble."

"No need," Elizabeth smiled, stepping away from the bed. "However will we explain those red, swollen eyes to John?" she added bleakly, convinced now more than ever that Mary must be given over to someone else.

The separation would be painful for both of them. But it must come. With love and regret she looked down on

the bed. Then, before her feelings incapacitated her, she
left the room. . . .

Behind the red brick façade of the Stanhope mansion
in Mayfair, John Thadeus Delane looked about and realized with amusement that this London house probably
was the only surviving island of Southern American aris-
tocracy left in the world.

With the keen eye that had made him the great journalist and editor that he was, Delane sat in the elegant
first-floor reception room, awaiting the late appearance of
Burke Stanhope so that they might start their journey to
Eden Castle. Tempering his impatience, Delane settled
back in his chair, feeling fully his fifty-four years.

In the splintered peace of an uncertain future and a
glorious past, he released his journalist's eye and surveyed
this luxurious room. Through the opened door he saw the
servants, American Negroes, in white jackets and white
aprons, scrubbing, polishing.

Shifting his tall frame on the chair, Delane hoped that
he would be spared the mad Caroline this morning. Now
he mused anew over his affectionate relationship with this
sad, exiled family.

He had met Jack Stanhope first—when had it been?
Late forties, not long after Delane had taken over the
editorial reins of the *Times*. That summer he had journeyed to America and upon his request to be shown a
flourishing cotton plantation he had been escorted to the
magnificent Stanhope Hall outside Mobile, Alabama,
where Jack Stanhope and his then-beautiful Caroline had
greeted him with such hospitality that his intention to stay
a fortnight had stretched on into a month.

Burke had been only a little boy, running through the
high summer sun with his Negro companions, the best of
Jack, the best of Caroline, the sole heir to a profitable
though doomed world. Strange, but out of the three, Delane felt the greatest pity for Burke.

He heard a step at the door and swiveled around, expecting Burke. Instead the white-haired old Negro man
named Charles, who served as butler, stood before him,
silver coffee service in his hands.

"Mr. Burke sends his apologies," he said in that Southern drawl which Delane found so pleasing. "He says to
make yourself comfortable and not to steal all the silver."

As the old man poured coffee, Delane was aware of the twinkle in his eye and marveled at the humor, which in a true English household would not have been tolerated. Not that Delane condoned slavery, and not that he hadn't in the past had heated arguments with Jack Stanhope. Still, there was an enviable ease between these people and their servants, and when Jack had made the hard decision several years ago to leave his ill wife in London rather than subject her to the horror of destruction following the war, his problem had not been to force certain Negro servants to join her in a foreign city. His problem had been how to choose from among the seventy volunteers who wanted only to continue to serve her.

"Thank you, Charles." Delane smiled, taking the cup of coffee. "And tell Burke that if he's not down soon, the silver will still be intact, but my patience will be missing."

The old man was halfway to the door when Delane called out, "And Mrs. Stanhope? How is she this morning?"

A quick sorrow crossed the old man's face. "She's well, sir," he said, then added a curious contradiction. "Not well, is what I mean. But she's happy most all the time, and that's a blessing."

Then, as though he'd said enough, he left the room.

What in the hell was keeping Burke? They should have been on the road by now. In a way, he looked forward to this fortnight, this grand unveiling of the restored Eden Castle. How the gossip had flown about London coffeehouses for the past year, all directed toward London's financial wizard and master builder, John Murrey Eden. According to the most imaginative tongues, Eden had spared no expense in the renovation of his ancestral home. One wild report had it that the windowframes were made of solid gold, but Delane would have to see that for himself, along with several other promised treats such as the massive Alma-Tadema painting of "The Women of Eden," a project which had attracted the attention of the art world as well as the financial world of London.

It promised to be a circus and Delane wouldn't miss it for the world. When the heavy parchment invitation had come over two months ago, Delane had accepted without hesitation, and sensing good journalistic sport, he had requested permission to bring along his young American friend. The request had been granted, and with delight

Delane had lived with the secret knowledge that he would be escorting Lord Ripples himself into the very bastion of British aggression, arrogance, and cunning.

"Lord!" Delane gasped, grinning. What sport it would be!

He strode the length of the reception room, searching the door eagerly for his protégé. What sane journalist would have done otherwise with a brilliant, natural-born writer, educated at William and Mary, trained to take over a world that no longer existed? Put him to work, of course, which is precisely what Delane had done, although in the beginning even he could not have predicted the success of the Lord Ripples column.

Smiling, Delane sat on the back of the sofa, studying the pools of sunshine eddying at his feet. There! He heard a noise outside the door and went eagerly forward, only to halt after three steps. It was not Burke. Instead an apparition in a pale yellow dressing gown slipped around the corner like a trailing cloud, her parchmentlike skin blending with the wispy folds of yellow silk, her emaciated body lost somewhere in the vapor. In her blue-veined hand she held a lace handkerchief which she waved before her face as though to rid the room of a noxious odor. In the process she saw him and drew sharply back, her eyes reflecting her fear.

"Caroline, no need. It's me," he soothed and stepped forward, aware that behind that white hair was a brain that had shut down on all images save pleasant ones.

Delane still remembered the day not long after the Southern surrender when an embittered Jack Stanhope had come to his office and had informed him of Caroline's "illness." And since Jack had had no idea of what conditions he would find on his return home, he was leaving his wife in the Mayfair mansion under the protective custody of his son Burke, and as soon as he could reconstruct their world he would send for both of them.

Delane had offered to look out for them. In spite of the differences in their ages, he considered Burke Stanhope a surrogate son as well as a fascinating companion. As for the ruin that was Caroline Stanhope, there was little he could do except be loving and polite and play her games with her.

He looked up and saw her standing just inside the door. Then came words, the floating image moving closer. "Is that you, John Thadeus Delane?" She smiled, the voice trailing off in soft Southern speech, the head turned demurely to one side, as though somewhere within the dead husk the young Southern woman was still alive and flourishing.

"At your service." Delane smiled.

"Well, my sweet stars!" Caroline gasped. "Now, why didn't Jack Stanhope tell me you were coming? Isn't that just like the man, to leave me to discover my houseguest wandering disconsolately through my front parlor?"

"I wasn't wandering, Caroline." He smiled lovingly down on her. "I just stopped by to call for Burke. We are leaving today for—"

She backed away as though a false note had sounded in her head. "Burke?" she puzzled. "Why, I think he took off riding for Mobile this morning. Did he know you were calling for him? He's really such a rude boy on occasion."

As her voice drifted, she commenced moving through the room, her lace handkerchief trailing over the mahogony furniture. He watched her, all the time keeping his ear turned toward the door, praying that Burke would arrive soon.

From the corner of the room, in a blaze of morning sun, she turned abruptly. "It's a disgrace," she began, "that the soldiers should be allowed to behave like this. It makes a bad impression on our visitors."

Struggling to keep up with the twists of her mind, Delane followed as far as the center of the large room. "What soldiers, Caroline?" he asked, knowing in advance that he might or might not receive an answer.

"Would you like coffee?" she asked.

"Charles has served me. And you, may I pour you a—"

Her eyes suddenly filled with worry. "Did you see Jack Stanhope when you were in Mobile this morning?" she asked.

"No. I—"

"He told me he was going to meet you there. He has such admiration for the English. He's really very fond of you, you know. Did I tell you, Mr. Delane," she called from the sideboard where she was pouring a glass of sherry, "that the prevailing dream of Jack Stanhope is to make his way to England and there to become an honored citizen?"

Delane laughed. "I doubt that, Caroline. The South and

Stanhope Hall mean far too much to him. He would never
be happy."

"It's true," she whispered. "Sometimes I have a nightmare. I see myself on a cold rainy street and I'm all
alone, quite alone, so cold, alone and so cold—"

"You're not alone, Caroline," he soothed. "You have
friends."

"Who?" she demanded.

"Myself for one." He smiled, taking the glass of sherry
from her hand before she spilled it.

"Did I show you what I've done in the rose garden?"
With a mercurial change of mood, she was on her feet,
her loneliness forgotten, tugging on his hand for him to
join her.

"Come, Mr. Delane, the darkies and I have been working for days to surprise you." She walked a few steps away
to the window where suddenly she bowed her head.
"Don't you agree, Mr. Delane," she began, her voice
floating, "that Stanhope Hall is the most beautiful place
on earth?"

He followed her line of vision out of the window and
saw only the gray pavement, wet from the early-morning
rain, and the endless red bricks of Mayfair and his own
carriage waiting at the curb.

Where in the hell is Burke?

"Of course you are planning to stay with us for a while,
aren't you, Mr. Delane? I can't bear it when visitors come
for just a week or two. Please say that you will stay with
us until Christmas."

"I don't know, Caroline."

"Of course you will. I won't hear otherwise."

She turned away, one hand pressed against her forehead as though in an attempt to contain the confusion
within. "How many times I've told Burke—" As she
passed by the sofa she spied the silver service on the low
table, sat primly on the edge of the sofa and poured a cup.

"Does Burke—have a lover, Mr. Delane?" she asked
politely.

Taken aback by the question, Delane laughed. "I'm
sure I don't know, Caroline. I'm afraid you will have to
ask Burke."

"Oh, I have," she said, smiling over the rim of her coffee
cup. "I know he doesn't have a wife, but I suppose he has
mistresses, plenty of them. A boy that good-looking—"

Suffering embarrassment, Delane looked back toward the door.

"Mr. Delane, I want you to promise me one thing. You must promise me that you will talk to Burke—"

"About what?"

"Tell him that he must never leave me, that he will kill me if he does." She was trembling, her thin arms wrapped about her.

"Caroline, please," Delane begged.

"No, you must listen to me!" she pleaded, gripping his arm with surprising strength. "I know what he's up to. Every night he rides away from here. I have spies working for me and they report back. They tell me that on occasion he journeys as far as Mobile for his whores—"

Delane wanted to move away but she continued to grasp his arm. "Please," she begged, "tell him that I can abide whores. But tell him what I cannot and will not abide is a wife. Tell him that for me, Mr. Delane. We must not have a wife here. No, no, never. No wife, no wife; not for Burke, no!"

Then at last, blessedly, he heard it, a firm step on the stairs. And in the next minute Burke was at the door, lines of fatigue creasing his face, as though he'd slept too hard or not enough.

"Ah, Delane . . ." He smiled, adjusting his gray waistcoat. But the smile faded as he caught sight of his mother.

Delane looked back at Caroline, expecting a reaction from her. But there was nothing. She sat on the sofa, her hands lying idly in her lap, a tuneless humming escaping from her lips.

He glanced up at Burke in time to see the small death on his face, as though he'd hoped to make his escape unnoticed. "Sorry I was delayed," he muttered, heading toward the drifting woman.

Delane watched as Burke knelt before his mother and took her hands between his own. He noticed the knuckles on Burke's right hand. Bruised they were, red and scraped. Obviously the young man had passed an eventful night.

Well, Delane was certain he'd hear all about it during the journey to Eden Castle. For now, he watched in sad fascination the scene between mother and son.

"I'm leaving now," Burke said, above the tuneless humming. "I'll be away for a fortnight, but Charles knows where to reach me—if you need me—"

Still no response from the humming woman. If she was even aware of her son kneeling before her, she gave no indication of it.

"Mother, did you hear me? I said I was leaving now. Promise me you'll be good and do as Florence says."

Slowly Burke stood and straightened himself. "She's worse," he commented quietly.

"Come," Delane murmured. "We should have been on the road an hour—"

Burke nodded, still standing over her, his eyes dark with worry. As he drew on his gloves, he frowned as though his injured hand had caused his discomfort. He tried once more. "Mother, can you hear me? I'm leaving now."

But still there was nothing from the humming woman except for a small smile that was vaguely triumphant as though she were pleased by his worry.

Then Burke turned about. "Again, sorry to have kept you waiting, Delane," he said, as he led the way to the door.

But as they were starting out into the entrance hall, words evolved out of that soft humming. "If you see your father on the road, Burke, please send him to me. Tell him that Caroline needs him. Tell him that she is alone—"

From where Delane stood it looked as though weight had just been lowered against Burke's neck. Without a word and as though eager to put distance between himself and the house in Mayfair, he led the way down to the pavement, hoisted his valise up to Delane's coachman and crawled inside the carriage.

Delane followed, his heart going out to the young man, wondering briefly about the limits of servitude that a father could legitimately place on a son. The last letter that Delane had received from Jack Stanhope had been well over a year ago. It had come from a hotel in Mobile and had stated that it would be best for Burke and Caroline to remain in London. Indefinitely. Of course they were well provided for. Sensing the coming hostilities a decade ago, Jack Stanhope had transferred a large portion of his fortune into foreign investments, a valuable portfolio that Burke had increased with skill and cunning.

As the carriage pulled away from the curb, Delane

watched his friend in the seat opposite him, his eyes closed. It was too long a silence. Yet Delane reproached himself about speaking first. He had planned to take advantage of the journey to Eden to inform Burke of specifics regarding John Murrey Eden and the relationships of the people he would meet at the Eden Festivities. But there would be time enough for talk later. For now, let the silence persist as long as Burke saw fit. Let him deal with his private grief in his own way.

Delane was certain of one thing. It would be an invigorating fortnight, filled with good food, good wine, beautiful women and elegant surroundings. And at the end of those two weeks, it was his considered opinion that Burke Stanhope and John Murrey Eden would either be fast friends or the bitterest of enemies.

Either way, Delane and the *Times* would serve to benefit.

Still disturbed by the memory of his mother, Burke glanced out the carriage window at Windsor in the distance.

Across from him, he was aware of Delane maintaining an unusually long silence. But Burke was not yet ready for words, his mind and heart still occupied with the last image he'd had of his mother. He knew that she disliked his prolonged absences.

And the overriding question in his mind was how long would his imprisonment persist? And worse than that was his ever-growing suspicion that his father would never send for them, would never release him to a life of his own. Jack Stanhope's letters were coming few and far between now, and when one did arrive, it presented a grim picture of corruption, rising prices in construction, scorched fields which seemed to refuse new crops, and primitive living conditions which would surely kill his mother. "But soon," the letters always concluded.

Soon, Burke brooded with rising anger. Each letter was scrawled on the elegant stationery of the Imperial Hotel in Mobile where, Burke suspected, his father was living in irresponsible luxury.

Without warning, Burke felt a mild discomfort in his right hand and looked down, surprised to see his hand a fist and that fist pressing with undue strength into the seat cushion. He tried to relax and examined the bruised flesh

of his right hand and recalled the beautiful little Maria of
the Mask to whose aid he had rushed last night.

The thought that he would never see her again was a
deprivation that he was ill-equipped to meet, and he
pressed his head back against the cushion and closed his
eyes.

"Are you well, Burke?" Delane inquired, the first words
of this infant journey, but significant in that they spelled
the end of the silence.

"Not well, Delane," Burke told him honestly, "but
functioning."

He took note of his old friend across the way. Indulging
in an old perception, it occurred to Burke that there was
his true father, a highly intelligent substitute to take the
place of that distant and undoubtedly drunken truant.

Under the effect of these thoughts, he sat up from his
slouched position and vowed to give Delane what he
wanted, a good conversation.

But as he commenced to sort through his mind in
search of a suitable topic, Delane sat forward. "Your
mother, Burke," he began, unaware that it was the last
subject in the world that Burke wanted to discuss, "she *is*
worse."

"I know."

"What you don't know is that she was talking quite
volubly before you came in."

This *was* surprising news. "What was she saying?"

"It was incoherent, most of it. She mentioned your
father. And you—she mentioned you as well—said that
you had ridden to Mobile in search of whores."

Burke saw the sly smile on Delane's face and at first
was not certain if the man was speaking the truth. Before
he could inquire, Delane asked, "Were you?"

"Was I what?"

"Searching for whores in Mobile last night."

"Not likely," Burke said, glancing out the window at
the passing countryside, "except perhaps in my imagination."

"It wasn't your imagination that left you with a bruised
hand, was it?"

Bemused, Burke realized that the old journalist was as
curious as a scandal sheet tattler. "No," he said, "this is
a badge of honor."

Briefly he recounted the events of the night before.

"How dramatic!" Delane smiled. "I wish I could have seen it firsthand. And what favor did the lady give you for your troubles?"

"Nothing," Burke confessed. "By the time I went to collect she was gone."

"Ungrateful wench."

"She's quite remarkable, Delane—"

"I'm sure of it."

"—though I'll probably never see her again."

"Sad."

"She is so—"

"Beautiful?"

"More than beautiful."

"More than beautiful?" Delane repeated, clearly baiting.

Embarrassed, Burke fell silent.

"So you *were* in pursuit of a whore last night!" Delane smiled.

"She's not a whore, Delane. In fact I doubt seriously if a man has ever touched her."

Delane laughed heartily. "Burke, how can you be so naive? Any female who parades herself before a club filled with gentlemen knows precisely what she is doing and how to do it."

"Not this one."

Again Delane laughed. "Lord, I wish I had been there! A true virgin is a rare sight these days."

Burke took note of the grinning face and decided to drop the subject, a bit regretful that he had brought it up in the first place. He felt like a schoolboy confessing his first love. It had been a private interlude in his life, but apparently it was not a memory to be shared, and now Burke hoped Delane would leave it alone.

Outside the window he saw the outskirts of the approach to Reading, and in his mind's eye he projected the journey yet ahead of them, all the way to the edge of England and the North Devon coast. In an attempt to turn his thoughts to the ordeal ahead, he asked quietly, "And tell me of John Murrey Eden. . . ."

Across the way, Delane shifted his position as though the cramped interior of the carriage were already beginning to bother him. "What's to tell?" He smiled with suspect innocence.

"Oh, come now, Delane," Burke scolded, "this is not a

pleasure trip and you know it! Apparently I'm to ferret something out at Eden Castle, and you can make my job a lot easier if you at least give me—"

The very picture of wounded self-righteousness, Delane lifted his hands in mock protest. "Really, Burke, what a suspicious mind you possess. Here I invite you to join me in what well may be the social event of the year, and what do I get for my troubles? Suspicion, doubt and accusations of deception."

Burke waited out the performance, amused by the protest, a talent which had turned John Thadeus Delane into the awesome journalist that he was, disarming sources which ranged from Lord Russell to Benjamin Disraeli to Lord Aberdeen with that same wide-eyed protest of innocence.

Well, it might work on those distinguished gentlemen, but not on Burke, who had known Delane too long and who had learned at his knee those selfsame tricks. In response to the façade of innocence, Burke rephrased his initial question. "What precisely is it that you want Lord Ripples to search out in John Murrey Eden's outpost castle?"

Delane's expression changed; the façade dropped away and only the glint of the journalist's eye remained. "Anything. Everything that strikes you as being of uncommon interest."

"For what purpose?" Burke prodded further. "Are we to bring Mr. Eden down or raise him up?"

"Neither. He's too powerful for us to do either."

"Then what's the point?"

Delane smiled. "Curiosity, Burke, that's all."

"Yours?"

"Mine and that of the sixty-five thousand readers of the *Times*." He leaned forward, warming to the subject. "You see, for all we know of John Murrey Eden, he still essentially is a man of mystery."

"In what way?"

"In every way," Delane retorted, as though mystery were the one thing a good journalist could not abide. "He appeared ten, twelve years ago, literally out of the ether, at an obscenely young age—"

"How young?"

Delane shrugged. "Scarcely twenty, at that time."

"Is youth a crime?"

"Not in itself, no. But for the pup to shake the Royal Exchange as though it were his private toy and launch forth into a series of building projects—on borrowed money, I might add."

"Still, what's the offense?" Burke persisted.

There was a pause. Delane said quietly, "No offense, except that he succeeded."

Burke stared out the window. "How dare he?" He smiled, amused and intrigued. "But so far you have told me exactly nothing," he went on, facing Delane. "Where did he come from, this man who has offended by succeeding?"

Delane adopted a mask of cooperation as though only too willing to share his limited knowledge. "Initially, no one knows for certain. Reliable sources informed me several years ago that he was the bastard son of the philanthropist Edward Eden, of whom I'm sure you have heard."

No, Burke hadn't heard of Edward Eden and he wasn't interested. It wasn't the father who was the object of this journey, but rather the son.

"And when Edward Eden was killed—"

"How killed?"

"An accident of some sort," Delane said, vaguely waving his hand in the air. "The boy John was sent to live with his uncle at Eden Castle."

Delane paused. Burke watched him, still not certain why Eden had been singled out as an object of Delane's journalistic zeal. Men made fortunes daily in America and were not punished for having done so. Was it some dictate of the English class system which frowned on bastards overstepping their bounds?

As though coming back to himself, Delane lifted his hands and smoothed back his thinning hair. "Oh, God, it's a muddle! For some reason he was exiled from Eden."

"For some reason?" Burke repeated, surprised at Delane's vagueness.

"I swear that I've never been able to find out why."

"And you've tried?"

Delane smiled. "John Murrey Eden has been my avocation for the past eight years."

"Why?"

Delane seemed loath to respond immediately, and when in the next minute he gruffly dismissed the question with, "My motivations are not important," Burke suspected that he had two mysteries on his hands, and that the solution of one was directly related to the solution of the other.

"Go on. After Eden's exile from North Devon, where did he go?"

"To London," Delane replied eagerly, as though grateful to be back on track, "where he lived with a woman named Elizabeth, who in turn had lived with his father, Edward Eden."

"Was she his mother?"

"No—or at least she's denied it repeatedly."

"You've asked?"

"My sources have. Several times."

Burke ran his fingers over his bruised knuckles, amused at how effortlessly they kept losing John Murrey Eden.

"And after the woman named Elizabeth?" Burke went on, trying to nail down the elusive Mr. Eden.

"Well, he did a turn in the Crimea as first assistant to Mr. Thomas Brassey, though there was a falling out there as well, a disagreement which sent Brassey back to London, and John Murrey Eden to India."

His fascination mounting, Burke mused, "India. About the mid-fifties? I shouldn't think that that would have been a particularly pleasant place to be."

Delane agreed. "He was there during the Mutinies and, according to my sources, just barely escaped with his life."

"Did he go to India with the military?"

Delane laughed. "Not likely. To this day his most offensive statements concern the British military."

"Then what *was* he doing in India?"

The blank expression on Delane's face was not encouraging. "Then after India, what?" Burke persisted. "Did he return to Eden?"

Delane shook his head. "No. According to my sources he took up residence with Elizabeth again." His mind seemed to drift again. "A unique woman, this Elizabeth," he murmured, his hands folded before him, his eyes fixed on the carriage floor.

Respectful of this new mood, Burke waited before questioning on. When still Delane seemed locked in some past reflection, Burke prodded, "How unique, this Elizabeth?"

"In the way that any woman is unique," Delane said simply, and was content to let it go at that.

But Burke was not content to let it go. "Oh, come now, Delane," he chided. "I'm not a schoolboy. Such a pause deserves explanation. I repeat, how was the woman Elizabeth unique? Did you know her?"

The question seemed to hang unanswered on the air. At last, as though honesty were a habit which it was hard to break, he saw Delane nod.

So! Somehow there was a connection to be made between Delane and the woman named Elizabeth. Warming to his role as sleuth, and having wondered for years, along with every other scribbler along Fleet Street, what John Thadeus Delane did with the excess sexual energy provided him by an ill and constantly hospitalized wife, Burke leaned forward. "You *did* know her, didn't you, Delane?"

"Know her?" Delane repeated, his voice scarcely audible above the rattle of the carriage, "Of course I knew her! At one point even fancied myself in love with her."

"Go on," Burke invited, respectful of the confession and the new mood within the carriage.

But abruptly Delane shook his head. "Nothing more to tell," he snapped. "She had been a prostitute in younger days, though quite respectable when I knew her. She was living in a fine house in St. George Street which had been given to her by Lord Kimbrough—"

The name was lost on Burke, though the reality behind such a generous gift was not.

"—and she was presiding over one of the most glittering salons in all of London."

"And you were a member of that salon, I take it," Burke probed.

"I was," Delane admitted, "and I can't tell you what it meant to me, meant to all of us, to know that there was a safe harbor waiting for us each evening, presided over by one of the most generous hearts it has ever been my good fortune to know."

"Go on," Burke insisted, feeling his affection for the man vault under the effects of this confession of frailty.

But the storyteller had reached the end of his tale.

"Nothing more to say," Delane said gruffly. "One evening the salon was opened to us and the next evening it was closed. All we heard was that the boy whom she had raised as her son had returned."

His voice fell silent. His eyes lifted to the ceiling of the carriage, then closed. "God, she was so beautiful," he mourned. "Difficult to describe, the manner in which she—she made everyone feel so—as though you were the only one—an inner harmony and goodness that was so surprising. Not educated, not formally, but perfectly refined, as though—"

Ultimately his incoherency took a toll and left him looking exhausted. Out of love and respect Burke waited, knowing all too well the pleasurable torment that was plaguing his friend. So! John Thadeus Delane *had* been in love, and now, ten years later, he was curious to the point of obsession about the young man who had wandered back to England from India and who had shut down the only source of love and warmth in Delane's life.

Burke was now as curious as Delane himself. Women did not easily break the patterns of their lives, as witness his own mother. "Will she be there?" he asked. "At Eden, I mean."

The direct question served its purpose. Delane looked up. "I don't know," he murmured. "Oh, I'm sure of it. But perhaps not. . . ."

As the incoherency persisted, Burke fought back a smile at seeing the normally disciplined man so undone, and endeavored to move on to other, safer subjects. "Whom else can we expect to find at Eden?" he asked. "Is there a wife for John Murrey Eden?"

"Indeed there is. Her name is Lady Lila Harrington."

"Titled?"

Delane nodded. "Her father is Lord Liam Harrington, who about twenty years ago made a jackal of himself by pleading for the Irish Cause from the floor of the House of Commons."

"Why a jackal?"

"Oh, for God's sake, Burke, don't show your American colors so readily!" It was a lighthearted reprimand and Burke ignored it.

"Any children?"

Delane hesitated. "Two, I think, or maybe three." He shook his head. "I've lost count and information does not flow readily out of Eden. A reporter sniffing out news is frequently met with a double-grilled gate."

Burke smiled. "Is that to keep the world out or the inhabitants of Eden in?"

"A bit of both, I suppose," Delane said. "Clearly John Murrey Eden has drawn a line of separation between his public life in London and his private life at Eden."

"I would scarcely call a fortnight of public display private."

"That's just the point." Delane smiled. "We can only assume that he is ready for us to see something, can't we?"

"And whom else might we find at Eden?" Burke asked.

"Lady Lila's father, Lord Harrington, I believe is in residence at Eden."

"No wife for Lord Harrington?"

"Dead. Eden moved him into the castle shortly after the funeral."

"A generous gesture, I would say, on the part of the son-in-law."

"Oh, he can be generous, Burke, to a fault," Delane conceded. "He looks after his various building crews of over five thousand workmen as though they were his children and, of course, in return they give him the best efforts of any workshop in London, plus large quantities of loyalty and affection thrown in. But"—and there was an ominous pause—"he can be a bastard as well. Ask anyone who has had the misfortune to fall on the wrong side of him."

"I'd like to know. Who would that be?"

"They're not around for long," Delane said. "There was an old solicitor, Morley Johnson, whom Eden accused of embezzling large portions of the Eden estate. Instead of bringing the case to trial, Eden systematically set out to ruin the man." Delane bowed his head. "The last I heard his family was in the workhouse near Croyden. About six years ago, unable to earn a living, Morley Johnson committed suicide."

The grim recital cast a new mood inside the carriage. "But there are others who enjoy the protection of Eden.

For one, there is a most mysterious Countess Dowager, Lady Harriet Eden, the wife of Lord James Eden, now dead, who was brother to John's father, Edward. . . ."

As the confusion of relationships filled the carriage, Burke took a brief respite by gazing out of the window, enjoying the clear fresh air. He was aware of Delane talking on, but it was not until he heard the incredible words, "She's blind now, the result of self-mutilation," that Burke turned his attention back to the grisly announcement.

"She's *what?*"

"Blind."

"Why?" Burke stammered, trying to deal with the macabre image of a noblewoman blinding herself.

But the answer was predictable. "No one knows," Delane admitted. "And there's more. There is an Indian woman whom Eden freely flaunts as his mistress, who, according to gossip, lacks a tongue."

Burke felt an element of disbelief sweep over him. Surely Delane was inventing all of this. "I don't—believe—"

"And that is truth, as well," Delane insisted. "Eden himself has told the story many times, in the presence of witnesses, about how the woman and her son helped him escape the Mutinies by lying to her own people. They cut out her tongue and sent her back to him, and as a debt of gratitude he has vowed to care for her and her son for the rest of her life."

As the bizarre story filled the carriage, Burke leaned forward, not wanting to miss a word. It was clear that John Murrey Eden had passed through crucibles which would have destroyed a lesser man. As a thousand questions filled his head, he found that he could only give voice to one. "A son, you say?"

"Indeed. A bright lad, about eighteen, on whom Eden dotes. He has seen to his education and has publicly proclaimed that the Indian boy will be his heir, or at least one of them."

Burke shook his head.

"And there's more." Delane grinned, pleased with the effect of his story. "Eden has two cousins, the offspring of Lady Harriet and Lord James Eden; a young woman, Lady Mary Eden, about whom we know absolutely nothing, and the present Lord of Eden Castle,

Lord Richard, Fifteenth Baron and Seventh Earl, who for the last few years has served as Professor of Theology at Magdalene College, Cambridge, a brilliant and respected scholar who has published two books."

Burke smiled wryly. "The white sheep of the family."

Delane shared the joke. "He lives in Cambridge, though I'm certain he'll be present for the Festivities."

"He exerts no control over his own inheritance?"

"There was no inheritance," Delane said, "except for the title itself. After the death of his father, the estate fell into the questionable hands of the solicitor, and by the time John Murrey Eden had amassed his first fortune, the estates were gone except for the castle itself, the Eden family facing bankruptcy."

Out of the particulars of the tale, a fascinating conclusion was beginning to take shape inside Burke's mind: the bastard son returning triumphantly with enough coin in his pocket to rescue the family seat and restore the castle. What a debt they all must owe to him!

But before he drew any conclusions, he looked across at Delane in an attempt to discern if there were any other chapters to the story.

Delane shook his head. "That's all I know, Burke. There is, of course, a vast army of devoted staff, and a solicitor named Andrew Rhoades. And there is an ox of a man named Alex Aldwell, who serves as Eden's bodyguard."

Again he leaned back, shifted to the center of the cushion and braced his hands on either side. "All that the public knows now is that Eden Castle has been renovated and restored, that the labor has occupied the better part of his energies for the last eight years, and that for the first time the gates of Eden will be thrown open to the most distinguished guest list of the century, including a representative of every titled family in the kingdom, large portions of both the House of Lords and the House of Commons, the Lord Mayor, who will appear as emissary from the Queen and several members of the Royal Academy, whose interests will focus not so much on the castle as on the highly secretive Alma-Tadema painting of 'The Women of Eden.' "

" 'The Women of Eden,' " Burke mused. "All of them?"

Delane shook his head. "According to my spies, only

four. The Indian woman named Dhari; Elizabeth; Lady Mary, Eden's cousin; and Lady Lila, Eden's wife."

"Are they beauties all?"

"Under Alma-Tadema's brush I'm sure they will be," Delane replied. "And I understand the canvas is immense, the pose most unorthodox."

Burke started to inquire how unorthodox, but changed his mind. He would see soon enough, and now found himself impatiently looking forward to their arrival at Eden Castle. Whatever the coming fortnight would be, it would not be dull. Burke smiled. "Then I'm to snoop—"

"—to your heart's content."

"—without causing offense, of course."

A sly smile crossed Delane's face. "You won't cause offense. Americans are expected to snoop. The English view it as part of their basic lack of breeding."

Again Burke refused to rise to the bait, although coming from anyone other than Delane he might have been tempted to do so.

As Delane described the beauties of the West Country, Burke leaned back into the cushions, his head spinning with certain specifics.

She's blind as a result of self-mutilation.

They cut out her tongue.

He closed his eyes and felt a curious unease, as though the torment of John Murrey Eden's life had invaded his own. Surely the man suffered from a battering isolation and loneliness. In this unexpected perception, Burke felt that at that moment he understood John Murrey Eden better than any man had a right to understand another.

"Burke?"

It was Delane, searching for a way into his silence.

But for a few additional moments, Burke kept all the doors locked, sensing falsely—he knew that much—that John Murrey Eden was in his power now. The scale of balance had been tipped in Burke's understanding of Eden's loneliness.

The advantage was all his. . . .

Eden Castle
North Devon
May 10, 1870

SUFFERING A DEEP dread, Lila Harrington Eden prepared herself to receive her husband. Seated before her dressing table, she glanced up at the clock on the mantel. A quarter to ten. Fifteen minutes to clear the maids from her chambers, to loosen her hair and conquer the fear which plagued her.

As her blond hair tumbled about her shoulders, she tried to soothe herself with rational thoughts. He wanted another child. Otherwise he would not impose himself upon her: The only times in nine years of marriage when she'd had to endure this hideous act had been when John had approached her politely and asked for a child.

"There, milady. The bed is prepared. Anything else?"

Struggling, she brought her eyes into focus on the reflected image of Molly, the lady's maid, who had seen her through two births and four miscarriages, and who knew better than anyone what John's repeated late-night visits to these chambers meant.

The sympathy that Lila saw in Molly's eyes almost undid her. She reached behind her and felt Molly grasp her hand.

"It's a wife's duty, milady," she whispered. "And think of the pretty babe that you will give to Mr. Eden to go with those two handsome little boys."

Lila nodded and thought of her two sons, ages four and two. Stephen and Frederick, the most beautiful children she'd ever seen. How she loved them, and what joy she had felt when she'd witnessed the pride in John's eyes! And she didn't object to the swelling pregnancies; she didn't even object to the pain of childbirth.

There was only one fear, when her maids would leave her, when she would wait for the sound of that footstep which at any other hour of the day was capable of filling her heart with joyful anticipation.

39

As she bowed her head against the realization of what was ahead of her, Molly leaned closer. "Be strong, milady," she whispered. "Close your eyes and think on God."

Embarrassed, Lila refrained from telling Molly that she had followed her advice every night for the last two months and that God, instead of seeing her through it, had deserted her altogether.

She lifted her head in an attempt to demonstrate to Molly that she was well, although the moment the room was empty she felt ill. There was a knife turning within her. She grasped the edge of the dressing table and held on until the room grew steady.

Seated alone, the lamps turned low, she tried desperately to fall back on her imagination, the flights of fantasy that had saved her from madness when John had first led her to the marital bed several years ago.

Without warning a deep shudder ran through her and she wrapped her arms about her in an attempt to warm herself against the coming ordeal, sick with the knowledge that she was no more prepared for it now than she had been when John had first approached and filled her with terror, with the literal fear that he was trying to kill her.

Of course she knew better now, knew perfectly well the point and purpose of the act, knew that it must be performed nightly until she conceived. She gave in to a soft moan and left the dressing table and went to the window, which in daylight afforded her a view of the headlands, but which at night spread before her like an abyss.

"Wolf?" she called, hearing the trembling in her voice. She looked about in the shadowy room for her cat, generally a source of comfort, but she couldn't find him and knew that he'd probably run out of the room with the maids.

In increasing desperation she thought of her father so far away in the west wing, undoubtedly content in a game of cards with Andrew Rhoades. Once, after the third miscarriage, she had turned to him with a plea to talk to John. But her father had scolded her, had informed her that she was no longer a child, that she was a wife now, and that instead of trying to avoid wifely duties, she should go down on her knees and thank God for sending her a husband as generous as John Murrey Eden.

The remembrance of that paternal reprimand caused her to bow her head in an imitation of prayer. She *was* grateful and God knew that, but why was God withholding another child from her? Why after two months had she not yet conceived?

Suddenly she could bear it no longer and went down on her knees, trying to control the fear which was building within her. She *did* love him; she *did* adore her children; she *did* revel in her life here at Eden. Then what was the matter with her? Why could she not endure this most basic act between husband and wife? According to Elizabeth some women enjoyed it as much as the male.

At this incomprehensible thought, she tried to wipe the tears from her eyes and slowly pulled herself to her feet. She didn't want him to find her weak and weeping.

This show of bravado sustained her as she went about the chamber, extinguishing the lamps. He preferred that the room be black. She heard his step in the corridor.

Outside the door the footsteps stopped. Poised by the side of the bed, she fought down a rising nausea. "Please help me!" she prayed quickly.

In blackness she sat on the edge of the bed, aware of the pain increasing. She mustn't let him see, mustn't let him know, and she shut her eyes tightly, creating a double darkness, and tried to send her mind away to the edge of the ocean, to that beautiful vista of salt spray and sunlight that she'd seen only this afternoon in the little cove at the bottom of the cliff.

With a surge of joy she realized that it was working. For the first time in months she felt herself leave the bed and run along the headlands, searching the tall grasses for her private path which led down to the ocean. Even Wolf was with her again, the high May sun shimmering across his gray fur.

"Lila—"

Who had spoken her name? Whose hands were moving down the front of her dressing gown?

"Wolf, look," she called, ignoring the hands. Quickly she scrambled over the side of the cliff, pointing out for Wolf's benefit the fishing boats just making their way back to the safety of the harbor.

"If we hurry," she whispered, "they will throw you a fat herring. Run, Wolf—I'll catch up."

As she slipped down the side of the cliff, she felt a sudden chill, as though her body had been laid bare. Someone was speaking to her out of the darkness, but she preferred to listen to the whistle of the wind, to feel the feathery sensation of the grasses blowing against her ankles.

Someone was coming closer, the dark of the room alternating now with brilliant sunlight.

"Wolf, please wait," she called, trying to retain the sunlight.

"Lila—"

No, that voice had not been with her on her afternoon walk, and it had no place here now. She would have to outrun it, and outrun as well the rustle of a robe being discarded, the sensation of hands touching her breasts.

"Wolf, be careful; you'll get wet!" she cried as the massive cat chased the waves that broke on the beach near the small cove. "I'll race you to the quay."

What was that weight crushing her? There had been no weight on the beach this afternoon.

There! She was almost to the bottom of the cliff now, feasting her eyes on the clean, wave-swept little cove that was her private domain. No one else ever came here except Wolf.

"Wolf, find a seashell for me, one that contains the ocean—"

Oh, it hurt, the pressure inside her.

"Run, Wolf, run while you can. I'll try to catch up."

"Lila, please—"

Her breathing stopped. She felt crippled, her legs useless, the weight on her midsection increasing, something drilling into her flesh, the entire weight jerking involuntarily from time to time while she, with a desperation born of terror, tried to follow after Wolf down the long, clean, white expanse of sand.

But she couldn't move, and as the pain increased, she opened her eyes to the blackness of her bedchamber, and in an attempt to keep from crying out, she pressed her fist against her lips until she tasted blood. . . .

John completed the act as quickly as possible, aware as always that he was causing pain. After one convulsion he separated himself from her, drew on his robe, fumbled in the dark for the lamp and looked down on the sight which had greeted him every night for the last two months.

My wife, he thought angrily. What wife? It was getting worse, leaving him with the guilty feeling that he had raped a child.

In spite of his disappointment he drew the folds of her dressing gown over her and tried to focus on her face. "Lila . . ." he began, trying to ease her fear. But with the exception of the tears rolling down into her hair, nothing moved. She might have been a statue, sculpted in a position of consummate terror. With tenderness he tried to withdraw her hand from her mouth, but she was rigid to his touch, as though at some point during intercourse death had occurred.

In despair, John turned away and sat on the side of the bed. He *did* love her, reveled in her sweet beauty during the daylight hours, counted her gift to him of two sons to be among his most prized possessions. But he wanted more, and he wanted Lila to bear them. Then what was he to do?

The question only served to increase his despair, and he pushed away from the bed and paced a distance away. How could women be so different? Dhari submitted joyfully to his approach, deriving as much pleasure from the union of their bodies as he did, while Lila—

At the thought of her, he looked back toward the bed to see her watching him, her breathing coming in sharp spasms. Then he could watch no longer and fled the room which unintentionally he had converted into a torture chamber. Outside the closed door he paused, thinking that perhaps he should return and see that she was well.

But he couldn't bring himself to do that. After the Festivities were over he would take her to London, where a qualified physician could examine her, perhaps determine the cause of her repeated miscarriages.

He knew from past experience that such an examination would simply cause her more grief. Last year after the physician from Exeter had examined her she'd been ill for a week. Still, it must be done. He wanted more children, and while he regretted the pain he caused her, he intended to impregnate her as often as possible until

there were ten filled cribs in the nursery, every room of
Eden exploding with the laughter of well-fed, rosy-
cheeked offspring, all his own.

For a moment he stood without direction or compass,
lost in the elegance of new Eden Castle. Slowly he
looked about him. So! It was finished. Suffering that
anguish of accomplished goals, he sat wearily on the top
step and drew his robe about him.

He bowed his head, his mind turning on what tomorrow would bring—the first carriages rattling across the
moors, bringing journalists for the most part, repre-
sentatives from every major newspaper in England and
a few from France and Germany as well, the first act
of the fortnight Festivities, during which time the world
at last would get a glimpse of the paradise he had created on the North Devon headlands.

He had created it, and with a self-satisfied smile he
leaned back against the step, his eyes falling on beauty
wherever he looked. Even the once crude stone corridors
of the old castle had been transformed into passages of
expressive beauty, tapestries everywhere, shimmering
brass lamps fixed in permanent standards every four feet
along the wall.

As his eye scanned the surrounding illumination, his
hand caressed the thick scarlet carpet which covered
every stone floor with the exception of the Great Hall,
which boasted Italian marble in parquet squares of
black and white. And the walls and ceilings of that
magnificent room were now covered with the gigantic
painted murals done by the French artist Ricard, de-
picting early scenes of English history.

In his mind's eye he saw it so clearly, and every other
splendid detail of the new Eden, for every decision had
rested with him, every command to carve, to chisel, to
paint, had come from him. For over eight years he'd
caused an army of artisans and craftsmen to move at
the lift of his hand.

In the delirious excitement of his own accomplishment,
he forgot about Lila and ran down the steps like a child,
taking delight in each turned corner, aware of the beginning of the marble pavement, bracing himself for the
magnificent new gilt staircase which took the place of
the old wooden one, a single majestic descent to the
Great Hall, the new gallery running out on all sides, its

gilt ironwork glittering under the six massive chandeliers, each supporting two thousand candles.

At the far end of the Great Hall he saw eight watchmen standing guard near the door. They looked up in his direction and one took a step forward. But apparently a second closer look had revealed his identity and now all eight men made a respectful bow and turned their backs, as though they knew better than to intrude into the privacy of their master.

Feeling a bit sheepish for having been discovered prowling about in his dressing robe, John started to retreat back up the stairs. But again the problem confronted him. Where would he go? He had no appetite for the emptiness of his own chambers, and Lord Harrington was probably abed by now.

Of course there was Andrew, loyal Andrew, but if Andrew wasn't asleep he should be. Only that evening at table John had noticed the look of fatigue on his friend's face. And why not? John had placed heavy burdens on Andrew, had placed the full weight of his London operations on him while Eden was being completed. No, he would not disturb Andrew on this evening though it baffled him how the man could sleep, how any of them could sleep on the eve of such a momentous occasion.

He walked aimlessly about the Great Hall, stepping with his bare feet schoolboy fashion on only the white squares of marble, aware of how foolish he must appear to the watchmen, but uncaring.

At the exact center of the Great Hall he lifted his head and looked directly up into the dazzling chandeliers, their illumination momentarily blinding him and causing a stinging about his eyes, his emotions close to the surface, as without warning he thought of that rain-drenched young boy who had stood in this exact spot over twenty years ago, fatherless, penniless, announcing to Harriet that his name was John Murrey Eden and that he had come home.

The memory, so unexpected, led to others, and suddenly he looked up the staircase as though someone had called to him.

Of course there was no one there, and he shivered in the emptiness. If only Elizabeth were here. Well, she *would* be tomorrow, and Mary would be with her, his adored cousin, who would have to play the role of his daughter until Lila could—

The thought caused a small death, and aware of the watchmen's eyes upon him, he moved out of the Great Hall and took refuge in the library, an equally elegant and massive room, with walls of leather-bound volumes, a black marble fireplace at the far end, and resting before the fireplace the enormous shroud-covered painting of "The Women of Eden," where next week it would be unveiled and raised to a position of honor above the mantel.

Settling into a nearby armchair, John stared fixedly at the covered canvas.

The painting *was* remarkable. After his initial shock, John had been forced to concede the point, still seeing, in spite of the shroud, the revolutionary rendering of four women, all recognizable as Lila, Dhari, Elizabeth and Mary. But there the recognition stopped, as in various sensuous poses they gazed out over a white marble parapet at a vast blue Mediterranean sea below, their Roman garb merely an ephemeral film which scarcely covered their bodies, and indeed Dhari's breasts were visible beneath the yellow transparency which clung under the pressure of a mild wind. Precisely how the Royal Academy was going to deal with those bare breasts, John had no idea, but what sport it was going to be finding out!

Relying only on his memory, he stared at the concealed painting and saw Elizabeth. Oh, yes, Elizabeth was certainly present, or at least her Roman counterpart, a delicate matured beauty who, in spite of her small stature, seemed to control the other three.

Next to Elizabeth in the painting stood Lila, her bare arms resting on the parapet, her body angled in the same direction, but her fair, childlike head averted, a pose which seemed to say that in spite of the common focus of attention, there was something else, just out of sight of the canvas, which had caught and held her attention.

Still suffering from his recent encounter with her, John sank deeper into the chair, impressed anew with the accuracy of Alma-Tadema's perception.

Sharply he lifted his head, thinking he'd heard footsteps at the door behind him.

But the doorway was empty and he chided himself for his annoyance. Settling back, he again focused on the covered canvas, searching his memory for the last image, that of his beautiful Mary. Slowly he sat up as though drawn to the invisible image, her form and face predominant on the canvas, a breathtaking beauty who seemed to be searching the horizon with much greater intensity than the others, as though she alone would benefit from the return of her lover.

In the clarity of his recall, John felt himself suffering from a kind of inarticulate affection for her. She was a jewel, as innocent as the day she was born, a treasured temple of purity, as Lila once had been.

Without warning he found himself gripping the arms of the chair, dwelling on Mary's purity, unable to say why it held such an attraction for him. Many times it had occurred to him that he would have been wise to leave Lila untouched. How ill-conceived society was. Every man should have the right to possess two women: one to worship and the other to use for baser purposes. What a felicitous arrangement that would be!

He sat quite still for several minutes, staring at the covered canvas. Suddenly his attention was caught by faint movement at the door behind him. He turned in that direction, ready to dismiss the prying watchman. Instead an apparition swung into the center of his vision and seemed immediately to become the focus of the midnight landscape.

A thin, darkly clad figure, a veil concealing her face, stood in the doorway, her hands reaching out in an attempt to clear unseen objects, her head beneath the veil lifting and turning as though after ten years of blindness, she still longed to see.

John stood immediately, as though an imperative hand had seized him by the shoulders and swung him around.

Harriet—

He tried to speak her name, but a strangling sensation rendered him voiceless and, as he stepped forward to speak it again, he saw behind her her constant shadow, her maid Peggy.

As Peggy came into view, John held his position without speaking, looking to Peggy, as did everyone in the castle, for guidance concerning how he should respond to Harriet's unexpected presence.

A ferocious watchdog Peggy was, who looked at him over Harriet's shoulder and slowly wagged her head from side to side, a wordless command that John was not to speak, was not to signal his presence in any way.

"Now tell me, Peggy, tell me all about this room. . . ."

At the sound of Harriet's voice, John suffered the painful shock he always felt at hearing her speak, her voice as lovely as ever, the only faculty about her that had remained unchanged during her crucible. Somehow he always felt that the mutilation of her face and eyes should extend to her voice, but of course it hadn't, and the woman who had just asked Peggy for a description of the library might have been the same woman who twenty years ago had lifted him out of the misery of the odd-boy cellar and into a luxurious bed and a treasured love from which his soul still had not recovered.

"The library, milady," Peggy began, "and here is a lovely lacquered cabinet. Come, feel for yourself." Lightly she pressed Harriet's hand against the smooth black enamel. "Can you feel it?"

"Of course I can," Harriet scolded good-naturedly. "Tell me of its color."

For several minutes, John watched as Harriet bent low over the cabinet, her hands moving out in all directions, while Peggy stood silently behind her, her eyes fixed on John as though again she were warning him not to move or speak.

Still amazed that her soul was intact and as beautiful as ever, John found for a moment that he could not watch her and averted his eyes, his memory punishing him with a recall of the one and only time since her self-mutilation that he had seen her unveiled, the morning almost ten years ago of his triumphant return to Eden, when he'd thought her dead and Richard had informed him that she was alive. He had entered her chambers alone, the weight of emotion almost unbearable, as his eyes had fought the blackness for a glimpse of this remarkable woman who had been his first love, perhaps his only true love, and who had blinded herself upon learning the news from Morley Johnson's corrupt lips that she was indeed the natural mother of John Murrey Eden.

Seated on the arm of the chair, he crumpled forward, the ancient burden of guilt as powerful as ever, as though the ten years of penance for both of them had never taken place. The lamplight had caught on certain specifics, the eyeless sockets, two small ovals of white, the rough jagged scar tissue covering her cheekbones, extending over the bridge of her nose, the entire grisly script scarcely recognizable as a human face, except for the mouth and chin, which had escaped the stabbing thrusts of the forks.

He bowed his head into his hands, involuntarily shuddering. The faint sound caused a cessation in Peggy's voice behind him. Simultaneously he heard a gasp and looked over his shoulder to see Harriet raised up from her inspection, her head lifting, her hands reaching out as though seeking Peggy's protection.

"Who—" she gasped. "We're not alone!"

With an accusatory look, Peggy glared at John from across the room. "No, milady," she murmured. "Mr. Eden is present. I thought it best if—"

"John?"

A portion of her fear seemed to be receding, replaced by apprehension as she reached up to her face to make certain that the veil was in place.

John gave her all the time she needed, glad that she was aware of his presence, pleased by the scolding she delivered to Peggy. "Why didn't you tell me?" she murmured.

"You said you wanted to see the new halls, milady. You said nothing about visiting."

"Oh, Lord! Peggy, please don't take me so literally in the future. You should know that John—"

As she turned in his direction, he put the past behind him and went forward and grasped her hand. "You look lovely," he said, and lifted her hand to his lips. "If I'd known that you, too, were suffering from insomnia, we could have prowled together."

She laughed. "It's not exactly insomnia that I'm suffering," she said. "As I told Peggy, we'd better go and see Eden's new grandeur for ourselves before the hordes arrive tomorrow."

"I would have been happy to escort you."

"I didn't want to bother you. You've had so much—"

"It would have been no bother. You know that."

After this brief and self-conscious exchange, they stood

silently, John aware of Peggy's hovering presence behind them.

"This is the new library," he began, trying to bridge the awkward silence.

"So Peggy told me."

"Have you visited the Great Hall?"

"I have," Harriet replied, "and Peggy's eyes didn't miss a thing."

At that moment the watchdog herself stepped forward, primly adjusting the collar of her black dress. "We've taken the complete tour, Mr. Eden," she said. "Now I believe Her Ladyship is fatigued and should be returned to—"

"Oh, Peggy, nonsense," Harriet intervened. "I'm not fatigued at all."

Encouraged, John suggested, "Then why don't you sit with me for a few minutes? You are right about tomorrow. Our daily visits may have to go by the boards for a while."

He suggested mildly to Peggy, "Why don't *you* retire? I'll see Her Ladyship back to her chambers."

But the protest on Peggy's face was nothing compared to the sharp "No!" which issued from behind the black veil. Harriet lowered her head and when she spoke again her voice was soft though determined. "I'll sit with you, John. But, Peggy, you wait near the door. I'll only stay a few minutes; then we shall retire together."

Reluctantly, John agreed to the arrangement, privately loathing the look of triumph on Peggy's face. But it had always been thus. Not once since his return ten years ago to Eden had Harriet ever occupied the same room with him alone. Others did. She spent hours alone with Lila and the children. And Elizabeth, when she visited Eden, enjoyed endless teas with Harriet, and even Dhari could seek her out in private. Everyone enjoyed Harriet alone except John.

He should have accustomed himself to the ritual by now, knowing full well the point and purpose behind it. The passion that had brought them together in physical union years ago must not be permitted to flourish again. The first penance had been costly enough and was still not complete.

As Peggy retreated to the door, John guided Harriet toward the armchair and dragged a second chair into place until they were seated side by side, facing the shrouded canvas of "The Women of Eden."

For a moment neither spoke, as though the insignificant movements had drained them of all energy. Just as John was on the verge of uttering something witless in an attempt to fill the silence, she asked quietly, "Why couldn't you sleep? I should think that you would be exhausted, and certainly you will need all the rest you can get in order to face the ordeals which you've plotted for yourself."

He smiled and shrugged. "If only one could will sleep."

"I have an elixir I'd be happy to share with you, a wicked concoction, Peggy's private recipe."

"No, thank you!" He laughed. "More than sleep, I need my wits about me tomorrow."

The small intimacy moved him and gave him courage to speak more freely. "This once was the Banquet Hall, if you recall."

She nodded. "It always seemed misplaced to me, so far removed from the Kitchen Court."

"And the painting," John went on, "the Alma-Tadema painting, has Peggy told you about that?"

Harriet leaned forward, sharing his excitement. "No, and it was curiosity about that painting that led me here. Tell me!"

"Most scandalous, it is," John whispered, enjoying the new ease between them. "If you hear an explosion on Friday, it will merely be the gentlemen of the Royal Academy."

"Tell me all about it, John. Describe it in full. Is it in this room? Is it near?"

As her head turned in all directions, John soothed, "Yes, it's directly before you."

"You've seen it, then?"

"Indeed I have." As he launched forth into a detailed description of the large painting, she stopped him several times in order to "see" a precise color or posture. When John's narrative reached its conclusion, she sat as though wanting more.

"Will it hang here?" she asked.

John nodded. "Over the mantel. There they will reside forever, our four, caught in a pose of classicism, a perfect setting according to Alma-Tadema, who is quite

skillful in viewing the English Empire against the back-
ground of the Roman—"

"Neither actually," she corrected quietly. "It's *your*
empire. Dhari and Elizabeth, Lila and Mary, all belong
to *your* empire."

"And you?" he asked, covering her hand, shocked at
how rapidly they had moved from the objectivity of the
painting to whispered intimacy.

"Of course."

"Then why did you refuse to sit for the painting?"

"Oh, Lord, John"—she laughed, shattering the intimacy—"I'm not questioning Alma-Tadema's genius,
but how could he have worked a black veil into that
stunning sea of color that you have just described?"

In a strong need to counterbalance her merriment, he
suggested, "He would have painted you as you once
were."

"That woman is dead," she said, and pulled away
from his hand and called sharply over her shoulder,
"Peggy, are you there?"

"I'm here, milady. Shall we—"

As Peggy started forward, John lifted his hand to halt
her progress. "Give us a few additional minutes," he
commanded.

Peggy hesitated midway between the door.

Aware of the impasse, Harriet turned in that direction.
"We'll sit a while longer, Peggy, but please stay close."

The words had been spoken in the manner of a re-
prieve. Loathing the feeling that he had been chastised,
but grateful for her continuing presence, John sat well
back in his chair and tried to change the subject.

"You know the guest list, of course," he commenced,
his voice now befitting the room, formal and cold.

"Simply all of England," she said, "or at least all of
influential England."

"The Lord Mayor is representing the Queen—"

"And Mr. Disraeli and Mr. Gladstone as well, I believe you said."

"Representing themselves, as always."

"What if their paths cross?"

John shook his head. "Not likely. Andrew has had a
staff working for months. I didn't go to all this trouble
simply to have the arguments of Parliament transferred
to the North Devon Coast."

"How clever of you," she murmured, "to be so considerate."

"It was Andrew's idea."

"Good Andrew."

"Yes."

It was as though they were pushing the words out, both of them insisting upon formality. He found it a source of pain, the realization that the once great love which had existed between them now lay impotent. If only there were a safe territory where they could meet and talk, as mother and son, safe from the storms of the past.

"And Richard?" she asked as though sensing danger in the silence.

"Due to arrive tomorrow sometime," John replied. "Late, I believe he said. And I have a surprise for Richard," he added, his mood lightening. Perhaps at last they had found a safe territory in Richard, Harriet's son and pride, who taught at Cambridge.

"A surprise?" she asked. "Our lives of late have been filled with nothing but surprises, thanks to you. Surely they must cease soon."

"A different sort of surprise, this, one he really should have seen to for himself, but then you know Richard . . ."

"Well, tell me," she demanded eagerly.

"Lady Eleanor Forbes," he said, and waited for her reaction, which never came except in the form of a confused silence.

"I—don't understand."

"Of course you do, Harriet. You more than anyone should understand. I've arranged a marriage for Richard," he went on, his sense of accomplishment dampened by her obvious state of confusion. "I've already spoken to Lord and Lady Forbes and they are delighted and have assured me that—"

"You had no right!"

"No right?" he repeated. "I really didn't consider it a matter of rights. Richard is of marriageable age and beyond it. With his head buried constantly in books, what effort will he make to find a wife?"

"If he wants a wife, I'm sure he's capable of—"

John laughed, amused at how quickly she'd forgotten how shy her own son was. "Then all I'm doing is placing

an imminently qualified young woman on his immediate
horizon. Eleanor is quite lovely. I've met her on several
occasions in London and in her parents' home in Kent.
She will produce healthy heirs."

When she seemed disinclined to say anything further,
he tried to restore her good mood. "Regardless of what
happens, it will be good to see him again, won't it?"

"Will Aslam be with him?"

"He will," John said, seeing in his imagination the
eighteen-year-old Indian boy whom he loved like a son.

"Will Bertie Nichols be coming with Richard?" Harriet asked.

"Yes," John said, staring glumly at the colors in the
carpet at his feet.

"Good!" Harriet replied enthusiastically, as though
she were settling a score. "I'm very fond of Bertie, aren't
you? A more thoughtful gentleman doesn't exist."

John kept silent. His opinion of Bertie Nichols was at
odds with Harriet's. No, he did not care for Herbert
Nichols at all, the Professor of Greek and Latin at
Cambridge, who over the years had become Richard's
dearest friend.

"I have a secret, John," Harriet said, keeping her
voice down. "Please don't think me a silly old woman,"
she whispered, "but could you, without too much effort,
see a relationship between our Mary and Bertie
Nichols? I mean they did seem to get on quite well together last Christmas, don't you think? And it *is* time that
Mary commenced thinking about—"

"Don't be absurd!" he snapped, at first not certain if
she was serious or not. Then, seeing that she was, he
stood and walked a distance away.

"Why are you opposed to the idea?"

"Because it does not become you to speak such nonsense."

"Why?" she asked. "Mary is twenty-one. It's time
she—"

"She's a child, Harriet," he interrupted, amazed at the
degree of anger he felt at the insane suggestion. Pacing
around the bureau, he decided that now was as good a
time as any to share his thoughts on Mary with Harriet.
"I *do* have a change in mind for her," he began. "I
think it's time she left Elizabeth and London. From all
I hear, Elizabeth is still deeply involved with her radical

friends, and I don't think that's a suitable atmosphere for Mary."

Now Harriet rose, her hands reaching out for balance. "You must be careful," she warned gently, "not to hurt Elizabeth. She adores Mary. If she thought—"

"She knows I don't approve of her friends or their cause. Where is her concern for me?"

Harriet was at his side. "I'm sure it's over now," she soothed, referring, as John knew all too well, to the public embarrassment that Elizabeth had brought down on him last year when she had lent her name and large portions of her bank account to the insane cause of votes for women. The circus had even proceeded as far as the floor of the House of Commons, with the support of the jackal, John Stuart Mill, where they all had been laughed out into the streets.

Even now John found it difficult to believe that Elizabeth would ally herself with such madness. Yet his spies continued to report to him the number of radicals, both male and female, who could be seen entering and leaving the house in St. George Street.

No, he wanted Mary out of that environment and said as much. "I will find an opportunity during the next two weeks to talk to Elizabeth," he said firmly. "Mary will not be returning to London with her."

"Where will she go?"

"She will remain at Eden for the duration of summer, and come autumn she will leave for Cheltenham." Not wanting to upset her further, John simply said, "A suitable place for a young lady."

But something about Harriet's stance suggested that she knew. "The school, the one you've mentioned before?" she asked.

He really didn't want to answer. But she was insistent and finally he said, "Yes," and moved away from her torrent of protest before it spilled out. "It's for the best, Harriet," he said. "She's still a child, you know."

"You have no right," came the cold voice from beneath the veil. "She'll refuse to go. She will simply—"

"On the matter of rights, Harriet, I see no margin for discussion. I have taken on full responsibility for this family and I feel a perfect right to insist upon certain courses of action.

"She must be protected," he said finally. "A few years in an isolated situation will—"

"—destroy her."

"Not likely. It will teach her discipline, the one attribute which according to Elizabeth she lacks entirely."

"She's a young woman, John. She needs—"

"The matter is closed. If she continues to enjoy my protection, she will do as I say."

Suddenly Harriet moved back from him. He followed a step after, regretful that these difficult subjects had come up.

"Harriet, I had not intended to—"

"It's late," she said, moving too rapidly through the crowded furnishings. Twice he saw her collide painfully with chairs, and he saw Peggy hurrying to her aid.

"Wait!" he called out as the two women met near the door.

Only Peggy looked up as he drew near, her sharp eyes as accusatory as ever. Uncertain what he was going to say now that he had their attention, he faltered. "Will you—" he commenced, regretful that he had angered her. "Can I count on your—assistance in welcoming our guests?"

"No."

"Why not?" he persisted, recalling the debate which had flared between them for the past several months. "As Countess Dowager, your proper place is—"

She lifted her head, the veil doing little to conceal her anger. "What is proper for me is for me to decide, John."

In the face of her anger he retreated, sorry that their time together had gone badly. "I only thought—"

Then, when he least expected it, she stepped close to him and lifted her hand to his face, her fingers tracing the outline of his features in a most intimate gesture. "I suspect," she said quietly, as though she had put all anger behind her, "that tomorrow will be a beautiful day, the road to Eden clogged with important people traveling in elegant carriages to see your beautiful castle. I'm afraid," she concluded, stepping back, "that I do not belong to such a day. How would you explain me, John?" She laughed. "Oh, I can just hear it now. 'Lord So-and-So, allow me to present my mother, the Countess Dowager, who once long ago was my—' "

Sharply John looked up. In all the intervening years

they had never mentioned it. Now she was about to reveal all to Peggy.

But she stopped short, though the echo of that one
unspoken word seemed to shriek about the room.

Sensing her fear at what she'd almost done, and feeling it blend with his own, regretful that he had angered
her, John went down on his knees and clasped her to him,
his arms about her waist, clinging like a child.

At first he was certain that she would reject him. But
she didn't. Instead he felt her hands stroking his hair,
drawing him closer. "There," she soothed, as though he
were an injured child, "you're merely tired. We both
are. You must realize that."

But he was realizing nothing except her simple act of
locking him in her arms, reminding him of that night
years ago when still innocent of their kinship they had
fled the castle and in the seclusion of the woods she had
shared with him his first act of love.

Then it was over. As she pulled free of his embrace,
he looked up, sensing the broken bits of his personality
scattered about him, still unable to determine why at
this particular moment she'd granted him such closeness.

"Good night, John," she said from the door. He saw
Peggy take her arm and lead her away.

Still on his knees he watched them.

"Harriet—"

But he was alone in the elegance of his new library.
The echo of the guardsmen calling the hour reached his
ears from a distance. He felt a breath of icy air and
shivered as he rose, her features still before him as she
once had been, the straight nose, the finely arched brows,
dark eyes which looked back at him with the willful yet
beseeching expression of a lover. . . .

He could no longer support the realization, and he
made his way like an invalid to the chair where he sat
heavily, his head fallen back against the cushion, and
tried to deal with it, the awareness that in spite of what
he had become, in spite of all his success, he was still
the sixteen-year-old boy who loved her, who had known
even then with premature wisdom that he would never
love any other as he had loved her, and who now would
willingly create new hells for both of them if he could
have her just once more.

The thought dragged him to his feet. Directionless, he

glanced around the room. He needed something, someone. He needed something, someone. Lila? No! Dhari?
Yes, Dhari would kindly give him what he needed.

He hurried forward, gaining the door, breaking into a
run, seeing nothing of the elegance as he took the steps
of the Grand Staircase, aware of nothing but the perception that all his victories could collapse into defeat
unless he could outrace the sixteen-year-old boy running
behind him. . . .

"Checkmate!" Andrew Rhoades exclaimed with weary
though undisguised glee. He couldn't believe it. After a
full evening of suffering defeat after defeat at Dhari's
hands he'd finally achieved victory.

"Aslam won't believe it!" He grinned across at her,
delighting in her dark silent beauty.

"Nor would I," Lord Harrington said, lounging to one
side of the comfortable sitting room of Dhari's private
apartment. "If I hadn't witnessed it for myself," he
added.

Andrew saw him look up over the heavy parchment
invitation which he'd been studying for the last hour.

"You let me win, didn't you?" he accused good-
naturedly, ignoring Lord Harrington, concentrating instead on the serene female presence which during the
last few hectic months had brought him such pleasure.

Silent, as always, she smiled at him, her attractive
rose-velour dressing gown knotted loosely about her
waist, reminding him that she'd been abed when he and
Lord Harrington had knocked on her door, seeking a
relaxed chamber in which to pass this last night before
the crowds descended.

"You did!" he accused, and watched as she left her
chair and stood behind him, massaging the tightness out
of his neck, the sensation so pleasurable that he closed
his eyes and felt gooseflesh on his arms.

To his right he heard Lord Harrington at the sideboard, refilling his brandy snifter. But Andrew concentrated on nothing but the skillful manipulation of
Dhari's fingers, her silence working an increasing magic
on him. In spite of his pleasure, he took care to guard
his feelings and keep them in check with a reminder of
who she was and whom she belonged to.

She was companionship, that was all, bearing the cross

of her own tragedy with a nobility of spirit which dazzled all who came in contact with her. Leaning into her gentle massage, Andrew thought what ancient history it all seemed. Dhari was more an Englishwoman now than an Indian, with a brilliant son at Cambridge and a protected position within Eden Castle as John's—

Slyly his mind canceled the word before it took shape, and reaching behind he caught her hand and lightly kissed it in thanks for the massage and pushed out of his chair, feeling it best to move away.

On his right, he saw Lord Harrington studying the invitation which, come morning, would convert the rural idyll that was Eden into a thronging social event.

"Have you studied this carefully, Andrew?" Harrington asked, doing nothing to mask his distaste.

Hiding a smile, Andrew took refuge at the sideboard, pouring two snifters of brandy and carrying one to Dhari where now she sat close to Lord Harrington on the sofa.

"I've not only seen it," Andrew confessed, "I plead guilty to having assisted with its creation. Not only did I assist with its creation, but I suggested many of those lunatic activities which you see listed there."

As always, Lord Harrington was invincibly polite, trying to conceal his shock in diplomacy. "Well, I'm sure you had your reasons, Andrew," he said, flipping through the invitation, which months ago had been hand-delivered by special couriers to two thousand Englishmen.

Of course it was tasteless. Andrew was the first to admit that. But in his opinion this entire public display was tasteless, and for the past year he'd tried to argue John out of the whole foolish conception.

But to no avail. Eden had been the dream and goal of his life. Now that he had accomplished it, nothing would do but that he throw open the castle gates and invite what he hoped would be an envying world in for a look.

Taking delight in Andrew's involvement, Lord Harrington sat up on the edge of the sofa, his distinguished features glowing with good humor. "Umbrellas, shawls, fans, sketching materials and embroidery frames will be provided for the guests?" he read with a smile of incredulity.

"In addition, there will be walking, boating, sketching, picnics and, for the energetic, archery contests, riding, bowling and lawn croquet."

His sense of humor overcame his sense of incredulity and he leaned back, laughing heartily.

Feeling the need for a mild defense, Andrew sipped at his brandy and asked, "Well, what choice do I have? If John insists on dragging two thousand people out here, we'd damn well better give them something to do."

Then Dhari apparently had found a mysterious item on the invitation and leaned close to Lord Harrington, pointing to a specific page, wanting edification.

Even before he spoke, Lord Harrington was regaled with fresh waves of laughter. "Milord," he gasped, "you can't be serious! A nigger minstrel show?"

Andrew lowered his head in embarrassment. "John's idea." He winced. "Nothing I could say would talk him out of it. He saw one at Brighton some months ago and paid them a fortune on the spot to appear here next week."

As Dhari's question concerning the nature of a nigger minstrel show still had not been answered, Andrew said with a laugh, "You tell her what they are, Lord Harrington. For myself, I think I need another brandy."

"They make jokes, Dhari," he heard Lord Harrington explain, "and sing popular ballads and plantation songs from America and play banjos and concertinas."

Obviously one mystery was leading to another and as she looked questioningly up at the word "concertina" Andrew turned to the sideboard, his eye falling on the opened door which led to her bedchamber, a pretty room, the corner of the rosewood four-poster just visible from where Andrew stood, the pink and lavender brocade coverlet mussed from where she had been abed.

Suffering undue fascination with the bedchamber, Andrew only half heard the laughing voice of Lord Harrington, and a moment later the voice faded altogether as Andrew concentrated on the chamber where John took his mistress and worked out the frustrations of his marital bed in Dhari's dark and receptive beauty.

The thought was extraordinarily unpleasant, and forcing his attention away from the bed, Andrew looked back at Dhari. He felt a need to go to her, and abandoning his need for brandy, he stepped past the clowning Lord Harrington, sat beside Dhari on the sofa and drew her near.

At first, surprised by his nearness, she merely glanced at him. Then one hand rested lightly on his knee.

"Enough," Andrew begged of Lord Harrington and retrieved the invitation and proceeded to thumb through it, although he knew it by heart. "Come, Harrington," he invited gruffly, "sit on the other side and we will study our coming ordeal together."

"It must be costing him a fortune," Lord Harrington muttered, studying the menus now, the lavish banquets which would be served four, sometimes five times a day.

Andrew nodded, though said nothing. Long ago he'd ceased trying to keep accounts and had simply turned the ledgers over to three of their London bookkeepers. Any suggestion of economy on his part had been met with outraged protest from John. So let him have his party, Andrew had concluded, get it out of his system in the hope that a portion of his normally good disposition would return.

"Well, there is some compensation," he said quietly. "Aslam will be arriving tomorrow, as well as Richard."

The reminder caused a smile to break on Dhari's face.

"And sometime tomorrow," Andrew went on, "Elizabeth and Mary will rattle across those double grilles."

As Dhari's smile broadened, Lord Harrington gave voice to her anticipation. "The family all returned for the great occasion." He sat up, resting his arms on his knees. "Lila is excited as well," he said. "I think she views Elizabeth as the mother she lost."

Andrew nodded, aware of the silence around him. Out of the corner of his eye he saw a portion of Dhari's leg where, in her curled position on the sofa, her dressing gown had fallen open.

Quickly he pushed himself up from the sofa and was on the verge of suggesting that they all turn in, when he heard footsteps outside the door. The other two heard them as well, and in the next moment the disheveled man filled the archway.

"John!" Andrew exclaimed, his voice a bit too loud, as he struggled to hide a curious sense of embarrassment.

On his feet between the two who were still seated on the sofa, Andrew lifted the abandoned invitation. "We were just talking about—"

The man in the archway did not move. "What are you doing here?" he asked in a low voice, where anger was kept in check.

Andrew laughed and moved toward him, taking in all

angles of his friend's face, his breathlessness, as though he'd run a distance. "Chess," Andrew pronounced simply. "You may not believe this, but with Lord Harrington as my witness, I defeated this brilliant lady here."

If John heard anything, he gave no indication of it. The frown of displeasure on his face grew until he commanded, "Get out! You have no business here, neither of you. Now get out!"

Before Andrew could respond to the shocking command, he heard Lord Harrington behind him, his voice calm. "We were just leaving, John. I'm afraid insomnia was a general plague this night."

"Get out!" John shouted again.

In rapid order, Andrew felt anger, then resentment, then at last understanding. He knew John well enough to know what had happened. Clearly the marital bed had been a disappointment as always, and with his nerves stretched taut, he'd come to Dhari, only to find her—

"Get out!" he shouted a third time, and in the face of his anger, Andrew saw Lord Harrington retreat. At the sight of that nobleman bowed with fear at the small-boy tantrum, all understanding deserted Andrew and he was left with a rage as great as John's.

"Your rudeness is not warranted and does not become you," he said, striving for control, longing to look back at Dhari, who had yet to move from the sofa, aware that when he departed after Lord Harrington, she would be left alone with John.

"Surely you know," Andrew went on, "that we frequently pass evenings in this sitting room."

"You have no right," John said. "These are Dhari's private quarters."

"The lady invited us, John," Andrew replied. "I looked for you earlier, but you—"

"Get out," John repeated in witless refrain. "You're not even—dressed;" he stammered, his outrage strong.

"Nor are you." Andrew smiled, sensing that the rational man who had created an empire had disappeared and had been replaced by a spoiled child. Based on past experience, Andrew knew that there was no reasoning with him.

"Good night, then," Andrew said pleasantly enough, and at last turned back to Dhari, saddened by her frozen state.

"Thank you, Dhari." He smiled. "And again I apologize for my victory, although I still suspect that you let me—"

"*Get out!*"

"Good night, John." Andrew again smiled as he passed him, his concern splintered, a portion of it going to John, who undoubtedly would apologize to all come morning, and to Dhari, who would be left alone with him.

As Andrew closed the door behind him, he saw Lord Harrington standing a distance away, his head bowed in embarrassment. Coming from the other side of the closed door, Andrew heard the sliding of a bolt.

"Come," Lord Harrington urged. "A nightcap in my—"

But the invitation was drowned out by a torrent of curses coming from behind the bolted door, the specific words lost, but a continuous stream of anger, the voice diminishing as the footsteps moved away from the door.

Andrew listened, struggling to catch individual words, and failing. As the tirade continued, it was punctuated by a sharp short retort as though a blow had been delivered, the voice never ceasing in abuse, the words interrupted only by another slap, and then another.

With a suffering akin to physical pain, Andrew pushed against the door. "Damn him!" he cursed, and was on the verge of pounding on the door when he felt Lord Harrington's hand on his arm. "Leave them be," the old man counseled.

"Leave them be!" Andrew repeated, amazed. "You can hear it for yourself. He's—"

"She knows how to handle him," Lord Harrington counseled. "She, better than anyone, knows what to do."

Still the voice spewed forth its anger, but though he listened carefully Andrew heard no more blows.

Then silence. The tension caused a cramp to knot in Andrew's right shoulder.

"Come." Lord Harrington smiled. "Nothing has happened here which should surprise or distress either of us."

In that calm acceptance, Andrew leveled an even greater indictment at John. How long would everyone permit him to work his will on them?

"Come, Andrew."

It was Lord Harrington again. "Every family has se-

crets and we're no different. We both will love him
again come morning."

Andrew looked up at the voice. Of course he was
right. With a tolerant half-smile, he walked with Lord
Harrington down the corridor, though a portion of his
heart remained behind in the closed and bolted room. . . .

Cambridge
May 10, 1870

As LORD RICHARD EDEN, Fifteenth Baron and Seventh
Earl of Eden, sat waiting in his carriage outside his flat
near Magdalene College, he felt a sense of well-being
settle over him. How calmly God had taken his life and
lifted it out of darkness, had given him a task to perform
and a love to reciprocate. Now the only cloud in Richard's existence was the occasional suspicion that he was
unworthy of such happiness.

God, or John Murrey Eden, had done all this, and smiling at his willingness to confuse the two, Richard leaned
out the window and looked up toward the second-floor
casement behind the green of fresh spring ivy to the study
where Bertie was giving a student last-minute instructions
in the translation of Homer.

The tutorial should have ended an hour ago, and
worse, they should have been on the road to North Devon
yesterday. In addition, they had yet to stop by Madingly
Hall and pick up Aslam. Richard hoped that the boy
was ready.

Well, no matter. John would understand, and Richard
refused to spoil this glorious day with anxiety. According
to John's letters, the Festivities would stretch on for two
weeks. What matter if they were a day or so late?

Ah, at last, there they were, and eagerly Richard
leaned forward, amused that though both Bertie and the
young student were juggling a trunk apiece, Bertie was
still talking, his strong face reflecting the intensity of his
instruction.

Richard considered himself a dedicated don, but his

dedication paled in comparison to that of Bertie. At the
end of the walk, they stopped again, Bertie, in his eagerness to make a final point, lowering the trunk to his feet.
The student, a lanky, dark-haired young man named
Todd, reluctantly did the same, as though it would have
suited him better to transfer luggage rather than deal with
the complexities of Homer.

Richard took advantage of the scene, confident that
neither participant knew he was being watched, reveling
in Bertie, seeing him as he'd first seen him years ago when
Richard had been a terrified undergraduate.

What his fear had done to him then! It had rendered
him mute, his face expressionless, his voice scarcely more
than a whisper, a slim, petrified boy who considered himself unworthy to breathe God's air.

Small wonder, then, his transformation on that day with
that miracle of a man, one Herbert Nichols, that fero-
ciously alive son of a Norfolk rector, with no connections
and little money, yet filling the door of their Cambridge
attic with a degree of love that had, incredibly, increased
from that day to this.

In an attempt to retain the good memory, Richard
closed his eyes. He had never known such a man and
knew he would never know another. God did not create
such men effortlessly or in quantity, filling their hearts
with that rarest of commodities, an indiscriminate love for
merely all mankind.

There Bertie stood now, still vigorous and handsome, a
few strands of gray flecking his sandy-colored hair, his
shoulders bent from the long hours spent over books,
though still exhibiting a grandeur in spite of his unfortunate propensity always to look mussed.

Out of habit Richard lowered his head and gave a brief
prayer of thanks for the world and all the people in it.
When he looked up he saw Bertie with his arm about the
young man's shoulder, giving him last-minute words of
encouragement.

"You'll do well, Todd," he called out. "I know you
will. Remember what I told you, and have confidence in
yourself."

The last command was issued with mock fierceness,
causing the boy to duck his head, walking backward
across the small courtyard, his eyes fixed in adoration on
Bertie.

Then the student was gone and Bertie was left alone at the end of the path. Richard thought he detected a weariness on his face. And why not? He had seen his readers last night until past midnight and had risen before six this morning in order to prepare for the journey.

Richard left the carriage, summoning the driver to help with the trunks. He was less than three feet from him before Bertie looked up, his expression one of thoughtful repose. At the sound of Richard's steps on gravel, he glanced toward him with a soft apology.

"Ah, Richard, I'm sorry for the delay." He smiled, one hand brushing back his hair. "The boy will founder, I'm afraid, unless—"

"Unless you throw him a lifeline," Richard interrupted.

Bertie nodded and started to object as the coachman, a strapping lad from the town of Cambridge, effortlessly hoisted both trunks onto his shoulders and started toward the carriage. From experience, Richard knew that Bertie disliked the sense of being served or waited upon. When he started toward the coachman to lend a hand, Richard let him go.

As Bertie lifted the final trunk up, he turned about, in the process stripping off his black robe, his attitude still one of apology. "You can place the blame squarely on my shoulders, Richard. Or better still, I'll explain to John myself."

But Richard merely smiled, taking note of the rumpled suit beneath Bertie's black robe. It bore not the slightest indication that it had ever known a press. As Bertie flung his black robe through the carriage window, Richard stepped forward and straightened his neck scarf.

"Am I a total wreck?" Bertie brooded. "And I dressed so carefully this morning!"

"You look fine," Richard soothed.

"Trunks secured, sir!" The voice came from the young coachman, who had just taken his seat, reins in hand. Suffering the excitement that always accompanies a journey, Richard took Bertie's arm and assisted him up into the carriage, the sense of holiday strong within him.

As Richard felt the carriage start forward, the shadows of Nevile's Court obliterated the sun on the handsome, bemused face across the way. In an attempt to control the love he felt for the man, Richard felt a compulsion to continue talking.

He did not take his eyes off the face he loved more than life itself. Nor did he alter his focus as he reached up and released the small window curtains on each side of the carriage. As the curtains slipped down, casting the interior into a shaded coolness, Richard gained the opposite side, gently smoothed back the mussed sandy hair, grasped the steadying hand which Bertie had extended to him, and kissed him, the scent of the man, the feel of his arms enclosing him in a reciprocal embrace.

As Bertie drew him close, Richard gave himself fully to the embrace, finding in the shelter of those strong arms all he would ever need of love and closeness.

"A pair we are," Bertie whispered.

Richard settled under the sheltering umbrella of Bertie's arm, regretful that they were not making the journey alone, reminding himself that they would have to move with much greater care during the fortnight ahead. In their life at Cambridge they enjoyed a limited freedom, no one mentioning openly that dreaded word, submerging their love in an atmosphere of High Anglican sexlessness. The physical union that they enjoyed within the privacy of their upstairs bedchamber was their business, two highly respected dons merely sharing quarters for economy and convenience.

But now that they had left that secure womb, and particularly at Eden they both would have to exercise great care not to let their glances reveal too much, their whispered conversations, their early retirements.

In defense against the coming deprivation, as though both their minds had been moving on the same track, Richard felt Bertie's arms tighten about him, felt his lips again.

"I love you so much, Richard. How bereft my life would be without you."

Richard closed his eyes, the better to hear the treasured words, and silently thanked God for this richest of blessings He had seen fit to bestow upon his life. . . .

Aslam, grown tall and slim at eighteen, the great-grandson of the last Emperor of the Moghul Empire, but now more English than Indian, stood waiting outside his room at Madingly Hall, some three miles from Cambridge, and searched the road for Richard's carriage.

They were late, though in a way he'd expected it. In all the journeys he'd made back to Eden with Richard and Professor Nichols, not once had they departed at the appointed hour.

Although he'd been standing for over an hour, his valise at his feet, he continued to stand, his back erect, head lifted, paying no attention to the parade of students who entered and departed the hall behind him.

In his two years here he had yet to make one close friend. It suited him, his aloneness, his awareness of his difference, which included the color of his skin, the vast wealth of his adopted father, John Murrey Eden, and the superiority of Aslam's mind, the natural isolation that a brilliant intellect always forces upon its possessor.

As a single bead of perspiration trickled down the bridge of his nose, caused by the high May sun and the heavy fabric of his dark wool suit, he made no move to brush it away.

He should have kept to his room until he'd seen the carriage from his window. But that would have only meant a further delay, another excuse for the boys to torment him, this time about his enforced ride with the "dear old Sodomites of Nevile's Court."

With relief he heard the Hall door slam behind him, the air quiet, and now he tried to concentrate on the days ahead, looking forward to a respite from the loneliness. How he longed to see John again, to try to convince him that he could read law as well in London as he could here, or better still, let Andrew Rhoades tutor him.

But to all his heartfelt entreaties, John had stood firm, insisting on the "respectability" of a Cambridge education.

For the first time since he had been waiting, his head inclined forward as though a weight of confusion had been lowered upon him, the mystery and contradiction that was John Murrey Eden, a man who had turned his back on respectability and who still operated largely with only one set of rules, his own, now foisting the appearance of respectability on Aslam.

The rigid stance maintained for over an hour began to take a toll. A curious high-pitched siren erupted in his ear, his eyes watered under the effects of the increasing heat, and the heavy weave of his jacket seemed to be encasing his arms in lead.

About ten feet from where he stood was the inviting shade of a yew tree. What a simple matter it would be to lift his luggage and walk the distance into that inviting shade. But he couldn't do that. Without looking over his shoulder, he knew that eyes were still watching him from the window of the second floor. Oh, how he hated them, the raucous, inarticulate students with whom he had been forced to waste two years of his life!

Where is Richard?

Again he looked down the road past the fields and low cottages, the crest of the hill covered by a hazel copse which sloped downward into a marsh.

Because his mind was in need of diversion, he tried to recall the landscape of his birth, the crowded streets of Delhi in which he had passed his early years, daily running with his mother between Fraser Jennings' Methodist Mission School and his grandfather's Red Fortress. Would he ever see it again? Did he desire to see it again?

No, of course not. What was there in Delhi for him now? It was only with the greatest of effort that he could recall his native language, a mix of Persian and Urdu, and even then certain words escaped him, having been replaced by English counterparts.

"Aslam?"

He looked up at the sound of the voice, having lost contact with who and where he was. With what ease he had woven the spell of memory and ensnared himself, a trap so complete that he had failed to hear the rattling approach of Richard's carriage.

"Aslam?" Richard called again, as he started across the road. "Are you—"

"Ready," Aslam replied, reaching for his luggage, trying to brush the effects of his recall away and meet the man with fair skin and light eyes who was coming to greet him.

Then Richard was upon him, clasping his hand, a torrent of apology filling the air. "Late, I'm afraid, as always. Professor Nichols had a last-minute reader who was foundering in the depths of Homer." He smiled. "I'm not certain John will understand that explanation, but you'll help us explain, won't you?"

Aslam returned his smile, grateful only that he would

no longer have to stand on the road exposed to the eyes at the window. "I suspect that John will have sufficient diversion," he said cordially. "Our late arrival will go unnoticed."

As they approached the carriage, Aslam swung his valise up to the waiting driver, then stepped forward to receive the hand of Professor Nichols, who was leaning forward through the opened carriage door, his full blunt features as sweat-soaked as Aslam's.

"Good morning!" The large man smiled affably. "In the event that Richard hasn't already placed guilt, I take it all on my own shoulders. I trust we haven't kept you waiting long."

Aslam shook his head and murmured something about being late himself, and for a moment the three of them jostled awkwardly about in the small interior, no one quite certain how the seating arrangements should go.

"You sit across from me with Professor Nichols," Richard said at last. "I shall be an attentive pupil at the feet of the two most brilliant minds in Cambridge."

As Professor Nichols scoffed at the compliment, Aslam took the appointed seat, moving as near to the corner as he could. He would have preferred for the two of them to sit together.

As Richard secured the door, he suggested, "Why don't you take off your coat, Aslam? You look wilted."

"No, I'm fine."

"Well, I need no second invitation," Professor Nichols said, and in spite of the motion of the accelerating carriage the large man commenced to strip off his jacket.

During the awkward maneuver, the carriage took a sudden roll to the right, in the process causing Professor Nichols to lean against Aslam. "Sorry," he murmured and pulled his arms free, tossing the jacket to Richard, who folded it and placed it on the seat beside him.

Aslam watched the procedure and pushed closer to the window until he felt a ridge of metal pressing against his arm. Across the way he took note of Richard's face, which seemed filled with gloom, as though he knew all too well the reason for Aslam's shy isolation.

As the painful silence within the carriage persisted, Aslam felt shrunken with humiliation. They knew that he knew, that everyone knew, everyone except John and a few other residents at Eden who refused to see.

"Aslam, you're very quiet today," Richard commented. "No trouble, I hope, in getting off for a fortnight?"

"No. No trouble."

"And your studies?" Professor Nichols asked, joining in the enforced conversation.

"Fine," Aslam replied, unable to look at either man.

"We hear only glowing reports," Professor Nichols went on. "By Professor Kelsey's own admission, you frequently leave him far behind."

Aslam could think of no response and offered none.

"Aslam, are you happy here?" The blunt question had come from Richard, who leaned forward in his seat.

Embarrassed, Aslam nodded. "Of course. Why shouldn't I be?"

"You have no close friends."

"I desire none."

He'd not intended for his voice to be so sharp. He glanced at Richard, sorry for the look of hurt on his face. "My studies keep me very busy, Richard, as you know. I don't believe that John sent me here to make friends."

"Still, a friend or two does help to ease our passage," Professor Nichols said.

"All my hours are filled and need no easing." He dared to hope that was the end of it, but it was not to be, for in the next minute Professor Nichols raised his arm and rested it on the cushion behind where Aslam sat and asked warmly, "Would you do me a favor, Aslam?" he began. "Out of all the countless times we have made this journey together, I've longed to ask questions, but have refrained. All you must do is say no and I'll retreat."

On guard, Aslam sat erect.

"Tell me of India," Professor Nichols asked gently. "I know you were only a child when you left there, but there must be certain strong memories. I would love to hear it all from your lips. Do I know you well enough to impose on you in this manner?"

In spite of himself Aslam smiled, feeling a breach in that wall of resentment he'd been building toward the man. "Not an intrusion, Professor Nichols," he said honestly. "My thoughts were of India when you—"

"Then speak!" the man invited again with enthusiasm. "I'm certain that you've talked endlessly with Richard on the subject, but—"

"No." Richard smiled. "Out of all the conversations

that I've enjoyed with Aslam, not once have we spoken of
India."

"Well, then"—Professor Nichols grinned—"we have
just defeated the tedium of this journey. Come, Aslam,
clear your throat and your head and take us back with
you to the origin of your birth. And leave nothing out, no
memory of sight or sound or smell or touch. Share everything. Please."

Aslam smiled. Never in all the years that he'd spent in
England had he been issued such an invitation. Warming to Professor Nichols' invitation, he leaned forward in
the seat and stripped off his hot jacket, a gesture which
was greeted with approving applause from the two men.

"India," he pronounced with soft bewilderment. . . .

Eden Castle
May 12, 1870

MARY SPOTTED THEM first, the turrets and towers of
Eden Castle, rising like a solitary jewel from its setting on
the headlands of the North Devon Coast. Briefly she suffered a curious mix of anticipation and dread.

In an effort to cancel the splintered feeling, she said,
"Look!" to Elizabeth, who sat opposite her and who had
been strangely quiet during the entire journey.

As Elizabeth leaned forward, Mary lowered the window
and received her first scent of sea breeze mingled with
heather. As a sense of homecoming swept over her, she
murmured, "How lovely it looks! Banners and flags at
every tower."

Elizabeth settled back in her seat, the prim feather on
her bonnet keeping time with the rhythm of the carriage,
as it had done for the past two days. In her lap was her
notebook, which she had studied since they had left
Bridgewater early that morning, going over her list of fifty
invited guests. John had granted all of them the privilege
of issuing fifty invitations to private friends.

The invitations had gone out months ago. Why was
there now a need to endlessly study those names? Yet all

of Mary's attempts at conversation had been blunted, and sensing that Elizabeth was still angry with her, the journey had been passed in silence.

"You'd best close the window, Mary," Elizabeth counseled. "Your hair will be—"

The sentence was never completed, and again Mary felt that silent anger. Mary was willing to make apologies, if she only knew what to apologize for.

Reluctantly she obeyed, drew up the window and smoothed back a wisp of hair that had been dislodged by the force of the wind. As she settled in the seat an idea occurred to her. Perhaps Elizabeth's mood was not aimed at her at all, but rather at her disappointment that Charlie Bradlaugh had not been able to accompany them.

Mary knew that Elizabeth was very fond of the man. Yet how surprised she had been when early Sunday morning Elizabeth had directed their driver around to Mr. Bradlaugh's rooms in Turner Street, Stepney. They both had taken morning coffee with him, while Elizabeth had practically begged him to accompany them *now* to Eden. But he'd declined, and Mary had thought wisely so. She was certain how John would have reacted to Elizabeth's arrival in the company of the notorious Charles Bradlaugh, radical, reformist, possessor of one of the most powerful personalities in all of England.

"Elizabeth?"

At the sound of her name, Elizabeth looked up, though her eyes merely skimmed over Mary's face before moving on to the passing moors outside the carriage window.

Now, as horsemen approached, the carriage slowed. One rider glanced in the window and, seeing the occupants, lifted his gloved hand in salute and waved the driver on.

As the carriage picked up new speed, Mary realized she had less than fifteen minutes to penetrate that cold mask which had fallen over those normally warm features.

"Elizabeth?" she tried again. "Would the presence of Mr. Bradlaugh have made this journey more tolerable for you?"

"It's been quite tolerable."

"No, it hasn't. Not for you." Mary reached for Elizabeth's hand. "Please talk to me," she begged. "Are you still angry over what happened at Jeremy Sims'? It was so innocent, and I said that I was sorry."

Elizabeth's forehead tightened. "Not innocent, Mary," she corrected sternly, "and I'm not blaming you entirely. A large portion of responsibility rests on my—"

"Why must anyone be blamed?" Mary asked. "Jeremy Sims runs a respectable establishment."

"I don't think John would agree."

"And who is John to agree or disagree?" Mary retorted. "If poor old Jeremy Sims offends John, think ahead to Friday and the arrival of Charlie Bradlaugh—"

At last Elizabeth looked directly at her. "They are my friends," she murmured.

"Exactly," Mary agreed. "Your friends and your life. What right does John have—"

"That's enough!" Elizabeth snapped, bringing the exchange to a halt. "The point of all this confusion has been carelessly ignored by both of us."

"And what would that be?"

"Simple," Elizabeth replied. "It is that I can no longer take full responsibility for your—well-being—"

Mary sat up.

"—that John must make other arrangements for you, that we each have our own lives to lead, and—"

Stunned, Mary only half-heard the words, but understood the meaning behind them, the pattern of her entire life, being passed from hand to hand, thinking at every turn that at last she'd found a secure haven, when in truth she'd found nothing.

"Mary, please try to understand," Elizabeth begged, apparently seeing something on her face that alarmed her.

"I understand," Mary said. "I'm in your way."

"That's not true."

"I seem to have an unfortunate propensity of getting in everyone's way. What precisely did God intend for young women to do? Why can't I have a cause and goals as you do, and friends as Richard does, as John himself? Why must I sit docilely and wait for someone's permission to live my life?"

At some point her voice had risen along with her emotions and, unable to deal with Elizabeth's abandonment, she gave in to anger and saw through a blur the outline of the Gatehouse drawing nearer. It reminded her of a prison, the prison of her childhood and now her adult prison. Elizabeth, the jailer, handing her over to John, the jailer. Where would they send her next? How many locked doors would she have to endure before—

No! She couldn't and wouldn't endure passively any longer, and though she lacked a scheme, she waited until the carriage slowed for the curved approach to the Gatehouse; then, without warning, she pushed open the carriage door, abandoning bonnet, gloves and Elizabeth, as she had been abandoned, not caring where she was going so long as her steps led her away from the coldness in the face opposite her and from the rising double grilles of the Eden Gatehouse, which now loomed before her as menacing as the double doors of Newgate Prison. . . .

"Mary! Come back, Mary!"

Elizabeth called her name twice and, without thinking, was just starting out the small door in pursuit when without warning the carriage started forward. Balanced half in, half out, she clung to the door.

Her cry of distress summoned the attention of the driver, who brought the horses to a halt just outside the gate. Still struggling for balance, she saw several guards running to her assistance, saw as well a top-hatted gentleman in the carriage ahead peer back at her predicament.

Her attention torn between her own narrow escape and the fleeing Mary, she scarcely took note of the score of men, led by the gentleman, who hurried toward her. Not until they were upon her did she realize the seriousness of her perch. If she had fallen to the ground while the carriage was moving, she would have been crushed under the wheels.

"I say, are you—" The gentleman arrived first, his hands reaching up in an offer of assistance.

Elizabeth took his hand, and it wasn't until she was standing on solid ground that she glanced up at the gentleman's face, seeing in the concerned features some element of recognition.

He shared the recognition. "Elizabeth? My God, it *is* you! What in the—"

Her attention still torn between Mary's sudden disappearance and the man smiling before her, she foundered. Briefly she closed her eyes and lost her balance and would have fallen had she not felt his arm about her shoulders.

"I'm quite well," she lied, and looked up into the familiar face. *John Thadeus Delane.* She hadn't seen

Delane in years, not since she had closed her salon upon John's return from India.

In an attempt to mask the awkward situation, she offered a weak explanation. "The carriage door fell open."

As she placed the blame on the door, she glanced toward the rise of land which led to the headlands, searching for a glimpse of Mary's dark blue traveling suit. The young girl was nowhere in sight. Elizabeth felt a strong compulsion to leave the gathering of concerned men and run after her in pursuit.

But it was clear that no one else had seen what had happened, and Elizabeth tried to still her rampaging nerves with the decision that it would be best not to compound the embarrassment with the stark announcement that Lady Mary Eden had been the cause of it all with her unannounced exit from the carriage.

Elizabeth saw the guards, led by Delane, in a close inspection of the carriage door. Behind her she saw that four other carriages had arrived, the congestion about the Gatehouse getting worse. In Mr. Delane's carriage she saw another man peering through the small oval window.

Enough! She'd not intended for her arrival to be such a theatrical. As for Mary, she wouldn't go far. There were steep cliffs in every direction. As soon as Elizabeth could disperse the excited men and get the carriages moving again, she would search for her, undoubtedly would find her weeping on some sandy beach, would offer her an apology, remind her that she loved her as though she were her own daughter, and while the decision that they part company had been difficult, it was for the best.

Glancing through the Gatehouse, she saw the mountainous form of Alex Aldwell, John's personal bodyguard, hurrying toward the confusion. Trouble there. Alex would not be as easy to deceive.

Struggling for control, Elizabeth stepped back to her carriage where the men, with mindless intensity, were studying the perfectly sound carriage door. "Mr. Delane," she called out, "please, I beg you. Return to your carriage. I did not intend for you to—"

"It appears sound, Elizabeth," the man announced. "Still, one can't be too careful. If I were you I would have a new latch put on. Narrow escape, that."

He stood directly before her, studying her closely. "What a pleasant greeting party for our arrival at Eden."

She laughed. "A bit dramatic, I'd say. Wouldn't you? Ladies tumbling hither and yon from carriage doors."

He stared down on her, something giving him pleasure. "I must confess," he said, "that when I received the invitation, I thought instantly of you, wondering if you would be present."

"Be present!" she repeated, seeing Alex Aldwell thunder through the Gatehouse arch, heading toward them, "I wouldn't have missed these Festivities for the world, Mr. Delane. As you know, John Murrey Eden is my—"

"What's going on?" The voice was strong and filled with the authority of the man who served John with blind love and who for his efforts was now one of the two men whom John trusted completely.

He was about to bellow again when he caught sight of Elizabeth and his manner softened. "Oh, it's you, Miss Elizabeth." He grinned. "We saw the pileup from the Great Hall steps, and John—"

As he waved toward the Great Hall across the inner courtyard, Elizabeth saw him, the tall, erect, fully bearded figure of the man whom she had raised as her own son and who now reigned over the entire kingdom of Eden and large portions of London as well.

Dear God, how can I ever explain Mary's absence to him?

The thought stirred her into action and she gave thanks for her ability to lace a secure public face over a disintegrating private one. "Alex—how good to see you!" She smiled, grasping the big man's arm. "I'm afraid I'm the culprit—or rather my carriage. The door gave way on the turn and I almost—"

"She almost fell to the ground," Delane concluded sternly.

"Lord," Alex muttered, shocked. "Well, I'll have a look at it. In the meantime, John—"

"Yes, John," she interrupted, informing Alex that she was aware of the man waiting on the steps.

"All right," Alex announced to the waiting guardsmen, "let's get things moving. Come, Miss Elizabeth, I'll ride in on the door with you. If it—"

"That's not necessary," Delane insisted. "I offer her the security of my carriage for the—"

Great Heavens! They were talking about a distance of less than a thousand yards. Elizabeth could have easily walked it and would have preferred it. But, looking up, she saw that Alex approved of the idea.

"Good," he said, studying the line of carriages behind them, six in number now and two more just leaving the moors.

Before she climbed into Delane's carriage, she glanced again toward that figure standing at the top of the Great Hall steps, movement all about him in the form of stewards with trunks hoisted upon their shoulders and an army of maids carrying hat and boot boxes.

"May I help you, madame?"

She looked up at the sound of the male voice coming from inside the carriage, a peculiar voice, not English. Her eyes, suffering the transition from bright sun to the shaded interior of the carriage, could not at first see. It was not until they all had settled for the short drive that she saw his face, a commanding face with even features, younger than Delane, with a full shock of dark hair, his handsome gray eyes watching her.

By way of introduction, Delane said, "Elizabeth, give me the honor of presenting Mr. Burke Stanhope, from America."

Elizabeth nodded, suffering a peculiar sensation that she had seen the man some place before. "Mr. Stanhope," she said, "let me apologize for my melodramatic entrance."

"No apologies are necessary," the man said gallantly, something in his easy, open manner that was very attractive.

"You're not injured, are you?" Mr. Stanhope inquired thoughtfully.

"No, not injured, except my pride." She laughed, detecting just a trace of a soft "r" sound in his speech. From the Southern part of the United States was her guess.

She was on the verge of asking what part of America he was from when she felt the carriage slow for the turn which would deposit them at the foot of the Great Hall steps and John Murrey Eden.

Hurriedly she adjusted her bonnet and tried to adjust her feelings as well, and said cordially, "Permit me to be the first to welcome both of you to Eden Castle. I hope you enjoy your stay."

"I'm sure we will," Mr. Stanhope said.

At last the carriage came to a halt. As Delane and Mr.

Stanhope drew on their gloves, Elizabeth's eyes remained fixed on John. How handsome he looked in his dark jacket, beautifully tailored to accommodate his broad shoulders, his fair hair flecked with gray now, still the image of his father!

She smiled at the steward who was opening the carriage door and realized that within moments she would have to confront John with the distressing news of the missing Mary.

Her head whirling with the complications of the awkward moment, she did not at first hear the voice calling her name from the shadows of the Great Hall. Only at the last minute did she look up to see Andrew Rhoades moving toward her.

"Elizabeth." He smiled, enclosing her in an embrace, the touch of a man who once had shared her bed and who had given up his plea that she become his wife.

Though she loved him dearly and would do nothing to hurt him, she had finally convinced him that such a marriage would be a disaster for both of them. Married, she would lose everything. As a spinster she enjoyed at least one or two male privileges, such as the right to own her own house.

She brushed her lips across his cheek and broke out of his embrace before their past intimacies were made public for all those staring eyes.

"Andrew, how good to see you," she murmured, one hand smoothing back his thinning hair, turning him to meet the two gentlemen behind her, who had observed everything.

"Andrew, allow me to present Mr. John Thadeus Delane, whom I believe you know, and this gentleman is Mr. Burke Stanhope, an American who has honored us with his presence."

Andrew shook Delane's hand. "Welcome to Eden, sir. I hope you will find everything here worthy of a good report."

"I'm sure I will, Mr. Rhoades," Delane replied.

Then Andrew extended his hand to Burke Stanhope. "And you, sir, welcome to Eden—though I must inform you that I am not an official host. That's him at the top of the steps."

As Andrew asked Burke Stanhope innocuous questions about the weather in London, Elizabeth found her atten-

tion fixed on the scene at the top of the stairs, John holding court as only John could, though something was
different, as though he were trying too hard.

Then she remembered. Only last month, when they
had gathered at Eden for a final meeting before the great
day, John had made it clear that they all were to be in
attendance during the welcoming of guests. Now she realized that with the exception of Andrew, John was alone.
Lila? Missing. Dhari? Missing. Lord Harrington? Missing.
Richard and Aslam? Missing.

Good! Then perhaps John would save a portion of his
anger for those truants.

Then there was no time to pursue the mystery further,
for Elizabeth saw John motioning one of the stewards to
take the guests to their chambers. The false smile on his
face faded as he caught sight of her.

"Andrew," Elizabeth whispered, interrupting the conversation behind her, "please do me the courtesy of presenting Mr. Delane and Mr. Stanhope to John. Alex has
sent my carriage around for repairs and I must fetch my
luggage."

A curious expression crossed Andrew's face. "A steward will—"

"Please, Andrew!"

At last he understood and turned to the two waiting
gentlemen. "This way, if you will."

Elizabeth held her position, a little annoyed by the
manner in which John was ignoring her. Though their
eyes met repeatedly, he had yet to acknowledge her in
any way.

To make matters worse, she saw him take Delane's
hand with stiff formality, not a smile on his face. Mr.
Stanhope received the same treatment and, suffering increasing annoyance, Elizabeth saw the two men being
ushered immediately away by a steward, John having dispatched them with cold civility.

How uncharacteristic of him, she thought, *to defeat his
own intent.* He had invited the journalists here today in
an attempt to woo and impress them. Didn't he realize
that John Thadeus Delane wielded the most powerful pen
in all of London?

As she started up the steps toward him, she realized
how often in the past they all had excused his heavy-

handed behavior on the grounds, "He's tired. Bear with him; he's doing it for us."

"John." She smiled, still worshiping, if not this man at least the little boy he once had been, Edward's son.

As she went up on tiptoe to deliver a kiss, she felt a terrifying lack of response coming from the man himself. She was aware of Andrew standing to one side, like a friendly keeper, ready to soothe John at the first indication that he needed it.

"Where's Mary?" John demanded, overlooking the fact that as words of greeting they left a great deal to be desired.

Elizabeth answered truthfully. "I'm afraid I don't know. She left the carriage while we were still outside—"

"What did you say?" he demanded, as though she'd said nothing.

Her hurt increasing, Elizabeth saw new carriages entering the Gatehouse. This was neither the time nor the place for a discussion of Mary's childlike stubbornness.

"She was upset," Elizabeth said. "She'll return soon, I feel."

"Upset!" The parroted words barely concealed the anger of the man who spoke them. "You act as though she's one of your female friends from Manchester, more man than woman, perfectly capable of taking care of—"

Out of the corner of her eyes, Elizabeth saw Andrew's hand lift to John's arm in a restraining gesture. "I'll go and find her if you wish," he volunteered.

"No, I'll go myself," John snapped. "Apparently no one in this household knows how to handle her or how important she is to this occasion."

With that he was hurrying down the stairs, impervious to the newly arrived guests left standing before their carriages.

Without hesitation Andrew stepped forward, ready to fill the vacuum, though he looked back at Elizabeth and whispered, "What happened?"

Elizabeth merely shook her head, beginning to feel the weariness of the journey, feeling as well a stinging across the bridge of her nose as she tried to deal with John's rebuff. Of course she shouldn't be hurt. Out of all the inhabitants of Eden, John favored Mary the most. In the past Elizabeth had tried to understand the intense relationship and had failed. He possessed a dear wife, a loving mistress. What inexplicable need had now sent him running after his young cousin?

The mystery was beyond her and she touched Andrew on the arm and in the last moment of privacy whispered, "I'll be in my apartments if anyone—"

As Andrew's voice rose into the tones of a substitute host, Elizabeth walked into the shadows of the Great Hall, distressed to see an even greater confusion than that in the inner courtyard. Enormous stacks of luggage rested everywhere, the stewards and house wardens doing their best to disperse the crowds, over a hundred men and a scattering of ladies standing about, openly ogling the rich interior of the Great Hall, a few scribbling notes on well-worn pads.

There was something about the scene of chaos that struck Elizabeth as obscene, working journalists who perhaps had difficulty meeting monthly expenses exposed to an opulence worthy of Midas. She gathered her skirts about her and commenced angling her way through the crowds, overhearing stray comments: "A nob's palace, that's for sure!" "Makes Buckingham look like an outbuilding." "Where's the free drinks we were promised? . . ."

Her face burned with embarrassment and, increasing her speed, she spied a familiar face, that of Hettie, the lady's maid who sometimes tended her when she was in residence at Eden.

"Miss Elizabeth!" the woman exclaimed, her voice raised above the noise. "Come—you've no business making your way alone."

Grateful, Elizabeth allowed the maid to clear a path through the jostling men. At the far end of the Great Hall they found a harbor of relative calm. "When did you arrive?" Hettie asked. "And does Mr. Eden know you're here? How eagerly he has awaited you! And where's Lady Mary? He was expecting her as well. Have you ever seen nothing like it?"

As the woman's mind turned in all directions at once, Elizabeth made no attempt to answer her questions. Instead she had one or two of her own.

"Hettie, where is everyone? Lady Lila—"

"Oh, not well this morning, Miss Elizabeth," the woman cooed. "Her maids tell us she'll be abed most of the day." Her sorrowful expression lifted as she added,

"But the babes is fine. You must see them, Miss Elizabeth; darling they are, and growing."

Elizabeth nodded. "And where's Dhari?" she asked, still trying to capture Hettie's scattered attention.

Hettie's eyes grew wide, sharing the mystery. "I don't rightly know. My guess is that she's making herself extra beautiful for the arrival of her son."

"Then Lord Richard has not—"

"No," Hettie replied, shaking her head, the prim white-lace cap quivering under the movement. "And Mr. Eden was fit to be tied early on, he was. But he settled down." She moved close to Elizabeth, her excitement growing. "Oh, Miss Elizabeth, I wish you could see the Kitchen Court! They got eight chefs working down there. The pantry's filled with cakes and puddings and trifles, and in the butchers', whole stags, dressed for roasting, and sides of beef the size of—"

"They all must be fed, mustn't they?" Elizabeth smiled, cutting the woman short, not interested in the excesses in the kitchen. "And Lady Harriet?" she asked, feeling the need to account for all the missing.

"Keeping to her chambers," Hettie whispered, a portion of her excitement dampened as though an embarrassing subject had been brought up.

Elizabeth started up the stairs without a word of parting. At the top of the first-floor landing she stopped, out of breath. She was getting old and, suffering one of those unexpected perceptions, she looked out over the magnificent Great Hall, amazed that she had a place here, that the pathetic little prostitute whose mother had sent her out at age thirteen in an attempt to earn a few bob had risen from that beginning to—this.

The perception didn't last long and was instantly replaced by her knowledge of the unhappiness which resided within the walls of this now elegant castle.

Slowly she turned about, her weariness increasing. There had been a time as recently as a year ago when her visits to Eden were interludes of deep joy, reveling in John's success. Now she was forced to admit that her greatest contentment—and she was willing to settle for contentment; happiness being the illusion of the young—took place in London, with her small circle of slightly off-center friends, lending what limited support she could to their worthy causes.

During these thoughts she walked slowly toward her chambers at the end of the second-floor corridor, looking forward to the privacy of her sitting room, where, with luck, she might nod off for a few minutes.

But as she reached her door she changed her mind. Her instincts told her that there were pockets of terrible unhappiness in this castle, and with the impulse toward compassion that she'd learned at Edward Eden's knee, she entered her apartment only long enough to remove her bonnet, gloves and cape; then she started out toward the third-floor landing, undecided whether the first object of her attention would be Lady Harriet, who must surely hear the sounds of guests arriving and regret anew her self-imposed blindness, or Lady Lila, John's vulnerable young wife, who, though ill-equipped for childbearing, was doing her best to provide John with the large boisterous family he had demanded, or Dhari, who must live in a perpetual state of silence, missing her son and locked in servitude to the man who was responsible for her inability to speak.

As Elizabeth started toward the third floor, she thought of the missing Mary and couldn't deny that there was need there as well. But somehow it paled in comparison to the anguish suffered by the three women whose apartments were scattered over the third and fourth floors of Eden Castle, women who, in their special ways, had given their lives to the glory, comfort and pleasure of John Murrey Eden.

As her sense of justice tilted dangerously out of balance, Elizabeth gained the fourth floor and started toward Lady Harriet's chambers. The others, Lila and Dhari, would have to wait until their respective husband and lover returned from his search for his beautiful cousin.

She hoped they would understand. She didn't . . .

Expecting the luxury to end at the public rooms, Burke was amazed to find a Persian carpet beneath his feet as thick as the ones in the lower corridors.

Standing in the door of his guest chamber on the fourth floor of the west wing, he saw the dark green velvet drapes beautifully framing the long window, the window itself covered with white lace, which blew gently under the pressure of a slight channel breeze. As the steward unpacked

his luggage, Burke listened to see if he could hear Delane
settling into the chamber next door. Curious to see if those
rooms were as luxurious as his own, he started through
the door, then changed his mind. He knew that his old
friend was still smarting from John Murrey Eden's cool
reception.

Well, he'll recover, Burke thought, and moved deeper
into the room, his attention drawn to all aspects of the
decor, observing upon closer examination that at some
point good taste ended and ostentation commenced. Burke
smiled. Lord Ripples could write three columns on the
decor of Eden Castle alone. Objects could be reassuring if
life refused to fit into approved patterns and, based on
this excess of things, Burke had reason to believe that life
below the surface at Eden clearly did not fit into approved
patterns. Surrounding all was the odious smell of com-
merce, as though John Murrey Eden were silently pleading with his guests to judge him on the presentation of
displayed objects.

Curious, but Burke had not expected this. Glancing
about at the frills and geegaws and velvet fringes, he'd
somehow expected to find a castle as rugged as the man
himself, a simple utilitarian statement in stone which
matched the pragmatism of John Murrey Eden.

"Will there be anything else, sir?"

At the sound of the voice, Burke glanced over his
shoulder at the steward standing in the door, several suits
suspended across his arms, among them Burke's dress
blacks.

"There's no need," Burke said, indicating the suits
which were about to be taken somewhere. "I'm sure you
have—"

Thinking to relieve him of an unnecessary service,
Burke saw the tall man shake his head. "They could do
with a bit of press, sir. That's what I'm here for."

The man stood in the door, looking uncomfortable in
his crimson and gold livery, clearly new, with high-
buttoned collar and tight sleeves. The rooms below had
been a sea of identical uniforms.

Following his journalist's instincts, which, based on past
experience, told him that servants frequently were good
informants, he moved closer to the man, aware that as a
guest he had no business engaging him in conversation but
doing so anyway. What the hell! He was an American.

Americans, according to most Englishmen, knew little of the modes and manners of civilized people.

"What's your name?" Burke asked cordially.

"Paul, sir," the man replied, his eyes never quite making contact with Burke's.

"Paul," Burke repeated. "I'm certain you have other duties to attend to. The suits are—"

"You are my only duty, sir—you and Mr. Delane. I have no other responsibilities, save those which entail your comfort and well-being."

"How long have you worked at Eden, Paul?"

The direct question caused the man's eyes to move to Burke's face. "I'm not permanent staff, sir," the man replied, coldly polite. "I was trained and brought in for the Festivities."

"How many are there of you?" Burke persisted.

"Regular staff, sir?" Paul replied. "Regular staff members around two hundred. With us extras, we're four hundred strong."

Shocked by the figures, Burke glanced back to see the man gazing at him. "Anything else, sir?"

Still trying to comprehend a domestic staff of four hundred, Burke did well to shake his head. "One thing more, Paul. Do we dress for dinner, and what are we supposed—"

"Begging your pardon, sir, but there is a schedule of events on the table. It will inform you of all your activities and the required dress. As for tonight, no, the gentlemen of the press will enjoy an informal buffet in the Great Hall."

"None of the family will be present?"

"No, sir, not tonight. The first formal banquet will be tomorrow evening."

Burke glanced over his shoulder at the large gold pamphlet with crimson tassel which he'd missed in the general clutter of the room.

Paul bowed and murmured, "If there's nothing else, sir—"

"No, that will be all." As Burke started to close the door behind him, he called, "Please ask Mr. Delane to join me after he has settled in."

He moved back into the room, lifted the heavy parchment containing the schedule of events and carried it to the light of the opened window, studying the Eden coat of arms on the cover, still amazed that a gentleman would purposefully create this carnival atmosphere in the privacy of his home, subjecting his family to such public display.

Suffering an unexpected image, Burke closed his eyes and saw the young woman with the beautiful voice at the Jeremy Sims Song and Supper Club. How bleak his evenings in London would be without her, and he was certain that he would never see her again. He remembered his fleeting glance at the middle-aged woman standing in the wings, whose face bore the look of—

Abruptly he opened his eyes, thinking that he had seen that woman someplace. Mystified, he drew back the curtains, as though fresh air would help to clear the cobwebs from his head. He *had* seen her. *But where?*

As he squinted down onto the headlands below, he was distracted from his confused memory by his first glimpse of the vista, the vast sweep of headlands stretched out below like a massive green carpet, the carefully tended lawn extending to the edge of the cliffs, then the blue-green of the channel itself, dotted here and there with small white fishing packets, Wales visible in the distance.

Just as he was breathing deeply of the refreshing sea breeze, he caught sight of a figure, reduced by the height and distance to miniature proportions, a man running along the edge of the cliff. Fascinated, Burke leaned closer to the window, his attention caught by some recognition of the gentleman which carried in spite of the distance.

Good God! Burke tried to shield his eyes from the sun. It couldn't be, yet it was! The master of the castle himself, John Murrey Eden, who apparently had abandoned his duties as host and who was now running across the headlands in search of something.

Burke leaned further out and searched the headlands in both directions, finding nothing but a row of stone beaches placed every fifty yards or so, where guests might sit and enjoy the channel view.

Then he saw something at the extreme right edge of his vision, behind a low clump of shrub and beach bramble, a dark blue something that appeared to be in hiding. A woman? From that distance it was difficult to tell. She appeared to be crouching on the edge of the cliff, her head bowed, her face obscured, as though the last thing she wanted was to be found.

It *was* a woman. He could see her dark blue skirts, which she'd gathered about her in her bowed, crumpled position.

He looked back toward Eden, who had ceased running and who now stood at the edge of the cliff, hands on hips, as though baffled. *What a peculiar position to be in,* Burke mused, enjoying his crow's nest view, enabling him to see what Eden was looking for but had yet to find.

Enjoying this unscheduled drama, he rested his elbows on the sill. If Eden turned about now he would never find her, and Burke found himself pulling for her concealment. "Stay quiet," he whispered, as though sending down instructions to her, his eyes fixed on the hesitating figure of John Murrey Eden.

Abruptly the man stopped. Less than twenty feet from where the woman hid, Burke saw him kick petulantly at the ground.

Then he saw her. "Damn!" Burke cursed under his breath, amazed at his involvement in the distant drama. Apparently having found her, Eden suffered no compulsion to go immediately to her.

As for the lady, she was still locked in her illusion of safety.

Suddenly there was a movement, though not from Eden. This time it was the lady who, sensing his presence, looked over her shoulder and was struggling to her feet, ready to flee again.

Then Burke saw Eden moving. She had just started down the steep embankment when he gained her side and held her fast, both of them partially concealed by the thickness of bushes.

Words were exchanged, Burke was certain, though all he could detect was the struggle. Then, without warning. Eden slapped her, a silent pantomime of violence, his hand shooting forward, the woman reeling under the force of the blow, her body crumpled awkwardly to one side, her arm still held rigid by Eden.

Burke continued to stare down on the drama rising noiselessly from so far below. Suffering a surge of witless chivalry, he considered leaving his vantage point, and going to the woman's aid. In all seriousness he was fully prepared to do this if Eden lifted a hand to her again.

But to the contrary, the only movement taking place now was one of reconciliation, Eden drawing the woman into his arms, the two of them from that distance blending into one.

Under the duress of his gaze, Burke closed his eyes, confounded as to the true nature of this strange domestic drama. Slowly he looked back down, confident that after the reconciliation he would be treated to a full glimpse of the two as they emerged arm in arm, the drama over.

Therefore he was in no way prepared for the emptiness which greeted his eyes as he looked back toward the cliff. Nothing. Not a sign of life or movement. He leaned further out over the sill. Where could they have gone?

Suffering a keen sense of disappointment, Burke raised up from the windowsill. Who was the woman? He had no idea and, having failed to get a good look at her, perhaps would never know. But of this he was certain: for all the elegance and surface polish of Eden Castle, there were forces loosed here that certainly begged for closer scrutiny.

Suffering a twinge of conscience, it occurred to him, who better to uncover a man living a lie than a man living a lie? As though he were suffering actual deprivation at not being able to witness the two beyond his vision, he leaned dangerously far out the window and searched the emptiness.

"My God, Burke, I apologize for the tastelessness of this occasion, but it does not warrant suicide."

As the sound of Delane's voice, rife with black humor, filled the room, Burke drew back from the window, sad to see the expression of hurt still on his friend's face.

He smiled at an attempt to ease the hurt. "If, after the events of my life, Delane, I've resisted suicide thus far, I doubt if anything I find here will—"

Though Burke's attention was still splintered between the events which he'd witnessed on the headlands and the grim look on Delane's face, he sat in a near chair. "Well, what now, my friend?" he asked, deciding at the last minute not to share the specifics of the little drama he'd seen.

Delane shrugged. "Join the others, I suppose," he muttered.

Burke stood and took his arm, turning him about with a

cheerful suggestion. "Then come. Let's find the bar. Surely in the midst of all this wealth our host has been thoughtful enough to provide us with an open bar."

Delane glanced up at the invitation. "I'm sorry for involving you in this—circus, Burke," he said. "I fear that we have nothing but boredom ahead of us."

Burke started to reply but changed his mind, secure in the knowledge that the fortnight ahead might be many things, but boredom would not be one of them. Unwittingly he'd seen enough from his window to know that John Murrey Eden wore many masks. What sport it would be to try to glimpse behind one or two of them!

Also it occurred to him that he had better enjoy the bounty of Eden while he could, for he knew that when Lord Ripples finished writing about the Eden Festivities, he would not be welcomed in any part of North Devon, or the West Country, or in England herself, for that matter. . . .

He had not intended to strike her. It was just that coming upon her so unexpectedly, suffering concern for her and being repaid only with her stubbornness, he had tried reason first, and that failing, he had struck her.

As she'd fallen forward into his arms, he'd held her close and had apologized. But with his apology her tears had increased and, as she'd clung to him, he'd looked up and for the first time it had occurred to him that they were visible to anyone who might be peering out the upper windows of the castle. Cursing the congestion of visitors that he himself had invited, he had escorted her down the incline to the secluded beach, where now he knelt in the sand at her feet, where she sat on a piece of shipwrecked timber.

In spite of her tears, he realized that she'd grown even more beautiful since he'd last seen her.

"Mary, don't," he begged, finding her tears unendurable. He'd caused enough unhappiness within the castle the last few days. He'd counted on Mary's irrepressible joy and youthful spirit to set a new tone, once more in keeping with the occasion.

"Please," he whispered, trying to remove her hands from her face, seeing between her fingers dull red marks caused by his blow. *My God, what possessed me?*

"Mary, look at me. Nothing is worth this. You'll make yourself ill."

He heard the first break in the racking sobs, saw her bend her head even lower, as though the vanity of the woman were equal to the grief of the child. As she commenced to search for a handkerchief, he provided her with his own.

In the quiet interim filled with the soft lap of waves on the beach and an occasional spasm of her leftover grief, he rested his elbows on his knees, mystified by the effect that female tears had on him. Without a doubt it was the most effective weapon.

"Better?" he whispered.

But she gave no response and he put his arm around her, their foreheads touching. "Shall we talk?" he asked. "We must talk. Here I look forward for weeks to seeing you, and what happens? Elizabeth arrives alone, telling me some absurd tale about your bolting."

Both his voice and manner were light, as though he were speaking to a child instead of a young woman. Gently he pulled back the long strands of soft hair that had fallen loose during her tears. Suffering a mix of brotherly/fatherly love, John found himself desperate to know the cause of her grief.

"Now, what happened?"

"We . . . quarreled," Mary murmured.

"Who quarreled?"

"Elizabeth . . ." She lowered her head as though she had been newly defeated.

John laughed at the simple explanation that had caused such grief. "You—quarreled?" he stammered. "My God, Mary, people quarrel every day."

"I don't," she said, looking up. "And Elizabeth and I have never—"

"All right," he conceded. "What was the nature of your quarrel?"

"She said that she was going to talk to you, that she could no longer—care for me in London and that you must make other arrangements."

From where he stood he saw her bow her head, as though the rejection hurt deeply.

"She said what?" he demanded. Although it was the subject which he himself had considered, he resented the fact that Elizabeth had initiated it.

She faced him. "She said . . . she has her own life, and that I must be sent . . . somewhere else. She's never spoken like that before, John. I try very hard to do as she says, and I thought that she loved me."

As new tears spilled down her cheeks, he was there to receive her, enclosing her in his embrace, his attention divided between her softness and his growing anger at Elizabeth. If only she'd left everything to him. He could have handled it with much greater diplomacy. "No need. Elizabeth will do as I say. If London suits you so, then you shall have it."

Slowly she looked up at him, a smile on her face. "Oh, John, how much I love you!"

Pleased by her new mood, he kissed her lightly on the forehead, seeing up close her dark blue eyes—Harriet's eyes before—

"Come." He smiled. "Let's return now. I have guests to greet and you must look your most beautiful."

He was aware of her watching him, though he had the sense that she was not listening to what he was saying.

She lifted a hand to his face, her fingers moving across his flesh, a feathery sensation which caused the skin on his forehead to tighten. "We're—cousins, aren't we?" she asked, moving closer.

He nodded, knowing better, but the secret was his. And Harriet's.

"Cousins sometimes fall in love, don't they, John?"

With her face so close, he saw his reflected image in her eyes. What was she doing? And how could he stop it, for stop it he must, and soon.

"Some do," he said, trying to move away. "But it would be impossible for me to love you more than I do now," he added, still bewildered.

She seemed pleased by this declaration and, before he could object, she was in his arms again, the most incredible words filling his ear. "Then let me stay with you at Eden, John," she whispered. "Let me be with you always. I promise I'll make you happy."

"Mary, don't—"

Shocked by her sudden change of mood, he pushed her away, seeing the innocence of that face corrupted by the conniving expression of a flirt.

She didn't know what she was doing and, convinced

that the intensity of her emotions were simply residual, the need for closeness after Elizabeth's rejection of her, he tried to deal calmly with the awkward situation. "Of course you may return to Eden if you wish," he began, "but there's nothing for you here."

"You're here."

"A few days out of each month. The rest of the time I'm in London."

"We never see you there anymore. You used to come every evening."

"I—have no appetite for Elizabeth's new friends."

"Nor have I."

He smiled back at her, striving to maintain the objective conversation between them. "Well," he began, "perhaps the truth of the matter is that you have outgrown both London and Eden. Perhaps you need a new environment, one which will offer you more of a challenge."

A look of suspicion crossed her face. "Where?"

"There's no need to discuss it now."

"Where, John?" she demanded.

Gently he took her by the hand and led her back to the timber where he sat, and thought that she would follow suit.

But she didn't. She stood before him, that guarded expression on her face.

Glancing up at her only once, then addressing his words to the sandy beach, John commenced speaking, with as much diplomacy as he commanded.

"Do you know"—he smiled—"that I've had nothing but good reports from your tutors? They tell me how quick you are."

"Of course they would say that."

He looked up. "Then am I to understand that it's not true?"

"I can read and write and do figures," she said. "Little more."

"I find that hard to believe. Look at how Richard has risen, a full professor at—"

"I am not Richard."

"You share the same blood."

"Nothing else."

She was making it difficult for him. In the new silence

he looked up to see her hands trembling. "Where are you sending me, John?"

He disliked the tension between them. "I'm not sending you anyplace," he said. "The decision is yours, as is the choice—"

"That's not true. You know as well as I that I have never made one decision in my life. Others have done it for me."

"Well, then," he commenced, aware of her standing before him, her manner like a prisoner awaiting sentence. "Oh, for God's sake, Mary!" he exploded, disliking her martyred stance. "It's for your own good."

"What is?"

He drew a deep breath. "There's a school, newly established. For females. Near Cheltenham. I've visited it," he lied. "It's lovely, tucked away in a secluded valley in the Cotswoods, run by a Miss Veal."

At last he dared to look up. "A school for women, Mary. Imagine. A place where you can pursue your education, where you can—"

But all the time he was talking she was shaking her head. "No," she begged, crouching before him, her earlier grief nothing compared to this new fear, the most incredible words filling the quiet beach. "No. Please, John, don't. I beg you," she wept, "don't send me away. Let me stay here with you. I'll do anything you ask. I'll be good to you; I swear it."

She was approaching hysteria, her hands moving down the front of her gown.

John tried to move away, but she reached out for his hand and placed it on her breast, pushing closer between his legs. "John, please," she whispered. "Let me stay with you. It can be our secret."

Coming to his senses, though reeling with shock and outrage, convinced that Elizabeth and her sordid past were responsible for this clawing young woman, John could only stare at her, seeing nothing of innocence now.

Without looking at her, he commanded. "That's enough. Get up! If only you could see yourself."

"I *have* seen myself," she wept. "You're the one who refuses—"

"I said, 'Enough!' " In anger he looked down to see her. "Have you any conception of your actions?" he de-

manded, amazed at how ugly her face was now, mucus
from her nose blending with tears and spittle. Suddenly
he grasped her arms and shook her, a violent motion
which left her suspended in his grasp like a puppet.

Without warning a thought occurred to him so grim
that it almost rendered him silent. "Look at me, Mary,"
he commanded, and when she refused he reached for
her face, grasped her jaw with such strength that she
moaned softly.

Anchored in his grasp, he forced her attention. "Are
you—" he began and could not finish. "Have you—received a man before?" he asked, keeping his voice down,
as fearful of the question as she was of the answer.

In spite of her suffering, she smiled. "H-hundreds,"
she stammered, the smile increasing. "Thousands!"

Although he knew she was lying, something in her
manner enraged him—her stupidity, if nothing else, her
ignorance, the manner in which she had toyed with him,
exhibiting no fear. What if he had lacked the control?
For both of them? It was this awareness of what might
have happened that caused him to lift his hand and
bring it down across the side of her face with a force
that spun her loose from his grasp and caused her to cry
aloud, half falling to her knees, then immediately struggling upward, looking back at him with an expression of
fear.

As she commenced running up the steep incline, he
called after her, "Mary, come back!"

But she didn't, and the last he saw was the hem of her
gown disappearing at the top of the incline. Wearily he
sat on the timber, suffering deep remorse. He closed his
eyes and rested his head in his hands, still seeing her before him, the lingering sensation of his hand on her
breast.

Not cousin, his thoughts raged. *Sister, half-sister.* What
penance he would have to pay for that, in addition to the
one he was still paying!

But the thought was too difficult and he moved directly
to the edge of the water. He'd struck her too hard. Why
had he struck her at all? He'd not intended to force—

As his thoughts whirled through his head, he looked
up, struggling for control. He'd have to make his apologies later. For now, for the duration of this important
fortnight, he'd place a discreet guard on her, two loyal

stewards who would watch her every move and report
back to him. Then, when the last guest had departed, he
would personally escort her to Miss Veal's school in
Cheltenham.

Breathing with relief, he strode back to the steep incline. At the top he brushed the sand from his trousers,
smoothed back his hair, straightened his neck scarf and
walked with confidence the length of his headlands,
around the west wing of the castle, past his watchmen,
who bowed respectfully, and into his courtyard, where
straight ahead at the foot of his Great Hall steps he saw
new guests waiting eagerly for his reception. . . .

On Friday afternoon, only hours before the unveiling
of "The Women of Eden," Elizabeth sat on the window-
seat of Lady Harriet's private apartments, the chubby two-
year-old cherub named Frederick cuddled in her arms,
watching for Lila as she coached four-year-old Stephen
in a sweet, piping nursery song for the enjoyment of Lady
Harriet, whose veiled head kept time with the melancholy
refrain.

To one side knelt Dhari, her dark eyes alive with
shared love, the entire sitting room bathed in a diffuse
golden glow of midafternoon sun.

Elizabeth kissed the crown of Frederick's curls and
smiled as Lila helped Stephen with a low note, the little
boy's face a solemn mask as he endeavored to perform
well for Harriet.

Curious, Elizabeth mused. Though both boys were fair
like John, they bore a much greater resemblance to Lila,
their complexions hers, like fine porcelain.

As the nursery song rose with sweet clarity, Elizabeth
contented herself with Frederick, his chubby fist wrapped
around her finger. How peaceful it was here; how different from the crowded public rooms below!

All at once she heard two voices joined in the song.
Looking across the room, she noticed Harriet had drawn
the child close, her voice in perfect harmony.

The duet pleased all. Stephen grinned at his mother
but never lost a beat, and Lila sat back on her heels, her
pretty rose taffeta skirt spread out about her, and clapped
her hands in undisguised glee. With a smile she glanced
across at Elizabeth, as though wanting to include all.

Moved, Elizabeth tightened her grasp on Frederick,

and thought sadly, here was John's painting. Here were the Eden women, with one notably absent, but here in their true domain. How much more appropriate this, as opposed to that ridiculous canvas concealed beneath the shroud in the library.

As they were approaching the last stanza of the nursery song, Elizabeth thought that all they lacked was Mary's voice, and the thought shattered the peace of the room and dragged Elizabeth's attention back to the problem with which she'd arrived at Eden.

Mary.

She'd not seen her since their arrival. The first evening she'd managed to steal a moment with John, and tersely he'd informed her that he'd located Mary on the headlands, had found her distraught and had personally assisted her to her chambers.

Two days ago, bewildered by Mary's prolonged absence from all public rooms, Elizabeth had climbed to her private apartments in the family wing, only to find two stewards outside her door who had informed her that Lady Mary was not feeling well and had asked not to be disturbed.

Nothing unusual there. Mary frequently took to her bed during extreme excitement.

Then today she'd again stopped by Mary's apartments and had been told by the same two stewards that Lady Mary was preparing herself for the evening's Festivities and had asked not to be disturbed. Again a reasonable request. Elizabeth knew that John had asked Mary to sing for his guests tonight and, wanting to do well, undoubtedly she was saving herself. For the second time Elizabeth had accepted the words of the stewards without question.

As the harmony at midroom was winding down, she found herself inclined to question everything. To impose three days of seclusion on herself was most unlike Mary Eden. But perhaps it hadn't been total seclusion. Maybe Harriet had seen her, or Lila, or Dhari. Perhaps that door had only been closed to Elizabeth, and as the thought caused minor pain, she moved away from it and joined the others in applause for the song which had just ended.

"Lovely," she called from the window seat, as Harriet enclosed the blushing Stephen in her arms.

At the conclusion of this embrace, Lila reached out for her son and drew him close.

Frederick, feeling left out, scrambled off Elizabeth's lap and ran to join the embrace, approaching his mother and brother with awkward two-year-old exuberance and almost knocking them over in an attempt to find his way into the shelter of her arms.

Laughing, Lila sat on the floor and took both her sons with her, a tumbling scene of maternal love which caused Elizabeth to suffer a twinge of envy. How she would have adored children, her own children!

In an attempt to throw off the mood, she left the window seat and joined the laughter, taking up a position behind Harriet's chair. "What a secret you've kept from us all, Harriet!" she said, smiling. "I had no idea you had such a lovely voice. Now I know where Mary derives her talent."

Harriet grasped her hand. "I amuse myself," she said modestly. "During my confinement I would sing to pass the hours."

Standing behind Harriet's chair, Elizabeth made eye contact with Lila, a shared surprise at the unexpected reference to the past, to that nine-year imprisonment when she'd blinded herself, shut herself away from all contact with the world.

Why?

Lacking an answer and suspecting that she'd never have one, she hugged Harriet and was just starting to join Lila and Dhari where they sat on the floor playing with the boys, when a knock sounded at the door, immediately followed by an aggressive voice. "Lady Lila, I've come for the children. It's their dinnertime."

Lila and Elizabeth exchanged a glance, their mutual loathing of Miss Samson, the nursemaid, clear. Aware that her time with the children was limited, Lila gathered both to her.

"Bitch," Elizabeth muttered.

"So soon?" Harriet whispered, her regret as deep as the others'.

Lila leaned forward, the happiness of her face annihilated by the imminent loss. "I can care for them, Elizabeth," she begged. "Why won't John let me—"

The knock came again. "Come, Lady Lila, you have exceeded the hour by ten minutes as it is."

As Lila grasped her children, Elizabeth stood, recalling the countless times she'd begged John to fire the harsh old nursemaid and return the boys to Lila.

But he would hear none of it. Proper children had proper nursemaids.

"You are in there, Lady Lila," the voice came again. "I know you are. Let's not have a scene. You know the rules, laid down by Mr. Eden himself."

"Oh, for God's sake, let her in," Harriet muttered.

At last Dhari stood, and Elizabeth saw the same perplexed look on her face, her inability to understand why a mother would be denied her own children.

As she approached the door, the knocks sounded again, and Elizabeth saw Dhari fling open the heavy oak door with such force that it crashed against the wall. Still Dhari stood, as though blocking the entrance of the massive woman who stood on the other side, flanked by her three assistants.

From where she stood, Elizabeth saw the confrontation hold, saw the stern face of Miss Samson assess the woman before her, that look of unspoken censure in her eyes with which most of the servants viewed Dhari. How Dhari endured it, Elizabeth had no idea, and frequently in the last nine years she'd begged the woman to return with her to London and, while Dhari seemed more than willing, John would not permit it.

She saw Dhari step aside before the glacial, condemning gaze of Miss Samson, a bland, broad, constantly redsplotched face which wore a mask of perfect confidence.

Without words the woman bobbed politely to everyone in the room, then moved to where her two small charges were clinging to their mother's neck. Without speaking, she lifted her hand in signal to her assistants waiting in the corridor. As they came forward, one reached down for Stephen's arm, the other Frederick's, while at the last minute both children protested the rude separation. "Mamma, let us stay!"

Then it was over, the nursemaids marching both boys out of the door. As the gloomy parade left the room, Elizabeth turned back to the window seat, grateful that she did not have to witness the separation daily.

Well, someone had to move. They all, with the exception of Harriet, were expected downstairs, fully groomed, in less than four hours. Not that Elizabeth was totally

dreading it. According to Richard, with whom she had
enjoyed a private luncheon, Charlie Bradlaugh, her good
friend from London, had arrived early this morning,
to John's annoyance, or so Richard had said. At first
he had refused to receive the radical free-thinker, but
the porter in charge of the guest list had pointed out
that Mr. Bradlaugh was listed as her guest and the man
had been admitted, though he'd been asleep all day, recovering from the journey.

Elizabeth would have to apologize for the embarrassment, a chore that was becoming habit with her where
John was concerned. But no matter. She greatly looked
forward to Charlie's company tonight, and she even
looked forward to the unveiling of that silly painting,
aware that the artist, Lawrence Alma-Tadema, had himself arrived about noon in the company of several distinguished gentlemen from the Royal Academy.

"Come, Lila," Elizabeth urged, the need to stir life
into the frozen room strong within her.

As Elizabeth led the way to the door, she looked back
at Harriet. "Are you sure you won't join us?" she asked,
knowing the answer in advance but issuing the invitation
anyway.

"No, thank you," Harriet murmured. "An invalid does
have rights, and with what relief I will now exercise
mine."

Elizabeth had just turned about when she heard Harriet's voice again. "One small favor, Elizabeth," she
asked.

"Anything."

"If time permits, would you ask Mary to come and see
me? I know she's in the castle. Peggy told me so. I had
thought she would come to see me today, but—" She
broke off and gave a self-deprecating laugh. "As you can
see, I'm without pride. I hunger for my daughter's company, and I'd go to her, if I could."

"She's—not been to see you at all?" Elizabeth questioned, baffled.

Harriet shook her head. "I've sent Peggy several times,
but she's always greeted by two stewards who tell her
that Mary is . . . indisposed, or resting."

Having heard those tales before, Elizabeth turned to
Lila and Dhari. "Have either of you visited with Mary?"

Dhari shook her head, as did Lila.

"Do you suppose she's ill?" Harriet asked, concerned. "She arrived with you, didn't she, Elizabeth? Was she well then? Did you see to her chambers?"

The mystery was increasing for Harriet as well. "You've not seen her either since your arrival?"

"No," Elizabeth confessed. "I'm sure there's no cause for worry," she comforted. "You know Mary as well as I. She's probably just—"

"Has John seen her?"

"I don't know," Elizabeth lied, knowing full well that John was the last to have seen her.

Apparently at that moment Harriet sensed the new tension in the room. "John informed me that . . . he was sending her away . . . to some school, I don't know. . . ." Agitated, Harriet was in the process of struggling out of her chair.

"No, you wait here," Elizabeth insisted. "I'll go right away and report back to you."

Dhari stepped forward, indicating that she would wait with Harriet. At the door Elizabeth looked back. "I won't be long." She closed the door behind her and turned to see Lila in conversation with Harriet's maid, Peggy.

At the end of the brief exchange, Elizabeth reached out for Lila's hand and the two started down the corridor. In an attempt to fill the worried silence, Elizabeth smiled. "We have yet to have our long talk," she said, recalling how on past visits she and Lila always managed to steal a day together.

A look of need crossed Lila's face. "I'd like that."

"Well, then," Elizabeth said, "you run along. Try to rest for a few hours."

Lila nodded and suddenly reached out and drew Elizabeth to her, an unexpected embrace of such need that Elizabeth could only cling to her and try, without words, to reassure her that any nightmare could be endured.

Then the woman broke free and ran down the corridor toward her apartments. As she disappeared around the corner, Elizabeth held her position. Coming from four floors below she heard the distant echo of men laughing, and somewhere musicians were tuning their instruments. Time was growing short and, as always, the main problem was—Mary.

As she started off down the corridor, she suffered remorse for her condemnation of the young woman. There
were forces within Mary, an incredible capacity to love
and be loved, a generosity of spirit unlike anyone Elizabeth had ever known. How wrong of her to have mentioned so bluntly to Mary her dissatisfaction with their
living arrangements. What an intolerable rejection that
must have seemed to the young woman after a lifetime
of rejection.

Her step increased and, along with it, her need to
apologize. As she turned the corner which led to Mary's
apartments, she looked ahead and saw the two stewards
guarding the door.

Elizabeth stopped and drew herself up. Well, she'd
dealt with servants before and, although generally she was
polite to a fault, she was not in any mood to brook their
excuses. In spite of everything, she was eager to join the
Festivities below, for she loved John dearly and always
would.

Through John's genius, Eden Castle stood today in its
present state, and all its occupants owed their well-being
to this one man, who had taken a musty portfolio of
seventeen ancient deeds and converted them into one of
the most dazzling empires that England had ever seen.

Moved by her own thoughts, Elizabeth hurried toward
the waiting stewards, determined to get past them to
Mary, if for no other reason than to personally see that
she was smiling, upright and beautifully groomed for her
benefactor, John Murrey Eden. . . .

Curled in an enclosed position on her mussed bed,
from which she could see no single horizon that offered
hope, Mary heard the voices outside her door, the two
stewards who had informed her several days ago that it
was Mr. Eden's desire that she keep to her chamber.

Although at first she had objected to the confinement,
she had at last acquiesced, her decision helped along by
her mirror, which by nightfall on that first day had given
back a reflected image of a blackened eye, caused by
John's blows.

For the last three days she'd not even bothered to dress
and had seldom left her bed. She'd passed the hours
staring up at the heavy timbers overhead, listening to the
hum of voices in the corridor outside her door.

But the two stewards had stood fast and, confident that they would stand fast again, she raised herself to her elbow and shook a strand of snarled hair from her face and looked down the length of her body, past the nightdress spotted with old porridge to her dirt-encrusted toes, where sand had filled her slippers on that day she'd tried to escape.

There had been no escape for her and she knew that there would be no escape—ever. After these two weeks, John would send her away to prison walls behind which she would rot, unless she could take her own life first.

How calmly the thought entered her mind, and she leaned back against the pillow, her hands caressing her breast, the sensation bringing her comfort. Her mind moved easily into fantasy, replacing the despair of the present with a faceless lover, who late each night approached her bed and who stood over her, looking down—

Suddenly she moaned and turned on her side, her knees drawn up against the pain of emptiness. The voices outside her door rose, the two stewards protesting something.

Elizabeth.

The fantasy abandoned, Mary sat up, alarmed. Elizabeth was an extension of John. On the edge of the bed she looked back toward the closed door, where someone was struggling for possession of the doorknob. Why didn't they leave her alone?

Irrationally she looked about as though there were an escape route in this room which she had failed to notice after ten years of occupancy. But she saw nothing except the dead-end of her own chambers. She looked back toward the door, the stewards and Elizabeth mysteriously silent at the sound of approaching footsteps, the rhythm of the man's gait conjuring up an image of the man himself as she'd last seen him, hovering angrily over her, his eyes sharp with accusation, his hand lifting—

In defense against the memory of bewildering pain, knowing that now the door *would* open, that she would have to face both John and Elizabeth, Mary stumbled backward, spying the open window, the place from which during the last three days she'd looked down four floors below into the Eden graveyard, that enclosed plot

where every Eden since the fourteenth century had been
buried.

Hearing the key turning in the lock and knowing that
she would have to face the two people who once had
loved her but who now hated her and meant her ill,
and knowing further that the future held nothing for her
but locked doors and increasing emptiness, recalling the
shaded peace of the graveyard, she said goodbye to reason, as recently she had said goodbye to her pride, and
ran toward the rectangle of late-afternoon sunlight,
amazed that there *was* an escape route in this chamber
and how dense of her not to have noticed it before. . . .

Still angered by her confrontation with the insolent
stewards and grateful that John had come along and dismissed them both, Elizabeth was the first one through
the door and was almost driven back by the smell of
soiled linen.

But the disagreeable scent faded in importance as,
looking about, she caught sight of Mary, though it was a
Mary she had never seen before, clinging to the windowsill in a soiled nightdress, her long hair matted about her
face, her eyes filled with terror as she looked back into
the room.

John pushed past her and started toward the window,
apparently failing to see the girl pull herself sharply upward until she was balanced precariously on the sill.

"Wait!" Elizabeth warned him quietly, terrified by the
tableau.

Having managed to freeze everyone at least for the moment, Elizabeth made an effort to steady her own nerves
and took a closer look at the young woman who was
obviously ill. From that distance Elizabeth saw a swelling about her left eye, the once-flawless line of her
cheekbone marred by bruised flesh. Also in this brief
interim, Elizabeth looked about the room, taking note
of the tray of uneaten food, the mussed bed, the dark
blue material in the corner which once had been Mary's
traveling suit.

"I'll call the watchmen," John said over his shoulder.

"No!" Elizabeth shot back, confounded by his stupidity. *Doesn't he realize Mary is fully prepared to leap to
her death?*

Then there was no time for further questions. Apparently unable to bear the weight of their eyes upon her, Mary moved further out onto the windowsill and swung one leg up.

"No!" John called out, and Elizabeth heard fear in his voice.

She stepped behind him and counseled him to go back to the door. When at first he refused, she took his arm and in the most unconcerned tone said, "You must leave us alone, John. If you want the women of Eden to appear at their best in a few hours, we must be granted privacy. Isn't that right, Mary?"

Aware of her own heart beating, she guided him toward the door, daring to turn her back on the window and the impending tragedy. He did not go docilely, but he went, and in amazement she felt his arm trembling through his jacket.

"I'll wait outside," he whispered, pleading with Elizabeth to make things right. How often she'd seen the same expression on his face when as a little boy he'd brought her his boat with the torn sail or his toy soldier with the broken leg.

Closing the door behind him, Elizabeth wondered if Mary could be as easily mended.

"Shall we be about it?" She smiled toward the window, her eyes refusing to focus on the terrifying image of the young woman balanced on the windowsill.

"I trust your gown is in order," she went on, walking to Mary's wardrobe. Secluded behind the wardrobe door, Elizabeth closed her eyes and listened.

"Oh, Mary; how beautiful!" She smiled again, withdrawing the pale pink silk gown embroidered with pearls, a masterpiece of a gown, cut low in the bodice to reveal Mary's lovely breasts and a small waist.

Elizabeth lifted the gown and held it against her for Mary's inspection. "You know," she confided, daring to take one step toward the window. "I think we should spirit this back to London, don't you? Can you imagine the effect of this gown on Jeremy Sims' guests?"

Although she wanted to look up and chart Mary's reaction, her instinct advised against it. Her only chance to lure the girl back into the room was to convince her that Elizabeth found nothing unusual with her precarious perch.

Midway across the room, she stopped and posed a direct question to the empty space before her. "Did we decide upon a hair style, Mary?" she asked. "No, I don't believe we did," she said, continuing on to the bed.

Sharply she looked up, thinking she had heard movement. But she saw Mary still staring back at her out of eyes which appeared to fill with desperate unhappiness.

Elizabeth could resist her no longer and took one step toward the window, drawn to her grief and filled with remorse for her own contribution to it. "Mary," she began, "I tried to see you several days ago, but I was told you were ill."

Though she was approaching slowly, she still could not discern a change in Mary's face. "Others have tried as well," Elizabeth went on. "Lila and your mother have—"

Mary turned about on the ledge, as though the mention of her mother had caused greater pain. "Don't come any closer," she warned, and obediently Elizabeth froze.

Under the force of Mary's command, Elizabeth was obliged to drop her pretense of innocence. They both knew what was happening here, and gowns and hair styles were no longer viable subjects.

"Why, Mary?" Elizabeth whispered. "Why didn't you send for me? I would have come." When she didn't speak, Elizabeth went on. "Nothing is worth this. Whatever the nature of our disagreement, it can be settled in more—"

Was she crying? With her face averted it was difficult to tell.

"Mary, please look at me," Elizabeth begged. "Please talk to me. If you'll just tell me—"

She *was* crying: "I don't want to live anymore," she said.

"Why? You, more than anyone I know, have everything to live for."

"What?"

Elizabeth tried to turn her attention to that difficult question and was at first tempted to list the obvious reasons: Mary's youth and beauty, her position in the world, John's adoring support. But something in that tear-streaked, bruised face suggested that if these reasons made any difference, she would not be clinging to a narrow ledge, contemplating a fatal leap.

So Elizabeth abandoned the obvious reasons and said simply, "I need you, Mary. Words cannot express how you've filled my life these last few years. I didn't mean what I said to you in the carriage. I was—still frightened, alarmed by the incident at Jeremy Sims'. But—"

She was aware of Mary looking at her, a look of disbelief on her face. With less than three feet separating them, Elizabeth extended her hand. "Mary, please, come back to London with me. We'll start afresh, I promise. Whatever the problems are, we can face them—"

To Elizabeth's embarrassment, she heard her own voice break. She heard a rustle of movement and looked up to see Mary moving back from the edge, one hand lifting to Elizabeth, until their fingers touched, and in the next instant Mary was in her arms.

Eagerly Elizabeth clasped her, not certain of the nature of her commitment or Mary's deep grief, but grateful for only one blessing, that Harriet's daughter had been drawn back from the edge and that now all they had to do was to find a future for her.

Still with no words spoken they clung together, Elizabeth stroking the matted hair, her fingers once brushing across the bruised area on the side of Mary's face. Gently she sat with her on the edge of the bed, assessing close at hand the nature of the swelling. Though on the mend, it once had been painful.

"What happened?" she asked quietly.

Mary tried to speak through her tears and couldn't, and Elizabeth again enclosed her in her arms, doubtful if she could ever restore her to the point that she could make a public appearance in less than three hours. Scolding herself for such considerations, Elizabeth rocked back and forth with her, a gentle rhythm which ultimately soothed, and at last Mary leaned back into the pillow, making an effort at control.

"I'm . . . sorry," Mary whispered.

"No need. Everything is going to be well. You'll see—"

"I . . . can stay with you . . . in London?"

"Yes. I said so, didn't I?"

"John said—"

With the sense of moving to the heart of the matter, Elizabeth urged the girl to speak. "John said what?"

Mary closed her eyes. "He—said that I must go away, that you had spoken to him and—"

Suddenly she heard a voice behind her. "I said nothing

to warrant this, I can assure you." Elizabeth stood immediately and saw John only a few feet behind her.

He moved to the foot of the bed and stared down on Mary with an expression of disappointment. "I came here this afternoon, hoping to escort you down to meet our guests—"

Abruptly he turned away.

In the new silence Elizabeth charted the expression on Mary's face, one of stunned recognition, as though at last she knew what the rest of them had known for years —that this man controlled her life.

There was John to consider as well, looking groomed and handsome in his dress blacks, the slant of his jaw, his eyes still bearing a ghostly resemblance to his father.

Distracted by the comparison of father and son, Elizabeth looked up to find Mary watching the man, whose steps had carried him to the open window. When at last he turned, Elizabeth was in no way prepared for his words or the expression on his face.

"Do you—hate me so much?" he asked quietly.

Elizabeth looked down at Mary. The tears had commenced again. "I—don't—hate—"

"What else am I to think?" he asked, moving back to the foot of the bed. "I try always to do what I think is best for you, as I try always to do what I think is best for everyone at Eden. You are my family," he went on. "Why would I want to do anything that would hurt you or cause you grief?"

The performance was skillful. And effective. Mary's hand moved up, covering her face.

Aware that she would have to pull this tearful creature into some semblance of unity, Elizabeth suggested quietly, "Not now, John, I beg you. Why don't you leave us alone, and I promise you a miracle in three hours, all of us at your side for the unveiling."

In a despairing gesture, he lifted his hand as though he needed no reminder of what the evening held. He stared down on Mary and walked slowly to her side, removed her hands from her face and whispered, "You must understand, Mary, my only defense is that—I love you, perhaps too much. You're so very special to me that I want nothing to disrupt your life or hurt you in any way."

It *was* a skillful performance, the weight of sympathy

shifting in the room from the sobbing Mary to the meticulously groomed John. Even Elizabeth wondered who precisely was the injured party here.

Elizabeth beckoned for John to follow her. Leading the way to the corridor, she steeled herself against that injured expression. It was her intention to say nothing except to reassure him that they *would* be down shortly and that his Festivities would proceed uninterrupted.

Thus she was in no way prepared for the desolate question which he posed. "Would she—have jumped?"

Fortunately, she couldn't give him an answer, and simply said, "She's high-strung. Something caused her to—"

"All I suggested was Miss Veal's school in Cheltenham," he protested. "She hasn't even seen it, and even Richard thought it would be a splendid idea. If your female friends are right, and women are due the vote, then they'd damn well better know what to do with it."

She started to respond. But better judgment intervened. Still, she was grateful for his sarcasm, for now it enabled her to step back to the door, certain in her mind that the injured party was Mary. "You go along," she said briskly. "There will be time later to discuss all of this. As you have pointed out countless times, our first responsibility for these two weeks is to our guests."

"Damn the guests," John muttered and leaned against the corridor wall, his head bowed.

At last she succeeded in closing the door, though her final glimpse of his face was a moving one, not a trace of that aggressive strength which was customarily at home on his features. It was a child's face now, painfully facing the consequences of his own actions.

Well, she'd have to deal with the man/boy later. For now the real challenge was the young woman who lay curled and enclosed upon herself, her face a script of quiet grief.

Vowing not to ask any questions that might provoke disturbing answers, Elizabeth drew a deep breath, tried to affix on her face a mask of serenity and started toward the bed, calling out with a cheerfulness she did not feel,

"Mary, come. . . ."

It was a significant testimony to the topsy-turvy nature of the last few days that John Thadeus Delane, editor of the conservative *Times,* was now engaged in a warm conversation with Charlie Bradlaugh, editor of the radical and free-thinking *Reformer.*

From where Burke sat in his position of relative obscurity in an upholstered corner of the Gentlemen's Smoker off the Great Hall, he watched in silent amusement the curious duo seated at the round table, both physically large and powerful, though there all similarity stopped.

At least John Murrey Eden could be credited with one achievement—the union of these two disparate voices, one arguing for tradition and monarchy, the other publicly advocating the formation of an English republic with an elected president and constitution, similar to that which America enjoyed.

Grateful to be excluded, Burke sipped at his brandy and felt satiated with too much rich food, too much ostentation, too much tension of the sort which suggested that beneath the expensive new veneer of Eden Castle were currents of feeling which as yet Lord Ripples had not been able to identify.

Then perhaps he'd better be about the task that had brought him here, which was to find out all he could about John Murrey Eden. Thus far he'd learned exactly nothing, as the great man himself always seemed to be involved with others, a negligence Burke had determined was not altogether accidental. There was no possible way that he, an American exile, could serve John Murrey Eden, and he had the distinct impression that this was a financial and political gathering as much as a social one. Substantiation of this private theory was in the fact that Burke had yet to glimpse any of the beauties who supposedly formed that exclusive club known as the Women of Eden. They had been promised to the largely male gathering tonight, the living counterparts taking part in the unveiling ceremony.

He drained his glass and started out into the crowd, moving toward the laughing threesome composed of Andrew Rhoades, Lord Richard Eden and Professor Nichols.

When he was still a distance away, he noticed that Andrew Rhoades had observed his approach. Burke saw him place a restraining hand on Professor Nichols' shoulder, apparently halting the man in midstory, and calling out to Burke with warm cordiality, "This way, Stanhope—come and join us. We were just speaking of your country."

Grateful that he had been remembered from that single luncheon, Burke drew near, smiling. "Then perhaps I'd best move on," he joked. "One seldom hears compliments for the Colonies from an Englishman's lips."

"Now, that's not true, Mr. Stanhope," Professor Nichols soothed. "I was just telling Richard and Andrew about a young student of mine, an American lad, so bright, far in advance of his English counterparts."

Burke nodded, though suspected that the man was lying. There was no aspect of that statement that warranted the earlier laugh which had first attracted Burke's attention. Still, it was a harmless deception, designed to put him at ease. Since his true host had not deigned to make that effort, Burke was grateful for the kindness, regardless of its nature.

In an attempt to cover his well-meaning deception, Professor Nichols abruptly changed the subject, stepping back as though not to exclude Lord Richard, who was standing on his right.

"I trust you are enjoying yourself, Mr. Stanhope," Nichols smiled, clasping his hands behind his back and standing at ease.

Burke nodded. "It's been an—interesting few days," he replied safely.

Lord Richard entered the conversation, a knowing look on his face. "I'm afraid you're not seeing us at our best, Mr. Stanhope," he said graciously. "In spite of its size, I've always felt that Eden was happiest with a limited population."

Considering that at that moment they were being jostled on all sides by laughing, talking gentlemen, awaiting the stellar event of the evening, Lord Richard's claim held great appeal. "Still," Burke added considerately, "it's quite spectacular—the castle itself, as well as what Mr. Eden has done with it." His journalist's instincts began to surface. "Since everywhere I look I see new and major renovation, I can only assume that the castle had been allowed to—deteriorate."

Lord Richard laughed. "That's a kind way of putting it." He stepped closer, a likable man, mild-mannered, very approachable.

"You probably won't believe this," he went on, "but there was a time when, owing to certain harsh circumstances, we tethered our cow and several goats in this very hall."

Andrew Rhoades now stepped forward with a fresh subject. "And where, may I ask, is your distinguished companion? I trust he is enjoying himself."

"I can't speak for him," Burke said politely, "but I think he's found the occasion as—interesting as I have."

Briefly he enjoyed a private amusement. If only the gentlemen knew that they were at this moment speaking with Lord Ripples!

Lost in his own thoughts, Burke was not at first aware of the three men staring at him, as though someone had posed a question he'd failed to answer. "I—beg your pardon," he murmured, embarrassed, and sent Lord-Ripples away—at least for a while.

Andrew Rhoades laughed. "I asked if you knew Mr. Delane's whereabouts. I believe we have a few moments before John—"

Burke nodded. "He's in the Smoker, though you may be surprised at his companion of the moment. He's in deep discourse with Mr. Bradlaugh." He was prepared to say more, but the look of disbelief on the three faces around him canceled the need.

"I don't believe it," Rhoades said flatly.

"I saw it with my own eyes," Burke said, nodding, and entering into the spirit of fun. "And I heard it as well. Mr. Bradlaugh was giving him a detailed lecture on the nature of republicanism when I left."

"My God," Andrew Rhoades marveled. "Well, I must see this for myself. Come, gentlemen," he said to Nichols and Lord Richard. "I'll need eye-witnesses. I have friends in Fleet Street who will say I've lost my mind."

But Lord Richard begged off, claiming, "I must wait here, Andrew. Professor Nichols and I are awaiting a late-arriving guest. He should have been here hours ago, but—"

Surprised, Rhoades looked back at them. "I thought everyone was here who was supposed to—"

"He's an ex-student of mine," Professor Nichols interrupted apologetically, "a bright lad by the name of Parnell, coming all the way from Ireland. But knowing

Charles, he's stopped at every inn and pub along the way."

"Shall I alert the watchmen at the gate?" Rhoades asked.

"I've already done so," Lord Richard told him. "No cause for worry. Charles follows his own timetable. I wouldn't be at all surprised if he didn't show."

"Well, then," Rhoades said, backing away from the group, "if John comes looking for me, tell him I'm in the Smoker."

As he was about to turn away, his eyes apparently fell on someone just descending the Grand Staircase. "Damn," he muttered beneath his breath.

As all heads swiveled in that direction, Burke looked up and saw John Murrey Eden. To his right was the artist, Lawrence Alma-Tadema. The Dutchman had arrived in the company of the gentlemen of the Royal Academy only two days earlier and had been invisible since, putting final touches to his new masterwork, or so the rumor had been circulated.

To Mr. Eden's left was a young man, dark-skinned yet garbed with equal fashion in classic Western black.

"Too late," Rhoades muttered. "It looks as though the main attraction is under way."

As the rumble of predominantly male voices settled into a low hum, Burke saw Andrew Rhoades signal Lord Richard. "I believe this is our cue," he said with a smile. "If you gentlemen will excuse us. . . ."

From where Burke stood he saw Lord Richard exchange a warm smile with Nichols, as though the one man were supplying the other with moral support.

In spite of the glance, Lord Richard needed further reassurance. "Where will you be—"

Professor Nichols stepped forward. "I'll be right here when it's over. With Mr. Stanhope's kind indulgence, I'll view the Festivities in his company. How fascinating it will be to glimpse our English pomp through his American eyes."

Looking beyond their shoulders, Burke saw John Murrey Eden and the young man gazing out over the audience, clearly in search of someone.

A pronounced hush fell over the vast room. Burke looked up to see Andrew Rhoades and Lord Richard disappearing at the top of the stairs. The young Indian lad was missing as well, though still standing at midstair was John Murrey Eden, while two steps behind him was Alma-Tadema, looking uncomfortable in the limelight.

"Can you see?" Professor Nichols whispered thoughtfully and, without waiting for a response, he guided Burke to a position near one of the columns which afforded a perfect view of the Grand Staircase and the corridor leading to the Library and the scene where the unveiling would take place.

All at once, when the tension of waiting could be stretched no further, Burke heard the musicians commence a waltz and he was conscious of all heads lifting in anticipation toward the top of the stairs. Still, nothing was visible but the elegance of the staircase itself. Behind him Burke felt Professor Nichols step close in soft alarm. "My God, no slipup, I hope."

Then the waiting was over. The tempo of the waltz seemed to increase as at the top of the stairs appeared a pale, fair woman beautifully garbed in lavender silk, her long hair done up and softened with a fringe of curls framing her face, and carrying a small nosegay of violets. She was on the arm of a very tall, distinguished-looking older gentleman, who seemed almost to be supporting her, their arms locked together.

"Who—" Burke began.

"Mrs. John Murrey Eden," Nichols whispered. "A charming lady," he added, "though of a weak disposition and not by nature, I'm afraid, designed for this occasion."

Burke detected a tone of sympathy in the man's voice, as though it distressed him to see anyone uncomfortable. Feeling his fondness for the man increase, Burke asked further, "And the gentleman with her?"

"Her father, Lord Harrington. You've not met him yet?" he asked, surprised.

Burke shook his head.

Again all talk ceased as the two at the top of the stairs started down. For some reason they seemed mismatched, one resembling a lion, the other a lamb.

Suddenly at the top of the stairs and padding down softly behind her there appeared an enormous gray cat. At the cat's appearance a rustle of amusement arose from the guests, pleasantly breaking the tension.

"Wolf." Nichols smiled. For Burke's edification he

added, "The cat's name—an enchanted cat, or so Lady Lila claims—over two hundred years old."

Confident that his mistress was under way, the cat disappeared into the Library, where shortly the unveiling would take place.

"He'll be assured of a ringside seat," Nichols added, laughing with the rest of the guests.

With the comic appearance of the cat over, Burke heard the audience fall into silence as the pair on the steps drew even with Eden. Burke saw the woman hesitate again and it appeared as though she would speak to her husband. But no words were exchanged and again her father seemed to tighten his grip on her arm and lead her steadily to the foot of the stairs, less than twenty feet from where Burke and Professor Nichols stood.

From this close proximity she looked as though she were just recuperating from an illness or on the verge of succumbing to one, though probably it was just the tension of the occasion.

With their disappearance into the Library, the musicians commenced a second waltz, and as the top of the stairs was again devoid of life and movement, Burke listened closely to Professor Nichols' succinct explanation of Mrs. John Murrey Eden.

"She has produced two sons and lost four in miscarriages. Richard fears for her health."

As would any sane man, Burke thought, consciously aware that he was storing up any excuse to dislike John Murrey Eden.

Then there was movement again at the top of the steps, a very different pair this time, Andrew Rhoades smiling out over the gaping faces, not only making eye contact with Eden but winking massively as though to say, "We two at least know what a colossal bit of rubbish this is."

On his arm was Delane's friend, the charming older woman named Elizabeth whom they had rescued from her near-tumble out of her carriage door on that first day. This woman looked as though she were quite at home at center stage, was never happier than when admiring eyes were assessing her.

Burke looked closer, suffering again that twinge of recognition. *Had* he seen her before?

He now saw her pull free from Andrew Rhoades and draw near to Eden where, standing on tiptoe, she delivered a kiss to his bearded cheek. For the first time since Burke had witnessed that glacial man, he saw him respond to the affectionate gesture, his hand caressing the side of her face, their mutual love displayed for all to see.

In spite of the public nature of the event, the moment was good because it was honest. Burke had the feeling that it would have been beyond her to suppress that kiss and now saw that her affection was spilling onto the artist, Alma-Tadema, who with courtly dignity accepted her hand and kissed it.

As Andrew Rhoades and the woman started down the corridor toward the Library, Burke stared closely after her, that mysterious recognition still plaguing him. He *had* seen her before; he would swear to it.

There was no time for further questions as a new pair had now appeared in the arena at the top of the Grand Staircase, a dark, lovely beauty who was being escorted by the young man whom Burke had seen earlier in the company of Eden.

Was it his imagination or were the musicians playing more loudly as though to mask the new silence which had descended over the guests? From where he stood, he saw heads leaning forward, as though the majority of those present knew all too well the relationship of this woman to John Murrey Eden, knew her tragic history as well.

Now, unlike Mrs. Eden, who had appeared shy to the point of collapse, and the woman named Elizabeth who had, with warm-hearted abandon "performed" her way down the lengthy staircase, this woman stood with remote serenity, as though she neither dreaded nor enjoyed what she'd been asked to do.

"Can you imagine," Professor Nichols whispered, "the courage it requires for her to appear here tonight?"

When Burke didn't respond, Nichols went on. "Eden's mistress, you know," he said.

Then Burke's attention was drawn back to the stairs, where mother and son had just reached bottom after navigating their way past John Murrey Eden. Their pace seemed to increase as they hurried down the lines of stewards, apparently eager to join the others who had preceded them.

Leaning against the column, he turned away from the stairs and looked out over the guests. As he turned back toward the stairs, he caught a glimpse of Professor Nichols' face, amazed to see a tender smile as the large man focused on some new sight at the top of the stairs.

He followed the direction of the man's gaze back to the top of the stairs, where he saw Lord Richard, looking vastly uncomfortable, his arm about the waist of a—

Dear Lord!

Suddenly he froze in an incredible aspect of recognition. No, it couldn't be! No! Of course it couldn't.

Gowned in pink she was, this gown more elaborate than that other one. In an attempt to regain a degree of control, he closed his eyes to clear the curious image which had just appeared before him.

When he looked up again the two were moving, Lord Richard's arm still about that slim waist, the flawless shoulders the same, the neck the same, the full breasts the same, the hair the same, the mouth the same, the nose— Of course, the eyes had been masked. Still—

No! It was impossible.

Struggling for composure, he was aware that the normally talkative Professor Nichols had become peculiarly silent.

Unable to resist a closer look, if for no other reason than to confirm his faulty recognition, Burke glanced toward the stairs again. What he saw made no sense at all. That fair image did not belong here, but back in Jeremy Sims' Song and Supper Club.

As the two reached midstep, Burke talked himself out of his foolish recognition. Little Maria of the Mask, who had captured his heart and moved him so, belonged to London.

No, the closer she came, the more convinced he was that his recognition had been a false one. For one thing, this young woman was painfully shy. Most of the time her eyes were either down, concentrating on her passage on the stairs or lifted in furtive glances at John Murrey Eden, who appeared to be paying closer attention to these two than the others who had preceded them.

"Now there's a portrait, don't you agree?" It was Professor Nichols again, his voice still bearing the stress of his emotional involvement with the participants on the stairs.

Burke looked up to see the three poised at midstep, Eden on one side, Lord Richard on the other, and between them—

"Who is she?" Burke whispered.

Nichols laughed softly. "You *have* been ill-treated these last few days, haven't you? Although in truth Lady Mary has been absent. Ill, according to Richard."

"Lady Mary?"

Nichols nodded. "Richard's sister, Lady Mary Eden. Once the ugly duckling who has now become the beautiful swan."

As Burke focused on the stairs, he saw Eden presenting a bouquet of roses to Lady Mary, saw a blush forming on those pale cheeks as she accepted it without lifting her eyes.

Damn! The resemblance was incredible—the stance, the carriage, the angle of the head. Of course those all-important features, the eyes, had always been masked and were masked now, in that she had yet to lift them. But the most overwhelming argument came in the form of a hard question. What would Lady Mary Eden be doing performing in a public arena such as Sims' Song and Supper Club? Since he could not even begin to conceive of a reasonable answer, he contented himself with watching them descend the staircase, where John Murrey Eden stepped forward to include Alma-Tadema in the entourage. Then the four proceeded down the corridor, followed by the gentlemen from the Royal Academy and ultimately by the guests themselves in an excited mood, as though all were aware that they were approaching the highlight of the evening.

But as they started off toward the corridor a breathless, red-faced steward gained their side.

"Professor Nichols," the man called out, and Burke looked back to see the man still trying to elbow his way through the crush of guests.

Coming up alongside them, the steward delivered a terse message. "There's a gentleman at the gate, Professor Nichols, without an invitation, who insists that he is a guest of Lord Richard's. When I told him that His Lordship was occupied, he asked for you."

"Charles," Nichols sighed in annoyance. "The man is a master at poor timing." He glanced toward the crowded corridor, a look of longing on his face. "Well, you go ahead, Stanhope," he suggested. "I'll go and identify the black sheep and we'll rejoin you."

Before joining the others, Burke looked toward the Smoker in the far arcade. Should he summon Delane? He, too, had expressed curiosity about the painting. Apparently Bradlaugh's company had proved a prolonged distraction.

No, Burke must at least inform him. He could hold a discussion any day with Charlie Bradlaugh in any Fleet Street pub. But the unveiling of "The Women of Eden" would only happen once and was more or less the sole purpose for their lengthy journey to this remote spot.

As he hurried toward the Smoker, he glanced back and saw the last of the guests just entering the corridor.

"Delane?" he called out, sending his voice ahead, hoping to rouse the two from their new fascination with each other. "The painting is about to be—" But as he gained the open doorway and peered inside, he found the room empty.

Damn! They *had* joined the company, and now probably were enjoying front row seats while he—

Turning about, he retraced his steps and saw an army of maids and stewards moving into the Great Hall, arrangements of tables and chairs being placed around the edge, baskets of flowers being arranged in the corners, several hundred men and women working silently for the pleasure of one man. Even in the halcyon days of the South, visiting at the large plantations such as Four Willows and Surrey Hill, Burke had never seen so large a staff. Of course these faces were white and those had been black, but the degree of servitude varied little.

His thoughts carried him to the door of the Library, where he realized that the crowded room was silent, over two hundred guests standing at attention, all focused on something at the far end of the room, a massive shrouded painting which sat on a slight elevation, Alma-Tadema holding forth, saying something about the juxtaposition of empires, Roman and English, and their differences, which were few, and their similarities, which were many, and the universal appeal of beautiful women to both.

As the man talked on, Burke tried to ease as far into

the Library as he could. But there was little room. The
rows of seats had been taken, with half the company
forced to stand in any spot available to them. After murmuring several apologies, he found a relatively good vantage point on the west wall and found a bonus as well, a
small stepladder which was used to fetch books from the
upper shelves.

Not wanting to call too much attention to himself, he
stepped up on the first elevation and discovered an uncluttered view of the Library, and was pleased to hear
Alma-Tadema winding down, interested to see John
Murrey Eden step forward, as though it were his turn
now.

"Ladies and gentlemen," he commenced, sending a
strong self-confident voice ringing out over his guests, "let
me thank you for visiting Eden. The walls of this ancient
fortress are happiest when they are filled with the companionship of good friends. I trust that you have enjoyed
yourselves and that there will forever be a warm spot in
your hearts filled with the memories of your stay at Eden.
Now—"

As his brief comments came to an end, he turned back
toward the group on his right. "Now you've seen the living women of Eden. It gives me great pleasure to present
their portrait for your approval and enjoyment."

Alma-Tadema drew the canvas shroud to one side, and
there before all, larger than life, in a most remarkable
setting were "The Women of Eden," the faces the same
but their garb and locale Roman, four languorous beauties
gazing out over a blue sea from a high marble parapet,
their attention focused on some spot beyond the frame
of the painting, all recognizable as the four who had just
descended the Grand Staircase—the pale fair beauty of
Mrs. John Murrey Eden and the more aggressive Elizabeth, and next to her the dark beauty and scandalously
bared breast of the Indian woman, and next to her—

There it was again, the first-glance recognition which
informed him that he'd seen the young woman before,
under vastly different circumstances.

Upon the instant of unveiling Burke heard a collective
intake of breath. The crowd seemed to push forward,
then hold still, as though it required a moment to assimi-
late both the beauty as well as the shocking nature of the
painting.

And it was both. The colors were dazzling, the marble parapet elaborate in its veined detail, the elements of sky, sea, sun and architecture dramatic, though unobtrusive, supports for the four central characters, those lovely women, two frankly sexual, all portrayed with that dewy silkiness of a woman's flesh.

Then how to account for the stunned silence coming from the company? All at once he saw the reason, saw the gentlemen from the Royal Academy step slowly forward in close inspection of the large painting, taking their time before issuing a judgment, the reaction of the entire company hinging on theirs.

In the tense waiting, Burke made his own judgment. It was a remarkable painting but not a great one, the work of a good artist but not a genius. Still the painting would be a joy to live with. How fortunate the generations of Edens to come who would enter this Library and feast their eyes on those four, the wind breathing gently over their gossamer robes, the honesty of that one dark, clearly defined breast, four unique female wills all focused on something beyond the vision of the viewer, and that stroke alone, in Burke's opinion, raised the painting above mediocre.

What were they waiting for? A communal lover? A stern master? There was tension in those faces, the same tension he'd seen paraded in the flesh on the Grand Staircase. Someone was coming who united them in a common focus.

With increasing enthusiasm Burke studied the large canvas, his eyes forever coming back to the young woman, almost a child's face on a woman's body, as though Alma-Tadema had seen through her chronological age and had chosen rather to paint her emotional age, the same paradoxical attraction which he'd felt for Maria of the Mask, a beautiful child out of the element which society had assigned her, full of life and daring.

As the gentlemen from the Royal Academy kept everyone waiting, Burke looked over at the four living counterparts. The embarrassment of three seemed to have increased. The only ones standing at ease were Andrew Rhoades and Elizabeth. The others stood in half-turned positions, heads down, as though they longed to flee the crowded room.

Torn between the painting and the reality, Burke

glanced away from both and observed John Murrey Eden standing by Alma-Tadema in silent support, their attention focused on the gentlemen still studying the painting with maddening deliberation. Burke had the feeling that a judgment would have been announced long ago were it not for that one bared breast. The austere gentlemen were obviously trying to convince themselves that the breast was "classical" rather than pornographic.

Then, their decision was made. After a final hurried conference among themselves, one gentleman stepped forward and motioned for Alma-Tadema to join them before the canvas. All at once the gentlemen were shaking his hand, while one announced to the waiting company, "I present a new light on the horizon of English art—Lawrence Alma-Tadema."

At last given permission to express their admiration, the company broke into warm applause. Those seated rose to their feet and lifted their applauding hands high into the air.

Sensing that the drama of the evening was over, Burke looked again at the partially visible pink gown of Lady Mary Eden, amazed at her resemblance to the little singer at the Sims' Song and Supper Club. And it was just that, a unique similarity and nothing more, for not even by the wildest stretch of his imagination could he conceive of Eden granting the young woman the freedom to perform in such an establishment.

Having recently read a piece of romantic nonsense about everyone in the world possessing a double, he let it go at that and stepped down from the small ladder, determined to avoid the crush of departing guests, all hurrying toward the next entertainment, the ball which was scheduled to take place in the Great Hall. It was his intention to find a safe harbor until the Library was emptied, then quietly return and allow Lord Ripples to study the painting close at hand.

As he moved across the back of the crowded room, he heard Eden's voice again, self-confident, as though he'd known all along that the painting would be a success.

Why did the man annoy Burke so? No answer except an honest one, which suggested that his hostility might be based on envy as much as anything. John Murrey Eden, at approximately Burke's age, had created an empire for himself. He had not inherited it or married it or in any

way stepped into it ready-made. In Godlike fashion he
had created it out of nothing, from the ashes of destruction.

In his movement through the congestion of guests,
Burke saw in his mind's eye a clear image of Stanhope
Hall as it once had stood. It didn't last long and was
replaced by new applause. Apparently some new activity
was taking place on the elevation at the far end of the
Library.

Whatever it was, it held no interest for him. His moment of honesty had left him with a need for privacy.
The past seemed to be staring at him with dead eyes,
the present reminding him of the uselessness of his existence. As those two specters combined, he increased his
step until he caught sight of the door, and he was just on
the verge of passing through it when he heard a female
voice raised in delicate song, the tones of such crystal
clarity, the upper reaches so sweet and vulnerable, a voice
he'd heard before, the same voice that—

There was the possibility that he'd made a mistake
again. And there still was no explanation for it. Why
should— But the question never had a chance. With his
eyes closed, he saw that other scene recreated perfectly,
all pieces of the puzzle save one falling into place; the
drunken student leaping over the stage, the young woman
watching his approach from behind her mask, the sound
of a woman's scream, not hers but someone else's.

The woman! Elizabeth!

That's where he had seen her before, in the wings of
Jeremy Sims' Song and Supper Club.

With his eyes still closed, he felt lightheaded. The mystery was solved and yet not solved. It had been the two
of them; he was certain of it now. But why? What had
brought them there, and did John Murrey Eden know?

Listening to the lovely song, he felt his spirits lift at the
realization that he had found her again. Or had he? Confined behind the protective barrier of John Murrey Eden's
affection, she could very well be even more unapproach-
able than she had been at Sims' club. No matter! He had
no intention of letting her disappear again.

As the beautiful song approached its conclusion, he
found himself transported back to Sims', old rotund Jeremy slyly presenting to his clients the bluest of bluebloods
behind the mask of a music hall entertainer.

Smiling at this sudden understanding of Sims' secret, he determined that what he needed now was a go-between who could bestow upon him a formal introduction. What was so unreasonable in that request? He was a guest and he wanted simply to meet the four women whose respective beauty had been fixed for all time by Alma-Tadema's vision. And if, after having met the four, one attracted him more than the others—

He glanced over his shoulder, hoping to catch a glimpse of Delane. But instead his eye fell on a much more likely candidate, a man who, by his own confession, had watched her transformation from duckling to swan. Standing with him at the door was the late-arriving guest, Charles something. He couldn't remember.

No matter. Burke did not intend to intrude on their society for long. He wanted one simple, proper introduction, then it would suit him perfectly if everyone would just disappear and leave them alone.

To that end, and over the burst of applause which erupted at the conclusion of the song, Burke pushed his way back to the door, calling out with a degree of enthusiasm which shocked even himself, "Professor Nichols, a favor, if you will. . . ."

It had not been her intention to remain with the company beyond her song. She felt she owed Elizabeth that much, and how pleasant it was to be back in her good graces. But now that her song was over and had gone well, now that the silly painting had been unveiled, the ball just under way, it seemed incredible to her that a few hours ago she had been perched on a window ledge, contemplating the end of her life. She must remember this lesson in the future, that a dark vista in one direction does not necessarily mean that the entire world has been plunged into darkness.

Standing at the edge of the Great Hall, she watched the gracefully twirling ladies and gentlemen, the lights from the multicandled chandeliers overhead catching on jewels and rich fabrics, the doors at the far end flung open, the mildness of the fragrant May evening filling the crowded hall.

To one side and standing behind her were Elizabeth and Andrew. They had been dancing until a few moments ago when they stepped out of the circle and rejoined her here, not paying the slightest attention to her, however, but rather engrossed in a lighthearted conversation.

To her left and seated in a chair which had been provided for her by John was Lila, poor dear Lila, who looked so uncomfortable in her gown, though Wolf was curled comfortably enough on her lap, impervious in his arrogant feline way to the human antics about him.

And Dhari was dancing with Aslam, the boy towering above his mother now, though Mary could remember well when it had not been so.

And John? Quickly she looked about, as though feeling a need to keep him forever in her sights, and found him near the door of the Smoker in the opposite arcade, still in close huddle with Alma-Tadema and the gentlemen from the Academy.

Beneath her gown her foot kept time with the music. She felt like dancing, would have settled happily for Andrew Rhoades, who perhaps was the worst dancer in the world, with the exception of her brother Richard.

She looked out over the crowded hall. Where were they, Richard and Professor Nichols? She'd seen them earlier and then they had just disappeared. She would have no objection to dancing with Professor Nichols. She adored him and, for a large man, he moved well on his feet.

But they were no place in sight and, since none of the male guests seemed to want to approach her, she had to content herself with merely standing on the side, imagining the sensation of an arm about her waist, a man leading her into the tempo of the waltz.

About twenty minutes later, when still no one had approached her, her foot beneath her gown ceased its tapping. Perceptions of the sort that recently had caused her such pain swept over her. She would not be asked to dance tonight. With anyone. As always, dressed and groomed, she was waiting for someone's permission.

As all of this combined with an irrational awareness that she was standing alone and therefore was surely an object for gossip and worse, pity, she turned and started up the stairs, at a slowed pace in the beginning but finally breaking into a run, convinced that the privacy of her apartments would be better than this humiliation. At least in her chambers she could close her eyes and conjure up the sensation of a man's arm about her.

"Mary!"

The voice, so sharp, yet distant, surprised her. Approaching the top of the stairs, she wasn't certain whether or not it had been a part of her fantasy.

"Mary! Wait!"

From the top of the stairs she looked down upon her brother Richard, and standing behind him was Professor Nichols, and behind him were two gentlemen she'd never seen before.

This was no fantasy. They were real enough and she felt suddenly shy, for all were looking up at her with intense interest, all except one, and he looked as though he were in pain.

She saw Richard whisper something to the others, then start up the stairs toward her. As he drew near, she reached out and stroked the side of his face. How she adored him, this brother who all her life had consistently loved her, no matter what she did!

In response to this affectionate gesture, he caught her hand and kissed its palm, and the expression in his eyes seemed to mirror her thoughts.

"You look lovely," he whispered. "I've been told that for the last few days you were not feeling well."

Beyond his shoulder she saw the other gentlemen in a huddled conversation. The third continued to stare up at her as though she were a ghost.

"Are you well now?" Richard asked.

"I was never ill," she admitted, fascinated by the intensity of that gentleman's stare. She looked back at Richard. "I quarreled with Elizabeth, or she with me." She shrugged. "At any rate, we've reconciled now."

Thinking that that would be the end of it, she was surprised to see the concern on his face. "You're not retiring so soon, are you?"

"I had thought I might," she said, and did not bother to explain her aloneness.

"Poor Mary," he murmured and gained the top step and put his arm around her. "Might I impose upon you for just a moment longer? There is a gentleman who would like to meet you. He's a friend of Mr. Delane's and I'm afraid we've done a poor job of making him feel welcome these past few days. Stay for just a short while longer and help me to welcome him to Eden."

"He—wants to meet me?" she asked, amazed at this turn of affairs.

"Come," Richard urged. "Just a few additional moments, please?"

She'd never been able to resist Richard. Aware now of all three men gaping up at her, she took Richard's arm and started down the staircase.

As they drew near the bottom, Professor Nichols stepped forward and gave her a light kiss, a familiar gesture based on an old friendship. "I trust that we are interrupting an errand of no great importance?" he asked, smiling.

"No. I was just retiring."

"So soon? Oh, come—you can sleep any time. Now you have admirers."

To one side she saw Richard smiling, though taking no active part in the encounter, as though having delivered her to Professor Nichols he had performed his duty.

She looked back to see Professor Nichols guiding a tall, lean man toward her. His face was quite gaunt, his chin fully bearded in a luxurious growth of red-brown beard.

"Lady Mary," Professor Nichols began, "allow me to present Mr. Charles Parnell. He only just arrived, having traveled all the way from Ireland, the dust of the road still on his boots, as you can see, but he insisted on joining the Festivities."

"Mr. Parnell," she repeated.

By the way of further introduction Nichols added, "He was a student of mine at Cambridge last year and I'm afraid he doesn't have very much love for English—"

"Is that true, Mr. Parnell?" Mary asked politely. "How have we offended you?"

Gallantly the man bowed. "You have not offended me at all, Lady Mary. I think Professor Nichols has reference to my fellow students at Cambridge, who fancied themselves country gentlemen and who succeeded in behaving like stableboys."

She was in no way prepared for this stern indictment and had no idea how she should respond to it. Fortunately there was no need, for Mr. Parnell stepped back, thus clearing the way for the second gentleman, who was equally as tall though not nearly so gaunt, the man who had viewed her so soberly at the top of the stairs and who, even now on the verge of introduction, was looking at her with a degree of intensity that caused the heat of a blush to rise on her cheeks.

"And this gentleman," Professor Nichols went on, "is Mr. Burke Stanhope from America, though now residing in London."

"Mr.—Stanhope," she repeated and could think of absolutely nothing further to say.

Apparently neither could anyone else and when the awkward silence stretched beyond the point of embarrassment, she was on the verge of bidding them all goodnight and retreating to her chambers.

"Lady Eden," the strange gentleman finally managed, "I just wanted to tell you how—lovely your portrait is. . . ."

His voice, so un-English, and his faltering manner caused her to smile. It was reassuring to see that someone else suffered as she so often did.

Buttressed by this thought, she asked, "Where in America is your home, Mr. Stanhope, and are you on holiday here?"

Two harmless questions, or so she had thought. Thus she was in no way prepared for the rude manner in which he ignored both and posed a question of his own. "I have not yet enjoyed a waltz, Lady Eden. Would you do me the honor of becoming my first partner?"

No! All her instincts resisted the invitation, although earlier it had been her most ardent wish.

"I—was just on the verge of retiring, Mr. Stanhope. . . ."

"Nonsense," Professor Nichols interrupted with characteristic bluntness. "Give the man at least one dance, Mary. After all, he specifically requested an introduction."

Behind her she heard Richard's voice urging, "That gown was designed for the waltz, Mary. Treat us all to your beauty in movement."

It was a gracious compliment delivered with affection. More to please Richard than anyone, she gave Burke Stanhope a smile and lifted her gloved hand. "Then come," she invited, "one is just commencing. I've never danced with an American before."

"The waltz is universal, Lady Mary," Burke Stanhope said, smiling—a very pleasant smile, she observed, altering his face, warming it.

As he led her forward, she glanced back at Professor Nichols and saw a self-satisfied smile on his face, as though he'd kept a promise or won a wager. She looked back again and saw Professor Nichols and Richard leading Mr. Parnell toward the chair where Lila sat. Suddenly Mary felt that they had purposefully set out to provide diversion for all the unoccupied women of Eden.

Sensing that she had been manipulated, or worse, "seen to," she felt Mr. Stanhope's arm about her waist, hands raised and, in her preoccupation, missed the first beat and would have stumbled had it not been for his immediate support.

He smiled down on her. "Shall we try again? I'm afraid it's been a while since I've—"

"The fault was mine, Mr. Stanhope," she murmured, grateful for his willingness to take the blame.

All at once they moved forward into the large circle of the waltz, and within the instant found the tempo of the music and matched it to their own, and a few moments later she felt herself swept along in a glorious whirl of gowns and graceful movement, always feeling his support about her waist, the subtle guidance of his hand in hers, the same sensations that she had planned to enjoy in fantasy in her chambers but now enjoying the reality more.

For the first complete circle neither spoke, as though both were concentrating on doing well. In the blur of passing faces she caught sight now and then of a familiar one, Elizabeth in the arms of Mr. Bradlaugh, who passed her by with a look of pleased surprise. She saw Andrew Rhoades and Dhari, though neither saw her, their attention locked on each other.

Once or twice, buoyed by the tempo and the delirious feeling of lightness, her smile grew into a laugh and she looked up at Mr. Stanhope to see him sharing her pleasure.

"The portrait *is* lovely," he said at last, as though feeling certain enough of himself to indulge in conversation.

"I'm glad you like it," she replied, "though speaking for myself, I'm afraid I find it rather silly."

"Why silly?"

"Have you ever seen a vista like that in England? Elizabeth tried to convince Alma-Tadema that the back-

ground of Eden Point would have been much more realistic."

"I'm not certain that his goal was realism."

"Then he succeeded admirably." She smiled. "And if
the painting pleases John—and others—then my opinion
is insignificant."

At first she thought he would refute her words, but he
didn't and proceeded to stare down on her with that same
intensity. And when he showed no signs of speaking, she
rephrased one of her earlier questions which he'd left
unanswered.

"What part of America is your home?" she asked,
finding him most attractive, a quality of warmth and interest which she'd failed to notice during their awkward
introduction.

"I live in London now," he said, again avoiding the
question.

Well, she certainly would not force the issue. She was
enjoying herself too much to spoil it with awkward questions.

Amazed at how lovely the evening had become, she
closed her eyes and gave in to the glorious sensation of
their bodies moving together, the flow of others around
them, the enticing floral odors which permeated the Great
Hall.

It was with a sense of regret that she heard the music
come to a halt. She opened her eyes to find him staring
down on her, as though he, too, regretted that it was
over.

"Would you care to—sit down?" he asked, as couples
shifted about them.

"Not really." She smiled, hoping that she wasn't being
too daring.

"Shall we try again, then?" he asked, laughing, his arm
still about her.

"Yes," she agreed, finding his face a continuous source
of pleasure, a rugged face with a few fine lines about
the corners of his eyes, a face quick with intelligence
and something else, a sober quality that spoke of—what?
Sorrow?

Then the music commenced again, the tempo slower
this time, and she felt him draw her closer and did not
object and discovered that by looking straight ahead her
eyes just cleared his shoulder, and by concentrating fur-

ther she was aware of his breath caressing the right side of her forehead.

"Lady Mary," he asked, his voice soft over the slowed tempo of the music, "may I—ask you a question?"

She looked up, amused by his formality. "Of course."

"Have you—ever seen me before?"

She thought at first that he was teasing. But she saw not a glint of humor on his face.

"Seen you before?" she repeated. "Where would I have seen you before?"

"Do you—know London?"

"Know it!" she exclaimed. "I live there most of the time when I'm not at Eden."

"Do you know of—an establishment called Jeremy Sims' Song and Supper Club?"

The words approached her steadily over the music. It was several moments before she realized that they had stopped dancing, hearing not the music but Elizabeth's fearful warning. *"What if someone should discover who you are, and tell John?"*

"Mr. Stanhope, I think I should retire now."

"No, please wait," he begged. "I did not mean to cause you distress." He led her toward the center of the Great Hall and out of the flow of dancers. "I simply wanted to tell you how much pleasure you have given me. Earlier I thought it was you, but wasn't certain until I heard your lovely voice."

Embarrassed, her mind turning on all the aspects of trouble he could cause for her, she tried to retreat.

But he protested a second time and held her close, and with no option except to make a public spectacle of them both, she remained in his arms.

"Please listen," he begged, as though he'd known beforehand that the announcement would upset her. "I have enjoyed your performances for the last six months, refusing to let anything interfere with my Thursday evenings at Jeremy Sims'." He drew so close that his face disappeared from her view and she was left with the sensation of his whispered breath in her ear.

"If your appearances there are a secret, then I swear that it will be my secret as well. All I ask is that you let me know in advance so that we can guard against a repetition of what happened."

She looked at him, recalling the gentleman who had come to her rescue. "It—was you."

He nodded. "I had hoped to gain an introduction that night, but when I returned to the stage, you were gone."

"Elizabeth was—"

"I know. Alarmed, as well she should have been."

"How did you recognize me?"

"Your voice, although I was fairly certain when I first saw you. I simply couldn't make a connection."

"And you've told no one?"

"No."

She continued to gaze up at him, only vaguely aware of the couples passing behind them. She softly laughed. "I had thought that the mask would—"

"It did, for a while. But you must remember I've studied you closely every Thursday night for months."

Flattered, she blushed. "Why?"

He paused. "Because I found you the most fascinating woman I had ever seen."

It was as though the rest of the Great Hall had gone dark about her and the only light available was that of his face.

"Mr. Stanhope, I—"

Though he had not interrupted her, she broke off, finding that she lacked sufficient breath to form words. All that mattered was this remarkable man, who continued to stare down on her with a degree of adoration she'd never seen in a man's face before. She had the most peculiar feeling that what was happening would have happened anyway, that no force in heaven or on earth could have prevented them from standing here at the center of this crowded hall, at a time approaching midnight, on a mild May evening in the year 1870.

Still no words from him, only that tender expression on his face, a look of relief, as though a long search were over.

"Is anything wrong?"

The voice came not from him but from behind her and belonged to Andrew Rhoades, who had interrupted his dance with Dhari long enough to make inquiry of the two who stood so still at the center of the dance.

"No," she murmured. "We—were just—"

"—trying to find the tempo," Mr. Stanhope said with

a smile, gently covering for her. "Come, Lady Mary," he invited. "Practice makes perfect."

Without warning he swept her away from the inquiring face and back into the waltz, Mary enjoying a sense of abandonment she'd never felt before, as in the rush of color, light and music, all of her old fears vanished, along with the past, and were replaced by the quiet strength and contagious optimism of the most remarkable gentleman she'd ever met.

"Mr. Stanhope," she gasped as his tempo increased, not really wanting to say anything but merely to speak his name. In the warmth of his smile, then his open laugh, she had no choice but to cling to him and follow after, and secretly pray that the dance would never end. ...

"Who is he?" John demanded of Andrew Rhoades, peering out over the crowded Great Hall from the door of the Smoker, where he'd emerged for a breath of air unpolluted by the pedantry of the Royal Academy.

"He's Delane's friend," Andrew replied.

"The American?"

Andrew nodded.

"How long have they been dancing?" John demanded, amazed at Andrew's laxness. John had left him in charge of the women. Shocked anew by the sight of Mary enclosed in the arms of a stranger, he glanced across the Hall to where he'd left Lila to find her in conversation with her father and—

Another stranger!

"And who is that?" he demanded. "My God, Andrew," he muttered, "I asked you to see them both to their chambers by midnight."

"It's a special occasion," Andrew replied quietly, though John thought he detected that hint of condescension in his voice that he'd heard repeatedly during this past year.

He felt a surge of resentment at such an attitude, and this, combined with the sight of Lila laughing as warmly as he'd seen her laugh in months, caused him to stride away from Andrew as though the man did not exist.

"John, wait," Andrew called, and caught up with him. "His name is Charles Parnell," he said in the manner of an apology. "He's a friend of Richard's and Professor Nichols', an ex-student, I believe, from—"

"I don't remember seeing his name on the guest list."

"It was there; I can vouch for it. Would you like to—"

John again cut him off by walking away, this time into the quiet arcade which encircled the hall. He was tired, his nerves stretched taut by the constant society around him. There were other problems, as well. The Academy was now in the process of withdrawing their initial praise of the painting by pointing out flaw after flaw to poor Alma-Tadema in the Smoker. The man had ceased even trying to defend himself or his vision.

There was one other overwhelming anxiety plaguing John, which as yet he'd not found the courage to share with anyone. Though his Great Hall was filled, these guests were cut from an inferior fabric, business associates, members of financial boards who had supported and encouraged the John Murrey firm in the days before his stock had soared.

But there were notable absences, as well. Earlier in the day he had ordered the banners raised for Lord and Lady Minden, for Lord and Lady Oreford, for Lord and Lady Berkely, for Lord and Lady Forbes and their daughter Eleanor.

Yet where were they? All he knew for certain was that they were not present, and he'd wanted desperately for them to be here. And the worst of it, those families were to have been only the beginning. More were scheduled to arrive on Monday.

Would they come? How dare they not?

The conclusion of the dance brought his attention back to the Great Hall, and through the crush of dancers he caught sight of Mary and—

"What did you say his name was?" he demanded of Andrew, who stood beside him.

"Charles Parnell. He's Irish and I suppose Richard thought that—"

"No. I mean the other."

"Stanford, I believe," Andrew muttered, "or Stanhope. Something like that."

His vagueness and lack of concern enraged John. "Really, Andrew, I'm disappointed in you. I had thought I could trust you."

"What have I done?" Andrew demanded, laughing.

"And what have *they* done? It *is* a festivity, John, one of your own planning. I doubt seriously if Lila or Mary knew that they had been forbidden enjoyment. Otherwise they might as well have stayed in their chambers."

"Which is now their immediate destination," John muttered, trying to restrain his anger.

As he started off, heading toward Lila, Andrew said, "What do you intend to do?"

"What you should have done hours ago. See that they are safely retired where they belong. I don't know why I must point certain facts out to you, but you know that my wife's strength is limited. She does not even possess the fortitude to carry a child to term. Am I to stand by and watch her deplete what little stamina she has left in a flirtation with—"

"She is not flirting, John. She is merely enjoying the company. As you can see, her father is present."

"And Mary," John went on, staring at the two who were commencing the next dance, their eyes locked on each other, "Mary is a child, an undisciplined, overemotional child. She would be amenable to the suggestions of anyone, even a fortune hunter."

Andrew laughed. "The gentleman does not look as though he's in need of a fortune, John."

Weary of talk and aware that he couldn't abandon Alma-Tadema forever in that lion's pit with the Royal Academy, John turned his back on Andrew's amusement and strode around the arcade until he was approaching the table where Lila sat laughing with her father and the tall Irishman.

"John . . ." She smiled, looking up. "I'm so glad you've joined us. Allow me to introduce—"

But he allowed her nothing and quietly commanded, "Come with me."

He saw the blush on her face, saw Lord Harrington lean forward as though to intervene. "John, I was just telling Mr.—"

"Come with me," John repeated.

From behind he felt a restraining hand on his shoulder and heard Andrew Rhoades offer courteously, "I will escort her to her chamber, John. You return to the Smoker. I suspect that you are needed."

The combination of the restraining hand and Andrew's voice blocking his will, and the sight of Lila pulling away as though fearful, all these things conspired against him, and he turned with a suddenness that dislodged Andrew's hand and was in the process of removing him further when another voice cut through his anger.

"John, I've been looking for you."

He glanced over his shoulder to Richard rising from a near table where he'd been conversing with Nichols. He, too, was smiling, though it was a taut smile, full of warning.

As Richard drew near, John closed his eyes, belatedly aware of what he'd almost done. Oh, what a tale that would have been for the journalists to take back to London—John Murrey Eden engaging in fisticuffs with his solicitor on the night of—

In the manner of an arbitrator, Richard put his arm about John's shoulder. Before directing him back to the gaping company he whispered, "Your nerves are talking for you. Don't let them spoil a triumphant evening."

He led John back to the small table, where John saw Mr. Parnell on his feet, a look of arrogance on his face.

"Charles"—Richard smiled—"it gives me great pleasure to present my cousin John Murrey Eden, your host and Eden's benefactor."

Still shaken by his eagerness to attack Andrew, John held himself in rigid control. He stared at Mr. Parnell's outstretched hand, then took it briefly, only half-listening to Richard's explanation of who the man was.

Beyond Richard's shoulder he saw Aslam and Professor Nichols looking his way. Had Aslam abandoned him as well?

"Now," Richard concluded, having said everything he'd wanted to say, "it *is* late, Lady Lila." He smiled. "Do me the honor of allowing me to escort you to your chambers. There is always tomorrow and—"

Suffering annoyance that Richard was doing so well what he had done so poorly, John stepped back from the table, thinking that perhaps after all this foolishness was over he'd go away for a while. The Continent, even America. Let them all see how they could get along without him.

He looked back to see Lila whispering to Mr. Parnell. While her invitation was muted, Mr. Parnell's reply was clear. "Tomorrow at noon, yes, I'd be delighted."

He saw her accept Richard's arm, stop and deliver a

warm kiss to her father, summon her cat Wolf and, without a word in his direction, start up the stairs, her head bent close to Richard, as though they were talking about him.

It wasn't until they had disappeared into the second-floor corridor that he came back to himself and observed that, where before all had been gaping at him, now everyone had turned about, Professor Nichols and Aslam walking toward the arched door which led to the night beyond, Lord Harrington and Parnell, their backs turned, engaged in conversation.

John closed his eyes, suffering the persistent feeling that he was in the midst of enemies. But of course that wasn't true. Richard had been right. It was his nerves and his various anxieties.

Then there was one to whom he owed an apology, Andrew Rhoades, and he turned to his left, where he'd last seen him.

"Andrew—"

But he was no place in sight, the arcade deserted.

Then he saw him at the center of the dancers, a plotting island of betrayal, Dhari on his arm, his head bent close to Mary and the American, obviously warning them.

He felt anger as raw as any he'd experienced in a long time. He would not abide it—was not obliged to abide it —this continuous effort on Andrew's part to circumvent his wishes.

Then he was moving, ignoring the voice inside his head which counseled prudence. Pushing through the rush of dancers, he was less than ten feet away when the four turned and saw him, a look of apprehension on Andrew's face and Dhari's, and something more complex on Mary's, a defiance. And on the other's—

"Ah, Mr. Eden . . ." The man smiled, extending his hand. "Though we met formally several days ago, I'm not foolish enough to think that you'll remember. I'm Burke Stanhope. Mr. Delane of the *Times* invited me as his guest, and permit me to express my gratitude to you for—"

Momentarily disarmed, John faltered. It had been easier to dislike Parnell's arrogance than this broadly grinning gentleman. In truth, John had no quarrel with the man himself, only his preoccupation with Mary.

At the thought of her, John glanced to one side, where

she'd moved in subtle retreat next to Andrew. He'd never seen her cheeks so flushed. She was so beautiful. Harriet must have looked like this when his father had fallen in love with her.

These thoughts, paradoxically, left him weaker and stronger.

"Come," he said, reaching out for Mary's hand with sudden force. Caught off her guard and finding herself ensnared, she tried to struggle free. Behind him he was aware of Andrew, ready to intercede.

To his right he was aware of the American gentleman, his earlier cordiality gone. "My apologies, Mr. Eden. We were just—"

But he wasn't interested in the American gentleman. His goal was, as it always had been, to secure Mary in some safe place, away from men's eyes and men's ambitions.

To that end, he stepped back, taking Mary with him, tightening his grasp on her wrist when again she made an attempt to struggle free.

The sound of her protest roused the American to some foolish state of misplaced chivalry, and with one stride he came down between Mary and John, dislodging her wrist from his grasp and taking her place before him.

"Mr. Eden, please," the man said quietly. "I must insist that you allow the lady to walk by herself. She has done nothing to warrant such embarrassment."

John ceased hearing the words. All he was aware of was the pleased look in Mary's eyes. And he was aware of the man's stance before him, defiant, the echo of his flat American voice reverberating about John's head, blocking him, as Andrew had done earlier. While he owed Andrew a degree of consideration, he owed this man nothing except the concentration of fury which was building within him. Although that voice was still counseling him prudence, he felt a need to strike something, a need which had taken root long before this actual moment. In spite of the vastness of his fortune, in spite of the degree of respectability which he'd tried to restore to this scandalous family, he was what he had always been, the bastard son of the great Edward Eden.

In an exaltation of rage, defeated by his own past, he lunged mindlessly forward, all his errors in judgment and missteps of the past joined in that one strong, unretreating face. If he could not master the respect of an exiled American, what chance did he have in the stellar gallery of lords and ladies?

Since in his entire life he had discovered that there was only one way to gain respect, and that was by force, he grasped the interloper by the jacket and was just in the process of drawing back his fist, fully prepared to deliver a killing blow, if necessary, when without warning the man raised both arms, dislodging John effortlessly, and followed through with a stunning blow to the side of John's jaw that sent him reeling backward, the chandeliers spinning above him in confusion, the rhythm of the polka interrupted by a woman's scream.

Though dazed, but still on his feet, John started forward again and this time made solid contact with the man's shoulder, spun him about and gave as good as he got, the blow dislodging the man from his center of balance, though he managed a brief look upward before John fell upon him, his hands moving to his throat, pressing until he was scarcely aware of the solid chorus of women's screams, the musicians' instruments silenced, only one voice predominant over the din, that of Andrew Rhoades' cry for the watchmen, who appeared within the minute, and the next thing John was aware of was strong hands lifting him bodily, drawing him away from the man whom he had pinned on his back and whom he joyfully would have murdered.

"My God!" Andrew gasped close to his ear. "Have you gone totally mad?"

Still, John was aware of little except the face of the man now rising to his feet, a thin trickle of blood slipping from the corner of his mouth, though his expression was as arrogant as ever, as though he too regretted the guards' rapid intervention.

"Get him out," John commanded, struggling for breath. "Escort him to his carriage. And I want two riders to see him across the moors."

"My—belongings, Mr. Eden."

"—will be sent to you. The hospitality of this castle is closed to you."

"No." The soft voice belonged to Mary and came from somewhere behind him.

John ignored it and went on in an attempt to convince the carefully listening company of his rightness in this matter. "I don't know how gentlemen behave in America," he said, full-voiced, "but this is England, where true gentlemen—"

"He did nothing, John!" Mary cried. "You were the one. You—"

"Get her out of here as well!" he shouted over his shoulder and saw Mary with Elizabeth's arm about her. Was he surrounded by enemies?

When he looked back he was pleased to see the guards obeying his command, one burly watchman on each arm, a subtle restraint but restraint nonetheless.

As the company parted for the embarrassing exit, he saw a familiar face step out of the crowd and confer with the American. John Thadeus Delane. John would have to deal with him later. Prestigious editor or not, the man must be made to understand that John did not appreciate him bringing rabble to these Festivities.

When the conversation stretched on, John shouted, "Get him out of here! If his companion wishes to accompany him, his belongings will be sent as well."

"John!" The shocked whisper belonged to Andrew, and he looked back to see his face drained of color and saw more, saw Dhari and Elizabeth escorting a sobbing Mary through the company, their arms protectively about her.

John suffered a brief remorse. Why couldn't she see that he was just trying to protect her?

Feeling a need to rest his eyes from the sorrowful trio just starting up the stairs, John looked toward the departing American. His conversation with Delane had ended, though John saw that old man peering at him with sadness.

But his primary interest was not Delane but rather the arrogant man who had successfully shaken off his guards and who was now strolling easily through the silent company, his head erect as though feeling neither humiliation nor regret.

Still watching him, as though he were a threat to keep forever in his sight, John was in no way prepared for the man's final gesture where, upon reaching the doorways which led to the inner courtyard, he turned and faced the entire company, a look of amusement on his face as he lifted his hand to his forehead in a salute to all, though his focus was fixed on John, something triumphant about his stance and manner.

Then he was gone, leaving all staring at the open door, a stunned quality enveloping the Great Hall.

Belatedly, John was aware of the shambles which once had been his magnificent ball. The musicians seemed incapable of starting together or on key, and there was no need anyway, for the company was departing in hushed groups of twos and threes, all making their way to the Grand Staircase, leaving the maids hovering over empty tables.

He glanced toward the Smoker and saw several gentlemen peering out, relaying the events to the others inside. Presently they withdrew into the room, their attack on Alma-Tadema undeterred by the events which had taken place in the Great Hall.

Looking ahead, he saw Mr. Delane still standing about twenty yards before him, his attention splintered between the empty doorway and John himself.

Weary of the evening and dreading the gossip which would whirl for months about the episode, John was in the process of retreating to the Smoker when Delane called to him.

"Mr. Eden—a word please, if I may."

While his quarrel was not with Delane, there were a few questions he would like to ask the man. He held his position, not deigning to look up at Delane's approach, and warned himself to move with greater diplomacy here. This man *was* powerful.

"Mr. Eden—my—apologies," Delane began. "I must confess I was occupied and did not see—" He broke off, struggling for articulation. "How—did it start?"

"With your friend, Mr. Delane," John replied without hesitation. "I have never witnessed such crude behavior, and he left me no choice." He paused, gratified by the remorse on Delane's face. "May I ask his name?"

"Stanhope," Delane murmured, "Burke Stanhope. I've known his family for years. I can't—"

"American, I believe?"

Delane nodded. "Though he lives in London now."

"Why?"

The blunt question merely added to Delane's confusion. "Why what, Mr. Eden?"

"Why is Mr. Stanhope living in London if America is his home?"

"There wasn't a great deal of his home left after the recent hostilities. His mother is too ill to return, and—"

"Then he has abandoned his homeland."

"It's not that simple, Mr. Eden."

"Why not? His behavior here tonight was certainly cowardly."

Delane stepped closer, as though they had come full circle back to the heart of the mystery. "What, precisely, did he do, Mr. Eden?" he asked again.

"He behaved rudely toward Lady Mary," John commenced, undaunted. "He detained her against her wishes and countermanded my orders."

He was aware of movement to his left and caught a glimpse of Andrew's shocked face.

Now in a conciliatory manner John extended his hand. "My quarrel is not with you, Mr. Delane." He smiled. "You have caused me no offense except perhaps an error in judgment which motivated you to bring such a man to Eden."

"He is a gentleman," Delane protested hotly.

"Not tonight he wasn't," John contradicted. "He behaved like a predator, as all Americans are predators. They simply lack the leavening wisdom of centuries of civilization. The present turmoil in their own country bears witness to that."

As he spoke, he was aware of a new expression on Delane's face, one of astonishment. "So you see, Delane, he didn't belong here, had no business here, and certainly no right to offend the members of this family."

"No, of course not," Delane murmured courteously, backing away from the encounter, "and whatever the nature of his offense, Mr. Eden, I do apologize."

Then he was gone, taking his astonishment with him, leaving John with the painful sensation that somehow he'd lost again.

Whatever the nature of his offense . . .

Hadn't he just stated the nature of the man's offense? How much clearer need he make it?

"Andrew—"

But as he turned he saw Andrew hurrying after Delane, catching up with him on the stairs, talking rapidly, though Delane in no way acknowledged his presence.

"Damn!" John cursed, and felt the sense of unrest increase within him. He stood at the center of the now empty Great Hall. Along the edges of the arcade a few guests remained, chatting nervously, their eyes lifting to him, then turning away.

In the sudden absence of noise, in those embarrassed half-glances, in the painful sense of betrayal and in the continuing sense that he had lost and the American had won, John looked about, his mind in chaos. Feeling a need for escape, he walked steadily toward the corridor which led to the Library and the painting of "The Women of Eden."

He closed the door behind him and felt the breath catch in his throat. Ignoring the sensation, he started through the clutter of chairs, not looking where he was going, never once lifting his eye from the four women fixed for all time in the painting.

Voices in the corridor outside the door went past, hesitated, then moved on. . . .

"What in the—"

Abruptly Richard stopped in the doors which led from the inner courtyard into the Great Hall. Less than an hour ago he and Bertie had left a formal ball comprised of over two hundred guests. They had taken a brief, mind-clearing walk along the headlands, enjoying the May evening, and had only just returned to find—

"This is the right castle, isn't it?" Bertie joked, a step behind him.

"I—don't understand. . . ." Richard faltered, leading the way into the hall, which was empty now except for the maids who were clearing the tables of half-filled wine-glasses.

About thirty yards ahead he spied Bates, the dignified old butler. "Bates," he called out.

"Milord," Bates murmured, after taking a backward glance at the place where a dozen stewards were lowering one of the massive chandeliers.

"Would it be possible for you to tell me what happened?"

Bates adjusted his white gloves. "I can't say, milord. An early end to the Festivities, that's all."

"For what reason?"

"I'm sure I don't know, milord," the man replied cautiously.

"Where is Mr. Eden?" Richard asked.

"I'm not certain, milord," Bates told him, standing ramrod straight. "I believe I saw him entering the Library. Would you like for me to—"

"Was he alone?"

"As best as I can remember, milord. I'd be happy to—"

"No. No, thank you, Bates. That will be all."

His alarm increasing, Richard led the way across the Great Hall, amazed at the rapid transformation. Behind him he was aware of Bertie. "Perhaps it's nothing," he soothed, "the company merely fatigued after several days of—"

While Richard appreciated this attempt, nothing he was saying made sense. John had said earlier that he expected the ball to go until dawn.

Outside the Library door he stopped. He leaned closer, trying to hear, but the large room gave back silence. As he listened he felt Bertie's hand on his shoulder.

"Come," he suggested quietly. "Let's retire early, as the others have done. The mystery can be solved come morning."

Richard looked back, having heard clearly the invitation. Both men stood motionless outside the Library door. Richard glanced about and, seeing the corridor deserted, he lifted a hand to Bertie's forehead.

"Would we be safe?" he whispered, recalling how in the past they had always denied themselves when in residence at Eden. The risks were too great.

"I think so," Bertie replied. "I suspect that the routine of the castle has been—"

They walked a few steps beyond the Library door, Bertie just reaching for his hand, when a steward appeared at the far end of the corridor.

Quickly the two men separated, Bertie striding to the opposite wall in an attitude of suspect ease, while Richard returned to the Library door and knocked, his heart beating too fast.

He glanced again toward the end of the corridor. The steward was gone. He exchanged a relieved look with Bertie and whispered, "Let me speak with John first, see what happened. Then—"

The postponement was as painful for him as it was for

Bertie. "Only a moment," he said, studying the beloved man who now leaned against the far wall, head bowed. Richard knew his thoughts, for they were his as well, a mutual sadness at the furtive nature of their love, a deep regret that in the eyes of the world they were worse than lepers, and if found out could be prosecuted and imprisoned.

Sodomites should be flogged and castrated, John had pronounced once.

But he and Bertie were not Sodomites. They simply shared a love, a rich companionship and a mutual need and respect. Was that so unspeakable?

Lacking an answer, he knocked again, then pushed open the door.

"John?"

At first glance he thought the room was empty. But just as he was turning about he saw a figure hunched over in one of the large wing chairs near the end of the Library.

Motioning for Bertie to follow, Richard made his way through the clutter of chairs where earlier the entire company had gathered for the unveiling. As he approached, he saw that it was John, though a very different John from the man who had proudly presided over the unveiling. This man sat in the chair, his head down and buried in his crossed arms, a posture of such despair that it occurred to Richard that perhaps he should depart without speaking.

But he couldn't do that. He'd loved John ever since they had been boys together.

"John, what—"

Then the face lifted with an expression of helplessness, as though he'd received a message of tragedy and had been forced to bear the sorrow alone.

"John, what—has—" Reeling from such an expression, Richard drew up a chair and sat beside him. He was aware of Bertie a few feet away, his concern as great as Richard's.

"Please," Richard begged. "Tell me what—"

With a despairing gesture, John brushed aside the inquiry and propped his head against his hands. "Too late, Richard."

"Too late for what?"

"To prevent me from—" But he could not finish and

Richard and Bertie were left with the spectacle of a man so weakened by grief that he could not speak.

Bertie drew even and, in a voice familiar and tender, said, "Mr. Eden, please. Surely nothing warrants such black—"

John looked up. He seemed embarrassed by Bertie's presence and walked to the end of the room, all the while fumbling in his pocket for a handkerchief.

Richard heard him call back, "My apologies, Professor Nichols. I thought Richard was alone, though I should have known better."

Was there an edge to his voice? Richard couldn't be certain. "We just returned from a walk, John, and found the Great Hall—"

"—empty, yes," came the voice from the mantel. With his back turned, Richard saw half-gestures, John wiping at his face, then studying his handkerchief as though his grief were visible. "My fault, I can assure you," he went on, his voice hardening as though cynicism were a healing balm. "Who else could ruin an evening as thoroughly—"

He looked back at them from the mantel and coldly suggested, "Go along, both of you. I have no desire to ruin the evening for you as well."

"John, please," Richard begged. "Whatever it is, I'm certain—"

Bertie interrupted. "I'll bid you both goodnight and take advantage of the early evening to probe a few of the books I brought along."

Richard's initial instinct was to protest, although he felt certain that John would do it for him. Bertie had been coming to Eden since their undergraduate days. There was no need for him to take himself out of any discussion.

But when John made no move to intercede, Richard watched, helpless, as Bertie started toward the door. In an attempt to cover the awkward exit, Richard called out, "Wait, I'll go with you." To John he added, "Perhaps you'd prefer to be alone."

"No. I wish you would stay."

Caught between the two men, Richard foundered.

"Good night," Bertie called from the door, his voice forced, as though he were trying to cover his own embarrassment.

Before Richard could respond, the door was closed.

"I'm—sorry," came the voice from the mantel. "I will

add him to the long list of people to whom I must apologize come morning."

Hearing that same tone of desolation, Richard settled back in the chair. "Please tell me what happened." With his concentration still focused on the absent Bertie, he was not at first aware of John drawing near to the chair where he sat, a new expression on his face.

"Do you think it wise?" John asked.

Richard looked up, struggling to make the transition. "Do I think what wise?"

"That you are seen so constantly in his company."

Alert to danger, Richard struggled for the proper response. "He's a good friend"—he smiled—"as Andrew Rhoades is your good friend."

"I do not live with Andrew Rhoades."

Richard laughed. "It's a matter of convenience and economy."

"I will buy you a house."

Puzzled, Richard looked up, not certain how the focus of attention had shifted. "John, I did not come in here to discuss my life. You're the one who seemed in need—"

"I'm sorry," John replied, sinking into the opposite chair. He leaned back into the cushions, his face in repose now, though still bearing evidence of his earlier grief. "I'm afraid I caused a scene," he murmured.

"Of what nature?" Richard inquired, relieved to be out of the spotlight, though shaken by John's subtle attack on Bertie.

"There was a man," John commenced wearily, eyes closed. "Possibly you met him—an American, a friend of Delane's—who was behaving aggressively toward Mary."

"What happened?"

"He challenged me, launched an attack, and I had no choice but to reciprocate."

Richard felt relief that he'd not witnessed such a scene. "Where is he now? The American."

"What choice did I have? I sent him packing."

It was Richard's turn to close his eyes, feeling embarrassment on his face. What morsels of gossip the guests would take back to London! No wonder John's despair. Still, what was he to have done? Mary was his prize. Richard knew that as did everyone else, except the hapless American.

"Well, it's done," Richard concluded. "I'm sure that

Mary is grateful to you. It isn't every day that a lady in distress enjoys—"

"No. She—loathes me," John muttered, assuming that hunched position, as though a weight had settled upon him.

"Surely not. If she was in a distressing situation, she must feel only gratitude."

"Distressing situation!" John repeated. "She is so innocent, Richard, she doesn't even know when to feel apprehension. The man was making fools of both of them, and she, instead of objecting, was responding, as though—"

Behind the barrier of his hands, he went on. "She knows no fear, has been so sheltered that she would go smiling to her own ravishment—" He broke off. "Oh, God, what am I to do? I would not cause her pain for the world, yet every time I try to—"

"Don't, John," Richard begged. "It will pass, I'm certain of it. It's as you said, Mary is a child in many ways. I'll talk to her if you wish. Whatever her mood tonight, she will be restored come morning."

"And then what?" John asked. "It will happen again," he said in a mournful tone, striding toward the painting which rested, ignored, on its standard, concentrating on one face. "I'm afraid that my fortune will be her curse. Men will persistently try to get to it through her, and she, in her innocence, will not even know what they are about."

Richard listened, not in complete agreement, yet not wanting to add to his mood by disagreeing with him. "Have you mentioned the school in Cheltenham to her?" he asked, thinking that it might be a solution.

"Yes. It was mentioned and instantly rejected."

Nothing very surprising there. Still, Richard was certain that he could convince her that it was for the best. With the sense of offering a final reassurance, he left his chair and drew even with John where he stood before the painting. He was prepared to speak, but the whispered declaration, "I love them all so much, yet I only succeed in hurting them," moved Richard until he felt compelled to reach out in a gesture of support.

"I will speak to her," he said. "And I promise further that what seems so black tonight will be forgotten come morning."

It was a generous promise and partly false, considering

that there was nothing he could do about the shocked guests who had witnessed the ugly scene.

Still, it seemed to comfort John, who sank heavily into the chair, as though he were approaching exhaustion. "Tell her," he concluded, "that she must be on guard against those who would ruin her."

"I will."

"And tell her that in your opinion the school holds the brightest future."

"I will."

"And tell her that all of my actions are rooted in love."

"I will indeed."

Richard hoped that the black mood was over. The hour was late. The encounter had left him exhausted. More than ever he needed Bertie's healing love. "Are you well now, John?" he asked, moving a step toward the door.

When at first John did not respond, Richard took a step further, praying that Bertie had not fallen asleep. "I'll see you tomorrow."

Still no response and, thinking that he was free to go, Richard increased his steps until he was approaching the door when at last John stirred himself to words.

"Apologize to Professor Nichols for me," John said, not turning in the chair.

Richard looked back. "Bertie needs no apology." He smiled. "The man was born with the gift of understanding."

"You're very fond of him, aren't you?" John asked, still maintaining his position, his attention fixed on the painting.

Richard felt a pulse in his temple, always the sign of fatigue and danger. "It's as I said, John, he's a good friend."

"Do you see women, Richard?" At last John turned, his arm resting on the back of the chair, his expression in no way revealing the nature of his question.

"See—women?"

"Socially, I mean." John smiled. "Has some heartbreaking beauty caught your fancy and you've kept her a secret from us all?"

Briefly Richard experienced the sensation of falling. "Cambridge—is not known for its—beauties, as you put it."

"Then come Monday I will have a surprise for you,"

John added, bearing little resemblance to the grieving man Richard had discovered earlier.

"A—surprise?"

"Indeed. Quite to your liking, I think." He paused, then added, "Will Professor Nichols be staying for the entire fortnight?"

"Of course. We were planning—"

"No matter." John grinned. "All I ask is that you are groomed and highly visible on Monday morning."

"I don't understand—"

"You will then, I promise," John added, and turned about in his chair.

Richard stood by the door, trying to sort out what John had said. *Do you see women socially? Will Professor Nichols be staying? Come Monday I will have a surprise for you.*

"John?"

"Go along with you," John replied. "And I thank you again," he added with kindness. "I'd be lost without you."

In the face of this declaration of love, Richard's anxieties were eased. John had meant nothing, and as for the surprise—

Without warning, John concluded, "You know as well as I what must be done."

"What must be—"

"Good night, Richard."

Dismissed, Richard stepped out into the corridor and closed the door behind him. His head felt dull, as if lead had been poured into it.

You know as well as I what must be done.

Surely John would not force him into anything. He had no right . . .

He stood a moment longer, suffering the sound of a shrill alarm in his head. He must talk to Bertie immediately, must tell him everything that had been said. They had discussed in the past the possibility of emigration, to Australia, to Canada, America, anywhere.

Bertie would know what to do. For an instant, a specific image of horror filled his mind. No! Perhaps Bertie should leave now, perhaps the two of them should bid each other a very public goodbye. If John had suspicions, then they must throw him off the track. Better a temporary separation than—

Yes, but he must not seek Bertie out tonight. He must let it be known to someone that he was retiring alone.

At the end of the corridor he looked out over the Great Hall at the scattering of servants still dismantling remnants of the once festive ball.

"Bates," he called out to the butler, who was directing a group of stewards in the removal of chairs.

"Milord?"

"A wassail, Bates," Richard requested. "In my chambers, if you will."

"Of course, milord. One or two?"

"One. I said one, didn't I?"

"Yes, milord. Anything else?"

"No."

As the man departed, Richard thought he detected a knowing expression in those normally expressionless eyes. *Did they all know?*

In the anguish of that possibility, Richard turned about, aware of the stewards staring at him. Exerting all the discipline at his command, he walked steadily up the stairs, grateful that no one could see his face. . . .

On Monday morning, from the door of Lady Harriet's sitting room, Elizabeth watched as Richard tried reason, though in the face of Mary's silence it seemed a weak tool.

"He meant nothing by it, I swear, Mary! You must understand how difficult this all is for him. Believe me, he feels worse than you."

As Richard's voice droned on, Elizabeth leaned wearily against the door frame, surprised to discover that she was almost envious of Professor Nichols' early-morning departure, though *there* was a mystery. As well as she could remember, Professor Nichols had never departed from Eden without Richard. Yet all he'd said at breakfast that morning was that duties were pressing upon him and he must return immediately to Cambridge. And, more mysterious still, an hour later, only she and Charlie Bradlaugh had been on the Great Hall steps to bid him farewell.

She closed her eyes to rest them from the bright spill of sun filtering through the casement windows. Mystery or no, she still wished she might have been in that carriage with him, escaping this hectic place, where guests seemed to be leaving willy-nilly, where only this morning she'd heard the house warden complaining bitterly about the lack of organization.

In spite of everything, Elizabeth smiled. At least Mary was no longer suicidal, as she'd been earlier in the week. Nor were there tears. Since her public embarrassment on Friday evening, she seemed to have acquired a simple resignation. She'd passed the weekend in a docile state, saying nothing, though repeatedly Elizabeth had tried to engage her in conversation.

Ultimately last night Richard had offered to speak with her. Now he'd been talking steadily for almost an hour, and Mary had at least given the impression of listening, though there was a distant look in her eyes.

"Are you listening to me, Mary?"

"I'm listening."

"Do you understand any of what I've said?"

"Of course I understand, Richard."

"Then I'm sure you will agree that it serves no purpose to bear a grudge toward John. It's as I've said. He meant well, and whatever actions he took on Friday evening, they were for your own good."

Elizabeth saw Mary bring her brother into focus with a strange expression. "Do you know how often in my life I've heard that, Richard?"

"What?"

"That something or other is for my own good."

"It's true."

"And when will I be capable of directing my own life, my own actions?"

"Never," Richard said, without hesitation.

Elizabeth looked up, surprised at the word, and felt something constrict within her. She knew Mary well enough to know that the word and the edict behind it were equally as unacceptable to her.

"Never?" she heard Mary repeat, shocked by Richard's pronouncement.

"Of course not," he replied without rancor. "Would you have it any other way? John's protection is a rich blessing. And when the time comes, he will cede that protection to another man · who is worthy to become your husband. But until that time, your only responsibility is obedience; cheerful obedience, I might add."

"Did you hear that, Elizabeth?" Mary asked with suspect calm. "Do you agree?"

A sense of being trapped engulfed her. "Yes, I heard," Elizabeth admitted, "but I don't think that my opinion is at issue here." It was a cowardly response and she knew it. Later she would have to try to help Mary understand that the issues which had been fought for in London applied every place but Eden. Here, for the sake of family harmony, it was wisest to play the docile role.

"The quarrel is between you and John," she said. "Listen to Richard and please, I beg you, leave me out of it."

The silence in the room was sharp, leaving Elizabeth with an impression that she had destroyed something.

Blessedly, Harriet spoke, her calm voice a soothing balm. "The incident was unfortunate, to be sure," she said, appearing at first to take Mary's side. "However, I'm sure it's as Richard said, Mary," she went on. "I can't conceive of John relishing such a scene."

"Then why did he cause it?" Mary asked.

"According to Richard," Harriet replied, "the man was insulting."

"That's not true!" Mary protested hotly. "Mr. Stanhope is a gentleman. And may I remind all of you that the Hall was very public. If there had been any real danger, don't you think—"

"Mary, you don't understand," Richard commenced. "John was not fearful of the man literally offending your person. He simply felt that—"

Abruptly Mary stood. "Do you have anything to say to me, Richard, that you haven't said before? If not, then I beg you to excuse—"

"There *is* one other matter, Mary," Richard cut in. "It is John's wish—and I agree with him—that you take up residence away from here for a period of time."

Unfortunately, Mary was less than three feet from where Elizabeth stood, and thus she was privy to an expression on that face that she'd never seen before, as though she'd been cut adrift.

"I—am planning to return to London with Elizabeth," Mary answered, looking directly at her.

"No," Richard said, "not London."

Without turning, Mary asked, "Where?"

"There's an institution—outside Cheltenham, a school run by—"

Mary closed her eyes. One hand seemed to lift toward Elizabeth as though for support, but was withdrawn.

"Mary, please. . . ." It was Harriet again, sensing her daughter's distress. "Please come and take my hand. This is all so unnecessary. And I'm not at all in agreement with Richard or John regarding that school. So, come back and let's talk of other matters."

An expression of relief covered Mary's face. "Mama," she whispered, and ran back to her mother's side, and was instantly enclosed in open arms.

Harriet whispered, "Oh, how I've missed you! Come, you must tell me everything. Tell me about the painting. Was it well received? And tell me about the American gentleman. What's his name? And how on earth did he get caught up in all this silly business?"

From her position near the door, Elizabeth saw Richard's shoulders sag with defeat. If he'd been sent with a message, then the message had been canceled by a loving maternal voice. How John would take this news, Elizabeth had no idea and didn't really want to know. Somewhere in the gardens that eminently sane gentleman, Charles Bradlaugh, was waiting to escort her on a morning walk. Dhari and Aslam and Andrew were out riding. Lila and her father and the attractive Irishman, Charles Parnell, were cloistered in Lord Harrington's room, and John was preparing to greet his second wave of guests this afternoon. And now Harriet and her daughter were blissfully locked in each other's company.

"Richard, come," she said, thinking to invite him to share the walk with Charles Bradlaugh, wanting only to clear the chamber.

Affectionately she took his arm and led him down the corridor, speaking the first words that came to her mind. "I'm sorry that Professor Nichols had to leave so unexpectedly. I know how fond you are of—"

Abruptly he drew away from her. "It had been his intention to leave early all along. He has other obligations."

"Of course," she murmured. She was about to suggest that he join her for a morning walk when he drew further ahead and called back politely, "If you will excuse me, Elizabeth—"

Did she have a choice? She watched, astonished, as he hurried down the corridor, turning left at the corner into the passageway which led to the Family Chapel.

Curious! What would he be doing in the Chapel?

Merciful heavens, how she would like to flee with Charlie Bradlaugh back to London! What a simple world that was compared to this.

Scolding herself for these thoughts, she hurried on down the corridor, hungry for sun, shivering from the permanent chill which seemed to be imbedded in the stone walls. . . .

In a significant way, John had hoped all morning that his business conference with Alex Aldwell would be interrupted by Bates' announcement of arriving carriages. *They should be here by now, Lord and Lady Forbes, Lord Russell. Where in the hell are they?*

"And in my opinion, the new building site on Portland Place will require additional crews. And here's the ledger you requested on the Circus Road site. It seems to me that . . ."

As Alex's voice droned on, John settled back behind his desk in the spacious second-floor chamber which he'd selected to be his office outside of London. Glancing about, he realized that the chamber more nearly resembled an antique market than a business office. What had possessed him to give his approval to Queen Anne furnishings, replete with pale pink roses and velour drapes? It was suitable for a whore, and no one else.

He leaned back as far as the delicately ribbed constriction of his chair would allow and tried to keep his mind on Alex's voice. There were matters under discussion that needed his attention.

Alex—

Thinking the name, he glanced across at the large man, quite the dandy this morning, in a dark brown plaid suit and bright yellow silk neck scarf. Powerless to halt the assault of memory, John recalled the first time he'd laid eyes on Alex Aldwell in that grim hospital ward at Scutari, Alex, an erstwhile soldier of fortune recently returned from India, ill with dysentery, and John, an equally erstwhile survivor of the madness known as the Crimean Engagement, young enough and foolish enough to listen to the rantings coming from the bed next to him.

They had gone separate ways. Alex back to England; John to India, yet fate had joined them together again when each had been in sore need of the other. Fifteen years ago that had been, and now viewing the man it occurred to John that Alex Aldwell might very well be the only person in the world whom he could trust.

"But we need Andrew," Alex was saying. "There are some legal matters that are holding us up, and I, for one, don't trust none but Andrew—"

John nodded. *Andrew Rhoades.* A small regret there.

"Do you think it would be possible for him to return to London soon?"

John rubbed his forehead, behind which beat a small pain, the result of a sleepless night. "I'll need him here for the rest of the week, but after that I see no reason—"

"Are you—well, John?" Alex asked considerately, closing the ledger.

"Of course I'm well," John scoffed, moved by the man's inquiry. No one else of late seemed to give a damn how he felt.

"And the various—fêtes?" Alex inquired further. "Are they going well?"

"Tolerably," he murmured.

"I've been searching the London papers for the first accounts," Alex said with a grin.

John looked up. "Anything?"

"No, not yet, but then it's far too early, isn't it?"

John stared at him, aware that Alex was trying to read his mood. Weary of his close scrutiny, John left the desk and took refuge by the window, which gave a perfect view of the inner courtyard below.

"And how is Lady Lila?" he heard Alex ask, still trying to penetrate John's silence, "And the babes," he added, his voice going soft at the mention of John's two young sons, whom he adored.

"Well," John muttered from the window. "Look in on them if you wish before you leave. Tell Miss Samson I gave you permission."

"I'll do it," Alex said warmly.

Weary of the awkward meeting, John said, "I'll sign these later," gesturing to the scattered documents which Alex had brought him from London. "Now I have a few requests to make," he added, and sat behind the desk.

"Of course. Anything." Alex smiled and, as was his custom when John was giving orders, he withdrew from his pocket a small leather notebook.

"No," John said, "there's no need for notes. I'm sure you can remember—"

He waited out the quizzical expression on Alex's face. "Private matters, these, Alex. I trust I have your loyalty."

As though hurt by the question, Alex leaned up in his chair. "As you have always had it, John, as you will always have it."

The declaration moved John, and he thought of the numerous times in the past when Alex had performed "private duties" for him: fetching a street woman for him when he'd awakened in the early hours of the morning in need of that particular breed of female, driving a competitor out of business in a hundred subtle ways. In the course of their long relationship, Alex had never questioned him or censored him or challenged him.

Torn between his new requirements and his overwhelming sense of gratitude, John looked up. "Your careful attention, then, Alex, and your vow that what we are about to discuss will never leave this room."

"You have it."

John found that he could not look at the man and turned about in the limited chair until he was gazing safely into emptiness. "I have the need, Alex," he began, "of the services of a private investigator. You are to find me the best. The man is to take up temporary residence in Cambridge and he's to report back to you on the daily, the hourly movements of Professor Herbert Nichols."

At last a faint sound, not a complete articulation at first, but slowly expanding into one. "Lord Richard's friend?"

John nodded.

There was a pause. "Done," Alex said, and John knew that it was.

"Then I want you to find out everything you can for me on a man named Burke Stanhope, an American presently living in London. Where I have no idea, but it shouldn't be too difficult."

"Done," Alex said again. "Anything else?"

"One thing more. When you return to London, I want you to send a donation of five hundred pounds to a Miss Veal, to a school for women in Cheltenham. Send it by special courier and make certain that my name is attached."

"Done," Alex said a third time, and John looked back over his shoulder to find the man grinning passively at him, not a sign of a question in that broad flat face.

"God, what would I do without you, Alex?"

"A better question is what would I do without you."

"Then take yourself off to whatever recreation you desire," John said gruffly, in an attempt to stay his emotions before they ran too high. "You've earned a rest, and the hospitality of the entire castle is at your disposal. I'll send a steward along to see—"

"No need," Alex said, declining the offer. "I don't need no man to wait on me, you know that. I take what I want."

"You do indeed." John smiled.

"A night's rest, John, and I'm on my way back to London." At the door he paused. "We miss you. I hope you won't be too long following after."

"As soon as all this is over, Alex, I promise you."

Then he was gone. For a moment longer John sat behind his desk, weary at midmorning. Why was everything becoming so difficult?

Lila

He wanted to see her.

In an attempt to offset the emptiness of the courtyard below his window, he pushed back from the desk and hurried through the door, thinking *Lila*, thinking not only of his rightful claim upon her but thinking how good it would be if she'd only smile at him as she'd smiled at the stranger. . . .

London
May 14, 1870

IN SPITE OF his efforts to pay attention to his mother's incoherent discourse, Burke's concentration was consistently dragged away by the persistent ache in the lower left side of his jaw. It was nothing much in the way of serious discomfort—in fact, it was rather pleasing.

By merely running his tongue over the bruised flesh,

he discovered that he was capable of resurrecting the entire evening—the orchestra, the scent of roses coming in through the doors, and ultimately that one remarkable face, the enchantment of Jeremy Sims' Song and Supper Club miraculously transplanted to an outpost called Eden.

"Burke, you must believe me. I don't think the darkies can be trusted."

In response to her accusation, he tried to offer comfort. "Why can't they be trusted, Mother? We've trusted them for years. They love you dearly as I do, and would do nothing—"

"No, Burke," she pleaded, half rising from her chair. "They refuse to—" Abruptly she stopped, spying Charles standing silently at the door. At the sight of him, she sat back down, the bow-shaped painted lips parted, and from them issued a soft moan.

Over the half-formed accusation, Burke saw Florence join Charles at the door. She stood as though assessing the situation, then moved steadily to his mother's side.

"Come, Miss Caroline," she soothed, "we'll walk in the garden if you wish. What pale cheeks my pretty has! Mr. Sun needs to touch them, that's what. Come."

As the maternal voice cut through the silence, Burke saw his mother glance up at her old maid, a combination of longing and resentment on her face.

"It *is* in my head, isn't it, Florence?" he heard her plaintively ask as they passed through the door.

"Of course it is, Miss Caroline. You trust old Florence, you hear. After all, who dressed you on your wedding day?"

"You did."

As the two female voices, one strong, one weak, drifted out into the entrance hall, Burke closed his eyes. Perhaps it was time to write to his father again, though a hell of a lot of good that would do. Gazing at the distorted reflection of the dining room on the side of the coffee service, he saw Charles step forward on the opposite side of the table.

"Will you be in this morning, Mr. Burke?"

"For a while, yes."

"To callers?"

"Depends on who they are, Charles. I have work."

"Mr. Delane, sir. He's waiting in the library."

Abruptly Burke turned. "My God, why didn't you tell me?"

"You were breakfasting, sir, and you need one good meal a day."

But Burke didn't wait for the rest of the boyhood lecture. He suffered a brief mental confusion. Who precisely had been "freed" in the recent hostilities? No matter. The one man he wanted to see more than any in the world was John Thadeus Delane. They had had the opportunity to exchange only a few words that last night at Eden before the watchmen had escorted Burke out. Burke had assumed that Delane would be staying for the entire second week of the Eden Festivities.

He moved out of the room at a rapid pace, and a few seconds later pushed open the library door, where he saw his friend standing in solemn scrutiny of the pavement beyond the lace curtains.

At his entrance, Delane turned and on his face Burke saw the same gloomy expression which he'd last seen at Eden.

Burke smiled, a little amazed that Delane had not enjoyed the theatrical as much as he. "You're certain you weren't seen entering this house?" Burke joked. "I suspect that Mr. Eden will see to it that I become a social leper."

Ignoring the joke, Delane took his outstretched hand and earnestly inquired, "Are you well? Have you seen a physician?"

"Oh, Lord, Delane—you're not serious."

"It was a considerable blow."

"It was nothing, and I enjoy my bruised jaw as a soldier enjoys his battle wounds, with the sense of danger past and hard-earned dignity."

Up close he saw that Delane was still reeling from the incident. In fact he looked worse than Burke, his eyes buried in hollows, his clothes mussed.

"Come," Burke offered kindly, "let me summon Charles. You look as though you could use—"

"No, no. I require nothing," Delane said. "Nothing, that is, except the ability to comprehend."

It was as Burke suspected. The foolish incident was weighing more heavily upon Delane than it was on him.

As they settled into the sofa before the dead fire,

Burke asked quietly, "When did you arrive, and why did you leave Eden?"

With a half-smile, Delane said, "I arrived late last night in a carriage borrowed from the madman himself, and I left the next day after your departure because no civilized man would—"

"Oh, civilization has nothing to do with it, Delane. The man felt compelled to protect what was his. I was the interloper."

"You bear him no ill will?" Delane asked in amazement. "My God, man, you were publicly humiliated!"

Burke laughed outright. "*You* obviously suffered greater humiliation than I did, my friend. In fact I thoroughly enjoyed it, wouldn't have missed it for the world."

Delane cast him a glance which suggested that he was in the presence of another madman. Confronted with such an expression, Burke tried to explain his feelings. "Ah, now you see we come to one of the basic differences between the English and the Americans. As tools of arbitration, a man's fists are hard to beat. There's something very honest about a good blow delivered in righteous anger. Of course, it seldom solves anything, but it does have a way of clearing the air and defining the game."

Delane shuddered. "Barbaric. And you're no better—"

"Nor am I worse." Burke smiled, saddened to see that the man had lost his sense of humor someplace along the road back from Eden. "Oh, come, Delane, it was great sport and you know it, and the prize was certainly worthwhile."

"The—prize?"

"Lady Mary! Surely you don't think I'd engage in battle without a prize."

Delane looked directly at him, a slow dawning on his face. "You're not—surely you don't mean—you're not going to try to see her again?"

"Of course I'm going to see her again," Burke replied expansively.

Aware that Delane was staring at him, he left the sofa, feeling momentarily weakened, as though the mere thought of her was capable of draining him. His steps took him to the window where, for the first time, he realized the incredible obstacles in his path. If she remained at Eden, he would have no chance at all of contacting her again. But if she returned to London in the company of—

"Delane, where did you say your friend lived?"

"My—"

"Elizabeth."

Delane turned around in the sofa, the confusion on his face mounting. "In—London?"

"Where in London?"

"St. George Street. Number Seven, I believe."

"Thank you."

"You *are* mad," Delane pronounced with conviction. "I expected to find you this morning in the company of your solicitor, preparing to bring suit against Eden. You have grounds, you know—unprovoked assault."

"There you're wrong again, Delane," Burke said from the window. "I worked very hard to provoke that assault, even threw a punch of my own."

"Why?"

"There are one of two ways you can come to know a man," Burke said. "Either through his love, which I'll admit is the most desirable, or through his hate." He approached Delane with the sofa between them. "From the manner in which we were being ignored, I determined early on that there was a strong possibility that John Murrey Eden was capable of loving no one but himself." He shrugged and leaned against the back of the sofa. "Then what was left?"

"Yet, you intend to take no action?"

"No, there will be no charges. Burke Stanhope will do nothing. But Lord Ripples—"

All at once the mystery left Delane's face and was replaced by a smile of astonishment. "Then you'll write something?"

"Write something!" Burke parroted. "Ripples is already hard at work, Delane, and if you'll get out of here, I can promise that he'll deliver copy to you that will cause shockwaves which will be felt all the way to Eden Point."

Delane grinned, as though in the heat of the melodrama he had forgotten the entire point of the trip to Eden, though he prudently warned. "No libel, Burke, nothing that will enable him to drag *us* into court."

As the man came around the sofa, Burke rested his arm affectionately on his shoulders. "Have you forgotten that I learned the libel laws at your knee, Delane, and forgotten as well the words of your predecessor, Thomas Barnes . . ." He lifted his head so that Delane might hear again the full quote on which he'd based his entire professional life.

"The first duty of the Press is to obtain the earliest and most correct intelligence of the events of the times, and instantly, by disclosing them, to make them the common property of the people. The Press lives by disclosures. . . ."

Delane listened carefully. At the end of the quote, he made a strange comment. "Then why do I feel like a traitor?" he asked softly.

Taken aback, Burke withdrew his arm. "I don't know. You're far better equipped to answer that than I." When doubt still raged across his face, Burke reminded him, "You are not obliged to print everything that Lord Ripples writes."

"No!" Delane said, as though enjoying a sudden resolution. "The man is arrogance itself, the worst combination of aggression and righteous zeal, which has left us with enemies all over the world. No," he repeated, "tell Lord Ripples that all I ask is that he write the truth as he saw it during those few days at Eden."

"He has never done less."

The two men stared at each other, as though in that instant they both were aware of the incendiary nature of their profession.

"Well, then, be about it," Delane concluded, hurrying toward the door. He stopped and turned back. "Your— mother?" he inquired politely.

"The same."

"I'm sorry."

Burke saw a look of sympathy on that weary face. How good it was to have at least one friend.

"And you're sure you're not injured?" Delane inquired further.

"A badge of honor." Burke smiled. "I will nurse it with pleasure."

There was another pause. "And you *will* try to see the young lady again?"

"As soon as possible."

Delane shook his head, then he was gone. Burke stood

on the closed side of the door, effortlessly seeing her face in the spill of morning sun at his feet.

Why the attraction? Because from the beginning, when he'd first seen her months ago at Jeremy Sims' and when he'd last seen her at Eden Castle, the one quality that she'd tried to keep hidden, and which even her beauty and sweet voice could not mask, was her own soul-shattering loneliness. For Burke it had been like looking into a mirror. . . .

❦

Eden Castle
May 16, 1870

LADY ELEANOR FORBES, daughter of a penniless English peer, knew precisely what she had to do. She'd been trained from birth to "marry well."

Seated in the Banqueting Hall of Eden Castle with Lord Richard on her left and John Murrey Eden on her right at the head of the table, she glanced about at the magnificent hall and decided with admirable pragmatism that there was money here, if nothing else.

A peculiar evening, she thought further, the vast table set for over seventy-five guests, yet less than twenty seated awkwardly about, their eyes never lifting to their host, strangers all as far as she was concerned, with the exception of Lord Richard, whom she'd met briefly at their arrival that afternoon. Of course she knew John Murrey Eden, that remarkable gentleman with whom she'd danced repeatedly during the London season and who was a friend of her father's and a frequent visitor at their country home in Kent.

She knew he was married and had looked forward to meeting his wife. But she was not present at this evening's meal. Only old women sat at this table, like her mother seated opposite her, more Grandmama than Mama. Both her parents were approaching seventy, Eleanor a "late mistake."

Preceding her had been three brothers, the eldest dead and buried in a place called Sebastopol in the Crimea;

the second, Peter, a gentleman sailor at Osborne; and the third, Percy, a charming though hapless gambler who had come close to exhausting the already depleted family coffers.

So it was left to Eleanor now, the "mistake," to please the Edens and convince at least one of them that she was "suitable" and would "breed well."

"Lord Richard," she said quietly, for the silence about the table seemed to forbid speaking aloud, "I noticed from my window upstairs a narrow path which appeared to lead down the side of the cliffs. Where does it go?"

"Mortemouth," the man replied, politely enough, though not raising his eyes to her, which she considered a waste, for with the help of her maid she had groomed herself carefully and knew that she was pleasing, and knew further the precise points of her attraction: a flawless white complexion complemented by coal black hair, lavender eyes the color of heather, and a full body which had been carefully sculpted by many missed meals. Her gown was white, French silk, fit for a bride, as her mother had hopefully pointed out.

"Mr. Eden——" She smiled, trying again to her right this time, the handsome bearded countenance of the man about whom all of London had gossiped at one time or another. "Forgive me if I'm forward, but I had hoped to have the pleasure of meeting Mrs. Eden. Is she——"

"Ill," the man replied, steadily eating as though the consumption of the lobster mayonnaise on his plate were the most important thing in the world.

"I'm sorry," she murmured and looked up, pleased to see Mr. Eden staring at her.

"Forgive my preoccupation this evening," he said, touching her hand where it rested on the table. "I'm certain that you did not travel all the way from London to be cast into gloom. Come, Richard, we're both failing as hosts and, in the presence of such beauty, that is unforgivable."

"I propose a toast," Mr. Eden pronounced, full-voiced with a suddenness which caused heads to snap the length of the table. "To all our guests who have done us the honor of journeying to Eden!"

He held his glass until the others followed suit and, to an uneven chorus of murmured approval, Eleanor tipped her glass and merely tasted the wine, aware that there

would be other toasts and, if she were to accomplish her
goal, she needed a clear head and a steady eye.

But she was wrong on the first count. There were no
further toasts, and she watched Mr. Eden sit back in his
chair, the gloom about him deep and spreading.

From the far end of the table came the unexpected
sound of laughter. Longingly, Eleanor looked in that direction and saw a warm foursome consisting of the woman
named Elizabeth, who earlier that day had greeted her
kindly in the company of the notorious freethinker
Charles Bradlaugh. Eleanor's father later claimed to have
recognized him and had sunk deep into new brooding
over the "propriety" of the Eden household.

But as her mother had pointed out, they had not come
to Eden for propriety. Propriety would not pay the
French dressmaker or satisfy Mr. Soames, the solicitor
for White's, who had been sent to collect just a gentleman's portion of Percy's twenty-seven-thousand-pound
gambling debt.

So propriety had never been mentioned again, not
even when Mr. Eden's silent Indian mistress had appeared on the arm of a gentleman named Andrew
Rhoades. And Eleanor knew she was his mistress. Who
in London did not know it after relentless caricatures in
Punch?

Now these four—Elizabeth, the Indian mistress,
Bradlaugh and Mr. Rhoades—as though impervious to
their own scandals, seemed to be the only pocket of
merriment in the entire hall.

There was more laughter, sharp and precise, and again
Eleanor peered down the table to see that a young man
had joined the fun. He was Indian as well, though the
cut of his dress blacks was English.

As though aware of themselves as spectacle, Elizabeth
and the man named Andrew Rhoades glanced toward
the end of the table, where Mr. Eden was glaring back at
them. A few moments later, while the distant conversation did not cease, it fell, the little group all bending in
toward one another, as though a wordless edict had been
issued.

Eleanor was aware that she was feeling tense, realized
that she'd been sitting with her shoulders hunched. Silently she scolded herself and sat up straight. She was
glad that the people laughing were enjoying themselves.

But it did not concern her. It was her task to please only one man, the brooding John Murrey Eden.

To that end she adjusted the pearls about her throat and filtered through her mind the proper subjects on which a lady could speak without causing male offense. She settled at last on, "Your castle is beautiful, Mr. Eden. I'm certain you know that it's the talk of all of London. And how sad that so few can see its beauty firsthand."

"Have you had the opportunity to see all the castle as yet, Lady Eleanor? No, of course not. We'll remedy that tomorrow. I will take you on a personally conducted tour. Would that please you?"

A peculiar offer, she thought, like a small boy wanting to show off his possessions. "Yes, thank you," she murmured.

The fourth remove was before them, smoked turkey and an enormous roast beef. And, gratified, she saw Lord Richard and Mr. Eden preoccupied with eating, the latter insisting with his mouth filled that the stewards give generous portions to all. Strange, but she did not remember the man being so cloddish.

There was a sudden burst of laughter coming from the far end of the table, sharper this time. Since there was nothing else happening at the table except the consumption of food, it was difficult not to look in that direction and wonder about the source of amusement and wish to be a part of it.

She was aware of Mr. Eden returning his fork to his plate, his eye leveled at the small group, most of whom were dabbing at their eyes after the last outburst of laughter.

She saw him lean back in his chair, his fingers folded over his mouth, only his eyes visible, an expression just barely containing anger.

"Elizabeth!" His voice, razor-sharp, cut through the residual laughter, and all heads turned first in his direction, then to the offenders at the end of the table.

"John?" The woman smiled back, something challenging in her smile, as though she knew him too well to be intimidated by him.

Then Eleanor heard Mr. Eden, his voice rife with suspect goodwill, say, "I was just wondering if it would be asking too much for you to share your amusement with the rest of our guests."

The Women of Eden

Unfortunately, the invitation seemed to provoke fresh hilarity, and as the others took refuge behind their napkins, Eleanor saw Elizabeth straighten herself. "It was nothing of great importance, John, I promise," she said smiling. "Mr. Bradlaugh was just relating a tale of—"

"And your friend could not share it with the entire company?"

"Hardly," Elizabeth murmured.

"Let us be the judges of that."

"John, please," Elizabeth begged.

"No, I mean it," Mr. Eden persisted. "Since the meal commenced the rest of us have been forced to witness your vulgarity. Now I think the least you can do is to inform us of the source and nature of your amusement."

Eleanor looked down into her lap, aware of the heat on her face, doubly aware of the other guests all frozen in their respective positions, as though if they only held still, the ugly scene would diminish.

But it didn't, and now into the stubborn silence came a new voice, strong yet apologetic. "I meant no offense, Mr. Eden, I swear it."

Eleanor looked up to see Mr. Charles Bradlaugh on his feet behind Elizabeth's chair, his hands on her shoulders in a protective gesture.

Hoping that this would be the end of it, Eleanor glanced up to hear Mr. Eden say, "Elizabeth, kindly tell your friend to take his seat. He is a guest in this house only under your auspices and I want the present company to know that and thus spare me any responsibility."

To her left she heard Lord Richard murmur, "John, please—"

Just as Eleanor was beginning to wonder if anyone would ever move again, she heard a chair scrape and looked up to see Elizabeth standing, the expression on her face one of hurt.

Elizabeth gazed steadily back at Mr. Eden, then murmured, "If you will excuse us—" and without another word she skirted the far end of the table, Mr. Bradlaugh behind her, the silence now punctuated by their footsteps.

As the embarrassment continued to spread, Mr. Eden said in a forced voice, "Please, my friends, let's continue. And eat heartily. You will have the chance to dance it off later. The musicians are tuning their instruments and the ball will take place as scheduled."

*A ball? With less than twenty guests? But perhaps
others are due later,* Eleanor thought. Down the table she
heard her mother make an attempt at conversation, and
feeling a degree of pride in that dignified old woman who
in younger days had served Queen Victoria as lady-in-
waiting, Eleanor began to hear a steady hum of voices
about her, the pulse of the party not exactly revived, but
at least still beating, though Mr. Eden seemed to have
sunk into new depths of brooding.

Eleanor tried to think of something to say and realized
that while her "finishing" lessons at her mother's knee
might serve her well in most situations, there were forces
in this Banqueting Hall tonight which were well beyond
her. If fate decreed that she would become Lady Eden,
she must remember that her true master would never be
her husband, the man seated on her left whose head was
bowed so low that he appeared to be at prayer, but rather
the man seated on her right, London's premier master-
builder, who now sat slumped in his chair, his head jerking imperceptibly like an angry bird of prey. . . .

Later that evening, watching the sad spectacle of eight
couples waltzing in isolation about the Great Hall, Eleanor glanced across the Hall and saw her father and
mother entering the small Library in the company of
John Murrey Eden.

Just before her father disappeared into the room she
saw him look back at her, his normally bland face set in
a hard way. It was only a brief glance, but the message
was clear. Fate was in the process of determining her
future.

No matter. She would make the best of it, for in her
twenty-one years she'd learned one lesson well, that the
world was gentlest with those who willingly played the
role that the world had assigned to them.

She had been trained from birth for this moment, to sit
passively beside a man she did not love, aware that
forces were being set in motion that would bind her to
him forever, and not to whimper or complain, and certainly not to cry, but rather to smile pleasantly and flatter
his ego with: "Lord Richard, tell me of your work at
Cambridge. How important it sounds. . . ."

By late Tuesday afternoon, the embarrassing script had

been written large and clear for all to see. No other guests
were coming. Out of the one hundred and fifty elegantly
engraved invitations which had been delivered to England's titled families, less than twenty had appeared.

Out of the habit of loyalty, Andrew Rhoades sat in one
of those beastly Queen Anne chairs which John had
chosen as decor for his office and watched apprehensively
as the man himself gazed out the window into the empty
courtyard below.

Andrew had not been summoned. He had taken the
initiative himself and had sought John out, though it had
required massive effort to do so. That John was suffering,
he had no doubt.

Andrew looked up from his thoughts to the brooding
man at the window, his hands clasped behind his back,
his head tilted at an angle which seemed to personify his
hurt and bewilderment.

"John, it isn't the end of the world,. you know," Andrew said. "It's time we got back to London. Alex tells
me there are matters requiring our attention. What
would you say to leaving tonight? Richard can take care
of—"

"Why didn't they come, Andrew?" came the mournful
voice from the window. "How have I offended them?"

Andrew pushed out of the uncomfortable chair, feeling
the need for movement when confronted with such a difficult question. "I wouldn't say that you've—offended
them, John," he began prudently, "although your success
may be a bone of contention." No, that wasn't the right
approach or the honest one. "For all the liberal rhetoric
sweeping across England now"—he smiled—"there are
still barriers between the classes."

That wasn't much better. In fact, Andrew turned, expecting a fiery rebuttal. But to his relief he saw nothing
but the man, fixed as a statue, still gazing out the window.

A moment later John stepped back to the desk. "Where
is Richard?" he asked.

The rapid transition caused Andrew to falter. "I—
don't know."

"Is he with Lady Eleanor? If he isn't, I wish him to be
so. Seek him out, Andrew, and inform him that it is my
wish that he pass the entire evening in her company."

Baffled, Andrew nodded, though he couldn't understand

how the pretty young woman could provide Richard with any diversion.

"And see to it that our guests have everything they require," John added, this last request even stranger than the first. The guests had at their command a staff of over four hundred. Surely they were being looked after in every sense of the word.

"And tell Miss Samson that I will visit the nursery within the hour and that my sons are to be dressed and informed of my coming."

Andrew smiled, amused at the thought of little Stephen and Frederick snapping to attention in their father's presence.

"And tell Mary that I would like to see her at dinner tonight."

Andrew stood alert. Trouble there. Mary had found a safe refuge in her mother's chambers and he doubted seriously if she would willingly comply with John's wishes —not after her recent humiliation. Still, he would try.

He glanced across at the man standing stiffly behind the desk. "Anything else, John?"

The direct question elicited no response, though a few minutes later he saw John come out from behind his desk and start wordlessly toward the door.

"John? Where are you—"

"See to it, Andrew. Everything."

"But I had thought that we might—"

"I'll be back within the hour."

"But where are you— May I—"

"See to everything!"

Andrew ceased his questioning. It didn't hurt so much to deal with this John.

But he was in no way prepared for the scarcely audible voice now coming from the door. "I'm sorry, Andrew, if I've tarnished your reputation. It was not my intention to be a stigma to those I love most."

Self-pity was there. But something else as well, the incredible realization that John was assessing his own worth in terms of those guests who'd spurned him.

Andrew stared at the bowed figure. When at last he'd found his tongue it was too late, John passing through the door, impervious to Andrew's repeated calls of: "John— wait—"

Mystified, the echo of that last ridiculous apology ring-

ing in his ears, Andrew went immediately to the window,
which gave a view of the courtyard below. A few minutes
later John came into sight, walking at that same steady
pace past the watchmen, who roused themselves long
enough to bow before their master.

But as far as Andrew could see, John was not
even aware of their presence, and continued walking, head
down, hands clasped behind his back, chained internally
by some overpowering drive.

It was alarm, coupled with curiosity, which suggested
to Andrew that perhaps John should be followed. That he
was caught in a deep depression there was no doubt.

Hurriedly Andrew left the room and traced John's steps
down the stairs through the Great Hall, past the servants,
who tried to look busy, on through the doors and out into
the late-afternoon sun.

*I'm sorry, Andrew, if I have tarnished your reputa-
tion—*

His thoughts took him the length of the castle, where at
the northwest corner he stopped, his eyes scanning the
gardens which stretched before him in colorful profusion.
But there was not a sight of John.

Whatever demons were at the moment grappling with
his soul, Andrew suddenly felt generously inclined to let
John deal with them alone. The mood would pass. They
always did. Next week, when they were back on familiar
London ground, rushing from one building site to another, then Andrew would find a way to tell John what
was in his heart, that though there had been difficult occasions on which his love had faltered, that love was still
very present, and, contrary to tarnishing Andrew's reputation, he considered his association with John to be the
richest aspect of his life.

He had just started back down the cool damp path
when his eye fell on movement coming from an unlikely
place, the graveyard, that cloistered area hidden behind
high walls where every Eden for the last six hundred
years had been buried.

He moved stealthily toward the black iron gate, wanting to see but not wanting to be seen until—

John.

He was standing before the marble headstone of his
father, Edward Eden. As Andrew's eyes grew accustomed
to the dim light, he stepped back behind the protection

wall itself and peered around the gate at John, who appeared to be merely standing before his father's grave, not in the attitude of mourning or prayer, but rather a defiant stance, as though he were asking questions of the grave.

It occurred to Andrew that he had never seen him here before. Elizabeth came often and on occasion Lady Harriet, but those were the only two who ever paid their respects to the Eden dead.

In the chill evening, Andrew shuddered. Of all the haunts of Eden he would have thought this one the last that John would have sought out. Surely he would find nothing of comfort here.

Feeling that he was intruding on an intimate moment, Andrew was in the process of turning away when he saw John take one step forward, his hands reaching out for the marble headstone bearing the inscription EDWARD EDEN 1798–1851. He seemed to grasp it, as though he wanted to rip it from its place in the earth. But at last his intent failed him and Andrew saw him go down onto his knees on his father's grave, his head bent low, a soft, childlike voice joining the sighs of waves coming from the strand, an almost soundless moaning which nonetheless Andrew heard clearly.

"Papa—"

Andrew turned away, unable to watch any longer.

Lord Liam Harrington, originally from County Kerry, Tully Cross, Ireland, sat back in his chair in his private sitting room, amazed that the long-dreaded public opening of Eden Castle should be so enjoyable and that the enjoyment was emanating from such an unlikely source— a tall, gaunt, attractive young Irishman who had kept them both captivated for the last several days with his humorous accounts of "Britishness."

Though it was approaching midnight, the three of them having dined alone because of Lila's indisposition, and though Mr. Parnell had held forth nonstop for over four hours, still Lord Harrington was loath to let the evening end.

To Mr. Parnell's thoughtful observation of, "It's late and you both look weary," Lord Harrington insisted, "No, not at all," though he glanced across at his daughter Lila, lying on the chaise in her dressing gown, and determined that while she didn't look particularly weary, she looked ill, her eyes darting to the clock. John would send for her soon, as he always did, and Lord Harrington would be forced again to witness her fear as her maid helped her to the door.

Yet what can I do? She was the man's wife. She had her duties and no choice but to perform them. In addition, Lord Harrington was too deeply in debt to John Murrey Eden ever to take Lila's side against him. The man wanted more children, a reasonable Catholic desire, and Lila must be the bearer of those children, whether she fancied it or not.

Strengthened by these thoughts, he redirected his attention to the irrepressible Irishman, Mr. Parnell, who had regaled them all evening with stories of his English classmates at Cambridge.

"Tell us more, Mr. Parnell, I beg you," Lord Harrington pleaded, rising from his chair to fill both their brandy snifters, in the hope that the man would talk on until Lila was sent for, and then remain for that next ungodly hour when Lord Harrington was forced to dwell on what she was enduring.

"I can't imagine what's left to tell, Lord Harrington," Mr. Parnell responded. "Suffice it to say that my Cambridge days were a disaster from start to finish. If it hadn't been for a few men such as Richard Eden and Herbert Nichols and my supervisor, G. F. Pattrick, my three and one-half years there would have been even more unproductive than they were."

"Then you count the experience for nothing?"

"Absolutely nothing." Parnell smiled.

"Why did you go?"

"My mother's idea," Parnell said, laughing. "God spare the world from ambitious mothers! She'd thought to make an English gentleman of me, but—"

Abruptly the man broke off and stared into his brandy.

As though hoping to guide the conversation away from that painful topic, Parnell asked, "Is it true, Lord Harrington, that your daughter has never seen Ireland?"

Embarrassed, Lord Harrington leaned back in his chair. "I'm afraid it is," he confessed.

"I don't believe it," Parnell said, standing. "I merely ask her when she'd last been home and she calmly replies that she's never been to Ireland!" He strode a few steps about the room, looking back at the two of them, only to conclude with a vigorous shake of his head. "I don't believe it; I really can't."

"You must understand, Mr. Parnell," Lord Harrington began feebly, "I married an Englishwoman and dissolved all my Irish holdings many years ago." He placed his snifter on the near table and locked his hands before him in defense against the memories of that bleak past. "It was during the Famine, Mr. Parnell. I was unable to care for my workers and I wearied of watching them die."

He closed his eyes against the assault of memory and guilt. Unable to face it, he'd run from it, had run as well from his Catholic faith. In a rush of grief he walked a distance into the shadows of the room and threw back a defensive, "No, Lila has never seen Ireland, and my last glimpse of it was not one that I would want her to see."

Softly he heard Mr. Parnell say, "The invalid lived, Lord Harrington. Surely you received news of that. The Irish heart beats as strong as ever and will continue to do so, despite British greed. I can't imagine that you will be contented forever within the confines of this English fortress, nor Lady Lila."

"She is an English wife now, Mr. Parnell," Lord Harrington replied, "as she was an English daughter."

"And an Irish one," Parnell added. Then, as though he too had sensed that the conversation had taken a disagreeable turn, he sat on the edge of the chair, that irresponsible grin seeming to light all the dark corners of the room, and cordially invited, "Then you must both come and visit me at Avondale. Oh, beautiful it is, you wait and see, Lady Lila, comfortable but not grand, set in a park of ancient trees and rolling grassland."

As Parnell rushed on in loving description of his home, Lord Harrington watched Lila, the changes on her face as Parnell talked about the small comfortable rooms, the cozy library, the three bay windows which afforded a breathtaking view of the lush parkland, every feature in direct contrast to what she inhabited here at Eden.

As Parnell's enthusiasm mounted, keeping pace with his voice, he left his chair and sat on the edge of Lila's chaise, as though his words delivered close at hand would have a greater effect on her. Lord Harrington found himself drawn forward by the man's passion, his determination to make the dream happen, to work alongside his

farmers, enjoying the dignity of labor, an experience not
totally foreign to Lord Harrington, despite his ten years of
pampered boredom here at Eden. In his youth he, too,
had worked alongside his father and knew the feel and
smell of Irish soil as well as any man.

"Ah, glorious it is, and glorious it will be," Parnell
concluded in a state of rapture, his hands clasped between
his legs, his strong patrician features lifted toward the
ceiling.

Suddenly Wolf awakened and meowed plaintively. The
animal sound, coming so unexpectedly after the torrent of
human words, set them all three to laughing, Parnell
claiming, "See? Even Wolf wants to come. Poor Wolf,"
he added, gently rubbing the cat's head, "condemned to
a diet of English rats."

There it was again, that coldness in his voice for everything English.

Lord Harrington had a question, indeed had postponed
asking it for several days. He drew near to the chaise and
tried to speak diplomatically. "If I may ask, Mr. Parnell,
why did you come here?"

A look of surprise covered the man's face. "I was invited," he said, "by both Lord Eden and Professor Nichols. I was on my way to London to visit my brother
John, and, if given a choice between the filthy roadside
inns of rural England and the cornucopia of Eden Castle,
which would you select?"

Lord Harrington smiled. It was as he'd suspected. The
man was a charming opportunist.

"Money, great masses of it, has an incredibly strong
odor." Parnell grinned. "And this poor Irishman couldn't
resist a good glimpse at one of England's truly great cess-
pools."

Aware that he'd said too much, Parnell delivered an
apology to Lila. "I beg your forgiveness, milady," he
murmured.

"No need, Mr. Parnell," she replied, the expression on
her face soft with reflective tenderness for the land of her
ancestry which she'd never seen. "My husband is—"

A knock came at the door, a light rap, not at all capable of eliciting the look of fear which covered her
face.

Lord Harrington saw Parnell glance toward the door
and offer kindly to open it.

"No," Lila whispered, drawing her dressing gown more tightly about her. In the next moment when Wolf jumped down from her side and darted into Lord Harrington's bedchamber, Lila cried out, "Wolf, please!"

In defense against the cry and the dread in his daughter's eyes, Lord Harrington summoned strength from some remote source and ignored Parnell's offer to answer the door, going himself, knowing full well what he would find on the other side.

There they were, precisely as he had imagined them, a strange party of executioners: Lila's maid, Molly, her expression in the dim corridor as fear-ridden as Lila's, and standing behind her, two strapping male stewards who had been sent to assist her with the completion of her duties.

"Begging your pardon, Lord Harrington," Molly whispered, "but Mr. Eden—"

"I know," Lord Harrington replied sharply and thought, *How barbaric!* Was the fault Lila's or John's, and how long could his daughter endure nightly rape, and why between husband and wife did it have to be rape?

Frustrated and despondent for lack of an answer, he commanded brusquely, "Madam, your husband is waiting."

He turned away from the conclusion of the ritual, Molly stepping aside to permit the two stewards to enter the room, the men, one on each arm, lifting Lila to her feet, a gentle assistance, simply acting as support for her weakness, no one paying the slightest attention to her soft plea of "No, please," the echo fading under Molly's encouragement of "Come, milady—"

Then they were gone, and Lord Harrington closed the door quickly behind them, fearful that she might cry out again, and took his regret to the window where in the comfort of night he thought again, *Barbaric!*

"With your forgiveness, Lord Harrington," Parnell said, a few steps behind him, "why do you permit it?"

"Permit what?" Lord Harrington replied, taking shelter in a feigned ignorance.

"Your daughter is ill," Parnell said. "That is apparent to anyone with eyes to see. Why do you permit her nightly to be subjected to—"

"Who am I to give my permission?" he countered. "They are husband and wife, Mr. Parnell," he pointed out, embarrassed to be discussing such an intimate matter with a stranger. "Mr. Eden wants more children. Doesn't he have that right? Tell me if I'm wrong, please."

He heard the entreaty in his voice and hated it, seeking consolation from a man he'd known for less than a fortnight.

But to his extreme pleasure Parnell gave it to him. "Yes," he said at last, as though his conclusion had been painful but nonetheless honest. "Yes," he repeated, "a husband has rights—even John Murrey Eden."

The two men stared at each other, a bleak, uneasy stare, as though something had been omitted, something left unsaid.

Parnell rallied first. "Come," he said, placing an affectionate arm about Lord Harrington's shoulder, "another brandy for medicinal purposes."

Comforted, Lord Harrington refilled their snifters and settled back in the easy chair opposite Parnell. And, in order to keep his thoughts away from the chambers two floors below, he asked with sudden urgency, "Please tell me more of Avondale, Mr. Parnell. . . ."

Like a monstrous and mortally wounded prehistoric creature, the Eden Festivities gasped a final breath on Friday morning and died, to the relief of all.

The comparison was John's own, muttered in private to Aslam during the last tortuous breakfast with no members of the family present save Aslam and less than ten diehard guests, including Lord and Lady Forbes and their daughter, Eleanor.

With the conclusion of that awkward meal, John had dutifully stood at the bottom of the Great Hall steps and bid all farewell, their expressions of gratitude for his hospitality sounding more like condolences.

As the last carriage belonging to Lord and Lady Forbes rattled through the Gatehouse arch, John watched with weary eyes and thought that at least something had been accomplished there. A marriage contract had been drawn up and signed with mutually advantageous clauses for both sides. John had waived the dowry from the impoverished family in exchange for their promise that Lady Eleanor would be patient with her intended, Lord Richard Eden. The "engagement" could stretch over an unprecedented five years if necessary, and during that time

Lady Eleanor was not to see or be seen socially with any other gentleman. She was to respond affirmatively to any invitation made by the Eden family and was to launch immediately into a correspondence with Lord Richard, persisting even if he failed to reply.

Of course John had assured them that he was confident a marriage would take place well within the five-year limit. But in the event that it didn't, Lady Eleanor was then free to pursue her matrimonial search in more promising directions. In return for this display of patience, John would provide the Forbes family with fifty thousand pounds per year, which would enable them to retire all of Percy's gambling debts, plus their household debts, thus achieving a degree of financial respectability when the ceremony did take place.

And it *would* take place, and with that conviction he had reassured both parents and daughter. The fact that the prospective bridegroom had not put in an appearance for the last two days was a bit harder to explain.

As the Forbes carriage rattled beyond the Gatehouse, John closed his eyes and tried not to dwell on the bitter disappointment of the last few days. In the heat of the late May morning, he felt a trickle of perspiration course down the side of his face. He opened his eyes and brushed it away and saw his hand unsteady before him. That they considered him a fool there was little doubt. That he *was* a fool there was no doubt. What need had he for any of them, those pampered bluebloods with their inherited and rapidly dwindling wealth, pathetic specimens like Lord and Lady Forbes, in outdated and musty-smelling clothes, and their pretty little practical-minded daughter, who had more sense than the two of them put together? She'd smelled a proper bargain right enough, and when they had faltered, she'd always been there to make them strong.

No, she would perform admirably for Richard, would provide him with children, a male heir specifically, keeping the line intact. And, in addition, she would be a pretty bauble to add to Eden, a healthy specimen to take the place of those sulking females who now plagued his life.

He stood a moment longer in the hot sun, his eyes fixed on a heat wave dancing across the inner courtyard. Briefly one specific memory engulfed him, transported him back to another May morning quite different from this one, cold,

raining, the sixteen-year-old boy with the mud from his
father's fresh grave on his boots.

*My name is John Murrey Eden. My father was Edward
Eden. I have come home. . . .*

In spite of the warm morning and all those intervening
years of tragedy and accomplishments, John realized that
he was as alone now as he had been then.

But a man must be stronger than his own solitude, and
he was master of Eden in every sense of the word. The
point was to take rejection and turn it into an exalted act,
the supreme expression of a life beyond rejection. It could
be done. He'd done it many times before.

As he turned about, already sorting through in his head
his immediate course of action, he saw standing in the
shade of the Great Hall arch a familiar and well-beloved
figure.

Aslam.

From the bottom of the steps he continued to gaze up,
making direct contact with those dark eyes, as aristocratic
as any Englishman's. What a treasure the boy was, and
how tall he was growing, and how straight, not a trace of
the frightened little boy who'd fled India with him years
ago.

"Aslam . . ." John smiled, starting up the steps, grateful
for the young man's presence. "Come," he added, placing
his arm about the boy's shoulders. "Let's steal a moment,
shall we? Two, if need be."

The boy responded with a smile and followed John into
the shade of the Great Hall, where together they stood and
watched the dismantling process, the chairs, which had
stood empty for the last few days, being carried away by
the stewards, the footmen lowering the banners bearing
the coats of arms of all the guests who had not appeared.

"A grand fiasco, wasn't it?" Aslam said with bluntness
which caused John to laugh.

"It was indeed," he conceded, deriving comfort from
Aslam's honesty. No one else was that honest with him
anymore.

"Come," John urged, "let's see if we can't find a quiet
haven somewhere. I've neglected you long enough. In
here." He smiled, standing back at the Library door and
letting Aslam pass before him. Of course there were
a hundred problems which needed his attention elsewhere:

the physician, who at this moment was with Lila, and Mary, whom he'd not seen for three days.

Looking up from his thoughts, he saw Aslam at the far end of the Library in close study of Alma-Tadema's painting, "The Women of Eden."

The boy possessed possibly the keenest intelligence that John had ever known, and he found himself awaiting his opinion with as much anticipation as earlier he'd waited the opinion of the Royal Academy.

"Well?" John prompted, seeing on that young face a sedate smile, like one who knows the stakes but is safely out of the game.

Slowly Aslam lifted a finger to his lips. His brow knit as though he were not quite satisfied with his own opinion. "They all," he commenced, "look sick to their stomachs."

"They—what?" John stammered.

"They look sick to their stomachs," Aslam repeated with conviction. "Come! See for yourself."

Stunned, John followed the boy's command, standing directly in front of the painting and seeing that he was right, all four women poised in angles of waiting, and on all four faces pained smiles of some unidentified discomfort.

John stared closer, trying to repress the urge to laugh. But the need was too great and as he felt the compulsion grow, he made a peculiar sound like a strangling chicken. As the juxtaposition of Aslam's brutally honest critique echoed in ridiculous counterpoint to the pedants from the Academy—*"excessively emotional, lacking dramatic restraint, vehemently romantic"*—John gave in to the long-needed release of unrestrained laughter, reaching out for the support of a near table, his eyes filling under the duress of his hilarity, the whole spasm lasting several minutes and leaving him gasping for breath.

"John, I—"

The bewildered voice came from behind. Fishing blindly in his waistcoat for his handkerchief, John tried again to stifle his laughter. "I'm sorry," he gasped, attempting to straighten himself for the boy's sake, who looked mildly hurt.

Restoring the handkerchief to his pocket, he stepped forward and unashamedly enclosed the boy in an embrace. "My God, how grateful I am to you!"

"I—don't understand," Aslam confessed.

"I know you don't and I'm sorry," John murmured.

"Well, it's true," Aslam persisted. "Look at them. The only time I've seen that expression on my mother's face is after she had consumed too much ginger and cream."

"Oh, God, don't!" John begged, still gasping for breath, more than willing to concede the accuracy of Aslam's judgment. How effortlessly the boy had punctured the hot-air balloon of pretense which only last week had permeated this Library.

Still wiping at the corners of his eyes, John circled the foolish painting and sank in pleasurable exhaustion into a chair. Without thinking, he murmured the first words that came to his head.

"When are you going to join me in London, Aslam? I have reason to suspect that I am in sore need of your leavening presence."

Not until he saw the expression on Aslam's face did he realize that unwittingly he'd spoken the words that were closest to the boy's heart.

"I'll return with you tonight," Aslam said without hesitation.

Sitting up, John altered his initial statement. "No, you're not ready yet. But soon. A year. Two at the most."

"In what way am I not ready?" Aslam protested. "I'm reading far in advance of my tutors now. And what I lack, Andrew Rhoades can teach me."

"I run a complex firm, Aslam," John gently reminded him. "My solicitors need to be fully prepared."

"But I'm accomplishing nothing at Cambridge," Aslam replied with conviction. "It's a—stupid place, the students more interested in rowing than—"

As he sank despondently into a chair, John watched him, aware of what the young man must be forced to endure in that English bastion of learning.

As the brooding silence persisted, John felt regret that he needed the assistance of anyone. But his own formal schooling had been merely adequate, and where the baroque complexities of English law were concerned, he needed trustworthy and reliable aides. Andrew Rhoades had served him well, but one day Aslam would serve him better. Andrew owed him nothing but friendship; Aslam owed him his life, and on a debt of that proportion, what an allegiance could be built!

"Patience," John counseled, reaching forward to ruffle the boy's hair, though he knew it annoyed Aslam.

Predictably, Aslam pulled away and continued to glare unseeing into the space before him. Impressed by his gloom, John asked, "Is it so bad, Aslam? Cambridge, I mean. From what I've seen of the place it looks idyllic, the little Cam flowing placidly through the green meadows—"

"It's hell."

"How so?"

Abruptly the young man looked up, as though aware that he'd said too much. "It's just that—"

As he faltered again, John sat up straighter. "Just what, Aslam? Tell me."

The young man sat with his hands clasped before him. "There are rituals—disgusting rituals—"

"Of what nature?" John asked, his mind moving to Richard and to the private investigator he'd recently turned loose on Professor Nichols.

When Aslam either couldn't or wouldn't speak further, John suggested the unthinkable. "Sodomy?"

That was all he said, but it was enough. An expression of bereavement crossed Aslam's face, as though he knew he's said too much.

A noble impulse, John thought, though in the next moment the nobility was shattered by Aslam's forceful suggestion, "Let me return to London with you, John, and I'll tell you all!"

John gaped at the boy. Disappointment was there, combined with a desire to "hear all." But the bargain itself reeked of self-interest, blackmail almost.

In an attempt to digest his disappointment, John turned away, increasing the distance between them. A sudden knock at the Library door eliminated the need for him to make a decision.

"Who is it?" he shouted angrily over his shoulder.

"It's Bates, sir. I was sent to inform you that the physician has requested a brief conference with you."

Damn! he thought. *But perhaps it is just as well. When did it happen? When did Aslam change from that honorable little boy to—*

"John?"

As Aslam called to him, John dismissed him with an edict which he knew would hurt. "Leave me now," he said coldly, "and prepare to return to Cambridge. I believe Richard is planning to depart—"

"No!"

By God, am I surrounded by disloyalty? "No, what?" he demanded, facing the young man down.

Aslam retreated first, colliding with Bates, who stood poised on the other side.

"Aslam?" John called after him, feeling the need to explain something.

But the young man was gone and John was left with a feeling of heaviness. He turned away from Bates, though he was aware of the man waiting patiently at the door.

Then he remembered. The physician, another incompetent, a stammering old charlatan named Dr. Cockburn whom John had brought out several years ago from Exeter and had ensconced in comfortable quarters in the Servants Hall to tend to the daily disasters that plagued Eden's over-large staff: fingers chopped off with butcher knives, broken limbs, vapors. The mewling and complaining had been endless, and Dr. Cockburn's job had been to quiet this chorus of lamentations.

It had never been John's intention to have the old man attend the family, but seeing Lila's weakened condition the night before, aware that at some point during intercourse she had lost consciousness, and determining that she could not await the more professional examination of a London physician, John had summoned the old man early this morning and had sent him to Lila's private chambers.

A futile exercise, he realized now. She'd been examined repeatedly by men more skilled than Cockburn. A prime specimen, all had pronounced, healthy and equipped to bear a sizable brood. Then *what?*

"Mr. Eden?"

"Show him in," John snapped and strode away from Bates' inquiry, his eye, in the process, falling on the ridiculous painting, finding it impossible to believe that only a short time ago he'd enjoyed a soothing merriment.

He heard a faltering step at the door and knew without looking that his patience was about to be sorely tried.

"Cockburn," he called out, and at last brought the old man into focus where he stood in the doorway, a stout gentleman with shaggy white hair and brows.

"That will be all, Bates," he added, amazed at the rising anger he felt.

"Well, come in, Cockburn, and close the door. You requested a conference and here I am."

"N-not a conference, Mr. Eden—"

"Then what in the hell?"

Seeing an expression of fear on the old man's face, and realizing that shouting was accomplishing nothing, he closed his eyes and tried to rein in his mysterious anger.

"Then if not a conference, your—report, sir, if you will," he invited with admirable calm.

The man drew himself up, as though aware of his lack of professionalism. "A d-difficult undertaking it was, sir, b-but I give it my best, I did—"

"And your diagnosis?" John snapped, finding that he was unable to even look at the man.

"Simple, r-really," the man stammered, unaware of his own contradiction. "It's j-just a matter of poisonous blood." He smiled down on John. "It h-happens most often to f-females—"

"Poisonous blood?" John repeated, repulsed by the man.

"Aye, sir. S-spotted it early on. Color of the face, if you know what I m-mean—"

No, John didn't, and experienced a deeper regret for having subjected Lila to—

"But n-not to worry, sir," the old man added. "Cure's under way."

"What cure?"

"Bleedin', sir, what e-else? On my life, it's the only solution. We'll let the little dears suck on her for a few hours. Then—"

On his feet, John reached across the table and grabbed the man by his throat and dragged him halfway across the table. "Have you lost your mind?" he shouted. "She's weakened as it is. What possible good will come from—"

"P-please, sir," the man gasped, his veined and smelly hands flailing in the air, "it w-will serve, I swear it, and it'll do the babe no harm either—"

John was on the verge of throwing Dr. Cockburn across the room when one word caught his ear. "B-babe?" he stammered, only half aware that he sounded like the doctor.

"Aye, sir." The old man nodded. "Bleedin's normal course for p-pregnancy. It benefits both mother and—"

"Babe?" John repeated, relaxing his grip on the man's throat.

Old Cockburn laughed with relief. "I'd s-stake me life on it, sir. I'm the f-first to admit I ain't proper and skilled, but I do know a swelling woman when I see one—"

Confronted with such conviction, John continued to stare, his mind reeling. A babe, if it was true, had been his most urgent wish. But there was something else. Lila. For the last few months she had begged a week of privacy for herself each month, claiming painful cycles. If she were truly pregnant then there would have been no cycles.

"Are you certain?" John demanded, coming around the table.

"N-never been more certain, sir. There's a growin' thing in y-your wife's belly. I'll s-stake my life on it."

For a moment longer John stared down at the flabby face. Then he was running, scarcely hearing the old man calling after him, "I h-had to restrain her, sir, for the leeches to do their work. But she and the b-babe will be the better for it."

The babe. That one word he clearly heard and took it with him all the way up the steps.

Babe! Oh, God, don't let this one terminate too soon, he prayed, taking the stairs three at a time, taking also his deep hurt that Lila had not told him, had continued to use the classic female defense against him.

Why?

But as he approached her chamber door, the question seemed less urgent in the face of this glorious news.

Another child, a daughter this time, please, John prayed, and pushed open the door.

"Who is it?" he heard Molly call from the bedchamber.

From where he stood with the sitting room separating them, John saw only the foot of the bed. Before he could respond to Molly's call, she appeared in the door, her eyes filled with tears.

Upon seeing John she burst into new weeping and with the hem of her apron pressed against her lips, she begged, "Oh, please help her, sir. Please put a stop to it."

Something in her plea warned him to harden himself to what he might find in the bedchamber. Then, recalling anew that Lila had recently deceived him, he moved forward, ignoring Molly, though the sight beyond the door stopped him with a force as though an invisible barrier had dropped down between him and the bed, a sight so distasteful that he raised his eyes to the safety of the velour drapes behind the bed.

"Sir, please make him take them off her," Molly wept behind him. "She's suffering terrible, as you can see."

Yes, he could see that, having found the courage to look back down on the bed. Lila was visible only in profile, her wrists drawn over her head and lightly trussed to the bedstead, her nightshirt lowered to her waist, approximately thirty black leeches attached to her upper torso, several nestled into the area of her armpits, others attached to her arms, the majority boring deep into the white flesh of her breasts and upper stomach. Small, black, curling, their bodies twisted with the satiation of her blood, appearing on the white field of her flesh like black commas.

Hardening himself to the sight, he recalled the numbers of times that he had submitted himself for bleeding. Even his London physician still recommended it, though it was considered old-fashioned in advanced medical circles. It was painless, and what he was responding to, and certainly what Molly was responding to, was Lila's restraint —that and the repulsive nature of the leeches themselves.

"I beg you, sir, do something. She's ill and growing worse."

Suddenly he'd had enough of Molly and, without warning, he slammed the door to the bedchamber, shutting out the hysterical maid, shutting himself in.

At the sound of the door slamming, Lila turned her head, and John's first glimpse of those pale features caused him to falter.

Drawing one step closer, he observed that the pillow on which her head was resting was soaked with perspiration and tears. But now there were no tears. In fact she appeared to be holding herself very rigid, her eyes fixed on the ceiling.

He stood beside the bed and waited for her to look at him. With almost unbearable grief he charted the changes which had taken place in this once lovely woman. He *had* loved her, loved her still as much as love could be present, burdened with the realization that every time he approached her, he caused pain.

When she still refused to make eye contact with him, he felt a portion of his armor weaken and leaned gently forward. "Lila—"

At last those eyes shifted from the ceiling and moved to his face, and he observed that they were brighter than usual, though more sunken and prone to dwell longer on what they saw.

"Lila," he began, feeling pity for her, wanting, in spite of her deception, to ease her suffering. "Not much longer." He smiled, trying to keep his eyes from the leeches. "And it's for the best," he added. "Dr. Cockburn says that it will serve both you and the babe."

At last he noticed that he had fully engaged her attention. Her thin rib cage, which earlier had been rising and falling with her breathing, grew still, then commenced to rise and fall at a more rapid pace, her agitation made manifest in the manner in which her hands, in spite of their restraints, clutched at the bedposts.

Was she still trying to deceive him? Did she take him for a fool? "Yes," he replied forcefully, "Dr. Cockburn has confirmed it."

He saw her struggle against the strips of muslin. Realizing that she could not free herself, she fell back against the pillow, her eyes closed.

He watched her, his own emotional state none too steady. Directly under her left breast a leech detached itself and slithered up, its small tubular body fat with her blood, leaving a small red path in its wake. The others were beginning to shift, barely perceptible movement, as each detached then reattached itself to her flesh.

Watching the shifting black slime, he experienced a wave of nausea and disciplined his eyes to stay safely on her face, his mind to occupy itself only with the mystery of her denial, which seemed to carry new deception with it. All those other miscarriages—had she forced them? It was not unknown. Whores purged themselves monthly. But was she so loath to bear his children that she would do this?

As the mystery grew, so did his sense of threat, and now he was aware of the silence in the room, broken only by her panting. Yet behind his anxiety was his joyful realization that she was again carrying his child and, if need be, he would have her watched day and night until the babe grew to full term and was safely delivered.

Of course he had no proof of his earlier suspicions, only the fact of two safe deliveries followed by countless miscarriages, and the repeated professional opinions, including Cockburn's, that nothing was wrong with her.

For the dead babies he grieved only a moment, then renewed, with purpose and impervious to her melodramatic reaction to simple bleeding, he informed her, "You *are* carrying a babe, Lila, and this one will see life. I swear it."

He discovered with regret that she was crying, her face bearing no resemblance to the beautiful young woman whom he had married in the apple orchard of Harrington Hall over ten years ago.

"Lila, please," he begged, hurt that she had deceived him. "Are my requests so unusual? I have a right to children, don't I? And you're my wife. Who else—"

"No—baby," she whispered, and appeared to want to say more, but the spasms had commenced again, convulsions which seemed to sweep over her every ten or fifteen seconds and cause her teeth to chatter.

He was sorry for her, but sorry for himself as well, and now it was his duty to inform her of certain necessary changes in her life at Eden.

"There *will* be a babe, madam," he announced, drawing the coverlet up over her, stopping short of her waist where the leeches were drawing the poisonous blood out of her. "And though I must return to London shortly, I'm assigning new maids to your chambers, women who will provide you with everything you need in order to produce a healthy infant," he went on, thinking that the loyal Molly would have to be dismissed. Most likely she was Lila's co-conspirator.

"And these four will be given strict instructions never to leave you alone. Is that clear? There will be no vigorous exercises. I prefer that you remain in these chambers for the duration of your confinement. Then, after the safe delivery of my child, you will be granted your freedom again."

She grew still. "My—father—"

"Not for a while," John advised. "You need isolation in order to regain your strength." It occurred to him that he must contrive to take Lord Harrington back to London with him. The old man was constantly begging to be of service. It would be a simple matter to assign him some useless duty, thus removing him from the close proximity to his daughter, in the event that his paternal concern got the best of him and caused him to forget his debt to John.

"Your father will be returning with me to London," he announced. "My work there has been neglected for too long, and he can be of service to me." A new idea dawned. Take everyone back with him. Clear the castle of all eyes and ears which might tend to frown upon a husband who imprisoned his wife. Mary, Elizabeth, Dhari—all would return with him, leaving only Harriet, whom he could trust not to venture out of her seclusion and who seemed to prefer it when the castle was empty.

Feeling comfortably hardened and justified, he took a final look downward, then moved toward the door, finding Molly on the other side.

"Is she—is milady—"

"Well." John smiled. He strode past the woman and maintained silence until he reached the door. Then he turned back with a simple announcement.

"Your services are no longer required here. You are to pack your things at once."

The look of shock on the plain face spread. "Sir, I—don't understand—"

"Of course you do," he countered genially. "How much clearer need I make it? See the housewarden before you leave and she will give you sufficient funds to tide you over until you can find another position."

"But, sir—what have I—done?"

"You've done nothing," he reassured her. "It's just that my wife will require special care in the future. She will be well looked after, I can assure you of that."

He saw the woman glance back toward the closed door, her confusion dissolving into sadness. "Does—Lady Lila know that I—"

"Of course she knows!" John snapped, losing patience. "Come now, gather your things and be off with you. I'm sure you'll find another position soon."

For a moment longer the maid hesitated, her eyes scanning the closed door lovingly, as though trying to see through it to her mistress.

"Molly, did you hear?"

The sound of his voice raised in anger jarred her loose

from her grief and quickly she ran past him and disappeared down the steps.

John listened to the new silence. He withdrew the key from the lock, closed the outer door and locked it. Until certain arrangements could be made, he wanted no one to see her in this state. He owed her that much. He would pass the key on to Dr. Cockburn, who shortly would remove the leeches and, because the old fool had brought him such joyous news, John would grant him permission to vacate the Servants Hall and occupy one of the more comfortable chambers in this corridor. After all, a physician must be near his patient.

In the meantime, John had much to do. He must select four reliable women from Eden's vast staff who would do his bidding in all matters, and the most joyous duty of all, he must inform the others of this miraculous news, that Lila was carrying new life, a sister, he hoped, for Stephen and Frederick, the third accomplishment in John's private empire, the creation of a large and boisterous family, all bearing the name of Eden.

Suddenly he smiled. A babe, a fitting end to this desolate fortnight, as though nature were informing him that he needed no one but himself.

Suffering a spasm of happiness, he hurried off down the corridor to spread the news. . . .

Through the two windows with their bright, lattice-figured curtains the sun fell on the soft rose carpet, and into the warm spaces. Mary stretched her hand, thinking that in spite of everything she felt at peace.

Seated on the floor at her mother's feet, she watched the bright red yarn which Harriet held taut between her outstretched hands while Dhari rolled it deftly into a ball.

A fascinating twosome, Mary thought, glancing up at her mother, the Englishwoman who had found a soulmate in the dark-skinned Indian woman who, in spite of her birthright, was more of an Englishwoman than any of them.

"What's it to be, Dhari?" Mary asked, watching the ball of red yarn grow larger.

At the direct question Dhari placed the ball in her lap and pantomimed a shawl, her eyes conveying more than most people's words.

"It will be for Lila," Harriet added. "She complained of a constant chill last winter, and Dhari thought——"

"Poor Lila." This voice came from behind Mary and belonged to Elizabeth, who sat with her feet up on the chaise, sipping tea. "I don't think there's a sun in the world that could warm that child. Her hands are perpetually cold."

"Then mittens." Harriet smiled. "If the yarn permits, a pair of mittens might be appropriate."

As the winding process commenced again, Mary nestled closer to her mother and thought how good peace was, both internal and external, after the recent turmoil during which time she had learned much about herself. Specifically, she had learned that she must "abide," as Harriet had phrased it. Anything could be borne, her mother had told her further, as long as one did not pit one's will against the world. If a course of action could not be acted upon immediately, then the wise woman bided her time, kept her silence and worked in harmony with those forces about her.

How simple it all sounded, and it must work, for never before had Mary felt such peace. Of course what she had confided to no one was that in large measure she was being sustained by memories of that one miraculous man who had danced with her and who had looked upon her with eyes which had suggested that he had found her equally miraculous.

Abruptly she drew her knees up, tucked her long skirts beneath her, rested her cheek on her upraised knees and gazed sideways at the patterns of sun and shadow on the floor. Out of the turmoil of a thousand contours gradually emerged his features.

Will I ever see him again?

When she came back to herself, she heard her mother asking Elizabeth, "When will you be returning to London?"

"Not for a while." Elizabeth smiled, placing her teacup on the tray. "I like Eden best without people. Now that all those guests have departed——"

"Did it go well?" Harriet asked.

"Not well," Elizabeth confessed honestly, and Mary knew she was thinking of her own humiliating exit from the Banqueting Hall in the company of Mr. Bradlaugh and that man's late-night departure from Eden. "Less than twenty of the scheduled guests arrived this week."

Harriet leaned back in her chair. "How sad for John," she murmured. "He's worked so hard."

In the silence Mary looked at Elizabeth, who sat with her head down. She expected her to launch forth in her usual loving commiseration for John, forgiving him all. "He'll recover," was all she said.

Mary smiled. How pleasant it was, this new alliance which existed between them. Outside the door she heard a footstep, the sound of boots, then Peggy's voice protesting, "She's occupied, sir."

There was another voice, more familiar. "Occupied, hell! I have news—" The door burst open and she saw an incredible sight: John smiling, filling the doorway, hands on hips, a lightness to his manner not at all consistent with the sullen man who had brought disaster down on his own house.

At last he spoke, his voice as expansive as Mary had ever heard it. "Ah, here you are!" He grinned. "All the ladies of Eden in hiding from me."

"Not hiding, John," Elizabeth corrected gently. "Just keeping out from underfoot."

"But that's precisely where I want you," he said laughing, closing the door behind him.

"I'm sorry, John," Harriet interrupted quietly, "about the—"

"There's nothing to be sorry for, Harriet," he said. "And now that I've found you all," he continued, stepping further into the room, "no one may leave this chamber until I've made my announcement."

Mary looked up to see him moving about the room like a small boy, dutifully delivering kisses to one and all, though he stopped short of where Mary sat and turned away, leaving her the only one in the room who had not received the gift of his affection.

Abide and be patient.

"All right. My news is this, and you are the first to know." He lifted his head. "New life," he murmured. "My announcement concerns new life, a new Eden, my third child!"

Elizabeth was on her feet, a look of joy on her face. "Oh, John, that *is* marvelous news! But are you—certain? It would be too cruel if—"

"I'm certain," he pronounced. "Old Cockburn has just examined her, and while he may not be much of a physician by his own admission, he claims that he does know a pregnant woman when he sees—"

Mary moved to one side, belatedly aware of Harriet trying to stand so that she might deliver her congratulations. "How happy I am for you, John," she said, grasping the arm of her chair. "Is Lila—"

"Well," John beamed. "I just left her. She is as delighted as I am."

"I must go to her," Elizabeth announced. "I must—"

"No!" The grinning man disappeared and was replaced by a face that Mary had seen before too many times.

"No," he repeated, the smile back in place, though not as broad as before. "She's—resting now. Cockburn's with her. He has informed me that she needs complete quiet."

"But is he—capable, John?" Elizabeth inquired. "I hear the servants gossiping about him. They say that he is—"

"He will serve for a while," John replied. "In time I will bring out a London physician. But for now—"

As his voice drifted off, Mary was aware of her mother settling back into her chair, the entire room suffused with the softening projection of a new baby. In spite of her own apprehension, Mary found herself smiling. A new child was what John had wanted more than anything in the world. Perhaps now he would not focus so harshly on her.

"I'm happy for you, John." She smiled, at last throwing her congratulations in with the others.

"We all are," Harriet repeated, "though I hope this one goes better than—"

"It will," John cut in. "According to Dr. Cockburn the secret is complete bedrest and quiet."

"Do the others know?" Elizabeth asked. "Richard and Andrew?"

John shook his head. "But I'll tell them before they leave."

At last Mary saw Dhari look up, her attention caught by something that had been said.

Elizabeth asked, "Are they leaving? So soon?"

John nodded. "Richard and Aslam will depart tonight, Andrew first thing in the morning." He stretched his arms and clawed toward the ceiling. "The ill-fated Festivities have at last come to an end," he announced broadly. "I've neglected my duties long enough. We all have."

With his hands laced behind his back, he walked slowly to where Dhari sat at the table, her hands manipulating the needles through the red yarn. "In fact," he began, stopping behind her chair, "my second announcement concerns us all. We all will be leaving Eden come Monday."

Elizabeth looked up. "I had thought to stay for a few additional—"

"No. I want no distractions for Lila, no late-afternoon tea parties like this—" He gestured about the room, the censure clear on his face. "You know as well as I that if you remain Lila will seek you out, and the stairs are the worst of all, according to Cockburn. No, I want everyone in London with me for a while."

He seemed to assess the female faces about him, then again a grin splintered those strong features. "I'll impose no hardships on you. Quite the contrary. Indulge yourselves to your hearts' content. Concerts, art galleries, dressmakers—"

From where Mary sat she saw his hand make its way down the side of Dhari's neck, an intimate gesture. For the first time the knitting needles went silent.

"You have no real objection, do you, Dhari," he asked, "to leaving Eden for a while?"

There was no response at first. Slowly the woman shook her head and the needles commenced a slowed but steady clicking.

"And you, Mary?" he asked. "Surely there's no objection coming from you."

"No," she replied without hesitation. "I'm happiest in London."

"Of course you are," he agreed, approaching her and extending his hand. As he lifted her to her feet she went willingly, seeing nothing in that generous countenance to cause her alarm.

"I tell you what we'll do," he said, putting his arm around her shoulder. "We'll entertain more often. Yes, we will. That monstrous house of mine has never known a decent ball. Elizabeth, you can help us," he added, drawing Elizabeth close beneath his other arm. "We'll dust off those chandeliers, polish the floors and give the most lavish balls that old London has ever seen."

In view of the recent disastrous Festivities, it seemed a generous offer and yet one which pleased Mary. Perhaps at last he would grant her just a portion of her own life. Still, based on experience, she knew that he was capable of saying something and not meaning a word of it.

"Are you—serious, John?" she asked.

"I've never been more serious."

He seemed determined to hold her in his gaze, as though aware of her doubt and his need to dispel it.

"If I've made you unhappy, Mary, I'm truly sorry. But you must understand that my impulses are weighted with love for you and nothing else."

His manner, his voice, the expression on his face were as honest as any she'd ever seen. She did love him very much, this strong, handsome cousin.

Without warning she found herself in his arms. In the quiet embrace she heard nothing but his own labored breathing close to her ear and the click of Dhari's knitting needles, and for a moment longer she luxuriated in his tenderness, like all deep feeling, concealing a melancholy strain. She must remember this lesson as well, that it was much easier to love than to hate.

"Then it's settled," he said at the end of the embrace. "We'll all return to London and leave Lila in the solitude she needs to properly nurture my child. Is it agreed?"

It was as far as Mary was concerned, though with surprise she heard a protest coming from Elizabeth. "But Dr. Cockburn, John," she murmured. "Now more than ever Lila needs expert professional—"

"I said he would serve for a while," John snapped. "Of course I'll be returning periodically to Eden. If I feel she needs more assistance, then I'll certainly provide her with it."

"Still, she's not well, and we are all aware of how—"

"What precisely is it, Elizabeth?" he demanded, confronting her where she sat on the chaise. "I thought that you, more than anyone, would look forward to an early return. Don't you miss your menagerie of friends? I assure you, I'd much prefer that you entertained them in your own house in London than here. I wouldn't be too surprised if you singlehandedly and your associates were not responsible for this last disastrous week. What gentleman or lady in their right minds would—"

The shocked look on Elizabeth's face silenced him.

Fresh from loving him, Mary was astounded by his outburst. Never had she heard him speak like that to Elizabeth.

"I'm—sorry," she murmured. "If you'll excuse me, I have much to do."

Not until she reached the door did he find his voice and the will to use it. "Elizabeth," he called out, a desolate quality to his voice. "Elizabeth—wait—"

But she didn't and, stunned, Mary watched her depart the room. In sympathy Dhari commenced gathering up her work and silently left the room without a glance at the man who stood near the chaise, his initial high spirits obliterated in the small death for which he was totally responsible.

Mary looked toward her mother and saw her seated erect in her chair, though her veiled head was turned several degrees to the left, away from the place of hurt feelings, as though in spite of her blindness she still saw too clearly.

When no one seemed inclined to move, Mary plunged her hands into the pockets of her skirts to hide their trembling and kissed her mother through the veil and whispered, "I'll come later and say goodnight."

Having decided that it might be best to pass John by, she drew even with him, and changed her mind. He appeared so pathetic, devoid of strength and consumed with regret, and with the intention of offering comfort, as he recently had comforted her, she touched his arm and whispered, "Elizabeth has a miraculous capacity for forgiveness. I know, for I have offended her many times."

He looked away. Then, with a sharpness which warred with the grief on his face, he said, "The offense is hers; not mine. I do not seek her forgiveness."

Then there was nothing more to stay for, except to try to sort out in her own mind the enigma named John Murrey Eden.

At the end of the corridor she looked back and saw Peggy just starting into the chamber. *A mistake that,* Mary thought, though in the next minute she saw John leave the room. He paused outside the door as though he wanted very much to return. But Peggy closed the door forcefully and left him standing alone in the corridor.

Quickly Mary slipped out of sight around the corner, not wanting him to see her. At the top of the landing she stopped, debating with herself whether to turn right toward Elizabeth's apartments or left toward her own. Dhari would be with her by now, and perhaps Dhari's silent presence was all she desired.

Later she would seek her out, when they both felt stronger. For now she longed for a closed and bolted door behind which she could still the turmoil of hurt and harsh words in that most healing memory of all. No fantasy this time, but a specific face, a specific form and a specific sensation of an arm about her.

Of course she would have to fill in the music out of her imagination, but what a simple task that would be, compared to the demands she had placed on her imagination in the past.

❧

London
June 1, 1870

"STILL READING?"

From the window of Delane's home in Sarjeant's Inn, Burke looked across at the man bent over the desk, the sheaf of papers in his hand angled toward the small lamp, nothing on his face to give the slightest indication of how he was reacting to Lord Ripples' latest offering.

Satiated with the delicious meal provided by Delane's French cook, Burke sipped at his brandy and looked out at the night beyond the window, the street emptied of all traffic, as well it should be at three in the morning.

Smiling in spite of his satiation and fatigue, he recalled Delane's absurd melodrama in setting up this meeting. In the past Burke had strode midmorning into Delane's office in Printing House Square, deposited Lord Ripples' column on his desk, then strode out again, greeting personally the assistant editors, most of whom he knew by name.

But this time it had been very different. At Delane's insistence Burke had been instructed to stay clear of his offices and not to come to his home until well after midnight, and then to leave his carriage at least a block away and come on foot, keeping his portfolio concealed under his coat and with every step making certain that he was not being followed.

Well, he had followed those instructions to the letter, though it had been a damned inconvenience to do so. Now, having overeaten because of the late dinner and consumed too much brandy while Delane deliberated over every bloody word, Burke abandoned his vigil on the window and walked about the comfortable study.

Distracted from his prolonged waiting, he amused himself by reading several framed letters, one from the war correspondent Sir William Russell thanking Delane for his courageous reportage of "the truth." Another from Gladstone commending a liberal stand which the *Times* had taken on some matter close to his heart. And a third addressed coldly to "The Editor of the *Times*," in stiff, blocklike handwriting on black-edged stationery, chastising the *Times* for daring to criticize her "protracted seclusion" as a widow, the scant though heated four lines signed, "Victoria R."

That Delane was a man of courage, Burke had no doubt. Then why was he faltering under the slight weight of Lord Ripples' justified attack on John Murrey Eden?

Beyond the column heading, *The Demi-God of Eden,* Delane had read in silence, as though in the locked privacy of his home there might be listening ears. In truth, Burke had not thought his material that incendiary. In past Lord Ripples columns he'd indulged in much greater irony and sarcasm. Not that his words were truly objective. The readers of the *Times* could get their objectivity from the financial section. They read Lord Ripples for different reasons. He gave them permission to hate, and only lately had Burke come to realize what a rare gift that was.

To be true, the opening paragraph was strong:

A guilty conscience was never betrayed by a more superior sniff than that witnessed at Eden Castle, North Devon, a fortnight ago. Under the guise of fellowship, London's master-builder, John Murrey Eden, opened his castle gates, hoping to humble the world with a display of riches unrivaled since the halcyon days of Roman decadence. The stench of poor taste could be whiffed across the Channel and into Wales—

Yes, a bit heavy, that, though taken all together and not set apart, as he had just done in memory, it did mesh. Consider the second paragraph:

> John Murrey Eden labors under the delusion that material goods are the outward sign of a conscious respectability, and respectability, as every good Englishman knows, is the name of that Common Level of behavior which all families ought to reach, and on which they can meet without disgust. In accordance with this philosophy, Eden presented a contradiction of material splendor and moral bankruptcy, though unwittingly he served as the most polished mirror ever held up to English society in recent times.

How well he knew it, even in memory, having lived with it, gone to bed with it and awakened with it every day for the last three weeks. It was good and he knew it was good, and more importantly, it was the truth. Not until he had commenced work on this particular piece had he realized how deeply he resented the English and all they stood for, their arrogance based on nothing of substance except a propensity to bully the rest of the world under the guise of their "Christian mission."

Still reading?

"My God, Delane," Burke said, shattering the silence of the room. "Do you want me to read it for you?"

But Delane lifted a restraining hand and with deliberation laid a page atop the other pages already resting on the desk.

He'd read it twice at least and, as far as Burke could tell, he was rereading certain sections. Well, let him! The words would stand up even to the critical eye of John Thadeus Delane. Yet in spite of this private conviction, Burke continued to wander restlessly about the study, running through in his mind certain passages that might be causing Delane discomfort.

There was that historical comparison near the bottom of the third page, culminating with:

> . . . we remember with surprise that we are dealing with a race which had once and not so long ago been famous for an independence and even an ec-

centricity, and we must now ask what has happened
to make it submit its behavior and its language and
its ideas to this untenable mediocrity. . . .

Too strong? Not strong enough, when placed against
the reality of that week at Eden, that swaggering, maudlin
public display which most assuredly had taken its tone
from one man.

> . . . for the most part, the Demi-God of Eden
> presented a face of reserve to his public guests, but
> we must remember that reserve is the defense of
> the wise and the refuge of the stupid, and in this
> case it appeared to conceal cynicism and super-
> ciliousness as well. . . .

Abruptly Burke drained his glass, recalling unexpectedly the Alma-Tadema painting, that incredible recognition of the pretty young girl who had held him in thrall
at Jeremy Sims' Song and Supper Club. He smiled into his
empty glass. He *would* see her again. But when and how?
Now what was left for Delane to read that he had not
read thrice before? Glancing back at the man hunched
over the desk he discovered with relief that he was reading the final page—again:

> . . . Let the Demi-God of Eden enjoy his marble
> castle while he may, for one day all his underfed,
> unpoliced, ungoverned and unschooled brothers
> will rise up against him and show him *their* code,
> not in bloody revolution, as England's neighbors
> across the Channel have done so often, but rather
> in slow assault, in subtle transfers of power, in allot-
> ments for the young, the old, the poor, until one
> day the descendants of the Demi-God will awake
> to find their castle stripped, their bogus "respect-
> ability" in shattered pieces about their feet.
> The Demi-God of Eden will receive no homage
> from this corner, nor should he receive homage
> from any quarter of England, for he and his breed
> are fast changing the English landscape from one
> of proud and sober confidence to something un-
> speakably grim. Into what patterns the emergent
> lines and angles will fall, we cannot tell. But a hun-

dred years from now when their culture and civilisa-
tion lay in waste about them, and if there is enough
energy remaining to look for a cause, there will be
no need for them to look beyond their own boundaries to the costly excitement of Imperial politics,
to annexation and debt, to the obscene excesses and
insensibility of conscience personified by the Demi-
God himself: John Murrey Eden.

There! Done! Across the flickering light of the study,
Burke watched Delane closely, ready to lodge a protest if
the man started back at the beginning a fourth time.

Fortunately he didn't. Instead, with almost mournful
deliberation, he placed the final page atop the others,
flattened his hand on them, as though to contain the
words written on the pages. Slowly he removed his spec-
tacles and placed them with equal deliberation atop the
piled pages.

Without looking up at Burke, still addressing the
stacked papers, he asked quietly, "Is that—really the
portrait we present to the world?"

"I can't speak for the world," Burke replied honestly.
"For myself, yes."

Delane continued to stare downward, his fingers gently
ruffling the edges of the pages, his ability to respond
either excluded or rendered mute by private thoughts. He
waved a hand toward Burke and commanded, "Draw
the drapes, please."

"Oh, good Lord," Burke muttered, suffering an exhaustion of his own. But he drew the drapes on the window and, hoping to lighten both their moods, he joked,
"There's no one about now but owls and rats, Delane, and
I doubt seriously if they have the slightest interest in anything that Lord Ripples—"

Another abrupt movement coming from the desk cut
him short. Delane leaned forward and drove his fingers
through his hair, allowing his hands to come to rest,
blinder-fashion, obscuring his face. From behind this barrier he spoke.

"One cannot be too careful. Our only protection lies in
complete secrecy."

All right, then, Burke thought, trying to rein in his impatience, "What is your opinion?"

"I think—" Delane began, then broke off, shaking his

head, looking at Burke with eyes which seemed to ask for patience. "Oh, God, Burke . . ." he muttered, leaning back in his chair.

"Were you expecting something else?"

"No," Delane admitted, "but there is something different about this one, and you know it as well as I." He leaned forward as though at last he'd found a negotiable train of thought. "In the past Lord Ripples columns, in spite of their content, there has always been a—a levity, sometimes satiric, sometimes ironic, but always in spite of the criticism a sense of fun."

"I did not have a great deal of fun at Eden," Burke replied.

"No," Delane agreed, "I know you didn't, and I have apologized repeatedly for—"

"It was not your place or obligation to apologize."

"Still, I can't help but wonder if perhaps you haven't lost a degree of—objectivity."

"Did you ask me to accompany you for my objectivity?"

"No, of course not." As the man waved his hand apologetically in the air, Burke retreated to a chair and sat heavily. Why was he so surprised? While Delane was many things, he was also an Englishman, and clearly he was seeing himself in the scathing indictment spread before him on the desk. Well, three weeks of effort for naught, but no matter. It had kept Burke busy, kept his mind off the slow disintegration of his mother and his own senseless existence.

Delane spoke again, posing questions as though he were a dimwitted schoolboy. "Do you really see so bleak a future for us, Burke?"

"Worse."

"Yet the Empire is flourishing."

"From whose point of view? And I can assure you it won't always flourish."

"But social changes are being made."

"Nothing of permanence or significance."

"We export over sixty percent of the world's goods."

"Using the resources of others."

"They are compensated."

"Justly?"

There was a pause, the rapid-fire give and take coming to a halt. Burke had uttered his rebuttals effortlessly, with no real hope of changing anything. In fact, it was now his intention to leave soon, at the first moment he could do so gracefully, without offending Delane.

"It's late," he announced, leaning up in his chair, thinking that he might send his carriage on ahead and walk home. Although the distance was great and he was tired, he felt a peculiarly urgent need for fresh air.

To that end he was in the process of pulling himself to his feet when Delane spoke again, his approach a different, though interesting one. "You know what bothers me most about this particular column, Burke?" Without waiting for an answer he went on. "Through all the coldness of the prose, the logical progression of thought, the massive declarative statements which stop just short of libel, I see an author unwittingly exposing himself."

Stunned, Burke froze in his half-raised position. An interesting twist, this. Apparently his writing was more effective than he'd realized, Delane putting *him* on the defensive. Interested to see precisely how the man would pursue it, Burke sat on the edge of the chair and invited: "I don't understand, Delane. Explain yourself."

The man shrugged and turned the pages over, his eyes racing across the lines, as though searching for specific ammunition. "It's quite apparent," he said patly. "In your zeal to catalogue our disasters, past, present and future, you reveal yourself to be a man who has had disaster heaped upon him."

In the face of this absurd statement, Burke could only gape.

"And further, in your need to create an entire historical case against us, culminating in the annihilation of our present way of life, it isn't too difficult to glimpse behind the words and see a homeless exile."

"Oh, my God, Delane—you can't be serious!"

"I'm not only serious, I'm concerned." The man leaned forward, an expression of paternalism on his face. "Burke, have you ever considered returning home?"

"To what end?" Burke replied angrily, moving away from the desk.

"I'm certain you could be of help to your father."

"I have no desire to be of help to my father."

"Then for the sake of your mother."

"My mother is insane. It matters little to her where she passes her remaining days, so long as they bear a resemblance to her girlhood. That duplication, as you know, is impossible at home. The theatrical can only take place on foreign soil."

"Then for your own sake," Delane concluded, a caring tone in his voice which momentarily unnerved Burke. When and precisely how had the focus shifted? And was Delane a complete idiot? There was nothing left in the Southern part of the United States now. Besides, Burke could make no significant move until the death of his mother, a reality which the physicians had been predicting for years, but which had yet to materialize. And God forgive him for such thoughts, because he did love her.

Unable to deal with the complexity of his emotions, he turned his mind to other matters. "Then by all means don't print it," he said, more than ready for that early-morning walk.

"I didn't say that."

"My God, Delane—you've said nothing but for the last fifteen minutes!"

"I've said other things as well, if only you had taken the time to listen."

It was the man's harsh tone more than anything that caused Burke to halt at the door. He looked back to see Delane on his feet.

"Primarily what I've been saying, Burke, if you could submerge your ego long enough to hear, is that the day after this appears in print we both may find ourselves thinking back to this night and wishing we had made another decision."

Astounded, Burke started back across the study. "Then —you are going to—"

"Of course I'm going to! In spite of the author's emotional involvement, much is said that needs to be said. I just feel that I should warn you."

Pleased by this unexpected development, Burke smiled. "Don't tell me that you are genuinely fearful of John Murrey Eden?"

"Not fearful. Apprehensive."

"But what can he do?"

"Sue!"

"Who? You? You didn't write the article and can swear so under oath. The *Times?* The paper has been sued before on more legitimate grounds and has always emerged triumphant. And the column will go on the Letters page, won't it, where Lord Ripples has always gone, in the company of all those other disgruntled and anonymous Englishmen."

"This is different, Burke." Delane leaned across the desk, his face taut with worry. "In the past Lord Ripples has written safely on very public London events: the opening of a new gallery, some particular madness in the House of Commons. But Eden will know that the author of this column possessed an invitation to his Festivities, occupied a chamber in the castle, partook of his hospitality."

"Hospitality!" Burke laughed, pleased that after all his words might find their way into print. "Delane, there were over two hundred guests that first week and, according to Eden's solicitor Andrew Rhoades, over one hundred and twenty-five of them were journalists of one stripe or another. Eden will have to commence his suits at Taunton and work his way back across the country to London before he can unearth Lord Ripples."

He paused, pleased to see that Delane was listening. "And I find it difficult to believe," Burke added quietly, "that the English courts have so little to do that they can pander to the shrill protests of John Murrey Eden."

The confrontation held, Burke feeling amusement for this man opposite him who in the past had taken on the British War Office, the inefficiency of the British Army and had faced down threats at Cabinet level, and yet who now seemed to be backing away from a single adversary.

"He will do nothing, Delane," Burke added firmly, "because there is nothing he can do. Oh, mind you, I'm not saying that he'll like it, but it was not composed to elicit the appreciation of John Murrey Eden."

"Why was it composed?" Delane asked gently.

Momentarily, Burke frowned. "To let the English see for themselves that the fiasco at Eden is merely representative of a larger ill—"

"Noble," Delane murmured, a hint of sarcasm in his voice. But it only lasted a moment and was quickly replaced by a limited degree of enthusiasm and another spate of commands. "Then we'll run it next week, and starting now and continuing for a month thereafter, I don't want to see you in Printing House Square. Is that clear?"

It wasn't, though Burke nodded in affirmation: "Perfectly."

"Nor are you to contact me or my editors in any way, either socially or professionally. Is that clear?"

"It is."

"We've been seen together too often in the past, and if Eden is as intelligent as I think he is—"

"I will disappear from public view, I swear it, Delane," Burke vowed dramatically. It seemed to bring Delane so much pleasure to play these little games, the least Burke could do was oblige.

"Then it's settled," Delane concluded. Still studying the papers in his hand, he muttered, "My God, this will cause ripples right enough!"

"Our very point, if I recall correctly," Burke said with a smile, reminding Delane of the entire purpose behind the conception of "Lord Ripples."

The man nodded, then sat down, withdrew a ring of keys from his pocket, unlocked the bottom drawer of his desk, dropped the pages in and quickly locked it again.

Aware of Delane's genuine concern, Burke extended his hand across the desk. "I thank you," he said simply.

Though Delane took his hand, he countered, "I'm not certain I thank you as yet. The increased circulation brought about by the column may very well be consumed in legal fees, though the unions will love your words."

"Well, then?" Burke grinned.

"And you may want to prepare yourself to be burned in effigy again."

"Nothing like a good fire to warm the bones on a chill London evening."

Delane stared at him. "Go along with you now, and stay out of my sight for at least the next six weeks. Is that clear?"

"Done," Burke called back. He was to the door and almost through it when a thought occurred. "Delane," he called, looking back to find the man still behind his desk. "That woman, the one who suffered the near accident outside the Gatehouse at Eden, do you know whether or not she has returned to London?"

From the look of confusion on Delane's face it was clear that the rapid transition had eluded him.

"Elizabeth?" he faltered.

"That's the one. Do you know whether or not she's returned from Eden?"

Delane muttered, "I—have no idea."

"Where did you say she resided? You told me once, but I'm afraid I wasn't paying—"

"Why?"

Burke smiled. "Just . . . curious, that's all."

Still unable to draw a parallel, Delane obligingly said, "Number Seven on St. George Street."

"Thanks," Burke called back and took his leave before Delane made the connection and issued another set of commands.

In the entrance hall he found Delane's manservant dozing in a chair. Not wanting to disturb him, Burke stealthily lifted his cape and top hat from the man's lap, where apparently he'd been holding them for several hours. Closing the door quietly behind him, he stood in the safe darkness, breathing deeply of the clean pre-dawn air.

Number Seven, St. George Street.

He knew the area well. Near Parliament, a quiet, respectable street, its inhabitants composed of prominent surgeons, a few solicitors and the woman named Elizabeth.

Without being able to say how he knew it, Burke suspected that where the woman was, Lady Mary would be also and, since there was nothing pressing upon him for the next six weeks, it might be fun to do a bit of sleuthing on his own, try to locate the beautiful young woman who had given him such pleasure at Jeremy Sims' Song and Supper Club, and later, briefly, at Eden Castle. . . . .

Out of the myriad tasks that Alex Aldwell performed for John Murrey Eden, he liked this one the least, though he understood the need for it and continued to perform it on the basis of that understanding.

So what if John sent him almost nightly over to Kate Hamilton's well-appointed brothel in Haymarket to fetch a young clean dolly-mop and bring her back to his mansion in Belgravia? John had needs like any man, and what was he to do with his wife ill in confinement at Eden, and his darkskinned mistress now ensconced at Elizabeth's house in St. George Street, paying more attention to Andrew Rhoades than her master?

This young girl must have pleased him well, for, grinning all the while he had followed her down the stairs tonight. Alex stood waiting to escort her to a carriage, deliver the *Times* to John, and retire after his weary day.

Tasks completed, Alex headed toward his apartments on the second floor, looking back once to see John proceeding up the steps, head down, slapping the folded newspaper gently against his leg.

Alex turned back and was just opening his door when he heard a voice. "Did I—thank you, Alex?"

He looked up to see John poised halfway up the stairs, still beating a gentle rhythm with the newspaper. Moved by the curious question, before he could respond Alex heard the voice again, as diminished and humble as he had ever heard it. "Do I—ever thank you enough," he added, "for your loyalty and friendship?"

"No thanks are needed, John," Alex said, gruffly, embarrassed by the show of emotion. "And if they were, then I'm the one who should be thanking—"

He had thought to say more, but saw that John was moving up the steps again. Alex pushed open his door, secure in his mind on only one point, and that was the simple fact that for all of his contradiction and inconsistency, he loved John Murrey Eden as much as it was safe for one man to love another. . . .

About twenty minutes later, just as he was adjusting his nightcap, he heard a crash, the muted and distant sound of glass shattering. From his position on the edge of his bed he looked up, trying to determine its direction and cause. But while he was still trying to work through this puzzle he heard another, then another—someone systematically destroying every glass object within grasp.

He sat forward in stunned alarm, then he was moving. He pushed open his door, thinking all sorts of things—that a servant, drunk with too much ale, had gone berserk, that the house had been invaded by a band of thieves, that whatever the nature of the disturbance which had shattered the peace of the quiet night, he'd better see to it before John—

Standing in the darkened corridor outside his door, he heard footsteps coming from the upper regions of the house, angry footsteps setting off reverberations which Alex felt on the floor beneath his bare feet.

"John?" he called out, as though he wanted to stay that force thundering down the stairs.

Then the man himself appeared, bearing no resemblance to the one who only a few minutes earlier had whispered a moving thanks to Alex. This man, standing less than ten feet from him, a wadded sheet of newsprint crushed in his fist, looked demented, his eyes glittering unnaturally in the semidarkness of the corridor, his form seeming to grow uncannily large in the flickering lamplight.

"Fetch Andrew Rhoades," came the voice, the words somehow finding their way out in spite of his clenched teeth.

"Fetch—" Alex tried to repeat and couldn't. "Do—you know the hour, John?"

Whether he knew the hour or not, Alex never determined, for in the next breath he repeated his initial command, louder this time: "Fetch Andrew Rhoades!"

"I'm sure he's abed, John," Alex tried to soothe. "Can't it wait until—"

"Goddamn it, fetch Andrew Rhoades!" John shouted, his voice resounding through the empty corridors.

Stepping back from the onslaught, Alex observed that the corridors were no longer deserted. Below in the entrance hall he saw the servants, all in nightcaps and nightshirts, a few holding candles, their eyes lifted fearfully toward the top of the stairs.

Resigned to his late-night errand, Alex retreated to his bedroom door, still trying to determine the cause and nature of John's outrage. "John, what is it?"

But the man said nothing, though on his face Alex detected a martyred expression, all the grief and unhappiness and disappointment of the last few weeks joining forces against him. Just as Alex was about to speak again, he saw John lift his head as though he were having difficulty in breathing. He whispered hoarsely, "Leave me alone. Send Andrew to me."

In bewildered alarm Alex waited until the reverberating footsteps diminished and disappeared near the top of the house, until a door slammed in the same vicinity with such force that it dislodged a fine rain of plaster particles which fell about Alex's feet.

Aware of the huddled servants looking up, Alex bent slowly to retrieve the sheet of newsprint, shocked by the display of fury, feeling the need to know more so that he could at least attempt to explain to Andrew Rhoades why he was being routed out of bed in the early hours of the morning.

Flattening the crushed newsprint as best he could, he tilted the sheet toward a near lamp and at first saw nothing but a blur. As his eyes began to adjust to the fine print and dim light, he saw a column heading entitled, "Rising Grain Prices," and another concerning the new franchise bill before Parliament, and others equally as innocuous, certainly nothing to warrant—

Then he saw the words: *The Demi-God of Eden. . . .*

He read only the first paragraph. That was enough. The content, so brutal and injurious, assaulted his senses and provided him with the momentum to dress quickly, drawing his trousers on over his nightshirt, saddling the fastest horse in the stable and setting out at top speed in his pre-dawn race through the city, hoping to return with Andrew Rhoades, who might, with luck, offer sympathy, experienced judgment and an avenging course of action. . . .

Cambridge
Late June 1870

FROM WHERE LORD Richard Eden sat in his study, surrounded by his books, the diffuse light of a mild June evening spilling in through the windows, the harsh London *Times* article spread before him, he leaned back and found his mind moving hungrily into Fenelon, the French Roman Catholic theologian, who two hundred and fifty years ago had created a very sensible movement called Quietism.

Man must make himself small and unresisting. A cross is no longer a cross when there is no longer a self to suffer its weight.

How he wished that he might send that philosophy to John—not that it would be received, let alone understood.

Richard leaned forward across his cluttered desk and lifted his eyes to the glorious evening beyond his window, one of those flawless, crystalline early-summer English evenings, when the perfume of the roses was intoxicating.

He closed his eyes in a prayer of thanksgiving, relieved

that after three weeks since his return from Eden the apprehension and despair and resentment which he'd brought back with him were at last subsiding. All three were expensive emotions and most detrimental of all had been his resentment of John, his attempts to thrust the young woman continuously before him.

A cross is no longer a cross when there is no longer a self. . . .

Of course there was the fact of the newsprint before him, picked up by Bertie earlier that day from the table outside the dining hall, a scathing essay signed by someone identified as Lord Ripples, whose sole journalistic intent seemed to be to inflict as much pain as possible without wholly killing the victim. Although John was the specific target, the writer had chosen as well to take on all of England, her past impulses, her present foibles and her future sins against merely God and all Mankind.

Slowly Richard lifted the newsprint and tried not to dwell on the hurt that John must be experiencing. He'd posted a letter to him earlier that day after his first reading with Bertie, though he feared that it had been an ineffectual letter, pledging anew his love and loyalty, and tactfully advising John to ignore the prejudiced words of the anonymous writer.

In retrospect, the advice seemed ingenuous at best and foolish at worst. As Richard knew all too well, there was not one single impulse in John to "let things alone."

Weary of the crisis which was raging so far away, Richard glanced over his shoulder through the partially opened door which led to the study, the place where both he and Bertie met officially with their readers. *Will he never finish?*

As though Bertie had heard his thoughts, Richard heard him say to the students, "That's enough for one evening. Go cool those fevered brains so that tomorrow they can absorb more."

Pleased that the session was concluding, Richard looked at the work on his desk that he'd failed to accomplish. What a propensity for daydreaming he'd suffered this night!

"So this is how you pass your time while I slave to bring enlightenment to young minds?"

At the sound of the voice, Richard turned in his chair

and looked over his shoulder to the warm, grinning face of Bertie Nichols, who lounged easily in the door.

Delighted that he was here and that the rest of the evening was theirs, Richard tried to arrange the mussed papers before him. "It's not a proper evening for Fenelon," he confessed quietly. "I'm afraid that my mind needs your strict discipline. Come," he urged, wanting both of them to clear their minds so that later that night they might approach each other with uncluttered attention. "I believe that Mrs. Pettibone has left us two of her fresh meat pies. A cup of tea and then may I suggest a brief walk? We really should take advantage of this perfect evening in defense against those long winters."

At some point Bertie left his chair and stood behind Richard's, his attention focused on something outside the window. From that angle Richard could not see his face, but sensed a change in mood, as though something besides students were troubling him.

"We've had a good life together, haven't we?" Bertie asked, and something in his manner set off a series of alarms in Richard's head.

"What do you mean?" Richard asked.

Bertie leaned forward and reached for the newspaper bearing the column heading, "The Demi-God of Eden." Passively he opened the news sheet. "Do you have any idea who this Lord Ripples might be?" he asked, looking up.

"None," Richard replied. He had thought to pursue the subject further, but Bertie asked, "How do you think your cousin has reacted to this?"

"How would *you* react to it?" Richard replied. "Needless to say he won't like it and probably will do everything in his power to force the anonymous writer out into the open."

"To what end?"

Richard shrugged. "Retraction, and apology."

"Yet he invited the journalists to Eden for the sole purpose of reporting what they found there."

"True. But he'd hoped for quite a different impression."

Bertie seemed to be listening carefully. "He's very powerful, isn't he, your cousin?"

Richard was taken aback by the simple question. Bertie knew John well enough. "Yes, he's powerful," Richard conceded, "but he's a good man and would never use his power to inflict hurt on others."

"Do you really believe that?" Bertie asked.

"Of course I do, and you do, too. You've conversed with him; you've been witness to his generosity."

"I was also summarily dismissed from Eden several weeks ago."

Richard fell silent, thinking how unusual that they had waited until now to discuss that awkward moment. "Why are we wasting time in this manner, Bertie?" he asked. "Those days have come and gone. We're back on track now and, in answer to your question, yes, we've had a marvelous life together and will have a marvelous life in the future."

It was a good moment except for the doubt which continued to mar Bertie's face, though ultimately he, too, responded by leaning forward and cupping his hand around the back of Richard's neck, the two of them very close now.

"Sorry for this damnable gloom," Bertie murmured. "I suppose I could manage a life without you, but I dread—"

There it was again, that ominous threat as though something were coming to an end. Because Richard couldn't deal with it and had no desire to understand it, he suggested quickly, "Mrs. Pettibone's tea will wait, as will the summer evening. Come," he murmured, his mind moving ahead to their bedchamber at the rear of the flat, cool linens, the comfortable bed.

Convinced that the need and desire were mutual, he was bewildered to see Bertie sit back down in his chair. Then there were words, incredible ones. "I was thinking, Richard, that it might be wise if we established separate residences."

Stunned, Richard demanded, "Why?"

"I had hoped that by now you would have perceived the reason for yourself."

"What are you saying?" Richard asked angrily, his hurt and confusion conspiring against him.

"I'm saying," Bertie replied calmly, "that someone has set a watchdog on us."

"A—what?"

"A watchdog," Bertie said, "I've seen him almost every

day for the last two weeks, and am amazed that you have not—"

"I don't know what you're talking about!"

"At first I wasn't certain," Bertie explained, "but now I am."

"Certain of what?"

"That we are being watched. This flat, you, me. . . ."

Richard tried to draw a deep breath in order to deal with the insanity of Bertie's words. "I—don't believe you," he stammered. "Who would—"

"I was hoping you could tell me that as well." Bertie smiled, his eyes fixed on that same spot beyond the window. "He stands—there," he said, pointing across the hedge in the direction of the fountain which fronted the building opposite their flat.

Apprehension was pressing so heavily upon Richard that he felt he could not stir. But feeling the need to see for himself, he glanced out the window and saw nothing but the deserted walk.

Slowly he raised up and looked down on the true mystery—Bertie himself. Was he speaking the truth? Were they being watched, and to what end? Or was this Bertie's way of informing Richard that he had found another source of affection?

Unprepared for the pain of that last thought, Richard felt himself go weak. He reached for the chair behind him and sank into it. Then he was aware of Bertie kneeling before him, grasping his hands. "Listen to me, Richard," he pleaded. "It isn't the end of things, though I must confess that at first I thought it might be. But it's simple, really. If someone has been sent to spy on us, then we must give them nothing to see."

Partially reassured by Bertie's closeness, Richard found the courage to ask, "But who? And why?"

"Who else?" Bertie replied, glancing back at the folded newsprint on the desk.

"But why?" Richard demanded. "And are you certain?"

Bertie sat back on his heels, his hands grasping Richard's legs. "Why?" he repeated. "Eden needs a legitimate heir, doesn't it? And who but you can produce that? And yes, I'm certain. I wasn't at first, but I am now."

"I've seen nothing."

"You want to see nothing, Richard. But believe me,

our future safety lies in us both seeing as clearly as possible now."

Bertie had been talking in feverish haste and was suddenly silent with a questioning look. "Do you trust me, Richard?"

"You know that I do."

"Then for a while I'm going to take rooms in town."

"No—"

"For a while, I said. Perhaps John's present ordeal will draw his attention back to London and the watchdog will retire and leave us alone."

Richard closed his eyes against the coming separation. "I have no life without you."

"Nor I you."

They clung to each other in the darkened study. It was Bertie who first moved away from the embrace. "Look," he murmured, holding back the edge of the drape.

Slowly Richard stood. Before he looked out he fought a silent battle with himself. Bertie was wrong. John would not do this. But as Bertie stepped back to make room for him at the window, Richard lifted the edge of the drape and looked out, his eyes moving instantly toward the small fountain.

A man stood there, leaning relaxed against a lamppost, one leg propped before the other. He was smoking a pipe or cigar—Richard couldn't be sure from that distance and saw only the wreaths of smoke curling about the man's head.

Still the dragons of doubt persisted. Couldn't he simply be taking the air, a tradesman from Cambridge curious about life here?

Richard was on the verge of presenting Bertie with these arguments when the man by the lamppost shifted positions, stood erect, looked in both directions, then moved stealthily into a new position directly behind the hedge, less than ten feet from their front door.

Angered by the invasion, Richard dropped the drape as though it were hot and confronted Bertie, who had retreated to the chair behind the desk.

"He has no right," Richard said. "John has no right—"

Sharply Bertie lifted a finger to his lips. He began to shake his head back and forth, thus reminding Richard that it was dangerous to speak now.

Richard started back toward the window, then changed

his mind, realizing that any movement of the drape would
signal the man's attention. In an attempt to ease his growing sense of being trapped, he started toward the door,
then again changed his mind.

His sense of entrapment dangerously increasing, his
sense of outrage and injustice keeping pace, Richard
turned away from the door. "He has no right," he repeated.

Again Bertie leaned forward, urging quiet. Stymied on
all sides and trapped within the confines of his own study,
Richard closed his eyes and leaned upon the desk and
tried to still the fear within him.

Before him on the desk he caught sight of his books on
Fenelon.

*A cross is no longer a cross when there is no longer a
self to suffer its weight. . . .*

How empty and sterile those words sounded now. He
sat slowly in the chair and returned Bertie's sorrowful
gaze. . . .

London
June 1870

TAKING CARE TO fasten her beaver hat with the flowering
veil, Mary inserted a second pin through the soft fur, then
lowered her arms and gazed into the mirror.

Without warning and for no reason that she could think
of, unless it was the resemblance about the eyes, she
thought of Richard. How often of late she'd done that,
wondering what Richard would think of that fabric, that
gown, this hat.

As she leaned forward to pinch color into her cheeks,
it occurred to her that she missed Richard and his quiet
ways because of the storm which had been raging below
in Elizabeth's drawing room, off and on, night and day,
for the last week—a silly melodrama with constantly
changing characters, one day Andrew, the next Lord Harrington, occasionally Elizabeth and Dhari, while the lead
actor remained the same.

Listen! She could hear him now and marveled at his capacity to sustain such outrage. And the cause of it all? A foolish newspaper article written by an anonymous journalist who had visited Eden during the fortnight's Festivities and had found it lacking.

Everyone had tried to soothe him in witless variations. But John's anger had increased in direct proportions to the offers of comfort about him, and late last evening when he had mentioned his desire to file a suit against the London *Times*, Andrew Rhoades, in angry resignation, had stomped out of the room, leaving the rest of them to absorb his fury until well after midnight.

Grateful for a chance to flee this madhouse, Mary took another quick glance into her looking glass, not pleased with what she saw, for she was too plump to look really well in the fashionable riding habits of the day. Nevertheless she adjusted her foldover skirt, grabbed her riding crop and gloves and hurried down the stairs.

She was to meet Doris, Elizabeth's maid, at the front door, a condition which Mary had agreed to two days ago when she'd asked Elizabeth for permission to indulge in the harmless activity of an afternoon's ride in Rotten Row.

Not only had Elizabeth granted it, she'd looked longingly at Mary, as though she wished she might join her. But that was out of the question. John's anger seemed to require Elizabeth's presence, almost as if he were punishing her instead of the anonymous journalist.

Midway down the stairs, Mary stopped. No sign of Doris at the front door. She held her position on the stairs, debating with herself whether to return to her room or proceed on into the drawing room and wait for the maid there. She would have preferred to wait on the pavement outside in the warm June sun, talking with Jason, Elizabeth's driver from the West Indies, about the various merits of her horse Bonaparte. She adored the dignified black man who treated her so courteously, though with a twinkle in his eye.

But it would never do to wait on the pavement. Anyone in the drawing room could look out and see her, and she had no desire to call attention to herself.

So she elected simply to wait on the stairs and settled near the banister, listening with detached interest to the voices coming from the drawing room.

No one had departed following luncheon. Andrew was

there, his weary-sounding voice a pronounced counterpoint to John's rising angry one. Lord Harrington was
there as well, in solid support of Andrew's point of view.
And Elizabeth, of course, whose shoulder Mary could
just see through the drawing room arch, a silent presence
saying nothing at all. And today Alex Aldwell was present
as well.

Safely out of sight and aligning the fingers of her leather
gloves, Mary heard John interrupt Andrew in midsentence.

"Why would it be so difficult?" he demanded. "The
man was a guest at Eden."

"One of over two hundred," Andrew quietly reminded
him.

"But the column appeared in the *Times!*" John
shouted. "I should think that would narrow the search
considerably."

"Not necessarily," Andrew said. "I've already made
an inquiry at the *Times*. No one knows the identity of this
Lord Ripples, and they all are prepared to testify to that
in court."

"Of course they would say that," John countered, "but
proclaiming that in the safety of an editorial office and in
sworn testimony in a court of law are two different things."

"I believe them," Andrew said quietly. "And I believe further that any Englishman could have written that
article and submitted it to the *Times*. They appear weekly,
you know, on the Letters page, an open forum, a legitimate place for anyone to say anything."

"But someone *must* know his identity," John bellowed,
"someone in authority."

"Not necessarily," Andrew repeated. "There are constant letters to the paper, signed anonymously."

"This is not a letter."

"No, but the *Times* always publishes a disclaimer to
the private opinions expressed on its pages, and this is
what I've been told in all inquiries. *They—are—not—
responsible.*"

As Andrew's words, measured out as though for a
child, filled the silence, Mary held still, her eyes focused
on the face of the old clock. Three-twenty. *Oh, Doris,
why couldn't you have been early?*

Then she heard Elizabeth's voice.

"John, please, let it drop. The words are offensive
enough without damaging yourself further in vengeful

action. Listen to Andrew. Ignore the column. I assure you that most of London has done so by now. Legal action of any form will only resurrect the matter and summon everyone's attention."

"I don't give a damn about everyone's attention!" John exploded. "I only care about the attention of one man, and that's the bastard who wrote it, a cowardly bastard, hiding behind—"

As John's voice rose, Mary glanced through the railing toward the kitchen door. If Doris didn't appear soon, she would go down and drag her up. How desperately she wanted to flee this place for the broad, tree-lined bridle path of Rotten Row, the sun warm upon her back, June fragrance all about, Bonaparte trotting easily past the ladies and gentlemen and heading, as though he had an appetite of his own, for the southwest corner of the park where the pretty "horse-breakers" rode, those hordes of kept women who paraded every afternoon for the pleasure of London's male populace.

Mary had ventured to the edge of the crowd yesterday and had watched along with everyone else, fascinated by their beauty and fashionable clothes and scandalous lives. She'd looked closely for the most famous horse-breaker of all, the beautiful Skittles, who was a near national figure and who once had been painted by Sir Edwin Landseer, an equestrian portrait which now was one of the main attractions at the Royal Academy. Mary had seen the painting many times and longed to see the woman herself, who was reported to have had over one hundred lovers.

"And just where might John Thadeus Delane be?" she heard John shout, his fury destroying her image of the woman who enjoyed such freedom.

"Out of the country," Andrew replied.

"Convenient," John snapped.

"It's true. His assistant claims he is on the Continent."

"When is he expected to return?"

"Mid-July is what I was told. But surely you don't think that Delane—"

"Yes, I do!" John cut in. "Delane *is* the London *Times*. Nothing appears on those pages without both his approval and consent."

"Oh, John, that's nonsense!"

As the battle continued to rage, Mary leaned back against the steps and tried not to hear the charges and countercharges and thought again of the horse-breakers of Rotten Row. Yesterday she'd had such an amazing compulsion to join them, to slyly enter their parade and see what it felt like to have men look admiringly at her. But what if one approached her, as they frequently did, hiring women on the spot, then leading them away through the dappled green of Hyde Park toward waiting carriages?

Abruptly Mary closed her eyes, simultaneously shocked and fascinated by the fantasies in her head.

Just then she heard the kitchen door creak open and looked down to see plump Doris emerging on the top step, her middle-aged face flushed from the climb and from her labors of cleaning up after luncheon.

Grateful to the woman and vowing to tell her so as soon as they were alone, Mary stood rapidly, caught Doris' eye and placed her finger to her lips, indicating the need for stealth and silence. She could make it undetected to the bottom of the stairs, but beyond that she would be in clear view of anyone within the drawing room. There would be about six steps of complete exposure, then the freedom of the door and beyond.

Slowly she moved down the steps, motioning for Doris to keep pace below her, the woman drawing level with her as she descended, comical in her prim little hat with the single pheasant's feather which stood erect and quivering. Clutched in her gloved hands Mary saw her basket of needlework where for the last two days she'd passed pleasant afternoons with the other chaperones under the shade of the trees at the edge of the park.

As Doris shifted her sewing basket to the opposite arm, Mary saw a look of annoyance on her face, as though to say that her day had been too busy to play games. And, to Mary's consternation, halfway across the no-man's land of the arch Doris announced, "I must be back by half past five, you hear? Them girls downstairs are dim-witted and don't even know how to—"

In spite of the chattering Doris, they had made it past the arch and were just approaching the front door when Mary heard a stern command.

"Wait!"

With her hand on the doorknob, she held still, hoping that the command had not been aimed at her. But the hope was short-lived, for she heard John ordering, "Come back, please!"

The "please" in that voice meant nothing, and resignedly Mary motioned for Doris to hold her position by the
door. She moved back to the arch and felt the weight of
all those eyes, Andrew the nearest by the mahogany table
near the window, a faint smile on his face, as though he
welcomed any distraction. Across the room near the fireplace she saw Elizabeth seated, and near the opposite
wall, Lord Harrington on the settee, trailing the gold chain
of his watch back and forth between his fingers.

Alex Aldwell was there, too, his face as alert as any in
the room, as though he felt it his task to monitor everything for his master.

At last there was John, standing near Elizabeth, his
hands laced behind his back, a posture of suspect ease
considering the flush on his face.

Would no one speak? He had summoned her. Wasn't it
his place to—

"Where are you going?" he asked.

"Riding, John," she said simply, hearing the echo of
her mother's voice: *Be patient and endure.* "It's a
lovely afternoon," she went on, smiling at the gloomy
faces looking up at her. "Far too pretty to pass indoors."

But her smile was lost on the man, who started toward
her with such speed that she was tempted to step out of
his way. He stopped less than three feet from her and
glared angrily down on her, as though she were the one
who had written the article about the Demi-God of Eden.

"Whose idea was this?" he demanded. "Who takes my
present distress so lightly that they willingly add to it?"

This self-pitying question was addressed to the room at
large and, seeing the distress on all their faces, Mary decided to come to her own rescue. "It was my idea, John,"
she said. "I often ride in Rotten Row." Thinking to distract him from his anger, she added, "I'm a good rider,
too, though I should be, for you taught me yourself. Remember?"

But the nostalgic recall was hers alone, for he continued to glare down on her as though the mere sight of
her offended him. "You ride—*where?*"

"I told you. In Hyde Park, Rotten Row. It's quite a
popular—"

At the mention of that name, as though delighted to
have found a new target, John whirled about in the di-

rection of the chair near the fireplace. "And you have permitted this?" he demanded.

From where Mary stood she saw Elizabeth try to meet both the question and his new shock. "It's a harmless sport, John," she said, "and a good form of exercise. Mary's right. I myself enjoy——"

"I don't give a damn what you enjoy!" he exploded, striding to midroom, his tone of voice seeming to alert Andrew Rhoades by the window.

But if John was aware of the slight movement by the window, he gave no indication of it. With new energy which dangerously resembled enthusiasm, he took several steps closer to Elizabeth, then stopped. "I don't believe it," he pronounced quietly. "I simply don't believe it."

As the confrontation between John and Elizabeth grew uglier, Andrew stepped into the fray. "I don't understand John," he confessed. "What's the problem?"

At the sound of the voice behind him, John turned as though he were being attacked from the rear. "Well, if you don't understand, Andrew, I'll be damned if I can explain it to you."

"Try," Andrew insisted calmly. "I've ridden in Rotten Row many times myself. It's constantly patrolled and quite pleasant."

"And you're not my cousin, either," John countered, "a ripe target for anyone interested in extortion. Nor are you a defenseless young woman. Nor are you aware of the numbers of whores who ride every afternoon in the park, soliciting."

"Oh, good Lord, John!" Andrew laughed. "Their activities take place in one small corner of the park, and Mary, I'm sure, stays well away——"

"Indeed she will stay well away!" John broke in. "As far away as her chambers on the second floor of this house."

At the sound of the edict, and no longer capable of hearing her mother's whispered advice to be patient and endure, Mary stepped forward, aware only that this last harmless pleasure was being denied her.

"I stay in my room all day, John, with the exception of these few hours, and I'm tired of it. And I'm equally sick of this foolish bickering. Surely you have a sizable enough audience for your anger. Why is my presence necessary?"

She'd not intended for her voice to be so sharp, and

curiously in the ensuing silence she focused only on Lord
Harrington, who had ceased to drag his gold watch chain
through his fingers and who was looking at her in apprehension. Concentrating on Lord Harrington, she was
not at first aware of the footsteps approaching her angrily
from the left, and only at the last minute did she turn to
see John reach out and grab her by the shoulders where
he held her in a viselike grip, then began to shake her, a
gesture of such violence that she felt her neck crack, her
head wobbling back and forth like a broken marionette's,
the drawing room growing blurred, though certain words
reached her ears with painful clarity.

"You are never to speak to me in that tone of voice
again. Is that clear? You will do what I say in all matters,
and in this matter I command you to return to your room,
take off that indecent costume and behave yourself in a
manner befitting someone of your station."

"P-please," she stammered, trying to wrench free from
his grip, dropping her gloves as she struggled to defend
herself.

Frightened, and knowing from painful experience the
damage he could do, she cried out, "Elizabeth!" and felt
his hands leave her shoulders, the force of the separation
whirling her about, where she collided with the table, seeing Andrew on one side of John, Lord Harrington on the
other, these two men daring to drag him backward into
the center of the room, impervious to Alex Aldwell, who
took one step forward, then held his position.

Still frightened, Mary pushed herself up from the table
and felt Elizabeth's arms about her, while over her shoulder she saw the curious tableau at midroom, John still being restrained by Andrew and Lord Harrington, though his
face was stricken, as though belatedly he realized what
he'd done.

Enfolded in Elizabeth's embrace, Mary heard Andrew's
voice. "I doubt seriously, John, if Mary will encounter any
threat on the lanes of Hyde Park as real or as potentially
damaging as your own actions toward her."

She saw John bow his head. He tried to wrench loose,
but sensing that his captors would not release him without
reassurance or apology, Mary heard him mutter, "Let me
go—I'm—sorry—"

At last the two men stepped away and watched as

John retreated to the fireplace where Alex poured a brandy from the sideboard and offered it to him.

"I'm—sorry," he whispered to no one in particular and yet to everyone. "It was not my—intention to—"

How was she to deal with it? Was she to apologize to him? No! Before the ludicrous thought took root, she hurried past Elizabeth and ran through the archway, past Doris' shocked face, stopping only long enough to whisper, "Come on, please!"

As she drew open the front door, she remembered belatedly that she'd failed to retrieve her gloves and her riding crop. No matter. Nothing could draw her back into that room, and she ran eagerly down the steps toward the waiting carriage, drawing sustenance from Jason's grinning face as he held the carriage door for her with a gentle scolding, "Old Bonaparte will be wondering—"

As she settled back into the cushions, she was vaguely aware of Elizabeth and Doris holding a brief whispered conversation at the top of the steps. Then she saw Doris settle laboriously into the seat opposite her, her face awash with concern.

"Miss Elizabeth wonders if you are—"

"I'm fine," Mary replied, keeping her eyes straight, still feeling the violence of his hands on her shoulders. "We're ready, Jason," she called out of the window and, with relief, felt the carriage lurch forward, speed increasing, putting distance between her and the madhouse that was now Number Seven. . . .

Within the concealment of his carriage, Burke Stanhope had maintained a constant vigil on St. George Street for the last two days, specifically on Number Seven, where the traffic passing in and out had been incredible, some of the faces recognizable from his brief stay at Eden.

Then yesterday at midafternoon the front door had opened and he'd been rewarded with the appearance of a lovely apparition, the young woman herself, John Murrey Eden's cousin.

He had watched, fascinated, as she'd chatted warmly with the tall Negro driver, had seen her joined by a squat woman with the unmistakable air of chaperone about her, and had followed their carriage to the stables at the edge of Hyde Park, where he had seen the chaperone settle on a bench under a near tree, while the young lady had emerged from the stable on a magnificent black horse and had started off at a trot down the bridle path.

Frantically, Burke had tried to hire a horse from the arch old stablemaster, who had informed him that "This here is private stables for English gints and ladies." By the time Burke had run back to the bridle path, the young woman had disappeared into the sun and shadows, leaving him with the painful sense of having lost her again the moment he had found her.

In an attempt to walk off his disappointment, he'd strolled through the entire park, ending up on the corner where the horse-breakers plied their trade. Only the English would combine the two great national pastimes—forbidden sex and equestrian skill—into one colorful spectacle.

But today he was ready, had been up since dawn, visiting the daily horse auctions at the edge of Smithfield's, where he'd paid an exorbitant price for a handsome gray stallion with a wild look in his eye, though possessing the promising name of Rendezvous. With the horse tied securely to the back of his carriage, he'd then stopped off at Tyler and Sons Leatherworks in Castle Street, where he'd paid another small fortune for a fine, hand-tooled English saddle and bridle, and thus armed had proceeded on to the stables at the edge of Hyde Park, where he'd soothed the arrogant old stablemaster with a five-pound note and had successfully penetrated that "private domain of English gints and ladies."

Now, seated in his carriage at the end of St. George Street, Burke kept a steady eye on the broad front door of Number Seven, hoping the young woman would elect to ride two days in a row.

The family enclave was in session again, and Burke smiled as it occurred to him that he would give anything he possessed to hear what was going on behind those broad front windows. With Delane in Paris, he'd had no report at all on Eden's reaction to Lord Ripples' words, though for the last several days the Letters page of the *Times* had been filled with a curious contradictory correspondence, a few writers outraged by the insults leveled both at Mr. Eden and the Empire, a few others, recognizable union leaders, in warm agreement. Burke had not expected to touch that social nerve.

He leaned forward as he saw the front door of Number

Seven open, saw *her* descending with undue speed, her head down as though she were running from something.

Rapping lightly on the roof of his own carriage, Burke signaled his driver to make ready to move. The driver urged the horses forward, simply setting them in motion until the other carriage had passed them by, then gathering speed for the discreet pursuit. Earlier Burke had told him all he needed to know, and the man had grinned— "Done, sir."

As they entered Serpentine Road, the foot and horse traffic increased, requiring that they break their speed, but Burke continued to keep the carriage in his sights and did not relax until he saw it stop a short distance from the stables, saw the driver leap down and open the door, saw her in brief conversation with the maid.

In the interim of waiting, and confident that his scheme was working, he leaned out his window and took note of her graceful movements, most becoming in her pretty riding costume, the little beaver hat with flowing veil, the becoming nip of her waist, the fullness of her breasts. A more attractive young woman he'd never seen.

The conversation with her maid was completed now. Looking beyond her beauty, Burke saw the driver just emerging from the stables, leading the black horse toward her, trying to quiet him from the activity going on around him.

As she spied her horse, she ran eagerly forward, abandoning the maid who stood by the carriage door. With only slight assistance from the driver, she swung herself up and settled prettily into the sidesaddle position and started down the tree-shaded path of Rotten Row.

Then it was Burke's turn to move. He took the double doors of the stables running, found his new horse stomping impatiently in the stall and, with the help of the old stablemaster, who clearly liked the feel of five-pound notes, rapidly adjusted his saddle, swung up and felt the horse commence to spin beneath him.

"Whoa, there," the old man soothed, keeping a tight grip on the bit. "I take it you ain't tested him yet." He grinned toothlessly. "Well, lead him gentle. He looks spooked, he does."

Burke nodded and thought belatedly that he should have broken in the animal in private and hoped now that he could pull it off, at least until he was safely out of

sight from the old man's critical eye. As he entered Rotten
Row he raised up in his saddle and looked the length of
the bridle path, hoping to catch sight of that beaver hat
with flowing veil.

He spied her at the far end of the path where it veered
to the right and passed beneath a solid canopy of yew
trees.

Urging the horse to greater speed, he passed the other
horses on the path, striving to keep the beaver hat in view,
but feeling beneath his boot now an ominous slippage, the
stirrups easing further and further down, the entire saddle
loosening. The horse, sensing trouble, began spinning.
Several riders passed him by, giving him a wide berth,
their English faces censuring a novice so amateur as not to
take the time to make certain that the saddle strap was
securely joined.

Sensing disaster moments before it happened, Burke relaxed his grip on the reins and was just attempting to
swing his legs over for a quick dismount when suddenly
the saddle slipped completely loose and, as he was in the
process of jumping, the accelerated movement pitched
him forward and down, where he landed unceremoniously
on his backside in the soft mud and dead leaves of Rotten Row.

A ruddy-faced and rotund old Englishman rode close
and grinned sympathetically down. "Really tough luck,"
he commiserated, failing to hide a smile. "I say—you're
not injured, are you?"

"No," Burke muttered, lifting his hands gingerly from
the damp mud and spying Rendezvous munching placidly
on an unscheduled feast of summer grass across the way.

"Faulty strap would be my guess," the old Englishman
added. "Can't trust the workmanship these days, you
know. Everyone's giving short shrift."

Aware that his audience was increasing, Burke pulled
himself up out of the soft mud, examined his backside
with new embarrassment and bobbed his head at the
gaping faces surrounding him.

"No damage." He smiled, lifting the saddle from the
mud. He backed across the bridle path, relieved to see the
small crowd dispersing.

The horse restored, he whispered, "Let's do it proper
this time," and the animal lifted his head, responding

beautifully to the reins, and started off down the long bridle path.

For almost an hour Burke rode up and down the paths of Rotten Row, straining his eyes through the sun and shadow, thinking, *That's her!* But it never was. Once he even returned to the stables on the possibility that she had completed her ride and had departed. But there was no sign of the black stallion in any of the stalls, and only the sly, slightly suspect smile of the old stablemaster, who sucked on his pipe and said nothing.

Where in the hell was she? Would she abandon the bridle path and take off into the heart of the park? If that were the case, Burke didn't stand a chance of finding her. There were hundreds of secluded walks and paths. He might as well return his horse to the stables and take up his vigil again on Number Seven.

Then that's what he would do, after one more brief turn about the path. There was always tomorrow and, in spite of his disappointment, he found himself enjoying the sport, this stately though leisured parade, surrounded by magnificent horses and graceful ladies and gentlemen, the entire ambience one of ripe summer luxury, a mild breeze blowing across him.

Amazed at the speed with which his spirits had risen, he looked up at the sound of voices and saw that he was approaching the place where the horse-breakers plied their trade.

Drawn forward by fascination and with nothing else to do, Burke guided his horse into the crowd of men, some on horseback like himself, others on foot, a solid line of waiting carriages stretching the length of the Serpentine. A marketplace, that's what it was, where gentlemen came to look and to buy.

Finding a good vantage point, Burke released his grip on the reins and settled back to enjoy the parade, the ladies in their ravishing riding habits and intoxicatingly beautiful hats, roguish wide-awakes and pretty cocked cavalier's hats with plumes.

From time to time he saw a gentleman step out of the crowd, walk toward a particular horse, exchange a few discreet words with the lady and, after a nod of her head, lead her animal to a waiting steward, assist her down, then walk a step ahead of her through the crowd toward one of the carriages.

Fascinated by this accepted form of bartering flesh, Burke watched a moment longer, thinking that in some future column it might be a suitable subject for Lord Ripples.

Now he was weary, having been up since dawn, and disappointed at the futility of the long day. How doubly frustrating it was to have had her so close and lost her. No matter. He knew where to find her again.

Just as he was guiding Rendezvous out of the press of gentlemen, he heard a disturbance on the far side of the circle, a gentleman on horseback reaching aggressively forward for the reins of another horse, shouting something which sounded like "Whore!" Several of the ladies halted their march to draw closer to the altercation.

From where Burke sat, half-turned in the saddle, he thought that some pretty someone had changed her mind or raised her price and now had a disgruntled client on her hands. As the unpleasantness continued to attract more attention, Burke hoped that they could settle it peacefully, for there were no police about, this being the one area in the park beyond their jurisdiction.

He was about to turn away when he heard the gentleman's voice rising in anger shout, "Bitch!" At the same time he saw several of the ladies angle their horses between the gentleman and the target of his wrath. Battle lines were being drawn.

Not until he had moved to a position of relative safety at the outer edge of the crowd did he look back, his curiosity getting the best of him, and from this line of vision saw the mane and head of a stunning black stallion, its eyes showing white, several of the ladies interceding in curious protection of the young woman who clung to her saddle, her pretty little beaver hat with flowing veil dislodged and knocked awry in the struggle, her eyes as white and as fearful as—

God!

Struggling to steady his horse, Burke brought him around until he was facing directly toward the disturbance. Briefly the interfering ladies obscured his vision of the young woman. Surely he'd imagined it. What would she be doing here?

But once again the crowd shifted, the gentleman trying to explain himself to one of the ladies, speaking full-voiced, his protest clear. "We struck a bargain, we did," he shouted. "I offered and she agreed. Now all I ask is—"

Burke did not wait to hear the gentleman's specific request, knowing full well its nature and seeing the young woman clearly for the first time. *Good Lord, does she make it a habit of getting herself into awkward, potentially dangerous situations?*

Suddenly he flattened his heels into the stirrups and galloped rapidly about the circle, not certain what he was going to do when he got to the trouble spot.

Approaching from the other side, he penetrated through the riders. Taking advantage of the element of surprise, he rode forward and grabbed the reins from the gentleman's hand and led the frightened black horse to the center of the circle, paying no attention to the young woman, concentrating instead on the protests coming from the gentleman.

"I say, you have no right!" he shouted, a rather elderly gentleman Burke observed close at hand, no real threat except for his indignant moral outrage.

"My apologies, sir." Burke smiled, guiding the black stallion into a position of safety behind him. "I believe if you had taken the time to listen to the young lady's protest you would understand. You see," Burke went on, not daring to look at the young lady behind him, "she struck a bargain with me late yesterday afternoon. Cash in advance, I might add, but as I had a pressing appointment and could not see our bargain through, she vowed to wait for me here today. The nature of her protest to you, sir, instead of being dishonorable, is quite the contrary, is honor itself."

My God, I'm even beginning to talk like the bloody English! he thought. Apparently it worked, for the old gentleman, while still grumbling, was retreating, and at that moment one of the enterprising young horse-breakers, spying the wad of pounds in his pocket which he'd been in the process of giving to Mary, moved close with a whispered offer. A few minutes after that, the old gentleman, smiling now, was leading the young lady triumphantly through the crowds toward his carriage, where a footman stood waiting to take possession of both their horses.

Thinking that now was the time to leave, and still without a backward look at the young woman behind him, he guided their horses through the crowds of grinning men, heading not toward the pavement of the Serpentine but following a narrow path which led into the heart of the park.

They rode in silence for several minutes away from the laughing men and at last, curious about his "bargain," he looked back and saw her head bowed, the little beaver hat clutched in one hand, the veil torn in the scuffle, her long hair mussed and loosed.

"You're not—injured, are you?" he asked softly, bending low in an attempt to see her face.

She said nothing.

"Do you remember me?" he asked, thinking that she might not.

Still no response, and he sensed a siege of gloomy embarrassment settling over her.

Although he had at least a hundred questions, he refrained from asking any of them and turned about in his saddle to plot a course for them. He didn't want to compromise her further by taking her into a deserted area of the park, yet he longed for an interval alone with her. Convinced that she was unable to give him a direct answer, he led her horse into a sheltered arbor beyond which a garden of summer flowers was in full bloom, a quiet, now deserted though public part of the park where an arrangement of stone benches flanked the gardens, and the generous branches of an ancient oak offered shade.

Quickly he dismounted and tied their horses to the trunk of a near tree and turned his undivided attention to her. For the first time he saw tears.

Moved, Burke lifted his arms to assist her down. "Please don't, Lady Mary. You're safe now."

Something, his tone of voice, the words themselves, caused fresh grief, and she accepted the offer of assistance, and more, clung to him once she was on the ground, burying her face in his jacket and pressing close, as though for admittance into the shelter of his arms.

Eagerly he provided it, though he felt as though his breath were failing him, never believing that he would be holding her so soon. Though he tried to think of additional words of comfort, words seemed entirely unnecessary. At last she stepped away from him, fumbling through the pockets of her skirts and producing a handkerchief.

She wiped at her eyes and walked a few feet around the garden, her head down, struggling for control.

He followed a respectful distance after her, wanting to give her all the time she needed, praying that this small, secluded garden would remain secluded, at least for a while.

"Are you certain you are not harmed?" he asked.

At last she turned. "I'm fine." She nodded, studying the handkerchief in her hand. "It—all happened so fast—"

Growing brave, Burke kindly suggested, "Here, why don't you sit for a while?" and was pleased as, without protest, she permitted him to take her arm and guide her toward one of the stone benches.

Once or twice she looked up at him, making eye contact, then concentrating on the embroidered edges of her handkerchief. She seemed to want to speak, but something was preventing her.

"You—do remember me?" he asked politely.

"Of course," She smiled. "Mr.—Stanhope, I believe—"

"Burke Stanhope, yes."

"And I am Mary Eden," she replied, a tinge of color warming her cheeks.

Oh, yes, Burke thought, amused that she was ignorant of the fact that for the last two days he had rearranged his life to fit her schedule.

Then the mystery itself loomed large before him. *What in the hell was she doing there? Surely she knew the purpose of that unique circle of females. Impossible to believe she had wandered into their midst by mistake.*

"Lady Mary," he commenced, moving a step closer, "if I may ask—one question—"

"I knew what I was doing, Mr. Stanhope," she said, anticipating his question. "What I did not know was that someone would take me seriously."

It seemed a weak answer, therefore probably an honest one. She seemed to have a propensity for underestimating situations. Apparently the vast stretches of boredom in her life had produced a capacity for vast amounts of witless daring.

"I am most grateful to you again, Mr. Stanhope," she said, seeming to relax for the first time. "How curious it is to know so little about the gentleman who seems to have a habit of rescuing me."

"No thanks are needed." He smiled, fascinated with the play of sun upon her face. Lord, how beautiful she was, the tip of her polished riding boots just visible beneath her dark brown skirts, the restlessness of her small hands as they continued to play with the handkerchief, the delicate fringe of stiffened lace about her throat, framing the face itself, wisps of fair, curly hair surrounding that perfect cameo of wide-set dark blue eyes and flawless skin.

"Please feel free to sit if you wish," she invited. "You, too, have had a strenuous afternoon. I see from the back of your trousers that I was not the first mishap of the day."

He laughed, seeing the humor on her face, having forgotten about his earlier spill on the bridle path. "A confession," he said, seating himself on the end of the bench, a safe distance away. "I am not by nature a horseman."

"Then why on earth—"

"As long as I'm forced to pass time in England, I decided that I might as well do as the English."

"Still, it could be dangerous, I mean, training is so important."

"Oh, I've ridden before, Lady Mary, but simpler beasts and under simpler circumstances." He decided that he had said enough. It was not his intention to delve into his own splintered past. The afternoon was too perfect for that.

Neither spoke, though the raucous conversations of the birds in the trees above adequately filled the silence.

Then, as bad luck would have it, they both started together, he thinking to ask if he could fetch her something, she saying something which was lost in the middle of their voices.

"I'm sorry." He smiled. "You first."

She lowered her head as though embarrassed. "I—just wanted to apologize again—"

"No need—"

"—for your recent embarrassment at the hands of my cousin."

He'd not expected this. Still he felt touched by her need for apology.

"It was a pleasant evening, in spite of all," he said.

"How could it have been?" she demanded. "He purposefully set out to humiliate you."

"I don't think so. We simply were at cross-purposes, that's all."

Suddenly her mood changed, became businesslike. "I don't mean to detain you, Mr. Stanhope," she said, starting to rise.

"You're not detaining me. Please. Rest a bit longer. You had quite a scare."

She laughed. "Oh, not really. I knew the gentleman would come to his senses sooner or later. It was just a harmless afternoon's sport, that's all, to counterbalance the—"

She stopped speaking and closed her eyes. He sensed a new emotion in her, very close to the surface.

"To counterbalance what, Lady Mary?"

"I'm afraid that the household where I reside is not a very pleasant one at the moment," she confessed quietly. She gazed out at the sun on the riotous flowers. "Have you ever felt, Mr. Stanhope," she asked, staring at the flowers, "that you have no true place in the world, that in spite of its vastness that, just when you think you've found a niche that might suit you, someone comes along and says, 'No, you can't stay there,' or 'No, that's mine,' or, 'No, that won't do for you at all . . .'"

Her voice drifted off into the sun, taking Burke's attention with it.

Slowly she went on. "Of course Elizabeth says it's just because I'm young, that in time—"

"Time has nothing to do with it," Burke said quietly.

She looked up at him. "Do you know what I'm talking about?"

"Yes."

Never had he seen such a look of soft sympathy in any eyes, particularly not in such beautiful ones.

"How selfish of me," she murmured. "How far away from home you are and—"

"No farther than you, Lady Mary." He smiled. "As age has nothing to do with it, neither has geography."

"Then what is it?" she asked earnestly.

He faltered. Although he knew precisely what she was talking about, he'd never analyzed it thoroughly. Part of the natural human complexity he'd assumed, something to do with one's expectations of life, with memories, with love. Yes, one's capacity to love and be loved certainly had something to do with it.

"I'm sorry I asked such a foolish question," she said, returning her handkerchief to her pocket.

"It wasn't foolish," he said, fearful that her movements signaled her desire to end the conversation. "It's just that I have no ready answer—at least not an infallible one."

She glanced over at him, something in her expression which suggested that each time she looked at him she saw something new. Under this close scrutiny, he felt as self-conscious as a schoolboy. In an attempt to break the mood yet retain the intimacy of the conversation, he walked a few feet away, resting his boot on the brick border which surrounded the flowers.

"Forgive me, Lady Mary," he began, not looking at her, "but earlier you said that the house in which you are residing is not a very pleasant one. Is there anything that I can do . . ."

For a moment she looked as though she would not speak further and sat worrying a loose stone with the toe of her boot. "You met my cousin, Mr. Stanhope. Surely in that one unhappy meeting you saw him to be a man who does not like to be challenged or offended."

"And someone has offended him?" Burke asked, knowing better.

She looked up from the loose stone. "You haven't heard?" she asked, surprised. "Or, more accurately, read—"

Not wanting to lie, Burke retained an interested silence and hoped that she would speak further.

And she did, seeming to warm to the subject. "A journalist wrote a column several days ago which appeared in the London *Times*. From his writing it was obvious that he'd been a recent guest at Eden. The article is—"

She hesitated and he waited, anxious to hear her opinion of Lord Ripples' words. "The article is—what, Lady Mary?"

"Devastating to my cousin," she replied, concealing her own opinion.

"And the words of—this anonymous journalist have upset him?"

"Upset him?" she repeated, rising from the bench and following after him to the edge of the flowers. "He has done nothing but rage since it appeared. He seems to demand an audience. *Everyone* must be present to hear and see him, and yet he listens to no one. Poor Andrew has been talking his head off for over a week, but John won't hear. And in the meantime life for all of us has come to a standstill."

She was very close to him now, less than a foot away, her hands relaxed at her sides.

"And this—Andrew," he commenced, under duress. "Does he suggest a course of action?"

"Oh, yes," she said. "His advice is to ignore it, that to do anything else would merely call more public attention to the affair and make it worse."

"And I take it your cousin does not agree?"

"No," she said and walked a few steps beyond. "No, not John," she repeated, her voice fading as she walked away.

Abruptly she bent over to caress a long stalk, heavy with royal blue delphinium. "In Lila's garden there is a dark purple variety, so lovely . . ." she said to no one in particular, her fingers gently studying the design of the flower.

Burke watched her, hypnotized, each gesture, no matter how small, appearing like a miracle before him.

"Poor Lila," she said mysteriously, her mood shifting from admiration of the flower to one of compassion. "Poor everybody." She smiled, lifting her eyes to Burke. "I'm sorry, Mr. Stanhope. I must sound as senseless and deranged as an old—"

"Not at all," he reassured her, and bridged the distance between them and, with a daring born from the need to be close to her, he suggested, "Would you care to walk?" and extended his arm.

"For a while," she agreed, though she looked apprehensively over her shoulder toward the bridle path.

As they strolled along the graveled path, Burke was aware of how small she was, barely topping his shoulder, not petite, for her figure was full. How attractive she must have appeared to the old gentleman who mistakenly believed he had bought her for the afternoon.

He had thought to guide her back to the subject of John Murrey Eden, but instead he spoke in a different vein. "No chance, I suppose, of your gracing old Sims' stage again in the near future?"

Abruptly she stopped and disengaged her hand from his arm. "No," she murmured, "and please, never say anything to—"

The walk so recently commenced was brought to a halt. Looking down he saw new fear on her face and felt a surge of anger, questioning the right of any human being to cause such a look on another human face.

"Your cousin?" he asked, knowing it was none of his business and knowing further that she was perfectly within her rights to tell him so.

But she didn't. "Were you at Jeremy's every night, Mr. Stanhope?"

"Every night that you were there." He smiled. "The pattern seemed to evolve into Thursdays, if I recall."

"The safest night, according to Elizabeth. The night when Jeremy's place was bound to be half-empty."

"It wasn't half empty when you were there."

"No," she replied in quiet self-satisfaction. She began to walk ahead of him, her head down as though lost in lovely though dim memories.

He followed after, content to watch her from all angles, and took careful note of new riches: the soft white canal which ran the length of her neck and disappeared into the ruffle of her jacket; the curious manner in which she took a step, then rose up on her toes as though she would have preferred, if it had been ladylike, to skip; the tiny shell of an ear just barely visible beneath the hair drawn loosely back into a knot.

As they were approaching the place where they had started, having encircled the garden once, he saw her glance toward their horses, placidly munching on summer grass.

"Do you come here every day, Mr. Stanhope?" she asked.

He shook his head, laughing. "I've never been here before in my life."

"I—don't understand—"

"You brought me here today, Lady Mary. Surely you were aware of that." It had not been his intention to make this confession, but as long as the explanation was partially launched, he might as well complete it.

He drew close. "With your forgiveness, I determined some days ago that you rode here in the afternoons. I went out at dawn this morning to Smithfield's, purchased that creature over there, who with one exception has served me well, purchased in addition all the necessary equipment to mount him properly, followed you along

Rotten Row and promptly lost you, only to rediscover you a short time ago."

He'd not looked at her during this explanation, and now that he had completed his confession, he found that he dreaded doing so. What if she misinterpreted his intentions?

At last he found the courage and looked slowly up to see her returning his gaze.

"I'm—not certain I understand—"

"I had to see you again," he replied simply. "Since Jeremy Sims' is now a barren place and since our waltz was interrupted at Eden and since I was fairly certain that I would not be granted the honor of calling on you formally"—he smiled and shrugged—"I took matters into my own hands."

"Then you did not appear by accident this afternoon?"

"Not at all."

"And what do you intend to do with that handsome horse which you have ridden only once?"

"Ride him daily, if you'll be here."

He was being very forward and he knew it, and knew further that she had a perfect right as a lady to walk away and not address him.

Stopping by the bench to retrieve her hat, she seemed unwilling to speak further.

How foolish of him. He'd spoken far too bluntly. Inexperienced and out of touch with matters of the heart, he'd forgotten that the pursuit must be delicate and subtle.

He watched as she adjusted her hat, ready to rejoin her maid and driver, who must not know or even suspect that she had just spent the last half-hour in questionable isolation with an American gentleman.

Praying that she would speak and somehow cancel out his blunt confession, he saw her walk wordlessly beyond the arbor to the tree where he had secured their horses. He followed after her, keeping his distance, convinced that he had caused her offense.

On the verge of calling "Wait," he saw her stop, a look of concentration on her face as she studied the reins in her hands.

"I thank you again, Mr. Stanhope, for your timely appearance," she said with disheartening formality, as though nothing at all had passed between them.

Apparently she'd said all she wanted to say and now

led the black stallion a good ten yards farther before she stopped and looked back in his direction. "Tomorrow afternoon, then, Mr. Stanhope, about half-past three, here in the garden?"

She didn't smile, nothing so warming as that. Then she was gone, a small determined figure making her way through the park, leading her horse behind her, as self-possessed as though nothing at all unpleasant had occurred that afternoon.

Tomorrow afternoon. Half-past three—

He stared as though someone had forbidden him to move, and watched her progress across the expanse of the park, moving toward the late-afternoon light of the street, where the carriages awaited the riders, one carriage in particular which would take her back into the "unpleasantness" of Number Seven, St. George Street.

A sharp regret there. Foolishly it had never occurred to him that Lord Ripples' pen would cause her grief, and he *was* sorry for that.

He looked up as though in need of one last reassuring glimpse. But she was gone, and her absence pressed against him like a major deprivation, as though something that his soul had not even known it required had been taken from him.

He tried to find a direction, something worthy of his attention. But there was nothing significant enough to distract him from the curious feeling of weakness which now crept over him.

In this mood and with no other options before him, he turned back into the garden and, in an attempt to re-create her presence by sheer force of memory, he commenced walking slowly along the gravel path, head down, holding himself very steady, as though he were an invalid recovering from a long and serious illness. . . .

There was a disturbance opposite her in the carriage, an annoying disturbance which shattered the quiet newly risen within her.

"Where were you? I sent Jason twice in search of you. If you think it's easy accompanying you here every day, you are very mistaken."

Mary tried politely not to listen. Somehow she had the feeling that, like John, the disturbance demanded an audience but not a response.

She wouldn't mind obliging the screeching voice, except that all her thoughts and feelings were actively involved with that most incredible revelation, that *he* had sought her out, had gone to great trouble and expense to follow her here, and that they would meet again the following day.

Effortlessly she conjured up his image. The only word that accurately described his face was beautiful. Something about his eyes, or more accurately the way he had looked at her, something very steady. She had never met anyone who had looked at her so—agreeably.

"There! That's a much more suitable expression," the disturbance pronounced, the voice less shrill. "What you must understand, Lady Mary, is that, what with all the present trouble, the two of us don't want to add to it, now do we? Poor Mr. Eden. I know he treated you badly today, but then he has his grief, too, now don't he?"

That was better, a pleasant tone of voice, sorrowful and compassionate.

He wanted to see me, went to great trouble to do so.

Mary closed her eyes and pressed her fingers against her lips, fearful that she would laugh aloud, some irrational behavior which would alert Doris and cause her to lecture again.

No, joy must be concealed, as though joy were not a respectable emotion. But no matter. Tomorrow *would* come, and she would see him again.

Near the end of the Mall, Mary glanced out the carriage window, amazed at how beautiful the world had become. Suddenly she shivered, unaccustomed to such perceptions. Then, as though fate were trying to remind her that happiness was the exception not the rule, she suffered a devastating thought.

What if he doesn't return to the park tomorrow?

"Are you well, Lady Mary?" Doris inquired, leaning close as though she'd seen something that alarmed her.

"Yes." Mary whispered, fighting off the hideous possibility. "Just tired, that's all," and wondered how she would survive until tomorrow.

Eden Castle
September 1870

"WHAT DID YOU say your name was?" Dr. Cockburn called from the top of the Great Hall stairs to the tall, arrogant-looking young gentleman who stood beside the carriage.

Damn! The watchmen shouldn't have let him in without first establishing his identity.

"Your name, sir?" he called again, aware of a few idle stewards watching the confrontation from the shade of the castle wall.

When still the young man did not deign to answer, Cockburn was on the verge of calling a third time, when the man shifted his position and shouted back up the stairs, "Parnell, sir. Charles Parnell. I've come to see Mrs. Eden, Lady Lila—"

"Not possible," Cockburn said, with a wave of his hand feeling a bit arrogant himself. And why shouldn't he? In the remarkably short time of three months he had risen from the Servants Hall to a position of respect at Eden Castle, now occupying comfortable guest chambers on the second floor, at Mr. Eden's insistence, with a brand-new wardrobe, again at Mr. Eden's insistence, who had kindly said that all he wanted in return for Cockburn's rise was a whole and healthy babe some months hence.

Inevitably that thought dampened his smug feelings and left him gaping down on that strong face, that refused to go away and that also refused to take no for an answer.

Now the knave dared to threaten him. "I think you'd better reconsider, old man," he shouted up. "Mr. Eden sent me," and with that blunt announcement caught Cockburn's attention.

He looked steadily down on the intruder. "Mrs. Eden —is ill," he pronounced, falteringly, sensing a breach in his wall of authority.

But the brash young stranger was feeling no such breach. "I'm aware of that," he said, nodding, daring to start up the stairs. "Not only aware of it—indeed it is the very purpose of my mission."

Dr. Cockburn knew he was lying. With that infallible recognition that one liar has for another, he knew instinctively that the man was lying. But most accomplished in the art was this gentleman who now stood before him at the top of the stairs, his eyes never lifting from Cockburn's face.

"I realize that I'm intruding unannounced," he said, a hint of apology in his voice. "I was here for the Festivities at the first of the summer, then attended to some business in London. As Mr. Eden knew that I was returning to Ireland, and as circumstances are keeping him occupied in London, he asked me if I might not stop off at Eden and visit with his wife, and send a report to him immediately."

"I—s-send him w-weekly reports," Cockburn stammered.

"Yes, but he finds them too technical." Parnell smiled. "He desired the simpler report that only a friend of the family might deliver."

If the man were telling the truth, then Mr. Eden would be furious if Cockburn refused him admittance to Mrs. Eden's chambers. If he were *not* telling the truth, then Mr. Eden's rage would be—

Gawd, I don't want even to think on that! "Credentials, Mr.—"

"Parnell."

"Yes, M-Mr. Parnell. Did y-you bring any papers, a letter of—"

"Great God, man, are you totally senseless?" The man's outrage was awesome. "I did not ask Mr. Eden for a letter, nor did he offer one. I'm certain that he assumed you would take a gentleman at his word. Of course I see now he was mistaken, and I'll trouble you no further. However, you can be certain that I will send a courier with a special message immediately, reporting in detail my reception here." *Lord, what am I to do now?* The man was retreating down the steps, taking his offended outrage with him. If Mr. Eden had indeed—

"Wait!" Cockburn called out. "Forgive my—caution, Mr.—"

"Parnell."

"Y-yes, Parnell. But y-you must understand the r-responsibility that Mr. Eden had placed on my—"

"I understand."

"She *is* ill."

"The purpose of my unscheduled stop."

"Her confinement is not going well."

The man seemed to look up at this, as though surprised. "Her—confinement?"

Cockburn nodded, relieved that the man was climbing the steps again, giving him another chance. "The b-babe is not securely anchored, I fear, and s-she's proving a most difficult patient."

"Take me to her," the man demanded, and strode past Cockburn as though to say he'd find his way with or without his assistance.

Trotting after the tall, forceful figure, Cockburn welcomed the shade of the Great Hall and felt the need to warn the man in advance of what he shortly would see for himself.

"She's—changed, sir," he panted, struggling to keep up. "Forgive the n-nature of this crude subject, but there is almost c-constant bleeding. And n-naturally she's considerably weakened."

"Is no one here with her?" the man demanded over his shoulder.

"Oh, yes, we're all here with her."

"I mean one of her family."

A strange question, Cockburn thought. *If the gentleman has indeed seen Eden recently in London, wouldn't he know that all the family have returned to London with him? Perhaps. Perhaps not.*

"This way, sir," Cockburn said, directing him to the right at the top of the second-floor landing, his anxiety rising. Was he doing the right thing? What if the gentleman was able to determine that the lump growing in Mrs. Eden's belly was not a babe?

Because, if he could determine that, then all was lost, Cockburn's carefully worked out scheme all for naught, his intention to keep the woman alive as long as possible, at least for another month or two, then have God intervene and take her, replacing the dead lump which would go with her to her grave with a fresh, newly born, blood-coated and squalling infant. There were several such womb-bound infants now down in the village, one in particular due to emerge shortly before Christmas, a whore's conception, a well-worn tart who had already given birth to seven bastards. For a pretty handkerchief and five pounds Cockburn was certain he could talk her out of this eighth excretion, and thus could he pacify Mr. Eden in the death of his wife with the gift of a child. In Cockburn's opinion, that was all Eden wanted anyway, the child. Wives could be easily replaced.

Approaching her chamber door, Cockburn called out to the stranger still striding ahead of him, "You must wait while I announce you. The lady herself may be unwilling, in which case—"

"Just tell her Mr. Charles Parnell from Ireland is here to take her home."

Alarmed, Cockburn blocked the door. "Take her—" he gasped.

"I don't mean literally, you idiot!" the gentleman exploded. "You take an Irishman home when you talk about the mother country. Now I command you, give me passage or that courier will be on his way to London by—"

Shaken by the man's words, Cockburn unlocked the door and backed through it, warning, "Hold your position. I'll summon you in a few moments."

Quickly he closed the door behind him and bolted it. Just emerging from the bedchamber, he saw two of the women who now sat in constant guard on his patient.

"Is she—"

"Not well."

He brushed past the expressionless face and gained the doorway and looked down on the woman in the bed.

Gawd! How can I ever explain that to anyone?

What precisely had drawn him back to this dreary place he had no idea. A compulsion perhaps, a fascination with the delicate little Irishwoman who had never laid eyes on her native land, who had seemed more a prisoner than a wife in her own castle.

That, and the all-pervading boredom with his brother in London and the peculiar sense that fate was making him wait offstage, husbanding his powers until the right moment in history came. In a way he didn't mind the waiting. At least it was peaceful. When the storm broke,

whatever its nature, his instincts informed him that he
would not know peace again.

Now he paced restlessly in the gloomy corridor outside
the bolted door, a bit regretful that he'd lied his way into
this place. He had thought to spend a placid day with
Lord Harrington before catching the ferry for Wales at
Kewstoke. Then an additional four days would see him
home, where he would have to deal with his mother's disappointment over his failed life.

Thinking he'd heard something, he looked back at the
closed door and saw two large, flat-faced Englishwomen
emerging. They gave him a brief glance, then strode down
the corridor, one carrying what appeared to be a bundle
of soiled linen.

God, but he loathed them—all aspects of them! Not
just the two waddling down the corridor, but all their
countrymen as well, their dull, self-righteous faces, their
frozen souls locked for eternity in the illusion of their superiority.

There *was* one exception, and he was forced to deal
with it—his affection for Lord Richard Eden, who, along
with Herbert Nichols, had been the only two civilized
voices he'd encountered during the ill-fated Cambridge
days. Thinking that Lord Richard's simple kindness was
representative of the entire family, Parnell had accepted
the fortnight's invitation several months ago, and had discovered too late that he had been sadly mistaken. If it
hadn't been for the hospitality of Lord Harrington and his
daughter, that miserable fortnight would have been even
more miserable.

It was with the sense of returning that kindness that
he'd stopped off at Eden and, in the process, had learned
for the first time of Mrs. Eden's confinement.

Well, he'd only stay for a few moments, long enough
to wish her well, then he'd follow the channel to the ferry,
shake the dust of England from his boots forever and start
the last leg of his journey home.

Momentarily lost in the anticipation of his departure,
he looked up at the sound of his name to see the idiot
doctor standing in the door.

"She's f-feeling poorly today, Mr.—"

"Parnell."

"Yes—Parnell. But she said if I would apologize for
her appearance and warn you—"

"Consider it done!" Parnell snapped, impatient to get the visit over with.

"Then this way, please, and only a few moments. Both she and the babe need all the strength—"

For the first time Parnell faltered. There was an odor in the room which alarmed him, and a sense of suffering so great that it had become a thing of substance.

Steeling himself against these irrational feelings, he straightened his shoulders, cleared his head of all other matters and strode to the bedchamber door.

And stopped.

Dear God, he whispered, confident that no one had heard, not even the Deity to whom his prayer had been addressed. . . .

In the beginning only Wolf had been there, and he was questionable company, having over the years grown fat and passive on the diet of Eden mice.

Then the pattern of the four women had evolved, two standing watch by day, two by night, tending her not cruelly, but not lovingly either, viewing her from time to time as though she were simply part of the bed linens, placing her under light restraint when she tried to sit up in an effort to accommodate the searing pain in her stomach.

Daily the old physician came to see her and prodded and poked, causing greater pain and fresh humiliation. And from time to time, when the pain caused delirium, she called out for everyone, but no one had answered, and one day one of the women had sternly suggested that she was merely doing penance for having been a reluctant wife. At that moment it had made sense and in a way still did, though she earnestly prayed that her penance would end soon.

Drawing substance from hope, she tried to breathe deeply, the better to accommodate the next wave of pain which seemed to start in her lower abdomen and cut through to her spine. At some point she was aware of voices around her.

"Make her presentable. Can she sit up?"

"I doubt it, doctor, but we can try—"

As the activity in the room whirled about her, she knew that something was different, and she tried to be cooperative, lifting herself as much as possible for a fresh night-

shirt and fresh linens, sorry that she could no longer
control her kidneys, thus adding to the burden of those
about her.

As the two women lifted her soiled nightdress, the old
doctor told them to wait and stepped closer and bent
over her swollen belly, distended as though in midpreg-
nancy.

Lila held still, submitting to his examination, hoping
that he would see what she knew to be the truth, what her
hands told her each night as she grasped the lump in an
attempt to ease the pain. There *was* something growing
within her, but it was an evil something, not the babe
that John expected, but rather something that must be
dealt with before it destroyed her.

"Please," she whispered, but no one was paying attention to her. The women had joined the doctor, bent over
the lower portion of her body and, as their hands moved
over her, Lila closed her eyes and hoped that whoever
was waiting to see her did not lose patience and go
away.

"I don't think she can sit erect, doctor," she heard a
woman say.

"Nor should we ask her to," the male voice replied.
"Can she speak lucidly, do you think?"

"Oh, yes," a woman replied. "On good days she talks to
her cat. Let's see. Mrs. Eden? Are you with us today? A
special day it is. You have a visitor."

She looked toward the door, trying to catch a glimpse
of who her visitor might be.

"Mrs. Eden," the doctor began, his voice kinder than
usual, "this gentleman has come to see you at the request
of your husband."

How remarkable was the degree of fear she experienced at the mention of her husband! While she
was trying to recover from it, she wondered when it had
happened, when love had died and fear taken its place
—for she had loved him once.

"Mrs. Eden, can you hear us?"

It was the doctor again. "Yes," she murmured, and
tried again to blink the stranger into focus.

"This is Mr. Parnell, milady. And I beg you to inform
him that you are being well looked after, as that is the
message he will convey to your husband."

Bewildered, Lila stared back at the two, who seemed more than willing to stare down on her.

"Leave us!" Mr. Parnell ordered. When at first the doctor did not move, he said again, louder, "Leave us, I say," in the tone of a man accustomed to being obeyed.

"Only for a few minutes," the doctor said, retreating to the door.

Alone with a man she hardly knew, Lila suffered embarrassment and, fearful that the lump growing in her belly was visible beneath the linen, she lightly drew up her knees and for her efforts suffered pain as excruciating as any she'd ever experienced. She clutched at her stomach and pressed her head back into the pillow.

A few moments later it blessedly receded and left her gasping. Glancing to her right, she saw that it was Mr. Parnell. "Please." She smiled, wanting him to come closer.

Out of that shocked face words evolved. "Mrs. Eden," he questioned, as though he, too, were having problems of recognition. "I was told you were ill, but—"

"Please come closer, Mr. Parnell," she said. Her energy was limited and she wanted desperately to speak with him before the doctor returned.

"Did you—come from my husband?" she asked, extending a hand toward him, which he kindly took and enclosed in his own.

"No," he told her, truthfully. "I've been in London, but I did not see your husband and, forgive me, but I had little desire to see him." He leaned closer. "Does he know that you are—ill?"

She shook her head. "He thinks that I am—"

"Then he should be informed. Obviously all is not well with your confinement. You need skilled attention if a healthy babe is to be—"

She closed her eyes. "There is no babe, Mr. Parnell," she whispered. "I've tried to tell them all that, but they won't believe me."

"But I was told that—"

"There is no babe," she repeated, wasting precious energy. She'd long since given up trying to convince the women and the doctor. But Mr. Parnell was different. Why didn't he—

"Then—you are not carrying a child?"

"No," she repeated, and felt her energy dwindling and

realized that she had to make her request while she still
could.

"Please, Mr. Parnell," she whispered, "you must listen
to me. Would you—find my father for me, and tell him—
I need him?"

"Lord Harrington?"

She nodded. "He went back to London with John. I
want to see him—before I die, and there's not much
time. . . ."

"Before you die?" Parnell smiled, trying to lighten her
mood and lift her spirits. "You've produced two healthy
babes, Mrs. Eden. There is no reason why—"

"Find my father, please, Mr. Parnell," she begged.
"Tell him I must—see him."

Something in her voice sobered him. He nodded,
though she couldn't tell if he meant it or not. The pain
was increasing again. She tried to lie still, but there was
no position of ease, and ultimately she had no choice but
to flatten her legs, the protuberance visible now beneath
the sheet, her hands supporting it, trying to cover it, to rip
it from her body, anything to bring her ease.

Throughout this new agony she was aware of Parnell
calling for the doctor. A short time later she felt her head
being lifted, was aware of a vial pressed to her lips, the
sweet, dark brown fluid which normally she refused because it plunged her into an endless sleep. But now she
welcomed it, swallowed deeply, uncaring of the trickle
which ran down the side of her chin.

As the substance burned into her throat, she opened
her eyes to see the doctor raising up from bending over
her, his white hair seeming to float about his head. He was
saying something to someone, but all she could hear were
unrelated words.

"She doesn't want the babe, you see—denies it constantly—Mr. Eden fears she will destroy it—must keep
her—quiet—"

"She appears to be in great pain."

"Imaginary—an interesting case—a woman refusing to
perform her duty."

"Then—she's—well?"

"Not well—a complicated delivery, I'm sure—but no
need to alarm Mr. Eden."

"She spoke of—dying."

"She won't die."

Then she had no more desire to listen. The elixir was beginning to take effect, a pleasant lassitude extending to all her limbs, obliterating the sensation of feet and hands, numbing the pain.

Her last clear thought was one of sadness. Mr. Parnell would not relay the message for her. No one would come until it was too late. She would be forced to enter that distant realm alone. If only she knew for certain—

Sad, too, was her realization of how ill-equipped she'd been for this world. Wolf had tried to warn her, but she hadn't listened, and now he, too, had abandoned her.

Someone was crying within her, but she was certain that the tears were deep and would never be visible to anyone in this world.

Everyone dies, she thought, and that simple perception eased her fears. If only she could see her garden one more time.

The numbness was almost complete, only one small portion of her brain still speaking to her, kindly reminding her that surely on the other side there would be flowers. . . .

Relieved that it was almost over, Cockburn walked to the carriage with the gentleman, lying with every breath to assure himself of a good report to Mr. Eden.

"It's a c-classic case, really, Mr.—"

"Parnell."

"Yes. A classic case of a reluctant wife. Not a very pretty one, I concede, as you have recently seen for yourself, but nothing to concern y-yourself with."

Unfortunately there still was a predominant expression of concern on the intruder's face which had to be eased before Cockburn could send him on his way.

"She appears to be suffering so," the man said falteringly, his head down as though trying to rid his vision of lingering images of the sickroom.

"All concocted, I assure you," Cockburn reassured him. "You see, it happens every time. I saw Mrs. Eden through her first two confinements and it was the same then, refusing to admit to her swelling belly, totally bedridden the last few months, r-refusing to eat. But"—and soundly he shook his head—"here is the paradox: once the babes have emerged from her womb, I've never seen a more loving m-mother. Dotes on them, she does, refused to let

a wet-nurse come near them." He shook his head for em-
phasis. "M-most curious it is."

The gentleman looked down on him, still undone, wiping his forehead with a large, mussed handkerchief. "I
don't think I'll return to London," he called down from his
carriage door. "I'm sure I'm needed at home, and I'll send
my report in writing."

Excellent! Cockburn couldn't have asked for more.
How calm a written report would be, nothing of the gentleman's undone expression to give himself away.

Now, as the man gave his driver the signal to start,
Cockburn called out, "A safe journey, Mr.—" Why
couldn't he remember the name? Then it made no difference, as the carriage was picking up speed, rattling
through the Gatehouse, veering sharply to the right, heading toward the channel road, London safely in the opposite direction.

Cockburn waved, though it was a perfunctory gesture.
Feeling the need to stretch his legs, he walked the short
distance to the Gatehouse, where just over the castle wall
he saw the dust stirred by the departing carriage.

He nodded to the watchmen, who were just lowering
the grilles, then he looked back at the immense façade
of Eden Castle and felt a flair of pride that his long and
generally undistinguished career had led him here. *God
saves the best for last,* he mused, and decided to forgo
his final check of the day on Mrs. Eden. Like the gentleman who had recently departed, he'd had enough of her
suffering for one day. The elixir would see her through
the night, and come morning he would examine her again,
see if he could discern any changes in her swollen belly,
try to determine how much life was left in her.

Just as he started up the Great Hall stairs, he heard a
curious noise, the sound of a carriage traveling at a tre-
mendous rate of speed down the channel road. He glanced
back toward the Gatehouse and saw the watchmen peering
through the grilles, their faces turned in anticipation of
the rising dust cloud.

What in the— At that moment a carriage traveling at
unsafe speed rumbled past the Gatehouse, it's specifics
blurred under the duress of speed, the dust clouds bil-
lowing through the grilles, causing the watchmen to turn
away.

Curious, Cockburn stood at the top of the steps and listened to the carriage as it rattled out across the moors, heading toward the turnpike road and London.

"Did you see who that was?" he shouted at the watchmen.

"No, sir, not clearly," one replied. "Looked like the gint who just left."

Cockburn stared down through the shimmering heat waves of the unseasonably hot September. It wasn't possible. Why should the gentleman change his mind and inconvenience himself with a prolonged trip to London?

No, it probably was just a traveler, lost, trying to make up time.

Satisfied, he turned back into the shade of the Great Hall, reminding himself that before long he must go down into Mortemouth and check on the progress of the whore's belly.

My Gawd, what a lot his was, for all his new wardrobe and fancy chambers! While other men went about important business, he was forced to mark time by the swellings of female bellies. If he had it to do all over again, though pray God no, he'd go to sea, he would, where there were no such embarrassments as suffering females. . . .

❧

London
Late September 1870

FROM WHERE ANDREW Rhoades sat, John resembled a storm which had at last raged itself out. Suffering an uncomfortable mix of sorrow and annoyance for his friend, Andrew stood by the fire in Elizabeth's drawing room and watched the man slump in the chair, his legs extended before him, his fingers forming a tent before his face, his eyes lost in shadows created by sleepless nights and misplaced fury.

After an obsessive three months, during which time John had neglected everything, at last the rage had exhausted itself, though Andrew knew from experience that a brooding John was frequently worse than a raging one.

Since luncheon and shortly after Mary had left for her

daily ride along Rotten Row—the young woman was becoming an obsessive horsewoman, riding daily, rain or
shine—John had sat in brooding silence, listening to
everything Andrew had said but not responding in any
way.

Elizabeth had gone out a short time ago, seeking refuge
at Charlie Bradlaugh's. And Lord Harrington had not even
bothered to appear today, though where he had sought
refuge Andrew had no idea.

The only person in the drawing room with him enduring John's silence was Dhari. Andrew glanced in her direction, feeding on her beauty.

Busily engaged in her needlework, she was not aware of
Andrew watching her. Then she was and, as her needle
came to a halt, she looked at him, her communication
clear, her eyes filled with their secret, the love which had
so unexpectedly flowered between them.

Having surrendered to it for the first time just since the
return from Eden, Andrew suspected that he had loved
her always, since that first night years ago when she had
appeared out of that cold December night at John's side,
starved and half-frozen.

During all those intervening years he'd mistakenly interpreted his love as pity. But after the initial shock, pity
had faded in importance. There was nothing pitiable in
that living portrait of serenity, nothing pitiable in her
courage and passive strength. And though once she had
been John's, now she belonged to Andrew by her own
consent, and as soon as a degree of equilibrium could be
restored to all their lives, it was Andrew's intention to
speak openly to John, ask him to release Dhari from
whatever bondage bound her to him, so that he might
make her his wife.

The thought rendered him numb with happiness. It had
merely been the dream of his life to acquire the stability
of his own home, children, a woman who loved him in
spite of his many faults.

So engrossed was he in this dream and the soft reciprocal smile on Dhari's face, Andrew at first was not aware
of the man slumped in the chair, his position unchanged
except for his eyes, which were now watching them.

Jarred back to the present by the intensity of John's
gaze, Andrew faltered, pushed away from the mantel and
tried to address himself to the matter at hand.

Not too difficult, that. The "matter at hand" was the same as it had been for the last three months and although he loathed himself for his idiotlike repetition, he said again, "So, as I've pointed out, John, it would serve no purpose, except do further damage to yourself and surely we don't want that."

He wasn't certain whether or not John had made the transition with him. They had, minutes before, been discussing the possibility of bringing charges against the *Times,* thereby forcing the editorial staff to reveal the true identity of Lord Ripples, which if successful would lead to a new round of suits aimed at Lord Ripples himself, charging among other things slander and character assassination. For the last several weeks John had insisted that Andrew, as his solicitor, launch such proceedings. Andrew had tried to point out the folly of such a step.

First he was not certain that there were grounds. Similar cases in the past had been leveled at the *Times,* as well as other London papers, more severe cases than this one, charges leveled at certain statesmen and even members of the Cabinet. A few weak efforts at restitution on the part of the injured parties had resulted in making them look like greater fools, while the editorial staff of the *Times* had emerged stronger than ever. The magistrates, while sympathetic, seemed to have greater respect for a free and unencumbered press.

In Andrew's opinion, any thinking magistrate would throw them all out of court on their ears, but not before other journalists had resurrected the entire affair in the current press, thus rekindling the fires of embarrassment, which after three long months had almost burned themselves out.

This, then, was the outline of the debate which alternately had raged and smoldered in Elizabeth's drawing room. Now Andrew was sick to death of it and hoped that this new and prolonged silence on the part of John indicated that he, too, had either come around or worn himself out.

In an attempt to prod him into some sort of response, Andrew repeated himself in variation. "The matter is totally dead now, John. I've not heard it mentioned for weeks in any corner of the city. Men of good sense and goodwill turned their attention weeks ago to more serious matters."

"It is serious enough to me," John muttered, a childlike quality to his slouched position, though there was nothing childlike in that gaze which he continued to level at Dhari.

From where he stood by the window, Andrew was in a position to see the expression clearly and was alarmed by it. There was something vengeful in it. Now he found that he wanted very much to keep John's attention on the ill-fated lawsuit.

"John, I have some reports here I want you to see," Andrew commenced, surprised by the strength in his voice, as he headed toward his portfolio on the far table.

"Look at her, Andrew," came the soft though taut voice from the wingchair. "Remarkable, isn't she?" he mused, his fingers rubbing the bridge of his nose, his eyes unblinking.

Suffering embarrassment for everyone, Andrew slapped the papers against his hand. "John, I beg you. There are matters which need your attention immediately."

"Indeed there are."

"For the first time in the history of John Murrey Firm we've suffered a loss last month."

"August was ever a poor month."

"Not this poor."

"Will it affect our stockholders?"

"No."

"Then it's a normal August."

During this brief exchange, not once did John lift his eyes from Dhari's bowed head, nor did that single index finger alter its methodical massage of the bridge of his nose. All at once there was radical movement, John pushing up out of his chair, stretching, then assuming a relaxed position, his hands shoved into his pockets.

"Do you want to hear something interesting, Andrew?" he asked, his manner deceptively kind.

Resignedly Andrew lifted the sheaf of papers into the air. "I would prefer—"

"I don't know her exact age. . . ." John marveled, as though it were an ancient mystery which had plagued him for some time.

Andrew commenced to rejoin the leather straps of his portfolio. Under the best of conditions for the last three months John had been difficult to endure. He felt no further obligation to put up with more.

"Where are you going?" This was the same imperious tone, and it fueled Andrew's desire to get them both out of the room.

"There's a great deal of work to be done, John," he replied. "I had hoped for your assistance. In fact, I need it, but—"

"Of course you need it, Andrew, as you have needed me from the beginning, as all of you have needed me. I support the lot of you and ask nothing in return except loyalty."

Andrew drew the last strap into place and lowered the portfolio to the table. "You have it," he murmured.

John smiled, pleased by his small victory. "Surely that loyalty will enable you to listen to the ramblings of an old friend."

"Of course."

"It just occurred to me that none of us know Dhari's exact age. Now I realize that that's not terribly pertinent to the time or the day, but I, for one, find it an interesting dilemma." He moved slowly to where Dhari sat and he stood behind her, his hands massaging her shoulders. As far as Andrew could tell, she had exhibited no reaction to his touch, but continued to sit, head down.

"If indeed, as Fraser Jennings said, she was mid-twenties when I first met her," John went on, mindlessly pursuing the subject, "then that would place her in her mid to late forties." He turned his head sideways at the revelation. "Imagine that, Andrew!"

"I fail to see—"

"Of course you fail to see, Andrew, as from time to time you fail to see other important dimensions in certain situations."

"Then I must rely upon you to point them out for me."

"Which I am always only too happy to do." John smiled, his hand caressing the back of Dhari's head, in the process loosening the French knot and pulling free the long strands of ebony hair streaked with gray.

"Considering all that she's been through, she's very well preserved, don't you think, Andrew?" As John methodically wrapped the long strands of hair around his hand, Andrew watched, uncertain how long he could merely stand by.

"And she *has* been through a great deal," John went on. "Of course I have no way of attesting to the number

of men she had received before I came along. She had
borne a son, however, and with my own eyes I saw her
with Fraser Jennings, and of course during our time together she has been nothing less than generous."

As he spoke he began slowly to pull back on her hair,
forcing her face upward, a frightened face, Andrew could
see now.

"John, I ask you, please—" Andrew said and was not
given a chance to finish.

"Of course, I have no way of knowing how many men
she's received since she's been in London. I don't set a
guard on her, you know. She's a free agent, so I really
have no basis for complaint."

He had drawn her head so far back that her neck was
arched, her line of vision forced up to the ceiling. Fearful
of losing her balance, Andrew saw her hands reaching out
on either side and, unable to endure the soft moan which
escaped her lips, Andrew strode across the room.

"Let her alone, John!"

In mock surprise, John looked up. "What concern is
it of yours?" he smiled, though simultaneously he released
her hair.

"You baffle me, Andrew," he went on. "In the areas
where I legitimately seek your advice and intervention
you give me no aid. In personal areas where you have no
right to trespass you are quick with both."

Andrew had heard enough. It would be best if he left
before more was said, damaging further their already
strained relationship. "If that's all, John, then I'll—"

"But it isn't all." John smiled. To Dhari he commanded, "Get your cloak and wait for me in the carriage.
It's been too long since I've enjoyed your company. Talking of the past has made me—nostalgic."

No one moved, though the meaning behind the command was clear. Andrew saw Dhari bow her head.

In the ensuing silence it occurred to Andrew that for
several weeks he had sensed the end. At the sight of
Dhari's bowed head, at the sight of John abusing her, Andrew stepped forward, ready to sever all aspects of his
long relationship with John Murrey Eden. The man was
no longer the man whom Andrew had loved. This man
standing by the open door had grown bitter, narrow, cruel,
a "demi-god."

But as Andrew stepped forward, Dhari looked at him,

a curious warning look, and at the same time one of reassurance, trying to convey—what? All he knew for certain was that she had asked him not to intercede further.

"Truly one of God's greatest blessings," he heard John
say from the door. "A silent woman. Wouldn't you agree,
Andrew? If only they all could be born thus, how pleasant our world would be."

When his shock and anger dragged him back around to
face the man grinning at him from the doorway, he saw
Dhari's chair empty, the woman gone.

"You're not looking well, Andrew," John said considerately, "and I won't keep you but a moment longer.
You're right on one score and I concede it as a gentleman.
It's past time that we put an end to these constant post-
mortems of what to do and what not to do. And all your
points are well taken on previous suits brought against
various newspapers. And the anonymity of the journalist
does keep him safe."

Curious as to the conclusion of his little speech, Andrew looked back toward the door to see him drawing
on his gloves, adjusting his cloak. "So," John concluded,
his manner light, "we'll bring no suit against the *Times*."

"Thank God," Andrew muttered.

"But what we will do is subpoena Mr. John Thadeus
Delane to appear at a private hearing to be conducted
discreetly in a magistrate's chambers where under oath he
will be forced to reveal the identity of his anonymous
journalist."

Andrew blinked, unable to believe what he was hearing. "You—can't be serious!"

"I've never been more serious."

"Mr. Delane is a prominent gentleman, highly respected."

"Delane is a bastard who hides behind the sanctity of
his newspaper, confident that he is beyond the law."

"It will gain you nothing but further embarrassment."

"Perhaps. But it may gain me the name of the man I
seek."

"For what purpose?"

John smiled. "For the purpose of destroying him, as he
tried to destroy me."

Sick at heart, aware that nothing he had said had made
the slightest difference, Andrew sank into a chair, shaking
his head.

Apparently the appearance of weakness stirred John to
new anger. "I'm not asking you to do this, Andrew," he
said, "I'm commanding you to do it, and if you refuse,
you leave me no choice but to seek the services of another
solicitor, someone more understanding of the relationship
which should exist between client and agent."

So! Both of them had been thinking in terms of ending
the relationship. Andrew was on the verge of telling him
to do just that, and would have, except at that moment,
beyond the opened door he caught a glimpse of Dhari,
her cloak over her arm as she came down the stairs and
passed the archway, heading toward the front door and
the carriage beyond.

Either his residual fear at what she would be forced to
endure, or his new awareness of what a consummate fool
John was on the verge of making of himself, and wanting
terribly to be on the scene when that happened, all these
thoughts caused him to lean forward from his slumped
position and nod, mourning the death of the love he'd
once felt for this man, no longer concerned with protecting
him but eager only to assist him to new humiliation.

"Of course I'll do it, John. In fact I'll get on it this very
afternoon."

Obviously his cooperation had been unexpected because, for the first time since they had been in the room
together, Andrew saw an alteration on that arrogant face.
John looked suspiciously at him and, finding nothing to
rail against, he muttered, "I'd be most grateful."

"It will be done."

"Then perhaps all our lives can return to normal. That
would be fine with me."

Since no response was called for, Andrew offered none
and continued to watch the man who had so completely
annihilated his capacity to love that now he could not
identify hate.

"Well, then," John said with dispatch from the door,
"I'll be at home for the rest of the day, if you need me."

Not likely, Andrew brooded, returning the man's gaze.
Unable to watch the disintegration any longer, Andrew
walked away toward the dying fire, feeling a chill in the
room.

So engrossed was he in private mourning that he was
not at all prepared for the petulant voice which cut
through the silence. "She *is* mine, you know, Andrew, and

has been from the beginning. You had no right, none at all."

As Andrew looked back all he saw was the hem of a gray cloak leaving the room.

In defense against the pain of his own cowardice, he retrieved his portfolio from the side table, tried to clear his head enough to determine his destination and settled on his private office, where he would draw up the subpoena which would bring John Thadeus Delane and John Murrey Eden into direct and inevitably bloody confrontation.

As he hurried through the open doors and out onto the pavement he stopped at the top of the steps and watched through blurred eyes as though it were the most fascinating spectacle in the world, a black-mustachioed organ grinder expertly manipulating his red-jacketed monkey....

The carriage had scarcely departed the pavement when John discovered that he was having difficulty swallowing. Perspiration broke out on his forehead and, no matter where he looked, whether inside the carriage or out, all he saw was that last expression on Andrew's face.

Adding to his distress was his awareness of Dhari seated opposite him. Remorse as deep as any he'd ever felt pressed down upon him and, using the last of his strength, he drew down the window and shouted up at his coachman, "Just drive for a while, anywhere."

The coachman brought the horses about and settled them into a leisured pace down the Mall past the early-autumn beauty of Hyde Park and Rotten Row. John leaned up, wishing that he might catch sight of Mary.

But beneath the reds and golds of September the riders blurred into a liquid ribbon and he was forced to admit that it was best he didn't see her. He had again offended *her* as well, and, as long as he was suffering from this mysterious heaviness and before he did any more damage, he'd best content himself with a quiet ride and Dhari's silent company.

Abruptly he pressed his head back against the cushions. With difficulty he tried to breathe deeply and felt a pain in his side and opened his eyes to see Dhari staring at him.

"I'm—sorry," he murmured. As he turned away he saw a movement coming from her side of the carriage, as though in spite of everything that had happened, she still felt an impulse to offer comfort.

With his face turned away, he waited, full of childish hope that she would come to him as she always had in the past, without requiring an invitation.

But she didn't.

He tried to concentrate on the reality outside his window, seeing everything with a strange brilliancy. He couldn't remember when in his life he'd felt such consummate fatigue.

There had been many times when he'd been tempted to agree with Andrew that the matter was simply not worth the effort they were expending on it. Yet it had not been Andrew's name or reputation that had been obliterated by that despicable column, and it was not the name of Andrew Rhoades that had been on everyone's tongue in snickering gossip, nor had it been Andrew's trust that had been destroyed by the realization that someone had taken advantage of his hospitality as a friend and then had tried to do him in as his worst enemy.

Someone was playing a very serious game at the *Times,* a game which, if carried to extremes, would mean that no public figure would have any recourse to self-defense, that anything could be printed, no matter how damaging or untrue, and the offending journalist could hide forever behind the protective barricade of anonymity.

Of course John had a private suspicion, so incredible that he'd never shared it with anyone, but after prolonged contemplation it made great sense, that Lord Ripples was John Thadeus Delane himself, that under the pseudonym the aging journalist had devised a capital way to sell newspapers and drive his competitors out of business.

If this were the case, a hearing under oath would reveal all and, if indeed the man's judgment had been impaired by senility and aging ambition, then John would simply request a public retraction, content to let the man's punishment be his own embarrassment. But if some other Englishman were responsible for those devastating words, then further action would be taken, a civil suit, financial restitution, and ultimately complete ruin.

Warmed by these thoughts, John began to relax into the cushions, enjoying the rhythmical rocking of the carriage.

In time they all would be restored to an even keel, the mutual love he shared with Andrew as strong as ever.

Thinking on love, he glanced across at Dhari, who had settled back as well during the prolonged ride.

She *was* aging, John thought sadly, seeing new lines about her eyes and the corners of her mouth. She'd served him well and perhaps it was time to release her. There were others, younger, to whom he could turn, and if Andrew wanted her, then John would give her to him as a peace offering.

"Turn back!" he shouted out the window on a burst of energy, at last beginning to feel the heaviness lift. There was the key, then. Certain bridges had to be mended with those he loved. He'd never intended to hurt them. He would return and show them a different face, his old one, the one which in the past had elicited love and respect and loyalty. He could be as repentant as the next man.

"No—keep going!" he shouted, seeing that his driver was heading toward the house in Belgravia. "We're returning to Number Seven, St. George Street," he shouted further, and was aware of Dhari's look of surprise. Her eyes were fixed on him as though she had just perceived his intent, his generosity.

With mild regret, he said a silent goodbye to her. He'd kept his promise to look after her. As the carriage drew up in front of Number Seven, he said, more gruffly than he might have wished, "Go find your solicitor and tell him that his friend John Murrey Eden wishes you both well."

He watched as she alighted the carriage and looked beyond her to see Elizabeth, fully dressed, just descending the stairs.

"Wait!" he called up to his driver. On the pavement he saw Elizabeth nod in his direction, as though he were little more than a stranger, and proceed on to her own carriage.

Ah, bridges in need of mending there as well, he thought. And, in the spirit of his newly made vows, he caught up with her in three broad strides.

"Going out again?" he asked, wanting desperately to heal this relationship.

She proceeded on a step or two, as though she had little desire to exchange words with him. "Briefly." She smiled, pulling at her gloves. "Why don't you go inside?" she added. "Alex Aldwell is waiting for you. He says it's a matter of some urgency."

Aldwell could wait. Again reminding himself that he must show all these people a new face, he took Elizabeth's arm. "Wherever you're going, can't it wait? I had hoped that we might take tea together as we used to, all of us, Dhari, Andrew, Mary—"

"You must excuse me, John," she said and moved a few steps beyond.

Then he must try again, truly humble himself before her. "Obviously Andrew has been talking to you," he began, "telling you how—badly I behaved today."

"I've not seen Andrew," she said, still walking away from him. "When I returned a few moments ago he was not—"

"You've just come in?" he asked, puzzled. "Then why are you going out again so—"

"I'll return shortly," she promised.

Whatever the nature of her distress, it was increasing. An affair of the heart? He seemed to be surrounded by them today. A lovers' quarrel with Charles Bradlaugh?

Looking up, he saw that she was still moving away from him, and, in an act of discipline, he repressed the urge to command her to return and instead called after her, "Then I'll have to make do with Mary's company for tea, though we will miss you."

Her hand, extended to pull herself up into her carriage, froze in midair. Slowly she stepped back down to the pavement. "Mary has not returned home yet," she said softly, as though wishing he would not hear the words.

But he did hear and looked up at the sky and determined that the hour must be approaching six o'clock, the sun beginning to set. Although his instinct was to rage, he tempered his reaction, still wanting to heal the wounds he'd inflicted in the past. As for Mary, while her thoughtless disobedience would have to be dealt with, he doubted if she were in any real danger. After all, Jason was with her, as was Doris. She'd probably ridden too far and in her witless way lost track of time.

He found himself thinking of the school in Cheltenham. How much easier he would breathe if he could place her in that fortress for a few years.

But this was neither the time nor the place to bring up that touchy subject. Consciously striving to fill his voice with merely kind authority, he said, "No cause for worry. I'll go and fetch her myself."

"No."

"Yes!" He looked back at Elizabeth and was tempted to say, *You allowed her to run free. How can I entrust you with bringing her back?*

As he shouted out the destination to his driver, he reminded himself that the control he'd needed in his dealings with Elizabeth was nothing compared to what would be required of him when he found the truant Mary.

As the carriage proceeded along the edge of Green Park, he looked out the window, amazed to see how rapidly dusk was falling. Deep in the park he saw the lamplighters at work, and only a few late-evening strollers, couples mostly, taking advantage of the fading light for a whispered intimacy.

"Stop up ahead," he called out, seeing to his right the beginning of Hyde Park and Rotten Row. He was amazed at how deserted the area was. Earlier, when he'd passed this way with Dhari, the pavement around the bridle path and stables had been clogged with carriages and cabs, people coming and going.

Now? Only four carriages stood at the pavement. One he recognized as Elizabeth's and, standing beside it, he saw Doris and Jason.

"Here," John called, and as his driver guided the carriage in front of the others, he looked back through the small oval window, hoping to catch a glimpse of Mary. But nothing and, as Doris and Jason recognized him, he saw them lean together for a whisper. Then Jason started toward him, an expression on his face which looked ominously like concern.

"Mr. Eden," he said, bobbing his head.

"Where is she?" John demanded.

"I don't know, sir. She's never been this late before. I've just returned from searching the bridle path and found nothing."

"Does she follow a set route?" he asked over his shoulder.

"I wouldn't know, sir."

"Of course," John muttered, aware of Doris creeping up on his right.

While he was certain that her female contribution would be a waste of everyone's time, still he summoned her forward. "You!" he called out. "Would you have any idea—"

"Oh, no, sir, I wouldn't, sir," the little woman gasped. "She's a wicked, wicked girl, though, I know that, sir, worrying old Doris like this—"

John nodded, taking comfort in one small fact. She was a superb horsewoman. The chances of her having had an accident were slight.

Then where in the hell is she?

"You go that way," he said to Jason, pointing toward the western extremities of the park, "and I'll follow the bridle path. And tell *her,*" he added, stabbing a finger at the quietly weeping Doris, "to wait here and, if Lady Mary returns, she is to secure her in the carriage and wait for us."

He glanced up at the sky and assessed that they had about an hour of light left. "If you find her first, say nothing. Just bring her back here and wait for me, all of you."

"Yes, sir," Jason said, nodding.

John plunged his hands into his pockets and started down the bridle path, trying in the faint light to avoid the piles of manure dropped during the day's rides. *Damn!* He'd not intended to pass the conclusion of this day in this manner. He desperately wanted a cup of tea, wanted to see the look of forgiveness and joy on Andrew's face after he had returned Dhari to him.

Anger and discomfort rising, the chill of evening beginning to penetrate his jacket, he increased his speed, aware of his once-polished boots becoming caked with smelly manure.

A short time later he looked up to find himself at the far end of Rotten Row, an intersection which gave an uncluttered view of the bridle path in all directions, not a horse or rider in sight.

Then obviously she'd ventured off into the interior of the park, an area of merely several hundred acres, which would tax the abilities of three hundred searchers.

Standing on the deserted path, an alarming thought occurred. The park at night was alive with thieves and footpads, whores and whores' bullies, a world wholly remote from any Mary had ever known. Perhaps a brief introduction to the dark side of day and those creatures who inhabited it would be good for her—life's first installment in that classic lesson of caution.

As though to retract the thought before it became a reality, John started off across the park at a walk that rapidly became a trot, then a run, no longer concerned with the condition of his boots.

"Mary!" he called, and heard his own voice in echo.

"Mary!" he called again, and spied ahead a place where two paths intersected, one leading back to the pavement beyond Rotten Row, the other leading down to an arbor, completely obscured in shadows caused by early evening and the dense foliage overhead.

He paused for breath at the intersecting paths, looking down toward the arbor. The path was narrow. Surely she would have had better sense than to lead her horse there.

He held his position, thinking he'd heard something. *Listen!*

The soft whinny of a horse? Not a sound of distress, rather satiation, as though he'd had his fill of grass.

Cautiously, in the event he'd stumbled into a den of night people, he took a few steps toward the arbor and the concealment of the garden beyond. From this new angle he saw that it *was* a horse. No, two horses, tethered to the trunk of a tree to give them grazing room. In the diminishing light he observed that one was gray, a sturdy well-built animal.

And the other—

He blinked, half-convinced that his eyes in the semidarkness had deceived him. No, he'd seen that one before at Eden, two, three years ago, a handsome black stallion.

Cautious! Be cautious!

He started slowly down, staying well behind the concealment of bushes, listening, his eyes fixed on the darkness ahead, half-afraid of what he might see, half-afraid of what he wouldn't see. . . .

If God elected to give her nothing but sorrow for the rest of her life, she would not complain, for at least He had been generous enough to give her one unbroken interval of happiness, a series of afternoons so perfect that she could feed on the memories for the rest of her life.

Looking up in the diminishing light of day, she wondered precisely when it had happened, when had this small garden become a temple and that gentleman strolling a few feet ahead of her, head down, a god? How

curious, the sense of pain which moved in tandem with
her sense of happiness.

Now it was late and they both knew it was late, but
neither was capable of doing anything about it. Would it
be asking too much to ask the sun to stop moving for just
a short interval, to turn back the clock to two-thirty, or
better still, go back to yesterday or the day before when
he'd kissed her?

"Burke?"

Was there ever a more remarkable name?

He didn't respond, though he stood less than ten feet
from her where she sat on their bench. And she didn't
want him to respond, for she'd simply breathed his name,
as though to test it against the man himself, the face, the
form, the name all conspiring against her these past
weeks, forcing her to view her entire life before now as
something fraudulent and bankrupt.

Her little pleasures no longer brought her pleasure
unless they involved him, and the hours away from him
were ordeals to be endured, and the hands on the rosewood clock in her bedchamber were frequently her most
deadly enemies, refusing to move except at a snail's pace.
Then at last it would be two o'clock and she could legitimately leave the house, with two albatrosses about her
neck named Jason and Doris. But no matter. She always
shed them quickly enough.

Then freedom, and the brief canter to the intersecting
paths where he was waiting for her, his horse already secured, where without words he would lead her down into
their garden and they would find themselves alone, and
he would turn sideways on the bench and kiss her hand
and she would brush back a strand of loose hair from his
forehead and allow her fingertips to linger on his flesh and
try as best she could to deal with the immense love she felt
for him.

She shivered in the cool of early dusk and spoke his
name aloud this time, in need of his warmth and closeness, and was not all prepared for the sight of his face,
like a beacon in the night as he looked back, perceived
her need and sat close beside her, his arm about her shoulders, his hand stroking her hair.

"It's late," he whispered. "The chill is bad for you."

"Separation from you is worse."

Then she was in his arms, that miraculous face oblit-

erating her view of all else. But it didn't matter. Nothing
mattered but his closeness, his lips, his hand pressing
gently on the small of her back, a feeling so glorious that
she was trembling, not from cold but from the sheer need
to record every detail against the day when she would
have to rely on memory alone.

At the end of the kiss he continued to hold her, her face
nestled sideways against his shoulder, the rough texture of
his jacket a pleasant sensation against her cheek.

"It *is* late," he reminded her, his voice close to her ear.

"I know," she murmured, bewildered by how complete
she felt with his arms about her, how bereft without them.
"Then what are we to do?" she asked, bringing his face
into focus, regretfully reminding him of the dilemma
which had plunged them into this prolonged silence and
which had kept them dangerously later than usual in the
park.

"We'll talk tomorrow," he said, lightly tracing her lips
with his fingers. "Perhaps winter will be kind and come
later than usual."

"Not likely."

Here, then, was the outline of their distress. With the
coming of winter this natural chamber would no longer be
conducive to their meetings. Yet where would they go?

When he drew her close again, as though he, too, felt
the need to fortify himself against the coming separation,
she whispered, "Oh, my darling," and felt their dilemma
like an intolerable burden.

He held her only a moment, then stood up, as though in
anger, but in truth his voice sounded more like a cry for
relief. "Then I'll simply announce myself, formally, to
Elizabeth," he said. "It's her house. Surely she controls
who calls, and will not object."

"No," she said, going to his side, "you mustn't do that."

"Why?"

"Why!" she repeated, amazed at his momentary lack
of prudence. "You were there," she whispered, her voice
falling low, as though fearful that there were listening ears
close by. "You saw my cousin at Eden and know him to
be a man capable of—"

"If Elizabeth permits me entry, I don't see how—"

Slowly she shook her head, aware that not only did he
not see but neither did he understand that unique bond
which existed between John and Elizabeth, a bond that

had been temporarily weakened by the last few weeks but
which, as far as Mary could determine, was still strong
and intact.

In an attempt to gain a moment's respite for herself,
the better to explain, she turned away and walked a short
distance to the edge of the path. The shadows of dusk
had turned the fringes of the park to solid black, a mass
of undefined lines and shapes in which effortlessly she
found the contour of what appeared to be a human shoulder.

Shivering with cold and apprehension, she scolded
her imagination. "They are very close," she faltered, dragging her attention back to the matter at hand. "Elizabeth
does nothing without John's knowledge and approval."

"Why?" he demanded. "She seems very fond of you.
You said yourself that she was the one who allowed you to
go to Jeremy Sims'."

"When John was out of the city."

"Won't he be returning to Eden again soon?"

"Not soon. There are other matters which are pressing
against him now."

He gazed down on her with new intensity, as though at
last she had said something that he had understood.
"What—matters?" he asked.

Drawing strength from his closeness, she said, "That
newspaper article I told you about, weeks ago, written
by someone who had visited Eden—"

She had thought to say more, but she was not given that
chance, for abruptly he walked a few steps in the opposite
direction.

"Burke?" she called after him, and either the sound of
her voice or the pleading in her tone brought him back to
her where within the instant he drew her close.

She lifted her arms about his neck and secured the
closeness and heard him whispering her name over and
over again in her ear. At some point the pleasant lassitude
changed. As a low painful throb erupted in the pit of her
stomach, she lifted her face to him and saw a similar need
in his eyes and with a force which at first alarmed her, she
met his lips, though the kiss was quite different this time,
his mouth forcing hers open, his tongue probing deep inside, his arms tightening about her as though he wanted to
draw her into him.

"I—will—see—you," he vowed, a curious tone of anger in his voice.

"And there is nothing for me but these hours only."

Then how was it to be accomplished? How could she willingly remove her hands from the back of his neck where beneath his soft dark hair she'd discovered the fascinating canal of his upper spine and, by the simple act of moving her hand forward, she had discovered his ear, her fingertips tracing its outline. And there were so many other rich discoveries as well, the taste of his flesh along the line of his jaw, the pleasantly scented skin of his neck, the manner in which his hands had moved down her back and were now pressed against her hips.

It was commencing again, stronger than before, sensations which could not be ignored, a mutual need so acute that she found herself cursing the barriers of their garments and, as his head went down to her breast, she lifted her eyes to the darkening sky and was conscious of a silent thankfulness.

She was loved! An extraordinary man had found something in her to love!

The strips of light overhead narrowed. Suddenly she heard something, a rustle in the underbrush nearby. As the embrace ended, both stared at the spot where the disturbance had occurred.

"What—" she whispered, and discovered that she lacked the breath to continue.

Without a word, motioning for her to keep silent, he took two steps in the direction of the thick bushes.

As Mary waited she tried to quiet the acceleration of her heart.

"Nothing," Burke said at last, returning to her, though glancing over his shoulder. "An animal; perhaps a rabbit—"

She saw him then look up at the fading light and pronounce those most dreaded words. "You must go," he said. "You're very late."

"I'll tell them—something," she whispered, retrieving her hat from the bench, smoothing one hand over her breast, which was still alive with the sensation of his lips.

He appeared to be watching her, concern in his voice and manner. "Come," he urged. "I'll walk back with you as far as I can and see you safely to your carriage."

"But they might—"

"It's too dark. I can keep to the concealment of the trees. Tell them a stirrup broke—"

"Yes, something. I'll think of something—"

"We've stayed too late—"

"Too late—"

"If there's trouble—"

"There won't be. I can handle Doris—"

"If it rains tomorrow—"

"It won't rain—"

"There's a small shelter not far from here—"

"But we'll meet here first, as always—"

"Yes—"

Only in that abrupt silence did she realize how frantically they had been talking. She adjusted her hat in order to give at least the appearance of normalcy while he untied their horses and withdrew a small penknife from his waistcoat pocket and slashed the leather stirrup strap.

At last they were ready, and all that remained was the walk across the park and their imminent separation.

Without daring to look up at him, almost afraid of the beauty of his face, she walked a few steps ahead, picking her way carefully up the narrow path. As they emerged into the clearing of the park she was amazed to see the darkness complete and thought what a fearful place it would be without him and thought of the disturbance in the bushes and wondered if it had been an animal.

It was while she was sorting through these thoughts that she heard his voice. "You are aware," he said quietly, "that I love you."

What simple words, and so simply delivered! As they closed about her, she shut her eyes against the unexpected embarrassment of tears. How often in the past she had wondered if she would ever hear those words from any man. Now to have heard them from this man. . . .

He came up alongside her, apparently concerned by her lack of response. "And I you," she whispered and suffered a peculiar lightheadedness as though her system, unaccustomed to such joy, did not know how to deal with it.

They walked for as long as it was safe, neither feeling the need for words. As the edge of the park came into sight, she looked ahead and saw only two carriages waiting, hers and his.

"You go ahead," he said. "I'll wait here. And tell your

driver of the broken stirrup so he can report it to the stablemaster."

She nodded to everything and, in defense against the empty hours when she would be forced to sit her bed-chamber and conjure up those beloved features through the sheer force of her memory, she stepped toward him and traced with her fingertips the outline of his jaw.

"My dearest," he whispered and grasped her hand and pressed it, palm opened, to his lips. Then he relinquished her reins, placed them securely in her hands and, with a nod, urged her to go ahead without him.

Summoning strength she did not even know she had, she increased her pace and, with an act of discipline, put together the fragments of the old Mary, laughing, frivolous, whom Doris and Jason could recognize immediately.

"A minor accident, Jason," she called out, resisting the temptation to look back just one more time. "No damage, though I'm afraid it's made me quite late and I do apologize."

Whoever that giddy young woman was spouting all those lies, she had no idea. There was not one tone or inflection of her voice that she recognized. Yet she was moving inside her skin, so there must be a kinship somewhere and, as she approached Jason, she was relieved and pleased to see his face as expressionless as ever. She pointed out the broken stirrup and explained in what she hoped was a coherent manner how the day had been so beautiful. . . .

Dear God, so beautiful. . . .

Suddenly it occurred to her that someone was missing. "Where's Doris?"

"Waiting inside the carriage, milady. The chill was increasing and she only brought a light shawl."

As Jason held the door for her, Mary looked up into the carriage and saw the old maid seated in the far corner, her face turned away. Well, there was work to be done here. As Jason secured the door behind her, Mary sat uneasily on the edge of the seat and tried to determine the best approach.

Unfortunately in the quiet interim she dared to glance back at the line of trees about one hundred yards removed. And, though she saw nothing, she saw everything and knew that he was still waiting in the confinement of the shadows.

"Doris?" she commenced, realizing that eye contact was necessary for a truly effective apology.

But the woman would not look at her and, baffled by this reaction and suddenly lacking the energy to pursue it further, she repeated the tale that she had told Jason and at the conclusion was rewarded with one simple sentence.

"Well, you're safe and that's all that matters."

That was that, although she suspected the scolding would come later with Elizabeth, and perhaps even John, more than making up for Doris' strange silence.

She would have to deal with it as best she could. For now she was grateful for the silence in the carriage that permitted her to lean back against the cushions and relive certain sensations. Paradoxically how strong she felt *and* how vulnerable. How well *and* weak!

But tomorrow *would* come. She would see him again and feel his arms about her, and together somehow they could plot a future.

In that faith she would survive. . . .

Although he had first glimpsed the horror over three-quarters of an hour ago, only now did he begin to feel the reverberations, that deadly combination of shock and betrayal, a sensation which curiously started in the calves of his legs, painful muscle spasms that seemed to move steadily upward, like a marauding army, crushing his chest, closing off the air in his lungs, forcing him to shout, "Wait! Stop here! Let me out!"

As his driver drew the horses sharply up on the pavement, John pushed open the door with such force that he heard the hinges break and he walked steadily, as though he himself were on the verge of breaking, across Westminster Bridge, stopping at midcenter, perspiration on his forehead, his mind as swirling as the waters below.

Aware of the seriousness of his disintegration, he shut his eyes and clung to the railing and tried to draw breath. But he could not think clearly, and suffered anew a distorted image of what he had seen earlier in that darkened garden—the whore herself, the eternal female, deceiving, corrupting. . . .

He bent over until his forehead was pressed against the railing, the cold metal gouging his flesh, supplying him with minor relief.

"Mated," he mumbled aloud. Of course they had mated. The last image he had seen before he had fled his concealment had been the man's hand pressing against her, and she responding as wantonly as though—

He raised up and braced his arms against the railing. Vaguely, as though it were coming from another world, he was aware of late-evening traffic on the bridge behind him, a few pedestrians passing him by, their voices falling quiet as though they sensed distress, then their steps quickening, as though they wanted to remove themselves from it.

Oh, dear God, perhaps I didn't see it! Had it been a dream, a familiar nightmare? For he had seen the man before, the entire hideous episode at Eden re-created in variation, for now apparently the closeness of a waltz no longer sufficed. Now, through deception, they had progressed to—

"Mated," he whispered. Of course they had mated. . . .

God, how dark it was—as though fate intended him to see nothing except what had transpired in that garden. He was aware of a trembling in his shoulders, and turned up his collar against the chill and tried to deal with the loss—of everything, his fondest hopes and dreams, the devastating loss of that last temple of purity in his life. Where could he cast his eyes now when he was in desperate need of innocence, something, one thing in his world untrammeled, uncorrupted?

Again he reached for the support of the railing. A thought more unbearable than all the others entered his mind. Was this the first, or had there been others? Under Elizabeth's lax guidance had she long ago sacrificed her virginity and in truth for months, years, had he been deceiving himself?

Whore!

Looking up toward the end of the bridge, he saw his carriage, the driver waiting beside it. All deaths must be dealt with, arrangements made for the disposal of the body, the charade played out to the end. He would find no solution in the middle of the bridge, and circumstances demanded a solution.

As for the man, he could be dealt with in any number of ways. The more difficult corpse was Mary. He wanted never again to be in her presence.

Then it was a simple matter: a corpse implied the need

for a tomb or grave. Decomposing flesh was an ugly sight, and it must take place away from the eyes of decent men.

What he was looking for was a tomb for a living corpse, a place of confinement where the killer of the dream could contemplate her actions and be removed from decent society.

Stunned by the immensity of his hate, he realized curiously that he could not distinguish Mary's face from Lila's, or Lila's from Harriet's, Harriet's from Elizabeth's. The enemy was simply one monstrous female with painted lips and spread legs, luring all men to their destruction.

He remained there a while longer on the bridge, staring at the rushing water below, a prey to those growing images. Punishment was due of the most severe kind. She must be brought down first, then entombed. As for the man, her absence would be sufficient punishment. In the last moments of his agony, John realized that he did not blame him as much as he blamed her. Nothing could have transpired between them without her consent, her flirtations, as John had seen her flirting the night of the ball at Eden, without shame, without modesty or fear—

Fear—

There was something in that word that caught his attention and held it. If she could be terrified, if terror could bring her down, then perhaps she would march willingly to her own tomb, thus sparing him the role of villain.

Fear—

There was the key, a degree of fear which would render her useless, some isolated terror which would leave her forever distrusting and contrite.

The conception was only half-formed. But even in this state it brought him the first relief he had known for over an hour. He needed time to think, to plot. . . .

Thus resolved, though lacking a specific course of action, he commenced walking back across the bridge. With a strict sense of discipline, he ordered his mind to stay away from the offensive image of their embrace. The irritant there was the whore herself. Then he would begin the grim inventory a few moments before that when the impulse to kill had driven him out of his place of concealment. Then what had he done? He'd run across the darkened path and had approached Jason with perfect control, had informed him that he had located Lady

Mary, who would return shortly, and further, he had asked Jason to say nothing to her of their search or worry. With what kindness he had asked it, implying that he did not choose to play the role of spying cousin.

Jason had knowingly agreed, as had Doris, both of them viewing him with new respect.

He looked up, amazed to see his carriage less than ten feet ahead, his driver staring at him in concern.

"Are you well, sir?"

"Not well," John replied honestly, accepting the man's assistance as he crawled up into the carriage. "Take me home, please," he added and closed his eyes, still trying to defend himself against a world filled with deceivers and liars.

"Shall I fetch your physician, sir?"

"No, I don't need a physician!" John snapped.

As the carriage accelerated, he bent over in the seat, astonished at how much it hurt, Mary's death. For the rest of the ride to the empty mansion in Belgrave Square he felt his mind going blessedly silent, as though at last it had worn itself out and needed an interval of rest.

A short time later as the carriage stopped before the darkened mansion, he called out to the driver, "Fetch Alex Aldwell."

Why Alex Aldwell? Because he would do John's bidding in all matters without question.

What was his bidding in this matter?

He didn't know yet, but he would soon, before this night was over.

At the top of the steps he rang the bell and waited and saw the glimmer of a lamp through the cut-glass panels. One of his stewards opened the door, still struggling into his jacket.

"Mr. Eden?" he stammered. "We—weren't expecting—"

"I shall require nothing," John said, striding past the gaping steward, climbing the stairs, heading toward the seclusion of his fourth-floor chambers. As he turned the first landing, he heard the carriage rattling away from the pavement.

By his own estimate he had approximately an hour to collect his thoughts, banish the hurt and plot a course. It could be done. In a way, the death of this last dream was a comfort, the world at last a consistent place.

Breathless from the climb up he stopped before his chamber door and contemplated the darkness on all sides. How black it was.

"A lamp, sir. I'll bring you one right away," came the voice of the steward on the stairs below him.

"I don't want a lamp!" John shouted down and closed the door behind him and took comfort in the blackness, even though it was not black enough.

He could still see her, clinging to the man, her hands clawing, a creature bereft of shame and pride. Whore, slut, liar, deceiver. . . .

He walked across the darkened room, knowing the terrain by heart, feeling his desk, then the security of his chair.

Carefully he sat, folded his hands on the desk and waited for inspiration, confident that it would come.

Gawd, what a topsy-turvy evening this has been! Alex thought as he climbed awkwardly out of John's carriage, ignoring his empty belly, and looked up at the darkened mansion.

There he had been, just settling down in Elizabeth's dining room to the most glorious steak and kidney pie, when Elizabeth had announced that they'd best not wait for John any longer, lest the crust turn moist and cold.

He started wearily up the stairs to the darkened front door, his mind moving in two directions, behind to the carriage just rattling away from the pavement and ahead to the darkened stoop, the entire house dark, for that matter, yet the old driver had assured him that John was waiting for him inside.

What was in the wind now? And what would be required of him beyond what he was already doing— which was just about everything, overseeing nine building sites and all those accompanying problems, though in the course of the last few weeks he'd managed to solve a few of the more troubling ones, like the petty thievery which now had ceased as mysteriously as it had started?

Mysterious, my ass! He grinned as he rang the bell and waited, proud of his brainstorm to set thieves to catch thieves. What an effective job his disreputable quartet had done, all four ex-convicts bearing the signature of Newgate on their backs, awesome-looking creatures hired by

Alex to keep a sharp eye out in the workyards, find the culprit and serve as judge, jury and executioner.

The culprit had been one Jack Dalkins, a trusted foreman, or so Alex had thought.

Not that Alex wholly approved of their tactics, for Jack Dalkins had not yet returned to work from his stay in hospital with a broken head, two broken arms and a crushed foot. Still, Alex's first and only loyalty had been to John, and he'd not intended to stand idly by while some bastard stole him blind.

Cursing the growling in his empty belly, he rang the bell again. Where was everyone? "Open up!" he shouted, seeing a light through the panels. He heard the bolt slide, the door swung open and he saw one of John's stewards, coatless, a dinner napkin stuck into his belt. *Lucky bastard*, Alex brooded. Seeing that the man would not give him passage until he'd identified himself, Alex snapped, "It's me, Aldwell, you idiot! Mr. Eden sent for me."

"I beg your pardon, sir," the man muttered, stepping back.

"In his chambers, is he?" Alex asked, striding past the steward and glancing up the darkened stairway, dreading the climb.

"He is indeed, sir."

Suffering a slight anger which affected his breathing and made the climb more difficult, it was several minutes before Alex gained the top landing, where he stopped to wait out a stitch in his side. He lifted the lamp toward the closed door and called ahead, "John, are you there?"

He waited, head down, listening. He started to call again, but with a wisdom based on his long association with John Murrey Eden he opened the door and saw nothing but more darkness.

"John?"

"Come in and shut the door."

There he was at his desk, at least a recognizable outline with shoulders and head, though the voice sounded different.

Closing the door, Alex tried to understand the nature of this peculiar meeting. "We waited dinner on you, we did, John," he said pleasantly, starting across the room toward the desk.

"Hold your position!" the voice commanded. "Come

no closer. If you require light, place the lamp on the table
and take a seat."

If you require light?

A curious statement, as baffling as the voice itself, as
though Alex were the enemy. Still he obeyed, retraced his
steps to the sofa, collided with a low stool, placed the lamp
on the appointed spot and sat with growing uneasiness.

"I'm sorry I had to disturb you at this hour," John began softly, the old John, his voice filled with concern.

"You didn't disturb me," Alex lied. "In fact, I'd been
waiting all afternoon to see you. Last week Andrew gave
me several new freehold leases that require your signature."

"Why didn't Andrew deliver them himself?"

The voice had gone cold again. Not wishing to enter
into the complexities of this disintegrating relationship,
Alex murmured, "He's been kept busy elsewhere. He
thought I'd see you first—"

"—elsewhere," came an echo, and, thinking that John
might say more, Alex waited. But nothing more was said.

"I'll—bring them around tomorrow, if I may," Alex
went on, his voice sounding loud in the quiet room.

Matter closed. From where Alex sat, the figure behind the desk resembled a statue, his hands rigidly folded
on the desk before him.

"John, we can discuss all this tomorrow."

"Go on," the voice commanded. "Tell me everything
that's been going on. I've been removed from it for too
long. Tell me of the progress on the various building sites."

Ah, that was encouraging, the first interest he'd shown
in his own firm for several long weeks. Having been issued
the invitation to speak, and in spite of the circumstances,
Alex took the floor, pacing in the limited area near the
light, looking up now and then as he spoke in the hope of
provoking a response from the silent man.

But somehow Alex had the disquieting feeling that
John hadn't even heard what he had said. He looked back
toward the desk. "John, why don't we just—" he began,
and was not given a chance to finish.

"Go on!" came the command. "Talk to me. Tell me
everything."

For the first time Alex heard the tone of alarm. *Talk to
me,* as though the silence had to be filled with words.

He faltered. What would he say now? All those pressing

business matters seemed to have deserted him in the face of this unspoken need. Still he had to try and, as he paced beyond the spill of light, a fitting subject occurred to him —the solved problem of petty thievery which had been plaguing the central workshop.

Warming to the subject, Alex returned to the sofa and began the tale. "On the matter of thievery, John, if you'll recall," he began, and talked steadily for several minutes, listing the missing items and the refusal of the local police inspector to do anything about it, being short-handed and informing Alex that thieves came third after rapists and murderers, thus forcing Alex to take matters into his own hands, which he'd done right enough by hiring a unique set of watchdogs, fresh from Newgate.

Alex grinned. "And they moved with the efficiency of their breed, they did, John, and escorted Jack Dalkins to a secluded spot on the Heath and told him in an unforgettable way that one man did not have the right to take another man's property."

Alex laughed, completely forgetting the silent man behind the desk. "Course old Jack Dalkins will never be quite the same," he concluded, "but we'll hire him on when he leaves the hospital and find light work for him, and in the meantime, the thievery has stopped."

At last he looked toward the desk, hoping for a shared laugh, some indication that there was life at that end of the room. But from where he stood he saw nothing but the outline of shoulders and clasped hands and, fearing that he'd overstepped his bounds, that John did not approve of such methods, he grew defensive. "Well, the problem was real and growing, it was, the thievery adding up. As for Jack Dalkins—"

"What did they do to him?"

Grateful for the direct question, Alex replied, "Taught him a lesson, that's what. Oh, there's a few broken bones which will heal right enough and when he comes back he'll be a better mate for it, I can promise you that."

All at once he saw movement behind the desk, a stirring, the shadowy outline standing erect, his arms braced against the desk. In the next instant John turned away and disappeared into the deeper shadows at the far end of the room.

Alex gaped into the blackness, which seemed to have

swallowed John whole. He waited, listening, worried that he had offended with his rough tactics.

"I had no choice, John," he called out. "You were occupied elsewhere, and I didn't think you'd appreciate a debit inventory sheet for the last three months."

"Tell me—again," came the voice from the darkness.

"Tell you—what?"

"Everything."

Alex sat wearily on the back of the sofa. "I said it all the first time. I don't see—"

"Tell me again!"

There was something heavy in the voice which suggested that Alex had better do as he had been commanded to do. Still seated on the back of the sofa, he launched into a repetition of the tale. A few minutes later he brought the tale to its identical conclusion. "Dalkins will survive," he repeated. "I warned the watchdogs to do no lasting damage, and he'll be a better man."

There! He'd said it all twice and still could not understand why he was here. If John wanted to lecture him, he'd best do it quick, for it was Alex's intention to be seated at Childe's within the next quarter of an hour, soothing his bewilderment in a quarter hind-section of good English beef and a bottomless bottle of port.

Still silence. What in the name of God was going on?

"John, I—"

"What are their names?"

"What are—"

"—the names, Alex, of your—watchdogs."

Names! Good Gawd! Is John going to place blame on them? "Call them what you wish," Alex muttered. "They'll answer to anything."

"I want their names," came the voice from the shadows.

"And I don't know them!" Alex shouted, his anger lifting him to his feet, where he stood foolishly confronting blackness.

Slowly a form evolved out of the shadows, returning to the desk. "What—did you pay them?"

"Enough to ensure their loyalty and continued service," Alex replied. "They enjoy working on this side of the law for a change."

"Where are they now?"

Alex laughed. "Probably cutting some poor bloke's throat for the cost of a pint."

"You don't know?"

Alex shrugged. "I told them they could use the old barracks down by the river. It seemed to suit them well enough, the first reliable roof with the exception of Newgate which they've had over their heads since lads."

"Then you do know where they are?"

"I suppose."

"Fetch them!"

"Fetch—"

Uncertain whether or not John was joking, Alex laughed. "I don't think you'd find them suitable—"

"I said, *'Fetch them!'* "

There it was again, that heavy dragging in his voice, as though someone were speaking behind John, or through him. Unable to believe the command, Alex offered a protest. "I'm accountable for them, John. If you object to their actions, then deal with me. They only did what I ordered them to do."

"I'm not questioning either your command or your authority. I simply want you to fetch them."

Relieved that there was no blame to be placed, Alex stepped closer to the desk. "If you need—help, John—"

Then rage exploded out of the darkness, the same fury that he'd overheard coming from Elizabeth's drawing room for the last several weeks, mindless anger which seemed determined to hit every target in sight, whether it was guilty or innocent. "I need no help, Alex—I need loyalty, and if you won't do my bidding, then I'll get someone who will!"

Alex retreated. "You could search the world over, John, and not find a more loyal friend than Alex Aldwell."

Moved by his own avowal, he was not prepared for the command which came in mindless repetition from behind the desk. "Then fetch them for me and prove your loyalty."

"What shall I tell them?"

"The truth—that Mr. Eden wishes to see them and that he will make it worth their time."

As his mind turned under the mystery of the baffling assignment, Alex walked slowly to the door, determining what he had momentarily forgotten—that the man seated

behind the desk operated within his own framework of
logic.

He was halfway out the door when he heard John's
voice again, as considerate as he'd heard it throughout
this baffling meeting. "Take the lamp, Alex. I wouldn't
want you to stumble on the stairs. I have no need
of light."

Wearily Alex turned back and retrieved the lamp. "I'll
return as soon as I can," he said.

He closed the door behind him and hurried down the
stairs, thinking curiously of a wounded animal, the manner in which it will crawl off into a dark place to lick its
wounds or to die. . . .

It was approaching four A.M. when Alex returned to
the house in Belgrave Square in a hired carriage with his
questionable cargo. There were only three of them; the
fourth had been too drunk to come.

With a handkerchief pressed against his nose in defense against their odor, he tried not to look at their hard
faces, the three of them blending into a nondescript gray
form across from him, their matted and snarled hair
forming jagged outlines about their heads, like an infinite
number of serpents twisting in the movement of the carriage.

Formidable in appearance, with square-built bodies
and massive heads, they stared back at him with curiously
calm faces, the unspoken arrogance of men who lived by
their own rules and who feared nothing.

As the carriage turned into Belgrave Square, Alex said,
"Follow me and do as I say."

"Right, guv," one said, grinning.

Alex told the driver to wait and saw the three gaping
upward at the impressive façade of the mansion, and regretted that this mysterious meeting was taking place
here. Determined to see the thing through as quickly as
possible, he led the way up the stairs, hoping that the
servant had not slid the bolt.

With relief he felt the door give and entered as stealthily as a thief, aware of the three behind him entering this
grand place as arrogantly as though they belonged here.

Suddenly his head felt hollow as his belly and he caught
a peculiar glimpse of himself, as though he were standing

outside himself, bringing two forces together, the result of which caused him to shudder.

Too late now and, without words, he motioned for the three to follow after him, though at the last minute decided it would be safer to follow behind *them,* and with a jerk of his head urged them forward with whispered instructions, "To the top."

As he passed the first-floor landing he retrieved the lamp, hearing nothing except his own labored breathing and the three ahead of him, one with a death rattle in his throat, the other two gazing back at him with bloodshot eyes.

Oh Gawd, what am I doing? Lacking an answer, he knocked on the door, then pushed it open to find the room unchanged with the exception of a single burned-down candle on the desk at the end of the room.

"Wait!" John called out and extinguished the small flame, plunging the room into its customary darkness, but not before Alex had glimpsed what appeared to be several envelopes in John's hands.

"Did you find them?" John asked.

"I did. Three of them, at any rate. The fourth was too drunk to stand."

"Where are they?"

Without speaking, Alex motioned with the lamp that they were just beyond the door.

"Leave them there and close the door."

"I don't think that's wise, John."

"Then bring them in."

Alex pushed the door wide and motioned the three to enter. As guardian of the only source of illumination, he waited until they had aligned themselves near the far wall and, for the first time, considered the absence of light a blessing.

"Come forward, Alex. I have one more request."

As obedient as the three creatures who stood dumbly against the wall, Alex moved to the end of the sofa, suffering a painful perception that there were four puppets in the room, three who did not know better, one who did.

"Several months ago," John began, "while we were at Eden, I asked you to launch a discreet investigation of a certain gentleman." He paused. "Do you recall?"

Alex placed the lamp on the table, searching his memory. Shortly after his return from Eden he had set two in-

vestigations into motion at John's request, one concerning
Lord Richard's friend at Cambridge and the other—

"Yes, I recall. The American gentleman, I believe it
was, the one who—"

"Good. And what did you find?"

More difficult, that, though Alex had compiled a file on
the matter. But, of course, he did not have it at his fingertips and said as much, interrupting himself once to look
over his shoulder where he'd heard an impatient rustling.

"I can bring you that information tomorrow," he said.

"I don't want it tomorrow, and all I want now is to
know whether or not you learned the place of his residence."

"Yes. In—Mayfair, if I remember correctly—"

"Could you find it again?"

"Of course, though I don't understand—"

"I'm not asking for your understanding. I'm asking only
for your cooperation. If it's too much, I can easily find
someone else. Perhaps one of these gentlemen—"

Behind him he heard a snicker, one of the "gentlemen"
delighted at Alex's embarrassment.

"What is it you want me to do, John?" Alex asked resignedly.

"Deliver this," John said, placing one of the envelopes
on the edge of the desk. "It must be in his morning post,
that's all I'm asking. Is it too much?"

There was a mocking quality to his voice which Alex
tried not to hear. "Of course not," he muttered and
started toward the desk with the intention of retrieving the
envelope when John stopped him again.

"One more favor, if you will, Alex, and then I'll let you
go."

Let me go? What about the three who—

"Do you know the stables at the end of Rotten Row in
Hyde Park?"

"I—do," Alex stammered.

"Good. Then you are to deliver this to the old stablemaster and give him five pounds to make sure that it is
delivered to the addressee. Is that clear?"

Nothing had been clear all night long.

"Anything—else?" Alex asked, and receiving no answer started toward the desk, amazed to see that now he
was permitted to go the full distance.

"See it done," John said simply, "and I will be forever in your debt."

"No need, though if only I knew—"

"Then you're free to go."

"Free—to—" Alex faltered.

"Leave us," John said. "I have business with these gentlemen."

"No, John," he begged. "Let me stay. You don't know—"

"They won't harm me, Alex," he said. "If harm is done, I suspect I will be the one who inflicts it on them."

From behind he heard approaching footsteps and whirled about to see the three shapeless creatures coming toward him. "This gintleman wants you gone, Maister Aldwell," one said with a grin, his massive, dirt-encrusted hand reaching out.

Alex retrieved the letters and sidestepped the hand, unable to comprehend the forces on either side of the desk, forces which, though totally disparate, seemed perfectly allied. He secured the letters in his pocket and moved in a wide arc around the grinning three and did not look back until he was at the door.

"Good night, Alex," John called.

"I'll wait outside and see them home," Alex offered.

This offer elicited snickers from the three and rising anger from the man behind the desk. "I daresay they require no help in finding their way home, wherever that is," John said. "Now go!"

Alex closed the door behind him, washing his hands of the whole affair. He started cautiously down the stairs, wondering if he would ever know, wondering if he would ever want to know. . . .

Will God forgive me?

He had never forgiven John that offense committed years ago at Eden, and this was nothing compared to that. This was warranted. With John's help, Mary could salvage what was left of her life.

But will God forgive me?

Surely He would, for otherwise, why had He given John the power to manipulate and control? A God's gift to a god, divine intervention on earth.

He sat behind the desk, aware of the three waiting before him. He did not know their names and did not desire to know them. Yet he trusted their instincts and knew that he could ask them to do anything and they would perform it.

"Gentlemen—" he commenced, and waited out their shufflings as they drew near the desk.

When the room was quiet, he said, "I'm in need of a—service. . . ."

If asked, on this high blue September morning, to account for the tidal waves of happiness rushing over him, Burke Stanhope would have answered with one name: Mary.

The word alone was capable of transforming him. Of course, there were incredible obstacles yet ahead of them, and the two most awesome ones were self-made, and that was an irony which was not lost on him. His own behavior at Eden and his subsequent Lord Ripples column had closed the castle gates to him and forced him into the clandestine activity of late afternoons in the sunken gardens of Hyde Park, an idyllic setting during the warm days of summer and early autumn. But shortly, with the imminence of winter, nature would close that chamber as well, and then what would they do?

While he had no direct answer, he had perfect confidence in his ability to find one. His motivation was simple. He could not live or function without her.

Momentarily lost in these painfully pleasing thoughts, he looked up as a grinning Charles placed a platter of turned eggs and sausage before him. At first he was unable to account for the grin and at last looked toward the end of the table, toward the source of another miracle, his mother, who had announced earlier that morning that she wished to breakfast with her son.

Although at first the servants had been skeptical, there she was, seated in her proper place, at least giving the appearance of rationality, though looking closer Burke thought that she looked even more ill now than before, as though she had derived a portion of her physical health from her madness.

"Mother," he said quietly, as though testing the word on the air, and saw her look up from stirring her coffee.

"I'm here, Burke," she said, and in that gentle way confirmed that at least for the time being the veils of her madness had lifted.

Strange how boylike he felt. "I couldn't quite believe it," he commenced, "when Charles told me that you would be down."

She sipped her coffee and leaned back in her chair, one hand playing with the strand of pearls at her throat. "I get weary of that room," she said.

"Eat, Mother," Burke counseled her gently.

Midway through breakfast he saw her place her fork on her plate and lean back in her chair and look up at Charles. "Enough"—she smiled "and please don't nag, Charles. I do nothing, and thus require little food."

"I only nag you, Miss Caroline, for your own good," Charles scolded, doing nothing to mask his pleasure at this proper family tableau.

"My own good," she repeated, looking up as he re-moved her plate. "You're the worst tyrant around, Charles. Far worse even than Jack Stanhope—"

Burke saw the change in her face, the new passivity faltering, the pain of confusion taking its place.

A few moments later he heard her ask, "How long have I been here?"

Here? Does she mean this house, or England? He an-swered both. "In this house about seven years. In England, almost ten."

She looked up, the confusion on her face mounting.

Burke exchanged a glance with Charles. He pushed his own platter away and folded his napkin. "You know very well where we are, Mother, and why we are here."

When she didn't answer, he glanced up and wished that he hadn't. Silent tears were running down her face.

"Your—father, Burke. Is he—?"

"He's in America."

"Doing what?"

Burke paused. The only one who heard from Jack Stanhope now was John Thadeus Delane, and that was no more than once a year, a curt, caretaker letter instructing Delane in certain business affairs.

Glancing up he saw her waiting for an answer. Burke gave her one, though he knew it was a lie. "Rebuilding, Mother, that's what he's doing—trying to put Stanhope Hall back together so he can send for you."

He saw a new expression on her face, as though she'd seen his lie for what it was. As she rose from her chair, Charles hurried to her side, but she waved off his assist-

ance and moved toward the fireplace. "He will never
send for us," she said to the fire.

"We don't know that for certain," he soothed, though
he knew it as well as she. It was apparent that Jack Stanhope could live very well without a wife or a son.

"And it's not that I mind for myself. My life is over.
But you," she added and looked back at him.

"You have no cause to worry about me, Mother," he
said, and considered at that moment telling her about his
new happiness.

But he didn't and, without being able to say how it had
happened, they were standing together before the fire and
she was in his arms, begging him, "Never leave me,
Burke. Promise me now. Never abandon me. I don't think
I could bear it."

As he enclosed her, he shut his eyes to a new anxiety.
Of course she didn't know what she was asking. Wasn't it
perfectly possible for a man to keep the love of a mother
and add the love of a wife?

Wife! For the first time he thought the word and saw a
specific face, specific and beloved features.

"There," he soothed, and postponed any mention of
Mary Eden. There would be time later when his mother
was stronger. For now, their reunion was sweet and the
future would take care of itself.

"Look at me," he urged, holding her at arm's length,
feeling that their roles had been reversed, that she was the
child, he the parent. "Let's plot our morning," he suggested. "What suits your fancy? A walk in the garden?
A game of cards? Tell me what you wish to do and it shall
be done; I swear it."

The pledge seemed to mean a great deal to her. Almost
shyly she looked back at him and proposed, "A carriage
ride, Burke, that would be lovely."

"Of course, I should have thought of it."

"This afternoon," she added, returning his gaze with
level eyes.

Burke faltered, sensing a trap. "Not—this afternoon,
Mother."

"Why?"

"I have an—appointment."

"What kind of appointment?"

"Business."

"What kind of business?"

"There are matters that require my attention."

She stepped closer. "Florence tells me that you have adopted the habit of riding every day in the park."

"That is true."

"You were notoriously bad with horses when you were a boy."

"I'm learning new skills."

"Then let me come and watch. Nothing would give me greater pleasure—"

"No," he cut in. The sacrifice of his private meetings with Mary was more than he was prepared to make. Their hours in the park were limited. They had to arrive upon a course for the future soon, or else—

"Please, Burke," she begged. "How I long for a vista of beauty! I'm not absolutely certain where I've been or when I shall be summoned back, but I would adore to watch you ride."

Even as she spoke, he could chart the changes on her face, and to make matters more difficult, he was aware of Charles moving up on her left, a clear alliance, with Burke cast in the role of villain.

Still he could not oblige her, though at the last minute a logical solution occurred to him. "This morning, Mother," he suggested. "Fetch your shawl. I'll send for the carriage and I'll show you morning vistas so dazzling—"

But all the time he spoke she shook her head. "Not this morning," she said. "I'm afraid I'm not up to it." She grasped Charles' extended hand as though it were the only reliable support in her universe. "Pay no attention to me, Burke." She smiled, the expression of a sturdy soldier. "Certainly I have no intention of intruding where I'm not wanted."

"Mother, please," he said, his voice sharper than he'd intended, caught between his need and hers. "You would not be—intruding."

"Then it's settled?"

"For this morning, yes. I can call for the carriage now."

But she turned away and accepted the full support of Charles' arm and left Burke to accept the full weight of Charles' condemnation. "Then you *have* abandoned me," she said to the floor, seeming to grow weaker with each step.

"I've not abandoned you, Mother," he called after her. "Please come back, and let's—"

But there was no response, and he was left to digest the pathetic sound of their movement to the stairs.

Damn!

He turned back toward the warmth of the fire. Perhaps he had been selfish. Surely Mary would have understood his absence for one day. But how could he have sent word to her? And the thought of her waiting, worried and alone, could not be borne.

No, he would have to make amends to his mother later, and now more than ever it was important that they make other arrangements for meeting. Perhaps his mother would not object if he brought her here, although under what pretext Mary would leave her house he had no idea.

As the obstacles pressed against him, blended now with an uncomfortable weight of guilt, he leaned forward until his forehead was pressing against the mantel, one image providing him with a degree of solace.

Her.

He saw her face, that quality of her soul which had initially attracted him as long ago as Jeremy Sims' Song and Supper Club. Curious how she was capable of both strengthening and weakening him. He looked up at the clock. Scarcely nine-thirty A.M. Centuries to go before two this afternoon. How could he pass the hours?

He heard the bell at the front door, the announcement of the morning post. He held his position, staring down on his mother's chair. How pleased he had been with her new rationality. Yet in a way his life had been simpler when she'd been lost in the maze of madness. If her new clarity of mind meant that from now on he would have to account for all his actions, his every move—

"Master Burke?"

He looked up to see Estelle, one of the Negroes who had agreed to accompany them into exile.

"The post, sir."

"Thank you, Estelle," he said, noticing the single envelope in her hand. Probably a stray bill to be forwarded to their solicitor. "Put it there on the table, if you will."

He'd look at it later. For now his only hope for surviving the hours ahead was to submerge himself in mental activity, one of the several books waiting for him on his desk in the library.

"I said I would attend to it later, Estelle," he said, looking up, surprised to see the woman still at the door.

She appeared to be searching for something in the pockets of her long black skirts. "This, Master Burke, as well," she began, smoothing a second white envelope.

"Put it with the other and I'll see to them both later."

"This one didn't come in the post, sir. It was handed me this morning, early, as I was sweeping the stoop."

Puzzled, Burke stepped back toward the dining table. "By whom?"

"A gentleman, Master Burke. He said it was most urgent that I place it in your hands personal, and for my troubles he gave me this." She reached back into her pocket and withdrew a guinea. "He—asked me questions, Master Burke—"

"What kind of questions?"

The woman shrugged. "Was you in residence here, and was you the gentleman from America, and was you at home at the time? I said yes to everything, and then he handed me this." And she held up the letter. "And he said I was to put it in your hand, personal."

He'd never heard the woman so garrulous. "Then do so, Estelle," he invited, and met her by the door.

As she gave him the letter, he noted his name written in a somewhat aggressive scrawl across the front. He studied it, turned it over and saw nothing on the back but a plain wax seal.

"And here's the other, sir," Estelle added hurriedly, placing both letters in his hand.

Satisfied that she'd done her duty, she left the room, calling back, "We'll clean the table when you're finished in here, Master Burke."

He nodded absentmindedly and took both letters to the window. As though saving the greater mystery for last, he split the seal on the first and discovered John Thadeus Delane's familiar handwriting. The message was short. He'd only recently returned from the Continent to find a barrage of rumors awaiting him concerning the legal actions which John Murrey Eden was planning to take against the *Times*. He would try to sort out rumor from fact and, as soon as he was able to determine the validity of the man's many threats, he would like to have a conference with Burke, possibly within the next two days, time and place of meeting to be determined later. There was a rather melodramatic closing instruction to

"Burn this letter, lest it fall into the wrong hands," thus connecting the two of them.

Burke smiled down on the letter. He suspected that Delane hadn't had so much fun since the *Times* had attacked Victoria for her prolonged mourning of Albert. There was nothing like a good fray to bring color to a journalist's cheeks.

Then on to the mystery of the second letter, and without hesitation he broke the seal, removed the note, and read:

> MY DEAREST,
>
> I will not be able to meet you today nor can I at this time explain why. Trust me and wait until you hear from me again,
>
> MARY EDEN

He stared down at the message, which seemed to dance across the page, the fixed letters turning liquid under the duress of the sun.

I will not be able to meet you today.......

Disappointment as deep as any he'd ever felt moved across him, blending with the mystery of the note itself. Feeling somehow that a connection was to be made between the message and the messenger, he called, "Estelle!"

He heard the kitchen door at the end of the corridor open, heard hurried footsteps and Estelle appeared, wiping her hands on her apron.

Burke held up the letter. "Who did you say delivered this?"

"A gentleman."

"Did he give you his name?"

"No, but I didn't ask for it."

"What did he look like?"

"Oh, he was a big man, Master Burke, but he was polite and never gave me no reason for alarm."

Stymied by her account of the incident, Burke retreated from the door, the letter still in his hand. He reread the simple note several times, as though he'd failed to comprehend its equally simple message.

It just occurred to him that he had never seen Mary's penmanship before and was amazed at the bold, broad strokes which had emanated from such a gentle hand.

But it wasn't her penmanship that interested him,

rather the nature and cause of the disappointing message.

"I hope I done right, Master Burke," Estelle murmured. "If you want me to give over my guinea as well—"

"No, you keep it, Estelle," he said, turning back to the door. "If the gentleman comes again, would you please get his name?"

"I'll ask for it, Master Burke, but I'm not certain he'll give it. He seemed in a hurry."

As the woman talked, Burke's mind commenced to move in a more fearful direction. What if Eden had found out? What if he had badgered a confession out of Mary? What if she had been forced to tell him of their meetings of the last few weeks? What if—

But the thoughts were too alarming, and, fearful for her well-being, Burke was on the verge of calling for his carriage, traveling to Number Seven, St. George Street, and confronting the man directly.

Fortunately, better judgment intervened. Perhaps it was nothing. Perhaps she had other duties that she had to attend to, though since early summer no duty had been pressing enough to keep her from their secret meeting place.

Then what?

Confused and worried and unbearably disappointed, Burke sat in his chair at the head of the table and flattened the note before him, reading it over and over again, hoping to find a clue.

Without warning, the most painful possibility of all occurred to him. Perhaps she was tiring of the arrangement, and tiring of him as well. She *was* young, almost fifteen years younger than he. Perhaps her eye had been caught by one her own age, though he found it difficult to believe.

If there is someone else, why didn't I detect it before now? Wouldn't there have been an indication in her manner and attitude?

"Master Burke, are you well?" Estelle asked.

"Yes," he said, aware that he was giving too much of himself away. "Fetch Charles," he commanded, and refolded Mary's note and slipped it into his pocket.

Even though the note had been put away, he still could see it, that strong penmanship, the block letters written without scroll or flourish. He would never have assigned that penmanship to her. . . .

I will not be able to meet you today. . . . . .

He kept hearing *her* voice speak the words and that made the message even more painful. He'd been so confident that she had returned his affection.

"You asked for me, sir."

He looked up to see Charles in the doorway, his features still bearing the imprint of condemnation.

Too distracted to deal with past offenses, Burke muttered, "Tell my mother that I will be at her disposal this afternoon, all afternoon, if she wishes. We can—"

"That will please her," Charles interrupted.

"See what her wishes are and then inform me."

"Very good, sir," Charles replied. "I think a ride in the open countryside would bring her pleasure. I'll arrange everything. Perhaps a picnic lunch—"

Burke nodded, still struggling with the mystery of Mary's note. Why did it disturb him, the sudden cancellation of a secret meeting?

But there was an ache which seemed to be boring deeper inside him, leaving him sitting at the table, suffering the feeling that without her, life itself were ebbing from him. . . .

Timing was all.

Aware of this, and equally aware that she must give no one a chance to scold her for her tardiness the day before, Mary kept to her chambers all morning, vowing to read thirty straight pages of Mr. Mark Twain's *The Innocents Abroad* without looking up at the clock.

Not that it wasn't an enjoyable book. It was, and doubly important as Burke had given it to her several weeks ago. All things American fascinated her now, the incredible vastness of the country, the numerous tales that Burke told her of the West. She could listen to him talk forever.

Sharply she scolded herself for doing what she had vowed not to do, to think of him, to torture herself with the recall of his face, the sensation of his hands, his lips. . . .

She lay back against her pillow, her incredible happiness pressing against her. She stared at her hand and thought of his, twice the size of this one, lightly covered with fine black hair, capable of enclosing, soothing. . . .

Several moments passed before she was aware of her

own foolishness. Yet try as she did, his memory would not leave her alone, and ultimately she abandoned Mark Twain and tried to relax upon the bed so that she might be fresh and rested later.

But it could not be done. Burke occupied every thought, every impulse, no matter how fleeting. Then dress! If she bathed slowly and took extra pains with her hair, perhaps the hands of the clock would move from one o'clock to two o'clock.

Safe in the delirium of anticipation, confident that in the blessed security of his embrace all problems, all obstacles, would be surmounted, she moved toward her pitcher and bowl, stripped off the dressing gown, plunged the fresh linen into cold water and pressed its coolness against her breasts, as though to temper the fever of her happiness. . . .

The old stablemaster handed Mary the note along with the reins of her horse. At first she thought there had been some mistake, but then she saw her name printed in broad strokes on the envelope and, fearful that Jason, waiting at the stable door, would see the letter and inquire into its nature, she quickly slipped it into the pocket of her riding habit and led her horse forward.

Now well beyond the watchful eye of both Doris and Jason, she guided her horse to one side of Rotten Row beneath a bower of autumn trees and retrieved the note, knowing before she opened it that something had happened.

She tore the envelope and withdrew the single page and read the message at one glance:

DEAREST,
I will be unavoidably delayed today. But wait for me, I beg you, in our appointed place. I have important news.
B. STANHOPE

She read it three times and even turned the page over, thinking there might be something of greater illumination on the back. But there was nothing and, as her horse grazed on the dying grass, she read it yet a fourth time.

I have important news.

There was a cause for hope and, in a moment of loving

inspection, she realized that she had never seen his penmanship before. How broad and strong it was, faltering a bit on the closing letters as though he were trying to write well.

In the cool shade of the trees, she shivered. She needed him now, not hours from now. And what would she do with the abyss of time which gaped before her? He had not said how late he would be. Obviously something had happened. Perhaps his mother had taken a turn for the worse. She was ill. Burke had told her so repeatedly.

Yes, that was it, and a man of Burke's loving consideration would not leave a mother's sickroom. And how else was he to contact her except through the old stablemaster, the one place where he knew she would be alone and thus able to receive his note?

Carefully and with love, as though the letter were the man, she ran the tip of her finger over that bold signature and returned it to its envelope and secured it inside her pocket.

He *would* come. That was the important thing to remember, and she *would* wait for him. That was important as well. The thought of returning to that unhappy house in St. George Street without the healing balm of his love was unthinkable . . .

The crowds had gone.

Mary watched the last of the strollers until, turning to the left, they were lost to sight. The sun was setting behind the ridge to the west and the twilight began to weave shapes in the secluded garden.

By her conservative estimate she'd been waiting over five hours.

"Burke—"

She whispered his name in an attempt to dispel her rising anxiety. How much longer could she wait before Jason came in search of her? True, she'd been late the night before, but then Burke had been with her and she'd taken no notice of how shadowy and isolated the garden was at this time of night.

It was so quiet. Hard to believe that all of London lay just beyond that distant fringe of trees. What would she tell them tonight? Another broken stirrup? Not likely, but perhaps Burke would have a solution.

I have important news.

"Oh, please come," she prayed quietly, wrapping her arms about her in protection against the chill.

For over three-quarters of an hour longer she sat in the gathering shadows listening, watching the small path which led down into the garden.

What was that?

She turned quickly toward the indistinct sounds. In the effort of listening, she was aware of her eyes growing blurred. All were shadows, impossible to distinguish anything. Perhaps it was her imagination.

But it was not her imagination. Around her now, coming from three sides, she was aware of movement, the surrounding bushes rustling as though they had a life of their own.

Suddenly she rose and tried to move away from the animate bushes, and at her first step the sound of gravel crunching beneath her feet made an indistinct noise.

"Burke," she whispered, trying to deal with her rising fear, the sense that she'd waited too long, the certainty that whatever was moving through the bushes—

She commenced backing away from the stone bench, still clinging to the possibility that all was well, that it was only a matter of finding her way out of this place and returning to the path where assistance would be available.

Then, too late, a single form emerged from the bushes, massive, faceless in the shadows, not approaching her yet but inquiring, almost politely, "Mary, is it?"

Out of the turmoil of her terror, a hope flickered. Another message? From Burke. Otherwise, how could he have known her name?

"Yes," she murmured, confirming her identity. Eager to make contact with her love, she stepped toward the specter. "Did he send you?"

Without warning she heard movement behind her too late, heavy boots stepping aggressively across the gravel path, and she'd no more than turned on the noise when she felt herself overpowered, her arms wrenched behind her, a monster with many hands twisting her head to one side, binding her eyes with a heavy, foul-smelling cloth, though the last image her eyes recorded was a fearful one, the specter from the bushes stepping free.

Futilely she struggled. A violent trembling seized her and, mustering all the strength at her command, she issued one single cry, and for her effort felt a knotted

cloth forced into her mouth, the tethered ends bound
tightly around the back of her head, her lips distorted,
her tongue useless.

Thus silenced and blinded, she felt herself being
forced down onto the gravel path, something heavy
pressing against her back, her wrists being tightly bound
over each other. As the rough gravel cut into the side of
her face, she tried to cry out around the gag in
her mouth, but all she heard was her own inarticulate
moaning, and she closed her eyes beneath the blindfold
and felt her heart stop.

Blessedly, she lost consciousness, but less blessedly
she revived too soon. As the awareness of what was
happening pushed back the safe blackness, she realized
that she was lying on her back, her arms twisted and
bound beneath her, though she was no longer lying on
gravel but rather she felt the softness of dirt beneath
her. In an act of discipline she tried to control her terror, at least long enough to determine what was ahead
for her next.

Listening carefully over the thunder of her own heart,
she realized that she heard nothing. Had they gone?

Laboriously she tried to lift herself. But at her first
movement she felt hands on her shoulders, forcing her
back down, and heard as well a guttural laugh.

"The pretty's awake now."

"Then let's do it and get out of here."

"Her hair, we was told, remember."

The voices seemed to come from all around her, flat
coarse voices. Repeatedly she twisted her head, trying
to see. But it was useless, and equally as useless was any
attempt to scream. The sounds of her moans were am-
plified in her ears, her saliva choking her.

"Get on with it," a voice commanded, and then they
were upon her, foul-smelling hands moving about her
head, loosening her hair, one hand lifting her to an
upright position with a painful jerk of her hair.

Inside her head a woman was screaming, begging
them to release her. She could hear it so clearly. Why
couldn't they?

Then she heard a new sound, metal teeth biting together, her head jerked first one way then the other,
growing lighter, the sharpness of a cutting edge once
nicking her ear.

Held rigid by the grasp of a single hand on her throat, she had no choice but to endure everything.

God help me! the voice inside her head was whimpering as they continued to jerk her head, the iron blades eating closer and closer to her scalp.

Mother—

Then they were lowering her again to the dirt, where she felt the customary cushion of hair gone, the coolness of dirt against her ear.

They seemed to retreat and she heard their voices in muttering dispute a short distance away and tried to hear what they were saying. But the listening part of her was dying; even the voice inside her head was silenced. No longer whispering or praying or entreating, it was merely sobbing at how ugly the world had become, and how terrifying.

The voices returned and stood over her.

"No marks, Mr. Eden said—"

"No marks'll show—"

"She's fair—"

"Better than whores—"

"Then be quick—"

"And we all git a turn—"

As hands commenced pulling back the layers of her garments, as she felt the coolness of dirt beneath her bare legs, as a head with grizzled beard and whiskers lowered itself over her, as something of indiscriminate size and force wedged itself between her legs, as the double pressure on her body crushed her arms bound beneath her, she calmly gathered the few remaining fragments of her soul and took them to a deeper level. In the last moments of consciousness she was aware only of the rhythmic rocking motions of her body, the fire burning deeper inside her, the awareness of what was happening rendering her brain useless.

Her last clear image was of a little girl with long hair running across the headlands of Eden, gathering wild flowers.

With strict instructions, she ordered her soul to stay with the child in that bright and safe world. . . .

In her first moment of privacy in the tragic bedchamber, Elizabeth sank to her knees beside Mary's bed and felt all life forces deserting her.

Morley Johnson. . . .

The name came like the assault itself, without warning, reminding her of her own ordeal of rape years ago. Had she ever truly recovered from it?

"Oh, Mary," she mourned, unable to look on the still face, though the only visible marks besides her butchered hair were two small rope burns on her wrists, suggesting more than one assailant, more than one assault.

In her grief, Elizabeth saw herself as she had been a scant two hours ago, beside herself with worry as the clock had devoured the minutes, then the hours. But not until the chime of ten had she taken matters into her own hands, had affixed her bonnet and started down the darkened stoop alone, prepared to flag a hired chaise in Jason's absence, to journey to Hyde Park alone and not to return until she'd found the lot of them and most of all, thoughtless Mary, for she'd still been angry with her then.

How disastrous, that postponement of time! If only she had launched her search at eight o'clock or, better, seven, when Charlie Bradlaugh had offered to go for her. But no, she'd permitted Charlie to leave and had sat alone for three more hours, the very interval no doubt when Mary had been enduring—

But the thought could not be borne, and almost angrily she pushed away from the side of the bed and took her grief to the darkness near the window where below on the pavement she saw Jason, still trying to answer the questions of the police inspector, three bobbies standing at attention, as though guarding the house.

As she wiped away her tears, fresh ones took their place and, aware that she must regain her composure, that as the alarm spread she would be forced to answer questions from the police inspector, from the physician, if he ever arrived, and ultimately from John himself, she sat stiffly in a near chair, withdrew her handkerchief and held it flat against her face.

From behind this barrier, with the bed blocked from her view, she forced her thoughts back to a scant hour ago, to that moment when she'd just descended to the pavement and, hearing the rattle of a carriage and thinking it might be a hired chaise, had lifted her arm in an attempt to catch the driver's attention, and had seen and recognized Jason and had felt a surge of relief.

It had only been on second glance that she'd seen the look of disaster on his face, one policeman riding on the high seat with him, another opening the carriage door even before Jason had brought it to a halt, running alongside for a few steps, then reaching back and assisting an hysterical Doris to the pavement.

Elizabeth recalled thinking, *Something has happened to poor Doris.* It was not until a moment later that Elizabeth had looked back toward the carriage and had seen a policeman emerge awkwardly with a lifeless form in his arms, a familiar figure with the exception of the head, which resembled a young boy more than—

Breathless with the horror of memory, she stood and stumbled over something on the floor, the ripped and soiled garments which she had stripped from Mary, a foul odor still emanating from them. She kicked at them, then lifted them gingerly and carried them to a seldom-used cabinet behind the screen at the end of the room. There she stuffed them as far back in the darkness as she could. Later, when there was more time, she would personally burn them.

She closed the low storage cupboard and raised up, thinking she'd heard something from the bed. But it was nothing. Mary still was unconscious, her hair damp where Elizabeth had tried to wash it, the horribly butchered ends plastered softly against her skull, her head turned to one side.

What in the name of God is taking the physician so long?

She'd sent one of the policemen to fetch him and she'd sent another for John. It was approaching midnight, the traffic of the city eased. They both should have returned by now.

In growing alarm at the still face on the pillow, Elizabeth wiped away what she hoped was the last of her tears and thought how mysteriously empty her house had been on this night—Lord Harrington still not returned from his day with Mr. Parnell, Andrew and Dhari among the missing as well, Doris finally released to weep herself dry in the privacy of her rooms below stairs, everyone missing or absent, as though they had sensed impending tragedy and had wanted no part of it.

Tenderly she caressed Mary's forehead, baffled by the specific mutilation of her butchered hair, as though

someone knew that rape would not show except on the
soul and there must be something visible.

"Mary?" Elizabeth called softly, hoping to revive her,
praying that she would remember enough, though not
too much, the faces, a name, though not sensations.

Appalled at the incoherency of her thoughts, Elizabeth gathered her in her arms and held her close, as
though to cancel everything that had happened.

But sense and logic intervened and informed her that
she could cancel nothing, that Mary must bear her own
weight of memory, as Elizabeth had, and that if there
was a God in heaven, there also was a demon in hell,
standing watch over one particularly fiery furnace that
was held in reserve for beasts who walked about dis-
guised as men.

Slowly Elizabeth lowered her back to the pillow, thinking that she had heard voices in the entrance hall downstairs. She hurried to the door and looked down to see
the police inspector still questioning Jason, poor Jason,
who had had the misfortune to find her, in a small dirt
clearing beyond the sunken garden.

From Elizabeth's position at the top of the stairs, she
could only see their boots, one seated, the other hovering close. It had been Doris' testimony that the West
Indian driver had been with her, Doris, all evening that
had prevented the police inspector from accusing him.

Over the monotone of the police inspector's voice, she
heard the door open, people coming and going willy-
nilly in Doris' absence. Trying by a sheer act of discipline to rise above the chaos, she peered downward
and saw a strange set of highly polished black boots.

"Who is it, please?" she called down, her voice sounding
repellent, like a curious old woman.

The ruddy face of the police inspector came into
view. "It's the doctor, madam," the inspector called up.
"Shall I—"

"Yes, right away, please," Elizabeth interrupted, still
puzzled by the boots. She'd been expecting her customary physician, a kindly Father Christmas gentleman named
Tidwell, who'd looked after her household for over a
decade, a lovable old-fashioned man who on numerous
occasions had sat socially at her table.

But those boots did not belong to George Tidwell, nor

did the hem of that dark velvet cloak, nor those slender pegtop trousers, nor—

He was at midstep, and Elizabeth found herself looking down into the face of a man she'd never seen before, a new doctor's valise of leather in one gloved hand, a shiny top hat in the other, a look of imposition on his lean features and an unwillingness even to glance in her direction.

As he approached the top of the stairs, and as still there had been no formal introduction, Elizabeth stepped forward.

"Sir," she called out.

"Madam," he responded, looking haughtily up.

"You are—"

"The physician, madam," he replied, halting one step short of the landing. "I assume that it was you who summoned me away from a most enjoyable dinner party."

"I'm—sorry—"

"And I as well." He took advantage of Elizabeth's retreat to gain the top of the landing, where he stood before her. Impatiently he announced, "My name is Dr. Arthur Canning."

"Where's Georgie?"

"Dr. Tidwell," he pronounced, "is far too old to go traipsing about in the dead of night. I have recently joined his staff for the purpose of assisting him."

"Of course," Elizabeth murmured, struggling to deal with the man's arrogance. Somehow he was making her feel unworthy, female. Attempting to regain the upper hand in her own house, she said, "This way," starting toward Mary's closed door, dreading the thought of this cold man examining Mary.

Inside the room she glanced at the bed, hoping that Mary had revived. But she had not and, as the doctor pushed past her, she murmured. "She has not stirred since—"

Unable to say the word, he said it for her. "The rape, madam. These things must be faced. The police inspector has informed me of all that I need to know."

Standing at the foot of the bed, Elizabeth watched as he shrugged off his cloak, then stripped off his gloves, pushed back the sleeves of his dinner jacket, hovered over Mary, lifting one eyelid, recording her pulse and stopping for a brief inspection of the rope burns about

her wrists. He retrieved a small vial from his valise, un-
corked it and thrust it under Mary's nose.

At first there was no response. He inserted the end of
the vial directly into her nostril and clamped a hand
over her mouth, forcing her to breathe deeply of the
acrid odor which was beginning to penetrate as far as
the end of the bed.

On the verge of objecting, Elizabeth started around
the opposite side of the bed, then held her position,
seeing faint movement, Mary's head beginning to push
against the pillow in a gentle thrashing movement, one
hand lifting toward the obnoxious smell.

The minor struggle persisted for several seconds and,
though clearly she was conscious, still the doctor held
her head fast, his hand clamped over her mouth, forcing
her to breathe again and again.

"Doctor, please," Elizabeth commanded. "She's
quite—"

"Be still or leave, madam!" he snapped.

Unable to watch, Elizabeth turned away, trying her
best to control her anger. How did this restraint vary
from the ordeal which had plunged her so deeply into
unconsciousness?

"There," she heard the doctor pronounce with a self-
satisfied tone, and she looked back to see Mary's eyes
open, wide and darting, her hands grasping the coverlet.

Reflexively, Elizabeth pressed a hand to her mouth
to keep from crying out. There was not one aspect of
the pitiful creature on the bed that resembled Mary
Eden. From the butchered hair to the expression of
terror in her eyes, it could have been a complete stranger
lying there.

Speak to her, Elizabeth thought in a wave of grief.
*Someone must speak to her—inform her that she is safe
and among those who love her.*

But as she started toward the bed, the doctor stopped
her with a dismissal. "Leave us, madam, please—"

"But she is my charge," Elizabeth protested, anger
rising. "Go ahead and conduct your examination. I'm
not a modest—"

"It's not your modesty I was thinking of," the doctor
said, "but rather that of my patient."

Defeated by consideration from such an unexpected
source, Elizabeth retreated. Though every instinct within

her said "Stay," there was nothing she could do to combat the aura of professionalism beside the bed. She closed the door behind her and stood close, listening, but she heard nothing. The worst sensation was her own sense of helplessness. There was nothing she could do —about anything.

She walked slowly toward the straight-backed chair on the opposite wall and sat erect, her hands clasped in her lap. The voices in the entrance hall below seemed to have diminished. And there was no sound at all coming from behind the door opposite her.

Then, it was over, or just beginning, and how much responsibility for this tragic night rested directly on her shoulders? And how much more would John try to place there?

"Oh, dear God," she groaned. She bent over and covered her face in her hands and, in spite of the darkness, saw one crystal-clear image of Mary's face as it had been, as it was now.

A short time later she heard footsteps on the stairs and looked up to see the police inspector approaching, his eyes slanted into circumflex angles of pity, in spite of his professional objectivity.

"Madam," he called out, "a word, if I may."

"Of course. I'm sorry. I'm just waiting for the doctor to—"

"He's still with the young lady?"

"Yes."

There was an awkward pause, the inspector standing stiffly at the top of the landing. "Madam," he commenced considerately, "is there no one I can summon to be with you? Sometimes just a friend—"

"No," she said.

"I'm afraid I must inform you that my man has just come back from the Belgrave Square address—"

"John?"

"According to the staff, Mr. Eden is dining out this evening, a business conference of some sort. We left word that he was to come here immediately upon his return, though no one could say when that would be."

"Thank you, inspector," she murmured. "You've been most kind."

"Kind perhaps, madam, though I'm afraid not too

efficient. I feel I must warn you in advance that investigations of this nature generally net few results."

Yes, she knew that, but hearing the hopelessness in his voice made it all the worse. "Surely there is some recourse to justice."

"As of now, very little, I'm afraid. The West Indian is innocent, I'm convinced of it."

Poor Jason. She would have to look in on him later, and Doris as well. She closed her eyes to the concerned expression on the inspector's face and started out of her chair, when at that moment the bedchamber door opened and the physician appeared, meticulously drawing on his gloves, his face as unrevealing as ever.

Elizabeth waited for him to speak, and when no words seemed forthcoming, she went to his side, loathing the entreaty in her voice for simple information which should have been freely given.

"Doctor, please," she begged, "is she—"

"She's remarkably intact," he said, closing the bedchamber door behind him. "Of course the hymen is shattered, causing minor bleeding, but the genitals by and large are undamaged. No lasting scars, I'm pleased to announce." He was addressing the inspector, to the total exclusion of Elizabeth. "If there is such a thing in your profession, sir," he said, "it was a most nonviolent rape, which should tell you something, and I'm sure it does—"

The man's ordinary manner was maddening enough. Now to have the mystery and a sense of coyness added to it was almost unbearable. Though she had been excluded, Elizabeth asserted herself. "I don't understand," she pronounced coldly. "What precisely is it that you are saying?"

The inspector tried to intercede, but the overbearing physician would not give him a chance.

"The young woman's assailants were not sadistic. Or if they were, they tempered that sadism in a simple act of vengeance. For instance, the mutilation of the hair is a lover's trick, certainly not a rapist's, who would have used the blades in other areas, her breasts perhaps or the womb itself."

Sickened, Elizabeth turned away, but the haughty voice went right on, as though sensing her weakness and wanting to contribute to it.

"We've both seen female victims, haven't we, inspector, that defied description. Severed ears, disembowelment. The Rapist of Larchmont, caught only last year, always cut off his victim's feet."

The semidarkened hall began to swirl about her.

"But that young lady was most fortunate," the male voice went on in a light tone of voice. "It would be my opinion, inspector, that either she knew her assailant or he knew her. Revenge is evident to be sure, but muted revenge, almost as though he merely wanted to frighten her and cause her temporary discomfort, rather than destroy her, don't you agree?"

Elizabeth couldn't tell if the inspector agreed or not. Clearly the doctor had planted a theory in his head that had not been there before.

"It's—possible," he stammered.

"It's not only possible, I'd say it's quite probable," the doctor countered. He paused. "Of course, one overriding question remains—"

Elizabeth looked back, her loathing for the man increasing with each word he spoke.

"What, we feel compelled to ask, was a gentlewoman doing alone in the park at that hour unchaperoned?"

"She'd been riding," Elizabeth said.

"Was she astride her horse when her assailant overtook her?"

The inspector shook his head. "No. Her horse was found tethered outside the garden."

"Then she had dismounted and was clearly waiting for someone."

"That's not true!" Elizabeth protested.

"And how can you be sure, madam?" he inquired, not looking at her, but glancing over her head. "Were you there?"

"No."

"Was she allowed to ride after dark?"

"No."

"Did anyone think to put limits on her, restrictions, as it were."

"She was told—"

"—and apparently did not heed—"

Obviously sensing Elizabeth's rising emotions, the inspector gently interceded. "I believe that will be all for now, doctor," he said, and took the man's arm and turned

him toward the stairs. "And I thank you for your theories
on the case."

"Case!" the doctor parroted sarcastically. "You don't
have a case, inspector. All you have is a headstrong
young girl who was allowed to run free and undisciplined, and who received precisely what she deserved."

"You have no right!" Elizabeth cried, unable to listen
any longer. How subtly the weight of guilt had been
shifted from assailant to victim.

Stunned and sickened, Elizabeth watched as the two
men made their way down the stairs. At the bottom she
saw them stop for another whispered conference, the
doctor shaking his head, then laughing, the inspector
responding with a smile. They might have been two
gentlemen merely passing the evening sharing jests.

Dear God, enough! She turned away and walked to
the end of the second-floor corridor and waited until she
heard the front door open, then close.

She knew there would be no further investigation unless John pressed for one. Yet in a way she was forced
to agree with the two who had just left. What purpose
would it serve? How would it comfort the young girl
lying "intact" behind that door? How would it ease one
millionth of one percent of her memories of this dreadful night, memories which she would carry with her for
the rest of her life?

Either she knew her assailant or he knew her. . . .

There was that troublesome fact as well. And had
she gone to the park to meet someone?

Deep in mourning for the spiritual death of Mary
Eden, she returned to the straight-backed chair, knelt
before it and, ignoring Charlie Bradlaugh's tenet that
there was no God, prayed desperately to someone to
ease her guilt. . . .

It had been his intention to stay out most of the night.
For this most important evening he'd selected a prominent arena, his London Sporting Club, watching a
series of rat matches, even managing to forget the
deadly pursuit that was going on elsewhere in London
in the excitement of witnessing an aggressive little bull
terrier kill thirty-seven rats, some almost as large as the
dog himself, a few even hanging to his nose which, despite his tossing, still held on. Ultimately the dog had

dashed the lot of them against the sides of the white pit, leaving patches of blood as if strawberries had been smashed there.

He'd remained at the Sporting Club until almost dawn, placing several large bets so he'd be remembered, even winning one hundred and forty quid, to the envy of the gamblers around him.

Then he'd gone straight home and had encountered a steward dozing in the entrance hall, as though he'd waited up to deliver a message. But as he was fast asleep and as John already knew the nature of the message, he'd walked silently past him and retired, uninformed.

Of course when he'd awakened earlier this morning, the message had been delivered by a distraught Alex Aldwell, who apparently had stopped off at the house in St. George Street for a generous portion of Doris' turned eggs. But, according to the man himself, he'd found the table unset, the stove cold, and Elizabeth weeping.

So! The pursuit had been successful. More than rats had been smashed against the side of the pit last night, though when John tried to quiz Alex as to the specifics, the man merely urged haste, pleading. "It's something awful, John, you must come!"

At least giving the impression of speed and trying to quiet the small flames of remorse, he left his bed and dressed, sternly reminding himself that it was too late for remorse.

"Hurry, John, I beg you!" Alex called from the door. "Elizabeth could hardly speak. She's in need of—"

A lesson there as well, John thought as he adjusted his neck scarf. For long ago he'd reached the conclusion that Elizabeth was in large measure responsible for Mary's defiance and disobedience. Then let her suffer, let them both suffer, as he had been made to suffer, seeing again the shadowy garden, Mary entwined in male arms, as wanton as a—

"The carriage is outside," Alex called out. "I'll go ahead and tell him you're coming. Hurry—please—"

"You do that," John said softly to his reflection in the glass. As the door closed, he took advantage of the moment's privacy to remind himself that harsh problems called for harsh solutions.

Not until he saw his hands trembling in the glass did he realize the full extent of his unspent rage. But he reminded himself that rage was not negotiable this morning. He must see the episode to its conclusion, then turn his mind to other matters. There was Lila, for one. He must travel to Eden soon and check on the progress of his unborn child, enduring the hostile womb of a reluctant mother. And there was Richard in Cambridge and that whole sordid business. With luck, there would be two causes for celebration at Eden come spring, a christening and a wedding. Oh, there were so many things to attend to, in order to create the world as it ought to be.

Dressed now, and firm in his convictions, he lifted his head and for a moment saw his father staring at him from the glass.

"Poor Papa." He smiled at the familiar weak reflection. "How pleased you would be with your son now."

Feeling lighthearted, he turned away from the image and went to attend to Mary. . . .

As he bent over to lay a fire in the grate, Andrew Rhoades found the juxtaposition of events almost too cruel.

Selfishly he and Dhari had left London late yesterday afternoon with the thought only of driving as far as the Heath. But the high autumn sun had lured them farther and farther beyond the noise of London and, with typical perversity, a rainstorm had gathered over them in the vicinity of Maidstone and, as they were riding in an open gig with only one horse, common sense had dictated that they take shelter.

The small, simple country inn and hospitable innkeeper had proved an even greater allurement than the unusual day. Yet more had been accomplished. Confronted with her healing serenity, Andrew had pledged his love, asked her to be his wife, and she had agreed.

He adjusted the kindling around the larger logs, sprinkled several drops of oil from the pitcher and thrust a lighted candle into the well. The flames commenced burning well, and hurriedly he raised up to see how else he could be of assistance.

Just entering the door, he caught sight of Dhari, a white apron tied hurriedly over her dark green traveling suit, a tray of steaming coffee and biscuits in her hands. Shortly after their arrival, after Elizabeth had incoherently informed them of Mary's ordeal, they had found

Doris, still shaken, in her room off the kitchen, clearly unable to function. Dhari had taken over.

Still keeping an eye on the fire, Andrew watched as she placed the tray on the center table and commenced serving, first Elizabeth, who lay prone on the sofa, one hand covering her eyes, her exhaustion and despair finally taking a toll.

As Dhari offered her coffee, Elizabeth shook her head and, suffering a rush of old love for this remarkable woman, Andrew urged, "Please, Elizabeth, you must eat something. It will serve no purpose for you to fall ill as well."

Finally she sat up, with Dhari's help, and accepted a cup and one biscuit, though made no move to eat.

As Dhari offered a second cup to Lord Harrington, who was seated by the window, the tall, distinguished man grumbled, "Where is John? Why is he never where he should be?"

Andrew considered responding, then changed his mind. It was his opinion that they all had better enjoy the silence while they could, for with John's arrival a storm more awesome than any they had ever weathered would break about their heads.

Rape.

It dawned on him that that obscene word had been avoided by everyone in the drawing room. Elizabeth had wept out something about an assault, had informed them as precisely as her state of mind had permitted the specifics leading up to the tragedy.

It had been a complete rendition, but that one word, rape, had been missing, the only word that John would hear.

Andrew gazed unseeing into the flames, trying to gather about him his most objective frame of mind, knowing now more than ever that his difficult friend would need the leavening effect of calm and rationality.

Then Andrew heard it—the rattling approach of the carriage. In this last moment of privacy, he hurried to Elizabeth's side. "Do you feel up to it or do you want me to—"

"No," she whispered, "I've lived with it all night. I will repeat it once more and then never again," she added fiercely, though Andrew felt her arm trembling. He'd never seen her so undone, and what she felt would be nothing compared to what John would suffer and, as though feeling the need to keep the man in his sight, he hurried to the window beside Lord Harrington and saw John alighting his carriage, saw Alex Aldwell already on the steps, the large man urging haste.

But, curiously, Andrew saw John hesitate, say something to his driver, one reaching up, the other leaning down in a prolonged exchange.

"Does he know?" Lord Harrington muttered, sharing Andrew's bewilderment.

"Obviously not as much as he will soon," Andrew replied, and left the window and saw Dhari and Elizabeth standing close together. He started to say something of reassurance to both, but heard the front door open and went forward to greet the storm.

From where he stood, he saw Alex taking John's cloak and hat, heard John inquire, "Where in the hell is Doris? I pay her enough. One expects—"

"John," Andrew called out and was not at first prepared for the coldness in John's eyes as he turned toward the door.

As though suspicious of everything, John ignored Andrew and strode through the drawing room arch to a position of confrontation about ten feet from where Elizabeth stood.

At the moment she commenced to speak, John spoke first in a curious calm. "Andrew, I waited for you yesterday. I want news on the hearing with John Thadeus Delane. I assume that you've been at work on the matter. I believe those were my instructions. Of course, if other matters"—and here he lifted his eyes to Dhari—"are occupying too much of your attention, I can easily send for Aslam at Cambridge and relieve you of certain duties."

Lord Harrington stepped forward. "John, please," he muttered, obviously feeling the need to serve as arbitrator. "There are other, more pressing—" he commenced and never finished.

"Ah, it's you." John smiled, craning his neck about, as though just now aware of the man's presence in the drawing room. "And you've been busy as well, or so I hear. Your Irish friend, I believe, wasn't it? And what was his news?"

Lord Harringtom nodded, losing track of the tragic

issue at hand. "He had news, John, disturbing news."

"I daresay. The Irish love hysteria. They dote on it."

"He had stopped at Eden—"

"He had no right," John interrupted.

"—thinking to find me there. Instead he saw my daughter."

From where Andrew stood he saw John turn slowly in the chair. "He—did *what?*" he demanded.

"His report was most disturbing," Harrington went on, casting an apologetic look toward Elizabeth, who continued to stand at midroom, suffering the weight of her own undelivered message. "He tells me that my daughter is very ill," Harrington murmured. "I was wondering—if I might have permission to return to Eden, only for a few days, to see—"

"Of course she's ill!" John snapped, leaning back in his chair. "She's pregnant, and a reluctant pregnancy at that. But she *will* bear the child and she'll do it best if we all leave her alone." He glanced up at Lord Harrington, his anger either dissipated or held in check. "I'll send word immediately, reminding the guards at Eden that the gates are to be barred—to everyone. Is that clear?"

Lord Harrington lowered his head. "I'm—her father."

"And I'm her husband."

Waiting by the arch, Andrew had heard and seen enough. Elizabeth seemed to be on the verge of collapse.

"John, I beg you," he called, moving toward the fireplace. "Elizabeth must talk with you. We sent Alex to get you because—"

But he could not continue and was further undone by a strange look of amusement on John's face. "Andrew. What precisely is it that you are trying—"

"It's Mary." The voice, or what was left of it, belonged to Elizabeth.

"Go on," he heard John invite. "What about Mary?"

The suffering coming from the center of the room was intense. Although Andrew would have preferred to stay out of it, nonetheless he stepped forward. "John, she's suffered a dreadful—"

"Why don't you let Elizabeth speak?" John interrupted. "You weren't here. She was. I prefer a firsthand account."

"Do you know what has happened?" Andrew persisted, in an attempt to end this game of cat and mouse.

"I know enough."

"What do you know?"

Incongruously, John smiled. "I know that her fool-hardiness has led her astray, as it were. And I know further that lack of supervision on the part of certain people has contributed to it, and I know that deception and dishonor will always reap a bitter harvest."

"She did not deceive you, John," Elizabeth protested, "or any of us, and she was always carefully chaperoned by both Jason and Doris."

"Not so carefully, I'd say," John replied, and sat back into the chair, propped his elbows on the arms and invited coldly from behind this barrier, "Now tell me what happened. You, Elizabeth, only you, from the beginning."

Andrew retreated back to the window, abandoning all hope of helping Elizabeth. Apparently the fact of her punishment was unalterable.

For several minutes she talked. Andrew had never heard her so shattered. Blessedly the account was brief and she concluded with her first glimpse of Mary in the arms of the policeman, a form which did not even resemble Mary, as her clothes were soiled and torn, and her hair—

For the first time she faltered. Andrew heard John's voice prodding. "What about her hair?"

"It has been—shorn, barbarously, by someone who—"

Obviously she had reached the limits of her endurance, for Andrew heard a rustle of skirts and looked back to see her seated upon the couch, the handkerchief pressed against her mouth.

There was no sound in the drawing room. From where Andrew sat he saw John in profile only, a man who appeared to be deep in thought, though when he spoke his voice sounded remarkably like Elizabeth's, as though he, too, were approaching the limits of endurance. "Her hair will grow back," he murmured. Then, on renewed strength, he asked. "And that, I assume, is the extent of the damage?"

Weeping, Elizabeth did well to shake her head. "No, John, she was assaulted."

All at once the man lounging in the chair was on his feet. "She was—what?" he demanded, staring down on

Elizabeth and, in the face of that countenance, Andrew knew that John had not known, that Aldwell had told him little or nothing.

"That's not true!" he insisted over and over again. "I don't believe it. I won't. How do you know?"

"It is true, John."

"No!"

"The physician was here last evening. He examined her."

"He's mistaken. She was not—"

As suddenly as the outrage had commenced, it ceased. He straightened up from his hunched position and strode back to the fireplace.

For the first time Andrew felt a wave of pity for him. "John, I beg you," he began. "Consider the blessings. Mary *did* survive, and so frequently women do not. She has suffered and will continue to suffer for a long time, but that only means that she needs us more."

He wasn't certain if his words were being received. Though he was standing close to John, he saw not one indication of what he was feeling. Still with the intention of offering comfort, Andrew added, "We'll launch our own investigation. We're sure to find—"

John shook his head. "There will be no investigation," he said, staring doggedly at the mantelpiece. "I'll handle the matter myself."

"You! But you have no idea where—"

"Take me to her," he commanded.

Andrew saw Elizabeth rise wearily, as though eager to play out this last grim act. "She has not—spoken," she warned, "not since they brought her home."

This last information seemed to halt John in his forward movement, as though for the first time he was aware of what he would shortly be forced to look upon. He glanced about the room. Almost shyly he asked, "Andrew, would you please come with me?"

Every nerve in Andrew said "No." But he'd heard that tone of voice many times before, the mask of the empire builder stripped off to reveal the reality behind it, a frightened young boy, as though at some point in John's life his emotional growth had stopped while the great engines of his intellect had forged ahead.

"Of course I'll come with you, John," he agreed. "I love her as much as you."

They left the room, John leading the way, Elizabeth waiting for Andrew to catch up, then grasping his arm as though without his support she could not accomplish the stairs.

In this manner, and leaving the others behind, John led the way by a good twenty feet. But as they reached the top of the landing, Andrew saw him stop outside Mary's door, his hand on the knob but lacking the will to turn it.

Elizabeth pushed open the door, then stood back to permit them passage. Even then Andrew preceded John, though he caught a glimpse of that once strong face which now appeared to be drained of color.

Then Andrew was no longer concerned with John or any other aspect of the room, though he did take note of how dark it was, the drapes drawn on the window, shutting out the morning sun, one lamp burning low beside the bed, but that was enough, providing Andrew with all the illumination he needed to see the young woman lying on the bed, a coverlet drawn over her nightshirt, two raw and purple rings about each wrist, the signature of the bondage which had rendered her helpless, her head resting on a pillow, her once-lovely hair lying in short, jagged disarray about her face and, worse than all else, the face itself, so small and white and drawn, like an injured child's, as though her soul, in an attempt to run from the ordeal, had taken refuge in her childhood.

He heard Elizabeth, her words controlled as though she knew that the last thing Mary needed was her tears. "Look, my dearest," she whispered. "Look who has come to see you. It's John. He wants very much to—"

But the man standing beside Andrew did not move, and at last Andrew found the courage to look in that direction and was instantly sorry for he saw John's face as he'd never seen it before.

In an attempt to escape that face, Andrew moved to the side of the bed opposite Elizabeth. "Mary, can you hear me?" he asked softly. "As soon as you are able, will you talk to me, tell me what—"

"Leave her alone!"

The voice came from the foot of the bed and bore no resemblance to the man himself.

Elizabeth protested. "No, John, let him speak. Perhaps he can—"

"I said leave her alone, both of you." Without moving from the foot of the bed, and without lifting his eyes from Mary's face, he said, "The future is clear for her now. She must go away."

"No!" Elizabeth protested.

"She can't stay here," John said. "What is there for her here but a constant reminder of her ordeal?"

"She needs us," Elizabeth begged. "Can't you see? She mustn't be shut away—"

"She needs nothing that we have to offer," John countered, "neither our sympathy nor the idle and permissive atmosphere of this house, which led her into trouble in the first place."

For a moment Andrew thought that Elizabeth would retreat. The accusation had been clear.

But instead, with an anger which matched John's, she rallied and offered an eloquent defense. "This is my house, John, not yours. The atmosphere is to my liking and one of my own choosing. I know it does not please you and, if you will recall, I have begged you repeatedly to take Mary out of it."

Dangerous words, those, Andrew thought, glancing down at the wide-open eyes. The silence on Mary's face was not so deep as to prohibit a listening ear. What she did not need now was the announcement from the woman whom she adored as much as her own mother that she had never been wanted.

"May I suggest—" Andrew began, and was interrupted.

"I beg you, John," Elizabeth went on, "do not try to place the blame on me. For Mary's sake, let's not talk of blame at all. She needs our love and support now more than—"

"I repeat," John said, "she needs nothing from us. She needs seclusion and isolation in new surroundings. She needs discipline."

"Discipline!"

"Yes. For her mind. The discipline of studies to fill the void of memory. She needs the association of decent people who know nothing of this, who will be capable of looking at her and not seeing—"

"What are you suggesting?" Elizabeth asked cautiously, as though she already knew the answer.

"It's clear," he said, "a step which should have been taken years ago perhaps. I will make arrangements for her in Miss Veal's school in—"

"No!"

"There, in a safe environment, controlled and guarded, she can rechart her life along more responsible lines."

Though Andrew had vowed not to speak, his incredulity matched Elizabeth's. "You make it sound as though it were Mary's fault."

"It is," came the calm reply.

"You have no right," Elizabeth murmured.

"I have every right," John countered. "I am responsible for this family."

"On whose authority?" Elizabeth challenged.

"On my own, for there is no one else even remotely capable, as that pitiful specimen demonstrates."

Again Andrew suffered misgivings. Far too much was being said, damaging words, as though they were in the room alone. "John, please," he begged, "it doesn't have to be settled now."

"It *is* settled, Andrew. As soon as she is able to travel, I will personally escort her to Cheltenham, see her safely ensconced in that institution and—"

Andrew saw Elizabeth coming slowly around the bed. "It's what you've wanted, isn't it?" she accused softly. "You've always wanted to lock her away someplace, away from all life, from all—"

"That's enough," John commanded.

Indeed it was. Andrew was beginning to feel as battered as though he'd suffered the assault along with Mary. Yet as the two voices continued to hurl accusations at each other he looked back down on Mary and saw her lips, dried, trying to form words.

"Wait!" he called to the two beyond the foot of the bed and heard a cessation of their voices and was aware of them returning to the bed.

He saw Elizabeth enclosing Mary's hand in hers. "Oh, my dearest," she murmured as the eyes from the pillow struggled to bring her into focus.

The lips were still working. "I— want—" Mary com-

menced and closed her eyes under the duress of effort.
"I—want," she whispered, "to go—away. Please, I want
to—"

The words, though barely audible, were plain enough
for all to hear and provided John with the victory he
needed. "Of course you do," he smiled, brushing past
Andrew and taking her hand in his. "And you shall.
You'll find it to your liking, I swear it. And in a few
years, perhaps no more than two, you'll emerge from
this ordeal stronger and lovelier than ever. And it will
have been forgotten."

As the voice droned on, Andrew listened, amazed at
John's stupidity, to think that what she had endured
would ever be forgotten.

"Rest now," he heard John whisper. "I'll return tonight with all the roses in London. We'll have dinner
here together, just the two of us, and speak only of the
future. Is that to your liking?"

But there was no further response. Apparently she'd
expended what energy she had left in her single announcement. *"I want to go away."* Now her eyes were
closed, and with tenderness, John kissed her hand, his
fingers lingering in examination of the bruises about her
wrists.

Like a man renewed, he stood up from the bed and
strode to the door, not acknowledging Elizabeth in any
way, calling back, "Come, Andrew, we've work to do. I
want to speak to you about the hearing with Delane,
and there are other matters as well."

But Andrew held his position in sympathy for the
woman who stood alone beside the bed. No longer
weeping, she resembled an abandoned husk.

Andrew was on the verge of going to her side when
John reappeared in the doorway, his monstrous confidence almost an obscenity in this room. "Are you
coming, Andrew?"

Andrew was tempted to say "No," but his reliable
voice of reason calmly informed him that no one in this
room was capable of clear judgment, and on that
thought alone he said simply, "I'm coming, John."

In passing he placed a hand on Elizabeth's shoulder,
though she did not respond. The last image he had of the
room was of two abandoned women, each having been

stripped of some essential life force, each left on her
own to deal with the vacuum. . . .

On the following evening, almost insane with worry,
Burke Stanhope paced the darkened pavement opposite
Number Seven, St. George Street. How simple his dis-
integration had been.

He'd taken his mother for her second carriage ride in
as many days. Then he'd returned her to the Mayfair
house at midday and gone immediately to Hyde Park.

He'd saddled his horse himself as the old stablemaster
had been busy with a group of novice riders. Then, with a
sense of anticipation, he had ridden immediately to the
garden, his need to see her after a single day's absence
acute and his own curiosity mounting over why she'd been
unable to keep their appointment the day before.

At two-thirty the garden had been deserted and had
remained that way until shortly after eight P.M. His
concern increasing, Burke had returned to the stables to
the toothless old stablemaster, who had viewed him
with curious sympathy and had asked an equally curious
question.

"Your young lady, sir—how is she?"

His young lady! Had they been that obvious? If the
stablemaster had been able to link them, what would
prevent—

Then the nature of the inquiry itself had dawned on
him and, though that had been the beginning of his apprehension, still he'd managed to inquire. "I'm not certain
I know what you are talking about."

But the old man had not answered him. Instead he'd
shaken his head and pushed the wheelbarrow full of oats
ahead of him on the rough dirt floor, methodically pro-
portioning out a lot for each horse, talking nonsense.
"They should brush off Tyburn Hill, they should," he
grumbled. "Nothing like a public spectacle of a man's
execution to put the fear of Gawd into faint hearts."

Burke halted his pacing on the darkened pavement of
St. George Street, recalling how many times he'd begged
the old man to speak clearly, then, unfortunately, he had.

"Pitiful, she was, your young lady, and the ruffians
who done it ought to be—"

Without warning, Burke felt weak and reached out
for the iron fence behind him, turning his back on Num-

ber Seven and the vigil he'd maintained for the last
three hours.

Something had happened, he knew that much. *But
what?* Earlier that evening in his frustration he'd backed
the old stablemaster into one of the stalls and not until
he'd seen the fear in the old man's face had he moved
away. Obviously the man had told him all he knew, that
a young woman had suffered injury, that the police had
been involved and that he couldn't talk any more because he didn't know any more.

Suffered injury—

The words beat an assault across his brain, the depth
of his worry drawing his attention back to the house
across the way, an establishment which seemed to reek
of disaster with its drawn curtains, its single lamp burning in the entrance hall, the wagon which had arrived
about an hour ago with dozens of roses, as though for a
funeral.

If only he *knew!* Then he suffered the most irrational
of instincts, to simply cross the street and demand entrance. Countless times during these difficult hours he'd
almost succumbed to this foolish action, which would
only succeed in alerting the entire household to his
presence and, worse, jeopardizing their secret, perhaps
putting an end to all future meetings.

It was that thought which had prevented him from
bridging the short distance from where he stood to the
door itself.

What had she been doing in the park alone after she'd
sent the note informing him that she could not meet him
on that day? And what precisely had befallen her? Had
she taken ill? No, ruffians had been mentioned, the need
for the restoration of public executions, as though a
crime had been committed.

In this tortured manner he continued to pace, searching each passing carriage, as though foolishly hoping
that someone would give him the news he so desperately
needed.

It was shortly after midnight when the first rational
thought penetrated his mind. He needed access to the
house and, lacking that, he needed the assistance of
someone who would not be barred at the door, someone who could intervene on his behalf and ask questions
with the hope of receiving answers.

The name was in his mind even before he posed the question.

John Thadeus Delane. Surely Elizabeth would not bolt the door to him.

On that note of hope, uncaring of the hour and impervious to Delane's strict command that they not be seen together, Burke took a last glance across the street and tried not to dwell on the phantoms plaguing his mind. He ran toward the end of the street and his waiting carriage, calling out, "Printing House Square," to his driver even as he swung precariously through the small carriage door. . . .

Though the hour was late and he was approaching exhaustion, John Thadeus Delane sat behind his desk in his editorial house in Printing House Square, rereading the official parchment spread before him.

Delivered by special courier earlier that evening, neither his repetitive reading nor the added illumination of another lamp had done anything to ease his sense of incredulity.

It was signed by Andrew Rhoades, solicitor to John Murrey of Eden, and signed as well by Sir Henry Aimsley, a prominent though not wholly respected magistrate in the Temple. The script informed Mr. John Thadeus Delane that on the tenth of December, 1870, he was requested to appear in the capacity of editor of the London *Times* in Lord Aimsley's chambers for the purpose of interrogation regarding recently printed material in the above mentioned newspaper.

Interrogation?

He shoved the document across the desk. How dare they? Were they all asses, including Lord Aimsley, whose official seal had given legitimacy to the farce? Well known in the Temple as a magistrate who would perform any judicial service for a price, it was obvious that Eden had bought him for his own petty purposes.

With his thoughts gaining momentum, he moved around his desk and walked halfway to the door, where he stopped, gazing up unseeing at the large map of the world which covered the wall to his right.

But it wasn't the world that interested him, but rather his awareness of the disaster that could descend upon him in that hearing on the tenth of December. If Aimsley put him under oath—and he would, to identify Lord Ripples, then Delane would have no choice but to answer. And Eden would then have precisely what he wanted. And God help Burke Stanhope!

Delane stared at the world map as though seeing disaster in every corner. With his duty clear, he grabbed his cloak and started toward the door. Though the hour was late, still Burke had to be warned. Perhaps he could go home for a while, back to America beyond the extension of Eden's power, anyplace, but he must leave London until the hearing was over and Eden's attention had been focused elsewhere.

He'd taken less than three steps toward the door when suddenly he heard footsteps on the other side, running footsteps, or so it seemed, and in the next minute the door was pushed violently open, and filling the doorway was Burke Stanhope, his hair mussed, cloakless in spite of the chill evening, his coat undone, indeed everything undone, including the expression on his face.

Startled by the appearance of the very man he'd been on his way to see, Delane gaped, both men staring at each other with the weight of undelivered messages.

"Burke." Delane smiled, dropping his cloak back onto the chair and stepping toward the man, hand extended to assist him to a chair where he might regain his breath and composure.

But Burke needed no assistance and stepped further into the room, slamming the door behind him, confronting Delane directly.

"I know you said I am not to see you," he commenced, "and I wouldn't have come if it hadn't been necessary."

"No need," Delane soothed, still trying to guide him to the settee and perhaps a settling glass of brandy. What had caused this unprecedented agitation in his normally contained young friend he had no idea. Suddenly a grim thought occurred to Delane.

"Is your mother—"

"Well, thank you."

"That's good. I've been meaning to call. But I've been busy since my return. Come, Burke, I was just in the mood for a nightcap. Will you join me? We have much to talk about."

To the brandy Burke said no, but as Delane went to

the sideboard he was aware of the man pacing behind him. Snifter in hand, Delane returned to his desk. He felt most comfortable there, ready to deal with any crisis, and as he sat his eye fell again on the parchment from Andrew Rhoades and, feeling a need to deliver his own message, he said, "I was just on my way to see you," and lifted the parchment toward Burke, who in his own anxiety either didn't see it or didn't care.

"I have need of a favor, Delane," he said urgently, dragging a chair directly before the desk, forcing Delane's attention.

"Name it. If it's within my power, it shall be done."

Slowly Burke shook his head. "I—don't know where to start," he faltered. "Do you remember that woman, Delane, the one who almost fell from the carriage door outside the gates of Eden? You knew her or said you had known her before."

"Elizabeth?"

"Yes, that's the one," Burke said hurriedly. "I want you to go and see her, tonight if possible. No, not tonight; it's too late. First thing in the morning, though, I want you to go and see her and—"

"For God's sake, why?" Delane managed.

"I—need information," Burke went on, stammering as though he knew he wasn't making a great deal of sense. "You—see, there was an accident of some sort, involving—"

"Elizabeth?"

"No, but the young woman who lives with her."

"Lady Mary Eden?"

"Mary," Burke repeated, as though it hurt to speak the name. He turned away, leaving Delane in a state of bewilderment, one hand playing with the stiffened corner of the parchment from Andrew Rhoades, baffled that both their problems involved Edens.

Delane noticed for the first time that he was wearing riding boots, the caked mud of a bridle path coating the heels. He'd never known Burke to show an interest in matters equestrian and, as each small mystery compounded the larger one, Delane pushed back his chair, took a long, mind-clearing swallow of brandy and, following the instincts of a journalist, calmly invited Burke to take a chair and start at the beginning.

At the invitation Burke appeared to draw a deep

breath, then finally came words, the most incredible
words that Delane had ever heard, an account of one
chance meeting and recognition of the beautiful young
woman who had held all of Jeremy Sims' Song and
Supper Club enthralled for months, the same fair face
with whom he had danced immediately preceding his
expulsion from Eden. And all of this merely prelude to
the larger madness ' of clandestine meetings in Hyde
Park, the fascination growing to affection, the affection
to—love, and finally, the most incredible of all, an
aborted meeting and the gossip of a stablemaster who
had implied that tragedy had befallen the young woman,
and, as it was impossible for Burke to penetrate the
fortress behind which she was confined, and, by his own
confession, going mad with worry, he was now enlisting
Delane's help.

The incredible tale concluded, Delane sat in a state
of mild shock, torn between laughing his head off, which
somehow seemed inappropriate considering the tragic
slump of the young man on the settee, or clearing the
residue of romantic nonsense from the room with a
display of rage.

Instead, without a thought to choosing his words,
Delane sat up in his chair and announced bluntly, "I'm
afraid you've made an ass of yourself."

He waited, certain that such an accusation would
arouse a response from the man. When it did not, he
tried again. "Are you listening to me, Burke?" he
prodded. "I frankly find it difficult to believe anything
of what I've just heard."

"It's true."

"If it's true, it's madness. Out of all the available
females in London, why—"

"I did not intend for it to go this far, nor did she."

"And how far has it gone?" Delane asked cautiously,
thinking of the powerful ammunition that Eden could
use against the man when and if Delane were forced
to reveal his identity.

Burke sat up and conveniently used his hands as a
shield for his face. "It's as I said, Delane. I—love—her."

"Touching," Delane murmured acidly. He decided to
let the point of their intimacy pass. Perhaps it was best
that he did not know everything. As it was, he felt that
he knew too much.

He was aware of Burke standing before the desk. "Will you do it, Delane?" he asked. "Will you go tomorrow? *I must know.* Something has happened. Otherwise she would have——"

"Has it occurred to you, Burke," Delane commenced, hoping if not to shock him into good sense at least to mildly hurt him, "that the young woman was merely playing a game with you?"

"No."

"Why not? It's a good possibility. Her entire life has been a prolonged exercise in pampered boredom."

"That's not true."

"She must take her sport where she can find it, and how better than with an American who so outraged her cousin?"

"That is simply not true," Burke insisted, his hands on the desk.

Dear God, he appears to be literally unhinged. "Burke, please," Delane soothed, trying to ease him back into the chair and a degree of rationality. In spite of the fact that he did not sit, at least he was quiet. "What exactly is it that you want me to do with this— tale you've just delivered? Surely you don't expect me to take it seriously?"

"I want your assistance with one small matter."

"Small?" Delane asked, anger rising. "At the moment I am the chief target of Eden's rage. Look," he commanded and shoved the parchment from Andrew Rhoades across the desk, thinking that now was as good a time as any. Let Burke see for himself the hazardous days ahead where the Eden family was concerned.

Distracted, Burke started to ignore the parchment, but then something caught his eye. Delane saw him lift the paper toward the light of a lamp.

"My God, is he still pushing it?" he muttered.

"Apparently."

"Is this a subpoena?"

"No, not exactly, but I'd be a fool not to be there on the tenth of December."

"What will they ask you?"

"What do you think they'll ask?" Delane snapped, astonished at Burke's sudden denseness.

"My—identity?"

Delane nodded.

"And will you tell them?"

"Under oath I'll have no other choice."

Their eyes held, the full consequence of the hearing dawning on Burke. He read the parchment again, then tossed it onto the desk as though it were a matter of unconcern to him.

"Then do it," he announced coldly. "Tell Eden what he wants to know. It will come out sooner or later, anyway. In the meantime, will you please do this one favor for me—seek out Elizabeth and try to find—"

My God! One man in this office was mad, and Delane knew who it was, and raged at the loss of his rational friend. "I will do nothing," he shouted across the desk, "for your own sake!"

"For *my* sake!" Burke replied, suffering anger of his own. "What am I asking that is so unreasonable?"

"If you don't know, there's no way I can tell you."

"Please do. I thought I could count on your understanding."

"In all matters, you can, except the ones that threaten to destroy both of us."

"How would a simple inquiry destroy us? The house does not belong to John Murrey Eden. Mary has told me so. What right does he have to tell your friend Elizabeth who calls or who doesn't?"

"John Murrey Eden does not need a right!" exploded Delane, slamming his fist down against the desk. "I thought you knew the man better than that. A Demi-God. Your words, not mine. He controls everything he touches. And for his enemies he reserves a special hell."

Slowly Burke stood up from the desk. "You're afraid of him," he accused softly.

Struggling for control and losing the battle, Delane scooped up the parchment, crushing it in his fist. "Do you know what this means?" he demanded, aware that he was trembling under the duress of his anger. "Not to me," he added. "I'm in a position of relative safety. My reputation will ultimately protect me. But to you!" He stopped, his mind moving to a piece of recent history, the gruesome suicide of a corrupt solicitor named Morley Johnson, who had abused the Eden fortune and, in the process, had incurred the wrath of John Murrey Eden. Perhaps the Divinity would say that Johnson had no right to live, but only a demon divinity would have hounded, pursued, humiliated and ultimately destroyed him as Eden had done. The man had been found hanging by the neck in a rat-infested flat near the docks, scarcely enough skin on him to cover his bones, festering sores on his limbs and a peculiar look of relief on his swollen face, as though it mattered not where he was going, heaven or hell, it would be preferable to this world and the pursuit of John Murrey Eden.

Unfortunately his memory, instead of tempering his anger, only served to increase it, as he replaced in his mind's eye Morley Johnson's face with Burke Stanhope's. He lifted the parchment for the inspection of the man opposite him.

"This could very well be your death warrant," he said quietly, aware of the melodrama of his words yet somehow feeling that they were not strong enough. "Quite obviously," he continued, "this could spell the end of my protection. Don't you see, it's not me they are after. It's you. And the fact that I'm in possession of this parchment at all should tell you clearly of the man's need for revenge. And how precisely do you think he'll react when he learns that not only have you slandered his name but that you have compromised his cousin as well?"

"There has been no compromise," Burke replied. "Our meetings have been honorable."

"And secret."

"There was no other way."

"And there still is no other way," Delane stressed. "For your own sake as well as the young lady's, I would strongly advise that you bring the entire episode to a close."

"I can't do that."

"You—have—no—choice!" Delane thundered, aware that nothing he had said had made the slightest difference.

"The matters are unrelated."

"God in heaven, Burke! Can't you hear yourself? You're not making sense."

"Perhaps not your kind of sense. But then you can't understand."

Delane started to say more but found that he couldn't. The young man standing opposite him had just made a strangely eloquent response, a look of resignation, a suggestion that all arguments were impotent.

Confronted by such a response, Delane felt for his

chair, which had been pushed back in anger, dragged it forward and sat like a man defeated.

Having drained himself of all argument, he asked, "Would you consider going home for a while? Back to America?"

"There is nothing for me in America."

Delane rested his head in his hands and closed his eyes. "Then what do you intend to do?"

"As soon as I can, to find out precisely what has befallen her. As soon as I can, to see her again. As soon as I can, to ask her to become my wife."

Hearing the path to self-destruction spelled out so calmly, a groan escaped Delane's lips. Not until he heard the office door close could he jar himself out of this lethargy, and then it was too late.

"Burke, wait!" he called out.

But no one waited and, in a fit of anger, Delane picked up the empty brandy snifter and hurled it across the room, where it struck the edge of the table and shattered, the noise of destruction setting a proper tone for the days ahead.

He remained at his desk all night, his mind trying to work through to a simple solution. It was in this distracted and confused state that his assistant editor found him the next morning and informed him of the events of the London night which might be newsworthy for an evening edition of the *Times:* a carriage accident near the White Bear in Piccadilly and a spectacular fire near the river in an old abandoned barracks. Three corpses had been found among the smoking ruins, their bodies burned beyond recognition. Transients probably, who had sought refuge in the old structure.

"Run them all," Delane said, only half listening to the news stories, which had nothing to do with his present burden, which was the need to know precisely how far John Murrey Eden would go in his quest for revenge.

Cambridge
Late November 1870

FOR THREE DAYS Richard had tried to shake the gloom brought on by John's letter announcing his imminent arrival sometime before the first of December, a perplexing letter where each sentence provoked a question.

Behind him where he stood at the window keeping watch on the road below, he was aware of old Mrs. Pettibone's quiet fussing at the table, setting service for three, the small informal dinner having been Bertie's idea, that since Aslam had been mentioned by John in detail, then perhaps Aslam could shed more light on the disturbing letter. To that end Bertie had taken the gig about an hour ago to fetch Aslam and bring him back for a subtle question-and-answer period.

Still holding John's letter, as though somehow he'd failed to perceive some vital clue, Richard glanced down on the road below, dreading the evening. Aslam had grown so distant during the last few months, as though Richard had offended him. Yet he'd done nothing but try to fill the void caused by Bertie's move into the private rooms in town, a move which had left Richard bereft. Gradually the rooms in town were used less frequently, and slowly Bertie was moving some of his clothes back, his fears receding with the disappearance of the strange man whom he'd thought was spying on them.

Finally, for the last two weeks with Bertie's good-natured laugh filling the daylight hours in the flat and his consistently healing love filling the night hours, life had resumed, as steadily and as rewarding as ever.

"Will you be taking wine, Lord Eden?"

The question had come from Mrs. Pettibone, who hovered over the table, three wineglasses in hand.

"Yes, please," Richard said.

From the window he watched, detecting something sly in her smile. Dear Heaven, he was growing as suspicious as Bertie. To be sure, the old woman was the worst sort of country gossip, but Richard paid her handsomely and doubted if she would do anything to jeopardize the source of her income.

"When you finish there, that will be all, Mrs. Pettibone. Professor Nichols and I can manage and we don't want to keep you too late in the evening."

He saw a look of disappointment on her face, as though she'd been looking forward to staying.

"Well, I'm not finished, Lord Eden," she pouted. "I have a few more things to do in the kitchen, then, I assure you, I'll spare you my company."

"Mrs. Pettibone, I—"

But she was gone and he would have to make his apologies later, perhaps in the form of a bonus. Repeatedly Bertie had told him how unskilled he was in the handling of servants.

Bertie.

How many times in the last three days he and Bertie had studied John's letter and, with the intention of studying it again, he took it to his desk in the alcove off the front parlor, flattened the pages, drew a lamp near and commenced reading the words that he knew by heart.

The opening was a simple salutation. It was the second paragraph where the mysteries commenced:

I will be travelling back to London from Cheltenham around the first of December, after having ensconced Mary in Miss Veal's establishment. I'm not certain whether or not anyone has written to you, but Mary has suffered an illness. . . .

There the questions started. What illness? And if she were truly ill, then the rigorous discipline of school would be the last thing she needed.

Then to the third paragraph:

I will take the time to come to Cambridge for the purpose of retrieving Aslam from that unproductive atmosphere. . . .

Cambridge had been John's idea. He'd forced it on Aslam several years ago. Now what had happened to convert it into an "unproductive atmosphere"?

I require his services here to work with me in the firm and he can conclude his studies within the

Temple. I count among my friends several prominent solicitors who will be happy to sponsor him.

Where was Andrew Rhoades in all of this? If Aslam was to be transplanted to London, why wasn't Andrew his sponsor?

As always, all his vague apprehensions gradually narrowed into one, the constant nightmare, the secret knowledge of what he was. It wasn't shame he felt. How could such a healing love be shameful or wrong? It was simply his awareness of the abyss between his self-concept and that of the world.

"Well, now I believe everything is in order, Lord Eden."

He looked up at the sound of the voice and saw Mrs. Pettibone standing in the door, adjusting her black bonnet. "Country cooking is all it is, but I hope it suits."

"It will," he said with a smile, joining her in the parlor. "And for your trouble, here's a bit extra," he added, withdrawing from his pocket a pound note and pressing it into her gloved hand.

"Lord!" she gasped, carefully tucking the precious note into her handbag. "Well, then," she said, looking up, "have a pleasant evening, sir, and I'll be back first thing in the morning to straighten up."

"I'm grateful," he said, nodding, and walked behind her to the door, eager to see her on her way.

At the door she stopped and looked back, that same sly smile on her face which he'd detected earlier. "I was—just wondering—will Professor Nichols be moving back in—a permanent way?"

"Yes," he said, hoping that an affirmative answer would make it come true, "though why do you ask? What concern is it—"

"What concern!" she echoed. "I'm the one who straightens up after the two of you, remember? Perhaps I'd better go back and put clean linens on his bed now—"

"It won't be necessary, Mrs. Pettibone," Richard interrupted. "We can attend to that ourselves," he added, thinking with sadness of the charade they had to perform, sharing the same bed, then mussing the other for appearance's sake.

Weary and anxious before the evening had even started, Richard pulled open the door in an attempt to speed the old busybody on her way. "Again, my thanks, Mrs. Pettibone. We'll try not to leave too much in the way of a mess for you in the morning."

With growing apprehension he kept her in his sights until the door below closed and still he stood, staring down the darkened stairs, bewildered by the curiosity concerning Bertie.

Not until he heard the sound of a carriage on the cobbles beyond the garden did he abandon his position at the door and hurry back to the window.

With relief he recognized the gig, saw Bertie climbing down, and saw—

Nothing else.

He hurried to the door and was there to greet Bertie as he climbed the stairs. "Where's Aslam?" Richard demanded. "Did something—"

"He couldn't come," Bertie said. As though to halt any further interrogation he lifted his head toward the kitchen and the good odors of Mrs. Pettibone's stew. "The smells of heaven!" he exclaimed.

"Bertie, what happened?" Richard persisted, taking his cloak, knowing him well enough to be alarmed by this evasion. "What did he say?" he prodded, trying to ignore the sense of alarm growing within him.

Slowly Bertie commenced shaking his head. "The boy was polite at first," he began. "He asked me to convey to you his apologies, said that you knew John better than he and knew his impatience when people were not ready."

"What else did he say?" Richard asked, his anxiety increasing along with the mystery.

Bertie turned away and began riffling through the papers on his desk. "I've told you, Richard."

"You've not told me anything."

The hands collecting the papers ceased. "No," Bertie confessed, and the ease on his face was obliterated. "Like you, at some point I became insistent, but the more I insisted, the more belligerent he became."

"Belligerent?" Richard found the image a difficult one.

"Although I knew I was pushing too hard," Bertie added, "I felt a need to push hard, knew that something was bothering the boy. Finally he announced that the truth of the matter was that he had no desire to come."

"No—desire?" Richard murmured, wondering what had happened to that affectionate relationship he'd once shared with Aslam.

"Finally," Bertie concluded, "I pressed one last time and was told in angry tones that he had been ordered to have nothing to do with us—"

Richard suffered a sudden heat on his face.

"—that he had been told to remain in his attic, prepare his belongings, and exchange no discourse with us."

The words, so bluntly delivered, had an air of unreality about them. Though he knew the answer to his next question, he asked it anyway. "On—whose orders?"

"John's."

In an attempt to remain calm, he walked the short distance into his alcove study, aware of Bertie following behind him, his voice calm.

"He knows," he said, and in that simple manner confirmed Richard's worst nightmare.

Clinging to the last vestige of hope, Richard asked, "How can we be sure? And what difference does it make?"

"To me, none," Bertie said. "To you, I'm afraid, everything."

"What will—he do?"

"Perhaps nothing," Bertie said quietly. "Surely there are enough other complications in his life. Why should he concern himself with us? Perhaps his only concern is that Aslam not be—corrupted." Bertie shrugged. "In that case, he will come and fetch the boy and that will be that."

There was something hollow in his comfort as well as his words. John, as Richard knew all too well, was not given to simple solutions. What would he do without Bertie and where would he go and how would he survive?

"Give me your hand," Bertie commanded gently.

Richard obeyed and the contact seemed to lighten the darkness, though their hands were motionless and did not press each other. Richard even moved slightly away. But his consciousness was focused in the perception of that small area where their hands touched. And he suffered the desire to talk about the beauty and the strange power of love, but to talk without violating the

silence. He thought that they ought to say something
and he wanted to, but he didn't dare.

"I'm here," Bertie whispered. . . .

Who would blame her?

Neither God nor man, for what was a sixty-seven-
year-old lady to do but take from any hand that was
prepared to give?

Widowed since she was forty, though that was a case
of good riddance if ever there was one, Cella Pettibone had had to fend for herself in a world hostile to
women and widows.

As she hurried through the night, her destination
clear, she felt of the crisp new pound note tucked inside
her purse, a new addition for the thirty-seven already
tucked safely away in the tin beneath her mattress.

Oh, she was a smart one, all right, as smart as the
half-males she served. Still, there was a twinge of conscience. She liked the gentle Lord Eden. Him was a cut
above the rest of the three-legged animals she was
forced to serve and clean up after.

But with thirty-seven—no, thirty-eight—pounds tucked
safely away in her nesty, and with the promise of more to
come, it wouldn't be too long before she could shake
the dust of Cambridge from her feet forever, buy herself
some decent clothes and travel to that paradise called
London, where she was certain that some good gentlewoman would take her on as a lady's maid, and she'd
never again have to smell a man's piss or farts for the
rest of her life.

Buoyed by the prospects, she hurried along the cobbles of Cambridge, heading toward The Barley Man
where, in exchange for information, the gentleman there
would give her another pound, perhaps more considering the importance of what she'd learned this night.

Didn't even know his name, she didn't, though she'd
asked often enough, only to have him respond like he
was talking to a barber's cat, the names weren't the
issue and all she needed to do was to bring him weekly
accounts of the goings-on in Lord Eden's flat and for
her troubles she'd be handsomely paid.

If it was proof the London man wanted, she could
provide him with it easily enough, particularly now that
the lovebirds were back in the same nest. Of course,

they were careful around her right enough. But still
there were ways, the soiled linens for one, which she
washed weekly for them, coated with the dried residue
of male slime. Going against the teachings of God, it
was, all that wasted seed which had to be washed out
with her strongest lye soap.

In spite of her moral outrage, she suffered a second
spasm of conscience. She really liked them both very
much and somehow could not make a firm connection
between their kind treatment of her and the obscene
tricks they performed on the bedsheets each night.

Oh, well, her head was weary with thinking. It didn't
make a bit of difference to her what happened, one way
or the other. Her only goal was to fill that tin beneath
her mattress so full of notes that she could take herself
out of this male place and spend what few years God
had left her in the decent company of a noblewoman.

To that end, she hurried into the warmth of The
Barley Man, past the three-legged animals guzzling at
the bar and on up the staircase which led to the rooms
above.

She found it effortlessly, Number Three, having been
here countless times before, knocked and, to her surprise, heard the buzz of male voices coming from the
other side.

Strange! The man had always been alone in the past.
Suddenly she heard a cessation of voices and held still
outside the door, listening, and was on the verge of
knocking again when the door opened a crack and she
saw the nameless man's face and saw more, beyond
his shoulder into the room itself, saw a second man,
younger, with dark skin, like an Indian nigger, seated
before the table.

"Ah, Mrs. Pettibone," the man said, beaming. "Come,
come in, please."

When she hesitated, the man laughed.

"Don't be afraid, Mrs. Pettibone." He grinned.
"We're all friends here."

Cheltenham
Late November 1870

THEY WERE DRESSED in black, like penitents, their faces pale, their hair pulled uniformly back in rigid knots, their hands folded in their laps. Twenty-five, perhaps thirty young women, varying in age from seventeen to twenty-six, all staring up at him like ghosts.

"The schoolroom," Miss Veal announced. "The desks purchased, Mr. Eden, if I may point out, with your last generous donation."

"It's chilly," he observed, and wondered how soon he could exit this grim place.

Nothing that he had seen thus far of Miss Veal's School for Females had been as he had expected, and when he'd caught his first glimpse of it from the road over an hour ago he had been convinced that his driver had made a mistake, thinking nothing human could inhabit that ominous old Tudor mansion sitting in the middle of nowhere, well beyond the edges of Cheltenham.

But a weathered sign at the end of the driveway had announced in fading script, MISS VEAL'S SCHOOL FOR FEMALES, and the driver had brought the carriage to a halt. As John had looked down the long avenue of overgrown trees, his first instinct had been to turn about.

But worse than his initial impression of Miss Veal's establishment had been the white face seated opposite him in the carriage, a face that he'd had to endure throughout the tedious journey from London, an image made doubly grotesque by the foolish wig which Elizabeth had affixed to cover her butchered hair, an image that had said nothing.

Fully aware that he could not endure too many more minutes in that presence, he'd been forced to give his driver directions to turn into the long driveway and had comforted himself with the rationalization that it was the storm and wind and rain that had made everything so ugly.

"Come, Mr. Eden," Miss Veal urged, "the young ladies must be left to concentrate, and I have yet to show you the refectory and the—"

"I believe I've seen enough, Miss Veal. About Mary—" Even as he talked he fled the room and tried to see down the corridor where he'd left Mary, seated on a wooden bench in the entrance hall in the company of a female attendant.

"No need to worry about your cousin, Mr. Eden," Miss Veal soothed, coming up alongside him. "I assure you, you've taken the right step and she's in her proper place."

As the woman drew closer, John stepped back, finding her as disreputable as her establishment.

"We pride ourselves here, Mr. Eden," she went on, "on being able to take headstrong young girls and convert them into proper young ladies, ready to take their proper places in the world. Most of our young women come from pampered atmospheres," she said. "Nothing more difficult than to refuse oneself anything when all the world would grant one everything." She stepped closer. "So, I suppose we really mustn't be too harsh on our young charges. Frequently they hear a firm 'No' for the first time in their lives from the lips of my staff."

He nodded—to everything, and wished that the passage were a bit darker, thus preventing him from seeing this macabre creature, dreadfully old, older than any human had a right to be. Also, she was as thin as a cadaver, her stick figure without shape, and she wore a badly cut dress of no color at all, but which appeared to be stained with bits of dried food and lightly flecked with a residue of white rice powder. Another repulsive touch was her white hair cropped close about her head.

"Say no more, Miss Veal, I beg you. I must be on the road immediately and request now that I be shown Mary's quarters."

He detected a look of peevishness on the woman's gaunt face, but she recovered and announced, "Of course, Mr. Eden. I fully understand. This way, please."

As they drew near the entrance hall he took momentary refuge in the winter sky just visible through the slit in the heavy oak door. It looked as gray and hard as metal, the mists blurring the black outline of trees that rose from the distant ridges. The cold was even more acute than it had been in the schoolroom, whistling in under the door in razor-sharp drafts.

"Ah, here's our young lady," Miss Veal pronounced, and John dragged his eyes from the desolate landscape to the equally desolate vision seated on the bench. As far as he could tell, she had not moved.

He saw Miss Veal encircling her, one blue-veined hand inspecting Mary's face, an intimacy from which anyone would have withdrawn. But as the hand moved across her lips, the expression on Mary's face did not alter.

"She looks—ill, Mr. Eden," the woman announced.

How much to tell her? John wondered. Thus far he'd told her nothing. "She's not ill, Miss Veal," he began, "though she had an unfortunate experience about a month ago. In the park, it was. She was riding and ruffians overtook her."

Miss Veal listened closely to the vague account. "And what precisely did these ruffians do?" she asked, suspiciously.

"Frightened her, primarily."

"And what was she doing alone in the park?"

"She was not alone," John replied, "though her chaperone was some distance removed."

"Then she was alone." Miss Veal smiled, as though she'd won a victory.

"In a manner of speaking, yes."

The inspection continued, the old woman prodding in an almost obscene fashion, loosening Mary's cape, her inquisitive hands studying the wig and at last, in brutal fashion, stripping off both bonnet and wig, leaving the mutilated hair clear for all to see, a sight which had become even more unattractive in the last month as the hair had started to grow out in jagged tufts all over the small, pink scalp.

"Well, now"—she smiled down on Mary—"haven't we gone and got ourselves into a fine pickle?"

In her cold objectivity John discovered a curious comfort. For weeks he'd been forced to endure not only the ghostlike Mary but Elizabeth's constant sympathy as well, the woman a fountain of tears. And Dhari had been little better, and Andrew even worse. It was a genuine relief to look down on the silent young woman and hear her ordeal described quaintly as a "pickle."

"Well, the hair will grow, won't it, my dear?" Miss Veal was saying to Mary, as though she were confident of a response. "But there will be no wigs here," she added, and handed the hairpiece gingerly to the large female aide with whispered instructions to "Burn it!"

She looked back at Mary and commenced speaking, lifting her voice as though she wanted John to hear as well.

"One of the most important lessons to be learned at Miss Veal's," she pronounced, "is the courage to face oneself as one really is. Cosmetics are against the rules, as are frills and ribbons, hair curlers and most certainly wigs. We must concentrate all our energies on identifying our vanities and ripping them out by the roots. Only in penance and self-denial can we hope to reach that high level of awareness which will make us responsible women and obedient ones."

John nodded in agreement and searched Mary's face for the slightest reaction and found none. Apparently Miss Veal had launched the same search with the same futile results.

"The girl is not—addled, is she, Mr. Eden?" she inquired.

"No, not at all," John replied. "The experience has sobered her. And, of course, these surroundings are new and she is, by nature, very shy. In time she will—"

"Good. Good." Miss Veal smiled. "Well, then—come, child, and I'll show you to your room. You, too, Mr. Eden. I want you to see it all."

With Miss Veal in the lead, John following after and the aide and Mary bringing up the rear, the grim parade started up the staircase, encountering an even deeper chill and two stern-faced women garbed in black just starting down the stairs, their beaklike noses causing them to resemble birds.

"Two of our finest instructors, Mr. Eden," Miss Veal called down as the women passed him by. "Miss Andrews, Geography, and Miss Leonard, History."

John pushed close to the wall to give them easy passage. They did not acknowledge him in any way, but slowed their descent as Mary passed them by, their eyes focused on the ruined hair.

If Mary was aware of their scrutiny, she gave no indication of it and continued on up the stairs, eyes down. John felt he could not look upon her a moment longer and hurried down the corridor after Miss Veal, consoling himself with the thought that in a quarter of an hour at most he would be on the road to Cambridge.

"Ah, here it is," Miss Veal pronounced, stopping before a low, narrow door identical to the others which lined the corridor. John glanced about and saw no wall lamp and thought how black the passage would be at night.

Miss Veal pushed open the door and stepped back to permit John first entry into the cubicle, which measured no more than six feet in both directions, with one small window reinforced on the outside with two crisscrossing bars, and containing in the way of furniture one low cot with a single rolled blanket, one straight-backed chair, one desk and one washstand.

It resembled a prison cell. As the wind whistled in through the panes of barred glass, John asked, "The— source of heat, Miss Veal, I see no fireplace."

"There are no fireplaces in the individual rooms," she replied. "Too much warmth is not good for the system. The girls are allowed to congregate each evening after dinner in the parlor and there we have a large fireplace burning constantly. They are permitted to warm their nightclothes and, on extremely cold nights, we provide them with the luxury of heated bricks."

Still, John stood at the center of the cubicle, suffering a sharp sense of doubt, thinking that he should take Mary and flee this place. He suffered a painful image of her private chambers at Number Seven, St. George Street, a lovely den of soft fabric and color, the massive rosewood bed which he'd purchased for her when she'd moved to London, with the white lace canopy and rose-embroidered coverlet, the mahogany wardrobe filled with gowns and furs.

"Mr. Eden, you must remember," Miss Veal said at his elbow, "we here at the school are not intent on duplicating the young ladies' home environment. If those indulgent atmospheres had produced the desired results, there would be no need to place them in our care."

The voice was confident and John could not dispute the truth of her words.

"What we must do here," she went on, "is to strip away the layers of artifice and ease and self-indulgence.

We must re-create what adoring parents and generous guardians have corrupted. And, in the case of young Mary there, I would say that the corruption has been devastating."

"Then see to everything, Miss Veal," he announced on renewed determination. "I'll leave her in your capable hands. And from time to time please inform me of your needs here and I'll see what I can do."

He was out of the door and a few steps beyond when Miss Veal caught up with him.

"You're not going to say goodbye?" she asked, obviously stunned by the fact that he was prepared to leave Mary without ceremony.

Reluctantly he stepped back to the door and suffered instant regret. Mary was standing precisely where the aide had left her, beside the low cot. Her eyes lifted for the first time since they had arrived and focused on him. He thought she would speak and prayed that she wouldn't, and, unable to endure that gaze any longer, he turned away, thinking that he'd seen tears in her eyes.

"Mr. Eden, wait and I'll escort you," Miss Veal called after him.

But he was in no mood for waiting.

"Mr. Eden, there are papers you must sign," Miss Veal called again.

"Send them to London."

"Mr. Eden, we would like you to stay for tea, if you will. We had planned—"

But he didn't give a damn what they had planned. All that mattered was to put as much distance as possible between himself and that last image of Mary standing alone in her cell, her mutilation visible for all to see, and the devastating awareness of the part he'd played in bringing it about.

She deceived me, betrayed me. . . .

Only by repeating those statements of fact could he find the strength which enabled him to gain his carriage through the steady downpour of rain, wave aside his driver's offer for help, simultaneously shouting, "Make for Cambridge!" as he hurled himself inside the small door, where he promptly closed it and drew down the window curtains.

As the carriage started forward he heard his own

breath coming in gasps, his hands still clutching at the curtains.

She *was* crying, though the tears were insignificant and had been provoked by that reoccurring and lovely memory which for days had played hide-and-seek in her mind. Sometimes at the most unexpected moments she caught a brief glimpse of a strong brow, a lock of dark hair. . . .

She sat down on the low cot, aware for the first time that she was alone in the cell. She should have said goodbye to the man who had brought her here. That would have been the polite thing to do, and she'd tried, but he'd not given her the chance and, although she would never have said it to anyone else, she was glad to be here, away from Elizabeth's constant weeping and Dhari's sympathetic eyes and the whispers of everyone around her, and sometimes they hadn't even bothered to whisper but had discussed her openly, as though she were dead and incapable of hearing.

But she'd heard everything and understood more, and knew better than anyone that she was ugly and soiled and must hide herself away.

Then here she was, and perhaps in the safety of this place she might cleanse herself and learn to forget the hideous odor that always accompanied her nightmare, the sensations which still descended without warning and left her terrified.

No! She mustn't even think on them, and quickly she lifted her head and spied the small window and the gray day beyond, and left the cot and looked down on a rank and overgrown garden, no pretense at flowerbeds or any manner of cultivation, straggling bushes matted together above the dead grass, the ceaseless wind blowing against dead fruit trees, their crucified branches rotting under the nails that held them up.

The landscape suited her. Surrounded by such ugliness, who would notice her?

She heard a disturbance at the door and looked back to see a large woman in black holding a black dress draped over her arm.

"Lady Mary?" she inquired politely. "I've brought you this. You'll be more comfortable in it. My name is Frieda. Come, let me help you change."

How kind she seemed, Mary thought, and with what straightforwardness did she look her in the eye, unlike others who recently had looked around her or over her.

Without objection, Mary allowed the woman to remove her garments, her dark blue traveling suit first, then her petticoat, then her chemise, stooping herself to remove her slippers and hose, shivering in the chill without protection of garments.

The woman named Frieda was just in the process of swinging the coarse black fabric over her head when from the door she heard voices.

"Not so fast, Frieda. Let's have a look at the goods before you put the shroud on."

Mary looked beyond Frieda's shoulder to two women in black. She'd seen them earlier on the stairs. They hadn't been smiling at her. They were now, and Mary liked their smiles. It had been so long since anyone had smiled at her.

But apparently Frieda didn't. "Come on, you two. Leave the lass alone. She's been ill-treated by someone, and recently, too."

"We have no intention of mistreating her, Frieda, you old scold."

"We just want a look. How will that hurt?"

Slowly the two women came forward, encircling her, touching her flesh, one cupping her hand about her buttocks, the other tracing a line with the tip of her finger, commencing on her lower abdomen and circling her breasts.

"A beauty," one murmured.

"Quality."

"What do you suppose happened here?"

Not until Mary felt their hands on her head did she find anything worthy of objection. One of the women had re-emerged in her vision and was no longer smiling, as though at last she'd seen the ugliness.

As Mary lowered her head, she heard Frieda step forward. "Come on, that's enough. Go pick on those who know you," she commanded.

"Oh, my," one said, smiling sweetly. "Frieda's got herself a new pet."

"Private property, eh, Frieda?"

"Get out, both of you!" Frieda ordered.

To Mary's surprise, the two obeyed, though both

stopped at the door and watched as Frieda lowered the
black dress over Mary's head and pulled it into place,
buttoning the endless buttons which led all the way up to
her chin, adjusting the sleeves which fell over her hands.
Too large, the dress hung on her in ridiculous fashion,
though she was warm and grateful for that.

Suddenly something caused the two women at the
door to break into laughter and, begrudgingly, Frieda
joined them, and though all three were staring at Mary,
the sound of their laughter was so good, such a blessed
relief after the weeks of constant tears, that Mary
smiled back at them, drawing the shapeless dress about
her, which caused them to laugh even harder. . . .

Eden Castle
Late November 1870

WELL ACCUSTOMED TO solitude and silence after the ten
years of her self-imprisonment, Lady Harriet Eden preferred the castle in this somnambulist state. But today she
suspected that something was wrong, for the schedule was
off, Peggy was late.

As the minutes passed, recorded by the ticking of the
clock, Harriet lifted her head toward the door, alarm
increasing. Curious. In the past she'd scolded Peggy for
adhering to so rigid a schedule. Yet now—

There! An unmistakable footstep, though more than
one. Peggy in the company of someone? Without precedent,
that, for Peggy knew better than anyone how Harriet
disliked visitors except the family, but there was no family
at Eden now except Lila, who was confined in her pregnancy.

Several times early in the summer Harriet had tried
to see her. But her invitations had been rejected each
time and finally Peggy had told her that on John's instructions Dr. Cockburn had confined the young woman
to her chambers without company.

With no desire to cross John or jeopardize in any way
the birth of his third child, Harriet had retreated into

her own solitude, the months had passed and most of the time she even forgot that she was not in the castle alone.

Harriet heard the door open and heard Peggy's voice as strained as she'd ever heard it. "Milady, forgive my tardiness, but I—"

"What is it?" Harriet demanded, hearing in the taut voice a confirmation that something was wrong.

"I was just on my way up with your luncheon tray, milady, when I was approached by—two women—"

"Who?"

"I don't know their names, milady. They were hired some months ago by Mr. Eden to look after Lady Lila. They live apart and keep to themselves."

"And why did they approach you?" Harriet asked, wondering briefly where Molly was, Lila's devoted maid.

There was a pause, Peggy reluctant to answer. "I would prefer for them to tell you, milady. They are right outside. With your permission—"

Standing before her chair, Harriet hesitated to give her permission. She disliked prying servants. Whoever these women were and whatever their message, she was under no obligation to have any dealings with them. Over the years John had hand-picked a large and trustworthy staff. The management of Eden was in their hands. She wanted nothing to do with it.

To that end, she was about to say "No," when she heard Peggy again, a peculiar tone of entreaty in her voice. "Forgive me, milady, but I think you ought to see them. Something terrible is happening and you're the only one—"

Though only a moment before Harriet had thought with pleasure on her lack of responsibility, now, hearing the tone of need in Peggy's voice gave her a good feeling, made her feel necessary, no longer an invalid.

Lifting her head to be certain her veil was in place, she said, "Show them in, Peggy, but warn them to be brief."

"Thank you, milady."

As she heard the maid leave the room, Harriet debated whether she should receive them seated or standing. But there was no time to reach a decision, for she was aware of a scuffle of steps and a sniffling, as though someone were weeping and trying to conceal it.

"Straighten up," she heard Peggy whisper, "then identify yourselves and state your message."

"Me name's Agnes, milady."

"And I'm Louise——"

Peggy interrupted. "One spokesman will be enough. You there, you do the talking."

It took the appointed "spokesman" a moment to collect herself, then at last Harriet heard, "My apologies, milady, for bothering you like this, and we put it off, she and me, as long as we could, but we got to live with ourselves, now, don't we?"

"Get on with it," Peggy ordered.

"Well, milady, we was hired, you see, and there's four of us, to keep an eye on the young Mrs. Eden."

"Who hired you?" Harriet asked. Lila had her personal staff. Why were four more needed?

"Oh, Mr. Eden himself done our hiring last summer, it was, after all the big goings-on——"

Where is Molly? Harriet wondered again and was on the verge of asking when suddenly she heard weeping in the room, heard Peggy moving toward the sounds of distress.

"Now, that won't accomplish anything, will it?" she asked, soothing and scolding at the same time. "Go ahead. Talk to milady. Tell her just what you told me."

The woman tried to speak around her tears. "Oh, milady, it's terrible, it is. I ain't ever seen anything so terrible in me life. And the suffering. And that poor lass tries not to cry out, but sometimes she can't help herself and——"

Alarm increasing, Harriet sat up on the edge of her chair. "What are you talking about?"

"Her, milady," the voice replied, half in anger that she wasn't making herself clear. "Mrs. Eden, that's who!"

"Is she ill?"

"Ill, milady?" parroted the flat voice. "She's dying."

Harriet stood and counseled herself prudence. Servants tended to hysteria. "Surely you don't mean——"

"I mean just what I says, milady, and more."

"She always has difficult pregnancies."

"This ain't no pregnancy, milady," the voice insisted. "Please explain."

"Oh, she's swelling right enough," the voice went on, "but there's no babe growing inside her."

As fresh sobs filled the room, Harriet stood motionless, trying to sort out the hysteria from the truth. An idea occurred and she voiced it, convinced that the woman was not qualified to pass medical judgment.

"Have you seen pregnancies before?" she asked.

"Seen them!" the voice replied. "That's why I was hired, milady. I'm a professional midwife, I am. I've delivered babes from one end of Devon to the other. I've seen 'em come into the world sideways, backwards and upside down, and I've guided and helped ever last one of them. Oh, I know new life, milady, the feel and smell and the sound of it, and I'm here to tell you that there ain't no babe growing inside Mrs. Eden, but a monstrous lump that is on the verge of killing—"

Harriet didn't want to hear that again and cut her off. "The doctor—I thought that the doctor was—"

"A jackass, milady, if you'll forgive me. I wouldn't let old Cockburn treat me dog for ticks."

Dying—

The word approached her stealthily. If something was wrong, John would expect her to take charge. Still, she'd tried in the past to see Lila and had always been turned back by the doctor. And was the woman telling the truth or was she exaggerating, placing Harriet in the middle of a power struggle with the doctor?

As the questions occurred to her, she was aware of Peggy beside her. "The castle is filled with gossip, milady," she whispered. "All the superstitions about death running riot. They seem to feel that something bad's about to happen, and I—thought you should know."

Harriet nodded. While the other two women might tend toward hysteria, she knew from loving experience that Peggy was a rock. If Peggy said something was wrong that warranted Harriet's attention, then on that basis alone she had better look into it.

Still, there was the obstacle of Lila's locked door. "If I go," she asked, "will the doctor let me pass?"

"You leave the jackass to us, milady," the voice responded. "He's stuffing his gullet now and he always treats himself to an afternoon nap. If you would be so good as to come at this moment, we will see that you—"

"Get my shawl, Peggy," Harriet commanded.

A short time later, after having descended two flights of stairs and made their way through the core of the castle, Harriet was aware that they should be entering the west wing.

"There it is, milady," someone whispered behind her. "Up ahead. If you will wait here, I'll see if the old fool is about."

Harriet was aware of Peggy guiding her close to the wall, the entire episode beginning to take on a rather exciting sense of stealth and melodrama.

Then she heard something that radically changed her sense of sport, a moan, so low as to be scarcely audible, but a sound of pain all the same, and worse, pain that had been endured for too long without respite.

"What was that?" Harriet asked, aware of Peggy hovering close before her.

"I'm—not sure, milady."

"What's taking them so long?" she demanded and was on the verge of suggesting that they proceed without the assistance of the maids when she heard Peggy announce, "There, they are motioning us forward. Come, milady, let's see this through and go back where we belong."

Harriet was aware that they were passing through a door, and was aware further of an atmosphere of pain so strong that it was a thing of substance, a magnetizing center which seemed to emanate from—

"Over here, milady," Peggy directed. "The bedchamber is in this—"

Harriet knew the direction and was convinced that with no assistance at all she could have found her way into the small room to her left, the air about her filling rapidly with a noxious odor, worse than merely unclean linen, but something poisonous.

The spirit of death was in this room, hovering close, fully welcomed, yet holding back.

"Peggy—"

"Here, milady," said a voice which Harriet did not recognize.

"Guide me to her and be my eyes, please."

She felt the familiar hand in hers, drawing her closer to the source of the suffering, a peculiar silence coming from the bed. Without speaking she was aware of Peggy taking her hand and placing it on a hard, misshapen lump of human flesh, feverish-feeling even through the thickness of a muslin nightshirt.

"It's not a pregnancy, milady," Peggy whispered.

Weary of the translation, Harriet took over for herself, pushed the shawl off her shoulders and stepped closer to the bed, both hands at work, relying solely on the "eyes" in her fingertips, which traced the lump the length and breadth of the abdomen, the skin stretched taut, something filling that small cavity at twice its normal capacity, her hands lifting the nightshirt to feel the skin itself dampened by fever, the waist lost in the swelling, the breasts heaving as though Lila were panting.

"Is she awake?" Harriet asked of anyone who cared to answer.

Receiving no reply, as though the sight of the suffering had shocked the others into silence, she commenced a gentle exploration of the face and neck and was aware of the matted hair upon the pillow, the parched lips, the dampness of perspiration coating everything.

Still unable to determine whether or not there was a consciousness behind the suffering, Harriet kissed the fevered cheek and whispered, "Lila, can you hear me?"

"I think she hears you, milady," one of the maids volunteered, "but she can't talk much."

"She asks for her papa, but that's all," another said.

Dissatisfied with both responses, Harriet leaned close. "Lila, please—can you hear me?"

The face beneath her fingers wrenched to one side. Harriet could feel the pressure behind the eyes as the young woman struggled to digest a fresh pain.

Hoping only to absorb a portion of the suffering, Harriet sat on the side of the bed and lifted Lila to her, cradled her, and tried not to concentrate on the wobbling head, mute proof of her weakened state.

The spasm passed and, as she lowered her back to the pillow, voices evolved behind her.

"It's a growing tumor, milady, that's what it is. I seen the likes of it before in my auntie down in Weymouth. She swolled up and it wasn't no pregnancy, we all knew that, 'cause she was an unmarried lady and never knowed a man—"

The voice broke. "It was awful, milady. It got to where she couldn't use the chamber pot—"

"And herself there hasn't either for several days—"

"All she passes is blood, milady."

As their voices blended, Harriet caressed the burning forehead and tried not to think on the beautiful young girl with hair the color of the sun.

The dried lips were trying to form words, but all she heard was a gasping.

"Harriet—"

"I'm here, Lila," she replied, clasping the small hand between her own. "I wanted to come earlier but they wouldn't let me see you."

The voice was trying to form additional words, and Harriet bent over.

"My—children," Lila whispered. "May I—see my children?"

"Of course you may," Harriet promised. "I'll send for them immediately."

"And—my—father?"

Harriet hesitated. She would not make a promise she could not keep, although she vowed, "I'll write to him this very day and send the message with the fastest courier."

The breath, slight to begin with, was fading. Still there was more. "And Wolf. Please bring Wolf to me. I've—lost the path—"

Harriet listened, baffled. Wolf, she knew, was the gray cat that had been given the run of the castle. It would present no difficulties locating him. But what did she mean, "I've lost the path"?

"I'll find him, Lila," Harriet promised. "Now you must rest."

"No, please," came the voice. "I won't be afraid if Wolf is here. He promised to go with—me—"

"Go where, dearest?" Harriet murmured. "You must get well first, then—"

"Please find him," Lila begged. "He knows the way."

Coming from behind, Harriet heard one of the maids. "She's not in her mind, milady. She says the most curious things."

Harriet felt Lila's hand insistently pulling her down. "Please find him. I—don't want to stay here any longer. Please—"

Harriet followed each contortion of those slim fingers until one by one they became powerless, as a new wave of pain overtook her. There was a gasp and then she was still. Terrified, Harriet called for assistance.

"Is she—"

"Not dead yet, milady, just unconscious."

Silence followed this announcement and, although she asked for forgiveness, Harriet caught herself wishing that death had descended and claimed her. As long as she was at prayer, she bowed her head and asked God for guidance, fully aware that the burden of action was upon her.

To that end she stood from the bed and commenced issuing orders, amazed that beyond the uncertainty of the first few words it was easy, an ancient ability instilled in her by centuries of breeding.

"Peggy," she commanded, assigning the first task to that reliable woman, "I want you to fetch my writing portfolio. I will write a letter to John and I want it dispatched immediately by two couriers riding the fastest horses, and there are to be no stops until they reach London and place the letter in John's hand."

"Yes, milady."

"When you have completed that, I want you to go to the nursery and tell Miss Samson that the boys are to be dressed and made ready. I won't have them brought down now, but as soon as she awakens."

"Yes, milady."

Good Peggy. Harriet softened her tone of voice, "And after that," she went on, "please have two couches moved into the next room for us. We will be staying here awhile."

Harriet waited until she heard the departing footsteps, then she turned her attention to the women behind her. "I thank you for summoning me," she commenced, recalling the days when she had been mistress of Eden and what a magical effect a little consideration had on the servants.

"We should have done it sooner, milady," one said. "I told the others that Mr. Eden didn't hire us to watch his wife die."

Harriet nodded. "You did the right thing," and felt bewilderment that Lila had not mentioned John once. How sad for both of them. Then, aware that she had the attention of the woman and must do something with it, she commanded, "I want one of you to fetch Dr. Cockburn for me. I am relieving him of his duties and want to tell him so personally in order to avoid any misunderstanding."

"Oh, a pleasure that will be, milady," one said. "I'll keep that little chore for meself, if you don't mind."

"And I want one of you to alert all the stewards to be on the watch for the cat."

"No watch is needed, milady. He keeps to the kitchen and suns himself every afternoon outside the kitchen door."

"Then fetch him," Harriet said. "I want him here. And I want one of you to fetch pitchers of cool water, and clean linen. We are going to bathe her and try—"

"We done that, milady," one interrupted, "but it got to where it was hurting her so much to move her, we decided—"

"Bring them again," Harriet commanded. "We won't move her. We'll simply try to cool her and make her more comfortable."

"Aye, milady."

Then the instructions were over. This was all that Harriet could think to do. It had occurred to her she might send for a more competent physician from Exeter, but there was that feeling in the room, the sense of imminent death that was so strong it belied all medical assistance.

Aware of the women hovering about her, awaiting either dismissal or further instructions, Harriet felt a question forming.

"One of you mentioned a relation earlier, a woman who had suffered a similar—"

"Aye, milady. My old auntie it was—"

"What—happened?"

"She died, milady, and the richest of God's blessings it was when she drew the last breath. I never heard such screams and I never want to hear them again."

"And what was the medical decision on your aunt?"

"The doctor said it was a tumor, a mal-ig-nancy, I believe he said, something growing where it ought not to be, and blocking everything that oughtn't to be blocked, if you know what I mean."

She did. Lila's fever was the result of her own body wastes. She was poisoning herself.

She asked quietly, "Was it—a hard death?"

"The hardest I ever hope to see again," came the

quick reply. "Our old sawbones was good enough to give Auntie opium. And it helped some, but she still died the death of the damned."

Harriet lowered her head. She despised opium. Still, if it would ease Lila's agony. . . .

"Then fetch some opium," she commanded. "She will not suffer more than is necessary."

"Yes, milady. I tried to tell old Cockburn that, but he said no, that opium would effect the babe."

"The babe!" Harriet gasped, overwhelmed by the man's ignorance, shocked by John's willingness to place his wife in such inept hands.

"Aye, the babe," one repeated sarcastically. "He claims to hear a heartbeat, and even suggested once—"

"Fetch him!" Harriet ordered. "Fetch him immediately, then see to the rest of it."

While she was aware of how awkward she must look, she didn't care. At this moment there was nothing in the world that mattered more than the fact of death itself, obscene in this case, a young woman who had committed no crime, no sin, whose sole reason for being had been to bring happiness to others and who now, by some whimsy of nature, had been condemned to death.

Harriet waited until she heard the outer door close. Then she sat on the edge of the bed and felt for the fever-dampened brow and caressed it, and wondered how it was possible that many human beings judged this world to be heaven when in reality it was hell. . . .

It was well after midnight before she'd accomplished everything she'd set out to do. Now, seated fully dressed on her couch in the room next to Lila, the sleeves of her gown still damp from the cool lavender-water with which she had bathed the young woman, she was awaiting Peggy's return from the kitchen with a light meal.

In the silence she listened for the slightest sound coming from the next room. Nothing. There had been nothing all afternoon. Several times, alarmed by the silence, Harriet had felt for and found a pulse, mute evidence that life was persisting.

She shivered, not from cold but rather from a combination of fatigue and grief. Would anyone arrive in time? At best it would take the couriers a day and a half to make London. Then would John and Lord Harrington leave immediately? She'd tried to make the message clear and had urged the greatest haste.

She lifted her head in the direction of Lila's room, thinking that she'd heard something. But she decided finally that it was only the cat, Wolf, who had been found midafternoon and lured upstairs with a bowl of rich cream and who, according to Peggy, had settled comfortably on the foot of Lila's bed.

Abruptly she stood. In this unfamiliar environment she suffered a collision with a low table, quickly righted both herself and the table and with both hands outreaching, she commenced to feel her way about the small chamber.

Near the mantlepiece a bleak thought occurred to her. A transient guest had occupied these chambers, a brief, though dazzling, ray of light which had illuminated all their lives and which now was on the verge of being extinguished.

Could it have been avoided? Is Lila's death unnecessary. . . . What was that? Looking up toward the footsteps in the corridor, she heard Peggy's excited voice even while the door was still closed: "Milady, someone is here, a miracle!"

She heard the door open and was on the verge of demanding, "Who?" when a deep, fatigued though familiar male voice broke in.

"Milday, it's me, Lord Harrington."

"Lord Harrington?" she murmured, and reached out her hand and thanked God for at least one favor.

"How did you—"

"Where is she?" he cut in.

Aware of their cross-purposes, she found his arm and tried to place a restraining hand on it. "Lila is quite ill, Lord Harrington," she warned, feeling the need to prepare him.

"I know."

"How did you know?"

"A friend, Charles Parnell, stopped off here on his way to Ireland some months ago."

"He was—permitted access to these chambers?" she inquired, amazed.

"He took access for himself," Lord Harrington said. "Charles asks for nothing and thus avoids the possibility of being rejected." He paused, waiting out her questions before he could move on to the next room and the source of his love.

"Then John knows as well?" she asked, struggling to put the puzzle together.

There was another pause. "He knows Lady Eden—"

"Then why isn't he here?" she demanded.

"He said he was too—busy."

The simple words fell like rocks about her head. While she was still trying to recover, she heard movement and knew that Lord Harrington was proceeding on to his daughter's bedside.

"Peggy, please," she whispered, but too late. As they reached the door, she heard a deep groan.

"Lord Harrington, let me help," she murmured. But Peggy exerted pressure on her arm.

"He's at prayer, milady."

For over half an hour the ritual of prayer persisted. At some point she heard the sound of a rosary, and when she was just growing accustomed to the silence, she heard a male voice so constricted that it sounded as though the man were undergoing torture.

"Lila, it's me—Papa. Can you hear me? Please look at me. I've come back, my darling, to take you home again."

For the better part of that long night she sat with Peggy at her side, neither speaking, for what could either of them say that would match the eloquence of that deep voice as he tried to work his way through his grief.

Harriet had just heard Peggy's whisper of "Dawn" when suddenly the male voice fell silent, followed by a moan, then a lament which lifted the hairs on the back of her neck.

They reached the door at the same time, but Peggy left and went forward to confirm what Harriet knew was true.

"She's dead, milady," came the soft announcement. Harriet leaned back against the door, thanking God, thinking, *Could it have been avoided?*

She was in no way prepared for what she heard next, Peggy's sharp cry coming from a far corner of the room, her voice laden with disbelief.

"The cat, milady! I thought he was sleeping. He's—dead."

As the wailing lament of Lord Harrington rose and joined Peggy's irrational announcement, Harriet suffered a sensation as though she were being torn in half.

For the first time since her own crucible over ten years ago she bowed her head and thanked God for her blindness. . . .

❦

Cambridge
December 1, 1870

BERTIE WRAPPED THE ROPE around the trunk which contained the last of his books and looked about the drab empty room, relieved to be seeing it for the last time.

Richard was right. He had proved nothing by moving out of their comfortable flat except what they both already knew, that neither had any life without the other, and if John Murrey Eden was determined to find them out, then let him do so. Together they had a chance to survive, whatever fate had in store for them.

The thought that Richard was waiting for him with the tea kettle bubbling spurred him on a final inspection. He didn't want to forget anything, for he planned never to return.

Well, then, hoist this one trunk out to the pavement, then lock the door to this dingy room in which he'd passed one of the most miserable intervals of his life.

Before hoisting the trunk to his shoulders, he swung his cloak into place and thought on their plans for the future: the south of France, maybe fifteen years from now, a shared masterwork, a detailed study of the effects of Christianity on pagan Graeco-Roman life, a project which would challenge both their disciplines.

He shook his head at his own enthusiasm. There was time. Life had to be lived in logical progressive steps. The masterwork, the south of France, would come in time. For now all he needed was Richard's quiet company and love.

"Then—go—home!" he said aloud and was just in

the process of lifting the trunk up onto his shoulder
when he heard a noise at the outer door.

Richard, he thought, smiling. Richard had come to
assist him with this last trunk. He was more than ready
to receive that beloved face when suddenly the door was
pushed open.

"Aslam!" he exclaimed, confused to see the boy standing on his threshold. He hadn't even been aware that
Aslam knew where he was staying in town.

"What a pleasant surprise." He smiled at the young
man, who had yet to say a word. "Well, come in," Bertie
urged. "I'm afraid I can't offer you the comfort of a fire.
In fact, I was just leaving. But I have a splendid idea.
Why don't you come with me to Richard's and we'll all
have a cup of tea?"

He was talking too much and he knew it. But why in
the hell was the boy standing in that defiant position,
his eyes assessing the small room as though he were
looking for something?

"Aslam?" he began, sensing something wrong. But as
he stepped forward he saw Aslam move out into the corridor and turn, as though someone were with him.

Again Bertie thought that it was Richard. The two of
them had come together. With a sense of play he called
out, "Come on, Richard. No time for hide-and-seek. I'm
bloody well frozen and in need of a—"

But Aslam stepped further back, and the figure that
appeared in the doorway was not Richard.

"Mr.—Eden," Bertie murmured, and tried to cover his
shock by stepping back and putting the trunk between
them. "How—good to see you."

As the silence expanded to an uncomfortable point,
Bertie said, "We've been expecting you. Several days ago,
actually. Richard is most anxious to see you. Your letter
caused him some alarm. You mentioned Lady Mary's illness, but did not specify—"

*Will the man never speak? And how did they find me
here?* He tried again to alter the silence. "Richard—is not
here, Mr. Eden. He's—"

"I did not come to see Richard, Professor Nichols,"
the man said. "Might I step in for a moment?"

Belatedly remembering simple courtesy, Bertie rushed
to correct the oversight. "I'm sorry. Of course, do come
in, both of you, although I'm afraid it's not much warmer

inside. As you can see, I was just in the process of vacating these premises."

"For more comfortable ones, I hope." Mr. Eden smiled.

Bertie counseled himself prudence. "Yes, more comfortable."

Torn between the young man at the door and the curious manner in which Mr. Eden was leaning against the opposite wall in a position of suspect ease, Bertie found himself in the middle, trying to look in both directions at once.

Struggling to disguise his fears, Bertie said, "If you want to see Richard, Mr. Eden, he's not here."

"I've come to see you."

"Then by all means, my attention is yours," Bertie said. "I will try to be of service in any way I can—" He faltered. The mask of ease was slipping. "I'm—sorry. I have no chairs to offer you."

"No need."

"We might, if you wish, walk the short distance to the pub. It's quite a good one and there will be a fire and—"

"No, this place suits me."

Again silence. Bertie felt the need to keep both of them in his sights, a difficult task considering their positions at opposite ends of the room. At last, growing weary of trying, Bertie moved back until the three of them formed a triangle, leaving the rope-bound trunk alone in the center of the room.

Eden spoke in a peculiarly gentle tone. "I feel compelled to warn you, Professor Nichols, that my errand here today is not a pleasant one."

Bertie heard the sharp staccato sleet pelting at the window. The storm was growing worse, the room darker and colder. "Please speak openly, Mr. Eden. It's been my experience that one can deal with anything—"

"I'm grateful for your reassurance, and my request is quite simple."

"Name it."

"I want you to leave Cambridge, Professor Nichols. I want you to leave England. I will give you one week to put your affairs in order. Then you are to come to my London offices and I will have traveling papers for you plus two thousand pounds to cover any inconvenience. A steamer will leave Portsmouth on the thirteenth of December for Australia. I want you on it."

Bertie looked at the quiet man speaking madness. Perhaps it was a joke. Yes, that's what it was, a bizarre icebreaker to warm the passage to the true subject. Bertie laughed and stepped farther back until he felt the support of the wall. "I—don't understand," he faltered, the laugh fading when he saw that no one had joined him.

"Of course you do," Eden went on. "For years Richard has done little but boast of the vast scope of your intellect. Surely you can grasp the outline of so simple a proposition."

"Yes, I can grasp it, Mr. Eden, but I don't understand—"

"Then let me make it clearer." Eden pushed away from the wall and walked to the window, obliterating what little light of day was left. "I must make a painful confession," he said. "For several months both you and my cousin have been under observation by a private investigator, one hired by myself out of London."

"For what purpose?" Bertie demanded, angry at hearing his theory confirmed.

Eden shrugged. "For the purpose of gathering evidence, for the purpose of proving my private suspicions, which I have harbored and kept to myself for many years, since you and Richard first formed an—alliance."

The word was sarcastically spoken. With what ease the scene had become his worst nightmare. "And what would those suspicions be, Mr. Eden?" Bertie asked quietly.

The words came as he knew they would. "That you are a Sodomite, Professor Nichols, of the worst exhibitionistic kind, that your one aim is to corrupt men, as you have corrupted Richard, and that England can do very well without your contagion."

A cold wind seemed to be blowing directly on Bertie's face, but cold as it was it could not extinguish the fires of pain at hearing the accusation stated thus. He turned toward Aslam, regretful that the young man had heard, and requested softly, "Aslam, would you be so good as to wait outside."

Eden laughed. "Don't concern yourself with Aslam, Professor Nichols. First, he is well beyond your corruption, and, second, he knows more about your questionable activities than I myself." The laugh faded to a sad smile. "You see, Aslam has been working in concert with the private investigator, as has a woman named Mrs.

Pettibone. Do you know her, Professor Nichols? Does the name mean anything to you?"

Bertie turned away. Mysterious whispers seemed to be filling his ear. The walls of the decaying room were closing in on him. Perhaps loneliness wouldn't be too hard to bear for a man who had taught himself to love life in its entirety.

Eden saw his withdrawal and claimed a premature victory. "Oh, come now, Professor Nichols—things could go much harsher for you. In essence I'm offering you a new life, and I hear that Australia is a promised land, and they need teachers. With two thousand pounds in your pocket you can set yourself up in any kind of life you wish, perhaps even find one of your own kind to share it with."

One of your own kind. How unworthy he felt, how empty. On the wall before him was a strip of loosened wallpaper. He pulled at it and saw it disintegrate in his hands. "What if I refuse to go, Mr. Eden?"

There was a pause, then the voice spoke with even greater regret. "I don't think you would be that foolish," Eden murmured. "You see, I have just come from the police inspector's office. I've provided him with impressive evidence of certain Sodomite activities in Cambridge, right under his very nose, as it were. Do you know the police inspector, Professor Nichols? He's a very righteous man, a pillar of support in the local Methodist Church and a Bible scholar as well. He quoted endless passages for me, didn't he, Aslam, on corrupt and unnatural behavior between men, called it the handwork of the Devil."

The voice came closer. "He begged me, Professor Nichols, for the names of the parties involved, so that he could move swiftly to wipe the sinners out. But I withheld the names on purpose, though I promised him that I would supply them later."

He stood very close now. "I'm sure I don't have to tell you what a trial would mean to both you and Richard, a public trial, here in Cambridge with all your colleagues in attendance, the evidence—and it is impressive—dragged out for all to see."

Bertie tried to move away from the threatening voice. "And neither do I have to tell you, Professor Nichols," the voice went on, "the outcome of such a trial,

the judgment, the swift sentence, the persecution of Sodomites by fellow prisoners. . . ."

To his astonishment, Bertie felt his eyes fill with tears.
Still there was a weakness in the fabric of everything
Eden had said, a flaw which, if only Bertie could find it,
might make a difference. There was something too calm
in the voice, some aspect to the threat that Eden was trying to avoid.

With effort, Bertie wiped his eyes. With the obstinate
egoism peculiar to trapped animals, he found the flaw
and turned on it.

"I have no doubt that you are prepared to bring
charges against me, Mr. Eden. But what of Richard? I
suggest that you consider the pain he will suffer if you
bring charges against him, your cousin, who, by his own
confession, loves you deeply."

As he talked, he watched for the slightest change of
expression on that self-confident face. But he detected
nothing, though Eden did concede, "It would be difficult.
But no more difficult than it has been to watch his steady
disintegration from full manhood to something weak and
unspeakable." His voice fell. "Thanks to you, Professor
Nichols, I can hardly bear my own cousin's company
anymore. Your malignancy has emasculated him. He is
half-woman now, and I would rather see him dead."

Shocked, Bertie whispered, "I—don't believe you."

"Whether you believe me or not is unimportant."
Eden walked back to the window, where Bertie saw the
storm raging, the sky blackened with boiling clouds.

The voice rose above the storm. "Only Richard can
produce a legitimate heir to the Eden name, Professor
Nichols, and since you lack a womb, then you must be removed from the scene. A young woman of good birth
has been selected, and with your departure I'm confident that Richard will recover his lost manhood and perform the function for which he was intended."

"If he doesn't?"

Eden shrugged. "Then I'll send him to prison, without
hesitation, for he'll be as good as dead to me, and I prefer
that he do his rotting out of sight."

Stunned, Bertie stared at him. He glanced toward Aslam, as though the presence of a third party might alter
something. Then all the horror and threats congealed
within him and, suffering physical weakness, he stumbled

forward and would have fallen except for the trunk, which he reached for just in time. Sitting heavily, he closed his eyes.

"Oh, come now, Professor Nichols," the voice chided from the window. "It isn't the end of the world. In fact, I would suggest that you view it as the beginning of a new one. Will you do that for me, for yourself, as well?"

He could not reply.

"Then I'll take my leave and give you the privacy which you so obviously need. Aslam and I are on our way back to London. We won't stop by to see Richard. Please tell him that I shall look forward to his company during the Christmas Festivities at Eden."

Bertie tried to lift his head, but it hurt to breathe.

"As for yourself," came the voice from the door, a gentle voice, "I would advise that you see to the conclusion of your affairs here and within the week I'll look forward to seeing you in my London offices." Here the gentle voice altered. "Don't forget, Professor Nichols, that you are still under close scrutiny. If you are not on one of the London coaches by the seventh of December, an envelope will be delivered to the police inspector, and on the morning of the eighth I can promise that both you and Richard will be behind bars. Is that clear? Do you understand everything I have said to you?"

Understand? Understand?

"Good day to you, then Professor Nichols," the kind voice said. "All pain can be borne. If you truly love Richard, tell him goodbye. It will be best for both of you."

"If you truly love Richard."

Fortunately the door had closed when the tears came. But what matter? Bertie had lost everything else before the man. What matter his remaining pride?

The grief did not last long, and in less than a quarter of an hour he was quiet. Seated on the trunk in a slumped position of defeat, he punished himself by hearing again in memory everything that had been said.

He tried to remember the tranquility of Richard's face, specific gestures, the bend of his neck as he dealt with his readers, all the thousand details which in mysterious combination fed his love and reminded him that it was over.

Where was it, his new destination? He couldn't re-

member. Life was shrinking away from him, and everything about him seemed dead and loathsome. There was
no future, here or any place else, and how could he ever
make it to safety in that raging storm outside? And
where was safety? Surely no place in this world.

The resolution to his suffering came to him like a
beneficent smile. He luxuriated in it. It promised both
release and relief and, since he could endure no more,
he stood with purpose.

With calm hands he unwound the length of rope about
the trunk and tested its strength. He climbed up on the
trunk, the better to loop and knot it around one of the
blackened beams. Effortlessly he fashioned a noose,
dropped it around his neck, shrugged off the cloak, for
he would not need its warmth where he was going, and
stepped off the trunk, filled with books documenting
the wisdom and folly of ancient philosophers, into a safe
abyss where neither wisdom nor folly counted for
much. . . .

It was approaching midnight when Richard, distraught
with worry, ventured out of his warm flat in search of
Bertie.

Where is he? He said that he'd be back in time for six
o'clock tea.

Knowing Bertie's propensity for a chat with lonely
students, Richard had waited patiently until the clock
had struck a quarter to twelve. Then he fetched his cloak
and a single lantern with a wind shield and made his way
through the bitter cold night and the deserted Cambridge
streets to the disreputable rented flat which had served
Bertie as home for the last several months.

He hurried up the walk, knocked on the outer door
and, receiving no answer, pushed through into the narrow
corridor.

"Bertie?" he called, his voice falling back on him in
echo.

"Bertie, are you there?" he called again, lifting the
lantern in an attempt to send the illumination ahead.

Still keeping to the door, he saw nothing at first but
the dim outline of the miserable room, a wretched place
to shelter a man as rare as Bertie Nichols.

He saw what appeared to be a blanket hanging from
one of the beams and he thought, how careless of Bertie

to leave it behind, and, in a way relieved that he'd not found the man himself, he stepped forward, thinking to retrieve the blanket and use its warmth for the cold walk home, when the skittering lantern light ran ahead and he saw boots evolve out of the shapeless blanket suspended off the floor, then trousers, then—

A strong instinct warned him not to take a step further. But he ignored the instinct and ran directly forward and faced the atrocity full-front.

The cry started low in his throat and, burning and scraping all the way up, exploded near the top of his head. There was no escape. The agony was constant, and there before him, that beloved face frozen in a macabre death mask, tongue slung sideways out of the mouth, eyes protruding, the neck twisted at an inhuman angle.

He was only vaguely aware of his collapse, his knees buckling, though he was very grateful to the darkness which obliterated the face and plunged him into an abyss which was deep, but not deep enough.

Cambridge
December 5, 1870

THROUGH EYES DIMMED with sympathy and a twinge of guilt, Mrs. Pettibone watched the silent man seated by the front window, apparently unaware of the activity which swirled about him.

She had really expected him to recover before this. In her opinion, the hardest part was behind him. The funeral had taken place two days ago, Professor Nichols in his final bed, in a pretty little graveyard at the edge of town in the shadow of the parish church. Quite a turnout there had been, too, so many students, some weeping openly. She'd thought that would have brought poor Lord Eden a degree of comfort.

But it hadn't. The man had given her instructions to pack his things, he was going home to Eden, and beyond those few words he'd said nothing to her at all.

Securing the top of the wicker packing case, she thought that things had taken a nasty turn. Who would have expected the man to take his own life? Of course, in a cruel way, and God forgive her, it *was* for the best. According to that investigator from London, a pretty tea-party had been planned for both Professor Nichols and Lord Eden, and she would have hated to have seen that, all the scandal of a trial, their aber-rations, as the investigator called them, paraded out and gossiped over.

No, God forgive her, but they both were better off, Professor Nichols in his grave, Lord Eden with a second chance to act like a man.

Quickly she emptied the last cupboard. In a way she was eager to see him gone. There were friends waiting for her at the pub who were dying to hear her firsthand account of the goings-on.

Hurry then! This was the last packing case and all she had to do was affix her bonnet, say her goodbyes and take her leave. Oh, there *was* one thing more. She'd prepared a tiny little giftie for Lord Eden, nothing much, a small basket of hot gingerbread for the road. She'd baked it early this morning to take her mind off things in general, most specifically her part in the sad doings.

She laced the last strap of the packing case into place, caught the eye of the porter and watched as the hefty man lifted it effortlessly to his shoulders.

Having seen more than enough, and since her job was finished here, Mrs. Pettibone drew on her winter cape, affixed her bonnet and lifted the basket of gingerbread.

She approached the man warily. "Lord Eden?"

When he didn't acknowledge her, she considered just leaving the basket, but something urged her to try again. The poor man looked dead himself.

"Lord Eden? I fixed you this for the road. It ain't much, but you ain't et nothing to speak of and a traveler needs his strength."

He stirred, looked up at her with a concentrated expression as if he were trying to remember something. "Mrs. Pettibone," he murmured, "thank you for your kindness."

" 'Tis nothing," she scoffed, and placed the basket in his lap. "You take care of yourself."

One of the porters appeared in the door. "The carriage is secured, Lord Eden. Whenever you are ready."

She saw him start to pull himself out of the chair. On his feet, he tried to straighten his cloak, which had become twisted. "Here, let me give you a hand," she offered, and stepped forward, adjusted the garment, trying to keep her eyes off the vacancy in his face.

Mrs. Pettibone took his arm and propelled him gently forward, relieved to see him at last moving under his own steam, at least as far as the door, where he stopped and looked back, his eyes seeming to canvass all corners of the comfortable flat, stripped of all furnishings and ready for the next tenant.

Then he was gone, the porter moving ahead down the steps. She stared at the vacancy of the door, then hurried to the window, determined to see the grim departure to its end.

Well, now, how nice, she thought staring down at the garden, where approximately thirty students had gathered to bid him farewell. *That should lift his spirits right enough.* But as she watched, she wasn't certain that he even saw the students. They moved back to give him passage to the pavement, where his carriage was waiting. Several reached out as though to touch him, but he made no response and moved slowly through their midst, his head down, still clutching her basket of gingerbread.

Then it was over, the carriage pulling away, the students disbanding in groups of twos and threes until the garden was deserted.

She held still. With a jerk she lifted her head and shook off the bleak feeling that two lives had been ended, one dead and buried, the other still walking upright but with the smell of death about him just as strong.

Gawd! She was in terrible need of a pint, of raucous company, of laughter and diversion.

Without a backward look, and vowing never to step foot inside this flat again, she hurried through the door and down the steps, her pace increasing until she was running to her friends as fast as age and girth would permit.

London
December 5, 1870

ON ONE OF the most dazzling December morns in the history of man, John stood at the top of a hill which gave a perfect view of the city of London and thought that he'd never felt so good in his life.

To his right, about thirty yards away, he saw his driver, who was the cause of this brief stop. A harness had become loosened during the last leg of the journey, and before they descended into the traffic of High Street and Shoreditch the man had requested permission to stop and fix the faulty strap. They were on Upper Hackney Road and, following repairs, it was John's estimate that they were less than an hour from his home.

To his left, stretching his legs after the confinement of the journey, he saw Aslam, the sight of the young man never failing to bring him pleasure.

It had not been John's intention to make a five-day journey of it between Cambridge and London. But events had conspired against him. A missed turn on the Cambridge road, which had sent them to Colchester; this beautiful weather; the fact that he was so enjoying Aslam's company; the grim events of the previous two weeks and the realization that more unpleasantness awaited him in London, all this had prompted him to give his driver orders to make for Clacton-on-Sea, a resort on the east coast which had been deserted at this season of the year.

For three glorious days he and Aslam had walked the beach, reminisced endlessly about India, partaken of delicious meals in the grand dining salon of the Shores Hotel, and slowly John had felt the gloom caused by Mary and Richard lifting.

In his new ease, he found that he had a great capacity in his heart to forgive them. As young children, what force had there been in their lives that might have established much needed self-discipline? None! A drunken father who ultimately had destroyed himself, an ill mother who had locked herself away in isolation. No,

Richard and Mary had been raised by a handful of semi-literate and self-indulgent servants. No wonder they lacked a steady hand to control their own lives.

He stretched forward in a way that made his joints crackle and fixed his eye on the city below. Well, the unscheduled holiday had been pleasant, but now it was over and there lay reality.

"About finished?" he called to his driver.

"A few more minutes, Mr. Eden," came the reply. "I'd rather deal with this here than down there."

Patience, he counseled himself. He would arrive in plenty of time. Professor Nichols was due about the eighth, the hearing with John Thadeus Delane on the tenth. If all went well, he'd remain in London for an additional week to see to certain business affairs, then he'd pack everyone up and take them to Eden for Christmas.

He was hungry to see Lila, ripe with their third child, and he was eager to see his sons as well.

Christmas at Eden. The thought enclosed him like a caress. A roaring Yule log the size of a full-grown tree in the Great Hall fireplace, wreaths and garlands everyplace. And Harriet would join them this year—he would insist upon it. It would just be the family, and Richard would come home, though not Mary, and she would be missed by all.

But to fill the vacuum caused by her absence, he would invite Lady Eleanor Forbes. With Professor Nichols removed from the scene, Richard might be more inclined to respond to her considerable charms. Yes, he would do it.

Overcome by these visions and feeling the need to share them, he shoved his hands into his pockets and walked the short distance to where Aslam was maintaining a curious vigil on sprawling London below.

"A bit larger than Cambridge, wouldn't you say?" John smiled, coming up behind the young man.

Without looking at him, Aslam murmured, "How often I've dreamed of this day."

John drew even with him, hearing a bitterness in his voice which somehow jarred with the joy there. "Was your life at Cambridge so terrible?"

"Just hell."

He stepped closer and offered a gentle reassurance.

"Well, that's all behind you now. A new life is beginning for you. You will live with me in my house, and I'll teach you everything you need to know about the firm. You'll complete your studies in the Temple, and one day after you've proven yourself, and I'm sure you will, I'll make you a full partner. What do you say to that?"

The look of adoration in Aslam's eyes prohibited him from saying anything. He stepped away, his face as rigid as his stance. "I will make you proud of me, John. I swear it. And further, I pledge to you my loyalty and constant devotion in all matters."

A bit excessive, that, and John could have done without some of the pomposity. Still, the words were pleasing as well as the depth of sincerity behnd them.

Caught in the emotion of the occasion, John faltered. He would have liked to embrace the boy, but something in those determined eyes warned him against it and, in the awkwardness of the moment, both spoke at once.

"We should be home in a little over an—"

"Do you think he'll come to London—"

"I'm sorry." John laughed at the muddle of their voices. "Do I think who will come to London?"

"Professor Nichols."

John walked a step down the incline. "I'm sure he will. We didn't give him much choice, did we?"

"I've never liked him, you know," Aslam said, trailing behind.

"Why?" John asked, curious.

Aslam shrugged. "He seemed to want to—touch me all the time. He was forever touching my arm, my shoulder."

John looked back, grateful that earlier he'd kept his distance.

Aslam caught up with him. "I hate Sodomites," he pronounced, his eyes focused on London below. "When I first arrived at Cambridge I was told I had to attend an initiation of Greeks." His voice fell. John sensed that he should stop him, but he didn't.

"I was taken with four other boys to a small shed out in the country somewhere. We were forced to remove our trousers and lie flat in the dirt while one by one the other boys—"

His voice broke. He walked a few steps back up the incline. John could see his shoulders trembling and, while his heart went out to him, he knew better than to say or do anything. Every man had to deal with his own nightmares.

The horror passed and Aslam looked back. "As you were talking to Professor Nichols, all I wanted to do was to tell him how I'd felt that night in the shed."

"I know," John comforted. "But take solace in the realization of where we are sending him. Australia," John pronounced broadly. "Let him play his filthy games with the convicts."

Aslam laughed, the mood lifted and the young man was back on track. "Tell me of this hearing, John," he asked, walking a few steps ahead across the crest of the incline.

Surprised, John called after him. "How did you know about that?"

"My mother wrote and told me. She has written almost weekly for the last two months, though I have not replied."

"Why haven't you answered?"

Aslam looked at him as though surprised by the question. "Surely you know of her—attachment to Andrew Rhoades?"

John nodded.

"Did you know that they plan to marry?"

"I suspected as much."

"And you're not angry?"

John caught up with him and tried to compose a suitable answer. It wouldn't do to tell the son that he was merely tired of the mother. "She's free to do whatever she wishes," he said.

The look of shock on Aslam's face was pleasing. "But she's being—disloyal to you!"

John offered comfort. "I've learned, Aslam," he said quietly, "that you cannot hold anyone's affection against their will. It is your mother's happiness with which I'm concerned, and if I can no longer provide her with that happiness, then I will not stand in her way of seeking it elsewhere."

His voice just barely topped the gentle wind, and he saw such a look of adoration on Aslam's face that again he felt himself moved to touch.

But he controlled the instinct and let Aslam come to him, faltering at first, then at last stepping shyly into his arms, where John received his awkward, boyish embrace and heard his whispered confession, "I love you so much, John. I will never leave you."

The embrace held for several moments, John looking sideways out over sprawling London. How good the moment was, how kind of God to send him this gift of a young man's love when he so sorely needed it!

Together they walked back to where the driver was just climbing aboard his high seat. "All secured, Mr. Eden," he called down. "She can withstand anything now."

So can I, John thought, as Aslam held the door for him.

It was approaching noon—the traffic had been worse than usual—when Belgrave Square came into view. Across from him sat Aslam. Since they had entered the city, the young man had craned his neck out one window, then the other, commenting, on the changes that had taken place since he'd last been there.

Thus it was Aslam, still leaning out the window, who spied the carriages parked before the house and sounded the alarm. "I thought you said my mother was staying with Elizabeth," he commented, the chasm between mother and son deepening.

John leaned forward, amazed by the number of carriages parked on the normally quiet pavement before his house. Dhari's was instantly recognizable, as well as Elizabeth's. In addition there was a sturdy black one with JOHN MURREY FIRM emblazoned on the side, which meant that Alex Aldwell was present as well.

As soon as his carriage had come to a halt, John jumped down, angry to see such a congregation. Usually they held their dreary family meetings in Elizabeth's drawing room.

"Come!" he shouted back at Aslam.

Even before he reached the steps he saw the front door open, saw a steward relay a message back into the house and, taking the steps two at a time, John pushed through the door in time to see the lot of them emerge from the drawing room, Elizabeth dressed in grim black, her eyes as swollen from weeping as they had been when he'd left her over a fortnight ago with Mary in tow.

My God, he thought. *Does the woman do nothing but weep? Perhaps it has something to do with her middle years.* But before he could solve the puzzle he saw the others behind her, an equally grim parade. There Dhari, also dressed in black, and behind her, Andrew, his face drained of color, and next to him, Alex Aldwell.

As his annoyance escalated into fear—something *had* happened—he held Elizabeth at arm's length and tried to force an explanation out of her.

"What is it?" he demanded. "What has happened?"

Through fresh tears, she wept, "The first courier came three days ago with the terrible news that she was ill. Then yesterday, only yesterday—"

As she covered her face with her hands, John tried to put the scant pieces together. *Who was ill? Mary? Pray God, no. . . .*

"Tell me, Elizabeth," he commanded, reaching out for her.

The voice came from behind and belonged to Andrew Rhoades. "It's Lila," he said. "The second message arrived yesterday, signed by Lord Harrington and Lady Harriet. I'm so sorry, John. Lila is dead."

The black and white marble entrance hall seemed to be filled with motionless, silent people. In spite of the sunlight streaming in through the windows, it resembled dark night. John turned away, taking in all the faces that stared back at him, fully expecting one to refute the message.

How can she be dead?

"John, come sit down. Let me help you." It was Andrew again.

But it wasn't assistance that John desired. It was explanation, denial. Vaguely aware that he was turning in a slow, stunned circle, he asked Alex Aldwell, "This— isn't true, is it? There's been a—mistake?"

"No mistake, John, I'm afraid. Let me fetch the message for you. You need to read it."

Why in hell is everyone telling me what I need? "Elizabeth?" he called out, as though still willing to give someone a chance to refute what had been said.

But her tears merely increased. "We didn't know where to reach you, John. Oh, we tried. How hard we—"

Suddenly a new horror swept over him. "The babe," he demanded. "The baby is—"

He saw Andrew approaching him warily. "There was no baby, John," he said. "According to Lady Harriet, Lila suffered and died from a tumor."

John glared at the face effortlessly spilling lies. They were all liars. What pleasure they were taking in taunting him! There *was* a babe. Hadn't the doctor said so? And if it was dead, then Lila had killed it, as she'd killed all the others.

"John, please," someone was begging. "Let's go into the drawing room and sit down. I'll pour you a brandy."

He didn't want a brandy. He didn't want anything that they could give him. They were not to be trusted.

"Aslam!" he called out, lifting a hand, knowing that the boy would respond.

"I'm here, John."

For one stunning moment John could not remember why he'd summoned the boy.

Lila— Not dead.

He seemed to be having difficulty drawing breath. Everyone around him was using up all the oxygen.

Deprived of air and fast losing reason and too proud to accept their pity, he struggled up out of his confusion and whispered a single command to the young man standing before him. "Fetch the letter from Eden and bring it to me."

Then, because he could not endure the congregation or the echo of their malicious announcement, he proceeded toward the staircase.

"Leave him alone," he heard someone whisper.

"But we must know—"

"In time. There's time—"

While the voices continued to whirl behind him, he continued on until he gained the support of the newel post, then commenced slowly to pull himself up the stairs.

All he had to do was to make it to the first landing. Then the disloyalty which was coming from those faces and which was draining him of energy would no longer have an effect on him. One must always be stronger than one's enemies.

As he rounded the second-floor landing, he was pleased to find his theory confirmed. He *was* feeling stronger. It had been their pity that had weakened him. At last he gained his door and stepped inside and began to consider what Lila would like for Christmas. A little ermine cape perhaps to offset her blond beauty. And a muff. Yes, he would see to it this very day, as soon as—

But at midroom' his knees buckled and the truth struck a blow through all the armor of his rationalization and, without being able to say how he knew, *he knew!* She was dead. There was no babe. Scarcely thirty-seven, and he was a widower, an object to be pitied.

Outside the door he heard footsteps and, in an effort to hide his weakness, he sat on the sofa. There was a knock, then a familiar voice. "John, I'm here."

"Come," he called out, hopeful that the worst was over. There was no need for prolonged grieving. He had grieved before in his life and would grieve again.

He looked up, aware of Aslam standing just inside the door, a parchment in his hands. "Good," John said, and motioned him to come forward. "Quite a homecoming, wouldn't you say?"

As though aware of John's scrutiny, he extended the parchment. "Mr. Rhoades said to tell you that you must make preparations to depart immediately."

"Read it," John requested, thinking he would like a brandy but not yet trusting his legs. He leaned back against the cushions and closed his eyes.

The silence was broken by Aslam's voice. "It is signed by Lady Eden, Countess Dowager, and co-signed by Lord Harrington," he began.

Treachery even there. John had forbidden the old man to journey to Eden. Another score to settle.

Aslam read:

MY DEAREST JOHN,

It is with grieving hearts that we convey to you this message. On the first of December 1870 in the early hours of the morning Lila died. Forgive the plainness of the words and please bear no ill feelings toward those who bear this terrible message. As we lack a competent medical opinion, we hesitate to tell you more, except that in the judgment of the midwife she suffered a tumor which prevented her system from performing its essential tasks.

We are sending this by the fastest courier. We will await your imminent arrival with instructions for burial. Lord Harrington has penned his daughter's obituary and will hold it for your approval. We beg you, come immediately. All of Eden has been plunged into the deepest grief and we desperately need your presence.

In the faith that God watches us all and sends us no burden which we cannot bear, I remain

YOUR LOVING HARRIET

Silence, except for the rustle of the parchment being folded.

John opened his eyes. The resurrected memories were almost over. She had been a miracle to him in those early years. But the later ones had been discordant and filled with suspicions. Perhaps Harriet's God was wiser than he'd ever imagined. What a hell it would have been to have grown old with Lila! The suspicions would have turned to distrust, the distrust to resentment, the resentment to hate. Now he'd been spared all that and could remember her only with that sweet sadness that had first invested their love.

Feeling strong, he pushed up from the sofa, took the death message from Aslam's hand and dropped it on the table. "Of course, a journey to Eden is out of the question," he announced making for his desk.

"Out of the question," Aslam repeated.

"Still, without my guidance, they apparently lack the good sense to bury her, so—"

He reached into his lower drawer for his writing portfolio and, as he arranged it on his desk, Aslam stepped forward.

"Let me do that, John," he offered kindly. "You dictate."

Dear God, what a joy the young man is! He waited until Aslam was ready, then commenced speaking, pleased to hear his voice restored to its normal power:

MY DEAR HARRIET,

Circumstances prohibit a journey to Eden at this time. Therefore I request that you adhere to the following instructions.

My wife is to be interred as soon as you receive this message. Place her next to my father. I will attend to the headstone myself when I arrive for

Christmas. There is to be no service. If the family wishes, there will be a memorial during the holidays. I forbid my sons to see her. I will inform them when I arrive. Instruct Miss Samson to keep them in the nursery and isolated from the rest of the castle.

I am, as always, grateful for your cooperation and assistance.

"I'll sign it," John concluded and waited for Aslam to finish the last sentence.

That done, he was just reaching for the document when a knock sounded at the door.

"Shall I send them away?" Aslam whispered, an expression on his face which suggested that he would relish such a task.

John's impulse was to say "Yes," but it was probably Andrew and the man's appearance had been inevitable and, since undoubtedly that grim crowd was still congregated downstairs and since they would not go away until he sent them away, John ignored the look on Aslam's face and commanded, "Let him in."

A moment later Andrew stood before him, his face sunk into angles of gloom. *Dear God, why does the world so relish grief?*

"Come in, Andrew," he called out good-naturedly.

"I'm sorry to bother you, John," Andrew commenced, "but we were wondering how soon you would be ready to leave. The letter urges haste, and the rest of us are prepared to leave immediately."

"I'm not going anywhere, Andrew."

"I—beg your pardon?"

"I said, I'm not going anywhere."

"I—don't understand," Andrew faltered.

"Here," John said, shoving the recently penned instructions across his desk.

He watched as Andrew read Aslam's meticulous penmanship and could see the protest forthcoming.

"But, John, you *must* go," he insisted.

"It's quite impossible," John replied, retrieving the letter, folding and inserting it into its envelope.

Andrew looked almost desperately about the room. "But she's your wife!"

"And she's dead now. There is nothing further I can do for her."

"You can be there," Andrew said, "out of consideration, out of decency."

"Both moot points," John replied, "at least where Lila is concerned."

"I—don't believe it," Andrew stammered, backing away from the desk. "I'm sorry," he went on, shaking his head. "Clearly I intruded too soon. I'll give you additional time."

"I need no additional time," John called after him. "My decision is final and rooted in good sense, which seems to be in short supply in my house at present."

"And what am I to tell the others?"

"The message was short, surely you can remember." Briefly he regretted the hurt he saw in Andrew's eyes. *But why, in God's name, does the man challenge me on everything?*

The hurt passed rapidly and was replaced by carefully controlled anger. "The women," Andrew pronounced coldly. "Dhari and Elizabeth will insist upon going."

"Then let them," John said. "It's a woman's ritual. They will relish every moment of it."

"I would like to accompany them."

"No! I need you here." John leaned across his desk, amazed at the density of this once-brilliant solicitor. "The hearing," he pronounced broadly. "Have you forgotten it?"

"The hearing can be postponed. I'm certain that under the circumstances Lord Aimsley will understand."

Outraged, John shouted, "The hearing will not be postponed! Is that clear? And how can you even suggest such a step? You know how I've suffered. The only throught that has sustained me these last difficult months is the hope, the dream of getting John Thadeus Delane in the box, under oath—"

He caught himself up, aware that rage was a poison he could do without. And why should he allow himself to be driven to rage? This was not a debate. The issue was settled.

Slowly he sat back down in his chair and tried not to look at the shock on Andrew's face. "I've been traveling for a fortnight," he concluded quietly, "on two most distasteful errands. I've neglected my business affairs; I've neglected my own health. Now it is my intention to see certain matters through to their conclusions. Then, when my mind is clear, my responsibilities executed, I have every intention of journeying to Eden where, if it pleases you, I will outmourn all of you. Don't forget. The loss is mine."

He'd not planned to put on such a performance. The words had simply come of their own volition. Only now was he aware of the positive effect his theatrical had had on Andrew. The man was drawing close to the desk.

"I am sorry, John," he murmured. "How selfish of me not to understand." He straightened up, his face still desolate, though tempered with understanding. "I will convey your wishes to the others, and I assume then that Dhari and Elizabeth have your permission."

"Of course, of course," John murmured, resting his head in his hands. "Tell them to go with my blessing. And send Aldwell with them. They mustn't be alone on the road."

This last consideration was a master stroke. "Send my message with them," he added, "and tell them that a large portion of my heart goes with it."

Andrew took up the letter which recently he'd dropped in angry disgust. "I'll see them safely off, John. Then, with your permission, if you are feeling well enough, I'll go over the specifics of the hearing."

"Very good." John smiled. "And by the way, I've brought you a new assistant. Aslam—" He motioned for the young man to come forward and charted the expression on Andrew's face.

Surprise was there, as well as confusion. John went on, "I want him to work closely with you, Andrew. He's wasted his talents in the backwaters of Cambridge long enough."

He watched the two men sizing each other up. How subtly their relationship had changed. And how potentially volatile it was. Aslam was now a professional threat to Andrew, and Andrew, in his new alliance with Dhari, was a personal threat to Aslam.

He grinned at the quietly staring men, then he caught himself in time. He was the grieving widower now. Determined to play his proper role, he stood with a weariness that was not altogether feigned and walked to the door which led to his bedchamber. "Leave me, both of you," he requested softly. "I need an interval alone. Aslam, go and see if you can assist your mother with her preparations for the journey. Andrew, give Jason instructions. Have them take Elizabeth's carriage; it's more roadworthy. Instruct them to travel without respite. Harriet is waiting. . . ."

As his voice drifted off, he grasped the door frame and without looking back concluded, "A few hours alone, please, that's all I ask. The three of us will take dinner here tonight. We must be fully allied and prepared for what the future may bring."

With that, he stepped into the chill of his bedchamber, closed the door behind him, then held his position, listening.

Ah, there were the footsteps he'd been waiting for, both men moving without question to execute his instructions.

Slowly he turned to confront his bedchamber.

Dead.

He'd not expected this and, in an attempt to dispel the word and the meaning behind it, he struck a lucifer and lit the lamp beside his bed. The flame caught, though it burned weakly.

He sat on the edge of his bed and began laboriously to remove his boots. A fire would help. The chill was intense.

Boots removed, he stretched out and tried to clear his mind by concentrating on the dancing shadows overhead.

Mary . . .

The name entered his thoughts without warning and dragged him over onto his side, where he clutched the coverlet and stared sideways into the darkness. It *was* for the best. No need at this time to inform her of Lila's death. They had been very close and such news would only serve to upset her further.

Lila . . .

He rolled back the other way, becoming entangled in the coverlet. Abruptly he sat up, as though to combat the force of memory that was moving over him. His self-diagnosis had been wrong. He did not need to be alone. In fact just the opposite. He needed companionship.

But the memories persisted, some luminous and full of sunlight, others filled with misshapen images, and at last he stumbled upward, barefoot, heading toward the sideboard and the decanter of brandy.

As he was approaching the bottle he heard a knock at the door and before he could reply he saw the door pushed open, saw a chambermaid carrying an armload of wood.

"Forgive me, Mr. Eden," she murmured, "but Mr. Rhoades sent me, said a fire would suit you. If I may——"

He nodded, embarrassed to be caught in this state, bootless. "Yes, a fire."

As the girl approached the firewell in the outer chamber, he redirected her. "Not there, please. In my bedchamber."

She raised up, precariously balancing the wood in her arms. He stood motionless by the sideboard, his hand on the decanter, ready to pour. Slowly he returned it to the tray and followed after her.

She was kneeling before the grate. He sat on the edge of the bed, watching her. She was new, like most of his ever-changing staff. He was certain that he'd never seen her before. Fairly young, not yet twenty was his guess, as he assessed her slim waist and fleshy upper arms straining against the fabric of her dress.

Clever Andrew! Good Andrew! To send him such an unexpected gift. Would Aslam have been so thoughtful? He doubted it, though the boy only lacked experience.

"What's your name?" he asked.

"Nora," she said, expertly laying the fire, inserting kindling at key points.

"Nora," he repeated, fascinated by the manner in which her breasts pressed against her knees as she leaned into the firewell. "How old are you, Nora?"

"Eighteen."

"Eighteen-year-old Nora," he repeated, pleased to see the fire catch with the first spark. She stood back and fanned it with her apron until the flames were blazing well.

She turned to him, a becoming blush on her cheeks. "Mr. Rhoades said I was to see if I could do anything else for you."

John smiled. Dearest Andrew. He would have to think of some suitable way to repay him. Slowly he stood up from the bed and commenced removing his garments.

Her face showed neither pleasure nor displeasure. She merely smiled back at him as her fingers brushed magically down the long row of buttons, leaving a track of white flesh in their wake.

A moment later the black uniform was a circle about her feet and she stood before him in the firelight, a vision of shoulders and breasts and prettily plump legs.

He had thought to move on her immediately. Certainly there was a clear invitation in her eyes. But he hesitated and slipped beneath the cover to hide his inadequacy. It was only the circumstances, that was all, the damnable sense of death that still permeated this room, his recent thoughts of Mary, all the teary females with whom he'd been surrounded of late.

"Come," he invited, and held the coverlet back, certain that the closeness of that young body would make a difference.

Without hesitation she nestled in beside him, her hands moving instinctively down to the source that hopefully would bring her pleasure.

He gasped at the first contact. She leaned over him, her eyes wide with astonishment. "Poor you," she giggled, and disappeared beneath the coverlet.

He shut his eyes as he felt her lips close about him. It would only be a matter of seconds. The need was suffocating him, and with all his senses at the ready he followed her skillful hands and lips as she manipulated, caressed, massaged.

But after several minutes he was aware of nothing but the perspiration which covered his forehead and the emerging face of the girl, cheeks flushed, hair mussed, as she smiled sadly down on him.

No! There had been enough death this day, and since the future promised more, he would have to confront all death now and defeat it. With a violence that brought a look of alarm to her face, he pushed her down and flattened himself on top of her, forcing her legs apart and with a massive effort thrust against her, his hands kneading her breasts continuously, the perspiration from his forehead rolling down his neck, blending with hers as she lifted her legs about his waist, trying to make it easy for him.

Still he persisted, his actions growing more violent, his need keeping pace. But it was no use. There was nothing with which to penetrate her, and he suffered a severe pain in the side of his head.

"No more, sir," she begged, and tried to struggle free. "Maybe later. I'll come back—later—"

Panting from his effort, he looked down on her, and in his confused state saw Mary beneath him, then Lila, then Harriet, her veil removed, her sightless eyes streaming blood.

"No," he groaned and clung to the opposite side of the bed, waiting for the horror to pass.

A few moments later he heard the door close, but he did not look in that direction or protest her departure.

He couldn't. For the time being all his energy was focused elsewhere, not on the tears which slid down his face. He'd wept before and would weep again.

But there was something else moving across and through him, impaling him.

Fear.

For the first time in his life, he was afraid.

※

London, Mayfair
December 8, 1870

OBEYING AN INSTINCT so ancient that it required no interpretation, Caroline Stanhope, sensing that her offspring was in pain, had completely thrown off the veils of her madness and now viewed him with crystal clarity as he sat slumped in his chair at the far end of the table.

Her second instinct told her that the cause of his pain was a woman, and her third instinct was the most powerful and primitive of all. It simply commanded her to identify the interloper and destroy her.

"Burke, my darling," she called out to him, "talk to me please. I was absent from you for so long, I'm afraid you've acquired the habit of silence."

At last he looked up, though in a way she was sorry. Never had she seen him so distraught. His beautiful eyes lay in dark shadows, mute testimony to many sleepless nights. His hair lay mussed about his head, as though he'd risen from the ordeal of his bed to join her for dinner. And the heavy stubble about his chin suggested that he'd not paid serious attention to his grooming for several days.

In spite of this ruination, she was rewarded with a smile. "I'm sorry, Mother," he said, and concentrated with undue interest on the hem of his napkin.

"Burke, we must talk," she urged. "I'm still recovering from my illness, but I'm well enough to determine that you are falling into one, perhaps more painful than mine."

But he shook off her concern. "It's nothing, Mother, I assure you," he said, and pushed back in his chair.

Remembering a lesson that she'd learned early in his childhood, that the surest approach to her son was a circuitous one, she tried to relax. "Burke, I've been thinking," she began. "Why don't we entertain?" Before the protest on his face grew into a verbal one, she hurried on. "Listen to me, Burke," she urged. "I'm quite serious. And the servants would love it. Wouldn't you, Charles?" she called over her shoulder, trying to rally support for an idea which she had no idea of carrying out.

"Yes, Miss Caroline," the old man replied, "if it pleases you."

"There, you see!" she announced triumphantly, pleased to see that at least a portion of Burke's attention was hers.

"You have been ill," Burke said, reminding her of the embarrassment of her own madness.

"I suggest that we continue as we always have, Mother," he said. "You are not well enough for an active social life, and consider it a blessing, for I'm afraid you'll find the English an indifferent people."

"Burke, wait—"

But he didn't, and she heard the front door close and she was left alone with Charles hovering behind her.

"Follow him," she ordered quietly. "Keep him in your sight. He's not himself."

"Yes," the old man murmured, and a moment later she heard the door open and close again. . . .

Burke knew he was being followed.

At the end of the street, he saw Charles just descending the steps. It was a simple matter to slip into the narrow alley which ran between Number Eleven and Twelve, and wait.

A moment later he saw the tall black man loping down the street in pursuit of nothing. Burke re-emerged in the night, not certain of his destination, but feeling the need for movement to counteract his deep anxiety.

Two intersections later he flagged a passing hired chaise, shouted up at the driver, "Number Seven, St. George Street," and climbed into the narrow compartment, aware for the first time that he'd come out without a coat and the night was cold, and what in the hell was he going to do at Number Seven that he had not done before, which was nothing except stand in the shadows and stare, as though if he stared long enough *she* would materialize.

A short time later he shouted, "This is fine," tossed up a few coins and waited on the pavement until all was quiet. As he approached Number Seven he moved into the shadows of the house across the way, his habitual stand near the black iron fence.

The house appeared different tonight, dark and closed. Through the windows on either side of the door he saw a faint gleam as though a single lamp were burning deep in the interior. But for the rest of it, it was solid black, the drapes drawn on every window, not a trace of smoke coming from any of the chimneys.

He stared, shivering. He couldn't go on like this. He felt as though he were being hunted, that fate was tracking him down. He had to know if he would ever see her again. He had to know—everything.

On that note of determination, fully aware that he was throwing caution to the wind, he left the shadows and started across toward Number Seven, trying to clear his mind, at least to the extent that he could be coherent. He was cold and shaking so badly that his teeth rattled.

He paused at the bottom of the steps, his determination not faltering but merely a last-minute attempt to pull himself together so that he did not wholly resemble the madman he felt he had become.

He knocked, timidly at first, though the slight sound seemed to reverberate through his frozen ears. He waited. The darkness did not alter in any way.

He knocked again, louder, so loud that the sound seemed to echo up and down the street. He looked behind him. If a watchman were to pass— But the street was empty.

Then he saw it, the slight alteration in the darkness,
the light shifting, drawing nearer. He murmured an indistinct prayer. "Dear God, please—" Then he heard the
sliding of a bolt and the door was pulled open a crack,
where on the other side he saw a middle-aged maid, her
nightcap tied about her double chin, one hand grasping
her dressing gown about her neck, the other thrusting the
lamp directly into his face.

"What do you want?" she inquired. "The house is
closed. You must have the wrong—"

Sensing that the door was about to be shut, he stepped
forward and with one hand grasped the outer door
frame. If she closed it, she would be forced to crush his
fingers.

"Please," he commenced.

"You got no business here," she snapped. "I don't
know you," and she peered closer at him, revealing eyes
that were red and swollen, as though she were suffering
a cold, or had been weeping.

In an attempt to offset her impatience, Burke tried to
speak calmly. "I was wondering if I might speak with
—Elizabeth?"

The intimate use of the name made a difference,
though she continued to study him, searching for a clue.
"Do you know Miss Elizabeth?" she demanded.

"I do. I was wondering if I might—"

"Gone," she pronounced flatly. "Not here—"

"Could you tell me where—"

"Gone to Eden," the maid answered, "the lot of them,
for the funeral."

The single word fell like a weight upon his head. He
tried to repeat it, but found that he could not draw sufficient breath into his lungs. Fearful that he had received the message for which he had come, he continued
to stare doggedly, at the mournful maid, another word
forming in his head. "Mary—"

Suddenly a torrent of tears spilled down over the plain
face. "Gone," she wept. "Please leave us alone, that's
all we ask. This is a house of mourning—"

Even as she spoke she was in the process of closing
the door. Now he did nothing to prevent it. How blessed
his state of ignorance had been.

*They have gone to Eden for the funeral. Gone. All
gone—*

Though the door was closed, the bolt slid, he continued to stare at it, hoping for a refutation of everything he'd just heard.

But there was nothing. He shut his eyes, only vaguely aware that it had begun to snow. At last he turned away, unable to make out anything on the street before him.

Gone. This is a house of mourning—

He walked on, not knowing where he was going, seeing her clearly in memory, her lovely hair, the forehead, the slant of eyes and nose, the mouth, the pretty manner in which she twisted her head slightly when puzzled, the lilt of her laughter.

Once or twice his reason tried to intervene. The message had been vague. Yet he remembered the ominous word "funeral." There was nothing his reason could do about that. It was as unalterable as the night and the cold.

He was conscious of a silent thankfulness, that he had known her, had shared just a moment of her life, stolen to be sure, and perhaps ultimately contributing to her—

No, he could not think on that and increased his steps. A short time later he looked up to find himself on the edge of Hyde Park.

At the top of the path he stopped. There was their bench, there the exact spot where they had first kissed, and over there on the opposite path the place where they had first discussed the need for a winter refuge.

Suddenly the reality of the night narrowed about him. She was gone. There was no need for a place of winter refuge, and never again would he see her approaching through the sun and shadow, and never again would he enjoy that look of trust in her eyes as she looked up at him. Never again any of it. He had found and lost her within the same stroke of time.

It could not be borne. Blindly he stumbled forward and sat on the bench and extended his arms on either side, as though to gather to him any residual memories which might be surviving beneath the blanket of snow.

But he found nothing except the hardness of the bench itself, winter's frozen dampness, and the deep conviction that his true state of loneliness had just begun. . . .

It was approaching midnight when, wept out, thought out, and dreamt out, he made his way like an invalid back to the house in Mayfair. During the last few blocks of this endless frozen walk he had counseled himself that from now on he must neither ask too much nor expect too much of life and fortune. He had been blest with one brief interval of paradise, the reciprocal love of an adored woman. If from now on he were less greedy, fate, perhaps, would be more kind.

To that end, all he asked for was a quiet and warm chamber, free of all intruders. He wanted to luxuriate in her memory, to recall specific occasions and write them down, record everything that he could remember about her as a safeguard against the day when, as an old man, his memory would fail him, and he would run the risk of forgetting that one beacon which had shone so brightly in his life for such a short interval of time.

Thus armed with this simple request, he turned the corner which led to his house, his feet inside his boots as numb as his mind and heart, and noticed angrily that even this small request was too much for fate.

On the pavement before his house he saw a familiar carriage, the driver buried under a mountain of rugs. He saw the drawing room ablaze with lamps.

Too weary for anger, he closed his eyes with a sense of letting fate do with him as it would, and slowly climbed the steps and knocked once and waited for the next ordeal to commence.

A moment later the door opened and Charles appeared on the other side. "Master Burke!" the old man gasped and extended a supportive hand, which Burke moved past, heading toward the drawing room and the voice of his mother, who called out, "Who is it, Charles? Please tell us that the prodigal has—"

His mother, catching sight of him, stood immediately. "Sweet Lord, Burke, have you lost your senses? Charles, hurry! Fetch him his dressing gown and a linen for his hair. Look at him, he looks like a ghost."

He stood in the doorway, giving them both all the time they needed, returning the close scrutiny of John Thadeus Delane, who apparently had broken his own rule by coming here.

"Delane," he muttered.,

In what appeared to be sincere concern, Delane started across the room toward him. "My God, Burke," he scolded, "you're frozen."

Burke brushed past him on his way toward the fire. There he stood for several minutes listening to the chattering voices behind him. Curious how, with his first contact with warmth, the sensation of freezing seemed to increase.

What was his mother saying? He must pay attention, at least for a few minutes more until he could take his leave and retreat into the comforting darkness of his own chambers.

"Caroline." The voice was firm but kind. "I—was wondering if you might leave us alone for a few moments. I must talk business with Burke and the hour *is* late."

Without averting his eyes from the fire, Burke listened to the voice, grateful to the man, who obviously had seen something in Burke's face which suggested that he was not altogether interested in reminiscences of his childhood.

Grateful for one small intercession on the part of fate, Burke heard his mother withdraw with characteristic Southern wile, somehow leaving the impression that withdrawal had been her idea all along.

"Well, I do agree, John Thadeus, the hour is late and I should have been in bed long ago. The doctor says I need my rest if I'm to complete my recovery."

"And a remarkable recovery it has been, Caroline," Delane said gallantly. "I can't tell you what pleasure it gives me to see you looking so well and beautiful."

Through it all, Burke continued to stand before the fire. How effortlessly he found her face in the flames, as it had once appeared before him in a fiery sunset, crimson and amber.

Mary . . .

He would never see her again, and in defense against the pain of that thought he leaned against the mantelpiece, amazed that there were tears left within him.

Their voices sounded far away now, though they still were involved with mundane matters. Dry garments had been produced by Charles and, as his mother's voice rose, indicating that she was on the verge of retracing her steps, Delane's voice again interceded.

"I'll take them, Caroline."

"And see that he gets out of those dreadful clothes immediately."

"I will, I promise."

At some point he became aware of a new silence in the drawing room. In the next moment he heard Delane close behind him, his voice filled with affection. "She's right, you know. Here, put this on."

At last Burke pushed away from the mantel, though he ignored the dressing gown, and sat heavily in the chair in a slumped position. "I thought we were not to be seen together," he muttered.

"I had to talk to you. But, please, get out of that wretched jacket."

"I'm well, thank you."

"You're half-frozen. Where in the hell have you been?"

"Walking."

"On such a night?"

"It suited me." Suddenly he leaned forward. The words came out of their own volition. "She's dead," he whispered. "Earlier tonight I went to St. George Street. The maid there told me—"

As his memory of that bleak exchange invaded him anew, he covered his face with his hands and tried to stem his grief at least until Delane left and he could be alone.

Instead of the sympathetic silence which Burke had expected, he heard Delane announce, "I know. We carried her obituary in the paper yesterday. I thought it might make a difference. So did my solicitors. We were hoping at least for a postponement of the hearing. But no. Word came this morning from Andrew Rhoades. It will take place as scheduled."

All the time Delane talked, Burke was aware of him pacing back and forth in front of the fire. Suddenly he exploded in anger, confronting Burke directly with, "My God, is the man a complete fiend? The death of his wife and he refuses to observe even the simplest decorum."

Death of his—

Burke looked up. The fire seemed to be burning bright, as though it were on the verge of leaping out of the fire-well.

"Death of his—" He tried to repeat the words and couldn't, confident that he'd not heard correctly.

"So tragic," Delane went on. "You remember her, of course," he asked, "from the fortnight last spring? So young, rather delicate. She didn't look well then, but who was to know she was so ill?"

As Delane spoke on, Burke pushed out of the chair, not giving a damn about anything but the discrepancy of one small word. "Wife?" he repeated, reaching out for Delane's arm.

In a new surge of anger, Delane shook off his grasp. "Yes, wife! My God, Burke, are your ears frozen as well?"

Stunned, yet warning himself against false hope, Burke momentarily retreated. "Mary—" he began, "I thought that—"

"Good Lord, no," Delane scoffed. "Where did you get that idea?"

Burke was aware of Delane staring sharply at him. "Are you still pursuing that lost cause?" he asked.

"Then where is she?" Burke demanded. "I was told by the maid that she—"

"I have no idea," Delane interrupted. A new tension surfaced on his face. "And what in the hell were you doing in St. George Street? I thought I told you to stay away."

"Not—dead?" Burke repeated, unable to move beyond those two miraculous words.

His state of confusion was more than Delane could bear, for suddenly the man stepped forward and grasped Burke's shoulder. "Will you please listen to me?" he demanded. "I have warned you once against such an impossible alliance, and I warn you again."

"Alive," Burke whispered, and the frozen state in which he'd passed this dreadful night thawed, and he could focus on nothing but the sweet revitalizing outline of hope.

"Burke, will you listen to me?" a voice demanded. "You are pursuing a phantom, nurturing a dream that can never be. Consider all the aspects of what you are doing, I beg you."

As the voice continued to assault him, Burke took his new happiness to the fire, where again he effortlessly found her face, more beautiful and full of promise than ever under this new patina of hope. Of course her whereabouts were still a mystery, but he would find her. On that quiet vow, he found the courage to face the man who was filling the air with such dire warnings.

But Delane had talked himself out, at least on this subject, and merely gaped back at him. "You're still— quite serious, aren't you?"

"I've never been more serious in my life."

"Do you—love her?" he asked, pausing before the word.

"More than I can state or you can comprehend," Burke said simply.

"It will come to nothing," Delane warned.

"We'll see." Burke smiled. More than ever feeling the need for privacy, he turned to face his old friend. "Come," he invited, making room for him beside the fire, "you said you wanted to talk to me. I promise to listen attentively, then we both can go to bed."

Reluctantly Delane drew near the fire, one hand massaging his forehead as though, taken all together, the night had been something of an ordeal. He turned his back on the blaze, his hands laced behind him.

"Considering your—present state of mind, I doubt if what I have to say will make much difference."

"Try me." Burke smiled, feeling indulgent and patient.

"The—hearing. It's upon us, you know."

"Ah, yes, the hearing."

Unfortunately his new attitude only seemed to enrage Delane further. "You must understand, Burke," he said grimly, "that if I am put under oath, as I surely will be, I cannot protect you."

"I know."

"Do you know what that could mean?"

"Of course." Burke laughed. "It means that Mr. Eden will at last know the name of the man who called him a Demi-God."

"And beyond that?"

"Beyond that what? You tell me."

"He could ruin you."

"What is there to ruin?"

For the first time Delane retreated, taking his worried expression and walking halfway across the room. "I'm surprised that you should even pose such a stupid question."

"Then tell me," Burke invited. "Tell me specifically why I should be alarmed by the wrath of John Murrey Eden? My God, Delane, if it hadn't been for Lord Rip-

ples I think there were times when I would have willingly
joined my mother in her madness."

"Still—"

"Still nothing. We both knew the risks we were running, and we both willingly took those risks. As far as I
am concerned, that is that. As for your apprehensions
concerning what Mr. Eden will do, dismiss them. In this
instance, my state of exile serves me well. I'm not obliged
to play by his rules. What he holds most dear, I view
with complete indifference."

"Except his young cousin."

Stymied, Burke gaped back at him. "Mary's love is reciprocal," he said. "If forced to choose—"

"Oh, Burke . . ." Delane groaned and reached out for
a near table as though he required support. "How is it
possible for a man of your intelligence to live among us
for almost ten years and still know so little about us."

There was a pause, then Delane pushed away from
the table, as though no longer needing its support. "If
John Murrey Eden represents the worst of the British
mentality, then he also represents the best. He has indeed
reshaped large sections of this London world to suit himself. And if he can disrupt entire blocks of mortar and
steel and replace them with his own vision, what do you
think he will do with you, mere flesh and blood?"

"Then tell me what you want me to do," Burke said,
"and I'll do it. Shall I attend the hearing and defend myself? I'm perfectly willing."

"No!" The single word exploded in the quiet room like
a cannon volley. "I want you no place near the Temple
on the tenth of December. Is that clear?"

"It is."

"You wait here," Delane concluded, his face suggesting
weariness amounting almost to illness. "If I'm forced to
speak your name, I'm certain you will be hearing from
Andrew Rhoades soon enough."

"A lawsuit?" Burke asked.

At the door, as though at last he'd talked himself out,
Delane smiled back at him. "If I could be certain that all
you would lose to Eden would be money, I would consider it a major blessing."

"Wait," Burke called after him. "What do you mean?"

Delane looked as though he would speak further. Then

something changed his mind. "I'll be in touch, Burke," he called back. "Don't bother. I can find my way out."

"Delane?"

But there was no answer and Burke heard the front door close. He stood near the fire until the rattle of the carriage diminished, then sat wearily in the chair, aware of an acrid smell about him as the clothes proceeded to dry on his back.

One nagging thought occurred. To the best of his memory he'd never seen Delane in such a state. Now the question was: Should the man be taken seriously? Or was he simply growing old and womanlike? And what were those veiled threats all about? What, beyond the limits of the law, could Eden do to him?

The questions continued to churn in his head, all unanswerable. Slowly he leaned back against the cushions. Undoubtedly he would have the answers in good time.

There were happier areas on which he could focus. Mary, lovely Mary, resurrected from a premature grave, and, of course, it all made sense now. The tragic death of the young wife had drawn them all back to Eden, all except the Demi-God himself, who apparently placed the need for revenge above the grief for his wife.

Burke shut his eyes. In a way, how he would relish an opportunity to be in the arena with John Murrey Eden. But Delane had asked that he remain invisible and, on the basis of their prolonged friendship, he would oblige.

After the foolishness of the hearing, after the young wife had been buried, they all would come streaming back to London, Mary among them, and, in spite of all obstacles, he would arrange to see her again, to rekindle the love which had blossomed between them, and under the sweet pressure of the reunion, they would plot the future together.

It would be so, and in that faith he could live and endure anything. . . .

Eden Castle
December 8, 1870

TOO LATE.

They had arrived too late and while Elizabeth was
certain that Harriet understood the reason for their delay,
she doubted if Lord Harrington did. But in his grieving
state perhaps he was incapable of understanding anything.

As the small black-clad procession made its way slowly
around the east wing of Eden Castle, taking the full stinging slap of the Atlantic wind in their faces, Elizabeth
bent her head lower and clung tightly to Harriet's arm.
The terrain was dangerous enough for a person with
sight. She had begged the frail woman to stay inside, but
nothing would do but that she and Dhari be shown the
fresh grave.

Looking directly up into the cold wind, Elizabeth saw
Dhari grasping Harriet's other arm. "Hold secure, Dhari,"
Elizabeth called over the gale, aware of Harriet's trembling steps. Walking behind them was the indomitable
Peggy, who kept a firm grasp on her mistress' waist, the
three of them leading the blind woman toward the graveyard beyond the north wall of Eden Castle, where
shortly they would have to endure the combined winds
of both the Atlantic ocean and the channel as well as the
greater punishment of the fresh grave.

But worse than all else was the pitiful man walking a
few steps ahead of them who, without the support of
Alex Aldwell, would be incapable of standing, let alone
walking. In all her years, Elizabeth had never seen such
a pathetic transformation. He bore not a single resemblance to the former Lord Harrington.

His bitterest disappointment, according to Harriet, had
been the absence of a Catholic priest and, as the nearest
one had been in Exeter and as Lila's burial would not
wait, Harriet had had to exert her authority and had
insisted upon immediate interment.

Elizabeth shuddered. In spite of her many garments,

the wind cut through as though she were naked. Looking
up, she caught her first glimpse of the black iron fence
behind which lay buried almost every Eden for the last
seven hundred years. Though it was noon, Elizabeth
felt as if she were moving through a cavern of night.

In spite of these discomforts, she offered Harriet solace.
"Not far. Just up ahead. Are you well?"

Beneath the black veil she saw Harriet nod. "I'm sorry
I'm such a bother."

Ahead she heard Alex Aldwell offering encouragement
to Lord Harrington as he supported the man with one arm
about his shoulder and another buttressing his arm. "Only
a few more steps, sir. You can make it, can't you?"

Elizabeth drew up her hood, blown back by the force
of the wind, and caught her first view of the graveyard
itself, her eyes moving to the large marble headstone with
the simple name carved upon it.

Edward Eden.

Abruptly Harriet stopped. "Are we—near?" she whispered. "We must be, for I can feel it."

"It's directly ahead," Elizabeth said, and knew precisely what it was that Harriet had felt—the presence of
death.

As the three of them guided Harriet through the gate,
Elizabeth looked ahead and saw the mounded dirt in
a corner of the graveyard, the grave itself seeming to sit
apart from the others, as though each generation of Edens
was assigned its own territory. The oldest markers, little
more than slate slabs, rested in crumbling disarray against
the far west fence, their carved names and the dates of
their tenures upon this earth almost obliterated by centuries of sea breeze and storms. Then, in a grisly cavalcade
the headstones marched slowly up through the centuries,
husbands, wives, children, all clustered together in death
as they had been in life.

They were less than twenty yards from the fresh grave
when Elizabeth looked ahead and saw Alex Aldwell and
Lord Harrington halt, their attention fixed on something.
As the surrounding headstones obscured her vision,
Elizabeth craned to one side to see what had halted their
steps. From where she stood she saw a black-clad figure
prostrate over the new grave, face obscured, weeping
audibly.

"Who is it?" Harriet demanded, sensing the intrusion.

"Someone is here," Elizabeth murmured. "I can't see who?"

Peggy released Her Ladyship and moved in a determined stride to the grave and the figure kneeling over it.

She called out, "It's only Molly, Lady Lila's maid."

"Molly?" Harriet repeated, puzzled.

All stood before the grave, looking down on the woman who either didn't know or didn't care that she was being watched.

As Peggy tried to rouse her out of her grief, Elizabeth saw Lord Harrington fall to his knees, rosary in hand, eyes closed. As his fingers moved over the beads, his face lifted directly into the cold wind.

She looked back at the little maid named Molly, who with Peggy's assistance was just struggling to her feet. Elizabeth saw a small covered basket clutched in her hand.

Having reached their destination, Elizabeth released Harriet's arm and moved a step to one side, concentrating on the freshly turned earth, unable to believe what lay beneath it. In fact, there was nothing in this cold graveyard which bore even the slightest resemblance to Lila. *There should be flowers,* Elizabeth thought angrily. *Mountains of flowers of every color and scent.*

But it was not the season for flowers, and she moved back from the barren grave and the man on his knees talking to Jesus' Mother, and saw Molly's tear-streaked face as she looked about her, aware for the first time that she was in the presence of the Countess Dowager.

"Milady," she murmured, drawing free from Peggy's arms and curtsying before Harriet. "I—hope I didn't—intrude. I wouldn't want to be someplace I shouldn't be."

Kindly, Harriet reached out her hand. Elizabeth saw the maid shift the basket and step forward until their hands touched, the contact seeming to provoke fresh tears.

"Oh, milady, I couldn't believe it," Molly sobbed. "I knew she was ill when I left, but—"

"Why did you leave?" Harriet asked.

"I thought you knew. I was—sent away, I was, last summer, just when Lady Lila needed me so."

Harriet drew the woman closer. "Who sent you away?"

"I was sent away by him, I was," she said. "By Mr. Eden."

There was no sound in the graveyard save for the wind and the muffled voice of Lord Harrington saying his beads. After the announcement Elizabeth saw Dhari turn away in an attitude of resignation.

Harriet was faring less well. "By—John?" she stammered. "I don't believe—"

"It's true, milady," Molly insisted. "I begged him, I did, to let me stay, but he was firm, said I was not fit company for his wife, not strong enough to handle her. Those were his very words, milady."

"Please, Molly," Harriet soothed, holding the weeping woman, "where did you go? If I had known I would have brought you back into the security of the castle."

"Oh, no, milady, I wouldn't have wanted you to do that. That would have been counter to Mr. Eden's wishes and would have only caused more trouble." At last the woman stood erect and withdrew a small handkerchief from the pocket of her coat.

"I'm being well looked after," she went on. "When I left Eden I took meself down to Mortemouth and was taken in by the old Reverend Christopher and his wife. Good souls, both, and could do with a bit of looking after. I clean and cook for them and it's not a bad life, though my heart never left her." And she looked down on the grave.

Suddenly there was the sound of a wrenching sob coming from the grave. All looked in that direction to see Lord Harrington collapsed, his rosary dragging in the dirt, as he clutched at the freshly turned soil.

Alex Aldwell had just stepped toward him when Molly interceded, went down on her knees beside the grieving man and put her arms around him. "Don't, sir," she said softly.

Distracted from his grief, Lord Harrington fixed on Molly as though she were a miracle.

"Here, sir," the woman said with dispatch. "Look what I brought." And she reached behind for the small basket. "Ain't much, but it will brighten the place, it will. Look!"

Elizabeth found herself leaning forward, trying to glimpse the contents of the basket. At last Molly produced a minor miracle of color in that gray slate day, a simple white china bowl with delicate fluted edges filled with a mound of yellow, freshly churned butter.

"Here, sir," Molly gently insisted. "You place it there, right in the center."

With hands that trembled visibly, though with childlike eagerness, Lord Harrington took the china dish and placed it lovingly in the exact center of the turned earth.

All stared down on the circle of color, the only voice that of Peggy, who was "seeing" for Harriet.

Elizabeth lifted her face to the wind. It seemed less cold now. The heaviness and pain were lifting. Of course the fact of death could not be denied, or the tragedy of it, but it had been softened somehow and made bearable by a serving maid and a small china bowl filled with butter.

As Elizabeth and Dhari took up their positions on each side of Harriet, the woman seemed to pull away from them. "Molly?" she called out, turning her head in all directions.

"I'm here, milady."

"Will you always be here?" Harriet asked. "Can you leave your present position and return to the castle? We —need you. Lila's sons need you."

Fresh tears, though different in nature, filled Molly's eyes. "Nothing—would make me happier," she whispered.

Then they were moving, the entire procession reversing their steps.

At the gate Elizabeth glanced back toward Lila's grave. Even from that distance the brilliant yellow and white of Molly's simple gift shone like a beacon in the bleak afternoon.

A short time later, as they were climbing the Great Hall steps, she found herself looking ahead with new dread to the evening. In the pressing urgency of Lila's death, Elizabeth had carefully avoided one subject.

Mary.

Harriet would have to be told, indeed had already made several inquiries about her daughter. In the rush of events Elizabeth had thus far escaped an explanation. But she was certain that John had written nothing, and a mother had a right to know, and though it seemed inhumanly cruel to force one tragedy after another upon her, still it had to be done.

Ahead at the top of the steps she saw several stewards and maids rush to assist the frozen family. Perhaps Dhari in her eloquent silence had been right. Anything could be borne so long as they felt love one for the other. It was the burden that one tried to carry alone that was unendurable.

Elizabeth breathed a quick prayer and added a plea for mercy. This family had suffered enough. Let fate plague someone else for a while.

As she was hurrying after Harriet through the Great Hall door she heard a shout from the watchman at the gate.

"Carriage coming!"

"John, do you suppose?" Harriet whispered, revealing for the first time her urgent need to see him and try to explain Lila's death.

Elizabeth did not reply, but kept her eyes fixed on the Gatehouse, the watchmen stirring out of their frozen lethargy.

As the carriage rumbled beneath the Gatehouse arch, Elizabeth looked more closely.

"Please, Elizabeth," Harriet begged, "who is—"

Elizabeth bowed her head and closed her eyes. If fate refused to provide her with respite, she would have to take it for herself.

With her eyes closed and lacking the courage even to speculate on what monstrous sorrow had rendered him thus, she said, "It's Richard. . . ."

❦

Forbes Hall
Kent
December 8, 1870

"IN MY OPINION, it is absolutely out of the question," Lady Forbes announced. "Is the man mad?" she fumed further. "Does he expect us to hop every time he snaps his finger?"

At the opposite end of the large Library, Lord Forbes called back, "I'm certain he meant nothing offensive by it, Mother. As we have observed before, Mr. Eden does things differently than we do."

Eleanor sat on the window seat at midroom, amused

by her parents. For as long as she could remember, whenever there was contention or disagreement her mother and father always sought out one of the larger rooms in the Hall; either the Library, where they were at present, or the Ballroom. With all due deliberation her mother would take up a position at one end, her father at the other, and over this vast distance differences would be resolved.

In amusement, considering that in her own mind the matter had been resolved, Eleanor listened to her parents' voices sail back and forth in a heated debate over the propriety of the letter from Mr. Eden, which had arrived only that morning.

It had requested—no, it had demanded—that Eleanor journey to Eden for the Christmas Celebrations, and it had insisted further that Eleanor come alone.

"Alone!" Lady Forbes exclaimed, echoing Eleanor's thoughts. "It's indecent," she went on, pacing at her end, looking far younger than her seventy years. Indignation was good for her.

"We did sign the premarital agreement," her father reminded wearily, "and we knew very well last summer precisely what it was we were signing."

Eleanor saw her father sit wearily at his bureau. Anger was *not* good for him. It made him look older, every inch the impoverished peer that he was, who was being forced to marry his daughter to the highest bidder in an attempt to cover his son's gambling debts, as well as his own.

Eleanor smiled at her melodramatic assessment of the situation. The present trouble stemmed from a difference in point of view. Her parents viewed her as a sacrificial lamb, while she viewed herself as the luckiest of all Englishwomen. There weren't many ladies from Newcastle to Kent who wouldn't give half their kingdoms for an alliance with the Eden family.

As her parents' voices continued to fly back and forth in proper debate, Eleanor tucked her slippered feet beneath the folds of her gown and nestled deeper into the cushions of the window seat and gave in to daydreaming. As long as the other parties in the room were enjoying themselves, why shouldn't she?

She looked through the small, mullioned windows and out across the green hills of Forbes Hall, her mind mov-

ing back to Eden. Eleanor hugged her knees and rested
her head upon them. To be mistress of such a place. . . .

Involuntarily, she smiled, amused by the ironies of life,
that she, the useless daughter, should now be facing the
noblest future.

Of course there was the matter of the man himself,
Lord Richard, but he was something of an unknown
quantity. What little she had seen of him last spring had
been pleasant. It would not be difficult to strike a bargain
with such a man, to give him love and children in return
for the security and prestige of his name. Besides, she
had learned long ago that love begins in earnest when
we love what is limited. There was a challenge about it
that appealed to her.

Then, it was time. The first step had been taken last
spring. Now the second step was about to begin.

Hurriedly, she swung her feet off the window seat and
heard her mother launch forth into the most ridiculous
argument of all.

"She has nothing to wear. She has a veritable paucity
of winter gowns and the man didn't even bother to state
the social functions. If I had a dozen dressmakers I still
wouldn't—"

"Mother!"

As her voice topped the aging one coming from the
end of the Library, she looked in that direction and saw
an expression of surprise on her mother's face, as though
a stranger had intruded into a private debate. *That is the
trouble,* Eleanor thought. *I've been uninvolved in my
own destiny for too long.* "Now come, both of you.
Enough polite shouting. There are times when it is best
to speak softly."

She waited until they were within arm's length of her.
"Please listen," she began. "I believe we all agree that
this discussion is both futile and foolish."

"Not at all," her father grumbled.

"Papa, you were there last spring. You and Mama both
signed the premarital agreement."

"Legally it is not binding," her mother interjected.

"But I want it to be binding," she announced. "I've
been waiting for Mr. Eden's letter since last spring. Now
that it has come, why the surprise or the discussion?"

"It isn't proper!" her mother snapped.

Eleanor laughed. "Oh, Mama, the Edens have been

improper for the last three hundred years. Why should you expect them to change now?"

"You have been raised according to certain strict standards, and I expect—"

"I have been raised to make a good marriage. Now that I'm on the verge of doing so, why are you standing in my way?"

"I forbid you to go alone," her father stated emphatically.

"I won't go alone, Papa. I'll take both Annie and Beulah, and you can send along a dozen stewards if you wish, to ward off highwaymen and other unidentifiable threats."

"It is not a matter for humor, Eleanor," her mother scolded. "I'm afraid that your—innocence prohibits you from understanding the real hazards."

"Which are?" Eleanor asked.

She saw her parents exchange a curious look, as though debating with themselves who would speak first.

Predictably her mother volunteered. "We are not speaking now of a childhood fête," she said. "Here, all of your life you have enjoyed the decorum and civility of Forbes Hall. At Eden you will be beyond our protection and, locked in marriage vows, you will be beyond our—"

"Mama, they are not monsters." She was expecting one or the other to interrupt her. When they didn't she moved to terminate the discussion. "Papa, would you please write to Mr. Eden and tell him that I accept his invitation with pleasure, that it is my intention to leave here on the eighteenth of December and, taking the road conditions into consideration, I should arrive at Eden on or about the twenty-second of December?"

All the time she talked she was moving toward the Library door, thus relieving herself of the worry on their faces.

"And you, Mama, if you care to come with me now, I'll show you that paucity of gowns of which you spoke. I think you'll agree that there are quite enough for ten women."

"Eleanor, wait!"

The voice was her mother's, bereft of intonation. She looked back and saw the two of them looking at her as though she were a corpse.

"Yes?"

"Do you have—sufficient black in your wardrobe?"

"Black! Now why would I want black, for the holidays?"

"Because Mr. Eden is in mourning," her mother replied. "Because his wife died last week. Did you know that?"

Stunned, Eleanor shook her head.

Her mother went on. "Don't you think it's strange that an invitation has been issued during a formal period of mourning?"

Eleanor stood in the doorway trying to deal with this new information. Though it cast an air of gloom on the days ahead, still it changed nothing. In fact, in a way it could even work to her advantage. "I'm flattered," she murmured, "to be included in the family at such an intimate moment. And I shall do everything I can to ease their sorrows."

Her determined manner shocked them anew. "You still insist upon going?" her mother asked.

"It's not a matter of choice."

"But you don't understand!" her father protested.

"I understand enough, Papa, more than you." She hesitated to see if there would be further rebuttal. "Well, then," she said, "come, Mama. Come help me select my gowns. But no black," she added, "not for this occasion. I'm not in mourning. If the Edens do things differently they must grant that right to others."

With a gasp of delight at her amazing self, she eagerly turned and took that first step. . . .

❦

London
The Temple
December 10, 1870

IN HIS PRIVATE chambers in the Temple, Sir Henry Aimsley stood over the naked female on his couch. *Judas, but she's beautiful!* he had thought. She had performed tricks for him all night. Fetched for him by his steward,

Arthur, Sir Henry realized that he didn't even know her name. What matter! As soon as he had dispatched with this foolish hearing he intended to return to this paradise where names ultimately might be important, though he doubted it.

At sixty-five, as he had been at six, Sir Henry was small, birdlike in all aspects. As his steward brushed his robes preparatory to this morning's hearing, he turned and engaged in his second-favorite activity, that of studying his face in the glass. For his troubles he suffered two regrets. One, that he'd not gone on the stage as a young man instead of burying his good looks in law books, and, two, that there would be no ladies present at the morning's hearing. It always made the time pass more quickly if there were a female or two about, a softly bulging bodice beneath which he could imagine the specifics of the female anatomy.

Peering into the mirror, Sir Henry saw his steward still brushing his "costume"—for what was the law but the grandest theatrical of all?

"Enough, Arthur," he scolded. "Leave the nap. It wouldn't do to appear threadbare before the richest man in England. Come, help me into my robes. Then fetch my wig. For one hundred pounds, Mr. Eden will get the full theatrical."

He turned about for a final look in the mirror. Pleased with what he saw and finding no room for improvement, he glanced longingly toward the small alcove and considered one more look at the sleeping female, but with strict discipline he reminded himself that the parties were already waiting in his chamber and that his superior judgment was needed and personal pleasure would have to wait.

In that frame of mind, he brushed past Arthur and walked through his library to the door which led to his public chamber.

Alone at the door, he paused, belatedly realizing that in the pleasure of last evening he'd failed to study the briefs which had been sent to him by Andrew Rhoades, a lengthy explication on the nature and purpose of the hearing.

Judas, can I bluff it? Of course he could. He knew enough from the gossip he'd heard in the Commons' dining hall and from what Rhoades had told him several

weeks ago when for one hundred pounds this hearing had
been arranged. The editor, John Thadeus Delane, was
involved, he remembered that much, and, of course,
John Murrey Eden.

Then he was ready, and drew a deep breath, and
pushed open the door and instantly took on the weight of
several male faces, including his two young clerks who
had already taken their positions, pads in hand, ready to
record the morning's boredom.

Oh, he *did* enjoy these opening moments of any
hearing, when his sense of theater was richly fed by the
respectful silence, all faces looking toward him, though
now he observed one face that was not looking toward
him. The lack of response was coming from the table on
his right, from the tall gentleman who sat next to Andrew
Rhoades.

Sir Henry knew who it was, the premier cock himself
in deep study of various papers spread out before him,
ignoring the pressure from his own solicitor to rise, as had
everyone else in the chamber.

For the first time Sir Henry observed another interesting face, that of a young man, Indian-appearing,
seated directly behind Mr. Eden. Probably the bastard
offspring of Eden's Indian mistress.

Sir Henry held his position behind his high bench, perfectly willing to give the man all the time he needed to
correct his bad manners. When the silence stretched to an
uncomfortable point, and when the man had yet even to
look up, Sir Henry took matters into his own hands and
set out to correct the miscarriage of tradition.

"Mr. Eden," he pronounced in a voice that had been
designed by nature for a proscenium, "it is tradition for
all parties to rise in the presence of—"

"I was prepared to rise a half an hour ago," Eden replied with matching imperiousness. "These other gentlemen, including yourself, may have time to waste. I
assure you, I do not."

The heat of embarrassment emanating from Andrew
Rhoades seemed to reflect the embarrassment of all,
though a moment later Sir Henry was pleased to see the
man half-rising, though with reluctance, where he held
himself suspended, then sat immediately.

The young Indian smiled, as did Sir Henry himself.
The morning might be of interest after all. Next to adul-

tery cases, he enjoyed most those cases where he could punish arrogance.

He glanced toward the table on his left and recognized the aging though noble face of John Thadeus Delane. A sad case, that. An alcoholic wife, though not a hint of scandal in the husband's past. Either he practiced celibacy or was a self-performer.

Sir Henry smiled at Delane and noticed that he was flanked on both sides by well-known solicitors, his own private staff no doubt, along with the legal staff from the newspaper. Of the two armed camps with which he was faced, if he had to choose a side Sir Henry would most definitely choose Delane's. Andrew Rhoades was outnumbered and perhaps outclassed.

Then to work, and in his best stage voice Sir Henry outlined the rules of the hearing. Both sides would have equal time to present their cases, though he made a plea for brevity. All parties were to understand that they were under oath, that they were to speak as objectively as possible, without emotion or exaggeration. And, since this was only a hearing, there would be no cross-examination and all questions would emanate from the bench. His judgment would be final and, if further litigation were required, then a new sitting magistrate would have to be found.

"Let us proceed," Sir Henry commanded, motioning for Andrew Rhoades to begin, the offended party by custom always taking the floor first. He noticed the young Indian on the edge of his seat.

Slowly Rhoades left his chair. "Milord," he began, in a voice that was scarcely audible, "our case is a simple one. Our premise is that a man, any man, is entitled to know the identity of his detractors. This"—and he held up the sheet of newsprint—"appeared in the *Times* several months ago, the date is noted, a vicious and, in our opinion, slanderous attack on my client, his heritage, his intent, his morals, his life in general . . ."

Here the poor man seemed to falter. He looked down at the newsprint as though struggling for direction.

"I request permission to approach the bench, milord, so that you may see for yourself."

"Granted," Sir Henry replied. He had some vague recollection of the attack on Mr. Eden, but was desirous of refreshing his memory.

As Rhoades placed the newsprint on the bench, Sir Henry stole a glance toward Delane. In addition to age he saw something else. Worry, perhaps. If only people realized how often they betrayed themselves through their faces. In the past Sir Henry had rendered decisions on the basis of who *looked* guilty and who did not. Unfortunately at this moment John Thadeus Delane looked very guilty.

Efficiently Sir Henry scooped up the newsprint and read the column heading: "The Demi-God of Eden." He scanned the first few paragraphs and found it increasingly difficult to conceal a smile. Thus he coughed conveniently into his hand and glanced down at the bottom of the column to find a name, someone named Lord Ripples claiming credit for the painful broadsides.

Well, what of it? Public figures were assailed every day in the press, every scribbler who could hold a pen seemingly dedicated to drawing influential and preferably blue blood. Not that Eden's blood was blue. But unfortunately bastardy, like adultery, was beginning to lose its hold on the public imagination. It simply was a case of excess. There were so many bastards and adulterers that they were no longer objects of interest.

"I beg your pardon, milord?"

Sir Henry looked up from his thoughts into Rhoades' face. Embarrassed, he realized that his mind had wandered. He thrust the newsprint back across the bench. "I fail to see the case, Mr. Rhoades," he said. "If you can please illuminate further."

He saw Rhoades glance back toward the table and the leveled eyes of both Eden and the young man. Deriving no help from his own camp, Andrew Rhoades turned back to the bench. "With your indulgence, milord," he murmured, "permit me to point out . . ." Again he faltered, as though he were constantly losing his train of thought.

The inept performance was being observed and recorded by the opposite table. Even old Delane seemed to be relaxing a bit. And Sir Henry was beginning to lose patience with the whole affair. True, he'd been paid well enough, but considering what was waiting for him back in his private chambers—

"I beg you, Mr. Rhoades," he said, "try to be as articulate as possible." In an attempt to get the solicitor back on track, he folded his hands and pronounced simply, "I fail to see a case. I *can* see a point of contention. The words printed there"—and he pointed toward the news sheet—"are unflattering and were undoubtedly painful for your client to read. But in my opinion, Mr. Eden is a public figure, and if every dignitary who had been offended by the press took his case to court, I'm afraid that Mr. Eden's building firm would have to construct courtrooms from one end of England to the other."

A polite laugh from Delane's solicitors was a nice reward for his humor. But Andrew Rhoades did not share that humor. Withdrawing a handkerchief and applying it to the palms of his hands, he stepped back toward the table, as though to align himself with his silent client. "Does that mean, milord, that a public figure has no recourse to—"

"It simply means, Mr. Rhoades, that a public figure is just that, available to the public and highly visible."

He saw Eden lean forward and summon Andrew Rhoades back to the table. The whispered exchange was brief. When it was completed Rhoades looked like a man who had suffered a fatal blow.

"Milord," he commenced, the white handkerchief in his left hand balled tightly inside his fist, "may I respectfully point out that my client's major contention is that this particular journalist is anonymous."

Well, by Judas, that small point did escape me. Sir Henry drew back the newsprint and studied the name at the bottom of the page. "There is a name here, Mr. Rhoades," he protested.

"A false one, milord, a coward who has taken refuge behind the protective shield of a respected newspaper and, from that secure point of concealment, is thus free to say anything he wishes about anyone, relieved of the possibility of ever having to face those whom he most grievously offends."

Sir Henry studied the name. It *was* a curious one. "Lord Ripples." Well, this changed the complexion of things a bit, offended his sense of justice entirely. Full disclosures, in his professional opinion, meant full disclosures for *all*.

"Is this true?" he demanded of the table on his left.

Poor Delane! Of course it was true. His face revealed everything. Yet one of his solicitors stood and announced with impressive calm, "We prefer not to answer any questions, milord, until both sides have had a chance to present their cases."

"Fair enough," Sir Henry agreed, "though I assure you the question will be asked again."

"And we are prepared to answer at the proper time, milord."

Sir Henry nodded, impressed. How smooth and professional they were compared to the zoo on his right. The young Indian was whispering continuously into Mr. Eden's ear.

"Well, Mr. Rhoades?" Sir Henry smiled.

Growing more distracted by the moment, Rhoades looked as though he were incapable of saying anything. Finally words evolved out of his confusion.

"Just this, milord," he murmured. "We feel that it is unfair for one man to be a target for another. And again let me remind you it is not the words or the circumstances under which they were written that we are challenging. The offense, the only offense, lies in the fact of the journalist's concealment. Today we respectfully ask you to pose a single question to Mr. John Thadeus Delane. We seek only the identity of the man who hides behind the pose of Lord Ripples."

Well, he *had* mustered a bit of showmanship there at the end. Still it was by and large a lackluster performance. As Andrew Rhoades was taking his seat, Sir Henry glanced toward Delane's solicitors. "Proceed," he commanded.

"Milord," one solicitor said, smiling. A young man, Sir Henry noticed, perhaps the youngest in the room with the exception of the Indian. Sir Henry disliked the young on general principles. "Our defense against this vague charge is simple. I present to you the facts. In our editorial offices in Printing House Square there are eighteen editors in addition to Mr. John Thadeus Delane. There are twenty-two editorial assistants, seventeen secretaries, nine permanent columnists and a fluctuating number of volunteer contributors."

He paused to let the numbers register with all present. His motive was clear. It required a small army to bring forth a single edition of the newspaper.

"Milord," the young man went on, "I think we can agree that it would be beyond the realistic expectations of any reasonable man to assume that Mr. John Thadeus Delane can be held solely responsible for the contents of this newspaper." His smile broadened. "Indeed there are times when, for various reasons, Mr. Delane's professional services are needed elsewhere and during those times he does not see the proof sheets at all."

The young man *was* clever. Not once had he addressed the opposite table. All his comments had been directed to the bench, a flattering focus as far as Sir Henry was concerned, surely a humiliating one as far as Eden was concerned.

The young solicitor stood directly before the bench, an apologetic smile on his face. "I respectfully submit, milord, that my client is being held responsible for writings that could have been executed and approved by perhaps fifty or sixty men. So, milord," he concluded, "in essence, as I'm sure you will agree, one cannot prepare a case if there is not a legitimate charge, and it is our opinion that Mr. Delane is innocent of any wrongdoing. In fact, we are baffled as to why we have been summoned here today and, as soon as Your Lordship adjourns this hearing, we will return to our respective and long-neglected duties."

Suddenly there was movement to Sir Henry's left. The young Indian leaned up and whispered something in Eden's ear. Eden appeared to listen carefully, nodding, then he was on his feet, ignoring the bench as though he had taken over his own defense.

"You know damn well what the charge is!" he shouted across at the young solicitor who had just taken his seat next to Mr. Delane. "You know perfectly well or you wouldn't be here now."

"Mr. Eden, I beg you," Sir Henry scolded, "please sit down. Direct your questions through Mr. Rhoades, who in turn will address them to the bench. We must maintain a semblance of professionalism, even in so unorthodox an arena."

Reluctantly and with Rhoades' assistance Eden returned to his seat, though there was a telltale flush on his face for all to see.

There was another brief whispered conference involving the three and at last Rhoades stood. "Milord, if I may rephrase the point of this hearing for the benefit of all, we are bringing no charges against Mr. Delane. We are here to seek information, a simple question. Who is the

man behind the Lord Ripples column? We are not even
questioning his right to print what he wishes. All we seek
is his identity so that my client may face him directly and
answer his charges—that is all," Rhoades concluded with
simple though effective weariness.

"Also, if I may respectfully point out, this is not the
first Lord Ripples column. They have been appearing ir-
regularly for several years and, almost without fail, they
have always been the cause of great agitation." His voice
fell. "We find it difficult, if not impossible, to believe,"
Rhoades went on, "that Mr. Delane does not know the
identity of the scribbler who increases the newspaper's
circulation every time he picks up his pen."

*By Judas, it's turning into good theater after all, com-
plete with pathos and dramatic pauses. Well, enough. It's
time for me to make sense of it all.* "In my opinion, the
matter is simple," Sir Henry pronounced, pleased to see
both tables look up, as though they had not expected a
decision so soon. "Mr. Delane"—he smiled apologetically
—"I'm afraid we must ask you for a name."

The look on Delane's face was not encouraging. All at
once his self-confidence seemed to have deserted him. His
young solicitor protested. "Milord, we fail to see—"

"Please sit down," Sir Henry commanded, though he
never raised his voice. It was more fun to humiliate youth
with the quiet dignity and authority of age.

Although it galled Sir Henry to admit it, Mr. Eden had
been right. There *was* a name to be had here, and they
knew it.

Sir Henry leaned forward, sensing that they were approaching the final act. He cleared his throat. "Having
listened carefully," he began, "it is my opinion that,
though the offense is a questionable one, nonetheless offense has occurred. To Mr. Eden I would like to say"—
and he looked in that direction—"that I am a staunch be-
liever in an open and free press. No shackles must be applied to these journalists in the execution of their duties,
which is to inform the public fully in all matters of public
concern."

He heard a premature murmur of victory coming from
Delane's table. *Not so quick,* he silently warned them.
The best drama was created by maintaining an equal
balance of tension.

"However," he proceeded, "I also believe that a man,

any man, has a right to his detractors' names. We cannot endorse anonymous journalism. We have only to look to history for disastrous precedents: the French Revolution, the Inquisition, the countless charges of witchcraft and heresy. . . ."

He shook his head. "No, while we must give to the journalist complete and unfettered freedom, we must also insist that they exercise these freedoms in a manner devoid of intrigue and hearsay."

Now the light of hope seemed to be emanating from the table on his right. What fun it was, playing with men!

"Therefore," he concluded, "and with all due respect, I request that Mr. John Thadeus Delane stand and answer one direct question which I will address to him from the bench."

With an air of sympathy he watched as one last hurried conference took place at the table on his right, though nothing came of it. The solicitors shook their heads at Delane's insistent questions. Apparently within the letter of the law there was nothing more to be done.

Thus it was that at last Mr. Delane bowed his head, then slowly pushed back from the table, rising wearily, a good man brought low by a scheming, vengeful bastard.

Hardening himself for the performance of his duty, Sir Henry sat erect in his chair and posed one simple question: "It is the request of this bench, Mr. Delane, that with clarity and truthfulness you reveal to all parties present the full name of the Englishman who writes under the pseudonym of Lord Ripples."

The request had been simply phrased and Mr. Delane was a man of keen intelligence. Then why the faltering look on his face? Why was he gaping toward the bench as though Sir Henry had addressed him in a foreign language?

"Come now, Mr. Delane," Sir Henry scolded. "Speak up!"

"Would you—" Delane began, and stopped. "Would you be so good as to repeat the question?"

Sir Henry heard the impatient murmuring coming from Eden's table and found himself in pained agreement. The man did appear to be stalling.

"I will be happy to repeat the question, Mr. Delane, but this time I must warn you. You must deliver yourself of a response. And further, let me warn you that you are under oath and must in all respects speak the truth. Is that clear?"

"Perfectly, Sir Henry."

"Then it is the request of this bench," Sir Henry repeated, "that with clarity and truthfulness you reveal to all parties present the full name of the Englishman who writes under the pseudonym of Lord Ripples."

There! He could not make it any clearer, though Delane's face seemed expressionless.

By contrast, the participants on his right were scarcely able to contain their anticipation. A glance in that direction revealed Eden to be on the edge of his chair. The young Indian had drawn closer, the strain clear on his dark features. Even Rhoades seemed to have stirred himself out of his lethargy and appeared to be squinting toward the opposite table, as though he were having difficulty hearing what was being said.

But nothing was being said. "Mr. Delane, will you speak, or will you force me to bring contempt—"

"No, no, Sir Henry," Delane muttered. He lifted his head and in a voice remarkable for its resonance said, "With all respect and sincere apology, Sir Henry, I'm afraid that I am unable to identify the Englishman who writes under the name of Lord Ripples."

There was sharp movement to Sir Henry's right, Eden on his feet, his face flushed with outrage. Sir Henry saw Rhoades place a restraining hand on his client's arm.

"Let me remind you again, Mr. Delane," Sir Henry said sternly, "you are bound to tell the truth, both by the tradition of the law as well as your honor as a gentleman."

Delane nodded. "I am aware of this, Sir Henry, and I can only repeat myself. I do not know and therefore cannot reveal the name of the—Englishman who writes as Lord Ripples."

"That's a lie!" The shouted accusation came from Eden, who was pushing his way through the clutter of chairs about the table, his face flushed with rage, ignoring the restraining hand of Andrew Rhoades.

"That's a lie!" he shouted again, "and Delane knows it, as does everyone in this room." As his fury increased, so did his steps and, though Sir Henry couldn't believe what he was seeing, he saw the deranged man lunge toward Delane, hands extended.

What happened next wasn't quite clear, for it happened

so fast and was so lacking in civility that Sir Henry could merely gape, as though he were watching the slow-motion movement of a nightmare. He saw Delane's young solicitor step forward, as though to come between his client and the rampaging Eden, and in the next minute Sir Henry saw Eden draw back his fist and deliver a piston-like blow to the side of that youthful face. The force of the blow sent the young man spinning backward into his colleagues, rendering them all useless as they struggled for balance, and for one terrifying moment there appeared to be absolutely nothing between Eden and the object of his rage, who continued to stand erect as Eden leveled a barrage of obscenity at him.

As the angry, crude voice rose about him, Sir Henry struggled to his feet. "Stop it!" he shouted. "I command you to—"

But at that moment he saw Eden lunge across the table toward the curiously placid Delane and, if it hadn't been for the rapid intervention of Andrew Rhoades and the Indian who moved swiftly up behind Eden and pinned his arms behind him, Mr. Delane would have received a blow that he most likely would have remembered all his life.

"Enough!" Sir Henry shouted, and belatedly realized that he'd taken no steps to provide this hearing with guards. Yet who would have thought that it would come to this?

"Get him out!" Sir Henry commanded Rhoades and the Indian. "Get him out before he commits an offense that will be truly worthy of a criminal suit."

He might have said more, but his voice was lost in the fury and outrage of Eden, who was literally being dragged from the chambers by Rhoades and the Indian, the intensity of the struggle reflected in their faces as both, allied now for the first time in the morning, dedicated themselves to the task of saving Mr. Eden from himself.

At last, and with monumental effort, they succeeded in dragging him to the door. With one hand Rhoades jerked it open. The last Sir Henry saw of John Murrey Eden was a face so distorted with animal fury that he scarcely resembled a man at all.

Blessedly the door was closed on the embarrassment, though all remaining in the chamber were treated to echoes of the rage, the man's voice diminishing only under the duress of distance, then suddenly falling silent, as though at last he'd either come to his senses or exhausted himself.

Sir Henry stared at the closed door. The only movement in the chamber was that of the young solicitor who had suffered Eden's fist. From the corner of his mouth spilled a small trickle of blood, which he dabbed at with his handkerchief.

Judas, what a terrifying turn of events this has been! And feeling mildly sick to his stomach at the barbaric display of physical violence, Sir Henry announced, "I believe this hearing is concluded."

All the solicitors were on their feet, clustered about Delane, murmuring their congratulations, a sense of victory to be shared by all with the exception of one, Mr. Delane himself, who continued to stare at the closed door as though an invalid had just been carried through it.

Sir Henry had had quite enough, thank you. The display of violence had offended his sensitivity and heightened his sense of a morning wasted.

"I beg your pardon, milord," one of Delane's solicitors inquired. "May we assume that the matter is closed?"

"As far as I am concerned you may," Sir Henry said. "I trust Mr. Delane as a gentleman and can only believe he spoke the truth. Whatever the offense caused by the mysterious scribbler, it pales in comparison to the human folly to which we were all forced to bear witness."

"Thank you, milord."

Shuddering at the thought of bodily assault, Sir Henry departed the chambers, leaving the victors to relish their victory. The matter *was* closed. Permanently. No bribe in England was large enough to force him to occupy a confined area with a mad dog. . . .

Cheltenham
December 24, 1870

WITH ONLY TWO exceptions, Mary found her new life within Miss Veal's school if not pleasurable at least endurable.

The first exception was this constant state of cold. The second hurt too much to think about. *Would they come tonight?*

As she huddled on the cot beneath her blanket, she sent her toes in search of the brick which earlier she had warmed at the parlor fire. It was cold now, and she tried to wrap the blanket more tightly about her, praying for sleep to come soon, then in the next breath praying that it didn't. Occasionally in sleep she found safety, but more often she found nightmares.

Tomorrow was Christmas and Miss Veal had promised them a packet of chocolate to follow the cabbage soup. Of course there would be prayers and lessons as always, but Mary was grateful for that. In the diversion of constant Bible study she'd managed to find a degree of relief from the terrors that haunted her. As Miss Maitland, the instructor, had pointed out, Mary had sinned and God had punished her.

Slowly she withdrew one hand from the blanket and reached up to her hair. It was growing out. She was certain of that, but it felt as jagged as ever. Fortunately there were no mirrors at Miss Veal's, so she was spared the agony of seeing herself. Though at first her fellow students had stared at her, now they no longer did so, and for that she was grateful.

Shivering, she turned on the narrow cot and tried to nestle deeper into the small pocket of warmth left by her own body. There was one interval each week when she was warm, the physical examinations which took place every Friday before the fire in the parlor.

At first these weekly examinations had alarmed her. Frieda, the woman who looked after her, had had a fierce argument with Miss Veal over Mary's participation in the examination. But Frieda had lost and Miss Veal herself

had patiently explained to Mary the awesome responsibility in the care and physical well-being of so many
young ladies, some, like Mary, from England's finest families. Infections had to be detected early, open sores that
might spread, chapped and chafed areas which must be
attended to.

Thus on that first Friday several weeks ago Mary had
taken her place in the line of students outside the parlor
door. Frieda had walked with her as far as the door and
had whispered a curious instruction. "Look 'em in the eye,
Lady Mary. Look 'em straight in the eye."

Mary had done just that, as she'd taken her place before the fire, facing a semicircle of eight teachers with
Miss Veal at the center, who had commanded her to remove all her garments and turn slowly before them.

She'd done this, enjoying the heat of the fire, and after
they had kept her standing for about five minutes, Miss
Veal had pronounced her well, had ordered her to put
her clothes back on and that had been that.

Now she found herself looking forward to that brief interval, standing naked before the fire. Over the weeks the
ritual had changed only a little. On occasion one of the
teachers would come forward and touch her, either on
the breasts or the buttocks, and once, last week, Miss
Maitland, the Bible instructor, ran her hand between
Mary's legs. But that was all, and Miss Veal had dismissed
her and, with reluctance, Mary had said goodbye to the
fire and had re-emerged in the cold corridor in time to see
a pretty young girl named Stephanie break into tears that
her turn was next.

Now she tried to huddle deeper into her cot and hoped
that the night would be quiet. Almost every night she
heard cries coming from someplace. At first they had
frightened her. But cries in the night, according to Miss
Maitland, were erring souls striving for forgiveness, and
they were blessed and should be received as such. Still,
Mary didn't like them.

Suddenly she glanced toward the door, thinking that
she had heard a step. As her dread of the inevitable increased, she covered her face with her hands and tried to
remember what Miss Maitland had said about welcoming
pain.

They *would* come tonight. She knew it, and there was
nothing she could do to avoid it. Then she must accept it,

as Miss Maitland had instructed her to do. Sometimes it
helped if she could concentrate on something else, a Bible
verse, a parable, a Latin conjugation.

They were coming. She heard them now and, in desperation, she shut her eyes and sent her mind deep into
her memory and found a familiar face which awakened
within her such feelings of warmth and happiness that she
was only partially aware of her door being pushed open,
lamplight filling the darkened cell, the four women standing over her, looking down, with that awful apparatus in
their hands.

"It's time, Mary. You know what to do."

Still she clung to the dream, all the time rising from her
cot, stripping off the muslin nightdress, scarcely feeling
the new chill.

If only she could hang on to the memory of that miraculous face.

Another female was hovering close beside her. "You
know why we have come, don't you, Mary?" this voice
asked kindly.

"Yes."

"Why? Tell us so we can be certain that you understand."

His hands. She remembered his hands, strong and
square with soft tufts of dark hair on the knuckles, remarkable hands that had—

"Mary! Pay attention."

"Yes."

"Why are we here?"

"To—rid my body of the poisons that are corrupting me."

"Good girl. Now—"

Yes, now. It could not be postponed any longer, and
Mary did not want to postpone it. Commence it now so
that it would be over soon and she could spend the rest of
the night exploring this remarkable memory. Had she
concocted it out of her imagination, or had such a man
really existed?

"Take your position, Mary," the female voice insisted.
As she still was fully occupied with her dream, she felt
hands guide her face down onto the bed, felt other hands
separate her legs.

Under the duress of the moment the face that had once
sustained her faded and, aware of what was about to happen, she reached forward for the iron bars at the head of

her bed and grasped them just as she felt the cold insertion into her rectum.

Compelled to look, though she knew the ritual by heart,
she glanced over her shoulder and saw Miss Maitland
standing over her legs, a full pitcher of cold water suspended in the air, which she now tilted into the end of a
long tube which led down into the insertion.

As cold water began to fill her bowels, Mary clutched at
the iron bars and tried to resurrect that face. Where was
he? She needed him now. The heaviness was increasing
as was the discomfort. And she had to hold it. They became angry with her when she couldn't hold it.

Out of the corner of her eye she saw another female
move a chamber pot into position.

Please, God, let me see him again, she prayed silently
and in defense against the increasing pain in her lower
abdomen, she clutched at the iron bars and buried her
face in the blanket and tried to send her mind to safer
ground.

But it could not be done. The pain was acute now and,
wiping her tears on the blanket, she looked back at the
pitcher still suspended, the water still coming.

In spite of her vow to keep silent, she cried out and
realized belatedly that she was alarming the other students
as they, when it was their turn, always alarmed her.

She was sorry for that, but the pressure on her bowels
could not be borne and she arched her neck and lifted
her head at an awkward angle and cried out for relief.

In defense against the unendurable she pressed her
face into the blanket. Surely purgation would come soon.
Surely one day God would forgive her. . . .

Eden Castle
December 28, 1870

ALTHOUGH THE ORDEAL of Christmas had been over for
three days, and although Andrew Rhoades had tried repeatedly to find John alone in order to speak with him in
private, thus far he'd had no success.

As he glanced about the grim Dining Hall, he debated the wisdom of speaking now. They were far from alone, but time was running out. He owed him that much, out of respect for the love they once had shared.

He looked about at these contradictory surroundings. The lovely hall bore all the external decor of Christmas jubilation. Bows of evergreen and spruce had been looped about the elegant plasterwork ceiling and a magnificent holly wreath adorned the marble fireplace where a massive Yule log still burned.

It was as beautiful as he'd ever seen it. Still, there was a poisonous air here and it was emanating from the family itself, everyone deep in private mourning with the exception of the young woman, Lady Eleanor Forbes. Why John had invited her into this misery, Andrew would never know. Even she seemed to be succumbing to the gloom. Only moments earlier she had excused herself from the table and had taken refuge at the pianoforte in the Great Hall and was now contributing to the gloom by sending back the plaintive echoes of a Chopin étude.

Andrew closed his eyes to the sorrowing faces about him and concentrated on the music. She did play well, and the musical harmony was soothing after the discord of the last few days.

Without opening his eyes, Andrew reached his hand out beneath the table until he found Dhari's. She responded to the pressure of his hand with predictable warmth, her fingers separating his until they were locked together.

Carefully he looked at her, amazed that now she was his, that at his request she had come back to London from Eden and that two days before Christmas she had done him the extreme honor of becoming his wife.

They had exchanged simple vows before the old vicar at St. Martin's-in-the-Fields. Then they had left immediately for Eden. Thus far they had told no one, not even Elizabeth, and Dhari kept the gold band studded with rubies that Andrew had placed briefly on her finger tucked away in the concealment of a white handkerchief.

Andrew had requested that she not wear the ring until he had told John everything. But as yet that opportunity had not presented itself. Not that Andrew hadn't tried. God, how he'd tried!

Wearily, he shook his head. After a relationship that

spanned almost two decades, he should be capable of understanding John Murrey Eden. But he wasn't, and his new awareness of this failure only reminded him of what he had yet to do, which was to inform John of his marriage to Dhari and their imminent departure on the second of January, when they would sail from Liverpool to Canada and, they hoped, a new and better life.

Abruptly he looked up, his senses sharpened by the awareness of this difficult task yet ahead of him. To his right at the head of the table he saw John, the food on his plate scarcely touched. He sat slouched in his chair, his dress jacket bunched about him, an expression of distance on his face.

Directly across the table from Andrew sat Richard. Anguish was there as well, though of a different sort, the suggestion of an invalid about the man. He seemed to move very slowly now and speak only when spoken to.

Next to Richard was Elizabeth, whose face bore the strain of the last few weeks. There were hollows about her eyes and she, too, maintained the silence that seemed to be the order of the day.

Next to Elizabeth sat Alex Aldwell, the only one at the table who was enjoying the culinary efforts of John's chef. But even that imperturbable man looked up from his plate with apologetic eyes, as though he felt guilty for enjoying himself.

Seated next to Andrew, of course, was Dhari, and next to Dhari sat Aslam, who kept a constant and adoring watch on John. Beyond Aslam there was nothing but the empty expanse of the table itself and two services, one which had been recently abandoned by Lady Eleanor Forbes, and one, unoccupied, which had been set for Lady Harriet. Someone had expected her this evening but, as always, she had not appeared.

This, then, was the setting into which Andrew was about to step with two difficult announcements.

"John," he began, and stopped, aware of how out of place a human voice sounded at this frozen table. He looked about and realized that he had gathered everyone's attention except the one he had addressed. That man did not so much as look up from concentrating on aligning his knife with his fork.

"John, I beg you, please give me your attention, for just a moment."

"You always have my attention, Andrew."

Relieved, Andrew was in the process of speaking when suddenly John shifted, sat up and abandoned his interest in his knife.

"She plays very well, doesn't she?" he commented, referring to the distant strains of Chopin coming from the pianoforte in the Great Hall.

In the absence of an immediate response, Elizabeth filled the vacuum. "She does indeed, John. She's charming in every respect, though I'm afraid we are neglecting her. Perhaps this wasn't the time to——"

"Then we must remedy that," John replied. "Richard, go and fetch her. Tell her we are in need of her charming presence."

Andrew protested. "Please, John. Richard can fetch her in a moment."

"But we have been accused of neglecting our guest," John protested.

Elizabeth tried to defend herself. "It wasn't an accusation, John. I just meant that . . ."

As her voice drifted off into a muddled silence, the tension and cross-purposes at the table increased.

Andrew waited for the air to clear. He was on the verge of speaking a second time when again John drew the attention to his end of the table.

"I miss—Mary," he murmured. "Mary always made it truly Christmas, didn't she? I remember how she would sing for us. Such a lovely voice . . ."

As his words drifted off, Andrew saw Elizabeth with her head bowed. *Dear Lord, what is the man doing to us all?* he thought.

"I had a letter before I left London. Did I tell you, Elizabeth?" John went on.

"From—Mary?"

"No, not from Mary. She's kept far too busy to write. My letter was from Miss Veal, who assured me in glowing terms that Mary was fitting in nicely. She said that she's a diligent student——" Here he laughed softly. "Can you imagine that? Our Mary a diligent student. Isn't that good news?"

"Indeed it is," Elizabeth murmured, looking up long enough to sip her wine. "Would it be possible to visit her? I thought that on my return to London I might veer in the direction of Cheltenham. I would like very much to——"

"No, it's out of the question," John interrupted. "Miss
Veal has made it clear. She wants no distractions, at least
for the first year." He leaned forward, as though to make
certain that his next words would be understood. "You
see, the whole point of the new regimen is to break old
habits of self-indulgence and lack of discipline. So I'm
afraid a visit is out of the question. In fact I forbid it."

Andrew saw the anger in Elizabeth's face, but instantly
it was replaced by quiet acceptance. He wished that
Elizabeth had challenged him. She, more than any of
them, had endured such continuous abuse at John's hand.
Through some misplaced sense of love and loyalty she
was prepared to endure even more.

With the renewed sense of preparing the way for his
own exit and that of Dhari's, Andrew tried again to speak.
The message was simple. Why couldn't he simply deliver
it and have done with it?

Then he would, though at that moment John stirred,
this time leaving his chair in a burst of energy which
dragged all the attention to that end of the table. "My
sons," he announced, full-voiced. "Lord Harrington has
requested the privilege of taking my sons to Ireland for a
brief visit in the spring. He says he has a woman, someone named Molly, who will care for them and he says that
it would please—Lila."

He paused, as though it had been difficult for him to
pronounce the name. "What is your opinion?" he asked.
"Do you think that I should permit it?"

Andrew tried to determine if he was addressing someone in particular. Apparently he wasn't. In the absence of
a response, Andrew tried to fill the void. "The decision is
yours, John."

"I know, but I'm asking for others."

"They are your sons."

"And his grandsons," John replied with a startling degree of largess. "He says it would help to heal his grief."

"You, Elizabeth," John went on. "No opinion from
you?"

Elizabeth looked up. "I agree with Andrew," she said.
"The decision is yours. In the end you'll make it, anyway,
regardless."

John laughed and stretched before the warmth of the
fire. "How well you know me, Elizabeth. Still, I was interested."

Sensing that the subject was closed, Andrew sat up on his chair, hoping that now it would be his turn. But unfortunately the stewards reappeared with arrangements of celery and cheese and dried winter fruit. Predictably, only Alex made a move toward the food and, as the last steward departed, Andrew summoned his courage and decided—now!

"John, if I may—" he began.

"Eat, Andrew." John smiled at him from the fire.

"I'm not hungry."

"No, that's obvious. No one seems to possess an appetite."

"John, I must speak," Andrew said bluntly.

"Speak!" he invited, slicing a piece of cheese vigorously, as though he had to kill it before he ate it.

It was not exactly the mood that Andrew had hoped for. Still, he could not postpone it any longer.

"John," he began, as though he were commencing a formal address, "and the rest of you as well, two days before Christmas, on the twenty-third of December, to be exact—"

"God!" The curse came from John, who pushed his plate away and was looking distastefully at it. "Is there anything more disgusting than the presence of food when you have no appetite?"

Over the taut silence he heard Elizabeth invite softly, "Please go on, Andrew. You were saying something about two days before Christmas."

Andrew gave her a grateful smile. "As I was saying, on December twenty-third at St. Martin's-in-the-Fields—"

"You know you are wrong, Alex," John interrupted from the end of the table.

"How's that?" Alex mumbled, his mouth filled.

"You said you'd never seen anyone grieve as Lord Harrington was grieving—"

"Aye—"

"Do you think I'm not grieving as well?" The question was posed with large amounts of self-pity laced in.

"Oh, I didn't imply that, John," Alex said. "Not any of us mean to imply that."

"You see, in my opinion," John began quietly, "it serves no purpose to give in to the weakness of grief. What is death but the endless laboring sigh of the earth?

The dead are—dead. They have moved on. There is nothing we can do."

Andrew was listening closely, not to the merit of the words, which sounded like every cliché he'd ever heard; rather he watched the reaction they seemed to be having on the others. Every face bore the circumflex eyebrows of sympathetic understanding.

Abruptly John sat up in a new burst of energy, as though a splendid idea had just occurred. He retrieved his glass of port from the table, a warm smile on his face. "Will you all accompany me to the Library where, before the Alma-Tadema painting of 'The Women of Eden,' we will toast my Lila and thank her for the brief joy she brought to all our lives? That"—he smiled—"would be a proper mourning."

The proposal caught on instantly, a splendid idea in the opinion of all who struggled to their feet, glasses in hand, the general movement leading to the door where John already stood.

Still desperate to deliver his message, knowing now that there would never be an appropriate time, and realizing that in a few days the reaction of John Murrey Eden would be a matter of monumental indifference to him, Andrew stood and raised his voice to full strength in an attempt to cut through the scraping of chairs, and pronounced loudly and clearly enough for all to hear, "My wife and I will remain behind, if you please. We have paid our respects to Lila and now we have much to do before we depart in a few days for Canada."

The silence seemed to whistle about his ears, and he heard his own voice in echo. *Good Lord—I'd not intended to shout it!* He was then aware of Dhari rising to stand beside him, willing to bear her share of the shock waves which seemed to be battering the large Dining Hall.

Elizabeth spoke first, drawing back to the table. "I— beg your pardon?" she stammered. "What did you—say?"

Eagerly Andrew repeated himself, all the time keeping his eyes away from the man who stood at the most distant point in the room. "I said that on the twenty-third of December, Dhari and I were married. And on the second of January we sail for Canada."

There! There was no way he could make it any clearer, and now he concentrated on Elizabeth's changing face. The shock had vanished and he saw the beginnings of a warm smile, as she hurried around the table and clasped Dhari in her arms. "Oh, I'm so happy for you both. Married! My goodness. Why didn't you tell me? How I would have loved to—"

Though Andrew's inclination was to join the chattering group behind him, Elizabeth admiring the ring which Dhari had brought forth from her pocket, still he knew that for all that had been said, nothing had been said, and there was no reaction in the room as powerful as the lack of reaction coming from the Dining Hall door.

With the thought of seeing it through to its conclusion, Andrew turned to where John was standing, glass in hand, where he'd been halted on his way to toast his dead wife.

He appeared to study the port in his glass. With his head still bowed, he commenced walking back toward the table. "Married," he whispered to the glass of port and placed it on the table as though it had displeased him.

"Yes," Andrew confirmed. "I wanted to tell you earlier, but—"

"When?"

"A few days ago, on the twenty-third."

John leaned back in the chair, a smile on his face. "So that's where you were on that day. I had need of you. I even sent Alex around."

If the words were unclear, the tone was not. They were being made to feel like misbehaving children. "How could you have looked for me, John?" Andrew inquired politely. "You left for Eden on the twenty-second."

Too late, Andrew realized his mistake.

"Twenty-second, twenty-third," John snapped, "what difference? You have seldom of late been where I needed you."

"I'm sorry. I assumed that with your departure—"

Suddenly John leaned up in his chair. "Why did you do it behind my back?" he demanded.

Be tactful, Andrew counseled himself, *and patient.* "It wasn't a matter of doing anything behind your back, John. We merely wanted it to be small and private, and we didn't think that you would be—"

"Interested?" John demanded. "Not interested in the marriage of my mistress with my solicitor?" His voice was rising, the words ugly. "What effective ammunition you've given my enemies to use against me, both of you," he accused. "As if the recent farce of a hearing wasn't enough, now you have made it possible for me to become the laughing stock of every public house and private club in London."

"We did not think," Andrew began, "that it would be—"

"No, you did not think," John mimicked. Abruptly he pushed back with such violence that the chair almost overturned, and strode angrily to the fireplace.

Elizabeth tried to intercede. "John, please. They have a right to—"

"To deceive me? To be disloyal to me?"

"It was not our intention to deceive," Andrew said.

"Then what *was* your intention? To simply disappear one day with her on your arm and send back word from —wherever in hell it is you are going?"

"Canada."

"Canada!" John retorted, hands on hips, his anger full-blown and still increasing. "What precisely do you think you'll find in Canada?"

"A new life."

"And what's the matter with this one?"

Andrew hesitated. "It's grown stale."

"England? Stale?" John parroted and slapped his forehead and turned away, as though he could not bear to face such stupidity. "Just the greatest empire the world has ever known," he said to the fire. "Just the only place in the world where a man can seize a future for himself beyond his wildest dreams."

"I'm not interested in seizing the future, John. I just want a peaceful present, that's all."

Slowly John looked back at him. "No, you never have been interested in the future, have you, Andrew? Your ambitions have always been limited to the moment. I would say, offhand, that it has always been the central bone of contention between us."

Andrew nodded. "Our visions *are* different."

"Indeed they are. Yours, limited."

Andrew closed his eyes.

It was while his eyes were closed that John's attack took an uglier turn. "Why in hell did you marry her?" he muttered. "She's used goods, Andrew, surely you knew that. Well used even before I took her on."

"That's enough, John," Andrew warned, tightening his

grip on Dhari's hand where she seemed to lean softly against him.

"Well, it's true," John replied innocently. "She's not the kind of woman you marry, Andrew. I thought you knew that. You take her to bed. You see she is well cared for, but you do not marry her."

The offensive words seemed to echo in Andrew's head. In a battle of fisticuffs he would lose, for John's physical strength was superior. But if he continued to speak, Andrew would be forced to find some way to shut his mouth.

Determined to end the encounter while he still was capable of a degree of civility, Andrew turned away and sheltered Dhari beneath his arm. "If you will excuse us," he murmured, and had just commenced leading Dhari toward the door when John spoke again, his voice strangely hoarse.

"Where are you going?" he demanded.

"To pack," Andrew replied. "We will be leaving tonight."

Elizabeth offered a whispered protest. "Oh, no, please stay a while longer. We'll never see you again."

"Let them go," John muttered. "I'm sick to death of the sight of them. They deserve that barbaric wilderness toward which they are headed. I predict in a year they will come running back to the security of England and Eden. Oh, you'll see them again, make no mistake of that!"

Throughout this tirade, Andrew and Dhari continued the length of the Dining Hall. Of greater concern to Andrew than the insane voice raging behind him was Dhari. She clung to him, her humiliation doubly tragic because she could not defend herself.

No, it was very important that Andrew not stop once in that seemingly endless journey to the door. He must take Dhari beyond the reach of John's voice, which still pursued them, the man's words incoherent now, a confusion of accusation and betrayal, of threat and revenge.

All at once, when Andrew was least expecting it, the voice fell silent. At the door he paused, trying to interpret the silence without looking back. But he couldn't.

Then he heard it, that same voice speaking his name, "Andrew—" the two syllables weighted with grief.

Although he had vowed not to look back, the cry struck something deep within him, the place where memory re-

sided, the good memories, the times they had spent together as young men prowling the streets of London,
enduring their apprenticeships at Thomas Brassey's. All
this and more conspired against him and caused him
momentarily to abandon Dhari and gave him the strength
to look back at the most remarkable man he'd ever known
in his life, a man who was capable of transforming the
world, yet who could not transform himself.

The splintered need he saw on that face was awesome,
the pain of regret, his expression suggesting to Andrew
that he, too, had suffered the same backward excursion
into memory.

Breathing heavily from his recent rage, John stood
alone by the fire, the red glow shimmering in the perspiration on his brow. "Are you—really leaving?" he whispered, a moving, childlike quality to his voice.

Andrew nodded, for he did not trust himself to speak.
At the first invitation he would have been willing to re-
trace his steps back to that suffering man and clasp him
in his arms one last time.

But the invitation never came. "Then I—wish you
well," John said. Abruptly he turned away, grasping the
mantel with both hands.

Was he weeping? Andrew couldn't be certain and now
discovered that his own strength was rapidly diminishing.
It was over. He had made his announcement and his wife
was awaiting him.

In a final shifting of loyalties, he turned his back on
John Murrey Eden, placed his arm about Dhari and
walked slowly through the door.

He did not look back again, and no one stopped him.

Richard knew.

He was the only one in that Dining Hall who knew
precisely what had happened this night. A friend had
been lost and, in spite of his own pain that had persisted
since Bertie's death, he was the first to recognize and respond to the grieving man leaning heavily against the
mantel.

Feeling his first selfless instinct since Bertie's funeral,
Richard rose slowly and looked about at the faces frozen
in shock.

*A cross is no longer a cross when there is no longer a
self to suffer its weight.*

John needed him, but first he must clear the room. "Alex," Richard whispered, "would you please take Elizabeth to her chambers? And Aslam, why don't you go and tell your mother goodbye? I'm certain she would appreciate it."

Amazed at how effectively the blind could lead the blind, Richard watched, grateful as everyone followed his directions. Unfortunately, long before he was ready for it, he found himself alone with John, and wondered briefly how he could offer solace when he was in such need himself. As though to further weaken his resolve, he suffered a clear image of Bertie's face, not distorted as he'd found him in death but whole and clear and full of love.

Grasping the table for support, he walked toward the man by the fire and placed an arm about his shoulders. "Come, John," he murmured. "We're alone now and I'm with you as I've always been with you. Come, sit. We'll talk for a while as we used to when we were boys. Do you remember?"

Though he was pleased with John's submission, he was most alarmed by his face. He continued to lend him the support of his arm until he was seated. Then he withdrew his handkerchief and commenced wiping John's brow, aware from his own experience with death and loss that the first step was to distract the mind.

"You've done this often enough for me in the past," Richard said, his voice gentle. "Herr Snyder used to say that you were better than Clara Jenkins when it came to playing nursemaid."

In the hope that the two references to their shared childhood would provide the necessary distraction, Richard continued to wipe the moisture from John's face, finding healing for himself by ministering to another.

Experiencing relief for the first time in many weeks, Richard drew a chair close and placed the handkerchief in John's hand. "Here, you do it. Remember, that's what you used to tell me. After you had cleaned me up and set me on the straight and narrow, you always said, 'A man must be responsible for himself.' Remember?"

To Richard's pleasure, John took the handkerchief, his eyes fixed upon the table. "Herr Snyder," he murmured, and shook his head, recalling the old German tutor who had kept them both on the straight and narrow. "Were we —ever that—young?" he asked.

"Of course we were."

Suddenly John looked up and Richard saw something he had never seen before in that face, a massive self-doubt, as though destiny were on the verge of defeating him. "I'm afraid, Richard," John confessed, "I no longer —see the point—to any of it."

It might have been his own thoughts of the last few weeks coming back at him. Stalling in a search for more than platitudes, Richard pushed back in the chair. The music coming from the pianoforte had started again. When had it ceased?

Abruptly John stood, tossing the handkerchief on the table as though to put that stage of his grief behind him. "My God, what a muddle," he muttered, striding past Richard.

Relieved that he was at least speaking and moving again, Richard closed his eyes. He was far from ready to offer significant solace to anyone. "We've lived through muddles before," he said quietly to the man pacing behind him.

"Who would have thought it?" John went on. "Canada!" he repeated, his mood now one of bewilderment.

Richard nodded. "I must confess I was as surprised—"

"It's madness!"

"To us. To Andrew it makes—"

"And what am I to do?" John demanded, reappearing on the opposite side of the table. "Andrew knows more about the John Murrey Firm than I do myself. He is the only one who is intimately acquainted with all the projects in progress as well as—"

It seemed a weak argument, and Richard said as much. "You have a large staff of solicitors, John. Surely one will be able to—"

"No! No! He will leave a vacuum that it will be impossible to fill"—he faltered—"in more ways than one."

There it was again, that uncharacteristic helplessness. Richard looked up at the man who was leaning heavily over the back of the chair where Andrew had been sitting. His face was disconsolate. "Oh, how I shall miss him. What would I do without you, Richard?" John whispered. "All my life, what would I have done without you?"

Because the moment required it, Richard found himself in John's arms, the two boys inside the grown men brushing aside their manhood and clinging to each other, children again, trapped in a world of grown-up terrors.

At the end of the embrace, John lifted his glass, half filled with port, and carried it back to the fire. "To our good memories." He smiled.

He drained the glass and seemed to study the empty crystal for a moment. "I—am so sorry for what I said earlier, to Andrew, to Dhari."

Richard nodded. "I think it would help all of you if you make a point to see them before they left, to wish them well."

"I will," John agreed. "I most certainly will."

"As for your business affairs, I'm certain that there are capable men who can fill Andrew's shoes. After all, you have Aslam now, and he's very gifted."

Then a small mystery occurred to Richard. He remembered how eagerly both he and Bertie had been awaiting John's arrival in Cambridge. But of course the visit had never materialized. Obviously John had come to Cambridge to fetch Aslam, but it was equally obvious that he had not lingered.

Richard looked up at John, who had again taken refuge by the fire. "Bertie and I had hoped for the pleasure of your company a few weeks ago. In Cambridge, I mean. We had quite a feast prepared."

Slowly John stood erect. He glanced once at Richard, then looked again into the fire. "I had—planned to stop," he said, "but I'm afraid that time did not permit it. I had lingered too long in Cheltenham seeing to Mary's well-being, and I had pressing business awaiting me in London."

"I understand," Richard murmured.

"Will you be going back to Cambridge, Richard?"

An easy question, an easier answer. "No, not for a while."

"Your duties there?"

"I asked for an indefinite leave, and it was granted."

There was silence between them, a silence altered only by the soft strains of the pianoforte coming from the Great Hall. As though the music reminded him of the musician, the new look of restoration on John's face faded. "Dear Lord, what will I do with her?" he moaned.

For the first time, Richard found himself ill-equipped to offer assistance. Trying not to be too blunt, he posed a blunt question. "Why did you invite her, John? You knew this would be a difficult time, in mourning for Lila and—"

"I invited Lady Eleanor here out of Christian charity, Richard," he explained, "for her sake as well as ours. I know her parents well, particularly her father. He was one of the few men in London who was kind to me after my return from India. Of course, he was in the process of systematically losing the remains of his inheritance. The old man has absolutely no business sense," he added critically.

"So, in exchange for certain introductions I tried to rally his fortunes and did to a certain extent. But unfortunately he has a son who has a talent for accumulating gambling debts."

He gestured toward the distant refrain coming from the pianoforte. "She always struck me as having had such a lonely childhood. Born late in life, she seemed more the granddaughter than the daughter—"

Abruptly he dismissed what he was saying. "But none of these are valid reasons, are they, for thrusting her into this household at this time. No, the truth now." He smiled wearily. "I invited her for a very special reason. I knew better than anyone the condition of Eden, the fresh grave—" His voice broke. "Lila gone, Mary absent. I thought it would be good for all of us to witness youth and beauty and warmth. I'm sorry. I was wrong."

"No need for apologies," Richard begged. "Not with me at any rate. I understand now and I agree. Your intentions matched your needs."

"No," John disagreed. "I had no right. It isn't fair to her or the family. No one here is capable of maintaining the charade of society. No," he said again, "I'll go this minute and apologize to her and kindly suggest that she—"

"You will do no such thing!" Richard said. He was on his feet, not at all certain of what he was saying. It was simply that he could not abide the expression of silent grieving in the face opposite him. "I'll go to the young lady," he offered quietly, a bit amazed at his own words. "I'm not certain that my company will please her, but—"

He had his reward in the look of gratitude on John's face, even though it was accompanied by protest. "I—can't let you do that," John argued.

Richard smiled. "I have enjoyed her music; I'll tell her

so," he said. "And why don't you go and speak with Dhari and Andrew, tell them what you have told me, that you love them both and that you wish them well?"

"I *am* grateful."

The two men gazed at each other. Richard felt stronger than he had in weeks. As he started through the door it was not his intention to look back. But concern made him do so, and love for the bowed man he'd left at the table.

He only glanced at first, then looked quickly back, amazed at what he saw. No longer was John slumped at the table. Now he stood erect, watching Richard as closely as Richard was watching him. Was that a smile on his face?

Surely not, though John turned instantly away, and Richard closed the door behind him and started off toward the music.

She knew that if she waited long enough someone would come.

Who, she had no idea. All of them had looked bereft, the tension in the Dining Hall so acute that she'd had to leave, suspecting in a way that she was contributing to it.

As she had taken refuge in the Great Hall, she had spied the lovely old pianoforte and, thinking to play softly enough to disturb no one, she'd settled herself before the keyboard and quite soon had lost herself in its mellow tones.

Unfortunately she had now played her entire repertoire twice and the thought had just entered her mind that perhaps she should retire, let this night pass, and wait for morning and hopefully an improved mood within Eden. With dispatch she concluded the Beethoven sonata, amazed at how much richer it sounded here than in the limited Music Room at Forbes Hall.

"You play beautifully."

The voice, so unexpected, came from behind. Quickly she turned, pleased that perhaps there would be no early retirement tonight after all.

"Lord Richard," she murmured, amazed at how quietly he had come up behind her. "I—hope I was not bothering—"

"Bothering!" he repeated, coming around beside her. "I can't remember when this old instrument has been played last. My Uncle Edward brought it for my Aunt

Jennifer and she was the last to play it."

"Did you know her? Your aunt, I mean. So many of my relations were dead before I was even born." She lowered her head and hoped that she wasn't saying too much. "I'm always a little envious when I hear words such as 'Aunt' and 'Uncle.' "

"I knew her very well," Richard replied, crossing his arms on the pianoforte. "She was—ill most of her life."

"I'm sorry."

For a moment it was as though the gloom of the Dining Hall had merely followed him here to the Great Hall. Eleanor considered trying to alter the mood but changed her mind. Let *him* set the pace and she would willingly follow.

She watched as he moved around the pianoforte, one hand caressing the highly polished rosewood cabinet. There was a tenderness about him that appealed greatly. Her brothers were rough and boisterous sportsmen. Even her father enjoyed a good hunt, coming home with flushed cheeks and bloodied gauntlets. She would have been most surprised to learn that this gentle man had ever killed anything in his life.

At the far end of the pianoforte he looked back at her. "I'm sorry for speaking so personally. You must think we—"

"I think nothing and see only a family that has suffered a tragic loss."

"How kind you are—and will you please play for us again tomorrow?"

"Of course I'll play."

She was embarrassed by the silence. It occurred to her that perhaps he had been sent to "see to her." In that case she must relieve them both of this awkwardness. To that end she walked a few feet away, looking ahead to the Grand Staircase.

"Lord Richard," she began, "I'm certain that you have other things to do. Please don't feel as though you must—"

"I assure you, I have nothing to do," he said. "In fact, I came to tell you that I am at your disposal. What would you like to do? I'm afraid that Eden can't offer much in the way of diversion. But there is always the Game Room and of course the Library."

"I remember the Library—" she smiled—"and that lovely painting of 'The Women of Eden.' "

He nodded and strolled easily beside her, his hands laced behind his back. "Quite a to-do, that was, wasn't it?" He laughed. "The castle filled with people we've never seen before or since, thank God."

"It was lovely," she murmured. "Very exciting, and how proud Mr. Eden was!"

She was aware of him nodding to everything, and was pleased by the fairly easy give and take between them. Curious, but he seemed so accessible now. Last spring he'd seemed so distant.

As they were approaching the Great Hall stairs, he stopped and issued an invitation. "Come," he said, "let me show you my favorite room."

Before she knew it, she felt his hand close about hers, an intimate yet innocent gesture, for she doubted seriously if he realized what he was doing. Swept up in his own enthusiasm, which blessedly included her, he had simply reached out to propel her forward, unaware that their hands had touched.

A few minutes later, "There!" he exclaimed, pointing ahead to the far arcade in the west wall of the Great Hall, to a small, low, Gothic arch, most unpretentious compared to the lofty arches of the Great Hall.

"It—looks like a cloakroom," she said.

"It was, originally," he said, nodding, and abandoned her to push open the low door, then stood back to let her pass before him.

From where she stood on the threshold, there was only darkness, though within the moment he had fetched one of the wall lamps, hurried past her and was now adjusting several lamps within the small chamber.

The faint illumination revealed little at first, but as the lamps blazed higher she saw what appeared to be a small library, the walls a solid array of books with rich leather bindings, a pleasant arrangement of simple furnishings, a charming window seat with drapes drawn, and a plain tile fireplace.

She noticed that the room was very cold. From all signs it had not been in use for some time. Without a word, she saw him expertly lay a small fire. She watched, amazed that the Lord of the Castle would be performing so menial a task. Not once had she ever seen her brothers, and certainly not her father, kneel down to lay a fire.

"You do that with great expertise," she commented, drawn to the warmth.

He laughed. "Bertie used to say I could coax a flame from a wet log—" Abruptly his hands froze in their activity.

Puzzled, she watched, and with relief saw his hands moving again, the fire blazing well. "At Cambridge," he said to the fire, "one learned to fend for oneself. No servants there, only—"

As his voice drifted off, she reminded herself to let him take the lead as he'd done all evening. To that end she stepped back and commenced looking about at this simple chamber which he had claimed as his favorite. In the new illumination she saw a large portrait over the mantel, the image of a woman, a most beautiful woman. "Who is that?" she asked, unable to take her eye off the face.

"My grandmother," he said. "Marianne, Lady Marianne—"

She had never seen such compelling beauty. Pity the poor females who had had to share a room with her. "She is—remarkable," Eleanor commented. "Did you know her?"

He shook his head. "She was ill for a long time and I was very little. I have a dim memory of an old woman, but, of course, she bore no resemblance to that—"

Behind her she heard him stirring and looked back to see him perched on the edge of the table, a look of amusement on his face. "You may find it difficult to believe"—he smiled—"but that lovely lady started life as a fisherman's daughter."

Eleanor looked up. "Surely not!"

He nodded emphatically. She was in service in the castle when my grandfather first saw her. Their courtship was launched in an inauspicious way. She disobeyed my grandfather in some small matter and in consequence he sentenced her to a public whipping."

Shocked, Eleanor looked back toward the painting. For what seemed an eternity they studied the portrait, his interest intense as though he were seeing it for the first time, or seeing a new dimension in it. She was forced to admit that she'd never felt more alive. Her proper, secluded existence at Forbes Hall fell away and suddenly she found herself in an arena with dazzling beauties and frightening horrors.

She shivered. What she had interpreted as life in the past had been merely sleepwalking.

Apparently their thoughts had been running along the same lines.

"I'm sorry," he murmured. "I did not intend to drag you back into the family history."

"No, please don't apologize. In fact I'd like to know more, everything."

Richard laughed. "Everything? I'm afraid that would take quite a while. The Edens have never done things simply or, I'm afraid, properly." He looked at her. "How kind you are."

"Kindness has little to do with it," she replied. "I've heard of Eden all my life and have been fascinated with it."

"Well, then," he said expansively, "starting tomorrow, a chapter a day for as long as you are with us. What do you say to that? And if I bore you, you have no one but yourself to blame."

"I promise I will not be bored"—she smiled—"and I look forward to it and beg you to leave nothing out."

For a moment they looked closely at each other. Though she longed with all her heart to stay, propriety and her sense of the moment urged her to leave.

"Now I'll bid you goodnight," she said.

At her words she saw disappointment on his face. "Must you? I mean, I know the hour is late, but—"

"And I've occupied far too much of your time."

"No."

"Besides, I have morning to look forward to."

He nodded, as though to say this was a sensible suggestion.

She paused at the door. "Good night, then, Lord Richard."

She had turned about when she heard his voice again with a simple request. "Please, just call me Richard. I've never quite known how to respond to the—other—"

She looked at him, strangely touched by this reluctant lord. "Richard," she repeated. The name sat well on her lips and tongue.

At some point, about a quarter of the way across the

Great Hall, she was aware of a curious sensation. He was watching her; she was certain of it.

It required all the discipline at her command not to look back.

❧

London
Hyde Park
January 8, 1871

BURKE SAT ON the frozen bench in the small garden, half-frozen himself, and heard echoes inside his head, a soft voice singing, then speaking his name as he'd never before heard it pronounced, taking those three syllables and transforming them into music. As long as she inhabited his memory he felt strong.

But where is she? What has happened? As those two questions cut through his memory for the thousandth time, he bent over and held his head, as though to keep it intact. At times he felt mindless with worry. Something had happened, something terrible and unexpected, and he *had* to speak with the woman Elizabeth. But in his repeated attempts in the past he'd always been rebuffed by the fierce little maid, who had kept a firm grasp on the door and who, on the last occasion shortly before Christmas, had threatened him with the police if he did not cease his harassment.

All he wanted was a brief audience with her mistress in an attempt to pick up the pieces of his heart, which had been shattered by a simple note informing him that she would be unable to meet him in the—

The note!

Her note, written in her own hand and addressed to him. He did have something which had emanated from her, indisputable proof of their acquaintance and, more important, his right to inquire after her. He closed his eyes and saw it in its place of security in the small chest in the third drawer of his bureau.

Amazed that the document that once had cast him

into such gloom should now lift him out of gloom, he ran up the path, plotting a new and, he hoped, successful assault on Number Seven.

He would place her note inside one of his own, thus eliminating the need for all but the simplest exchange with the old maid. He would request simply that she give both notes to her mistress and that he would await her reply with patience and civility on the stoop.

It has to work. It has to work! he repeated to himself.

And if it didn't? But he did not linger in search of an answer.

It was no longer a question of happiness. It was a question of life.

London
Number Seven St. George Street
January 8, 1871

FEELING MORE RELAXED than she'd felt in weeks. Elizabeth stretched before her drawing-room fire, toasting her toes, so glad to be home, and looked across at Charlie Bradlaugh, whose face seemed to reflect her contentment.

"Like a couple of old marrieds, we are, Charlie," she murmured. Fearful that she had said too much, she added, "Pay me no mind. I like to dream now and then. No harm."

As she leaned forward to refill his teacup she was aware of his eyes upon her. "I've never been opposed to dreams, Elizabeth," he said, "but I do try to recognize them for what they are."

At that moment the bell sounded at the front door. "Damn," she whispered, resenting the interruption. She had hoped to pass the entire afternoon with Charlie.

"Were you expecting anyone?" he asked.

"No, of course not," she said, and turned in her chair as she heard Doris emerge from the kitchen steps. "I'm not at home," Elizabeth called out. "Take their card, if you will, and tell them to come around another time."

Confident that she had taken care of the matter, she turned back in her chair and tried to ignore the cold draft coming from the opened front door.

"Miss Elizabeth?" The exasperated voice came from the doorway. It was Doris. "I wash my hands of it," she went on peevishly. "I swear I can't do all my duties as well as fend off—"

Elizabeth turned about in her chair, feeling peevish herself at this second interruption. "What *are* you talking about, Doris?"

"Him!" the maid said in a loud stage whisper, simultaneously pointing toward the front door. "I've told him repeatedly that you've got no business with him or he with you. But now, look!"

In exasperation she lifted a white envelope and wagged it back and forth before her face. "All he's asking is that I deliver this to you and he'll be more than pleased to wait for a response."

Mystified, Elizabeth glanced toward the envelope and beyond to Doris' martyred face. "What gentleman is it you are speaking of, Doris?" she asked.

"Him!" the old maid repeated, "The same one I was telling you about, the American who pounded on that door every night while you were at Eden."

"What does he want?" Elizabeth asked.

"You!" Doris replied bluntly.

Elizabeth looked back toward the fire. Charlie was leaning up in his chair, obviously intrigued by the mystery.

An American? She knew no Americans. She took the envelope from Doris, broke the seal on the back and withdrew two pieces of paper, one quite worn, the second fresh and white.

She opened the worn parchment first and saw something familiar about it before she'd read a word. The handwriting, that was it. Rather similar to—

She commenced to read the message, something to do with a change of plans, someone being told not to come to a certain place with the promise that all would be explained later. And it was signed by—

Mary?

How was that possible? Still absorbed by the confusion of the first note, she hastily opened the second and found a totally unfamiliar penmanship, an urgent plea from one

Burke Stanhope, who was respectfully requesting a brief audience concerning the person who had written the first note.

"May I be of service, Elizabeth?" It was Charlie, who apparently had detected her bewilderment.

Vaguely she shook her head. There was nothing Charlie could do. But on the other hand, she couldn't very well dismiss the notes or the mystery or the American gentleman who had brought both.

Gently she put a hand on his arm. "Charlie, would you excuse me briefly? I think that perhaps I'd better see—"

"Of course," he said, nodding genially. "I have an appointment myself within the hour."

"Will you return?" she asked, loathing to let him go.

"Whenever you say." He smiled graciously.

"I say dinner tonight at nine."

"I'll be here."

"Then tonight. Doris, see Mr. Bradlaugh out, then show the other gentleman in."

As both disappeared into the entrance hall, Elizabeth lifted the two notes. Burke Stanhope. The name was familiar. But the greatest mystery of all was Mary's name attached to a note which bore the handwriting of—

She felt another chill draft rush across the floor and moved back to the fire. Then she heard Doris' voice. "Miss Elizabeth, this here is him, the one who don't give up so easily."

Elizabeth looked back and saw a tall, well-built man with dark hair, who was just handing Doris his cloak and top hat and who was returning her stare with matching intensity.

"Mr.—"

"Stanhope," he said. A good voice, deep, relaxed-sounding in the manner of Americans. "Burke Stanhope," he went on, "and thank you for seeing me."

She nodded and was aware of Doris lurking in the hall, eager to stay and hear everything.

"That will be all, Doris," she called.

Doris muttered something, but Elizabeth couldn't hear. She waited until she heard the kitchen door slam shut, then kindly she invited Mr. Stanhope to join her by the fire. "You must be frozen." She smiled, trying to remember where she had seen him before. Quite a handsome man, he was.

"I was just having tea," Elizabeth said. "Would you like a cup?"

He shook his head. "No, please, and I am sorry for this intrusion. I saw the gentleman leave. It was not my intention to—"

Before such heartfelt remorse, she had no choice but to offer comfort. "It's not necessary," she said. "He's an old friend and I more than made up for his interrupted tea by offering him dinner later. He's probably very grateful to you."

He smiled and stood with his back to the fire. He was cultivated, she was certain of that. There was something else as well that she'd only now noticed about him a look of distraction on his face. And fatigue. He looked tired. Again she suffered that strange sense of having seen him. But *where?*

Seated in her chair before the fire, she realized that she had been rudely staring. "Forgive me, Mr. Stanhope," she murmured, "but I've seen you before."

"You have."

Surprised, she looked up. "Where?"

"At Eden, at the Festivities last spring. I was with Mr. Delane," he went on, "John Thadeus Delane. I believe you are an acquaintance of his. We shared a carriage for about three minutes, and you appeared to be under duress."

Then she remembered—the approach to Eden, her argument with Mary raging, trying to draw her back and almost tumbling headlong through the opened carriage door.

"I'm afraid it was not one of my better moments"— she smiled ruefully—"and, since I've not tumbled out of any carriage doors of late, to what do I owe this—"

"I have—come," he began, "on a matter of great importance, a matter which has almost driven me to distraction." His hands were interlaced so tightly that they appeared to tremble. "I have come to inquire about— Mary."

"What about Mary? Do you know her?"

All at once another veil of memory lifted. *Of course he knows her,* from that same occasion, the Eden Festivities, the disastrous ball. This was the gentleman with whom Mary had been dancing when John had—

"You do know her, don't you, Mr. Stanhope? It was the night of the ball."

"I know her," he admitted softly. "I knew her long before my journey to Eden."

"May I ask where?" Elizabeth went on. "Mary was living here with me at the time, and I thought I knew all—"

"I—never called on her," he said. "I didn't even know who she was. I just knew that every Thursday night there was only one place in London for me, and that was Jeremy Sims' Song and Supper Club."

Moved by the tribute and eager to understand all, Elizabeth walked briskly to the fire. Without warning, a grim thought intervened. The Mary who had captivated this gentleman and the Mary now in residence in Cheltenham bore no resemblance one to the other.

"Those days at Jeremy Sims' are over," she said firmly, "and it was my hope that they had been forgotten as well."

"They haven't," he said with matching firmness. He, too, stood. "And, as you know, I saw her again at Eden Castle."

Elizabeth laughed, trying to ease the tension. "Indeed I do remember. A bit of unscheduled excitement, I believe someone called it." She paused, noting that he did not share her amusement. She felt compelled to offer a belated apology. "I am sorry, Mr. Stanhope. I can imagine your humiliation, and over so slight a cause, a harmless dance."

"The cause was not slight, nor was the dance harmless."

"I don't understand."

He drew a step closer. "Halfway through that dance with Mary I knew what was happening, and she knew it as well." He bowed his head. "We were—forgive me—falling in love," he said simply.

Elizabeth gaped. *Falling in love!* How innocent that might have sounded if it had been pronounced in any other fashion and by any other man. But this was not a callow youth standing before her, or a pampered dandy or a self-centered young lord.

"Sweet heavens," she murmured, and suffered a pang of grief. Obviously he did not know the fate that had befallen his beloved. Was this the purpose of his visit? If so, God help them both.

"Mr. Stanhope," she said, "why are you here? Why are you telling me this?"

"I have lost her," he confessed. "We had made—arrangements upon our return to London, arrangements built on deception, I'll admit, but what choice did we have? I begged her repeatedly to let me announce myself and call for her here. But she was terrified—"

"Of what?" Elizabeth asked.

"Of her cousin, Mr. Eden, and in a way, of you."

She bowed her head.

"I'm sorry."

"Please," she said and took advantage of the digression to gain the sideboard and the reinforcement of a small brandy. Without words she lifted the decanter to him, but he declined.

"She felt," he went on, "that the two of you were in collusion against her. Of course, she knew that you both would remember me from the unpleasantness at Eden."

"And what were these—arrangements of deception?" she asked, holding her position by the sideboard.

"We met daily, every afternoon, under the pretense of riding."

Elizabeth looked up. Of course. It made sense now. How happy Mary must have been each day as she descended those stairs, knowing that shortly she would be in his presence. "May I ask one question, Mr. Stanhope?"

"Yes?"

"Did Mary—return your love?"

"She said that she did; and I believed her."

Elizabeth nodded. It had been a foolish question. Shaking her head, she returned to the fire. "Mary was right. It would have been pure disaster for you to come here."

"I conceded as much, though the seasons were against us. We knew that we couldn't meet forever in the park, and the last time I saw her I begged her to let me introduce myself to you." He paused. "For some reason, I sensed in you—an ally."

"So now you've lost her."

"Yes. I was to have met her one day as usual when I received this note"—and he retrieved the folded piece of stationery which Elizabeth had placed on the tea table. "As you read, she instructs me not to come, informs me that certain circumstances have arisen and that she would explain later."

"You didn't go to the park as usual that day?"

"No. Knowing that she wouldn't be there, I had no reason to do so."

Elizabeth studied his face. She knew nothing about him. He was, in all respects save one, a stranger. Yet that one exception was of vast importance and consisted of little more than an emotional recognition. He had told her the truth; she was certain of it. In spite of the overpowering odds against him, he obviously was deeply in love with Mary Eden, to the extent that he had disrupted his entire life.

Then she would test him to the fullest, and her next step would depend upon his reaction to her tragic message. "It was—an appointment you should have kept, Mr. Stanhope, in spite of the message."

She was aware of him approaching her, drawn by her mysterious manner.

Then inform him! "You see, Mr. Stanhope, she waited for you that evening, too late, and under the veil of darkness was—attacked by assailants who are still unknown."

His face seemed to grow pale, though he did not take his eyes off her. "Go on."

"She was brought home shortly after ten that evening. By the police. Her hair had been cut off. She had been raped."

His lips moved, though no words came out. She saw him lift his head as though to accommodate a sharp pain, and the momentum seemed to drag him about where he returned to the chair by the fire and sat heavily, his hands covering his face.

Not faring so well herself, Elizabeth turned back to the window, aware that she must give him time. At least it was over now. Undoubtedly he would digest the truth and leave and start the slow healing process, striking Mary from his mind and heart. It was for the best. In spite of the "good reports" which John claimed to have received from Cheltenham, Mary would never fully recover, was now headed for safe spinsterhood or safer madness.

"No!"

The angry word came from behind her. Startled, she looked up to see Mr. Stanhope on his feet, the piece of paper bearing the false message in his fist.

"No," he repeated, apparently accepting nothing. "It makes no sense," he said, lifting the note to her. "Why would she send me a message telling me not to come, then go herself?"

Sharing his bafflement, Elizabeth hurried toward him, trying to offer comfort, even if it was illogical. "I—don't know," she stammered. "Perhaps she—changed her mind."

"Then she would have sent a second message."

Suddenly Elizabeth stopped, remembering her confusion when first she'd read the message. "Let me see that again," she demanded, and took the page from him.

"This—is not Mary's handwriting," she murmured and looked up, aware of the man hovering over her.

"Then who wrote it?" he demanded.

Again she looked down at the note. She couldn't be absolutely certain, but the similarities were astonishing.

"Who wrote it, Elizabeth?" he demanded again.

"I—can't be certain," she stalled. It was not possible.

"Elizabeth?" Suddenly he grasped her arm. "I beg you."

"It resembles—John's handwriting."

The hand that grasped her arm held on, as though she were a lifeline. She was wrong. Of course she was wrong and, in an attempt to confirm her own tragic error, she glanced down again at the writing.

But she was not wrong. The slant of the letters, the letters themselves, were all too familiar. She'd seen the same penmanship countless times before, on letters from Eden, on notes requesting a special favor, on deeds which she had cosigned.

"Then—there should be another note," Mr. Stanhope said quietly.

"I don't understand."

"A second note," he repeated, "addressed to Mary, telling her to wait for me."

"No!" Elizabeth protested, his implication unbearable. John might have found out about their clandestine meetings and interceded in an attempt to bring them to a halt. But a second note to Mary implied—

"I must ask you to leave me, Mr. Stanhope," she said abruptly.

In response to the dismissal he held his ground. "I have no intention of leaving, Elizabeth. I have nothing to lose by offending you, and we both have everything to gain by uncovering the truth."

"There was no second message," she declared angrily, his persistence becoming offensive.

"How do you know? Have you searched her chambers, the garments she was wearing when—" He turned away. "Believe me, this is no easier for me than it is for you."

She *did* believe him. Still, what he had implied was criminal. Of late John had been guilty of many things, from crass thoughtlessness to arrogant high-handedness. But not this.

"Again, Mr. Stanhope," she said, moving away from the fire, "I must ask you to leave. I'm sorry for whatever grief you may have suffered, but—"

"Then tell me where she is," he asked, confronting her across the distance of the room as though she'd said nothing.

"I can't do that."

"Why not?"

"John has requested—"

Suddenly anger as raw as any she'd ever witnessed erupted from that corner of the room. "John—has requested," he repeated, and scooped up the note which bore the suspect handwriting and thrust it at her as though it were a weapon. "My God, by your own assessment John Murrey Eden was the one who wrote this message that lured her into the park that evening. And, since you refuse to assist me with the rest of the mystery, at least tell me where she is so that I may go to her."

"That is precisely why I'm not going to tell you," Elizabeth said, sick of the afternoon. "It is John's opinion that she needs—"

"*Damn John's opinion!*" he shouted. Then the rage seemed to subside as quickly as it had surfaced. He appeared to study the note in his hand, then resignedly tossed it back onto the table. "Mary was right," he said, as though at last he'd exhausted himself. "She was accurate in her inclination to fear both of you, though on several occasions I tried to convince her that *you* meant her no harm."

Elizabeth heard the accusation and started to respond to it, then changed her mind.

He stood before her, having halted his progress to the door. "I *will* find her," he vowed, and the vow was all the worse for the manner in which it had been delivered. "Wherever she is, whatever she has endured, I will find her and offer her again my love and my protection."

Incongruously he gave a soft laugh. "She was so— lonely, you know. The most foreign emotion in the world to her was happiness. She was suspect of it, certain that it would not last."

He shook his head. "How thoughtful of you both to reinforce her vision of the world."

Elizabeth tried to confront him, convinced that she did not have to endure either him or his accusations. But at that moment, her façade broke. Suffering an image of Mary as she'd been brought home that night, she stepped back from his accusations and reached for the sofa, where she sat and stared into space. "What—do you want me to do, Mr. Stanhope?"

"A search, if you will, please. I think, for both our sakes, we need to find the second note."

"There was no—" she began and ceased speaking. Words were useless when confronted with that determination. Wearily she rose and was almost to the door when she looked back to see him standing where she'd left him.

"Aren't you coming?" she asked, giving in to a bit of sarcasm. "You seem so certain. Perhaps you can lead us directly to the place of concealment, thus shortening both the search as well as—"

"I do have an idea."

"I thought as much."

"We had never exchanged messages," he went on, impervious to her comment. "In spite of its disappointing nature, I recall that for several days I carried her note around with me, deriving pleasure from its presence. After all, it had come from her, from her hand, or so I thought."

"What is it that you are trying to say?"

"Don't you see? If I responded in that way to a message from her, why would she not do the same?"

"I don't understand."

"Her garments," he said bluntly. "Do you still have the garments she was wearing that day?"

"No, of course not."

"Are you certain?"

"Of course I'm certain. They were torn and soiled and still bore—" Without warning she remembered. She had undressed Mary that night. She had been alone. She had stripped those foul garments from her and—

"You *do* have them, don't you?"

"I remember—but Doris was to have burned them—" She looked up from the staircase. "They were so—terrible," she whispered. "I remember I—hid them in the small cupboard behind the screen, thinking—"

Then they were moving. Halfway up the stairs she was aware of his hand on her arm, whether in assistance or to speed her along, she couldn't say. She gained the top of the stairs, lifted the lamp from the wall standard and led the way down the shadowy corridor, stopping before Mary's door.

She had thought that he might grant her a moment to catch her breath, but instead he took the lamp from her and pushed open the door and was halfway across Mary's chamber before she called out, "No. Over there, behind the screen."

He dropped to his knees and placed the lamp on the floor beside him, its flame casting grotesque shadows over the limited cubicle. He pulled open the cupboard door and bent low, his hands exploring the dark recesses until at last they stopped.

The garments had not been burned.

Elizabeth closed her eyes. She needed a respite, both from the appearance of the clothes, as well as from the man who knelt on the floor cradling them.

Then there it was, the second note, exactly as he had predicted, though she thought she detected an expression of regret on his face as he handed it up, as though all along he had hoped that he would be wrong.

She took the note and angled it down toward the lamplight and saw what she knew was there all along, the identical handwriting, the salutation, "My Dearest Mary," the message itself short and as cryptic as the first, mentioning an unexpected delay and begging Mary to wait for him, no matter how late.

"Elizabeth?"

It was Mr. Stanhope again, still kneeling. "I'm so sorry," he murmured, grasping her hands as though to assist her with the burden of her new knowledge.

If only she could understand. But even if John had his reasons, no reason in the world would be acceptable to—

"I know that you—love him," Mr. Stanhope went on, speaking intimately.

Love! Elizabeth thought on the word and felt herself grow cold.

"You must listen to me, Elizabeth," Mr. Stanhope said urgently. "You've helped me thus far. Help me to the very end. Where is she?" he begged. "Tell me so that I may go to her. Is she at Eden?"

"No. She's not at Eden. She's—in a school outside Cheltenham, an establishment called Miss Veal's." She closed her eyes. "John took her there."

"One last favor," he whispered. "Perhaps the most difficult. Say nothing to Mr. Eden. Do nothing that might sound the alarm. Give me at least a fortnight to find her and transport her to a place of safety. I beg you."

She nodded to everything. "When—will I know?"

"I'll keep you informed."

She had hoped that he might say more. But without another word he ran from the room, the clatter of his boots in the corridor bespeaking the urgency of his departure.

She listened carefully to his descent down the stairs. Then silence.

Everything in that cold room seemed to whirl about her. Looking down, she noticed that he'd placed the note in her lap and, though her first impulse was to brush it aside, instead she read the deceiving words, seeing clearly John's handwriting, the very message that had lured Mary into the park and had kept her there until—

She pressed her head back against the cushion.

Had he staged Mary's crucible? Had he placed those assailants in the park, fully aware of what they would do, perhaps even acting on his instructions?

But the thoughts were insupportable, and she bent over until her forehead was resting on her knees, her hands laced over her head, as though to ward off unseen blows.

London
Mayfair
January 8, 1871

AWARE OF THE need for haste, Burke gave his driver instructions to fetch the large carriage and four fresh horses, to pack what belongings he would need for a fortnight's trip and to have carriage, horses and himself waiting outside the house by midnight.

Hoping to arouse no one, Burke fetched his own valise from the storage beneath the stairs and carried it up to his chambers, grateful that his mother and the servants were sleeping soundly.

Stealthily he bolted his door and moved to the task at hand. A short time later his valise was packed with a minimum of garments, four hundred pounds and a letter of credit from his bank. He hurried to the sideboard, poured a glass of brandy as fortification against the chill evening and took a final look around his room, seeing the two letters he'd left which would explain his absence, one to Charles and one to his mother.

As all was ready, and the need for movement strong within him, he gathered up his cloak and valise, extinguished the lamp and started out into the darkened corridor. In a way it had been easier not knowing where she was or what had happened.

He was halfway down the stairs when at the top of the landing he saw a flicker of candlelight and heard a drifting, familiar voice.

"Burke? My darling, is it you?"

He glanced ahead. He could easily make it to the door before she reached the top of the stairs. In an attempt to outrun the voice, he took the carriage running, secured and bolted the door and pressed back against the seat.

As the carriage started forward he realized that he had yet to give his driver instructions. He drew down the window and suffered a blast of cold January wind. "Make for the North Road and High Wycombe!" he shouted. "I'll give you directions from there."

As his driver turned in the appointed direction, Burke drew the heavy fur rug out from beneath the seat and arranged it over his legs.

Cheltenham. In school. Her hair had been cut. . .

Slowly he bent over and tried not to see the image of that pale white cheek, those dark blue eyes which once had looked up at him with such trust and love.

How would he find her? Would she even remember him? Would she come with him, or would she remain blindly loyal to John Murrey Eden? And if she did come with him, where would he take her, to what location of safety beyond the reach of the madman's grasp?

As the questions, all unanswerable, continued to assault him, he sat back in the seat, pressed his head against the cushion and offered up one startling prayer.

His request was simple. He entreated God never to let him come within close physical proximity of John Murrey Eden, for if he did, he would surely kill him.

Cheltenham
January 13, 1871

AT THIRTY-SIX, she was an old maid and likely to remain one. God had seen fit to give her a set of features so ugly that childhood companions had laughed at her. Then He had sent a plague of smallpox, which kindly had taken most of those cruel childhood friends, but He had let her survive and had covered those already ugly features with a mask of pockmarks which still on occasion ran pus and scabbed over.

As though this weren't enough, He had given her an adult form which resembled the local blacksmith's and He had crowned the entire grotesquerie with the cruelest gift of all, a degree of intelligence so that she knew precisely how ugly she was and how barren her life would always be.

Small wonder, then, that on occasion Frieda Langford

looked about at Miss Veal's collection of unhappy females
and selected one as a pet. Kindness was in short supply in
this establishment, and if now and then, in exchange for a
moment's kindness, one of the girls was prompted to give
Frieda a crust of love, she would grab it eagerly, knowing full well it might be the last she would receive.

Now she stood in the dead winter garden behind the
crumbling Tudor mansion, well bundled in her thick
black cape, and looked out over the fiercely cold winter
day at her fifteen charges, all moving like spiritless ghosts
up and down the paths.

No one spoke. It was too cold for speaking. Their daily
ritual of an hour's fresh air was another of Miss Veal's
strident commands and, like the weekly enemas and
physical examinations, it was there to be endured.

Not that Frieda had any real quarrel with old Miss
Veal. She'd taken Frieda on, hadn't she, when no one else
in Cheltenham would have anything to do with her. Hired
six years ago as a "helper," Frieda had passed what possibly had been the happiest years of her life. No one here
seemed to mind that she was ugly and, while on occasion
her heart went out to the young ladies who were imprisoned here, still she agreed with Miss Veal's philosophy
that life was hard and only those survived who knew how
to accept their daily dose of pain.

Like that one. Frieda lifted her head and stared down
the length of the garden at the small solitary figure seated
on the stone bench, wrapped in the heavy black cape
that was standard issue for all the young ladies.

For some reason that one appealed to Frieda, had from
the beginning when the London gentleman had deposited
her several months ago. Oh, it had been clear even then
that someone had gone over her with heavy boots on.
From her butchered hair to the lingering bruises on her
legs, it had been painfully apparent that someone had
taken what he wanted without a thank you.

In those first few weeks Miss Veal had warned Frieda
to look for telltale signs of pregnancy in Mary Eden. But,
blessedly, there had been nothing and her cycles were regular and, while she didn't have to contend with a growing
seed, there was still grief aplenty plaguing the young
woman, and Frieda would give anything to ease it, to
cause just a semblance of a smile to color those pale lips.

Well, what harm in trying again? There was still about

twenty minutes left of the enforced hour. Her other charges were behaving themselves right enough, moving at a steady pace up and down between the dead flowers, rubbing their hands to keep warm.

Only little Mary Eden was seated and alone, and this was a legitimate reason for Frieda to approach her. On Miss Veal's orders, all the young women had to keep moving. Thus armed with a reason to speak, Frieda drew her own cloak more tightly about her and walked in a steady line down the garden path.

"You there," she called out, bridging the few feet that separated them and, though she stood directly over her, she was alarmed to see that the girl had yet to look up.

"Mary?" she said, her voice softening, and as she sat on the bench she bent forward in an attempt to see the face that was almost obscured by the hood.

Then she saw too clearly, the small face drawn and colorless, a stream of old grief which apparently was so powerful it required no sound.

"Here, now," Frieda comforted. She reached into the folds of her pocket and withdrew a handkerchief and lifted the girl's face. All the time she worked at restoration, she was aware of Mary's eyes on her, was aware of the girl's hands like two blocks of ice, while her forehead—

Frieda stripped off her glove and placed her bare hand against Mary's forehead. *Dear Lord, she is on fire!*

"Mary? Are you feeling well?"

The girl nodded and with the back of her hand wiped away the last of the tears.

Distracted from the feverish brow, Frieda counseled, "You know it doesn't pay to think on bad things. How many times have I told you that before?"

"I wasn't thinking on the bad, Frieda," she murmured. "I was thinking on the good. They are the hardest."

"Well, good or bad, you're letting something do damage to you, and it's my advice to—"

"Frieda, how long have you been here?"

The question caught her off-guard. "Well," she began, lifting her head to the sky, "to the best of my recollection, going on six years. Yes, about six."

She looked back at the young girl and didn't like what she saw there, the pupils of her eyes glittering unnaturally, a rigidity to her chin as though she were trying to keep her teeth from chattering.

"Come on," Frieda urged brusquely, "let's get you up and moving. You'll be warmer."

"Six—years," Mary repeated as though awed by the number.

"Aye, come—"

"Will you—stay here all your life?"

Half-risen from the bench and beginning to shiver herself, Frieda sat back down, amused by the question. "I suppose I will 'less something better comes along, and since that's not likely—"

All at once she noticed fresh tears on the girl's face. "Here, now, I thought I told you to keep your mind off those ghosts."

Slowly Mary shook her head. "I don't mean to cry. I really don't, and I wasn't thinking of anything."

In an attempt to stop the tears, Frieda announced. "It's letter-writing day," remembering that in all the months since Mary had been here she'd never written a letter to anyone. The young ladies were permitted one correspondence a week, and most of them considered it a high point.

Of course, what they didn't know was that all those letters containing such private thoughts to loved ones provided Miss Veal and her staff with a full evening of jolly good entertainment. The letters containing any sort of complaint were read and burned. A few were sent on, those claiming contentment, and certainly those which praised Miss Veal or any aspect of her institution.

But not once had Mary felt compelled to use her single piece of writing paper. Now Frieda felt it was time she made contact with her past.

"Your—mum," Frieda prodded gently. "Let's write to your mum this afternoon. I'm sure she worries—"

"No," Mary said, returning the handkerchief. "She—wouldn't read it, anyway."

"Now, why?" Frieda chided. "If you were mine, I'd—"

"She's blind."

Silence. The bough of the old tree overhead creaked in the pressure of the wind.

"I'm sorry," Frieda muttered, thinking that she'd take her scarred face any day if she could keep her eyes.

"Then the gentleman that brought you here," she said. "Surely he would like—"

All at once the young lady stood. She took one step toward the end of the bench as though to put distance between herself and the suggestion when suddenly she faltered, one hand reaching out for support.

"Mary? Are you ill?" Frieda demanded.

"No, I'm fine." But as she started to her feet again, her head seemed to lift as though she couldn't draw enough breath. Frieda stepped forward, her alarm increasing at how suddenly pale that face had gone and, just as she was reaching out to lend her the support of her arm, she saw the young woman collapse.

Lord—

Frieda stared down, shocked at the lifeless figure. "Fetch Miss Veal!" she shouted ahead to the other young ladies, who had just noticed the unconscious girl in Frieda's arms. "Hurry!"

As she carried Mary up the path, she bent over and placed her cheek against that pale forehead and immediately withdrew. It was as though she'd pressed against an oven.

As the girls reluctantly parted to make way, Frieda grimly remembered the time—when had it been, two, three years ago?—when one of Miss Veal's young ladies had died. In order to avoid a fuss, late one midnight Miss Veal had taken the body away. What she'd done with it, to this day Frieda had no idea, though she had been within earshot the day the alarmed family arrived, had overheard Miss Veal's lies, the old woman informing them convincingly that the young lady had simply run away.

Although she was out of the cold wind now, moving rapidly down the darkened back corridor, Frieda shivered and drew her lifeless charge more closely into her arms. Pray God that death would spare her. But if it didn't Frieda would not lie again. There were just so many compromises that even an ugly woman could make and still keep her soul intact.

She tightened her grasp on Mary Eden and held her close as though she were an injured pet and braced herself for the gargoyle of a woman who stood at the far end of the corridor, with arms crossed, viewing their approach with condemnation.

Due to impassable winter roads, the journey from London to Cheltenham required five difficult days. Impatient and worried to the point of madness, Burke had tried to endure the delays, had tried and failed to keep his mind off her, so near and yet so unreachable.

As they approached the outskirts of Cheltenham, Burke found momentary distraction in the beauty of the place. He'd been expecting a plain rural village. Instead he found a lovely Georgian spa with a wealth of Regency houses on elegant squares, tree-bordered open spaces and a grand promenade with a double avenue of horse chestnuts.

At the far end of the promenade he discovered the Queen's Hotel and checked in under the false name of Mr. Robert Stow. In the event that Elizabeth weakened and he was followed, the anonymity might provide him with a few additional hours.

The helpful desk clerk provided him with directions to Miss Veal's establishment about three miles north of town and, thus armed, Burke grimly realized that he had not one plan in his head.

As he hurriedly drew on his cloak, he was aware for the first time of his new proximity to her and suffered unbearable anticipation at the thought of seeing her again. These thoughts caused him to increase his speed, cloak adjusted as he took the stairs running, not stopping until he saw his carriage and driver.

"Just a brief trip," he called up, "three miles north, then the rest of the evening is yours."

The driver nodded. "Whatever you say, sir. The horses, though, they could do with a bit of a rest."

"And they shall have it, I promise. Soon." As he drew himself up into the carriage he called back, "Go slow once out of town. I'm not absolutely certain what I'm looking for."

And he wasn't. In fact he'd passed it by when he glanced out the rear window and saw the deserted dirt road, the beginning of a crumbling driveway and a small weathered sign, obscured by overgrown brush, which read: MISS VEAL'S SCHOOL FOR FEMALES.

He drew down the window. "Wait! Turn about."

As he swung down out of the carriage, he looked up at the mystery on the driver's face and said simply, "I won't

be too long," and headed at a rapid pace back to the beginning of the driveway.

He had gone about thirty yards when he stopped and
tried to peer ahead into the fast falling dusk. From where
he stood he saw nothing but the black traceries of dead
trees against the darker sky, and suddenly it occurred to
him that Miss Veal's establishment, whatever it was,
could be located miles ahead. Even now his sense of isolation was acute. Hard to believe that less than three
miles away lay Cheltenham.

About ten minutes later, just when he was convinced
that he was following a dead-end, through the thick winter foliage he caught sight of a single light, proof that
someone was residing in these impenetrable woods.

He increased his pace to a trot, keeping well to the
shadows, took a final turn and there it was, an immense
structure, Tudor was his guess, the entrance flanked by
pinnacles with domed caps which shot up like the mina-
rets of some Persian mosque.

He moved as close as he dared and saw that the
crumbling driveway culminated in a cobblestone courtyard, hardly visible beneath the carpet of dead and blowing leaves, and the most awesome aspect of the spectral
mansion was that, for all its size, only one lamp was burning behind the drawn drapes of the first floor, casting a
diffuse light.

Twice he surveyed the grim façade and on the second
inspection made another bleak observation. Out of all
those rows of chimneys on the roof, not one showed signs
of smoke. There was no fire within, no warmth.

No, Mary was not here. Elizabeth was wrong. Even so
consummate a bastard as John Murrey Eden would not
abandon his cousin in this frozen and isolated prison.
Convinced of this, he turned away, stepped back to the
pavement and had taken about four steps when his
thoughts stopped him.

He had to make certain. He'd traveled a great distance
under difficult circumstances. Why would Elizabeth lie to
him? He remembered well her reaction when she had discovered the second note. She had been convinced of
Eden's manipulative hand behind Mary's ordeal.

No, Elizabeth had not lied to him. Of course, there was
always the possibility that Eden had lied to *her*, had
merely told her that he had deposited Mary here.

For several minutes the battle raged. Occasionally he glanced back over his shoulder toward the mansion, as though perhaps he'd failed to see an important clue. But each time he saw nothing that he'd not seen the first time. Certainly no human life could exist within, not for long.

At last the battle was over, terminated by a simple though dreaded resolution. Come morning, in some fashion, operating on some deception, he would seek entrance and see for himself and, as desperately as he wanted to find her, he prayed silently that he would not.

Then he was running, not even bothering to keep to the shadows, for shadows covered all now, his mind moving in a hundred directions at once, the problem simple.

All he needed was for that front door to swing open to him and one hour in which to launch his search. Surely he could accomplish it. He *had* to accomplish it.

But how?

❦

Miss Veal's School for Females
January 14, 1871

SICK WITH WORRY over the condition of Mary Eden and outraged that Miss Veal had refused the night before to send for the doctor in Cheltenham, Frieda took a last look at that feverish face, saw her shivering beneath the single coverlet, grabbed the two bricks, now cold, from the foot of the bed and decided to take matters into her own hands.

She looked down on Mary and saw not one aspect of hope. Her eyes were closed as they had been all night, though not in sleep, the mouth partially open in an attempt to breathe over the rattling congestion in her lungs. But the worst of all was that constant shivering, as though in spite of her raging fever she could not get warm.

"Damn her!" Frieda cursed aloud, seeing in memory Miss Veal's face the night before when she had glared at the lifeless figure in Frieda's arms and had pronounced, "Malingering, that's all. Give her a dose of salts and oil and she will be on her feet come morning."

On her feet, Frieda thought, still angry. It was her untutored opinion that Miss Veal's "malingerer" was on the verge of becoming a corpse.

"I'll be right back," she whispered to the girl, aware that she couldn't hear but saying it anyway. Carefully she tucked the two bricks under the concealment of her apron and started out into the corridor, pleased to find it empty.

At the top of the stairs she paused, stymied by one enormous obstacle. How could she discover if Miss Veal was in the front parlor? Sometimes she took her morning tea there, but occasionally she spent the early-morning hours in the kitchen, badgering the kitchen staff. Well, if she encountered Miss Veal she would tell her straightway that the "malingerer" was not on her feet this morning and she'd best come look for herself.

Firm in her resolve, she started down the steps, keeping her eyes on those closed parlor doors, certain that at any moment they would swing open and the harridan herself would appear.

Suddenly the front bell rang. Frieda froze. What in the name of— Obviously she'd been so busy concentrating on her own mission she'd failed to hear a carriage. Who could it be? No one ever called on Miss Veal's school unscheduled, and Miss Veal had said nothing about expecting visitors.

Gawd! There was Miss Veal, just pushing open the doors, her teacup still in hand, glaring at the ringing. In the next minute she swiveled her head about, her eyes falling directly on Frieda, who was just starting back up the stairs.

"Wait!" Miss Veal called out.

Trembling, Frieda obeyed and turned back, concealing both bricks behind her back.

"Answer it," Miss Veal commanded, "and tell whoever it is to go away. I am expecting no one."

Frieda bobbed her head, the two bricks becoming objects of incredible weight.

"Well, move!" Miss Veal ordered as the bell rang a third time.

"Yes, ma'am," Frieda murmured and, still concealing the bricks beneath her apron and thanking God for her misshapen body, she proceeded down the stairs, aware of Miss Veal watching.

As Frieda approached the door, she shifted both bricks

to one hand, slid the bolt and with some effort drew back the heavy door a crack.

On the other side, in the gray, drizzling morning, she saw a gentleman, quite handsome he was, fashionably dressed, with a silly grin on his face. "Good morning." He smiled, obviously unaware that he was standing on the threshold of a place where smiles did not flourish.

He looked different and sounded different. But as the awkward weight of the two bricks caused her hand to cramp, she said brusquely, "We are not receiving this morning. Good day."

As she started to close the door, to her surprise he stepped forward and with one hand forced the door open. "You might let me state my case," he said in a voice that definitely was not English. She glanced over her shoulder to see Miss Veal still watching.

Spurred on by the awareness of that grim face, Frieda threw manners to the wind. "Look, I don't give a damn what your case is. We ain't receiving this morning, and that's that!"

As she tried to close the door again he stepped forward. "Could you tell me this, then," he persisted, "do I have the pleasure of addressing Miss Veal herself?"

At that Frieda smiled. "No, I ain't Miss Veal. But if I were, the answer would be the same. Now, I must ask—"

"Then would you take a message to her?" the gentleman insisted. "Tell her that Mr. Robert Stow from the London *Times* is here. Tell her that he is doing an article on the new progressive schools for young ladies, and that this establishment was highly recommended to me as being the finest—"

Gawd! Where did he get his information from? "I suggest, Mr. Stow," she said archly, "that you put that pretty speech in writing and address it to Miss Veal."

But at that moment Frieda heard a voice behind her, a voice so different from the crow's voice which generally filled these corridors that she was compelled to look about.

"Who is it, Frieda?" this new voice called out, filled with suspect goodwill.

"A—gentleman," Frieda stammered. "Says—"

"I heard what he said, my dear. Here, take my teacup for me and I will attend to the matter myself."

As Miss Veal addressed her false voice to the gentleman at the door, Frieda stepped back out of the line of vision, placed the teacup on the hall table and eased the bricks to the floor, where with the toe of her shoe she slid them beneath the table itself.

She looked up in time to hear Miss Veal at her wheedling worst. "Your name, please," she demanded of the gentleman, though Frieda was certain she'd heard it the first time.

She heard his voice again, a most peculiar voice, foreign, she was certain of it.

"Mr. Robert Stow. From the London *Times*," he repeated.

"And the nature of your business, Mr. Stow?"

As the gentleman launched forth into the reason for his appearance here, Frieda glanced back up the stairs, her mind moving toward the ill young woman. She'd hoped to have accomplished her mission by now and been back attending the girl. But here she was, the bricks as cold as ever, while she was caught between the fawning Miss Veal and the equally obsequious gentleman, who was filling the air with the most absurd flattery she'd ever heard.

"And while I left London with several addresses, Miss Veal, I came here first, having heard nothing but the highest praise for your establishment, and convinced that the readers of the *Times* would enjoy a firsthand account of such an advanced institution."

From where Frieda stood she could see Miss Veal in profile only. But that was enough. "You're not—English, Mr. Stow," she accused.

"By adoption, I am," came the swift reply. "My native country is America. But we should never have turned our back on England's stabilizing influence. This is my home now, Miss Veal. A wandering son has come to his senses, you might say."

America! Frieda had never seen an American before.

"Need I point out, Miss Veal," the American gentleman was saying now, "that it might be—how shall I put it —that it might be mutually beneficial for you to grant me a brief audience. The readership of the *Times* is vast. Such a story as the one I would like to write about your school would undoubtedly reach many eyes, families who perhaps are looking for a place to situate their young women."

He paused. Never had Frieda seen such intense interest on the old bitch's face. She looked transformed. "Well, do come in, Mr. Stow. It's a death chill in the air this morning, and I'm certain that we'll both be more comfortable discussing matters before a toasty fire."

Within the instant the gentleman had cleared the doorway and stood in the entrance hall with what appeared to be a smile of relief, though his eyes were moving everywhere at once. Frieda had never seen such searching eyes.

"This way, Mr. Stow," Miss Veal invited, leading him to the front parlor and motioning him inside.

Still holding her position by the front table, Frieda caught only a glimpse of the roaring fire and with longing saw the gentleman move directly toward it.

Discouraged, she waited for Miss Veal to follow after him. At least then she could retrieve her bricks and return to her charge, where perhaps she might warm her with her own body.

Instead she heard Miss Veal call out to the gentleman, "I'll be with you in a moment, Mr. Stow." Then she closed the door and started toward Frieda, her normally chalklike face flushed with color.

"Well, don't just stand there like a dumb cow," she snarled. "Go immediately and alert the staff. And lay a fire in every fireplace and see that they are burning well. Then go to the kitchen and tell Cook to add a joint to the stew and extra vegetables, and warn one and all that there is to be no punishment of any kind for the next few hours."

Stunned by the barrage of instruction, Frieda protested. "It would take ten women to do all that, Miss Veal. I can't—"

"Then get them!" the old woman whispered fiercely. "And be quick about it!"

"One moment, please, Miss Veal, if you will—"

"I don't have a moment," the old bitch snapped, "and neither do you."

"It's about Mary Eden—"

"Did you hear me?" the old woman practically shrieked, the veins in her neck popping out like thin blue cords.

Before such mindless anger, Frieda retreated. If the gentleman from the newspaper had cared to listen, he would have heard all, might have heard for himself how two-faced the old shrew was. As she backed away toward the kitchen door, Frieda found the courage for one more

comment, a warning this time. "She's worse, Miss Veal,
she is. 'Less you get help soon, she's—"

But the old woman merely followed after her with arm
raised as though if Frieda uttered one more word she'd
get her ears boxed.

Frieda had seen these bursts of wrath before and
wasn't too alarmed. Still she didn't waste any time retreating to the kitchen door, where she flung it open and momentarily hid behind it.

She was still watching a moment later when Miss Veal
drew open the parlor door and sent her false voice
ahead. "Ah, Mr. Stow—now tell me precisely what you
want to know about our humble establishment and I'll
most certainly try to oblige."

About two hours later, when it was approaching noon,
after having foisted most of the duties off on the four
scullery maids, Frieda stood over Mary Eden and saw
something that alarmed her even more than the constant
shivering.

The young girl lay absolutely still, her mouth partially
opened, lips dried, in an attempt to breathe over the rattle in her lungs. Her eyes were closed and she responded
to nothing.

Lord, what am I going to do now? Slowly she sat in the
straight-backed chair, never taking her eyes off the still
face, and ran through what were at best limited options.
If the hazards weren't so great she'd bundle her up and
carry her on foot the three miles into Cheltenham. But the
hazards were monstrous. The entire school was alive with
the excitement of the gentleman who had demanded to be
shown everything.

Commencing with a tour of the basement rooms, including the kitchen, proceeding to the first-floor reception
rooms and classrooms, they were, at his insistence, working their way systematically through the house, Miss
Veal's screeching voice floating up now and then in some
raucous artificiality, the others, staff and students alike,
giggling and blushing like idiots.

No, escape was out of the question—at least for now.
Then what? Sit here with folded hands and watch her die?

Suddenly Frieda was on her feet, ready to announce
before God, the gentleman and all, the tragic facts of
what was going on in this cell when at that moment she

heard chattering coming up the stairs. She opened the
door a crack and saw a sizable entourage just climbing the
stairs, Miss Veal in the lead, the gentleman a step behind, his hands laced easily behind his back, but his head
swiveling in every direction, his eyes missing nothing. Following behind him were five of the staff, with insipid grins
on their faces, all trying to speak at once.

Hurriedly Frieda closed the door, losing her nerve. Perhaps this wasn't the time. From her position inside the
closed door she listened as she heard doors opening and
closing, the gentleman insisting upon seeing every cell,
and over all was Miss Veal's singsong voice pointing out
the cleanliness and neatness, the physical order which was
a primary tenet in her philosophy and which always led
to mental and emotional order.

"They are inseparable, don't you see, Mr. Stow?"
Frieda heard now.

"I do indeed," the gentleman replied, "and most impressive it all is."

As their voices passed by the door, Frieda closed her
eyes to rest them from the still figure on the bed and
wished that she might close her ears as well.

Will he never leave?

What a din it was out there! What was going on now?
As best as she could hear, someone was frantically calling
for Miss Veal to "Come quick!" She heard running footsteps, then heard the reverberations of several people
taking the stairs at great speed.

A few minutes later the corridor outside the door was
silent, all apparently drawn away by something of greater
interest. In this new quiet, Frieda sat on the edge of the
bed and enclosed Mary's feverish hands in hers. Still, how
beautiful she was! Had God created such beauty to let it
expire here on a cot in this cold prison?

Suddenly the grim thought was interrupted by what
sounded like a single step outside the door. She'd just
turned in that direction when the door burst open and a
most remarkable sight appeared before her.

"I—beg your pardon," she sputtered, trying to rise to
her feet, angered by the intrusion.

It was the gentleman, but a very different expression on
his face than the one she'd seen downstairs. Now he
looked almost deranged as he closed the door behind him,

his eye falling on Frieda, then moving instantaneously down to the bed where his vision held.

"I must ask you to leave, sir," Frieda announced angrily, trying to come between her vulnerable charge and the gentleman's intense gaze. "You'll find nothing of interest here, I assure you, but a very sick young lady who requires only—"

Abruptly she stopped talking for two reasons. One, it was clear from the expression on his face that he was not hearing a word, and two, that same expression was now speaking volumes as he moved slowly toward the bed, only tenderness and sorrow in his manner.

Frieda held her tongue. She walked to the foot of the bed, her mind churning with a thousand questions, but one predominant which begged to be asked, even though she knew the answer.

"Do—you know her, sir?" she whispered.

There was no response. There was no need for one. He sat on the edge of the cot and grasped the hand which earlier Frieda had held and pressed it to his lips, then to the side of his face, and finally bowed his head over it.

Still suffering confusion and knowing that their time was limited, Frieda asked, "Where are the others? How did you know to look here?"

"I heard you speak her name downstairs. And, as this was the only cell they refused to show me, I knew she had to be here." He paused. "I—did not know she was ill."

Suspicious, Frieda stepped closer. "You ain't from no newspaper, are you?"

He shook his head.

"And you ain't no Robert Stow either."

Again he shook his head.

"Then who are you?" she demanded. "And what do you want here? You ain't her kinsman, are you? No, I can see that. Then who are you and what business do you have here?"

She thought he'd never answer. He seemed content simply to sit on the side of the bed and clasp the still hand, as though at last he'd found the object of a long search. She was just getting ready to go for help when the gentleman lifted his head and showed her for the first time a glimpse of his remarkable face, weakened by a depth of emotion.

"I love her," he said simply.

I love her! Lord, what words! To hear them spoken was a treat, even though they were intended for someone else.

"Well, then," Frieda said at last, "what do you intend to do about it?"

Her businesslike tone, and apparently the conviction that he'd won her trust, seemed to work miracles on the gentleman. No longer seated in a position of passivity, he was on his feet. "I've come to take her away," he said, hurrying to the door, opening it a crack and peering out. "Could you dress her for me? I'll take her to a physician in Cheltenham, but we must—"

"Where are the others?" Frieda demanded.

"Someone said something about a fireplace smoking. They all ran off, but I'm certain—"

Frieda smiled. "It's a wonder they all ain't smoking like locomotives. They are never used, and they were lit now for your benefit."

The gentleman stared at her. With renewed purpose he returned to the bed. "Please help me to dress her warmly. I must take her out of—"

"I'm afraid, sir, you wouldn't get as far as the top step," Frieda said, not enjoying putting out the fire of his enthusiasm, but as a plan it lacked even the rudimentary elements of good sense.

"Then what?" he demanded.

Confronted with the direct question, Frieda turned all her concentration to the problem, aware, along with the gentleman, that their time to plot was limited.

"Do you have a carriage?" she demanded, a plan beginning to take shape, though a hazardous plan it was.

"Of course."

"Well, then," Frieda went on, keeping her voice down in the event someone was lurking outside, "every afternoon from two to three the young ladies exercise in the back garden. I'll dress Miss Eden as warmly as possible and try to get her on her feet long enough to walk her to the garden." She leaned closer, stunned by the insanity of her own words. "There's a small path, overgrown but I think you can find it, at the rear of the garden. You will have to leave your carriage on the access road directly north of the school. Shortly after two this afternoon you find that path and walk along it until you come to the edge of the garden. Wait there!" She added sternly, "Out of sight. If the other young ladies see—"

"Go on."

But Frieda had come to the end of the madness which she called a plan. "I'll bring her to you. You'll have to carry her the distance back to your carriage, then you must leave immediately. Do not return to Cheltenham. You should make it to Oxford by this evening and seek a physician there." She looked back at the pale young woman. "If she requires one," she added, ominously.

He saw the direction of her gaze. "Is—she—"

"She's very ill, sir," Frieda snapped. "You can see that for yourself. Go along with you," she urged, "before the dragon returns and ruins everything." As she walked him hurriedly to the door, she added the most important point. "With luck and a little help from God, I can conceal her absence until four this afternoon. But no longer. When the young ladies file back there's always a count. So by four o'clock alarms will be sounded."

"What will she do?"

Frieda shrugged, wishing he would be on his way and stop asking questions to which she had no answers. "That's not my concern, nor should it be yours. If you love her, just take her away from here and put as much distance as possible between yourselves and this place."

He appeared to have listened closely to all she had said, and now a new expression covered his face. "What's your name?"

"Frieda."

"You're jeopardizing your own position by helping us, aren't you?"

She hesitated and thought she heard steps on the stairs. "Hurry," she said softly. "They can't find you here or all is lost before we start."

At first reluctant, then at last agreeing with her sense of urgency, he drew open the door and peered out. "Two o'clock," he confirmed. "I'll be there."

Frieda closed the door but heard him lift his voice into the tone of an inquiring guest. "Ah, there you are. All's well, I trust?"

She heard Miss Veal's voice, at first rife with suspicion, though lifting into its customary falseness. "I do apologize. Mr. Stow, for abandoning you in this manner. I really thought that you were right behind us."

As their voices dwindled down the corridor, Frieda relaxed for the first time. She closed her eyes to rest them from the impossible task she had set for herself. How would she ever get that ill figure on her feet and into the garden? And what if, in the altered routine of the day, the exercise period was canceled?

No, she had no fears on this last count. No diversion, not even the handsome Mr. Stow, could divert Miss Veal's regimen.

I love her.

Lord, what she wouldn't give just once to hear those words directed at her! Appalled by her own foolishness, she hurled herself into action, flinging open the wardrobe and withdrawing Mary Eden's two black muslin dresses. The point was to keep her warm and alive while awaiting her rescuer. It wouldn't do to place a corpse in his arms.

To that end, and in an attempt to keep her mind off everything that could go wrong, Frieda moved toward the bed.

"Mary?" she whispered, trying to nudge a sign of life from the still face. "Can you hear me?"

But apparently she couldn't. All her energies were being channeled into the effort of breathing.

No matter! Frieda could do it. On the hope that some of that residual love splashed over onto her, she would do it all.

Shortly after two-fifteen, and murmuring a prayer to God for His divine intervention in all matters, Frieda sat at the lower end of the garden, one broad arm around Mary Eden, who was so bundled inside her double garments that she looked twice her normal size.

Moving up and down the paths were the other young ladies. One or two had inquired about the curiously relaxed Mary Eden, who had journeyed to the garden totally under Frieda's strong support. But now they had lost interest and were concentrating on the task at hand, which was to keep warm.

Lord, let him come soon, she prayed, and in the tension of waiting recalled his departure shortly before noon, his disguise firmly in place, loudly thanking one and all, particularly Miss Veal, for having received him with such hospitality. Shortly thereafter, and exhausted by the encounter, Miss Veal had retired to her private chambers, where she'd remained for the rest of the afternoon.

There! She *did* hear a step, unmistakable this time, the sound of a boot crushing winter leaves. As she turned eagerly in that direction her eyes, skimming the rear of the old Tudor mansion, saw a second sight which caused her heart to stop.

"Wait!" she called in a low voice to the bushes behind her, having seen a man's shoulder. "Get down! Hurry!"

She only had time to make that single warning when the familiar figure framed in the back door started toward her. Frieda held still, her arm clasped about her lifeless cargo, feeling her heart in her mouth.

"I thought you said she was ill," Miss Veal challenged when she was about ten yards away. "If so, I shouldn't think—"

Remembering the skill with which the gentleman had played his false role earlier, Frieda, rigid with fear, launched into a theatrical of her own. "Oh, she's better, she is, Miss Veal," she called out. "No cause for alarm. This fresh air will make her right as a fiddle soon enough."

The old woman stood directly before her, her stern face a map of suspicion. "She doesn't look none too well," she accused.

"Sleeping is all," came Frieda's breezy reply. "She was up half the night, you know, trying to get me to do special favors for her. Well, I told her right off that I wasn't here to fetch and carry for her."

How much longer Frieda could sustain the pose she had no idea. At last Miss Veal moved back a step, the suspicion on her face replaced by begrudging admiration. "You're a good girl, Frieda," she pronounced coldly. "You continue to serve me well and you'll always have a place here. And you should get down on your knees every night and thank God for making you ugly. Look what happens to them with fair faces—" And she jabbed her finger toward Mary Eden.

"Aye, Miss Veal," Frieda whispered, amazed at the stinging tears in her eyes, provoked, no doubt, by the bitter wind. She watched as the old woman made her way back to the door.

At last she disappeared, the door closing behind her,

the dead garden silent except for the wind. Frieda bowed her head. *Thank God for making you ugly....*

The grief did not last long. Somewhere behind her was the gentleman, still waiting to receive his precious cargo. And it was up to Frieda to transfer that cargo from this bench to the concealment of bushes without attracting undue attention. She began whispering, "Come, Mary, help me walk you to freedom. There's someone waiting who—"

Laboriously she lifted the girl to her feet and realized that she would have to support her wholly and, as the expenditure of energy increased, she concentrated on the ten or twelve yards ahead, spying the gentleman crouched down into a place of concealment, his face colorless as though he were aware of their recent danger.

"Has she gone?" he whispered.

"For now," Frieda replied, still struggling to support the young girl.

Seeing her effort, he stepped forward and lifted Mary into his arms, cradling her close as though perfectly willing to carry her forever.

Moved by the sight and pleased at her involvement in the escape, it required all the discipline at Frieda's command to urge, "Go now—and hurry! Take her away while there's a breath of life left in her. And remember. I can only give you till four o'clock, and then I'll have to sound the alarm."

He stood before her, the intensity of those remarkable eyes focused on her instead of Mary. "And you," he asked, "what will you do?"

"My duty." Frieda smiled. "Like I've always done."

"Will things go hard for you?"

"They've gone hard all my life, sir." As the sense of urgency pressed down upon her, she whispered, "For Gawd's sake, we ain't got time to chat! Get out of here, both of you, and I'll pray for you, and if she—survives," she added softly, "tell her that Frieda Langford had a hand in it. I'd like her to know."

The gentleman continued to stare down on her as though seeing her for the first time. "Here," he said, fishing something out of his pocket and pressing it into her hand. "If there's hell to pay, this will make the paying easier."

He leaned closer and kissed her on her cheek, a
lightning-fast movement which caught her unaware.

It was several moments before she recovered, and
even then she looked up in a blur to see him running
through the cold afternoon, his head bent low over
Mary, carrying her as though she were the most treasured object in the world.

For a few minutes longer Frieda stood, literally paralyzed by the strangest feelings she'd ever experienced.
Only as an afterthought did she look down at the note
in her hand.

Fifty pounds!

Thus she suffered her second shock of the day, though
even that paled in comparison with the first, a memory she
would carry with her for the rest of her life.

No longer would she have to bow her head in embarrassment before anyone. She had been kissed by a
handsome gentleman and, though no one else had seen
it, she would guard that memory and feed on it and
thank God for it.

She looked down the frozen path. Gone!

"Pray God go with them," she whispered, and secured the note in the pocket of her dress, and wiped
away the tears, lest the young ladies see them and
think her weak.

Once Burke had entertained the foolish notion that
they could make it all the way to London. But by nightfall, and on the outskirts of Oxford, he took another
look at Mary and drew down the window and shouted,
"Stop here! At the first decent public inn."

Hurriedly he raised the window and cradled her close,
as he'd done all afternoon, alternately thanking his good
fortune for having found her and cursing the obvious
abuse which had been dealt her, and suffering a degree
of hate for John Murrey Eden that left him breathless.

If she dies . . .

But he could not even think on such a thought, and
concentrated on that beloved face, studying all aspects
of it, as he'd done all afternoon. It was thinner, the eyes
lost in black circles, the cheeks pale, the once luxurious
hair short and jagged about her head.

Still it was the only face in the world that held any

meaning for him, the only face for which he would plot a future.

But the only future that made any sense now was one of pressing need. He must find a warm chamber for her, a comfortable bed and the services of a physician.

To that end he looked frantically out the window, his eyes skimming over the outskirts of Oxford, the low cottages, lamplight burning within, a scattering of commercial shops, and finally—

"There! Stop there, please!" he shouted, spying a small country inn, a neatly lettered sign bobbing in the wind, which read THE NEW HOPE.

"There's better up ahead, sir!" his driver shouted.

But he didn't want better. If Miss Veal launched a pursuit, as she was sure to do, or worse, if she sent word by fast courier to London to inform John Murrey Eden that his cousin had escaped her prison, then he hoped they would not think to look in a small, plain country inn.

"No—here," he called out, having allowed the carriage to pass the inn by for a closer inspection.

As Burke was crawling down, shielding Mary from the wind, he called back to his driver. "See to the horses, then come inside. There will be a room for you."

Bending low over Mary, he pushed through the door and saw half a dozen men on his right seated before a roaring fire, pints in hand. Burke realized what a spectacle he presented, his hair windblown, a woman in his arms. In an attempt to ease the shocked faces before him, he launched forth into what he hoped would be a succinct explanation.

"My—wife is ill," he began, feeling that perhaps that piece of information was the most important. "We were traveling to London from Scotland and she took ill. I was wondering—"

But a few minutes later he realized that something was causing them even more distress as they whispered among themselves. Then he realized what it was—his voice, distinctly un-English, causing their suspicions to vault.

Angry that nothing he had said had made the slightest difference, he demanded, "Where is the publican? If you would be so good as to—"

"Behind ye, mate, if you'd open your eyes and take a look."

He whirled on the deep voice and turned to see a giant, partially concealed in the shadows at the end of the pub, only his white apron and a massive bald head visible from that distance.

Startled by the apparition and convinced that he would be met with further opposition, Burke strengthened his grasp on Mary and wearily started speaking. "We only seek a chamber. As I was saying, we were traveling back to London after holiday in Scotland, and my wife took—"

"What's she got?" the publican demanded, coming steadily forward, though stopping about ten feet away.

Burke blinked at the giant. A more massive man he'd never seen. In answer to his question, he replied, "I'm— not certain. It's congestion of some sort. She's having difficulty breathing. She needs—"

"Wait a minute," the man commanded, drawing closer. "You—ain't English, is you?"

"Oh, God!" Burke cursed, hoping that his driver had not found a stable, for he was certain they would be leaving here immediately. "No, I'm not English," he said, doing nothing to disguise the sharp edge in his voice.

"Then what are you?" the giant asked.

With a sense of nothing to lose, Burke confessed to his lack. "I'm an American," he announced, loud enough for all to hear, and was just turning about when he heard an explosion of laughter and looked back to see the publican drawing nearer, wiping his broad hand on his apron and extending it to Burke in what appeared to be sincere warmth.

"Then you're most certainly welcome at the New Hope." The man grinned, revealing missing front teeth. "And your wife there, she'll have the best chamber in the inn, which ain't saying much, but we can make her comfy, we can."

He saw the look of shock on Burke's face and shoved his beefy hand even closer. "Giffen's me name, guv, Giffen Radcliff, and I never thought I'd live to host an American, but right proud I am, so take me hand and let's make a bond, then we'll get your angel there up to bed where she belongs."

Stunned by such hospitality, Burke took the hand as best he could and, disarmed by the man's grin, he almost spoke his true name but caught himself in time and invented a second one, as "Mr. Robert Stow" was no longer viable. "I'm Mr. Peter Bennett," he said, "and this is my wife—"

"Whether she is or ain't"—the man winked massively —"she does look a bit the worse for wear. So bring her along, Mr. Peter Bennett, and we'll tuck her in, then I'll send around for old Dr. Thatcher. He ain't much, you understand, but he's all we got and he charges fair."

The man led the way up darkened, narrow steps and looked back down on Burke. "Here, let me help you with her," he offered.

"No!" Burke said and saw hurt in the man's eyes. "I'm—sorry," he added. "It's just that I'm so—"

"—worried. Of course, you are, mate, and I apologize for intruding. Whoever she is I can tell she means the world to you. So old Giffen will just keep his hands off and his tongue still if, as soon as you're rested, you'll tell me all about your gorgeous country."

Burke nodded, his arms beginning to tremble with fatigue, his attention torn between the voice ahead and the lifeless face in his arms, and his increasing fear that she would not survive.

As Giffen led the way into an even darker corridor, Burke glanced ahead, wondering if he shouldn't have followed his driver's advice and proceeded on to a more respectable place. But Frieda's words still echoed in his ear—"*I can only give you till four o'clock, and then I'll have to sound the alarm.*"

Well, the alarm had been sounded for almost four hours, and, if a pursuit had been launched, it wouldn't be too far behind him, and it would not be too difficult for the most simpleminded rural authority to establish that Burke Stanhope had no legal or moral right to the woman in his arms. Since he would not give her up short of death, then concealment was the only alternative.

"Too many sacred cobwebs, mate, that's what we have here," Giffen was saying, as he stopped before a low door at the end of the passage. He removed a lamp from the wall standard and, in his anger over what he was saying, waved it about with such force that the flame was momentarily extinguished. "A dying bitch, she is, England. You know? Any which way a man turns he bumps his head against a law that says you can't do that, or you can't do this."

He shook his head, then laughed heartily. "As you can see, Mr. Peter Bennett, I'm a man who needs space, I do." He pushed the low door open, still talking, casting the lamplight ahead. "So I'm saving me bob, I am. And when the time comes, I'm shaking this miserable dust from me feet forever and joining up with me brother Harry in that Boston town."

Burke tried to appear sympathetic and impressed, but all the time he was taking grim note of the small chamber, not much larger than a storage closet, with one bed, one chair, one washstand and one table.

In addition to this bleak inventory he felt chill in the air which varied little from the one he'd just left outside. Giffen saw his look of distress and moved to dispel it. "Never you mind, sir. It's clean, it is. I can vouch for that, and in no time I'll have a fire going and a pot of tea, or something stronger if you wish, and I'll send one of me mates to fetch the doctor, and before you know it, you and your lady will be cozy and warm. And anything you want, all you'll have to do is ask old Giffen and he'll come running." He grinned. "How could he do anything less for a fellow American?"

Before such an infectious smile, Burke had no defense. "Then be about it," he said softly and moved past the man and gently placed Mary on the bed, her face unchanged, eyes closed, only that terrible rattling which sounded in her chest with every breath.

The voice came from behind him, an aggressive yet gentle voice. "She'll be all right, mate. You just have to tell her that you love her and that you got more to offer her than old man Death's got on the other side."

The sympathetic voice, the long and tense escape, the uncertain future, all these things conspired against Burke and, impervious to the watchful eyes of the innkeeper, he gathered her in his arms and held her close and tried to hide his tears in her soft hair.

"That's it, mate," Giffen whispered. "Love the sickness away. It can be done. . . ."

It was approaching midnight and, though weary beyond description, Burke could not sleep. Through dimmed eyes he looked about at the small, though now warm, chamber and felt curiously as though they were not even on this earth but had been isolated on some distant galaxy where beyond the low door he would not find one point of identity or relationship.

If only she would open her eyes.

The old physician said she might if the fever broke and some of the congestion cleared. He'd pronounced it pneumonia and had placed an oil of clove compress on her chest, had advised Burke to make her more comfortable by changing her to a nightdress, and had perhaps partially believed Burke's story that their luggage had been stolen in an inn outside Newcastle. Burke had removed her slippers and loosened the buttons around her throat and had sat for the last three hours with a cool linen pressed against her forehead.

But her silence was as deep as ever, her breathing as labored. Weakened by fatigue and despair, Burke sat back in the chair at her bedside and thought of the first time he'd seen her.

The memory, instead of pleasing him, only punished him further and he looked up, recalling the ordeal which she had suffered at the hands of John Murrey Eden.

But hate was a poison he did not need and, because he was confident that there would be no more interruptions this night, Giffen having come and gone for the last time, he went down on his knees at bedside and, though a relative stranger to God and prayer, he asked the silence in the room to spare her on the logical basis that she could serve better here than in Heaven, where surely warm and loving spirits abounded.

It was while he was on his knees that he heard the door open behind him, heard a single step, which seemed to pause, then retreat, the door closing as quickly as it had opened.

Annoyed at this interruption, he looked over his shoulder and saw a neatly folded white muslin nightdress on the chair. A gift from old Giffen, he was certain, a man of infinite resources. He pushed to his feet, retrieved the nightdress and stood over her.

No, he wouldn't disturb her. If Death paid a visit during the night, she was more appropriately garbed in black than white.

In defense against the thought of death, he clasped
her hand and held it tightly, and vowed that even so
awesome a force as Death would have to wrestle him
for possession of that hand.

❧

London
January 15, 1871

To THE BEST of her recollection, Lady Eleanor Forbes
had never been happier. As she stood in the receiving
line in the drawing room of Mr. Eden's Belgrave Square
mansion, she knew better than anyone the meaning of
her place there.

Though this grand reception was being given by Mr.
Eden for the purpose of introducing his cousin Lord
Richard to London society, her place between the two
men made a bold announcement without words. Lacking the presence of any other female bearing the name
of Eden, she had been asked to fill the position as official
hostess, and never had anyone rushed to fill a role more
graciously. And her rewards were all around her, in the
beautifully gowned ladies and elegant gentlemen, mostly
from financial London but impressive all the same, in
the self-satisfied smiles on her parents' faces as they reflected in her glory, and, most important of all, in her
heart of hearts, for the man with whom the secret marriage contract had been arranged had turned out to be a
splendid man, gentle, considerate, thoughtful, all qualities
she'd never known before in a man.

Wanting to confirm the reality and, as there was a
pause, in the line of well-wishers, she turned to her left
and saw him in profile, looking ill at ease in his dress
blacks, though striving valiantly to be everything that
his cousin wanted him to be.

"Are you surviving?" she whispered playfully, engaging in a pleasant intimacy with him, though they'd
never even kissed, but rather an intimacy based on
companionship.

"Not surviving," he whispered back, "as much as enduring."

At that moment she heard music, the musicians in the second-floor Ballroom tuning their instruments for the ball which would follow the reception. As she smiled at the guests of the moment, she wondered if at last Richard would dance with her. In the fortnight since their return from Eden they had attended a party or a ball almost nightly and, although occasion after occasion had presented itself, Richard had always demured, claiming incompetence, claiming that he was a better witness than participant.

"Only a few minutes longer," she heard Mr. Eden whisper on her right. "Then I shall release you both, I promise."

She glanced in his direction and thought that he looked very tired. Indeed, that had been Richard's primary objection to this reception, which had first been suggested shortly after their return to London. Richard had claimed that it was not the time for a social function, less than a month after Lila's death. But Mr. Eden had insisted.

There were other mysteries as well. For one, the curious schism which had developed between Mr. Eden and Elizabeth. She had flatly refused to come. Yet the greater the opposition to the evening, the more determined Mr. Eden had been to see it through.

"It's a lovely party," Eleanor murmured, certain that he had his reasons for everything.

"It is, isn't it?" He smiled as though pleased with himself.

To her left she was aware of Richard leaning closer. Obviously he had heard their whispers and now joined them, in the process abandoning Aslam, who stood stiffly in formal dress to his left. "Who are they all?" Richard murmured, as though amazed that so many would be interested in greeting him.

"Friends," Mr. Eden replied expansively, "a few business associates." He paused, a heaviness in his voice. "Not everyone wishes us ill, Richard."

He was on the verge of saying something else, but Eleanor saw Alex Aldwell signaling him from the door. Mr. Eden excused himself, promising an immediate return whereupon they would lead all their guests up to the Ballroom.

Eleanor watched him as he made his way through the crowds, finding him as dramatic now as she had years ago when her father had first brought him as a guest to Forbes Hall. So many legends surrounded him that it was difficult to separate fact from fiction. But the general aura that went with him was that he was a man who could accomplish anything. While she was impressed with such power, she found that she preferred the humanity of Lord Richard Eden. Again she glanced in that direction to see him in close huddle with Aslam. Not wanting to intrude on their conversation, she contented herself with standing erect, receiving many admiring glances—her dark green velvet gown was exquisite —and wondered how long she would have to wait before she became Lady Eleanor Eden.

"Speaking of survival," came a voice next to her, "you don't look too well yourself."

She lowered her head in an attempt to hide any revealing emotion. "I have never felt better, Richard," she said to the floor.

"I don't believe a word of it," he countered playfully. "Aslam and I were just plotting an escape. Would you care to join us?"

Shocked, she looked up at the two male faces before her. "You can't do that, Richard! John would never forgive you."

Aslam stepped forward, a willing accomplice. "Not now, Lady Eleanor," he said. "Later. A midnight supper somewhere. Just the three of us."

Still confused, she glanced from one to the other. "Of course. Why not?" she said, and wished that their numbers might be reduced by one. While she was fond of the young Indian and aware of his importance in this family, there had been times in the past when she would have preferred his absence. Quickly she scolded herself. Richard adored him and insisted that he go everyplace with them, and Eleanor understood. After all, the boy was his only connecting link with his old life at Cambridge.

Then she would endure him for Richard's sake. "A midnight supper it is"—she smiled—"on one condition."

"Name it," Richard invited.

"You must dance with me."

"Oh, no, please," he begged, lifting both hands as though to hold the suggestion at bay. "I've told you repeatedly, Eleanor, I'm really not very good."

"Didn't anyone teach you?" she asked.

"Who would have taught me?" Apparently he detected something in her face and moved away from it. "You go along, Eleanor," he suggested kindly. "John will dance with you, as will every other gentleman, for you have captured all their hearts."

Retreating with Aslam at his side, he called back, "We intend to pass the rest of the evening in the Game Room over a chessboard. But at the stroke of midnight we shall come and fetch you and spirit you away to some exotic Soho restaurant and claim you as ours for the rest of the evening."

Her confusion mounting at the series of compliments, which added up to a rejection, she tried to call him back. But they were gone, like two schoolboys, slipping rapidly through the guests, Richard's arm draped across Aslam's shoulders, their heads bent together in anticipation.

Alone, she suffered a painful deprivation and considered joining them. She was just starting after them when suddenly she heard Mr. Eden's voice. "Lady Eleanor, where did they go?"

She looked back, wishing she had left earlier. "They—didn't say," she lied, protecting them. "I'm sure they will be along—"

"Then, come," he commanded, taking her arm. "Someone must remember their social responsibilities."

She thought she detected anger in his voice and did not particularly enjoy the manner in which he was propelling her forward, as though she were the one who had been remiss. Still, she enjoyed the sensation of eyes upon her as they led the way up the staircase, the other guests following behind, the entire company moving toward the Ballroom and the strains of a Strauss waltz.

At the top of the stairs they looked down through the glittering chandeliers on the equally glittering company, every face upturned in varying expressions of admiration and envy.

It might have been a scene out of her dreams, with only one exception. The wrong man was at her arm, the wrong hand was clasping her waist, and the wrong voice was whispering, "You are so lovely. I demand a dance...."

Three hours later, when it was approaching midnight, John looked out over the crowded Ballroom, feeling extremely pleased with himself. By God, it was a good evening, with only one or two exceptions, namely Richard's damnable shyness. The man had been sequestered in the Game Room all evening with Aslam. "A chess battle royale," according to the steward whom John had dispatched three times to fetch the recalcitrant Lord Richard and bring him back where he belonged.

But all three times the steward had returned alone, though Richard had sent his apologies. *Damn his apologies,* John thought, his good mood over, though he tried to mask his anger from Lady Eleanor, who sat in hurt silence beside him.

"Come," he invited, reaching for her hand. He'd lost count of the number of times they had danced together, and not just obligatory dances either, for he was certain that their enjoyment had been mutual.

To his surprise, she declined, and he saw fatigue on her face as well as disappointment, the overly warm room causing her hair to cling to her neck in becoming ringlets. She was so young. And innocent, he was convinced of that as well. Was Richard blind as well as shy? Could he not see the treasure that John had thoughtfully placed at his feet?

"Come," he repeated, not an invitation this time. He stood before her and observed that her breasts were so full that they pressed lightly against her inner arms and, feeling an old excitement and feeling as well that her objections had been token at best, he lifted her to her feet and guided her to the center of the crowded floor and, in the process of finding the rhythm of the music, allowed his knee to brush against the dark green velvet gown.

In an effort to cancel the startled look on her face, he softened the intimacy with an apology. "I can't account for my cousin's rudeness"—he smiled—"but I assure you I will speak to him about it."

"Please don't," she said. "He told me that he'd never had any instructions in the art of dance, and I—understand."

"Then why do you look so sad?"

"I'm not—sad," she countered, a blush on her cheeks.

"You're stiff."

"I'm tired, that's all."

"Then I shall escort you to the side immediately."

"No."

Her protest pleased him. Clearly she did not want to disappoint him. On the face of it, she owed him a great deal and, on the basis of this one-sided debt, he drew her yet closer, playing with her, enjoying the new blush on her face.

"Richard said—" she began, and did not finish, for at that moment he pressed his leg against hers, delighted at the current of excitement which raced through him, a deep-drawing sensation which he'd not felt for so long.

"Richard said what?" he asked, wondering how far he dare pursue it.

"My—parents," she murmured distractedly.

"Your parents left an hour ago," he said calmly. "I bid them goodnight and promised that I would see you home."

She looked up. "Then it seems I've been twice abandoned."

"Not abandoned," he countered. "I'm still here, and one day soon I hope that this will be your home."

"I'd like that," she confessed, a most becoming smile on her face.

For the duration of the dance nothing more was said, though John's entire consciousness was concentrated on those places where their bodies touched. To his extreme pleasure he felt his desire steadily increase, the curse of impotency beginning to lift, though the thought of taking action left him strangely motionless.

Not until the waltz came to an end did he release her, and only then begrudgingly, wondering how willingly she would go to his fourth floor chamber for a bottle of champagne. A brief respite. How could it hurt? If Richard came looking for her, perhaps jealousy would spur him into action of his own.

He reached for her hand in the same playful manner that had marked the entire evening and, knowing that she would not register serious protest with the guests milling about them, he led her without a word to the Ballroom door.

Not until they were in the privacy of the upper corridor did she pull free and grasp the banister. "Aren't we abandoning your guests?"

"They will manage without us for a while."

Then it came, almost a whisper, as though she knew the answer even as she posed the question. "Where—are we going?"

"We're taking a brief respite, that's all," he said, trying to make light of her apprehension. "A comfortable chamber, a warm fire and a bottle of champagne. Is there anything to object to there?"

For one fearful moment he thought she'd answer "Yes." "Good Lord, Eleanor," he scolded, "we'll be kinsmen soon. Come, let's lift a glass to the future, then we'll return to our guests and I promise I shall produce Richard for you, if I have to go and drag him away from that damnable chessboard myself."

All the way up the stairs he talked lightly of inconsequential matters, of Aslam, listening for the light pressure of a footstep behind him. Then he heard it, heard as well her contribution, as though as an imminent member of the family she was justified in speaking her mind. "Of course, I didn't know him when he was at Cambridge, but he seems happy here. And Richard adores him."

"Then you think it was a wise decision?" he asked, luring her forward one step at a time with innocent conversation.

"For now," she said, almost catching up with him at the fourth-floor landing. "I'm afraid his studies have suffered since Richard and I have been in London, but—"

"Do you enjoy London?" he interrupted, spying his chamber door, aware that he must keep her talking for at least a few more steps.

"Oh, yes!" She walked even with him now, not a trace of apprehension on her face. "Compared to the isolation of Forbes Hall it's merely the world."

"And Eden?" he persisted. "What are your impressions of Eden?" He had his hand on the door and pushed it open, delighted to see her move through it, propelled forward by the enthusiasm of her own response.

"I admire it," she said, "even though it is overpowering. It will take me forever to learn every passageway. But I shall do it, I promise you that, and——"

At the sound of the door closing, she ceased talking and looked about, as though unable to determine how she had arrived here.

With his hand out of sight behind him, he turned the key in the lock, then moved forward to soothe her apprehension before it grew to damaging proportions.

"Ah, there it is," he smiled, spying the champagne on the sideboard, cork conveniently removed, the entire setting courtesy of Alex Aldwell, who had followed John's instructions to the letter. As he presented her with a glass of champagne, he observed a faint trembling in her hands and retreated to the safety of the sofa, vowing, within reason, to give her all the time she needed.

When a few minutes later she had sipped once and placed the glass on the mantel and still seemed disinclined to say anything further, John settled back and started a considerable distance from the heart of the matter.

"Spring," he announced. "I think a spring wedding would be nice, don't you?"

She bowed her head, pleased with the subject, though hesitant. "Spring would be lovely," she agreed, "but——"

"But what?" he teased. "You're not having second thoughts, are you?"

"No, of course not. It's just that—Richard seems—reluctant."

"Oh, my God!" he scoffed. "Richard was born reluctant. A firm push from me and he'll come around."

"I really wish you wouldn't, Mr. Eden," she said with a formality that appalled him.

"Mr. Eden?" he parroted. "Is that how one cousin should address another?"

"We're not cousins yet."

"No, but we will be, I promise you."

The chamber was silent except for the crackling fire. She stood before it as though presenting herself to him in lovely silhouette against the gold and red glow. That implacable force was still moving through him, the need to act strong and growing stronger. In a way she reminded him of Lila, her youth and innocence, and in another way of Mary, her bravado under most tenuous circumstances. He had a feeling that she could bluff her way through any challenge.

"Are you—a virgin, Eleanor?" he asked, and recorded the embarrassment on her face. "It's a legitimate question. I have a right to know."

"Yes."

The news worked an incredible effect on him. Though he'd known it all along, having posed the same question to her parents before he'd signed the marital agreement, hearing it from those lips caused him to suffer a pronounced and identifiable sensation. He had endured its absence too long to lightly ignore it.

Slowly he rose, abandoned his glass on the table and approached her. "No cause for alarm," he soothed, taking her hands in his. "Less than a century ago I would have had the right to check for myself, a clinical examination to ensure health and purity of line."

She tried to pull away, but he held her fast. "I said, no cause for alarm," he repeated, mourning the loss of her bravado.

"Please," she whispered, "let's go back. Richard will be—"

All he had done was simply place his hand over one breast, a gentle, cupping gesture. But her voice halted in midsentence and she stepped back, dangerously close to the fire.

Unable to play the charade any longer and fast losing what little control he had, he grasped her by the shoulders and begged, "Let me be the first. Then you will know what to expect, and—"

Suddenly she was weeping before him. The image reminded him of another time, another place, Lila begging to be relieved of marital duties.

"Please," she begged, "let me go."

He stared down on her, his need blending with disappointment, both accelerating into rage, that the world was filled with cold women. Lacking the appetite to take her by force, he pushed her roughly to one side and strode past her, heading toward his bedchamber where he slammed the door and bolted it, and conjured up the image of a nameless, faceless woman and placed her naked on the bed and was about to mount her when suddenly he felt the tension leave his body, the desire diminish until, limp, he sat on the edge of the bed and stared, unseeing, at the floor and heard the sound of weeping.

Whether it came from beyond the door or inside his own head, he couldn't tell.

"Have mercy," Richard protested, as Aslam commenced to arrange the chess pieces for the fourth game. "Three defeats in one evening are enough for any man." He smiled and glanced toward the clock beyond the Billiard Room.

"Good Lord!" he exclaimed, on his feet and stiff from the sedentary position. "A quarter until twelve. Come, let's rescue Eleanor and make for White's. I'm starved."

Reluctantly Aslam concurred and began carefully to arrange the small ivory chess pieces in the velvet chest. "You play very well, Richard," he said generously. "Up to a point. And then your mind wanders. At the very moment when you should be most alert to my queen you seem mentally to drift off."

Richard laughed at the accurate assessment of his chess capabilities and settled into the chair again. "The story of my life, I'm afraid," he said, enjoying the companionship of the young man, watching with bemused resignation the meticulous manner in which he was storing the chess pieces. Based on experience, Richard knew they would be detained for at least another quarter of an hour. Every piece had to go in just so, a few receiving a loving polishing from the young man, who at eighteen could qualify as a chess master.

In the distance, coming from the Ballroom, Richard heard the sounds of a waltz. Strange how he looked forward to seeing Eleanor again and he hoped she wouldn't be too angry with him. Of course he'd have to tender countless apologies to John as well. But no matter—he was feeling well, better than he had a right to feel, considering the bottomless pit of grief out of which he'd recently climbed.

Bertie.

The man still went with him everywhere, but in Lady Eleanor's constant companionship the pain eased. He did like her company and he enjoyed as well the ease of their comings and goings. In public places, restaurants, galleries, no one looked askance at them, those weighted looks which he and Bertie had received so often. Somehow now he felt "proper," and after years of fear and apprehension it was as though a weight had been lifted.

Of course there were awesome questions in his relationship with Eleanor. For one, there was no physical attraction on his part and he hoped that she would not press for more.

"Richard." The inquiring voice belonged to Aslam. "Are you well?"

Richard nodded and walked away, in an attempt to cancel his emotion while he could still control it. "Put your treasures to bed," he called back. "We have an apology to tender and a lady to rescue."

After having aimlessly circled the room twice, he returned to the chess table to see Aslam absentmindedly polishing the head of a queen. "Let me help," Richard offered, convinced that they both needed movement and the distraction of Eleanor's warm personality.

"I'll do it," Aslam snapped.

Richard lifted his hands to stay the annoyance and leaned back in his chair and tried to fill his head with safe thoughts.

"Richard?"

He looked up at the voice. "Yes?"

Aslam bowed his head as though now that he had Richard's attention he didn't know what to do with it. It was while his head was still down that he asked a peculiar question. "Are you—happy?"

Richard almost laughed, but didn't, seeing the seriousness with which the question had been asked. In an attempt to honor that seriousness, he answered truthfully, "No, not happy. But I'm reasonably content, more so perhaps than I have a right to be."

Aslam looked up. "Were you happier at Cambridge?"

Although baffled by the questions, Richard responded honestly, "Yes, happier than I've ever been in my life."

"Why?"

"I felt, rightly or wrongly, that I was being productive, was contributing in a small way."

"And you don't feel that now?"

Richard smiled. "What am I doing here but living a life of pampered luxury? You at least have your studies in the Temple, and John calls on your services from time to time." He rubbed his eyes as though to dismiss the vision of a useless life. "All he asked of me is that I smile on cue and dress properly and be charming to pretty ladies."

"Will you ever go back to Cambridge?"

A most peculiar line of questioning! "I don't know. It has occurred to me. But—"

Again the past and all its pain rose up before him: Bertie laughing; Bertie racing across the Commons, late as always; Bertie counseling a young reader with wisdom and tenderness; Bertie's hand; Bertie . . . He lowered his head, aware of the emotion of his face and equally aware that he lacked the will to hide it.

While he was still struggling for control, there came another question. "You—miss him, don't you?" Aslam whispered. "Professor Nichols, I mean."

Sweet God, what is the boy doing? "Yes," Richard said, angry at the senseless conversation. "Now hurry. Eleanor's waiting and—"

"Then why didn't you come?" Aslam persisted.

Still recoiling from the earlier questions, Richard looked baffled across the table. "Come—where?"

"John said that you would be there, said that all he wanted was to speak to you, to both of you."

Bewilderment increasing, Richard confessed, "I haven't the faintest idea what you are talking about, Aslam. Come where? Speak to whom?"

Aslam ceased to lavish attention on the chess set and returned Richard's stare. "That night in Cambridge," he said, "that terrible night at Professor Nichols'. John told me that he had stopped by your flat earlier and that you had promised to be there."

Richard looked up. The room had gone still around him. "Be—where?"

"At Professor Nichols'," Aslam said impatiently.

Richard wasn't faring so well himself. All the fragments of half-information seemed to assault his mind, and he had the curious sensation that if he rose to his feet he could not stand. "John saw—Bertie?" he asked, hoping that something would be denied.

"Of course," Aslam explained, "and you were to have been there as well. John said—"

"What did John say?"

Aslam appeared to be suffering embarrassment. "He —knew everything—"

"What do you mean, 'everything'?"

"You know," the boy protested, "that you were Sodomites." His face flushed, his eyes became confused. "Neither of us had any idea that Professor Nichols would—"

At that point in the room where earlier the fire had blazed there now, in silence, crept masses of shadows which consumed all the light and warmth. In the manner of a self-flagellate, Richard wanted to know more. He tried to speak and thought he had, but as there was only silence about him, he tried again with all the remaining strength at his disposal.

"What—did John say to Bertie?" he whispered, trying to fight off the image of the noose.

It was Aslam who felt that enough had been said and, as he closed the chess case with a snap, he said, "No matter. John did what he thought was best and, of course, he had no way of knowing—"

Suddenly Richard felt himself driven forward by a force that literally lifted him to his feet. His hand, which never in his life had been raised in violence to anyone, moved as though of its own accord, grabbing Aslam's jacket and holding fast. "Tell me," he demanded, "what was said." When the boy either couldn't or wouldn't speak, Richard shouted, *"Tell me!"*

Aslam stood motionless, terrified. "He told Professor —Nichols to—leave England," he stammered. "He said it was for the best, for both of you. He said no charges would be brought if—he left right away. If he didn't he said he would have both of you—arrested—"

The darkness steadily thickened. It was as though a ragged wound incompletely healed had been opened and the pain and odor of infection had been loosened. Stumbling on the leg of the chair, Richard stepped back.

He would have both of you arrested. . . .

"Richard, please. It's over. I—thought you knew."

"No!" Richard whispered in an attempt to digest what was now a double horror. Bertie dead and John behind it. John the cause, John— He took another step backward, then turned and ran, his initial instinct to seek out the fiend himself and relieve him of life, as he had relieved Bertie.

But as he reached the Entrance Hall he changed his

mind, and chose the direct path which led to the front door, pushing past gaping stewards and Alex Aldwell, intent only on putting as much distance as possible between himself and this place of evil.

The first blast of cold January air greeted him like a slap in the face. He found his carriage and shouted up an indefinite direction of "Drive!" and, just as his strength deserted him, he fell across the cold cushions and wept openly for the double loss of the two main supports in his life, Bertie Nichols and John Murrey Eden. Both were dead to him now and would remain so for the rest of his life.

Alex Aldwell stood in the doorway of the Belgrave Square mansion and tried to make sense out of what was going on. *Damn—I have to straddle two worlds, that's the trouble!* He glanced back up the stairs where the music was going on, then turned his attention to the lower entrance hall where the disintegration was going on. As always, John was no place in sight, leaving it all up to Alex to hold the pieces together.

He stared glumly down at the letter in his hand which had just been delivered by a road-dusty courier all the way from Cheltenham, or so the bloke said. In consideration, Alex had sent him down to the kitchen for food, and now peered out at Lord Richard's rapidly departing carriage.

Something was going on, but what in the hell he had no idea. First, about ten minutes ago, that young lady— what was her name? Lady Eleanor—had come running down the stairs without a goodbye, hello or thank you, and had disappeared into the night. Alex had tried to stop her but she'd not even taken time to fetch her cloak.

While he'd still been pondering that mystery, here came Lord Richard, almost knocking down a couple of stewards in his speedy exit.

A moment after that Aslam had appeared, looking like something passed over, though unlike the other two who had raced out the front door, the boy's goal had been at the top of the house, for he'd taken the steps upward three at a time.

Just as Alex had started up the stairs after him, a steward had summoned his attention to the front door and the courier, who had informed him in rural dialect that "This here were to be placed direct in the hands of Mr. John Murrey Eden."

As he started again up the stairs, he wished that John would release him from all these "socializing" duties. He didn't do them well, and they exhausted him. He was best suited by nature and training to be a foreman of men and he was never happier than when he was watching the giant shovels break virgin ground for some new building project for John Murrey Firm.

His thoughts took him all the way up the stairs to the fourth floor, where behind the closed door he heard John's voice raised in anger. Alex lifted his hand, knocked once and peered in to see John in his dressing gown hovering over Aslam, who was seated on the sofa with bowed head.

"You idiot!" he shouted. "Dolt!"

"I—thought—he knew," Aslam stammered.

"Get out!" John commanded. "The sight of you sickens me. Get out!"

As the young man stumbled upward, then past him, Alex moved to one side, and his heart went out to him. He looked bereft. Alex made a mental note to seek him out later and remind him that John's rages frequently meant nothing.

"What do *you* want?" John demanded, summoning Alex's attention back to the chamber.

Experienced enough not to be intimidated by this complex man, Alex smiled. "How did the lad err, John?" he asked.

"That's none of your business!" John snapped. "What is it?"

He *was* testy tonight. "This was just delivered," Alex said, approaching the fireplace and the man brooding before it, "by special courier. I was told to place it in your hands direct."

John looked up. "What is it?"

"From Cheltenham it is. Do you want me to read it?"

John stared at the letter as though it were a curse from God. "Please do, Alex," he murmured and pushed away from the mantel and made his way to the sideboard, where he poured a brandy, downed it in one gulp, then leaned heavily forward.

Considerately Alex waited, thinking that the brandy would fortify him. But when he continued to stand in that stiffened manner, Alex slipped his finger beneath the seal, withdrew a single piece of paper and read the brief message for himself.

Dear Lord—

He glanced back at John. What were the fates trying to do? Destroy him? "It's from that—Miss Veal," he said, wishing that he'd sent a steward up with the letter. "She says she is compelled to inform you that—Lady Mary Eden has run away from the school and, while she is exerting every effort to locate her, the search thus far has been fruitless and she wishes for you to release her from any further responsibility."

Alex braced himself for new outrage, suspecting that this time it would be aimed at him. There was always a point of confusion between the message and the messenger. Thus armed with understanding, Alex continued to wait. Well, where was it? The outrage?

But it never came, though what did occur was worse. John lifted his head to the ceiling, as though he were silently entreating the Divinity to have mercy. "I'll leave for Cheltenham tomorrow. See that my carriage is ready."

That was all. He walked slowly into his bedchamber and closed the door behind him, and Alex was left alone, staring at the closed door, searching his memories of his long association with John Murrey Eden trying to recall a similar reaction.

But he couldn't. The fury of a lifetime apparently had been depleted and in its place was—what?

Though weakened by shame, Eleanor had retained enough strength and presence of mind to know that she must flee the house, and accordingly she had run cloakless out into the night and had taken refuge in one of the waiting hansom cabs.

Shivering from cold and her recent humiliation, she had drawn the fur rug up about her and had just been on the verge of giving the driver the address of her father's town house when, looking back, she had seen Richard leave the house.

In desperate need, she'd dared to hope that he was coming after her. But no. Something in his manner suggested a crucible at least as great as her own and, motivated by love, she'd waited until his carriage had passed her by, then had given her driver instructions to follow after.

For over an hour the carriages had cut an aimless path up and down the London streets and, just when she had despaired that he would ever select a destination, she saw his carriage roll to a stop on a high plateau on the outskirts of London overlooking the Heath.

Certain that he had seen the cab and must know that he was being followed, she waited about twenty yards away. When there still was no sign of life coming from within the carriage, she left her cab and walked across the brown stubble of grass, the wind even sharper up here, until she stood at his carriage door, trying to see him through the darkness.

"Richard?"

Then she saw him and saw too much, saw a face which resembled a dead man's, his eyes staring at her as though in his mysterious grief he didn't recognize her.

Unable to abide such a look, and forgetting her own recent ordeal, she climbed up into the carriage and was instantly rewarded with the most treasured gift of her imagination, his arms about her in embrace, the two of them clinging to each other, comforting and being comforted.

For several moments they held each other with no words spoken. It was clear to her that twin nightmares had brought them together and, while the specifics of his were still unknown to her, all that mattered was that they were together.

"Let's leave London," she whispered, and while there was no positive response there were no objections either.

In spite of everything that had happened, with the practicality and strength that was basic to her nature, she took control, sensing that he would always let her take control.

"Let's go to Forbes Hall," she murmured, smoothing his brow as though he were an injured child. "You'll like it there, I know."

Still, when there was no objection coming from the drawn face, she took matters into her own hands, extended her purse out the window to his driver with instructions to pay off the cab, then, with a daring which left her breathless, gave him directions to her childhood home in Kent.

"Make an easy drive of it," she called out. "Noon tomorrow should see us safely there."

As the carriage rolled forward she drew up the fur rug over both of them and looked again at his face.

"Oh, my darling," she whispered and drew him close and felt his hand tighten on hers beneath the rug.

Giving herself wholly to the rocking motion of the carriage, she closed her eyes, impressed with the ability of the world to transform itself so rapidly from a nightmare to a dream.

❦

Oxford
January 17, 1871

FOR THREE DAYS and two nights Burke maintained a constant vigil at her bedside, never once leaving the small room, never leaving his chair except to receive fresh linen and a bit of food now and then from Giffen at the door. Approaching the third night, his hope diminishing in exhaustion and fear, he sat on the edge of the bed and stared down on her, searching for the slightest change in that premature death mask.

But there was nothing, even less today than yesterday when she'd passed through a restless period, crying out several times in her delirium. It could not persist. The old physician had said as much. Tonight, tomorrow at the latest, the fever would either break or kill her.

"No," he whispered and shook his head, as though to postpone the inevitable. Fearing the night, he turned up the lamp and, as it flared brightly he allowed himself the luxury of closing his eyes and tried to remember the circumstances which had led him here to this death watch.

In need as acute as any he'd ever experienced, he stretched out his hand in another direction, toward her, and let it rest on her arm. He prayed silently that if Death came for her, let it take him as well.

How long he remained thus he had no idea. He must have lost consciousness, though it could scarcely be called sleep. Now what was that dragging him back from that safe darkness?

With his face pressed against her hand, he felt movement, so slight as to be hardly discernible, some force moving her hand, the fingers extending . . .

He raised up. Had he imagined it? Had he wanted movement so desperately that he had conjured it up by himself? He continued to stare with such intensity at her hand that it grew blurred before his eyes and, as though viewing it under water, he saw it again, the fingers straightening, the entire hand lifting.

On his feet, he pressed his head against her heart. It beat faintly but evenly. In spite of his own thunderous pulse he called quietly to her. "Mary? Can you hear me?"

He held his breath, then cautiously smoothed her cheek. First he kissed her closed eyes, then her lips, then he drew back and waited.

Her hand was moving again, as was her head, a faint shifting on the pillow.

"Mary, look at me, please," he begged. "I'm here. Can you—"

Slowly her eyes opened and moved unfocused about the room and at last stopped on him. "Burke—"

He lifted her to him and felt the back of her nightdress wet from the breaking fever.

So there was to be a path beyond this simple country inn! Then Burke ceased thinking and listened to the voices that seemed to be talking joyfully within him.

Two days later, though still weakened to the extent that it was an effort to hold her eyes open, Mary lay back against the pillow and tried to make sense out of this heaven into which she had awakened.

Beyond the foot of the bed a blaze of bright winter sun cast a glow on the specifics of the unfamiliar chamber. She'd never been here before, but she confessed to herself that she would be content to pass the rest of her life here so long as one face remained constant.

His—

Slowly she turned, wanting confirmation of his presence, though not needing it. He was always there, seated in that worn chair, looking equally worn, frequently dozing like now, rising to tend to her or receive a few necessities which were brought to the door by the man named Giffen. She had met him only that morning and he'd seemed so pleased to find her awake.

She gazed upon Burke's sleeping face and tried to recall the incredible story he'd told her in patient repetition, once yesterday, twice today. It was like the stories old Aggie Fletcher used to tell her when she was little, repetitious fairy tales, so familiar that Mary knew those parts of the narrative that would please her, the parts that would frighten her.

With only one or two exceptions, Burke's story in its entirety had frightened her. She liked the part where he'd posed as a London journalist to gain admission to Miss Veal's· school and, though it made her cry, she always enjoyed hearing about Frieda's efforts and loyalty on her behalf.

But the rest of it terrified her: Burke's account of his visit to Elizabeth, the discovery of the second note, John's hand behind it, behind everything.

As the specifics of the nightmare pressed against her, she opened her eyes and found Burke again. Though he'd talked long and hard, he'd never once asked about her ordeal and she'd never mentioned it. If it had mattered to him, he'd shown no indication of it.

She looked toward the chair and the man sleeping and offered up a simple prayer, that she never again be separated from him, that for the duration of the days God had allotted to her she be allowed always to move around him, to look upon him, to touch his hand and care for him, to comfort him, to love him in all the ways that it was ordained for a woman to love a man.

Was it asking too much?

As she wiped away tears she saw movement, his head twisting from the awkwardness of his position. While she was trying to restore her face, he came up out of the chair and hovered over her in alarm, having seen the tears and assuming that they meant distress.

"Mary? May I fetch—"

She shook her head and reached for his hand. "No."

He sat on the edge of the bed. "Giffen promised beef broth today." He smiled. "He said it would give you strength of an ox. Perhaps I should go and see—"

"Not yet," she begged.

"Did you sleep?"

She shook her head. "According to you, I've been asleep for the last five days. That should serve for a while."

"It wasn't sleep. You were ill."

As he talked, she lightly caressed his face, tracing with one finger the line which stretched across his brow and down the bridge of his nose, then his lips, where gently he kissed her fingertips.

Moved by the tender inspection, he bent over and kissed her. Without warning she thought of the nightmare in the park. "Burke—"

But she found she couldn't speak, and in the silence her ordeal became clearer, sensations she thought she'd banished forever, the heavy weight, the odor of which she would never cleanse herself.

Unable to say how it happened, she was crying and in his arms, aware of his fear as he held her, begging, "What is it, Mary? Please tell me—"

Then he knew. Without a word from her he knew, for he held her even more tightly. "It's over, Mary. It doesn't matter."

In relief she cried herself out, fortified by three words: *"It doesn't matter."* A short while later he lowered her to the pillow, his hands smoothing her hair. She marveled at the flow of strength coming from him to her and she found the courage to say, "I will tell you about it—someday. I want to speak of it."

He nodded. "Someday, when we are walking with our grandchildren and they are running ahead of us, then you can tell me."

"Grandchildren?"

"Of course!" He grinned. "Following children and both following the day you become my wife."

A dog barked outside the window. A carriage rattled past. Then all the street sounds fell silent as though in awe of his simple words. Mary tried to speak. But she could find nothing to express the joy in her heart. Then she was in his arms again, marveling at the word.

Wife. His wife—

"Will you," he asked shyly, "marry me?"

Did he require an answer? Then she would give him one and, separating herself from his embrace and taking his face between her hands, she kissed him and confessed quietly, "I have no life without you. Of course I'll marry you."

He enclosed her in his arms. With a thought of returning just a degree of the comfort that he had given to her, she drew his head down until it was resting on her breast. . . .

❧

London
St. George Street
February 1, 1871

FOR TWO REASONS, and two reasons only, Elizabeth had agreed to see John this evening. Even then, after responding "Yes" to Alex Aldwell's eloquent plea on John's behalf, she now found herself regretting her decision.

One, she was worried sick about the missing Mary, who was still missing, despite the five private investigators whom John had turned loose on her trail. She knew, for Alex had told her, that John had returned only yesterday from Cheltenham. Perhaps he had news.

She sipped at her sherry and tried to clear her head for the impending encounter and, without warning, a fragment of old love surfaced and forced her into a painful collision with her second reason for having agreed to receive John this evening.

Love! It was that simple. In spite of everything, she *had* raised him and in a way was responsible for what he was, though Charlie Bradlaugh had tried to talk her out of that "bit of foolishness."

Still, there was the truth of it, and with Richard's mysterious departure, Andrew and Dhari's emigration, Lila's death and now Mary's absence, she could understand the degree of pain he must be suffering.

"He's here, Miss Elizabeth." The voice belonged to Doris, who had done little to hide her feelings in the announcement.

"Show him in immediately."

Then the bell sounded and, as Doris hurried out of sight toward the door, Elizabeth drained her sherry and offered up a quick prayer for patience, for understanding, in the name of the deep love they once had shared. Still looking toward the archway, she started forward, baffled.

This side of the archway she stopped, having found him wearily removing his cloak and gloves at the pace of a man twice his age. For just an instant her heart went out to him. "John—" she began, and fought the impulse to go to his side, and stood back as he passed before her without acknowledging her, and moved the length of the room toward the fire.

When he still did not speak or recognize her in any way, she went to the sideboard, poured a snifter of brandy and carried it like a peace offering to the fireplace.

"Here," she said, "it will warm you."

He looked down on her, as though surprised he was not alone. As he took the snifter he spoke his first words. "Thank you for receiving me."

The simple expression of gratitude moved her and she caught a glimpse of the old John, capable of great love and consideration. As she sat in her customary chair before the fire, she was on the verge of asking if he would like food.

But before she could speak he looked out over the drawing room. "I understand there was quite a large reception here earlier this afternoon."

A harmless comment, though it did imply that his spies had been busy. "Yes," she confirmed. "A Frenchwoman visiting London for the first time. Her name is—"

"I know her name," he interrupted, "and I know the guest list as well, and I know the purpose of the meeting."

Elizabeth laughed. "Well, then, there's little need to discuss it, is there? Tell me what you found in Cheltenham? Did you see—"

He looked directly at her, the fatigue on his face hardening into censure. "Are you getting involved in that nonsense all over again?"

Taken aback by his change of mood, she stammered, "What—nonsense?"

"You know perfectly well. Less than three years ago you brought embarrassment to the entire family with your public involvement in that stupid franchise. My God, I would have thought you had learned your lesson."

He was ranging broadly back and forth before the fireplace. She watched as long as she could, then tried to force his mind to the matter at hand. "Please, tell me what you learned in Cheltenham. I've been so worried."

"Why?"

"Why?" she repeated, astonished at the question. "Because Mary is missing, God knows where."

"God may not know," he said, facing her, "but I think you do."

In the face of this accusation, she found herself incapable of a reply. She abandoned her chair, feeling a need for distance. As she retreated he started speaking again, pursuing her halfway across the room. "I had an interesting conversation with Miss Veal," he said. "It seems that on the morning of Mary's disappearance an American gentleman posing as a journalist with a London newspaper paid a visit to the school. He was there, or so he said, to do a story on the various institutions for young ladies."

His voice fell. "Don't you think it curious, Elizabeth, that he should start with a remote school buried in the Cotswolds?"

With her head bowed against his unspoken accusation, she briefly regretted her decision to see him alone. Then, angered by the realization that she was frightened by his presence, she turned to face him. "I don't know what you're talking about."

"I believe you do," he said. "Since my return to London yesterday I've sent inquiry to every newspaper in this city. No one was assigned to do a story on schools for women. What does that tell you?"

Anxiety increasing, she moved away to the sofa, still feeling the need for distance. "It—tells me nothing. What should it tell me?"

"Betrayal," he said flatly, rising from his chair and walking toward her. "You see, I know everything. I know it was the American, the same one who was at Eden last spring. I should have killed him then," he added calmly. "The same man whom Mary met repeatedly in the park last summer, another betrayal," he added, his voice rising as though he were warming to his subject, "and the same man who paid you a visit not too long ago and obtained precisely the information he needed and who now has spirited her off somewhere, the Eden name trampled underfoot in the process, Mary's whoredom complete."

"John, please—"

As she tried to blunt his rising anger, she saw that she'd only fanned the flames and, as he strode rapidly toward her, she grasped a small pillow as though that soft object would provide her with a degree of protection.

"Of course, I have only myself to blame," he said, standing less than two feet away. "How foolish I was to have entrusted her to you. A whore can only create a whore, isn't that right? With what efficiency did you make her into your own image! All the time I was trying to protect and defend her, you were working against me, giving her dangerous freedom, filling her head with romantic rubbish, turning her against me."

The words were hard enough to bear, but when she felt his hand tighten on her arm, she gave a soft cry and felt herself being drawn violently toward him, his face close, a deranged face intent on inflicting pain.

"Slut!" he whispered. "First you betrayed my father with every cock in London. Then you corrupted the only pure thing in my life. Why?" he demanded pathetically. "What did I ever do to you but try to lift you out of your own degradation?"

Response was beyond her, her terror so great that she tried to wrench free from his grasp. But he continued to hold her, dropping the brandy snifter to the floor, holding her with both hands, in spite of her pleas that he let her go.

"Go where?" he demanded sarcastically. "To Mary? Oh, I have no doubt that you know precisely where she is, that you stood silently by and allowed her to make a fool of me. Where is the love nest? I'd like to know. Do you watch them as they copulate? Have you given her careful instructions on how to discard the unwanted seed, or can the Eden family now look forward to an American bastard?"

"John, please," she begged. "You don't know what you are saying."

"I know very well what I'm saying. You asked me to speak my mind. Would you like to hear more?"

"No."

"Can you deny the truth of anything I've said?"

"I do not know where Mary is."

"Do you deny that the man came here and that you told him where she was?"

"They are—in love—"

"Then you did see him! You did betray me!"

"Yes!" She was only half-aware of his hand lifting, and when the blow came, a stunning blow to the side of her face, she fell backward into the sofa, her hand moving reflexively to the pain.

Half-turned away and fully prepared to cry out if he struck her again, she clasped her face and tasted blood where her teeth had cut into her tongue and saw him at last retreat, though now he was looking down on her as though she were something dead to be discarded on the refuse heap.

In defense against such a look, she drew herself up, in spite of her trembling, and delivered herself of a simple announcement to the man walking away toward the door.

"You should know one thing more, John," she said. "Mr. Stanhope has in his possession two notes: the one that he allegedly wrote to Mary and the one that she wrote to him."

Because of her own disintegration, she could not with accuracy discern his reaction. But he appeared to be unconcerned and astonished that she would delay him with such insignificant information.

"The night he was here," she went on, "we determined with little difficulty the false nature of both notes and the true hand behind them."

She paused, still unable to believe the accusation she was about to level. "We were left with only one conclusion, that you—arranged Mary's tragedy, that you were responsible for—"

Incredibly, he smiled. "Of course I was. And I would do it again. My only regret is that the villains did not finish the job and kill her, for she's dead to me now, along with all the hopes I once had for her."

Then he was gone. In a state of shock she listened to

his footsteps on the front stairs, the sound of the carriage
starting forward, then diminishing, then silence.

A half an hour later she still was seated on the sofa
where he had left her, her lower lip rimmed with dried
bood, a swelling bruise on her cheek, though all these discomforts were nothing compared to the silent battle she
fought with herself. On one side the impulse to hate, on
the other the need to forgive, on the insistent basis that
the once vulnerable little boy was now pitifully, tragi-
cally insane.

Almost paralyzed with fear for what the future might
bring, she bowed her head and begged God's forgiveness
and begged Him further to have mercy on John.

***

Oxford
February 5, 1871

Burke stood on the pavement before his carriage in
front of the New Hope Inn and tucked the fur rug about
Mary's legs and for his effort received her light kiss on his
forehead, and a look of joy in her eyes, despite her
pale complexion and the residual weakness which still
attended her.

"Are you certain you are capable of traveling?" he
asked, concerned, recalling the debate which they had
held for the last three days.

"Yes"—she smiled with conviction—"anywhere, as
long as you are with me."

He grasped her hand and tried to determine if she
really was capable of traveling, or whether she had urged
their departure after having heard him express concern
for his mother.

During one of their long afternoon talks he had told
Mary everything, commencing with the war which had
destroyed his home in America, his mother's illness, the
apparent abandonment of his father, and his exile in
London. Confident of her love, he'd even confessed to his
role as Lord Ripples, claiming full credit for the newspaper column which had so angered John Murrey Eden.

At first she had not believed him. But then she had, and she'd laughed at the irony, though she'd grown quiet at the mention of her cousin's name. Burke suspected that she had yet to fully believe his involvement in her ordeal.

No matter. They would deal with that later. The first priority had been to nurse her back to a semblance of health, then to make for London, where they could take safe refuge in his Mayfair house and there, enjoying a degree of security in comfortable surroundings, allow Mary a slow and leisured recuperation, so that together they might plot their future.

Lost in his own thoughts, he was unaware of the manner in which he was mindlessly arranging and rearranging the fur rug over her.

Not until she grasped his hand, thus summoning his attention, did he look up. "Enough," she whispered. "Old Giffen is waiting to say his goodbyes, and I'm most eager to meet your mother."

Recalling the condition in which he'd last seen his mother, and suffering a small sinking of spirits, he withdrew from the carriage and turned to face the grinning man standing in the door of the inn.

"Giffen," he called out, summoning the man forward. He saw a small basket clutched in his host's hand and knew that it probably was the last of the many thoughtful considerations the man had showered on them both for the last three weeks.

Burke wondered how he could ever say an adequate thank you. As Giffen came forward, Burke noticed a shyness in his manner that he'd never seen before, as though he, too, were moved by their imminent departure.

"Just a little something for the road, Mr. Bennett." Giffen grinned and extended the basket. "A nice round of Cheddar and two freshly baked meat pies."

Burke took the basket and regretted his false identity. Perhaps honesty would be at least partial repayment. "I'm not Mr. Bennett," he said.

"Oh, I know that, sir. Been a publican for too long, I have, seen too many 'Mr. Bennetts' come and go not to know a false one when I see him. But what I don't know, sir, is who you really are."

Burke shifted the basket and extended his hand. "My name is Burke Stanhope," he said, "and she," he added, gesturing toward the carriage, "is Lady Mary Eden. She's not my wife yet, but she will be soon."

Giffen laughed. "Well, I could have told you that as well," he said. "And you suit one another, you do." He leaned closer. "Now what I want to know is this: are all them babies going to be English or American? If you take my advice, you'll make them babes American, 'cause there's nothing for 'em here but boundaries and rising taxes and the glorification of a past which weren't much when it was the present."

He looked about the pavement, then extended his vision to include the road, the traffic, the clutter of surrounding shops. "It's space I hunger for, don't you see? A man needs space to dream in."

He seemed transfixed by his own words and in the interim Burke was aware of time passing, Mary waiting.

He reached into his waistcoat pocket and withdrew a fifty-pound note. While the man was still gazing in a generally western direction toward America, Burke pressed the note into his hand. "Then apply this to your passage," he said. "You helped me with my dream. Let me help you with yours."

Wordless, the man blinked down at the note and started to protest. But Burke didn't give him a chance. "Thanks, my friend," he called back as he swung up into the carriage, "and I wish you well."

Within the instant his driver flicked the reins and the carriage was pulling away from the pavement. Giffen was running alongside now, his face a map of gratitude, the note still clutched in his hand. "See you in America!" he shouted above the clatter of the carriage wheels.

"Is he serious," Mary asked, "about America?"

"Completely serious. His brother emigrated several years ago and has established a pub in Boston. Apparently his letters home have described a paradise."

"Is it?" she asked quietly.

"What?"

"A paradise."

Burke adjusted the fur rug over them both, tucked in the edges in protection against the chill wind and sat quietly at last, his eyes fixed on the shadows dancing across the opposite seat. "No," he murmured.

Mary saw something in his face and pushed closer. As he drew her near he rested his cheek atop her head and, while he was moved by her nearness, the future suddenly loomed before him like an abyss.

He had found his life and brought her back from the dead. Now what? He could not envision a life for them in the house in Mayfair, and what would his mother's reaction be? And Eden? Whether or not Mary had faced the inevitable—and he was fairly certain that she had not—her days there were over as well. Her cousin would not retreat so easily. Having been duped in more ways than one, he undoubtedly would come storming up out of a rage that would make his earlier performances seem like a child's trantrum.

Then where? And how? And when?

He continued to stare doggedly at the dancing shadows on the seat opposite, the questions coming faster than he could deal with them.

"I love you, Burke," a soft voice whispered close to his ear.

While the proclamation solved nothing, it moved him and provided him with strength and left him with the illusion that he could face and endure and triumph over anything the future might bring.

❧

London
Mayfair
February 7, 1871

IN SPITE OF Burke's loving presence and the day-and-a-half journey during which they had done nothing but talk quietly and hold one another, now for the last hour Mary had feigned sleep, feeling a need to clear her head for the next obstacle, and a formidable one it was.

His mother. Caroline Stanhope.

As a thousand and one little problems of female vanity presented themselves to her, she shivered beneath the fur rug and kept her eyes on the passing streets outside the window. It wasn't far, she knew that, less than fifteen minutes was her guess, and look at her.

Sweet heaven—what a portrait she must present, still garbed in the crude black dress she'd worn at Miss Veal's. Giffen had kindly had it laundered, but that had done nothing to alter its ugliness or the manner in which it hung on her after her loss of flesh during the illness.

And there was the illness itself, which had left her with a complexion the color of chalk, and her hair which had not known a curling iron or grooming brush for weeks. And her hands and nails, which were equally disreputable, her lips still chafed and dried from the fever and, worse than anything, was the persistent weakness. Though she'd kept it secret from Burke, it had taken all her energy simply to walk down the steps of the inn and into the carriage.

As the problems mounted, real and imagined, she thought with longing of her familiar chambers on the second floor of Elizabeth's house in St. George Street, her wardrobe filled with lovely gowns.

She must have made a sound, for Burke was bending over her. "You're—not asleep?"

"No," she murmured and found her way into his arms, finding in his strength at least partial relief from all problems, all horrors.

"Don't think about it," he urged, pressing her head close to his chest, knowing precisely the turn of her thoughts. "We're almost there," he added, clearly unaware of the other half of her terror.

"I'm frightened," she confessed.

"Why?"

"Look at me," she invited, smiling at her own vanity.

"I have been looking at you almost continuously for the last three weeks."

"Well?"

"Well, what?"

A little puzzled that he could not understand, she begged, "Please let me return to Elizabeth's first, Burke. I have fresh garments there. Let me—"

"No!"

The rebuttal was swift and left no room for debate. Only after he had turned away and settled back into the seat did he speak again, and then it was part apology, part warning. "I'm sorry, Mary," he said to the window, "but you must believe me when I tell you it is not safe.

And I'm certain that Elizabeth herself would say as much."

A thought occurred. "Then I'm never to see any of them again?" she asked, afraid of his answer.

"I didn't say that. We must first see to your recuperation and then we must chart a plan."

"What kind of plan?" she asked, curious about the future he had in mind for them both.

Without hesitation he replied, "Marriage, of course. As soon as possible; as soon as you are able. Until then your cousin has every legal right to reclaim you, to do with you as he sees fit, including sending you back to Miss Veal's."

"No," she whispered, unable to deal with the memories of the dreaded place.

That was all that was said. The mood was not broken until a few moments later when above the traffic sounds of noontime London, they heard his driver shout, "Mayfair ahead, sir!"

The suddenness with which he disengaged himself from her and peered anxiously through the carriage window informed her again that this next obstacle could well be the most awesome and that, while she possessed his love now, she shortly would be in the presence of the woman who had possessed his love all his life and there was a remote, though real, possibility that she would not take kindly to sharing it with anyone.

"You look as lovely as ever," he said hurriedly as the carriage drew up before the pavement. "Come. We're both home. And safe. At least for a while."

In spite of all her anxieties, she made an attempt to straighten her hair and thought with a wave of bleak humor that if her unborn son ever brought home a woman who looked like herself she would throw the baggage out. Pray God that Mrs. Stanhope possessed a more loving and understanding nature.

Clinging to Burke's arm for support in the face of her persistent weakness compounded by fear, they made their way slowly up the steps. As she heard the front door open, her heart almost stopped and quickly she looked ahead, expecting to see a stern-faced American matriarch.

Instead she saw a tall, razor-thin elderly Negro man in meticulous black jacket.

"Charles"—Burke smiled—"the prodigal has returned."

Without a word the old man stepped to one side. "Luggage, sir?" he inquired, his speech the same as Burke's, soft and musical.

"No," Burke said, trying to mask the embarrassment of travelers without luggage.

During the brief exchange Mary withdrew a step and found herself in a handsome entrance hall. From where she stood she could see into the library, the warmth of a small fire crackling in the firewell, the entire house in its quiet elegance reminding her of Elizabeth's house in St. George Street.

Suffering a pang of homesickness, she looked up to see Burke at her side again, the two of them now confronting a small group of Negroes.

"Allow me to present Lady Mary Eden," Burke said, his arm about her waist, as though it were his intention to demonstrate his affection, thus setting the tone on how the others should receive her.

Nothing more was said, and she was painfully aware of all eyes upon her. Now Burke was singling out specific servants for personal identification. "And this is Florence," he said, gesturing toward a dignified woman. "She raised me," he added, in a tone of affection, "and knows all my faults."

If the humor registered with Florence, she gave no indication of it but continued to stare at Mary, those alert eyes taking in everything.

Under such a gaze, Mary bowed her head. Burke, sensing the awkwardness of the moment, added sternly, "She will be our guest here indefinitely. She is recovering from a severe illness and I would appreciate any kindness that you can bestow upon her. If the guest chamber is in order, Florence," he went on, "would you be so good as to escort Lady Mary there and see that a fire is laid and that she has everything she needs."

Slowly Mary looked up to see the stern old woman's face as neutral as though she were wearing a mask. As she started up the stairs, the other servants dispersed. In a ragtag procession, those remaining started up the stairs, Florence leading the way, Burke with his arm securely about Mary's shoulder, and directly behind came Charles, the metal tips of his shoes hammering out a small dirge.

It wasn't until they were midway up the stairs that

Burke asked the question that was predominant on his mind. "My—mother, Charles," he inquired. "Is—she—"

"Well, sir," the old man interrupted, as though it embarrassed him to discuss such matters in the presence of strangers.

"Is she—"

"She is in her sitting room," Charles interrupted again. "Shall I tell her—"

"No, I will."

During these taut half-sentences Mary's alarm vaulted. Then they were moving again down a smaller corridor on the right, though Burke's attention seemed to be focused on broad closed double doors at the head of the stairs. The throne room, Mary suspected, and felt the presence of the invisible mother.

"Only a few more steps," Burke urged, and then they were inside the guest chamber, a small though lovely room, with a high, broad window obscured by heavy drapes, though Florence threw them open and the entire room was suddenly warmed by an explosion of high-noon January sun.

Without words, Burke led her to a comfortable chair and stood beside her while they both watched the preparation of the room. With what little energy she had left, Mary tried to marshal a degree of understanding. After all, she had arrived unannounced and unexpected, and this household was not an ordinary one in any sense of the word. Burke had told her enough to confirm that. All these people were exiles, driven to London by a war which had destroyed their homes. Though it saddened her to think it, she suspected that London had not received them with warmth. Small wonder that all appeared suspicious.

Then the burden was on her, the task of proving to them that she was not a threat.

"You must rest now," Burke whispered.

She nodded, not looking up.

"I'll go to my mother," he added as the servants were leaving the room. "I'll come for you in a while and we'll have tea with her."

Long before she was ready for it the room was emptied, a small fire burning in the firewell, the bed freshly made with clean linens and a full pitcher of water resting on the china stand.

After this brief inspection, she lifted her head in an attempt to draw breath and tried to rise from the chair so that she might cleanse herself and perhaps work a miracle of grooming, as Elizabeth used to say.

But the mood and the moment were too bleak. Without the support of Burke's presence she discovered that momentarily she could not move and was forced to remain seated, her hands curled in her lap, her shoulders bowed, her vision fixed on a future which seemed as hazardous as the past.

At four o'clock that afternoon Mary stood before the mirror and stared back at a sparrow in black.

The dress, of course, had been unalterable. Like death, it had to be endured. But she'd managed to cleanse her face and pinch a degree of color into her cheeks and, with the help of a comb and brush she'd found in the top drawer of the dressing table, she'd brushed her hair vigorously and had been pleased to see it falling into soft waves which framed her face and seemed to fill it out.

Though still weak, a brief nap had taken the edge off her despair. Well then, she thought with dispatch, turning away from the mirror, she'd done all she could do, at least to the exterior creature known as Mary Eden. As for the interior woman, that she could control completely and, in spite of everything, she found herself looking forward to her meeting with Caroline Stanhope.

Standing at the window in a blaze of late-afternoon sun, she vowed to bring to the meeting all the love and understanding that she could muster. For Burke's sake. It was not implausible to assume that all would go well. She'd learned one lesson through her various ordeals, the all-important one that few people in this world were blessed with such an abundance of love that they could afford to turn their backs on offers of new love. For now, that was all she could offer Caroline Stanhope—a rich love and gratitude for her son.

Deriving strength from these thoughts, Mary leaned against the windowsill and, as she'd been thinking on mothers, she thought on her own and her heart ached for that remote woman who resided in the third-floor chamber of Eden Castle. She felt a second surge of homesickness even more painful than the first, for Eden, for her mother, for the place of her childhood. Perhaps in time they might return there. Surely the threats of London would not extend to North Devon. How her mother would adore Burke and how pleased she would be for both of them in their newfound love!

She heard a knock on the door, heard a familiar voice call, "Mary?"

In a rush of love, as though they had been separated for days instead of hours, she hurried to the door.

"Burke, come in," she invited, grasping his hand, feeling that lovely surge that accompanies all love, the sensation of being needed. "Your mother—" she whispered, the top of her head just touching his chin, his powerful arms wrapped about her, providing the only shelter she would ever need in this world.

"—is expecting us." He smiled down on her and kissed her forehead.

"Is she—well?" Mary inquired, reluctantly stepping away from his embrace, aware of more pressing matters.

"Surprisingly, yes."

She took his hand. "Then come," she urged, "I look forward to meeting her."

In the corridor she saw they were not alone, saw Florence just departing through the double doors at the top of the stairs. The woman glanced in their direction, then wordlessly descended the stairs.

Taking his arm against the sudden chill, Mary leaned against him and whispered, "Any last-minute advice? Shall I be talkative or demure? Aggressive or passive?"

He drew her beneath his arm. "I've told her everything. Who you are, the circumstances under which we met, and that I've asked you to be my wife."

"Perhaps you told her too much."

"No. I wanted her to know everything."

Then he drew open the doors and stepped back to permit her passage and, as she moved forward, she took note of an immense and lovely chamber, a sitting room-bedchamber combined, a massive four-poster dominating one end of the room, while to one side near four large windows was a comfortable arrangement of furniture, a dark green velvet sofa flanked by wing chairs, the walls on either side of the windows covered by enormous tapestries. Her initial impression was that of an oversized room filled with oversized furnishings, yet void of any human being.

A moment later that impression was obliterated. She

saw at the far end of the room a small figure, dwarfed
by the size of the chair in which she was seated, garbed
in a dressing gown of ivory velour, her head surrounded
by a halo of thin, fly-away white hair, her attention focused on what appeared to be a large ripe pear, all her
concentration angled downward on the silver paring
knife which she was guiding expertly around and around
the fruit, producing an unbroken tail of peeling which
was falling into a small silver bowl nestled in her lap.

Burke seemed content to hold his position just inside
the doors, considerately giving Mary time to adjust to the
setting and give his mother time to look up and acknowledge them.

But this she never did, and continued to guide the
knife around and around the fruit, holding it up at an
angle, as though her fading eyesight were making the
simple task difficult.

When after several minutes there still had been no direct invitation to come forward, and when the pear had
been completely peeled, and after she had gazed upon
the paring knife as though it were a miracle of invention,
and when the tension of waiting had become embarrassing, Burke took matters into his own hand, grasped Mary's
arm and with a look of annoyance started them both
moving across the distance which separated them from
the woman sitting placidly in the spill of sun.

"Mother, this is—"

"Do you have any idea who sent this lovely fruit,
Burke?" she asked, holding up the pear as well for his
inspection. "They arrived yesterday without so much as a
card. Now who do we know who would be so thoughtful?" she went on, her voice striking the silence like something soft and boneless, her words a liquid stream, each
connected to the other.

"If you ask me," she said, "it was that nice Mr. John
Thadeus Delane. Yes, that's who, I'm certain. Did I tell
you he called twice during your rude absence? He did.
Quite an attentive gentleman, even though he is foreign."

Mary held her place several steps removed from the
woman, aware that she was being ignored, yet fascinated
by the remains of what once must have been a dazzlingly
beautiful woman. All the evidence was still there in the
high, classic cheekbones, the curved angle of the jaw, the
violet eyes imbedded in equally violet shadows that con-

tinued to study the pear as though it were the most fascinating object in the world.

In a rapid movement she lifted the pear and sliced it in half, the sun catching on the fast-moving knife.

"Here." She smiled sweetly, extending half of the pear to Burke. "You look wretched."

Taken aback by the offering, Burke started forward, then stopped, retraced his steps, grasped Mary's hand, this time taking her with him.

"Mother, this is Mary Eden," he said, his voice forceful, as though trying to cut through the foolish subject of fruit.

Those violet eyes were upon her, though they appeared to have gone blank. Struggling against a temptation to turn and flee the awkward encounter, Mary ventured forward until she stood less than three feet before the woman.

As the reciprocal inspection stretched on, she was on the verge of retreating when the woman motioned for her to come closer and, without hesitation, Mary did so, only to see that blue-veined hand which still clasped the knife reach up for her face, two bony fingers possessing surprising strength holding her fast.

"Forgive an old woman, my dear"—she smiled, their faces only inches apart—"but my failing eyesight makes this rude inspection necessary. I have a right, don't you agree, to see the face of the woman who has stolen my son."

Embarrassed, Mary did well to murmur, "I hope I didn't steal anything, Mrs. Stanhope, I—"

"No, of course not!" The woman laughed lightly, at last releasing her and turning her attention back to the fruit, slicing off a smaller portion and popping it into her mouth. Everything in the room seemed to wait upon her chewing. Mary felt herself almost mesmerized by the ugliness and the tension.

"No, of course you didn't steal anything," Mrs. Stanhope repeated. "From what Burke tells me, he's the thief. He's the one who kidnapped you and—"

"Mother, we would like tea," Burke interrupted. "Will you pour, or shall I?"

Waving the knife before her, Mrs. Stanhope murmured, "You do it, my dearest. My hands are unsteady of late. I'd more than likely spill it and embarrass you."

As Burke moved toward the table, she added not unkindly to Mary, "And do help yourself, child. You both look as though you forgot altogether to eat during your escapade."

Wordlessly Mary accepted a cup of steaming tea from Burke and read the message of encouragement and love in his eyes and selected a small sandwich from the platter and stood, as self-conscious as she'd ever felt in her life.

With the half-eaten pear still suspended in one hand, Mrs. Stanhope seemed to sit in a state of suspended animation, her eyes fixed on Mary. "You were pretty once," she said, "and you might be again, though it's hard to tell."

"Come, sit here near me," Mrs. Stanhope said, pouting. "I must see who has stolen Burke from me."

There it was again, that pouting, small-girl quality. And, to Mary's distress, he saw Burke arrange a second chair directly in front of the old woman.

As she sat in the appointed place, Mary felt a hot flush on her face. Burke offered her another cup of tea, but she said "No" and felt his hand close about hers in reassurance.

His mother saw it, as well, and from where Mary sat she saw the façade drop, the old woman looking as stricken as though someone had driven a knife into her breast. Not wanting to inflict hurt, Mary withdrew her hand and searched her mind for a safe topic of conversation. Her eyes fell on a small basket of needlework half-concealed beneath the skirt of the table. "Yours?" Mary smiled, pointing toward the basket, convinced that it was a harmless topic.

But the woman failed to respond. She seemed to be studying the knife, the delicate ivory handle, the joint which connected the handle to the blade.

"How long will you be here?" she asked.

Burke replied. "I told you, Mother. She's here for purposes of recuperation, as my guest."

"She doesn't look ill."

"I assure you she has been very ill. She needs rest and peace and—"

"Why does she have to come here? Has it ever occurred to you that her family may have good reasons for not taking her back?"

As the voice rose it became less soft and musical. Mary bowed her head. She'd never known such mortification. It was not working. It might tomorrow, or the day after, but not now.

"Burke, may I be excused?" she asked, starting to her feet.

"No!"

The harsh word, so unexpected, slammed against her. Shocked, she looked up to see the full weight of his anger directed at his mother.

"No," he repeated, softer this time, sitting on the edge of his chair, reaching for Mary's hand. "I want to say something and I want you here when I say it."

He renewed his grasp on her hand, as though fearful she might flee the room prematurely. "Look at us!" he commanded his mother.

When at first she did not, he repeated: "Look at us, Mother, and grow accustomed to the sight. I mean what I said earlier. I intend to marry her just as soon as possible and, while I would like your blessing, I do not require it."

He paused, as though giving the words a chance to register with that wandering mind.

"Did you hear me, Mother?"

Then she did, for she looked up, her face contorted with grief, and suddenly the handkerchief was pressed into service, covering her eyes, as the tears came.

The sound and sight of grieving resurrected other memories within Mary and represented all the losses she had ever suffered and, much to her surprise, she felt a bond of affection for the old, half-mad woman. Without knowing what she was going to do, she went down on her knees before her and grasped her hands.

"Mrs. Stanhope, please," she begged. "There's no need. Burke's love for me does not in any way affect his love for you. You must understand that and believe it. I have no desire to displace you in his affection or come between you in any way. Instead of cutting off his love for you, please let me contribute to it. I would very likely be dead by now if it weren't for him and, since you gave him life, then my debt of gratitude is to you as much as it is to him. Do you understand what I am saying?"

She wasn't certain whether the woman had heard or not. Then the tears seemed to subside. The old woman looked down on her, an expression on her face which was impossible for Mary to read.

"You are—very kind," she said. Then she looked at Burke. "When—will you marry?" she asked.

"As soon as possible."

She stared at him for ever so long. "Then it shall be." Her head fell back against the cushions of her chair. "You both must forgive a very rude and thoughtless old lady. If I've inflicted pain, I'm sorry. If I've caused—"

"No need," Mary said, trying to relieve her of the need for an apology. "I'm certain that in time we will become fast friends. I would like that very much and I would hope—"

All at once that thin hand lifted and began another inspection of Mary's face. No longer weeping, Mrs. Stanhope viewed her with quiet melancholy.

"You *will* be beautiful again!" She smiled sadly. "Under the effects of my son's love you will become ravishingly beautiful."

In spite of the blush on her face, Mary held still, something within her suggesting that it would be best to let the woman talk herself out.

"Leave me now, both of you," Mrs. Stanhope whispered. "I'm not fit company. Perhaps tomorrow I'll make a fresh start. I'm good at fresh starts, aren't I, Burke?"

"Yes, Mother." He smiled, lifting the bowl from her lap.

Mary moved back, weakened by her kneeling position and the tension of the occasion. She watched as Burke bent over and kissed his mother. "Sleep now. Tomorrow we'll talk some more."

"No more talk," she said. "I'm tired—so tired—"

As her voice drifted, Mary watched, amazed at how rapidly sleep had descended. Neither spoke until they were in the corridor outside. Then, as always, words were not as effective as the closeness of an embrace. "I'm so sorry," he murmured. Sensing new weakness in her, and in a way apologizing for the recent ordeal, he lifted her into his arms and carried her back down the corridor to her chamber.

Inside the room he placed her on the bed, remained bent over her long enough for a kiss, then almost paternally he counseled, "You sleep, as well. I'll send Florence to you. If you need anything—"

"I need only you," she said, wishing that he would sit on the side of the bed forever. Then she saw the fatigue in his face and remembered the countless nights when he'd not closed his eyes at all.

"Oh, my dearest," she whispered, and he was in her arms again, the nature of their closeness changing rapidly. She felt his hand on the small of her back, as though he were trying to lift her to him, his face buried in her neck, his breath warm against her flesh. As his hand commenced a loving caress of her breast, she shut her eyes. Though close, they were not close enough and, in spite of their mutual fatigue, or because of it, she drew him yet closer, cursing the barrier of their garments, unmindful of anything but the need within her.

His suffering was as acute, she was convinced of it, and with night breathing peace on all sides, he raised up and stared down on her.

He had just loosened the top buttons of her dress when suddenly a knock came at the door. Their eyes met in a moment of shared desolation. "Who is it?" he called out.

"It's me, Florence. I thought the young lady might enjoy—"

Mary tried to hide a smile, and tried even harder to still those sensate points within her.

"I'm afraid they're determined to keep us proper," he muttered. "Wait a minute," he called out to the closed door, then returned for a final kiss and whispered plea. "Marry me soon," he begged, "and I'll put a bolt on that door, and anyone who knocks will do so at their own risk!"

"Mr. Burke, are you in there? I know you are!"

In answer to Florence's insistent voice, Burke stood up from the bed and shouted, "I'm coming!" At the door he looked at her, the longing clear in his face. "Sleep well. Tomorrow we'll make plans."

She nodded and rejoined the loosened buttons, sensing that a puritan would shortly enter the room.

And she did. As her sharp old eyes darted about, Florence stepped briskly past Burke and carried a dinner tray to the side of the bed. "Soup," she pronounced flatly. "And I brought you a nightdress."

"Thank you," Mary murmured, pushing up to a sitting position. At the door she saw Burke still watching.

Florence saw him as well. "You run along now, Mr. Burke," she scolded, as though he were a boy of five. "Charles is waiting to tend you."

Burke nodded, though he lingered long enough to throw her a kiss, which she received gratefully before turning her attention to the fussy old woman who was moving a small table to the edge of the bed, then placing the dinner tray on it.

"Eat!" she commanded. "Ain't enough flesh on you for a man to grab hold of."

As she finished the broth and permitted Florence to undress her she felt a curious lassitude extend to all parts of her mind and body. For the first time in her life she enjoyed an almost dazzling simplicity of vision. There was only one path that led to only one future. And both led to Burke. Her days as a fugitive were over. She was connected in heart and soul and mind and, one day soon, body. Never again would the world change its shape. It was fixed and she with it, and, while there might be hazards like Caroline Stanhope, there would never again be terror or defeat.

Garbed in the clean white nightdress, she lay back against the pillows, her eyes heavy with sleep.

"Thank you," she murmured to the woman standing at the foot of the bed. She had wanted to say more, but her mind called a recess and she slipped instantly into a healing sleep, the long nightmare over, her head filled with luminous dreams.

She awakened to darkness, though beyond the window she saw the first pale streaks of light altering the night sky. She lay still, not absolutely certain where she was. As the familiar contours of the room appeared before her, she sat up, feeling remarkably restored.

She dressed quickly in the chill room, drawing on the black dress for what she hoped would be the last time. Never had she felt so suffused with love. She wanted to explore everything—the house, the gardens, the closed rooms which she'd observed the night before.

Thus dressed and groomed to the best of her ability, she stood and pondered the miracle of her resurrection. The clock was ticking on the bureau. Six-thirty. From someplace in the house she smelled the good odor of breakfast. She was starved. And was Burke still abed? *He won't be for long,* she thought, and smiled mischievously as she pondered the countless ways in which she might awaken him. How was it possible that her existence less than a month ago had been unbearable? How was any of it possible, that she would be standing here, her heart filled to such an extent that she felt tears in her eyes. Happiness was as great a hazard as grief. Both had to be assimilated gradually.

Ready for movement, for the sound of human voices, for the touch of a specific hand, she took a last look in her glass and saw her face bathed in the rosy light of dawn and hurried out into the corridor where she saw Florence just climbing the stairs, bearing a heavily laden tray which gave off irresistible odors, and heading toward the closed double doors which led to Mrs. Stanhope's chambers.

"Florence, wait!" she called out, and saw the old woman glance surprised in her direction.

"You're up and about early," she scolded, climbing to the top of the stairs, where she paused for breath.

Mary smiled. "I slept the night through, and I've never felt better, thanks to you and your kindness."

Embarrassed, Florence ducked her head and covered the moment with characteristic gruffness. "Well, you'll have to wait your turn for breakfast. This here is for Mrs. Stanhope. She's—"

An idea occurred to Mary. "Let me take it in," she suggested.

"Oh, no, I couldn't—"

"Please, Florence," she begged. "I used to take my mother her breakfast and nothing pleased her more."

Still the old woman hesitated. But the idea had taken root in Mary's head. Perhaps in the kindness of an early-morning encounter, the harshness of last evening would be forgotten.

"Please, Florence. It's important to me."

At last the old woman relented. "Well, I'm not saying she's going to like it," she muttered, passing the tray over to Mary. "She likes things the way she's been accustomed to them, but maybe—"

"Thank you."

"See to it that she eats, you hear?" Florence added, pushing open the door for Mary to pass through. Without warning the stern face softened. "She always wanted a daughter. I've heard her say it thousands of times."

Grateful for the supportive words, Mary smiled her thanks, renewed her grasp on the tray and turned to face the large chamber which, to her surprise, was aglow with every lamp burning.

Mary glanced at the four-poster at the end of the room and saw only a mound of down comforts, three or four at least, and remembered how her mother used to complain of night cold, something about the blood thinning with age, she assumed.

The weight of the tray was beginning to make her arms tremble and she moved toward the bed, never taking her eyes off the still head resting on the pillow.

Carefully she placed the tray on the bedside table, monitoring that face closely for signs of consciousness. Still sleeping? Then how to awaken her gently with news of breakfast and soft reassurances that she'd come in love?

She stepped back from the table and was just approaching the side of the bed when her foot struck something. Looking down, she saw a glint of silver, a familiar carved ivory handle, the paring knife which she recognized from the night before. Stooping to retrieve it, her hand was just going down when she noticed what appeared to be moisture, something red and glistening slipping out from underneath the comforts, culminating in a slight though steady stream.

Her hand, still moving toward the knife, altered its course. Two fingers moved toward the curious moisture, touched it, then slowly drew back and presented themselves for her inspection.

It was sticky, quite thick, like—

Suddenly she looked up to the side of the bed, traced the river to its source someplace beneath the comforts, her mind unfortunately moving ahead of her hand, connecting instantly the presence of the knife with—

No!

Had she screamed? Someone was screaming. Yet why did she seem blanketed in silence, and why was she drawing back the comforts to see what she had already seen, those thin arms lying limp beside that skeletal body, the comforts, the ivory dressing gown, everything, floating in blood, the wrists severed, turned upward at a rigid angle, as though she were a supplicant presenting evidence of her deed to a higher authority.

Reflexively, Mary stepped back from the horror, though the sight followed after her, boring into her brain. Quickly she reached out for the bedposts in need of support. As she grabbed hold, the bed moved, the head on the pillow stirred, as though she were awakening from a night's sleep.

The mysterious screams inside Mary's head had grown silent and all she heard now was a child whimpering, a sound so slight that it could not begin to drown out the terror coming from the bed, the old woman staring up at her from out of a sunken face. Her eyes opened and fixed on Mary. "I—had hoped you would come in time, and now you have."

In response Mary shook her head, as though with that simple movement to deny what she saw, what she heard.

"You see, my dear," the old woman went on with effort, "I could never compete with you alive. But dead—" A radiant smile covered those colorless features. "Dead, I'll defeat you. My ghost will lie between you and my son every night. At first he will blame himself. But he will blame you in the end, and how wretched you both will be!"

"No, please—"

"I—wish you only—heartache." The woman sighed. Suddenly her fingers curled in a convulsive movement, the blood spilling out from her wrists increased. In a final effort she turned her head until she was facing Mary directly, her eyes opened, though fixed and staring.

Clinging to the post, Mary tried to back away from that gaze. But she seemed to be locked on the horror, all breath deserting her, as recently it had deserted the old woman.

The child was whimpering again, a mindless repetition of one word. "No. No. No—" The rest of the chamber fell away, and she was left suspended on one small high pinnacle, clinging to the post, knowing that if she moved in any direction she, too, would fall.

Yet, given a conscious choice between those staring eyes and that dead face smiling, she willingly chose the abyss and took the distressed child with her and felt herself spiraling through a black emptiness which, though frightening, was preferable to the world she'd left behind. . . .

Two weeks after Caroline Stanhope's funeral, John Thadeus Delane sat in the library of the Mayfair house and silently thanked whatever God had looked over him all these years for sparing him the agony of a passionate love.

The face opposite him on the sofa bore no resemblance to the man he'd known as a boy. This face, lined with recent grief and new worry, belonged to an old man who had, on too many occasions, been pushed to the limits of endurance.

"What precisely is it that you want me to do, Burke?" he prodded gently.

When Burke did not answer, Delane leaned back against the cushions, relying on the philosophy that had served him well all his life. Put everything into perspective, then form as objective a judgment as possible.

This, then, was Delane's dispassionate judgment: with the exception of Caroline Stanhope's suicide, the whole affair had all the melodramatic aspects of a penny novel —the abducted female spirited out from under the nose of her keeper, a romantic illness in a country inn, the invalid brought back and ensconced in her lover's house, where now she suffered a setback, a mysterious illness beyond the diagnostic powers of modern medicine.

Pleased with his sensible assessment, Delane looked at his friend and felt his pleasure diminishing. There was nothing false or melodramatic about that face, his jaw lined with a stubble of rough beard, his hands visibly trembling as he shielded his eyes from the midmorning sun.

Moved by the sight in spite of his objectivity, Delane leaned forward, ready to help in whatever way he could, though his initial impulse was to lecture. Hadn't he warned Burke months ago against any involvement with the Eden girl? "What can I do?" he asked simply. "For your own good you must find relief soon."

Burke lowered his hands, revealing every detail of his face, the eyes heavy from lack of sleep. He had been a model of strength at his mother's funeral. The disintegration had commenced later with the girl's mysterious illness, the inability of the doctors to help her.

Standing before Delane, he requested, "Will you see her? Please?"

Everything in Delane resisted. "I'm not a medical man."

"I trust your judgment."

"I don't even know what to look for."

"I did not bring her all this way to lose her!"

"You should never have become involved in the first place."

"I had no choice."

There was something helpless in Burke's voice that suggested he had never spoken a greater truth.

Then nothing to do but go and play medical man. As he rose from the sofa it occurred to him that he *was* curious about this cousin of John Murrey Eden's, this remarkable young woman who had captured the heart of one of London's most pre-eminent bachelors.

With a look of gratitude Burke led the way up the stairs, where they encountered Florence just coming down, her normally neutral face showing the strain of this household for the last few weeks.

"I bathed her, Mr. Burke," she said, "but she wouldn't eat."

Burke nodded, a resignation in his manner which suggested he'd heard those words before. Halfway up the stairs, his pace slowed and, with rising sympathy, Delane tried to move him rapidly past the closed doors which had been his mother's death chamber. The young Eden woman had discovered her, or so Burke had told him the day of the funeral.

Delane stared at the closed doors, suffering a sudden understanding of Mary Eden's illness. He'd seen severed wrists before. Only last year Lord Addison had chosen the method rather than facing the scandal of adultery. Delane had been one of the first on the scene. The image had stayed with him for weeks.

Then they were standing before a smaller door at the end of the corridor, and the sense of the moment grew strong within him. If another death occurred—and what a spectacular death this one would be, John Murrey Eden descending like a wrath from God, the scandal of Mary Eden ensconced in Burke's household.

As the potential for disaster thundered down upon him, Delane pushed open the door of his own accord, though just inside the door he stopped and allowed Burke to take the lead, as he willingly did, the small figure on the bed drawing him forward like a magnet.

Delane followed as far as the foot of the bed and

stopped, staring down on the young woman, her eyes closed.

"Mary?" The voice was Burke's, who sat on the edge of the bed and lifted one hand and enclosed it between his own. "Mary, can you hear me?"

Watching, Delane had the feeling that she could. Her head turned in the direction of the voice, her eyes opened, then closed, as though the voice were a part of her nightmare.

For several moments Burke spoke softly to her, trying to coax her into speaking to him. But she never did, and Delane detected a stubbornness in her silence or, more accurately, a protective device. As long as she didn't respond, no one could involve her in any further horrors.

As these thoughts filled his head, he saw new suffering on Burke's face, saw him bend low over the young woman and take her into his arms, cradling her head as though she were an infant.

Before such intimacy, Delane turned away. As for a solution, he was bereft of ideas. Perhaps a woman would make a difference, draw her out of her silence. But what woman? An impersonal nurse? Old Florence?

Suddenly he looked back toward the bed as though someone had called to him. *By God, why didn't I think of it before? Why didn't Burke think of it? Elizabeth!* Good, sweet Elizabeth, who had raised the girl, who must surely by now have heard of Mary's disappearance and be sick with worry.

"Burke," he whispered, trying to draw the man's attention. He watched as Burke released her to the pillow. "Elizabeth," Delane suggested quietly as Burke joined him at midroom.

Slowly he began shaking his head. "No. I thought of her, but I'm not certain I can trust her."

"You don't have much choice."

"She's fiercely loyal to Eden."

"She raised Mary. There must be a bond of loyalty there as well."

Again Burke shook his head. "I can't risk it. If Eden were to learn of her whereabouts—I have no legal claim—he could take her away."

Delane nodded ruefully and wished that Burke had considered all these points of loyalty earlier. "If I can bring her here without detection, will you let her see the girl?"

"Of course, but—"

"Then I'm gone," Delane called back.

"He'll follow you," Burke warned, "and if he does, all is lost."

"It's going to be lost in another way if you don't—" But at the door Delane ceased speaking. The degree of pain on Burke's face was sufficient. It needed no more.

After Charles had helped him on with his cloak and seen him to his carriage, Delane settled back, feeling like an actor in a theatrical, the go-between, the loyal friend who brings help at the last moment.

Smiling at his foolishness, he closed his eyes to rest them from the glare of winter sun. He hadn't a plan in his head on how he would lure Elizabeth out of her house or if he would even find her at home. Compounding this vacuum was his remembrance of how tenderly Burke had held the young woman.

Well, lacking a great passion in his own life, perhaps the best he could do was to serve those more fortunate than himself. With longing he thought, *How would it have inconvenienced God to send me one small case of that irrational illness known as love?*

The meeting had been a good one—twice the number in attendance than they had counted on, a fair scattering of men among the women, a new coalition forming around the not quite dead corpse of the old feminist movement.

Stimulated by the afternoon at Lydia Becker's, Elizabeth gazed out the window at the passing London streets, aware that in about three more blocks the good feelings would desert her and be replaced by the depression which she'd come to associate with her home in St. George Street.

Perhaps she should sell Number Seven and move. Too much had happened there. Disappointments, tragedies unresolved, like Mary's continued absence.

Where is she? Elizabeth tried to discipline her thoughts. It served no purpose to torture herself. If Mary had wanted to contact her, she would have by now. Human beings change. The relationship that was so vital yesterday proves itself to be extraneous today.

As the maddeningly true cliché inundated her, she looked up and saw St. George Street ahead and tried to prepare herself for another empty evening, with only old Doris for company. The others, Aslam and Alex Aldwell, both of whom she was so fond, had stopped coming around, clearly on John's orders. She'd considered just last week making a trip to Eden to visit Harriet and try gently to apprise her of her daughter's mysterious and continued absence.

But she wasn't certain how welcome she would be there either. Eden, even more than London, was John's domain, and she could not endure the hurt of being turned back at the castle gates.

As these thoughts pressed against her, she braced herself for the turn into St. George Street, her driver brushing dangerously close to a large carriage parked on the right side of the street, curtains drawn.

Suspicious, she glanced back at it. Why was that one parked, with curtains drawn, the driver dozing in his greatcoat, as though someone within were maintaining a vigil?

John? Pray God, no. Yet, as her carriage circled wide for the approach to her house, she looked again and saw the driver stir, as though someone had given him orders and, even before her carriage had come to a halt before the pavement, that one was in motion.

Quickly she gathered up her belongings and was just alighting her carriage when she saw the other circle wide for the turn, its speed increasing. As she hurried up the stairs she prayed that Doris would respond immediately to the ringing of the bell.

Behind she heard the second carriage rattle to a sudden halt. With trembling hands she jerked on the bell cord, but still no Doris.

Damn! Alarm increasing, she looked at the large carriage, expecting to see John approaching. Instead she saw a gloved hand draw back the curtains almost timidly. She saw a man peering at her through the curtains. *Not John.* She breathed a sigh of relief and saw the man still staring at her, as though confident that she would recognize him.

Then she did. John Thadeus Delane.

"Elizabeth? A moment, please—"

As she approached Delane's carriage, she saw him push

open the carriage door, his face and manner conspiratorial.

"Forgive my—rudeness," he began, talking rapidly as though he must get it all said as quickly as possible. "Are you—alone?" he inquired foolishly, for he could see that she was.

"Of course," she replied. "May I ask why—"

"I beg you, ask nothing now," he broke in. "Please, are you certain there is no one awaiting you in the house?"

"Only my maid, and I'm not so certain of that. Now, what—"

"Please come with me," he said rather brusquely. "I have news."

Why should I accompany him—and news of what? "Mr. Delane, I must know the reason for this."

He leaned forward as though to draw her bodily into the carriage. "I have news," he said, "concerning Mary Eden."

"Mary—"

"Please come, I beg you. We haven't much time, and we mustn't be seen or followed."

He reached forward and clasped her hand, a new earnestness in his manner. "She needs you," was all he said, but that was enough.

With his help she pulled herself into the carriage and observed how quickly he locked and secured the door, then drew the curtains. Even after the carriage had commenced to move, he continued to draw back the curtains and peer out both windows. She'd never seen him so agitated.

Not until they were several blocks distant from St. George Street did he relax, and then a smug smile appeared on his old face as though he'd executed a great feat. "I think we did it, don't you?"

But Elizabeth's mind was still turning on that one name. "Where's Mary?" she demanded. "Is it far? You said she needed me. What has happened?"

In defense against her barrage of questions, he lifted both hands. "In time," he said. "First I want to ask a few questions of my own."

"What questions?"

"About John Murrey Eden."

"What about him?"

"How often do you see him?"

"I can't see what business that is of yours."

"If you want to see Mary Eden it is."

She stared across at him, trying to understand. She recalled a distant alliance, during the Eden Festivities almost a year ago, Mr. Delane in the company of the American.

"Mr. Stanhope—" she asked, trying to draw a connection.

"—is safe."

"Is Mary with him?"

Stubbornly he refused to answer and then she understood. Yes, Mary was with him—and how important it was that they conceal the fact from John or from anyone who might be loyal to him!

"Mr. Delane," she said, "my relationship with John has been severed. I've not seen him for several weeks and would prefer never to see him again in my life."

Dear Lord, how the words hurt! When she looked up, she was surprised to see him staring at her, as though in disbelief.

"Please take me to Mary," she begged. "I've missed her terribly. I promise I'll tell no one. Why should I? I'm more concerned for her safety than I am my own."

Finally he smiled, lifted his walking stick and tapped it three times on the ceiling of the carriage. "I don't know why I'm so worried," he murmured. "If their hiding place is discovered, they will simply find a new one. They *will* be together and only God will separate them."

"Tell me everything. How far is it? How long must we—"

"Not far, and I can only say that she's ill and that Burke is beside himself. We thought—that is to say, I thought—that your presence might make a difference."

Ill! She looked impatiently across the rocking carriage, wanting more. But obviously the stealth of the afternoon had taken a toll on the old man and he sat with his eyes closed, that self-satisfied smile still on his face, as though he'd performed his part and now it was left to others.

In an effort to calm her nerves, she closed her own eyes and envisioned Mary as she had been less than a year ago, full of life, willing to run any risk, taking the stage at Jeremy Sims' as though it belonged to her.

Reflexively Elizabeth shuddered. No more. A portion

of that warmth had been extinguished in a darkened garden, and the flicker that had remained undoubtedly had been quenched in the cold region of Miss Veal's school.

— What was left?

No need for an answer. Soon she would see for herself.

Delane had not dozed. He'd given the appearance of dozing in an attempt to avoid all her questions, feeling that Burke should answer them.

Yet her concerned impatience was difficult to watch, and when the carriage pulled up before the pavement in Mayfair, he saw her quickly alight. At the last minute he caught up with her and led the way up the stairs, where immediately the door was opened and he saw Charles on the other side.

"Come," the old man commanded. "You are to go directly up."

As they drew near to the top of the stairs, Delane looked down the corridor and saw Burke just emerging from her bedchamber. His face alone should have provided her with a fair indication of the seriousness of the moment.

Apparently it did. "Mr. Stanhope," she murmured.

He grasped her hands. "Thank you for coming." He looked beyond Elizabeth to Delane. "Were you followed?"

Before Delane could reply, Elizabeth answered for him. "No, I'm certain we were not. I've not seen John for several weeks. Our relationship has been severed."

From where Delane stood he saw the two staring at each other in a moment of assessment.

"Take me to her," Elizabeth said, breaking the spell of the quiet corridor.

Burke led her to the door with a succinct explanation. "She suffered pneumonia about three weeks ago. But she was well on the road to recovery. Then"—his voice fell, the explication became more painful—"two weeks ago my mother took her own life. Mary witnessed it—"

Edging closer, Delane saw Elizabeth's face, her expression one of shocked sympathy. She led the way into the room, her attention drawn to the young woman on the bed. Delane saw her sit on the edge, one hand brush-

ing lightly across the pale forehead. "Mary? It's Elizabeth."

Delane saw Burke step closer, drawn inevitably to his
love, the tension in the room manifested in his posture.

"Mary?"

It was Elizabeth, sitting back, appearing to be at ease,
her tone almost conversational. "This won't do, you
know," she scolded lightly. "Have you come this far only
to surrender? And so many are fighting for you!"

She glanced toward Burke. "Mr. Stanhope is here,"
she went on, addressing the silent face. She leaned close.
"Don't turn your back on us, Mary. We are all dealt suffering for a purpose. To strengthen us, to make us
more compassionate."

Still there was no response, yet Elizabeth went on. "Of
all the people I met at Eden so long ago, you and you
alone impressed me as possessing that degree of courage
which life demands. Of course, I could have been wrong,
but—"

All at once the head on the pillow stirred. Delane
looked closely, fully expecting Elizabeth to respond to
the movement, but she did not. She held her position on
the side of the bed and watched, along with everybody
else, as the eyes opened and moved directly to the face
of the woman who had just accused her of cowardice.

"Eliz—"

The half-formed word was scarcely audible. Then
Elizabeth reached out and lifted her into her arms, and
the last Delane saw before he turned away was the two
of them, Elizabeth's face buried in young Mary Eden's
hair, her arms locked about her, holding her. . . .

London
March 15, 1871

FOUR WEEKS LATER Mary sat by the rain-swept window
and wondered how many more resurrections were due
her. Like a cat with nine lives, did she have several to
go? She hoped not. Not that she wasn't grateful. It was

just that, surrounded by love as she had been for the past month, she doubted seriously if she could survive its loss.

Feeling the need to confirm the reality of that love, she glanced across the room toward the two who had drawn her back from the recent nightmare. They were like bears, the three of them. Burke, Elizabeth and herself inhabiting this small chamber in the house in Mayfair as though it were a safe cave against the chill of winter and other less easily identifiable threats.

Lovingly, her eyes focused on Elizabeth, who had, for all intent and purpose, moved into the house and now occupied the small chamber adjoining Mary's. Seeing her bent over her needlework in studied concentration, Mary smiled. She knew that Elizabeth hated needlework and undoubtedly had taken to it only in defense against the idle hours that always accompany recuperation.

From there Mary looked across the room toward the fire, to the true font of her rebirth, Burke, his legs stretched out toward the warmth of the fire, the London *Times* propped before him.

As the rain outside the window turned to stinging sleet, she drew the coverlet up about her and wondered how long it would be before they talked openly of his mother's death. She closed her eyes. She'd never told Burke about his mother's last words. She would have to one day, but not now.

"Mary?"

It was Elizabeth, her keen eyes missing nothing, in spite of the complicated needlework in her lap. "Are you certain it's not too cold for you there by the window? Why don't you return to bed, a brief nap before tea."

"I'm tired of bed," Mary murmured.

She was just reaching out for the nearest support when she saw Burke drop his newspaper and come to her aid. As his strong arms lent her support, she leaned against him, marveling at how appealing that hollow was beneath his chin.

"You're not ready to dance yet," he smiled, sitting with her on the edge of the bed.

"I'd just like to be able to walk."

"You will be soon," he soothed, lifting her hand and kissing it. In the manner of a loving father trying to deal with a bored child, he glanced back toward his abandoned newspaper. "Shall I read to you? I'm afraid it's dreary news for the most part—riots in France, Canada fears an invasion from America . . ."

"No," she said, neither willing nor able as yet to deal with the problems of the world.

Without warning, she thought of Eden, her mother, the headlands, those familiar corridors of her youth. "How long must we remain here?" she asked, gently forcing her fingers between his.

"Until you are stronger."

"And then?"

He shrugged. "Whatever you want."

She looked at him, this warm and handsome man who had pursued her with such zeal. How her mother would adore him! And suddenly how very much she wanted to show him Eden. Not just the pretentious castle he'd half-glimpsed almost a year ago, but all of Eden Point, the headlands, the tiny blue coves hidden at the foot of the steep cliffs, the carpet of wild flowers in the spring, the dramatic convergence of the channel with the ocean, a consummation of such force that the waves leapt high in a shimmering cascade of silver water. . . .

She bowed her head, overcome with remembrance of her home. "I—want to return to Eden," she announced tentatively.

"No!"

In the silence of the room she was aware of Elizabeth behind them listening. No matter. They had no secrets.

"Why not?" she asked, drawing free of his hand.

"It isn't safe," he said, his manner softening, though not his decision. "The risks are too great. I have no legal claim to you. Your cousin could—"

"He needn't know," Mary protested.

"How would we keep it from him?"

"My mother is there. Can't I ever see her again?"

"Not until—" He stopped speaking, his hands cupped about her face. "Marry me first."

She covered his hands with hers, an idea occurring, so right that she wondered how long it had lain in her subconscious. She leaned forward and lightly brushed his lips with hers. "I'll marry you at Eden."

He looked down at her, the indecision clear on his face. "Elizabeth?" he murmured, a soft cry for help, his love fighting a difficult battle with his better judgment.

As Mary turned she saw Elizabeth put her needlework aside, her face a neutral mask. Burke was looking toward her, the battle still raging. "The risks are too great," he said, even before she had spoken.

As she drew near to the foot of the bed, Mary saw her nod and feared that they would join sides against her. To her surprise, she heard Elizabeth say, "Still, it *is* her home."

"And John Murrey Eden's as well."

"But, as I told you, he knows that we are aware of his hand behind the conspiracy."

Burke shook his head. "Just because he has taken no action doesn't mean that he won't."

As the voices moved back and forth, Mary tried to keep up. Obviously they'd held long conversations, had explored all aspects of the hazardous situation.

"No," Burke said with renewed conviction. "The risks are too great, and we would have no protection there. The guardsmen would act on his command."

"Only if he were there to command them."

"And how do you propose to keep it a secret?"

"As I told you, he's quite involved here for now, has launched himself into a dozen building projects simultaneously. I can't imagine what would draw him back to Eden."

"No!" Burke said with greater force. "Here at least we have the safety of the city, the concealment of our position."

Elizabeth nodded. Then she added, "But at Eden you would have the support of the Countess Dowager, Mary's mother." She drew near, a smile on her face. "And a spring wedding at Eden would be lovely, good medicine for all of us."

Mary listened, daring to hope, not wanting to make things difficult for anyone but desperately wanting to see her home again, her mother, to share all with this man who occupied her heart.

"May I make a suggestion?" Elizabeth asked, a dispatch to her voice as though a decision had been reached.

"Please do," Burke muttered.

"I propose that we wait about three weeks, for the roads to clear, for Mary to regain her strength. Then I'll journey to Eden alone, talk with Lady Harriet, sound her

out, try to determine if we can count on her loyalty and
support. If I find out that all is well, then I'll send word
back to you and you both can proceed to Eden."

Mary gave a brief prayer of thanks. "You will love
it!" she exclaimed, reaching for Burke's hand, trying to
ease this new mood.

"I have no doubt," he replied, "but I love you more
and will do nothing to jeopardize—"

Elizabeth intervened. "If I don't feel that it's safe, I'll
return to London immediately."

"Then we'll wait for word," he concluded, not wholly
pacified but at least no longer objecting.

"It shouldn't be leisurely waiting." Elizabeth laughed.
"Look at you," she added, pointing to Mary. "Not a de-
cent gown to your name, at least not one that fits.
And now, in addition, you need a wedding gown."

Silenced by joy, Mary smiled up at the two looking down
at her. Through the muss of bed linens she found Burke's
hand and felt it close about hers.

"Come," Elizabeth ordered, reaching for his arm, moving effortlessly from the role of arbiter to that of mother
hen, "Mary needs her rest and we have plans to make."

There was no arguing with her. As Burke bent over
to kiss her, she wrapped her arms about his neck and
held him fast.

Then he was gone and she was alone.

Eden—

In spite of the chill gray day, that one word warmed
her. Never had she felt its pull so strongly. She saw in
her mind's eye an image of the family chapel filled with
flowers, saw herself in a white gown, Burke waiting
for her at the altar rail, her mother there, and Elizabeth
and perhaps Richard as well, and—

Suddenly she lost the image in a sudden chill. A door
someplace slammed shut.

John—

Tightly she closed her eyes and drew the coverlet up
over her head and tried to obliterate the faceless prem-
onitions with happier visions.

If Burke were with her, it might have been easier. But
alone, it was impossible.

Eden Castle
April 15, 1871

LADY HARRIET LIFTED her head and mourned the end of winter and solitude, and addressed the man who by her best estimate was standing about five feet in front of her.

"Then you have done all you can do, Lord Harrington," she said, wishing that the still grieving man had not involved her in his problem.

"Do I have your permission?" Lord Harrington asked, that same urgency in his voice that she'd heard for the last two days.

"You have it," she replied, "though I'm not certain that it's mine to give."

"What more can I do?" he demanded. "As I told you, I tried every day, sometimes three, four times a day, to see John. I even waited outside his house on occasion, like a spy. But I was always told that he'd either just left and would not be returning soon, or that he'd just come in and was in conference."

"Did you see Elizabeth?" she asked, vowing to keep her mind on the problem at hand. Not that it was a severe problem for anyone but poor Lord Harrington, who had returned from Ireland a fortnight ago for the purpose of reclaiming his two small grandsons and taking them on a grand tour of the mother country. He had journeyed to London in an attempt to find John and seal the promise which had been vaguely made immediately following Lila's death.

"Elizabeth?" Harriet asked. "Surely she would know."

"Gone," came the man's voice.

"Where?"

"Her maid couldn't or wouldn't say. I was simply told that she couldn't be reached."

Good, steady Elizabeth beyond reach? Well, undoubtedly Harriet would know all in time. The Eden family had a way of disappearing during the fierce North Devon winter months, only to come trailing back one by one with the first warming rays of the spring sun,

541

presenting Harriet with their various failures and victories.

"Take them with my blessing, Lord Harrington," she said, recalling the first and last time several months ago when she asked Miss Samson to bring the children to her chambers. Never had she been aware of two more spiritless little ghosts. Obviously she had frightened them with her black veil, and the entire afternoon had culminated in disaster, the boys weeping, Miss Samson scolding Peggy for serving them ginger cookies.

"Take them, Lord Harrington, and enjoy them, please, for their sakes as well as yours."

"John—"

"Leave John to me." She paused, other considerations following her first judgment. "You have help, of course."

"Yes. My friend Mr. Parnell will accompany us. And Lila's maid, Molly—"

"Good," she broke in, having heard enough.

While the boys were no longer infants, Stephen was now five and Frederick three, still they needed a woman's hand. There was one other question and she raised it, her mind running ahead to the day when she might have to answer John's questions.

"Your—destination, Lord Harrington. I should know that as well."

"We are going first to Mr. Parnell's home, Avondale in Wicklow. He says it is a perfect place for children— broad meadows, four new colts by his last count, and several sisters who have a tendency to view all children as their own."

"It sounds like paradise."

"I agree."

"Then take them with my blessing, Lord Harrington."

"Tell John that I tried to see him," he murmured. "And tell him that his sons will be protected by my life."

She felt his lips pressed against the back of her hand and he was gone, his steps sending back a good positive echo, like those of a man who was moving toward a desired goal.

It was approaching nine o'clock that same evening, and Peggy was preparing Harriet for bed, after having read to her Mr. Wordsworth's long, autobiographical poem, *The Prelude,* when Harriet heard the sound of a carriage in the inner courtyard below.

Peggy heard it as well and abandoned the hairbrush in Harriet's lap and hurried to the window.

"Who is it?" Harriet asked. Lord Harrington's party had departed around seven o'clock. Had something happened to force their return?

"I can't see, milady," Peggy called from the window.

"Then go immediately and find out," Harriet commanded.

She heard steps outside in the corridor.

"Milady," the old maid gasped, winded from her sprint down and up the stairs.

"Who is it?" Harriet demanded.

"It's Miss Elizabeth."

As the name registered, and the face of the loving soul behind it, Harriet felt relief.

A new fear surfaced. "Is she alone?"

"Quite alone."

"Come," Harriet requested in rising good spirits, "help make me presentable. I must—"

"No, milady," Peggy said. "She said she'd not disturb you this evening. The hour is late and she's exhausted. She said that a good night's sleep would serve you both for your reunion come morning."

"How I shall look forward to it," Harriet murmured. Oh, what a chat they would have—about everything.

"Good night, Peggy," Harriet replied. Then she added, "Tomorrow will be a glorious day."

Earlier that morning in the privacy of her chambers Elizabeth had prayed for strength, fully aware that she was facing one of the most difficult ordeals of her life.

God had generously obliged and had given her strength to climb to Harriet's third-floor chambers, to receive her loving greeting, to share breakfast with her, then, when she had deemed the time right, to ask for Harriet's attention.

God had sustained her throughout all of this, had even given her the power to speak succinctly yet honestly, omitting nothing, as she'd felt that for the sake of Mary's future Harriet must know all.

Unable to determine the effects her words were having on Harriet, the woman's face obscured, as always, by the black veil, Elizabeth had left nothing out. On and on in a steady voice she had catalogued the tragedies of the winter. It was approaching noon when she finally talked herself out and felt for the first time the departure of that strength which earlier had sustained her.

"Harriet, I felt you must know everything—for your children's sake, for your own."

For the first time in over three hours there was movement coming from the chair, one hand lifting as though to hold at bay any more words. She rested her head against the back of the chair. "Poor Mary."

Elizabeth was on the verge of telling her the joyous news, the impending wedding, the love which she shared with Mr. Stanhope. But before she had a chance, Harriet grasped her hand. "I must ask, Elizabeth. Have you—spoken the truth in all respects?"

"Yes."

"And the notes, the forged ones, are you certain that John—"

"Yes. On the occasion of his last visit to me he confessed as much."

"Where is he now?"

"Still in London, though I haven't seen him since—" She broke off. "I must confess, Harriet," she said wearily, "I don't understand. I've tried. Oh, how I've tried! But all I can see is Mary as she was brought home to me that night after—"

Harriet spoke softly. "In all of us, our creative urge is always linked to our self-destruction mechanism. In John, as in all great men, that link is even more insistent." She bowed her head. "How—unhappy he must be."

In that moment, Elizabeth felt for the first time the comfort of understanding. Having built his empire in London and his world at Eden, the incredible force known as John Murrey Eden had to turn his energies elsewhere. Unfortunately he'd tried to remake human beings in his own image, and had found flesh and blood to be less malleable to his will than iron and brick.

Now there was the future to consider, the remains of those shattered lives. To that end, Elizabeth raised up and posed the single question that had brought her to Eden. "Will you receive them?" she asked. "Mary and her young man? They want to be married. Here at Eden. Yet they are fearful that John will—"

"Of course I'll receive them," Harriet said without hesitation. "And tell Mary I'll give her the most beautiful spring wedding in the history of Eden." She paused. "This—American," she whispered. "You know him, of course."

"Yes, I know him. I lived in his house during Mary's recuperation."

"And?"

"And I found him to be one of the most remarkable gentlemen I have ever known. And most remarkable of all his deep love for your daughter."

"And it's reciprocal?"

At that Elizabeth laughed, recalling the light in Mary's eyes each time he'd entered the room. "Oh, yes." She smiled. "I assure you it is reciprocal."

"Good!" Harriet said briskly, her mind moving ahead to the future. "Then tell them to come, as soon as possible. I long to hold my daughter."

Confronted with the joy that once again had triumphed over tragedy, Elizabeth clasped Harriet to her. At the conclusion of the embrace, Harriet touched her cheek. "I am forever in your debt. Mary might have—"

"Rest now," Elizabeth counseled. "I'll send Peggy to you. We'll have dinner tonight together and indulge ourselves in that greatest of female pastimes, the planning of a wedding."

"I'll look forward to it." She said nothing more until Elizabeth had opened the door, then, "One last favor, Elizabeth."

Elizabeth looked back, ready to grant the woman anything.

"Will you help me write to Richard?"

"Of course. Anything else?"

"Yes. When you write to Mary and Mr. Stanhope, tell them they will be safe here. Tell them I will see to it. I do not fear John. We've done all we can do to each other. . . ."

In spite of the firmness of her manner, her voice drifted off. Quietly Elizabeth closed the door behind her and leaned against it.

"I do not fear John. We've done all we can do to each other."

What had she meant by that? In need of respite herself, and eager to dispatch the fastest courier to London with the letter to Mary and Burke, she hurried down the corridor toward her own chambers, amazed at the persistence of life.

❧❧

London
Mayfair
April 12, 1871

As FLORENCE WAS packing the last of her trunks, Mary stood by the window in the warming rays of the April sun and stared down at the curious old beggar she'd seen standing in the exact spot at various intervals during the last few days.

"Florence?" she called out. "Do you know him?" she asked, pointing down at the disreputable figure whose face was wholly obscured by the broad brim of his crushed, worn hat.

"Now how would I know him?" Florence scolded, annoyed for having been dragged away from the chores at hand.

"He's been standing there for ever so long," Mary murmured, feeling sorry for him, whoever he was.

"And he'll be standing there waiting for a handout long after you've gone!" Florence snapped. "Now, if I were you, I'd look to myself. Mr. Burke said he wanted to leave by six o'clock." She stabbed a finger toward the clock on the mantel. "One hour you got to make yourself presentable."

"Where is Burke?" Mary asked, her eyes still fixed on the old man across the street.

"I'm here," came the voice from the door.

She turned about, embarrassed to be in her dressing gown still. He'd left over an hour ago for the purpose of her dressing. As he met her at midroom in an embrace, she saw beyond his shoulder to Florence, who averted her eyes. "I'll finish," Mary called out, in an attempt to relieve the woman of her embarrassment.

"Finish!" the old woman pronounced dourly. "And I'll give you ten minutes," she added, "then I'll be knocking on the door ready to dress you."

As she slammed the door behind her, Mary laughed. "Has she always been like this?" she asked, as Burke sank into the bedside chair.

"Always," he confirmed, "or at least as long as I can remember, which is the same as always. My mother always said that it was Florence who ran Stanhope Hall, not her."

Standing before him, Mary saw it again, that sorrowful reflection when he mentioned his home. A moment later the reflection was gone, displaced by a fixed stare.

Gently she knelt before him, alarmed by such an expression. The bridegroom must be as joyous as the bride. Of course she knew what part of the trouble was. She was going home. He would never see his again.

"What is it?" she asked, drawing his legs close on either side, a provocative support. "You're not still worried, are you? About Eden?"

He shook his head. "If Elizabeth says it's safe, then I trust her. And it's what you want."

"Then what is it?" she prodded.

He looked down on her, his fingers moving through her hair, a pleasant though absentminded gesture. He laughed as though at his own foolishness. "Having plotted our lives up to this moment, I find now that—I've lost my direction."

"What do you mean?"

"After Eden, then what?"

"Then—back to London," she said vaguely. "Back here to—"

"To do what?"

"To do whatever you wish. Mr. Delane said—"

At the mention of the man who had been such a frequent and supportive visitor during the last three weeks, Burke laughed. "I think we all know that my days as Lord Ripples are over. I have no desire to inflict further pain—on anyone. Not even John Murrey Eden."

Then it was Mary's turn to retreat, the ghosts of the past still strong within her. Slowly she sat on the edge of

the bed and wondered if she could find the strength to
speak the words. For both of them.

"Then why don't we go to America?" she asked
simply, finding it easier than she'd ever thought possible.

He looked at her as though she had spoken in a
foreign language.

"Well, why not?" she went on. "It's your home and
soon it will be mine. And you're right. There's nothing
for you here in London."

"Are you—serious?"

"I've never been more serious." She smiled, amazed
at the shock on his face. Clearly the idea had not occurred to him. "And besides, I don't want you to have
to hide behind a false name ever again. I don't want to
be Mrs. Lord Ripples," she chided. "I want to be Mrs.
Burke Stanhope."

Her voice fell as the sense of her proposition fully
dawned on her. "And neither do I want either of us to
spend one minute of our future looking over our shoulder. We might conceal our marriage from him for a
while. But he'll find out, as he finds out everything,
and—"

As the possibility of a future as grim as the past
washed over her, she again knelt before him, her visions
of the future now fixed on America. "Please, Burke,"
she begged, and hoped it would suffice.

But he continued to look stunned. Instead of solving
the problem, apparently she'd only compounded it. "It's
—out of the question," he said flatly.

"Why?"

"This is your home."

"And America is yours."

"I—have no idea what we would find there."

"Whatever, we'll find it together."

"Everything was destroyed, in flames."

"Surely they have been extinguished by now."

"What—would I do?"

"What would you do here? You said yourself there
was nothing for you."

Suddenly he stood and brushed past her. For all the
quickness of his movement, he stopped at the foot of the
bed and looked back down on her.

"It—would be difficult."

"The past has been difficult," she reminded him gently.

"I can promise you nothing."

"I ask for nothing except your love."

"You would miss your home, Eden."

"In a few days Eden will no longer be my home. My place is with you."

As he leveled objection after objection, she tried to disarm them, gently though firmly. At last she saw a new expression on his face, one of old wounds being healed, one of possibility, of hope. "Perhaps—"

"Of course, perhaps," she said, rising to her feet. As she drew near to him she said with quiet conviction, "There's nothing here in England for either of us now, Burke—or rather too much, too many memories, too much grief—" She drew closer. "Then let's take ourselves away. Andrew did it, and Dhari—" She reached up and smoothed back that one errant strand of hair from his brow. "And remember old Giffen?" She smiled. "His last words were, 'I'll see you in America!' We can't disappoint him, can we?"

Then she was in his arms, locked in an embrace that was so tight it rendered her breathless. No matter. In spite of his strength she sensed a new calm within him, as though in that splintered fashion his mind had reached the decision that his heart had made years ago. The two forces were now joined.

There was a sharp rap at the door, immediately followed by Florence's voice. "Unless you want her to go to her wedding in her dressing gown, Mr. Burke, you better let me in now."

Abruptly he laughed, a curious sound, for in his eyes she saw emotion. "Hurry," he whispered. "I want to pause in front of Jeremy Sims' Song and Supper Club on our way out of London and thank God for directing my steps to that door."

She watched him leave the room and scarcely heard old Florence's grumbling, "Never seen such goings-on."

At precisely six o'clock, with the last trunk secured atop Burke's new roadworthy carriage, Mary descended the stairs in a beautiful traveling suit of dark green silk edged in black piping, a low-brimmed bonnet of curled peacock feathers on her head.

Burke was waiting for her on the pavement before the carriage. How pleased she was by the look in his eyes, the look of a man for whom the dream was on the verge of becoming a reality! Before she entered the carriage she lifted her eyes to the soft rose hues of early dusk. The world had never been so lovely.

He assisted her into the carriage and settled beside her. Not until the carriage had pulled away from the pavement did she think to look back.

Good! The old beggar had disappeared She hoped he'd find a home soon. She nestled closer beneath Burke's arm, grateful that she had at last found hers. . . .

The old beggar had not disappeared.

Alex Aldwell saw what happened. Perched atop his high carriage seat at the far end of the street, Alex had kept him forever in his sight. As young Mary had descended the stairs, Alex had seen the "beggar" dart down into the concealment of the kitchen entrance of the mansion across the way.

What in hell is going on? he thought. They had played this bizarre game every afternoon for the past week, John seeing to business affairs in the morning, then changing into the garments which he'd had Alex buy from the ragman.

Then they would come here to this quiet street where John would give Alex instructions to hold his position a block away while he pulled the worn hat low over his face, then hobbled up the street and took his place directly opposite the mansion.

Holding still, Alex watched as the last trunk was loaded and secured atop the carriage down the way, still wondering why John was hiding from the one person he wanted most in this world to see.

Well, there she was, standing on the pavement, and looking pretty as a picture for all the world to see. Then why hadn't John approached her? Why instead had he dashed down into the kitchen entrance, leaving Alex sitting high and stranded like a visible target?

Oh, Gawd! They would be passing directly by him, and quickly he lowered his head, pulled the collar of his jacket up about his face and tried to give the impression of a dozing coachman, all the while keeping one eye fixed on that approaching carriage, on the two in the back seat looking at each other as though there wasn't a sight in this world that held greater fascination for them.

Then they were gone, the carriage safely past, the horse picking up speed as they crossed the intersection, heading west toward the turnpike road.

Alex glanced back down the street in time to see the "beggar" emerging into the fading light of dusk and lift one hand, a signal that Alex was to bring the carriage forward.

As John pulled himself slowly inside the carriage, Alex waited patiently for directions. But they never came and, assuming that silence meant home, Alex flicked the reins and kept to the side streets and thought that at least it was over now, Mary and the gentleman on their way out of London to somewhere. Maybe now John would let Alex burn the ragman's clothes and they both could turn their attention to certain pressing business responsibilities—three litigations tomorrow alone involving the purchase of new properties.

A short time later Alex guided the carriage to a halt before John's house in Belgrave Square, with a sense of having seen the mystery through. "I'll take the carriage around back, John, and meet you in the office. There are some papers I want you to—"

Still no response, just those eyes staring up at him from out of the muss of rags and that soiled, crushed hat. "John—"

"We will be leaving for Eden in the morning," John said, his voice a monotone, nothing moving on his face.

"Eden?" Alex parroted, thinking he'd not heard correctly.

But there was no further response. Slowly John turned and commenced walking toward the steps, his head down.

"John, wait!" Alex called after him. If he lacked good sense, then someone had better provide him with it. "We—can't go to Eden," he protested. "You're due in court tomorrow, both in the morning as well as—"

"Aslam can handle it," came the vague reply.

Alex started to call after him again, but something warned him against it. He stared at the closed door, then lifted his head and stared straight up into the evening sky. He felt an internal tremor, a premonition of disaster.

"Gawd," Alex whispered, and for the first time in his life hoped with all his heart that He had heard.

Forbes Hall
April 15, 1871

LORD RICHARD EDEN sat at the bureau in the library of
Forbes Hall, Elizabeth's hastily scribbled note before
him, and looked about at the quiet domestic scene and
thought it interesting that he should feel so at home
among relative strangers.

Near the mullioned windows he saw Eleanor arranging a massive bouquet of early-blooming lilacs in a gleaming copper urn. The way the afternoon sun struck the
copper caused a flare of unearthly light to illuminate her
face.

"Remember symmetry," her mother counseled quietly
from the chair before the fire. "They prefer it when
no single blossom rises higher or falls lower than the
others."

Aware that he was staring, Richard looked down
upon Elizabeth's letter. Received only that morning by
special courier, it demanded a reply. But what?

Stymied, as he'd been for the better part of the day,
he leaned back in the chair and drank deep of the peace
which seemed to permeate the room: Lady Forbes' knitting needles performing a soft rhythmic clack over the
crackle of the fire, the occasional rustle of the London
Times as Lord Forbes shifted it in search of sufficient
light, nothing momentous occurring except that blessed
state where human beings surfeited with love were content to sit at peace.

It was a condition he'd searched for all his life, and
when he'd least expected to find it, indeed when he'd
given up all hope, it had appeared before him in the
guise of a kind, intelligent young woman, her equally
kind parents and their country seat of manageable proportions, scaled down to accommodate the frailty of
human beings.

What had started as merely an interim step, a safe
refuge in which to recover from Bertie's death and his
new awareness of the man who had caused it, had stretched

enjoyably into a stay of unlimited duration. He had tried to leave several times in the past. Not that he wanted to, but simply afraid that he was overstaying his welcome.

But all three, Eleanor and her mother and father, had dissuaded him in the most gracious of manners, persuading him that his absence would be a loss to all of them, that having raised three sons for better or worse, they enjoyed a male presence in the hall and his most specifically.

So, of course, he'd stayed, for where would he have gone? Back to Cambridge and all those memories? Hardly! To London? What was there in London for him? To Eden? And here was the most powerful denial of all. No, not to Eden, never back to Eden, not as long as the castle was in the hands of John Murrey Eden.

He must have made a sound, for Lady Forbes inquired gently, "Are you chilled, Richard? Bring your writing pad closer to the fire. The spring weather in Kent can be perverse at times. Sunny and warm, then chill."

"No, I'm fine, Lady Forbes," he said. "Thank you."

As he picked up the point, determined at least to write the salutation, he saw Eleanor watching him. "Would a walk help, Richard? A bit of fresh air to clear the head?"

"And postpone the ordeal." He smiled. "No, let me say what I must say, then I'll walk with you."

She nodded, more than willing to wait as long as necessary. Having made a promise, and grateful to her for her loving presence during these last difficult weeks, he dipped the point into the inkwell, shook it once, began the salutation, and hoped the rest would follow effortlessly.

MY DEAREST ELIZABETH,

I received your word only this morning on Mary's impending nuptials. All her life my sister has been in sore need of a loving and responsive heart, and I thank God that she now has found one.

As for attending the ceremony, I can only say that my heart will be there, but I will not. I plead with you to share this message with my sister and my mother. I ask only for their understanding, and yours. My mind and soul are such now that I find it impossible just to think of Eden Castle. In my imagination I see the Gatehouse and I can go no further. Though it grieves me to say it about the place of my birth, I can find no location, no single chamber or corridor in the vast castle that does not in some way contain a memory of pain.

Please understand, dear Elizabeth, what I will say now, and even as I write I am begging God's forgiveness. But as long as John Murrey Eden is connected in any way with Eden Point I will not return home. I do not wish him ill. I simply do not wish to place myself in his company.

Again I ask for your forgiveness and beg you to embrace my mother for me and tell Mary to write to me of her new life and love and convey to Mr. Stanhope my deep gratitude for loving my sister. And look to yourself as well. The cloud of darkness that enveloped my life hovers very close to you. You must be aware and vigilant.

And, dearest Elizabeth, I pray that this separation in no way affects the deep love which we have for one another. For now, I beg you not to think too harshly of me and please write again. I will be in residence here at Forbes Hall for a while longer. I realize I must chart a new course, but for the time being, I've been offered a safe harbor.

Please kiss Mary for me,

With deep affection,
RICHARD

He completed the last word and stared down on the parchment. Old habit suggested that he reread it for content and clarity. But new need insisted that it was not necessary. He knew what he had said and what he had done as well, cut himself off from his birthright, from the castle whose name he bore, from an unbroken line that stretched back to the twelfth century.

So be it! That pain was nothing compared to the projected pain of being in the presence of John Murrey Eden.

"Finished?"

The inquiry had come from Eleanor, who stood a short distance away, her cape over one arm, his over the other.

"Finished." He smiled, folding the parchment and

sealing it, vowing to send the special courier on his way by nightfall.

"Then let's walk," Eleanor suggested, handing him his wrap. "Come!" She laughed, running ahead.

Willingly, he followed.

❧

Eden Castle
April 16, 1871

ELIZABETH AND HARRIET had been on the steps of the Great Hall since early morning awaiting the arrival of Burke's carriage. They should have arrived yesterday, last night at the latest.

But thus far the horizon was clear, and watchmen stationed at half-mile intervals across the moors had all ridden back with the blunt announcement, "No one coming. No sight of a London carriage."

At noon, and aware that the waiting was beginning to take a toll on Harriet, Elizabeth kindly asked one of the stewards to fetch a chair for the Countess Dowager.

Though Harriet protested, Elizabeth saw her settled just inside the shade of the Great Hall arch, then went back to the top of the steps to resume her private vigil, not overly concerned but still anxious for their safe arrival. One source of her worry was standard. The condition of the roads in early spring was treacherous, deeply rutted and soft.

The second source of her worry was standard. *John.* The name took root in her mind and spread, causing a painful collision of emotions. How strange it was to dread his presence, to expect the worst from him and never to be disappointed.

Standing in the blaze of noon sun, she shivered at the unpredictability of human nature. Yet, in a curious way, what more could he do? He had wreaked havoc on every life at Eden save her own.

In the future she might even find a way to avoid that. Before she had left London, Lydia Becker had invited her to go to Paris with her, "a learning exercise," Lydia

had called it, a chance to witness the dedication of
French feminists, who were willing to be imprisoned for
their beliefs, as Louise Michel was now imprisoned at
Versailles.

Why not? Elizabeth thought courageously, and for one
incredible moment her mind went back to her past, that
frightened young girl who had crawled across the Common Cell in Newgate Prison and had offered herself to
Edward Eden.

The worlds between then and now! Paris with Lydia
and Maria! Why not indeed! That was the purpose,
wasn't it, of the new movement, the need for boundaries?

Suddenly she heard the sound of a horse approaching
rapidly beyond the castle gate.

In her excitement, Elizabeth started forward, then
turned back, remembering Harriet, who had heard the
sound as well and was now on her feet, seeking guidance.

"Here," Elizabeth soothed. "I'm here," she added,
grasping the woman's hand, feeling it tremble under the
duress of the moment. "We've time yet."

But at that moment the thundering approach of the
carriage filled her ears, led by two watchmen who had
ridden out to give them escort. In that brief instant before the carriage itself came into sight Elizabeth suffered
a painful fear. What if it wasn't them? What if something
had happened? What if John—

Again that single name caused her heart to accelerate,
and she grasped Harriet's arm with such strength that it
was difficult to tell who was supporting whom.

All at once she heard the clanging of the grilles as the
guards drew them up, saw the small dust cloud beyond
the opened gates, saw the guardsmen leading the large
carriage forward, and at last saw a beloved face at the
small oval window.

"They're here, Harriet!" she whispered excitedly. "It's
Mary."

As the carriage swung wide for the turn, she abandoned
Harriet at the top of the stairs and went forward to greet
the man who was just emerging from the carriage door,
that remarkable man who had pursued his love with
such diligence.

"Burke," she murmured, and kissed him, and saw his
face as restored as she'd ever seen it, the fatigue and
worry caused by Mary's illness gone, his eyes alert as

they swept the massive façade of Eden Castle, lingering on Lady Harriet still waiting at the top of the stairs, then turning immediately back to the door where, with moving gentleness, he reached out his hand to Mary and led her forward into the bright April sun.

Sweet Lord, but she looked beautiful! Elizabeth had never seen her more beautiful, her hair completely restored and turned expertly into a French knot, the pert bonnet of curled peacock feathers with their vivid blue eyes mirroring the blue of her own.

"Elizabeth—" Mary smiled and, as they came forward in embrace, Elizabeth clung to her and prayed silently that all her ordeals were behind her. Though she would have been content to hold her forever, she remembered the woman waiting at the top of the stairs, unable to see the rare beauty of this daughter and her handsome bridegroom.

Slowly Elizabeth released her and without words looked up toward the top of the stairs and the waiting Harriet. Then Mary started the steep ascent, her eyes fixed on her mother.

In spite of the rush of stewards removing the trunks from the carriage, Elizabeth heard Mary whisper one word, a simple word which somehow demolished the image of the confident young woman and left a vulnerable five-year-old child in her place.

"Mama—"

At the sound of the word, Elizabeth saw Harriet lift her head, heard a single soft cry of joy escape from beneath the black veil. Then she reached out and found her daughter and drew her into her embrace.

Elizabeth retrieved her handkerchief from the sleeve of her gown and saw Burke waiting by the carriage, faring none too well himself.

Thoughtfully she recalled the recent death of his mother and did not have to wonder at the nature of his thoughts, and stepped close to offer distraction. "Was the journey uneventful?" she asked, keeping her voice down, aware of a few servants sniffling near by, their face focused on the reunion at the top of the stairs.

"It was"—Burke nodded—"and very pleasant. We stopped by old Jeremy Sims' club on the way out of London."

Elizabeth looked up. "I don't have to ask why"—

she laughed—"and did Mary sing for the gentlemen?"

"No," Burke said. "Old Jeremy wouldn't permit it. But we all shared a bottle of champagne, and Sims said he'd played many roles in his life but he'd never played Cupid before."

"Did you have any difficulty in London?" she asked, knowing that he would understand the meaning behind the words.

"No, though I must confess I was expecting it daily. Do you think we have managed to elude him?"

"No," Elizabeth said without hesitation.

He stared down on her. "Do you think he will leave us alone?"

"No," she said, again without hesitation. Fearful that Burke would see the anxiety on her face, she took his arm and led him to the foot of the steps with a comforting reminder. "In a few days Mary will be yours, legally and forever. Then he can do nothing."

Aware of the falsity of that statement, she was on the verge of amending it when she looked up the stairs and saw Mary and Harriet whispering together. Mary looked down and wordlessly extended her hand to Burke. "Come."

He took the steps two at a time and was at her side within the instant. Elizabeth followed and heard Mary's introduction, "Mama, this is Burke—"

She might have said more, but at that instant Burke reached for Harriet's hand and kissed it, while Harriet in turn made a request.

"Mr. Stanhope—Burke," she amended, "may I see you in the only manner available to me?"

At first Elizabeth didn't understand, but Burke did, for immediately he took a step back, thus reducing his height, then lifted both her hands and placed them on the sides of his face, where her fingers began a tender exploration of his features, starting at the broad brow, moving down over his eyes, caressing the bridge of his nose, then fanning out on either side to encompass the line of his cheek and jaw, and concluding with his lips.

Twice she performed the inspection while Mary stood to one side. Softly from beneath the veil came a voice filled with delight. "Oh, Mary, how fortunate you are!" Then, to Elizabeth's surprise, Burke enfolded Harriet in his arms with the greatest intimacy, as though they had known each other forever.

With Burke at center, Mary tucked protectively under one arm, Harriet under the other, Elizabeth trailing behind—she did not mind, for a person could drown in the waves of joy washing over the three ahead—they proceeded into the shade of the Great Hall, then on up the steps to Harriet's chambers to focus on the promising future.

On April 18, Thursday, at three o'clock in the afternoon in the year 1871 one of the most beautiful weddings in the history of Eden took place in the small family Chapel buried in the heart of the castle.

Lady Mary Eden, only daughter of Lord James Eden, Fourteenth Baron and Sixth Earl of Eden Point and Lady Harriet Powels, wed Mr. Burke Stanhope of Mobile, Alabama, the United States of America.

By general consensus the only regret of the day was the fact that so few witnessed it: The Chapel filled with coral colored roses; the bride indescribably beautiful in a simply cut gown of white silk, her veil anchored by the diamond coronet of her station, and carrying a single white rose; the groom in dress blacks, viewing his bride with the expression of a man who had just glimpsed the shores of paradise.

Bishop Arthur Walsh of Exeter Cathedral presided over the High Anglican ceremony. As a special favor to Lady Harriet, and aware of the grief which this unique family had suffered, he made the journey to Eden, performed the ceremony, then returned to Exeter that evening.

Though the witnesses were few in number, their hearts were filled with happiness for the couple. Elizabeth was there, and Lady Harriet, and Harriet's indomitable maid Peggy, and Bates, the old butler, and five other upper-level servants who over the years had earned the affection and respect of the family.

As the groom placed the heavy gold band on the bride's finger, the witnesses felt the mysterious power of love. It invaded and conquered everything, and for all concerned nothing mattered but the two pledging their lives one to the other.

As they knelt before Bishop Walsh for the final

prayer, only the discerning eye could see their hands at their sides, a subtle movement, their fingers seeking, finding, intertwining. . . .

"America!" Elizabeth gasped, apparently having heard only the key word of Burke's announcement.

Seated across the table in the Banqueting Hall with the remains of her wedding feast before her and the reassuring clasp of her husband's hand beneath the table, Mary looked up at Elizabeth's shock. Curious, she'd expected that reaction from her mother, not Elizabeth.

"Why not?" Mary challenged lightly, hoping that Elizabeth would try to understand. She wanted nothing to mar this day, not even a polite disagreement.

"But—America," Elizabeth murmured. She looked across at Burke. "You told me once that you had no desire to return there."

"Once I didn't—" He smiled, and Mary felt his hand tighten on hers beneath the table. Though he spoke on, she lost track of what he was saying, distracted by the lovely realization that she was Mrs. Burke Stanhope, that there was no power on earth which could separate them now.

"So, in a way it was inevitable," she heard Burke saying. As he launched forth into a comparison of futures in England and America, Mary settled back in her chair, only half-listening. Why not? The decision had been made and Elizabeth would come around. For now she was fascinated by certain new feelings.

Husband. Was there in the entire language a more powerful word?

A protector, a friend, a companion, a lover. What a masterful design of God's to enable His creatures to face the world by twos.

Slowly she bowed her head. Over and above her deep feelings of gratitude she continued to hear the soft hum of voices, Elizabeth no longer protesting but merely sad.

As Mary looked up she realized that they had yet to hear from her mother. At the first break Mary posed a direct question.

"And you, Mama—you've kept still. What is your opinion?"

At first there was no response, though Mary was aware of both Burke and Elizabeth watching along with her.

Then all she said was, "It sounds like a great adventure, and you both know that I wish you well."

"But it's so far away!" Elizabeth protested.

"Not far," Harriet countered. "Peggy keeps me well informed in daily sessions with all the London papers. Not so long ago she was reading to me of the new steamships, capable of crossing the Atlantic in eleven days. So it's not that far, Elizabeth, and think what fun we'll have sharing letters. You will write, both of you?"

"Of course we will!" Burke broke in, "and you both must come and see us."

Harriet laughed. "No, I think not. I do well to navigate these familiar corridors."

"Don't make a decision now," Mary said, not wanting a final answer. She glanced across at Elizabeth and saw an expression of tender resignation on her face.

"Well, don't count me out," she said as though in mock warning. "I've lived all my life confined to this island. If you two can go traipsing across the ocean, then I very well may follow you one day. If I'm invited, of course."

"We shall construct special guest chambers"—Burke smiled—"just for you, Elizabeth."

"Let me know when they are ready," she replied, and Mary sensed a deep bond of affection between the two, which pleased her.

At that moment the stewards re-entered, two bearing a magnificent wedding cake four tiers high and adorned with roses and white satin streamers.

"Oh, how lovely!" Mary gasped.

As the steward placed the confection on the table, Mary took the silver knife and sliced four small pieces from the top tier. As she was performing this duty another steward filled the champagne saucers, and ultimately the servants departed and left the small but select wedding party alone again.

Feeling suddenly shy, Mary watched as her mother stood. "A toast. To my beloved daughter and her husband, who have been granted the most precious gift in heaven or earth, the reciprocal love of a desired mate." Her manner changed, became almost stern as she added, "Do not accept the gift lightly. It is given to so very few."

Mary thought Harriet would say more. But she did not. Slowly she sat back down in her chair in a new mood of sadness.

Then it was Elizabeth who took the floor with her customary self-confidence and said, "You both know I love you. You both know that my heart goes with you—" She paused, though Mary detected a twinkle in her eye as she added, "And I will not descend upon you until the birth of the first child. Then, if need be, I'll swim the Atlantic!"

Burke laughed, easing the tension, and all four glasses were lifted.

"Well, then," Elizabeth said, nibbling on the corner of her cake, "when do you plan to leave? Have arrangements been made? Have you set a date for us to dread?"

Burke leaned forward and was on the verge of replying when suddenly the door opened and Mary looked up to see Peggy. Without waiting to be summoned forward, the woman hurried to Harriet's side. "Milady, I must speak with you," she whispered, loud enough for all to hear.

Awaiting Burke's reply concerning the date for their departure, Mary saw her mother brush the woman aside. "Not now, Peggy, please. Can't you see—"

"I *must*, milady," Peggy insisted, leaning over the back of Harriet's chair.

"What is this?" Harriet demanded, angry. "Can't you see that we are—"

Then something caught her ear, a new sound, impossible to identify at first, then growing louder through the opened door, a shout, the sound of hooves reaching across the Great Hall and into the Banqueting Hall.

Mary saw Elizabeth slowly rise to the edge of her seat. "What is it, Peggy?" she demanded, unlike Harriet wanting a direct answer.

Peggy looked fearfully in her direction, then bent over Harriet's shoulder. "You told me to keep an eye out," she whispered. "Well, I did, and—"

Then they all heard it, the rattling stop before the Great Hall steps of a large carriage, the distant shouts of the watchmen, a steward calling for assistance.

"Who—is it?" Harriet asked in a dull voice, as though she knew the answer.

"It's him, milady," Peggy whispered.

The lovely golden glow left the room and was replaced by something cold and threatening as all four focused on the sound of footsteps coming across the Great Hall, a heavy-booted aggressive stride.

Beneath the table Mary reached for Burke's hand. Why couldn't fate have permitted them one small interval without interruption, without—

Then he appeared before them, stopping in the doorway, the specter from Mary's nightmares, the man who had wanted her destroyed and who had almost succeeded. So involved was she with her own dread that she was scarcely aware of the silence emanating from everyone else. In the stillness she thought how old he looked and how ungroomed, his clothes mussed and dusty, his eyes buried in deep hollows moving slowly over certain specifics, the wedding cake, the half-filled glasses of champagne, Elizabeth, Mary, Burke, Harriet, as though he were silently calling the roll.

As the silence stretched on, Mary felt the heat of embarrassment on her face and looked at Burke, who seemed to be the only one at the table capable of returning the man's steady gaze.

What does he want? Why does he come now?

As these questions assaulted her mind, Mary looked across at Elizabeth, who appeared to be studying the empty place before her with sad reflection, as though she had known that sooner or later it would come to this.

With weary determination, as though to end the tension before it destroyed them, Elizabeth leaned forward. "John," she began, not looking at him "we are celebrating a very joyous occasion here, the occasion of Mary's wedding. Would you care to join—"

"I did not journey to Eden to attend a wedding," he said, winter in his voice despite the warm April evening.

"No," Elizabeth persisted patiently, "but as long as you are here—"

"I came only to fetch my sons," he interrupted, holding his position in the doorway, "which I shall do immediately. I feel that they will be better served in London than here."

Mary saw her mother's head incline suddenly forward. But the prevailing interest for her still stood in the doorway, that awesome figure of a man whom once she had considered godlike.

As she bowed her head she heard his voice, mocking,

filled with hate. "So don't let me interrupt this private occasion," he went on, "I will be on the road back to London within the hour."

"John—"

Mary looked up at the sound of her mother's voice. But the man was gone. Mary saw him striding across the Great Hall, heading toward the stairs, and saw as well the ample figure of Alex Aldwell, who seemed torn between John's direction and the Banqueting Hall.

Predictably, he hurried after his master, and Mary's attention was drawn back to the table, to her mother, who appeared to be bent over with mysterious grief.

Elizabeth was at her side, her face still bearing the strain of the encounter. "It's all right, Harriet," she soothed. "I think he'll keep his word. He just wants the boys, that's all. Then he'll leave again, I'm certain of it."

For all of Elizabeth's words of comfort, Mary saw her mother still bowed as though physically ill. Burke saw her distress as well and tried to ease it. "It's over, Lady Harriet," he said kindly. "I'm certain that he knows what happened here today, and is wise enough to know that he has no power—"

But nothing that was said had eased her mother in any way. And when a moment later Harriet started up from the table Elizabeth caught her. "What is it, Harriet?" she demanded, "and where are you going? I think it best if you wait—"

"The boys are not here."

Elizabeth grasped Harriet by the shoulders. "What do you mean?"

"What I said." Distractedly she shook her head. "Several days ago I gave Lord Harrington permission to take them to Ireland. He had just returned from London where he had tried repeatedly to see John."

Stunned by the announcement, Mary saw Burke and Elizabeth exchange a glance. "Leave now," she whispered. "Leave immediately, both of you. Don't stop to collect your things. I'll bring them when I—"

"No!" Burke's response was strong.

"There will be trouble," Elizabeth warned.

"Then all the more reason to stay."

As Mary watched, she saw her mother seated at the head of the table, the uneaten wedding cake before her, the spirit of the wedding party in shambles. Privately

Mary agreed with Elizabeth. They should leave now. It would serve no purpose to inflame John further by their presence.

She was on the verge of joining forces with Elizabeth when she saw Burke settle into the chair next to her, signaling by his mood and manner that he had no intention of leaving.

"Burke, please," she begged, "Elizabeth's right."

"No," he repeated a second time. "I've avoided the man long enough," he added. "His quarrel is not with you," he said to Mary, "or with you," he went on to Elizabeth, "and not even you, Lady Harriet," he concluded. "I'm the offender, and as such—"

Then they heard footsteps, someone descending the staircase at a rapid pace.

Suffering a premonition of disaster, Mary sat on the edge of her chair and kept her eyes focused on the opened door, saw two servants dart past as though they were running for safety.

"John, I beg you," she heard Alex call, the man's voice drawing nearer.

Then there he was again, bearing no resemblance to the man who had stood in the doorway a short time before. Now his coat was unbuttoned, revealing a soiled shirtwaist. But it was his face that alarmed her. She'd never seen such a face, save for the demented victims who were hauled through the streets of London inside iron cages on their way to Bedlam.

"Madam!" he shouted, his rage manifesting itself in every feature, all his attention focused on Harriet. "I believe we have need of words," he went on, and for the first time ventured beyond the threshold of the door, moving forward in a straight line until he stood directly over Harriet where she sat in her chair.

Mary saw Alex Aldwell take his place in the abandoned doorway, an expression of regret on his face.

"Did you hear me?" John demanded, hovering over the bowed woman. "I have just returned from the nursery, where I was given distressing news."

"Yes," Harriet whispered.

"Is it true?"

"It is."

Suddenly John grasped her shoulders. Under the duress of physical contact, Harriet tried to draw away.

But he held her fast. Across the table Mary saw Elizabeth ease stealthily up.

"On whose authority do you send my children off with a lunatic?"

"He is not a lunatic, John," Harriet said calmly, sitting erect as though aware that she must not reveal her fear. "Lord Harrington was in London and tried to see you. You did promise—"

"I promised nothing—"

"Last Christmas—"

"*I promised nothing!*" John raged, and renewed his grasp on her shoulders with such force that she moaned and turned away.

Sickened by the cruelty, Mary closed her eyes and wished that she could block the sound of his voice as well.

"When did they leave?" he demanded.

"Several—days ago."

"Were they traveling alone?"

"No. Molly was with them, Lila's maid, and Lord Harrington's friend, Mr. Parnell."

"And their destination?"

Harriet paused. "I—do not know."

"You are lying!"

"I'm not. Lord Harrington wasn't certain—"

"And when will they return?"

"I—don't know that, either."

Suddenly in a violent gesture he half-lifted her from the chair. Elizabeth was on her feet, as was Burke, the two of them running toward the end of the table, Burke arriving first, dislodging Harriet from John's grasp and taking her place before him.

Mary went to her mother's side and guided her a distance away and looked back in time to see a crimson rage on John's face. As he lifted his arm, apparently willing to do battle with the man before him, she saw Burke counter with superior speed, his right hand converting instantly into a fist and landing squarely on John's left jaw, a blow that sent him reeling backward, where he stumbled and fell.

"You never cease to surprise me, Mr. Eden," he said quietly to the man on the floor at his feet. "I've never seen a man threaten a woman before. How does it make you feel?"

From Mary's position she could not see John. But she heard coughing and saw Elizabeth approach him on the opposite side of the table, a clean linen in hand, ready to extend it to him in assistance.

She saw Elizabeth stop suddenly, the linen still in her hand, her eyes focused on something out of sight beneath the table. Mary heard her whisper, "No," then saw her in slow retreat. She glanced toward Burke and saw him standing at the head of the table, an expression on his face which mirrored Elizabeth's, all his concentration fixed on something beyond Mary's range of vision.

"I don't believe that will solve anything, Mr. Eden," he said.

From the doorway Alex Aldwell found the courage to speak. "John, I beg you. Think what you are doing—"

Everyone in the room seemed frozen on some aspect of recognition that still eluded Mary. She was just starting toward the end of the table when she saw John rising to his feet, a trickle of blood slipping from the corner of his mouth, and in his hand, a gun, one of his dueling pistols, leveled at Burke.

"John, please," she begged, understanding now the fear in the room, the madman armed, the pistol ready for use. "Alex!" Mary called out.

Abruptly John stepped back, as though to bring them all within his sight. "Hold your position, Alex!" he shouted. "I warn you. Stay where you are!"

The man halted his forward progress and looked helplessly at Mary, who in turn took note of the position of the gun, raised and leveled at Burke.

"Elizabeth," Mary whispered, "make him put it away."

"Put it away!" John parroted, rubbing his jaw with his free hand. "I have no intention of putting it away. And I assure all of you that it is in sound working condition."

Incredibly, Burke smiled. "I have no doubt of that, Mr. Eden. You are not the sort of man who would let his weapons grow rusty. Your good sense, perhaps your judgment, but not your weapons."

"Burke, please," Mary begged.

"No, let him speak," John cut in, his manner almost at ease, as though at last he were facing his true enemy. "I've waited a long time for this moment," he went on, his missing sons forgotten, everything forgotten but his contempt for the man standing before him. Suddenly his voice fell, though he continued to hold the pistol level. "I should have killed you last spring," he muttered.

"You should have," Burke replied, almost genially, "for look what has happened now," he added, gesturing about the table at the remains of the wedding feast.

But John never once altered his line of vision and, still holding the pistol level, he advanced one step, shortening the distance between them. Mary stood motionless. At the very moment she thought she had endured and survived her last nightmare, here was the most terrifying one of all, the pistol aimed directly at her husband's heart.

"John, please," she begged again.

Witlessly she drew his attention toward her and suffered the full weight of his hate as he sarcastically demanded, "Who speaks? Is that the bride?"

Though he was addressing her, he never lifted his eyes from Burke's face. *"Your* bride, sir?" he questioned, a lightness in his tone which belied the seriousness of the moment.

Burke did not reply, though John needed no response. "Damaged goods, you know," he said, his tone as calm as though he were discussing the weather. "You've just bought yourself some well-trod territory, sir." He smiled. "She was raised by a whore, you know. That one standing over there—" And he jerked his head toward Elizabeth, who stood with bowed head.

"And prior to that," he went on, his voice raising as though he were warming to the subject, "she was brought into this world by another whore. That one seated there—" And this time he looked toward Harriet.

"Whores, both of them," he repeated, stepping closer to Burke as though to share a confidence, though still holding the pistol between them. "So you see, it's in her blood, you might say. But if you don't mind, I don't know why I should object. You might want to have her cleansed before you move in. The last three who used her were none too clean. Just a warning, you understand."

Weakened by embarrassment and humiliation, Mary found that she could not even look up at the confrontation. Then she heard Burke's voice again, strained, in spite of the silence in the room. "May I ask your intent,

Mr. Eden? If you are going to use that, I suggest you do so. Otherwise, I'll take my wife and leave."

"You will move when I tell you to move," John said, retreating a step himself, as though in need of greater distance. Suddenly he shouted, "My God, what more need I say or do? I've called your wife a whore, have in truth assigned the same designation to every female seated at this table. Are you totally ignorant in all respects?"

Above the shriek of his voice, Mary heard his message and suffered new horror. Apparently Burke had heard it as well.

"You want—a duel?" he inquired.

"Want one? I *demand* one!" John shouted, "and no one here can deny that just cause has not been given. There are witnesses. Aldwell there, and servants just outside the door. And now I repeat myself. Your wife is a whore, sir, as was her mother before her, who slept with her husband's brother and bore him a child—"

His voice echoed in outrage about the room. It was suddenly joined by Harriet's cry of, "No! Please don't—"

"Why not, madam?" John demanded. "I say, let the truth come out, all the truth."

"No, John. I beg you." Harriet was weeping openly.

As the sounds of human agony rose about her, Mary was torn between her own weakening state and that of her mother. Elizabeth was pushing past her, trying to turn Harriet away. Beyond the door Mary saw Peggy, aroused by her mistress' cry of distress. At the same time Alex Aldwell stepped forward and for a moment it seemed as though the entire room was in movement, revolving around one vortex, John Murrey Eden, who lifted the dueling pistol and again demanded, "Your response, sir. I have another of these in my chambers. Say the word and Alex will fetch it and within the hour one of us will be safely removed from this brothel."

The room fell silent except for Harriet's weeping as Elizabeth led her back to the chair and stood over her. But Mary was no longer concerned with either Harriet or Elizabeth. All her attention was focused on Burke's reply.

"No," Mary whispered.

"I did not ask you!" John shouted.

"No, Burke," Mary begged, ignoring John.

"You see how they corrupt us?" John cried. "She'll share her well-used body with you and share her coward-

ice as well. Women are contagions—all of them, Mr.
Stanhope."

Then it came, his voice as soft as John's was shrill.
"No, Mr. Eden. I will not accept your challenge."

"Then you are a coward."

"No. It's just that recently I've developed an overwhelming appetite for life."

Weak with relief, Mary clung to the table.

"Then I'll leave you to your own decay," John pronounced contemptuously, backing away and lowering the
pistol for the first time since he'd entered the room. "This
place should suit you very well, Mr. Stanhope, for this is
a woman's castle, designed to harbor the weaker of the
species. Men have never felt at home here, but I suspect
that you will be perfectly at ease."

At the door he handed the pistol to Alex, who received
it gratefully, his normally strong face reflecting the ugliness of everything that had been said.

Just as Mary was settling weakly into her chair, she
heard Burke, again.

"Mr. Eden, wait!" he called out. "I said I would not
fight you with pistols. But I will fight you. Willingly."

Before she could protest, she saw John turn back, new
interest on his face. "Name your weapons."

Burke paused, then lifted his hands. "These," he said.
"Bare fists. And to heighten your enjoyment permit me to
introduce myself properly." He stepped forward, reducing
the distance between them. "Lord Ripples, Mr. Eden, at
your service. The author, the true author of 'The Demi-
God of Eden.' "

The expression on John's face was fearful. No longer
arrogant, no longer armed, he appeared to crouch before
Burke, staring up at him as though in doubt whether or
not to believe him.

Mary followed every movement of his face, saw two
small feverish spots on his cheeks, his gaze unbroken, his
thoughts struggling in the depths, unable to rise to any
clarity.

"Lord—" he commenced, strangely breathless.

"—Ripples," Burke said, completing the name and re-
stating his identity. "I worked very hard on that piece of
writing, Mr. Eden, I can promise you that. And for every
accusation that I wrote, ten were left unwritten, and,

based on what I know now, the content of that essay pales in comparison with what I should have written."

Still John stood before him, stunned. Suddenly he whirled about and reached for the pistol which recently he'd placed in Alex's hand. But the big man moved back, concealing the weapon behind him, shaking his head. "No, John. The game's got new rules now and you must abide by them."

Though Mary was expecting another violent confrontation, John's perennial stance when his will was blocked, he seemed willing to abide by Alex's judgment. He looked back toward Burke. "Bare fists, then," he agreed readily. "Where?"

Burke shrugged. "The courtyard."

"When?"

"Now?"

John hesitated. "In a quarter of an hour."

"I'll be there."

Without another word, John left the room. Alex stayed long enough to show them his distressed face, as without words he begged for everyone's forgiveness. Then he too was gone, leaving the four of them alone.

Although she was no longer openly weeping, Harriet had yet to lift her head from the table. Now and then a single spasm caused her shoulders to shake, but for the most part she resembled a woman who had been beaten into submission.

Elizabeth, though standing upright, seemed incapable of looking directly at anyone and instead chose to focus on the floor at her feet.

But as always Mary's pressing concern was for the man standing alone at the end of the room and, as she moved toward him, she lightly touched the two wounded women in passing, then ran the rest of the way into his arms, where he received her warmly, trying to ease her tears with soft entreaties, "Don't, please. It will be all right."

Though locked in his embrace, which generally provided her with all the comfort she needed, she heard the madness of his words. *All right?* Nothing in the world would ever be all right, not after all that had been said and done here tonight. And the worst of it was that it was not yet over.

"Please don't, Burke," she begged. "It will serve no purpose."

"Oh, but it will," he soothed, trying to help her to understand. "It will serve his purpose as well as mine."

She looked up at him, bewildered by his words. Beyond his shoulder she saw Alex Aldwell giving the watchmen instructions of some sort. Their plain faces seemed to reflect her own confusion.

"Go with Elizabeth," Burke ordered. "I'll come for you shortly."

"No."

When she refused to obey, he looked down on her, then left the room.

"Burke?"

Though she called after him twice, he refused to stop. She called a third time, though her voice sounded weak and far away.

He wouldn't alter his course, she knew it, any more than John would alter his. In desperate need of understanding, she looked over her shoulder toward the two women at midtable.

But there was no understanding to be shared, only new grief blending with old.

Mary stared at the two, then reached out for the back of Burke's chair, empty now. Though lacking, it was the nearest support, and she was in need. . . .

Recovered, at least to the extent that she could function, Elizabeth summoned Peggy out of her stunned state and with the aid of two other maids instructed them to assist the Countess Dowager to her chambers and to remain there with her for the rest of the night. Under no circumstances were they to permit anyone to enter the room. Peggy nodded, understanding.

Then Elizabeth turned her attention to Mary, who continued to cling to the back of Burke's chair, still in her wedding dress, though now she looked merely foolish.

"You, too," Elizabeth commanded gently. "I'll take you to your chambers, where I want you to—"

"No!"

"It will serve no purpose," she counseled, hearing in her words the exact echo of Mary's words to Burke. "If they must fight—and I believe they must—Burke's decision was wise. And I'll ask Alex to stop them before—"

"No," Mary repeated, not looking up. Her voice suddenly grew hard. "Let them finish it. I want to see what it looks like—the sight of two men beating each other senseless."

. Against the hardness, Elizabeth had no defense. "Mary, please. Spare yourself—"

"No. I want to see it all." Then she added with complex female cunning, "And I want them to see me watching them."

That was all she said. Slowly she pushed away from the chair, took a last look at the remains of her wedding banquet and proceeded through the door at the end of the room.

Elizabeth knew that she should follow after her immediately. The appearance of strength was impressive, but in the event it was just façade, someone should be with her. Suddenly she suffered a deep dread. On the sideboard she spied a decanter of brandy and hurried toward it, confident that she would never have greater need for it.

She drank quickly, several burning swallows. Her eyes watered. As the warmth entered her throat, she lifted her head and looked toward the door, saw a steady parade of servants, upper level as well as lower, all hurrying toward the courtyard. Apparently the word of this grand theatrical had spread.

Then she must join them, though she wished with all her heart that someone in authority would send her up to her chambers, as she'd recently sent Lady Harriet.

She found Mary at the top of the Great Hall steps, looking out over the incredible scene. About forty watchmen had formed a large circle directly at the center of the inner courtyard. They stood in perfect symmetry a distance apart, each supporting a standard topped with a flaming torch. Though it was black beyond that ring of fire, it was as bright as day within it.

Around the outer edges of the circle stood the entire staff of Eden Castle. On the right was the Keep and what once had been the Charnel House and, beyond that, Elizabeth saw the solitary black finger of the whipping oak.

In quiet despair she compared the two barbaric visions: one ancient and imperious, the fight ring as old, yet more democratic, though the purpose of both was identical, two arenas where one human being could inflict senseless pain on another.

In an attempt to escape her own thoughts, she moved into position behind Mary. "You're chilled," she whispered, observing a faint trembling in her shoulders. "Shall I fetch a shawl for—"

"No," Mary said, though she never altered the direction of her vision to the spot where Burke stood, coatless, his white shirtwaist like a gleaming eye in the red-black scene, talking quietly with Alex Aldwell. They seemed so calm. They might have been indulging in little more than a quiet post-dinner conversation.

Elizabeth noticed a distinct silence falling over the courtyard, the once chattering servants standing at attention, their heads swiveling in several directions, up to the top of the steps where Elizabeth and Mary stood, back to the center of the ring where Burke and Alex were quietly chatting. A few even looked over their shoulders, bewildered by the missing half of this macabre show.

If Elizabeth had felt so inclined, she could have informed them that John Murrey Eden would not appear until he was certain of everyone's undivided attention.

As though to prove her thoughts, there he was, appearing in the Great Hall arch less than ten feet from where Elizabeth stood. He was coatless, as was Burke, his trousers tucked into highly polished black boots, his long hair slightly mussed.

Compelled to make one last effort to alter the inevitable, Elizabeth went to his side. "John, please," she entreated, "please call this madness off. I'm certain that Burke would agree. Whatever differences you have, you share many similarities as well. For Mary's sake, please!"

Standing close to him, she was certain that he'd heard every word. But he walked past her and Mary as well, never looking to the right or left.

The earlier silence of the night was nothing compared to that which descended on the inner courtyard now, the only sound that of John's boots as he strode across the gravel and entered the circle.

Lifting her eyes to rest them and searching for a safe vista when the time and the need came, Elizabeth saw Alex Aldwell approaching John, saying a few words to him. If there was any response, Elizabeth could not detect it. John's attention, like Mary's, had never lifted from the man standing at the exact center of the ring, still relaxed-appearing, his arms hanging easily at his sides.

In the last moment of sanity, Elizabeth found herself trying to assess the two men according to height, body weight, strength. Physically, they appeared to be perfectly matched. Then victory would go to the most determined, the one who had been the most deeply offended. Yet even there the match was equal, John aware of Burke's hand behind the Lord Ripples column which had caused him such grief; aware, too, that he had in fact stolen Mary away from him.

And Burke, of course, avenging Mary herself, the forged notes that had lured her into the park where the assailants had been waiting, the violent attack which would leave her permanently scarred, in spite of the richness of Burke's love for her.

The motivation on both sides was powerful, and there was a good possibility that neither would cease until one or both was dead. Her last thought was one of regret, that Burke had refused the offer of the duel. On reconsideration how clean and simple it would be, over in less than a minute, whereas this—

Then it was time, and her attention was drawn down to the arena where she saw Alex Aldwell retreating, the two men confronting each other with less than two feet between them. She saw Mary stiffen and stand more erect as though to fortify herself for the first blow.

Then it came, John leveling the first, moving forward with singular speed, a sharp jab to the side of Burke's face which unbalanced him, his body twisting in the process, both arms raised now for protection.

Both men began a slow encircling, arms extended. John lunged forward again and missed, and for his efforts received Burke's first stunning blow. As John's neck snapped back, Elizabeth heard Mary gasp, but no other sound escaped her lips.

They continued to circle each other, as though sizing up the potency of each blow, practical men, both of them, even in such base matters as the supremacy of the foe.

Elizabeth now observed something almost polite about their movements, as if in that first exchange a curious respect had sprung up between them. Each apparently knew now that the other was capable of inflicting damage, thus strategies were being altered.

Then, as though he'd heard a command to break free from the encircling, John sprang forward, pummeling

Burke with blow after blow, a relentless attack which
drove him almost to the edge of the ring, his head lifting
grotesquely with each thrust until finally he fell backward
onto the gravel, first blood spotting the white shirtwaist.

Even though Burke was still down, John lunged forward, though Burke was ready for him, reaching out
quickly and grabbing his wrists, twisting him over, his
body landing heavily, his arms flailing uselessly against
Burke's assault, both men grappling each other, rolling
over and over. Burke pushed to his feet first and dragged
John behind him, holding him at arm's length and delivering a blow that sent John reeling into the circle of watchmen, who calmly moved back in accommodation, then, as
John dragged himself forward, re-formed the circle as
tight as before.

Elizabeth closed her eyes to rest them and opened
them as she heard the crowd in a collective gasp and
looked down to see John lunge for Burke's legs, toppling
him, then straddling him, his knees pinning Burke's shoulders, leveling several blows directly into his exposed face.

Both men were wounded now, blood flowing from their
noses, their shirtwaists speckled. Beneath the repeated
blows Burke seemed to go limp. Suddenly his knee lifted
with such force that John was instantly dislodged and for
the first time a sharp cry punctuated the curious silence.

On his hands and knees, John allowed his head to fall
limp while he waited out the discomfort, momentarily
paying no attention to his opponent who, though on his
feet, was trying to repair his own damage. As Burke
wiped his sleeve across his mouth, Elizabeth saw the
sleeve turn crimson, the blood running down his chin now,
one hand covering his ear as though that were the main
center of his discomfort.

As though by tacit agreement, each man gave the other
a few seconds, though, as John was rising to his feet,
Burke stepped forward with a blow of such force that it
seemed literally to lift John into the air. His body whirled
around in a half-turn and as he fell forward Burke delivered a second blow to his midsection, which caused
him to buckle, his arms clasped about his stomach.

Though Elizabeth fully expected to see John collapse,
instead she saw him lift himself out of the downward
spiral, his fists continuously pounding as he drove Burke
around the perimeter of the circle, the two men now a

blur of white and red, exchanging blows of equal devasta-
tion, yet both somehow miraculously still on their feet,
each exposing the other to the most severe and prolonged
attack.

Elizabeth looked away and in the process saw several
female servants do the same, one completely obscuring
her face behind her apron, another pushing toward the
back of the crowd, searching for a place where she could
not see as well.

For herself, Elizabeth focused on the darkness beyond
the circle of torches, but she could still hear the impact
of fists, the boots scuffling over the gravel, the single cry
now and then, bespeaking pain.

For over three-quarters of an hour the battle went on
until the gravel within the ring was red with blood, until
both men no longer resembled men but rather half-
butchered animals in a slaughterhouse. Repeatedly Elizabeth looked away, thinking, *Now surely it will end!* But
each time they dragged themselves upward, their lunges
and thrusts less meticulous now, clinging to each other as
often as not, their hair matted with blood, their shirtwaists
torn, Burke's almost completely gone, the endless blood
coating his chest.

Still it went on, though most of the females in the
audience had long since turned away. Only the males
were loyal, with their wagers clutched in their hands.

Concerned for Mary, Elizabeth tried twice to lead her
away. But the girl refused to leave, though now she presented a spectacle as pitiful as those two bloodied, still-
encircling men. Elizabeth looked toward her and saw
tears on her face, though there was not one sound of grief
as she watched them in their final agony, both men so
exhausted they could scarcely stand, yet summoning energy from someplace to land another blow, then another,
and still another, their movements so erratic that they
appeared inebriated.

Enough! Elizabeth decided, sickened by the sight. It
had to be stopped. As she started down the stairs she saw
Alex Aldwell break through the circle, heading toward the
two men, his hand outstretched as though he, too, had
had enough.

But as John staggered forward he shouted, "Stay back!
I warn you. Stay back, all of you!" And he turned quickly

as though fearful that some of the watchmen might be approaching to assist Alex.

None did, and finally Alex retreated. Elizabeth, alone at midstep and helpless to alter the edict, watched close at hand as the two men staggered toward each other, bearing down on the advancing enemy and striking each other again and again amidst showers of blood.

Simultaneously they fell, though both lifted their heads, prepared for treachery, and, as though not to disappoint each other, it came. John crawled forward, half-wrapping himself around Burke, a curious, almost loving stance except for the fist which was shattering against Burke's ribs. For one instant a prolonged scream escaped Burke's lips, though he dragged himself away and turned back and lifted John by the hair and held his face suspended before him, then delivered a monstrous blow. The force sent both of them sprawling in opposite directions, Burke lying on his back, his legs and arms askew, his face a mass of blood, his knuckles bleeding, his bare chest heaving.

John lay sprawled opposite him, on his side, one arm extended toward his enemy as though even now he wanted to inflict more damage.

But for both it was over. Each lay upon the gravel, not cleansed of their malice but simply too injured and too exhausted to see it to completion.

Elizabeth stared down on the arena, no one moving, not even the crowd of witnesses, as though all were trying very hard to figure out precisely what had been accomplished here in this blood-drenched circle.

She saw Alex Aldwell start forward, but he stopped short of the two battered men, as though up close the sight would be even more grim. Then, remembering Mary, Elizabeth shook herself out of her horror and climbed back up the stairs, never taking her eyes off the young woman who had endured it all, who, to the best of Elizabeth's knowledge, had never averted her eyes or made a single cry beyond that one small gasp which had escaped her lips with the first blow.

It was Elizabeth's intention to block her path down to that scene if she were entertaining thoughts of that nature. But obviously she was not. As Elizabeth drew near she heard Mary say, "They will both require a physician. Send for one in Mortemouth. I'll be in my mother's chambers."

That was all she said. She turned her back on the grisly

scene and walked steadily through the Great Hall, her movement almost serene.

"I'll be in my mother's chambers."

Not a very promising place to begin a wedding night. Slowly Elizabeth looked back to the arena where the two men still lay, unmoved and unattended.

Then, because someone had to move, to disperse the servants, to lift the two "noble gladiators" to their feet and cleanse the area of spilled blood, she drew a deep breath and plunged directly into the circle and saw the hem of her gown growing red-splotched with blood, and began issuing orders.

He had not once lost consciousness.

With a stubborn pride that refused to acknowledge the pain, John lay on his bed in his chambers and watched through swollen eyes the ministrations of the physician. The damage was more severe than he had guessed: a fractured right wrist, a broken finger on his left hand, countless deep lacerations on his face, his lower lip split open, and a persistent agony in the small of his back, which had eluded the doctor.

Now, patched and splinted, he saw the physician leaving the room and longed to call after him for a report on his opponent. But he couldn't open his mouth for fear of reopening his lip, and, helpless, he watched Alex show the man out, then turn back, the censure clear on his face, though blended with what looked dangerously like pity.

John wanted neither and, in spite of his discomfort, he muttered, "Get out. Leave me alone."

At first Alex held his position, anchored by love and loyalty. "Can I fetch you anything, John? The physician said no solid food for a while, just—"

"—want nothing," John muttered. "Go on with you."

Still Alex stared down to the bed. Then he left, clearly eager to find a more pleasing vista on which to rest his eyes.

Good riddance, John thought, and for the first time, with no need to keep up a front, dared to relax into the pillow, although for his efforts he felt a burning pain in the small of his back and with his good hand clasped the bed linens in an effort to wait out the discomfort.

A few moments later it passed and left him with the belated realization that he did not really want to be alone.

Alex was good company and the night would be long. The
physician had warned him of that.

In increasing loneliness he glanced toward the door and
tried to call Alex back. But he could scarcely raise his
voice above a whisper. Damn! He *was* alone, while undoubtedly someplace else in his castle the American bastard was receiving the loving attention of Mary and Elizabeth and possibly even Harriet. As hate rose within him,
he closed his eyes and regretted only that he'd lacked the
strength to kill him.

Overcome with longing and need, he tried with his good
hand to drag himself upward. The shadowy chamber
whirled about him. He clung to the side of the bed for fear
of falling and felt a pulse in every wound.

Still he persisted until he was sitting upright, though
every nerve in his body resisted the position. His mind,
impaired by effort and pain, moved in a bleak direction,
back to the Banqueting Hall, Harriet's scream and collapse
as he'd almost revealed their secret.

Gasping with delayed terror, he lifted his head in an
attempt to accommodate the pain in his back which, for
all its intensity, was nothing compared to the pain in his
head, the realization of what he'd almost done.

As his thoughts blurred under the duress of effort, he
began to doubt his memory. Had he stopped short of complete revelation?

Propelled forward by an urgency which defied common
sense, he reached out with the intention of seeking
Harriet's chambers just down the corridor. He had to know
he had to ask her forgiveness.

Someone had to forgive him.

He stumbled forward, suffering a sensation in his back
as though a spear had been driven into it, yet persisting,
until through blurred eyes he located the doorknob and
found himself in the darkened, chilled corridor.

Grasping the wall and leaning heavily against it, he
made his way slowly forward, his eyes lifting to Harriet's
chamber door about twenty-five yards removed. Twice
he had to stop for breath. The corridor walls seemed to
be pressing closer. Shivering in his nightshirt, he heard
his teeth rattling together.

Suddenly at the far end of the corridor he saw a light.
Thank God! Someone was coming. Someone would assist
him, take pity on him and lead him into her chambers.

Standing motionless, still clinging to the wall, he looked up. The light was increasing, a curious illumination, not localized in the specific beam of a lamp but seeming to emanate from the floor to the ceiling, a solid column of blue-white light which hurt his eyes.

"Who is it?" he called out feebly, trying to shield his eyes with his good arm. "Who comes?"

Receiving no answer, he squinted into the brilliant illumination and saw the column of light moving steadily toward him.

"Please answer," he begged, cowering against the wall.

Still there was no response and, with fear vaulting, he looked directly into the unearthly light and saw the dim outline of a figure, a phantom which faded, then reappeared, the image of a woman, the face growing clearer, her eyes two enormous black concentric circles in the center of the light, something moving beside her, a monstrous animal of some sort, a high-pitched, ethereal voice filling his ear which seemed to issue from the phantom.

"Help—" he gasped, staggering backward, grasping at the wall for support.

The image was clear before him, the last shrouded mists lifting, revealing the face, though the form was horribly mutilated, the white gown torn open revealing a split abdomen, red slime coating white flesh, a disemboweled specter who nonetheless smiled at him.

Lila!

At that instant the immense cat crouched low. Thrice his size in life, he now fixed his gaze on John with blood-red eyes, awaiting the command of his mistress.

Before the horror, John stumbled backward, and, as he tripped, Lila laughed and simultaneously Wolf sprang forward. Feeling the sharp claws digging into his face, John blessedly lost consciousness, dragging a living piece of Hell with him.

Eden Castle
April 26, 1871

MORE CONVINCED THAN ever that there was a wisdom in sorrow, Elizabeth stood on the Great Hall steps in a blaze of early-morning sun, watching the steward load the last of Mary's and Burke's luggage atop the carriage.

Not wanting to intrude on the intimacy of their final goodbyes to Harriet, Elizabeth had promised to wait for them here. She closed her eyes and lifted her face to the healing rays of the sun and tried to keep her thoughts in order. It was, as always, a matter of priorities. First she would deal with the farewells, then she would try to confront the mystery that was taking place in the Library, John barricaded within that book-lined room, refusing to return to his bedchamber on the third floor, Alex tending him on the makeshift couch, though repeatedly Aldwell had begged Elizabeth to intervene.

What exactly she could do, she had no idea. But she would try. For Edward's memory and for the love she once had shared with John, she would make one final effort. Then she would turn her back on this castle and leave, Harriet secluded in her upper chamber, John self-imprisoned behind the Library doors. Some ancient passion bound those two together; what, she had no idea, but it was her considered opinion that neither would ever recover from it and both ultimately would be destroyed by it, and that was a spectacle she had no desire to witness.

She heard approaching footsteps moving across the Great Hall, and in her last moment of privacy warned herself against any undue show of emotion. It was the last thing that any of them needed.

Then she turned to face them, that strikingly handsome couple who, to the best of her knowledge, had yet to consummate their wedding vows. With what loving patience Mary had tended to Burke's various wounds, the most serious of which had been three broken ribs. He was still heavily bandaged and walked slowly.

But every night Mary had returned to her mother's

chambers, had slept on a small couch, only to awaken, refresh herself and return immediately to Burke's bedside.

Elizabeth still didn't understand it and, in a way grateful that she did not have to, she went forward to greet them and saw strain on Mary's face, the emotional stress of telling her mother goodbye, knowing that she probably would never see her again.

In an attempt to lighten the moment, Elizabeth stepped between and took their arms and announced calmly, "There is really no need for us to say goodbye now. I'll be seeing you in London."

"We'll be leaving as soon as we can make arrangements," Burke warned, his face still bearing the marks of the fight.

"Oh, but that will take time," Elizabeth chided gently. "You said so yourself. There's the house to be dismantled, passage booked, the servants to look after."

"Delane will help."

"I'm sure he will. Still, you'll be there when I arrive," Elizabeth added, aware that she was lying and hoping that no one else was.

As they approached the carriage, Burke went to confer with his driver, leaving Elizabeth facing the ordeal she dreaded most.

"My dearest," she whispered, turning to Mary, still seeing that hardness in her eyes as though she'd served warning on the world that nothing it could do would ever hurt her again.

Elizabeth clasped her tightly. "No tears," she counseled them both softly.

The advice seemed to soothe the young woman, who at last released her grasp on Elizabeth and turned to face Burke, who was waiting by the carriage door.

Struggling for control, in spite of earlier vows, Elizabeth stepped toward him. "Make an easy journey of it, Burke. I'm not even certain that you should be walking about. Everything in London will wait; I can promise you that."

He nodded and she thought that it was almost over, but without warning he reached for her hand, then his arm was around her shoulder and she found herself in a second embrace, as moving as the first, considering the two simple words he whispered in her ear.

"Thank you."

Laughing in an effort to keep from crying, Elizabeth ordered sternly, "You'd better take him away, Mary, before I steal him from you."

With relief she saw the laugh spread like a welcome contagion, and gently Burke assisted Mary up into the carriage, then with greater effort followed after her, leaning heavily into the discomfort of his injured side.

Settled at last, they looked down on her. "Then we'll see you in London," Mary called out, hopefully.

"Of course you will," Elizabeth lied again, and tried to memorize their faces against the day when she would be hungry to see them and they would be half a world away.

Blessedly, Burke gave the signal for the carriage to move and, congratulating herself prematurely on her splendid control, Elizabeth was in no way prepared for Mary's final cry, scarcely audible over the rattle of the carriage, but clear enough.

"I love you, Elizabeth . . ."

Then the dam broke, but fortunately the carriage had swung wide for the turn which led to the Gatehouse and no one saw her as she leaned against the banister, storing those words in her heart, as she would treasure them every day for the rest of her life.

She would not see them in London. It would be too difficult for all. She might one day journey to America and see them in their new home. For now, she was content to live with the echo of those words.

"I love you, Elizabeth . . ."

What remarkable words they were, capable of lifting her heart and sending it soaring toward the sun.

Seated in a straight-backed chair in the corridor outside the Library, in an uncharacteristic position of helplessness, Alex Aldwell kept a close eye on the goings-on beyond the Great Hall door. Thus he knew immediately when the carriage had departed and he stood, ready to confront Elizabeth, and drag her bodily, if necessary, into that place of need.

When at first she did not reappear, he waited patiently and tried to clear his head so that he could speak effectively. Not that he objected to the burden which had been placed on his shoulders, the burden of a clearly terrified and weakened John Murrey Eden, imprisoned behind those doors, refusing to return to his bedchamber, refusing almost all food and drink, passing the days and most of the nights in fixed concentration on that bloody painting, "The Women of Eden," even talking to it on occasion. Yes, Alex had heard him.

Gawd! He'd seen John through some rough waters, but these were the roughest, and on top of everything that was going on here was Alex's painful awareness of how much they both were needed back in London.

With Andrew Rhoades gone, the only one looking after "family interests," so to speak, was poor Aslam, who still needed a few years to do his growing up in and who now found himself holding the reins to the largest private empire in all of England.

Almost in anger, Alex stared across the Great Hall. *Where in the hell is she?* He'd heard the carriage leave over ten minutes—*Ah, here she is*. Alex started forward, spying her now, her head bowed as though—

He held his position at the end of the corridor, watching her slow approach. Too bad that Alex couldn't share her emotion, but as far as he was concerned the departure of the carriage was simply a matter of good riddance. Not once during the last few tense days had Elizabeth or Lady Harriet inquired after John, all their attention focused on that upper corridor where the American had been recuperating from that godawful fight. Clear to see where their sympathies resided.

"Elizabeth?" he called out, his voice echoing strangely across the Great Hall.

Slowly she turned about, altering her direction toward the Great Hall stairs and veering toward him. "Yes, Alex?"

"It's about—John," he began. "He's—"

"What about John?" she asked, moving alongside him. Annoyed, he said, "You know. We talked earlier—"

"And you told me he was residing in the Library now."

"Yes."

"Why?"

Annoyance increasing, he said, "If I knew that, I wouldn't need your help, now would I?"

Slowly she bowed her head. "I'm sorry, Alex. I didn't mean—"

"Talk to him, Miss Elizabeth," Alex pleaded, more

interested in solutions than apologies. "You go talk to him. He cares about you."

"He did once, yes."

"And he still does. I don't think I've ever understood him. Oh, I love him, that's a true fact, but as for understanding—"

He broke off, aware of the peculiar expression on her face, one of sadness, as though his confession of love had moved her.

In at attitude of new efficiency, she folded her arms and demanded, "All right. Tell me everything, Alex. When did he insist upon this move to the Library, and what reasons did he give?"

Pleased by her interest, he tried to turn his mind to the questions. "It was the night after the fight," he began. "He told me to leave him alone and I obliged, though later, about midnight, I thought I'd look in on him again. I knew he must be hurting. And you know where I found him? In the corridor on the floor outside his chambers."

Still amazed at his memory of that bizarre night, Alex paused to let the words register with Elizabeth. "What— did he say?" she asked, bewildered.

Alex shrugged. "He said nothing, but as I was lifting him back to his chamber he got very angry and said, no, he didn't want to go back in there, he wanted to go downstairs where the lamps were burning bright."

Before the Library door they both stopped. Alex felt talked out, though obviously he'd said nothing that had made any sense to either of them. "Please go to him, Elizabeth," he begged. "You'll make a difference, I know."

She looked at him with a curious expression, as though on the verge of challenging his words. She seemed to stare at the closed door, a battle raging within her. Finally she grasped the door and said simply, "Leave us alone. Let no one disturb us."

"Yes." Alex smiled, delighted to follow her instructions.

She bowed her head against the door. Then she pushed it open and disappeared behind it.

After she had closed the Library door, she was struck by two perceptions: the darkness of the large room after the brilliant sunlight outside and the odor, an unpleasant blend of old linen and an uncleansed body.

From where she stood she glanced down to the far end, to a curious sight, the heavy oak library tables pushed aside, chairs stacked atop them, a small area cleared to accommodate a low, mussed couch, a washstand and a large easy chair which had been angled about to face the massive oil painting of "The Women of Eden."

While the rest of the room was cast in semidarkness, the area surrounding the painting was illuminated as bright as day by a dozen lamps, all flaming brightly, casting shadows over the women in the painting, occasionally giving the impression that they moved, the painted wind catching in their pastel gowns.

She lifted her eyes from the painting and looked about at the disarray for the man she'd been sent to comfort. She found him, or rather found his hand, hanging limply off the arm of the easy chair, the rest of him obscured behind the high wing-back.

Then there was nothing to do but approach and see if he was in a mood to be rescued from this pit.

Slowly she made her way through the misplaced furnishings, debating whether she should speak and identify herself. Less then ten feet from the chair she stopped, appalled at the profile which appeared before her. What precisely had happened to the man known as John Murrey Eden, she had no idea. This man was old; his hair, mostly gray, lay mussed about his face; his beard mottled with old food; his face still bearing the scabs of the recent fight; his right arm still wrapped in splints; a dressing robe knotted loosely about his waist, the lower half fallen open, revealing bare feet and legs.

Shocked by the apparition, Elizabeth closed her eyes. How to begin? Where to begin? While she was pondering these questions she heard his voice, hoarse, subdued.

"Have they gone?" he asked, never lifting his eyes from the painting or acknowledging her in any way, yet revealing a certain knowledge of activities within the castle in spite of his seclusion.

"They have. Just a few minutes ago."

"Good riddance."

She started to respond, then changed her mind. She

stepped closer, taking note of his ruined face. "Are you —feeling better?"

"I feel like hell."

"I'm sorry. Wouldn't you be more comfortable in your own—"

"No!" At last he altered his position. She saw his hands grasp the arms of the chair, as though fearful that someone would force him to leave.

Saddened by such fear, she ventured closer. "John, what is it?" she asked, trying to take his hand, but he pulled away.

"I can't go back upstairs," he whispered, his head pressed against the cushions.

"Why?"

"Lila's up there."

"Lila?"

"Yes," he repeated sternly. "I saw her. And that cat. She wishes me ill. I know she does." Suddenly he grasped her hand, his injured face pitiful to behold. "Talk to her, Elizabeth," he pleaded. "Tell her that I loved her. I did, you know."

Stunned by this outburst, incapable of response, Elizabeth moved back. *Dear God, help us both.* As she walked away, needing time and distance, her eye caught on one specific face in the painting, beautiful Lila. "It wasn't— Lila you saw, John," she said. "The physician had given you something to help you sleep. You only thought that —"

"No!" The rejection came again, stronger than before, agitation covering that previously lifeless face. "It *was* her; I swear it. I won't go back, not until she returns to her grave where she belongs."

She saw him shivering. In the lapses between his words she tried to understand. What *had* he seen, and why had his mind been incapable of dealing with it? And why his fierce concentration on the painting, his face covered with bewilderment, as though he didn't understand anything he saw.

She took a few additional moments to still her own accelerated pulse, then drew a straight-backed chair close and sat, wanting only to accomplish what she'd been sent to accomplish and leave.

"John, Alex wanted me to ask you when you would be ready to return to London. He says—"

She broke off speaking, aware that he wasn't listening to her. "John, please look at me. It will serve no purpose for you to stay here. All those women are gone now. Lila to her grave, Dhari to Canada, Mary with her husband—"

When she was least expecting it, he smiled. His manner changed, became arrogant as he shifted in the chair, sitting upright, as though the images in the painting were enemies which must be confronted. "They will come," he said patly. "It's only a matter of time. All of them will come back."

Where only moments before she'd felt pity for this man, now she felt anger. "I think not," she countered. "Why should they?"

"Then you think wrong. They all will come back because of me." He leaned closer. "They need me, you see. I created them all, lifted them out of their inferiorities and elevated them to positions of supremacy."

He sat on the edge of the chair, excited by his own words. "Look at the painting," he commanded. "You see that all four females are looking for someone, waiting for the arrival of someone, someone who is very important to them."

"And who would that be?" she asked quietly, knowing the answer, but curious to see if he had the nerve to speak it.

He did. "Me," he said brightly. Broadly he shook his head. "Oh, no, it's only a matter of time. They all will come back, begging for my forgiveness. And, of course, I'll give it, because I do love them, you see."

"I'm sorry, John," she said kindly, though firmly, "but they won't come back. Before I left London I received a letter from Andrew and Dhari, a letter in which every line revealed blissful happiness. They've settled in Toronto. Andrew is building a good practice"—she paused—"a baby is expected in late summer."

It was as she'd expected. The last information had been the deadliest. With unblinking eyes he continued to stare at the painting, though she saw a pulse in his temple.

"No, John," she repeated, "Dhari and Andrew will not be back, nor will Lila, except perhaps in that tortured state in which you recently saw her, an unhappy ghost, seeking in death the love and understanding that you denied her in life."

"I—loved her," came the whispered reply.

"You did not," Elizabeth countered firmly. "You loved only your own will."

"Then Mary," he argued. "Mary, more than all of you, loves and needs me. And I'll forgive her betrayal. She carries with her all the hopes of Eden."

"Then pity Eden"—Elizabeth smiled—"for shortly those hopes will be sailing across the Atlantic for America, where they shall be devoted to her new husband."

"No!"

"Yes!" Elizabeth replied with matching strength. "She's gone, John, and you might as well face it."

He covered his face with his hands. From behind this muffled barrier she heard him mutter, "Then it's up to Richard."

She debated the wisdom of sharing with him Richard's last letter from Forbes Hall. Why not? Perhaps true healing could take place only under the cleansing influence of truth. "Richard may move the line forward, John, but he will not do it at Eden. He sent his regrets last week concerning Mary's wedding and told me in private that as long as you were here he would not be returning to Eden."

It was a harsh message, and momentarily she regretted having spoken it. Never had she seen such desolation on a human face. He leaned forward in the chair, his hands still obscuring his features, and for one terrible moment she thought he was weeping.

What she heard next was that voice, as arrogant as ever. "Then let them all go, and again I say, good riddance." Abruptly he reached for her hand. "You'll stay with me, I know, good Elizabeth, the only true mother I've ever known."

Abruptly he leaned back in the chair again, his eyes lifted to the ceiling. "Yes, just the two of us. That's how it should be; that's how it's been from the beginning. Good, loyal Elizabeth"—he smiled at the ceiling—"how I love you; how I've always loved you."

She had no words, no outlet, and felt an insufferable weight. No! Her days of servitude to this man were over. Although she had no clear-cut view of the future, her clarity of vision for the past more than made up for it. If she didn't know where she was going, at least she knew where she'd been, and knew that it was a landscape she could not pass through again and survive.

"No," she said simply and charted the shock on his

face as he lowered his eyes from the ceiling and focused on her.

"What do you mean?" he demanded.

"What I said. I think for both our sakes we should not see each other again."

Abruptly the shock on his face altered. He laughed once. Then came a second laugh, then a third, until he was speaking over his laughter, a sputtering incoherent sound, a thin stream of spittle running down from the corner of his mouth. "Not see each other again?" he repeated. "What nonsense! And where are you going?" he added, a heavier tone of sarcasm in his voice. "Has one of your lovers offered to become your husband?"

"No."

"Then what? Where would you go? Who would have you, an aging well-worn whore—" He waved his hand in the air as though to erase the ugliness of his last remark. "Forgive me, Elizabeth, but we belong together. We— understand each other," he added, slyly, "the needs of the flesh, if you know what I mean."

No, she didn't know and was in no mood to try to understand. Wise enough to realize that if she stayed they both would say far too much, she stood abruptly, ready to leave the room, except that he reached out and grabbed her hand and held her fast.

"Of course, you'll stay with me, Elizabeth," he begged.

With only minor effort she wrenched her hand free and confronted him, shocked that she should detest those features that once she'd loved.

"I'm going to France, John," she announced.

"France? What in the name of God are you going to do in France?"

"I've been invited."

"By whom?"

"You wouldn't know her."

"Her!" He settled back, a mocking expression on his face. "Well, variety is good for the soul, though I'd be surprised if it satisfied you for long."

She bowed her head in an effort to hold her tongue. She wasn't certain what it was that welled up within her, some ancient need to justify herself, to erase the humiliation of her past. "I'm going to France with Lydia Becker," she said. "We have been invited by Louise Michels to observe the French feminists—"

"I don't believe it," he interrupted. "Wasn't your last mortification enough? Do you and your—friends enjoy being the laughingstock of London?"

"Goodbye, John," she said, backing away.

"You don't even speak French," he shouted up at her.

"I can learn."

"And Bradlaugh will be going with you, no doubt. For all your rhetoric you still enjoy a good English cock, don't you?"

"Whether I go alone or not, I'm still going."

"Then you'll be the laughingstock of Paris as well as London."

"Perhaps."

"And what am I to do?"

As she circled the chair, he dragged himself forward, his voice, manner, words totally incoherent now. "You can't just leave me!" he cried out.

"I'm doing it." She smiled, deriving enjoyment from his disintegration.

"You're a whore, and that's all you'll ever be. Without my protection you cannot survive."

"We'll see."

"Elizabeth! Wait!"

The pathos of this last cry caused her to halt, and she looked back to see him clinging to the back of the chair, his face glistening with tears or perspiration, she couldn't tell which.

"What—do you want?" he whispered, on diminishing breath. Slowly he turned about and sank heavily into the chair. "What did any of you want that I was not prepared and willing to give you?" he muttered, staring at "The Women of Eden."

Elizabeth looked back at him, stunned by this wholly naive and ingenuous question coming from what had been the most brilliant mind in London.

Although she had vowed never to look upon him again, she retraced her steps until she was standing beside him, seeing him precisely as she'd first seen him, lumped in the chair, his eyes on the painting.

"What do we want?" she repeated, looking down on him, still amazed by the question. "What do *you* want?" she asked, pleased that she'd recovered so rapidly from his earlier abuse. Obviously he no longer had the power to hurt her.

"What have *you* always wanted, from the very beginning, John," she went on, "even when you were a little boy?" Failing to elicit a response, she provided him with one.

"Freedom, dignity, the right to pursue your own destiny, the opportunity to make those decisions that affect and influence your spirit and soul and body." She paused. "We are no different from you, John. Oh, our physiology is different, but that's all. And the difference does nothing to alter our hearts or our minds or our needs. For years, centuries, we've tried to convince each other that it does. But it doesn't, not in any fundamental or profound way."

Momentarily lost in her own thoughts, she forced her attention back down on the man who sat as though transfixed by four painted images. "John?" she said, hoping that he would respond in some way to what she had said.

But he did not. In fact, if anything the pain on his face seemed to have increased, his focus on the painting even more intense, as though he saw in it all the world's mysteries combined into one. If he'd understood a word she'd said, he gave no indication of it.

Then it was over. There was nothing more to stay for. She looked down on him a final time, amazed to see not one resemblance to his father, Edward Eden. Once they had been mirror-image reflections, the only difference residing in their souls. Now that difference had surfaced with a vengeance, annihilating even their physical similarities. What chance did mere flesh have against the power of the soul?

"Goodbye, John," she said, and without a backward look left the room.

Two hours later, with her luggage loaded and secured atop her carriage, she stood in the inner courtyard and took a final look at Eden Castle. How it had intimidated her once! But never again. In fact, she had good reason to believe that nothing would ever intimidate her again as long as she lived.

Before she climbed into the carriage she looked back toward the Great Hall, thinking briefly on two pieces of unfinished business. After she'd left John she'd gone in search of Alex, had found him quite drunk in the Kitchen Court. Perhaps it was just as well. She had no message for him, no instructions. He would have to find his own way, as would John. The April air was ripe for liberation, but the effort would have to be theirs.

Then she'd gone immediately to Harriet's chambers to say her goodbyes, only to be greeted in the corridor by a weeping Peggy, who had informed her that her mistress had slid the bolt from within; the ancient imprisonment had commenced immediately following Mary's departure. Again, though regretful, there was nothing Elizabeth could do about it. Perhaps for Harriet, with her ruined face and sightless eyes, the greatest freedom came with imprisonment.

Now there was absolutely nothing more to stay for, and accordingly she climbed aboard her carriage, took a last look at Eden Castle, then turned her vision toward the broad, unbroken horizon line.

She would find a future for herself somewhere. She was certain of it, as confident as she'd ever been in her entire life.

❧❧

Liverpool
May 3, 1871

BURKE LOOKED OUT over the crowded dock, and in this moment of inactivity made two fervent wishes: one, that he had made the right decision to return to America, and, two, that the crossing would allow them the degree of privacy that had consistently eluded them during these past hectic weeks.

He'd never gone through such days, and hoped that he never would again—the dismantling of the house in Mayfair, the transfer of funds, the complex task of booking passage for fourteen. All the servants had leaped at the opportunity to return "home." *Home.* There was a nagging anxiety.

He had tried repeatedly to warn them that the home they had left over ten years ago would not be the one to which they would be returning. His reports coming out of the South had been sketchy, but none of them had been good. Corruption and greed apparently were flourishing, the victorious Yankee "liberators" exploiting the Negroes in ways that would make Southern paternalism pale in comparison.

Still, nothing he had said had dissuaded them, and the eagerness with which they had hurled themselves into preparations for departure suggested to Burke that perhaps they had not been blissfully happy on free English soil.

Home—

As the confusion and mystery of that small word pressed down upon him, he altered his line of vision, turned slightly to the left and saw John Thadeus Delane with his arm around Mary's shoulder, pointing up at the immense steamship, *The City of Paris,* clearly an expert on ships as he was on everything else.

Enjoying a good reflective moment for a change, Burke leaned against the wooden shed where he was awaiting the army of porters with their luggage to clear Customs, and lovingly studied the two about thirty yards ahead.

Delane. What would Burke have done without the man? Generously Delane had offered to take charge of all the loose ends which Burke was leaving in London, and there were several, such as the disposition of the house itself. The man had been simply a bulwark during these hectic weeks, a curious reversal of position, considering that during the past year he had challenged Burke in every step of his pursuit of Mary.

Now look at them. Of course, Burke knew what had happened. Delane had fallen under Mary's charm, like everyone else who met her. After devoting his full energies to their departure for several days, Delane had insisted upon journeying with them to Liverpool and seeing them off in proper fashion.

Then Burke rested his eyes on his bride, still not quite able to believe that she was his. How he wanted to be alone with her, to erase that distance that had grown up between them since the night of the fight at Eden, a distance which had been compounded by his injuries and by the frantic activity of the last few days!

His eyes blurred under the intensity of his vision and the weight of his emotion. Gowned in deep rose velvet with fur trim and clasping the bouquet of red roses which Delane had presented to her upon their arrival at the dock, she resembled a living portrait, high color in her

cheeks, her hair once again her crowning glory. Pray God
their destination did not destroy her, as it had destroyed
his mother.

Submerged in a depth of old emotion and new, he was
only then aware of them coming toward him, Mary clasping Delane's arm, laughing over something he had just
said, and Delane responding with all the flushed enthusiasm of a schoolboy.

"Do you know what Mr. Delane told me, Burke?"
Mary said, laughing. "He said there would be concerts
on board, and all sorts of games and theatricals, like a
small London."

Confronted directly by her beauty and excitement,
Burke drew her close under his arm as though to reclaim
her, and in the manner of a mock threat said, "And we
shall attend none of them."

"Why?"

At that, Delane laughed heartily, understanding, his old
face ruddy with sea air and rising good humor. Then at
last a deep blush on Mary's face told them both that she
had understood as well. She buried her face in the roses
and left them all standing about in a muddled silence.

"Perhaps I should see how Florence is faring, and the
others," she said hurriedly and moved away, leaving
Burke with mild regret for having spoken so intimately.
There was a limit, however. He'd had a wife for almost
three weeks, yet they had occupied separate rooms in the
Mayfair house, his wounds from the fight still taking a toll.
Then, too, there was that regrettable distance, as though
she were angry with him for having challenged John
Murrey Eden.

"She is so beautiful," Delane murmured, watching
along with Burke as the vision in rose velvet made her
way toward the group of servants near the gangplank.
"Do you think she'll take to America?" he added, looking back toward Burke.

"She'll probably take to it better than I will," Burke
said honestly, still following her with his eyes, seeing
her safely delivered to the servants, who were greeting
her warmly.

"Do I hear doubt in your voice?" Delane asked.

"Yes."

Burke had hoped for quick reassurance from this old
friend. Instead he watched closely as Delane walked a

few steps past him, then turned back, his face reflecting his apprehension. "I wrote to your father some weeks ago," he said. "I sent the letter to his last known address, and—nothing. No response at all, I'm afraid."

While Burke appreciated the tone of apology, he was not surprised at the response. Still focusing on Mary, feasting his eyes on a positive vision, he muttered, "Well, we shall soon find out, won't we?"

Respectful of this mood, Delane nodded sympathetically. "I'm sure it's only a matter of—" But then he, too, broke off, obviously unable to present any logical explanation.

At that moment the door to the Customs House opened and a parade of porters streamed through with trunks hoisted atop their shoulders. Burke stepped forward and gave the man in the lead the numbers of the various accommodations on board ship.

When the last porter had passed them by, heading toward the gangplank, Burke turned back to Delane for the farewell he'd dreaded for days.

In an attempt to disguise his emotions, he smiled and said, "What's to say?" In a low tone, he answered his own question. "Simply that I could not have survived without you during these difficult years."

"Nonsense," Delane replied gruffly, apparently not faring any better than Burke. "You served me as I served you, which is the true mark of friendship. Did you know," he added on fresh breath, as though to lighten the mood, "that circulation of the *Times* has dropped since the demise of Lord Ripples?"

Burke laughed, grateful for the new mood. "Well, if you get really desperate, let me know and I'll send you columns from America."

Delane's face brightened even more. "Not a bad idea," he exclaimed, as though the foolish notion had actually taken root in his imagination.

"Enough!" Burke laughed. "If I do any critical writing, I'm certain I'll find plenty of material in my own garden. I'll give England respite for a while, and you as well."

For a moment his laugh hung between them, the old man's face cast in shadows of sorrow. Moved by such an expression, and aware that this stern stubborn man might have been the only true father he had in this world, and remembering his childhood when the long days of summer tedium had been so pleasantly broken by a visit from this Englishman, Burke at last succumbed, and without embarrassment reached out and drew Delane to him.

"Thank you, my friend, for caring," he murmured.

He gave them both a moment to restore their faces. Then he looked toward the gangplank, surprised and pleased to see Mary closely watching.

"Come," Burke said, taking Delane's arm, "there is someone else who would like to say goodbye."

As they drew to where Mary stood, he saw a becoming blush on her cheeks, as though she, too, were aware of the occasion. "Thank you, Mr. Delane," she said, "for being such a good friend to my husband."

Then old Delane had enough. "What in the hell are you using past tense for?" he bellowed. "You just give me word when you are ready to receive an aging and very tired Englishman and I'll be on your doorstep sooner than you can imagine."

The promise seemed to please Mary immensely. Without warning, though quite predictably, she leaned forward on tiptoe and kissed the old man lightly on the cheek.

The three of them exchanged a final awkward embrace. Then, with the captain's call to board echoing in their ears, Burke grasped Mary's arm and guided her carefully up the gangplank.

When they reached the upper deck, they went immediately to the railing and looked over and down. Burke observed that the chaos on the dock was clearing, most of the passengers aboard, the only ones left those who were saying goodbye.

Wordlessly he watched Mary in profile, still saw the high color in her cheeks, one strand of hair worried loose by the wind falling softly across her brow.

Privately he dealt with his last anxiety. How would she fare when she saw her homeland slipping away? She must have brooded on it at length, the realization that quite possibly she would never see England again, or Eden, or her mother or her brother, or Elizabeth.

As the great engines built up a solid head of steam and the bow lines were withdrawn, he saw her gently remove a single rose from her bouquet and toss it lightly back onto English soil. She closed her eyes, grasped the railing, then lifted her face to the wind.

He leaned closer, trying to read her expression. Was it sadness? Would she pass the entire voyage in premature homesickness?

"Mary?" he inquired, concerned.

But there was no answer.

She was aware of Burke's concerned inquiry, but she could not answer in the excitement of the moment. Then, too, she was a bit disturbed that she felt so little distress. She'd feared once that she might weep, but now there was not a single inclination toward tears, not tears of grief, at any rate.

As the ship got under way, the excitement mounted even more, and she found her attention torn in so many directions that she scarcely knew where to look. Behind them and all around them were promenading passengers, the dock of Liverpool almost gone from sight now.

Curious, her lack of regret. No sense of loss, either, but rather the simple realization that she was embarking on the greatest adventure of her life.

Looking up, she saw old Florence hurrying toward them across the deck, her stern black face peering neither to the right nor to the left. In her hand she clutched a sheaf of white envelopes.

As she drew near, Burke went forward to meet her and, before she could speak, he inquired thoughtfully if everyone was settled in.

She nodded in her typically efficient manner, as though to say, Of course, and why shouldn't they be? "I thought I'd better bring you these," she said. "I was in your stateroom unpacking your trunks and these were waiting for you."

Still standing by the railing, Mary saw Burke take them, a dozen envelopes, at least, all bearing the ominous look of invitation.

"Damn," she heard him mutter, after having opened one or two.

"What is it?" she inquired, drawing near, trying to see for herself.

He held one up with clear contempt. "An invitation to

join the captian for dinner." He held up another "An invitation for tea tomorrow with Lord and Lady Haldane; an invitation for sherry later that evening with Mr. and Mrs.—"

She watched with patient amusement as he thumbed angrily through the various social invitations, understanding both his mood and lack of patience.

Suddenly she took the invitations from him and handed them back to Florence. "Dispose of these," she said quietly. She ignored the old woman's shocked expression "And leave the rest of the unpacking to me. I can handle it."

"But—"

"Thank you, Florence," she said, smiling.

Puzzled, the old woman retreated and left her with the weight of Burke's surprised expression. Gently she took his arm and without words guided him toward the main deck, where the foot traffic was dense. She stood a moment looking out over all the ladies and gentlemen, many of whom had penned those loathsome invitations. Then, with the innate cunning of an actress who carefully chooses her audience, she whispered to Burke, "In honor of the skill which I acquired during my days at Jeremy Sims' Song and Supper Club, I'm about to faint. All I ask is that you catch me."

Without further warning, and greatly amused by the confused look on Burke's face, she feigned a most effective swoon, and only at the last minute as the deck was rising up did she feel the reassuring support of his arms about her, heard as well the rustled concern as people rushed from all directions.

Safely "unconscious," she rested her head against his chest and tried to conceal a smile as she heard his sputtering explanation to the shocked voices around them. "It's—nothing serious," he faltered. "Just let us through, please."

Then she heard another voice, a ship's officer. "I will fetch a physician, Mr. Stanhope. There's one on board. I'd be happy to."

"No, I don't—think that's—necessary," Burke said nervously. "Just give us passage and I'm certain that—"

Whatever he was certain of, he failed to say, and again Mary buried her face in his coat to hide a giggle, hoping

he didn't whisk her away too soon, before all those people could clearly see the indisposed Mrs. Stanhope and
thus eliminate them from their various guest lists.

All the way down the narrow corridor which led to
their stateroom she was aware of a trailing parade of
excited and concerned voices.

As she heard Burke's stammering attempts to get rid of
them, her repressed hilarity grew to dangerous proportions and, none too soon, she felt herself being carried
over a high threshold, felt his awkward movements as
he tried to close the door behind them, all the while
cradling his "ill wife."

When she heard the sliding of the bolt she slipped from
his arms, almost doubled over with laughter, as amused
by his puzzled expression as anything.

At last the fog lifted from his face and was replaced
by a look of loving amazement. "Wicked, that's what you
are," he scolded gently.

"Did you really want to attend all those dreary functions?" she gasped, still laughing. "If so, I can effect a
miraculous recovery."

"No!"

"Well, then—" She smiled and looked about at the
lovely wood-paneled room, complete with enormous bed
with red velvet curtains, a bouquet of spring flowers on
the table and two small, curtained dressing rooms on
either side.

She was aware of him waiting, watching, not knowing
quite how to approach her after the last difficult days.
Almost shyly, she approached him. With one hand she
reached up and loosened his neck scarf. "It's all behind us now, Burke," she said quietly. "Everything," she
added, confident that she'd said enough, that at last the
time for words was over.

He stared down on her. As if by mutual consent they
parted, each taking refuge in their private dressing room.

A few minutes later they returned to the bed without
the bother of dressing gowns.

"Come," he invited, a compelling intensity in his face
and manner as he drew her toward him and lay back
with her on the bed.

Still plagued by the nightmares of the past and the
question mark of the future, she hesitated. Her world

had been annihilated so many times before. But as Burke approached her in love and need she felt a new strength, a new hope that, although in the future her world might be severely shaken, it would never again be destroyed.

With a certain pride, she looked back on her share of outlived sorrows. Then she drew her husband to her.